Sic Semper Tyrannis

A novel of liberty and the future of America

Seamus Branaugh

SILVER LAKE PUBLISHING

ABERDEEN, WA ♦ LOS ANGELES, CA

Sic Semper Tyrannis
A novel of liberty and the future of America

First edition, 2010
Copyright © 2010 Silver Lake Publishing

Silver Lake Publishing
101 West Tenth Street
Aberdeen, WA 98520

For a list of other publications or for more information from Silver Lake Publishing, please call **1.360.532.5758**. Find our Web site at **www.silverlakepub.com**.

All rights reserved. No part of this book may be reproduced, stored in a retrieval system or transcribed in any form or by any means (electronic, mechanical, photocopy, recording or otherwise) without the prior written permission of Silver Lake Publishing.

Library of Congress catalogue number: Pending

Seamus Branaugh
Sic Semper Tyrannis
A novel of liberty and the future of America
Pages: 594

ISBN: 978-1-56343-906-3

Author's Note

Individual liberty is a fragile thing, relying as it does on the perfectly-timed interaction of the complicated machinery of government and society. Just one wrong move here or there and people end up living as slaves under the horrors of collectivism or corporate statism. Most Americans, like most people, say that they value liberty and individualism. Yet they show little appreciation for its complexity or rarity.

My goal, in telling this tale, is to restore some of that appreciation.

I have many acknowledgments, apologies and appreciations due to scores of people and groups of people for helping me along the way to completing this project.

My family, first. I've tried to treat these characters and plots with a professionals detachment. But the people nearest to me may see flashes of themselves and have probably heard bits and parts of arguments you'll hear here; and, for that, I owe them thanks. And, to extent I've cribbed from their lives, some apology.

Stories with ambitions of political relevance work best when they're mirrors of the societies from which they spring. Two writers have inspired me to build *this* mirror. Those writers are Robert Heinlein and Ayn Rand (not the center of the cult-like group but the author of two big, idiosyncratic novels). If my work here even approaches the standards those two set, I will be a happy man. And I apologize in advance to any of their enthusiasts who end up disappointed with this effort.

Lastly, to explain in part how this particular story chose me, I'd like to describe a conversation I overheard some years ago between two people that I knew, but that didn't know each other, at a popular holiday party. One person had been born and raised in Manhattan, only to move to Los Angeles for work. She proceeded to become more Angeleno than the Angelenos. The other had been raised in the suburbs of a southern city and fled as soon as possible to Manhattan. Their conversation bounced quickly from business (both worked in the same industry) to art to politics. Dangerous terrain. They might have started out flirting; but that didn't go very far. Despite their similarities, they couldn't find any conversational common ground. And, finally, the new New Yorker literally threw up his hands and said "You'll never understand. I mean, I assume you're a smart person; but you'll never *really* get my point. You have to be from New York."

The native New Yorker said nothing. Maybe because, in that moment, she thought the fellow was right. Or maybe, as a *real* New Yorker only *acting* like an Angeleno, she had contempt for the recent convert.

As I stood next to them, eavesdropping on their talk, several things struck me. First, how much people identify with Cities. Second, how often City dwellers insulate themselves from anything that happens outside of their "walls." Third, how certain some people are that their experiences must be shared directly in order to be understood.

The first point is generally true. The second is sometimes true, sometimes not. The third, no matter how certainly *believed*, is false. Or, as my college logic professor might have corrected, it's both false and invalid. True or false, valid or invalid, these points make for provincial perspective. And provincialism is a handmaiden of tyranny.

When I was young, one of my first really good teachers said, "There are great stories in the things people think are true."

So, Mrs. Murphy, here's one. I hope.

Seamus Branaugh, Winter 2009/2010

Sic Semper Tyrannis

Sic Semper Tyrannis

One

Crowley took a long drink of ice water. For a moment, in the middle of swallowing, he felt removed from the crowded room. He felt like he was swimming in the cold water off of Sanibel Island.

He did this during mark-up sessions. Drinking cold water energized him. And he needed that more often lately.

"What I'm worried about is this section sounding like we're being defensive. We tick off all of our economy and jobs points. Then we move into the problems. It just sounds...nervous. Shouldn't we mention the problems first and then the solutions? Isn't that normal speech structure?"

The lawyers and finance guys looked like they were struggling not to check their screens. The technical work and all supporting textlinks were finished. But company practice was that everyone needed to be in the room for the last meeting on the annual report. The PR people had waited through the first hour; the lawyers would have to wait through the second.

The annual report was important. It was the reason five of his six direct reports were together in one place—a rare thing. There was always some tension when all of these competitive personalities were in the same room at the same time. The City's corporate structure meant a rigid hierarchy. Crowley's word trumped that of any of his C levels. Or all of them. And none of them liked that. Most of these senior managers could be CEOs in smaller Cities; and each probably thought he or she could be CEO *here*.

There was an animal sense to these power dynamics. Although Crowley knew intellectually that his authority as Tampa's CEO was solid, he couldn't shake the gut-level fear that his lieutenants might try to band together and convince the Board of Directors to toss him out. Things like this had happened in other places.

He trusted gut feelings more than he trusted intellect. He'd studied the parallels between animal dynamics and executive competitiveness in his organizational psychology courses in school. The animal stuff had seemed silly to him then; he wished he could remember more of it now.

Matthew Chambers was the Chief Financial Officer. He was the closest thing Crowley had to a second. But Chambers had two things working against him. First, he was the newest of the C level executives. Second, like most CFOs, Chambers had come up through the banks—so his loyalty to the City was always slightly suspect.

But Chambers was clearly the smartest of Crowley's reports, intense and precise. Crowley had said many times that Chambers could analyze a set of facts more quickly and more completely than any person he'd ever known. This mental quickness could be intimidating.

Crowley's glass was filled again. He drank more cold water.

For generations, CFOs in City governments had complained that the presumption of divided loyalty had unfairly kept them from being promoted to the top spots. The career managers never quite trusted them, believing moneymen served the markets—which inevitably meant the Brahmins—first and most.

This was the constant tension in being a City executive. The Brahmins wanted smooth market performance; but the citizens wanted security. And security didn't just mean walls and guns. It meant food and energy. And no City had enough of those. The CEO had to make sure that the deals were in place to keep tax revenues high enough to keep food and energy flowing. And the Brahmins were always looking over his shoulder to make sure their markets and their money weren't disturbed.

Chambers wasn't a Brahmin. In fact, his family hadn't even been citizens. They'd been admitted to Tampa as displaced people after the Second Baltimore/Philadelphia War. So, Crowley trusted his CFO. No one who'd come so far in a third of a lifetime would betray the City for the markets and the greater wealth of a few Brahmins.

Armand Haupt was the Chief Technology Officer. He was Tampa's longest-serving C level and a true engineer. No bullshit, few games. Always interested in the nuts and bolts of the situation. He'd done a few things that had helped Tampa keep ahead of the other cities in the region. He'd suggested the Nordsk Telecom core communications system when other cities went with Asian shit. So, Tampa had completely avoided the NTT frequency conflict meltdown. And he'd always argued against the extreme surveillance systems that other cities used. This had allowed Tampa to earn a valuable reputation as a City that respected citizens' privacy.

Haupt had been CTO for decade before Crowley arrived—and would, as net pundits liked to point out, probably still be there a decade after Crowley was gone.

J.C. Sandoval was the Chief Legal Officer. "The Shark" had also been serving from before Crowley's appointment. He was a ruthless politician—as CLOs tended to be. With so many sharp minds in his department, Sandoval concentrated on keeping in close contact with his equal numbers in the private sector. He also had lots of ties to lawyers in Miami and Havana. He wore loud suits and a shaved head; both designed to make him seem younger and less jowly.

The Shark's move from Miami to Tampa some 20 years earlier was a human reminder to both Cities of Tampa's emergence. It was no secret that he had lobbied for the CEO position before Crowley had been chosen. But he didn't seem to mind working with the *wunderkind*. He also didn't seem to mind his name surfacing any time a major City in the Americas was looking for a CEO.

(Bertram Barrett, the Chief Security Officer, was the one C level missing from the room. True to his profession, Barrett didn't like all senior executives to be in any one place at one time. He was listening in on the meeting from his office in the Ybor City district. And, frankly, he probably wasn't listening too carefully. Annual reports weren't his strong suit.)

Andrea Fournier was the Chief Marketing Officer. She was a polished woman, an excellent manager. There were few women who had C level jobs in major cities; and those who did were usually CMOs. But Crowley had appointed her himself, so he didn't think of her as a token. She was efficient and loyal.

Since Crowley had come out of marketing himself, efficiency and loyalty were the qualities he wanted most in a CMO.

In some ways, this was Fournier's meeting, as much as Crowley's. But writing wasn't her strength. On these matters, she deferred to Thornton Ryan. Or was it Ryan Thornton? Whatever the order of his names, the old fellow had been a journalist in his youth, switched over to public relations in his middle age and settled into this particular niche once he realized he'd never be a C level executive.

Crowley stole a quick look at his watch and took a shorter sip of water. He wasn't sure why he was so thirsty. Maybe the heavy lunch. Or maybe all the red wine at dinner the night before.

Like many lower level executives who kept working after their career momentum had stalled, Thornton dressed and acted eccentrically. His gray suit, white cotton shirt and red silk tie were out of a history book. Of course, his clothes weren't actually so old. This meant that he had to find a tailor somewhere who specialized in old-fashioned suits. And he probably had to go to New York or London to find that.

The waste of time and money that went into such self-indulgence bothered Crowley. All to create the impression that the system hadn't rejected him—he'd rejected it. Maybe. But Crowley suspected that Thornton forced other quirks. Wrote with a pen and paper. Didn't use a screen. Rode a bicycle. Paid cash.

Thornton wasn't alone in this kind of behavior. Big Cities spawned a certain number of colorful oddballs. They found their niches as teachers, journalists or entertainers. Bohemians.

"Well, sir. In my opinion, the best way to handle a hard transition is to explicate it. State right out, 'Those are the good things that have happened this year. But we also have some problems.'"

Explicate. Perfect word for a willful oddity.

Together, almost like an old church chant, three of the younger PR people chimed in "Don't want to say 'problem.'"

Thornton corrected himself, "Challenges."

Crowley looked down at his draft. It appeared on the big screen in a special, oversized type—the easier to read as everyone went along. In a smaller insert on the lower right-hand side, the page appeared as it would when the report was finally released.

The style and structure of these annual reports were set. The report could never be longer than four standard screen pages. It had to summarize the successes and failures of the previous year. It had to explain the strengths and weaknesses of the current moment. And, finally, it had to predict the risks and opportunities that lay ahead in the coming year.

He had to cover all of this, using enough detail so that he didn't sound evasive...but not so much detail that average citizens would be bored. Crowley was very good at striking the right balance. The human touch was always important: So one or two pointed references to specific people were always good. And a joke—aimed at an unthreatening news story or, even better, aimed at himself—would usually help.

"No, I like 'problems.' We're going to make some pretty bold suggestions in a few paragraphs. I think it's reasonable to say we've got some problems. They'll make our solutions seem justified. I mean, no one needs to fix a *challenge*. But everyone wants to fix a problem."

One of the junior PR people added the words, which appeared simultaneously on Crowley's small screen and the large screen against the far wall in his office.

The editor highlighted the new text in bright green and then placed a green arrow several paragraphs below, after the succinctly-worded and neatly bulleted problems.

Thornton piped right up, "Ah, yes. We need a balancing transition into your proposals. Since we've explicated our strengths and weaknesses, we need to explicate that we're moving to our solutions. It's easy enough. We simply add 'These are our strengths and weaknesses. We have them every year. What makes this year different is that I have a bold proposal for handling them.'"

One of the chanters rushed to add, "Shouldn't characterize our own proposal as *bold*."

Crowley agreed. It did sound arrogant. The word was smoothly removed from the green text. "OK. This looks pretty good. Let's take a look at what we've got."

As he said this, the green text shimmered several times and dropped into the same black type that filled the rest of the screen. A second after that, the smaller insert to the screen shimmered twice and expanded, taking over the whole display. It blinked from the third page back to the first page; and the other pages appeared in inserts along the bottom of the screen.

Crowley took a quick look around the room. Fournier, Chambers, Haupt and Sandoval were reading their own hand-held screens. So did the two young Brahmins—one interning with Chambers in finance and one with Sandoval in legal. The other eight people in the room were all reading from the large screen against the far wall. This was a hierarchy thing. Everyone *had* personal screens, of course; but, in a staff meeting, only C level executives and Brahmins used them.

Sic Semper Tyrannis

"Okay. Let's give this thing a go. I'll take my first crack at reading it and you all can groan when it sounds terrible."

Polite giggles as everyone got set.

"I've got…what…two days to get this thing down." Crowley didn't deliver the annual report live. But, in two days, he would make a digital video in the morning that—after a little minor editing and shaping—would be released globally at noon. There was no law about it, but a hundred years of tradition dictated that the president record and release the annual report on the same day. And Crowley was very much a traditionalist.

His screen shimmered to a teleprompter format, which he could read easily. The other screens all stayed on the "final" version. He drank more water and started.

Fellow citizens of Tampa, valued stakeholders and interested parties around the world,

My name is Michael Crowley. I am Tampa's President and CEO and, today, I am pleased to present the City's annual report.

This is the one-hundred and fifty-fourth annual report since Tampa's founding as a sovereign City and my sixth report as the leader of its management team. I serve at the pleasure of the City's Board of Directors which, in turn, answers to citizens and stakeholders.

I believe that Tampa's results from the past year—and this management team's plans for the immediate future—give everyone good reason to continue enjoying life in one of the world's premier locations.

Let me take a few moments to offer you some of the details about life in Tampa.

First, this City is thriving. But all standard measures, Tampa's economy is one of the strongest in the world. For the twenty-eighth year in a row, we have enjoyed a net increase in the Gross Domestic Product. That means there is more money being made, spent and saved here (if you are interested, please click through for a databox with more details).

And even our rate of growth is growing. Our GDP growth was 1.8 percent—an increase from 1.5 percent the year before.

The number of tax-paying jobs in the City reached an all-time high—2.635 million. There have never been so many contributors to our City's well-being! Our communications tech industry is the envy of the world. We make the best energy storage devices anywhere. We export phosphate, nanotech and seafood.

And our jobs number this year has been helped a lot by SpielbergDisney Media's decision to consolidate its corporate functions in Orlando. As anyone who scans the entertainment dailies knows, Orlando—our media borough—is on a winning streak. We've lured major media studios from cities like Vancouver, SoCal, Hong Kong and Bangalore in each of the last five years. But none is more important than the SpielbergDisney move. I have to give SpielbergDisney CEO Than Tran Everett much thanks for making that decision. She and her team have found the Creative Light in Orlando!

No discussion of Tampa's commercial power would be complete without some mention of the Tampa Space Agency's Pegasus XIII satellite program. More than 1,200 media satellites positioned to allow telecom anywhere in the world. We finished the placements two years ago—and WorldTelComm made good on its promise of "One Screen. One Net. One World."

Last year, we started recouping on this massive investment. Cities and states around the world—from Tokyo to Sydney to the Caliphate to Paris, London and New York pay us for access to the Pegasus system. This will keep Tampa in riches for generations.

The Caliphate doesn't threaten us with energy cutbacks because its people don't want their screens to go dark!

Our Space Agency is the best in the world. Our City can place satellites with incredible precision—for security or commercial purposes. There's simply no competition for the TSA's aerospace power. Working with our corporate partners at Cazanove and Boeing, we are developing a quantum field propulsion system that will give us faster-than-light-speed space travel by the end of the decade. That will make interstellar travel a reality. This year, we will begin to replace our older spaceplanes with the Crusader class. These ships are designed to use the quantum engines when they become available. But, in the meantime, the Crusaders will serve many purposes—from managing the satellites to servicing our moon station to establishing a permanent colony on Mars. Interstellar flight and a permanent Mars colony. These have been dreams of mankind for hundreds of years. They will be realized by this City within the next decade.

Back here on Earth, one of the other important metrics that measure a City's financial health is the number of applications for immigration that it receives. This year, our Immigration Service received 161,358 legitimate applications for immigration to Tampa. Another record! And these are quality applications. Almost 140,000 were from other Cites; only 20,000 from the wasteland. And, to those people waiting for immigration to Tampa, I say "Thank you." And I wish you the best in coming here to create a better life for yourself and everyone else here.

Another major metric of civic financial health is the net trade balance with other Cities. There's been a lot of debate among economists in recent years about this best way to measure net trade balances. Here in Tampa, we measure this in the simplest way. We ask: How much money have our people and businesses invested abroad, compared to the money people and businesses from abroad have invested here? The answer: Much more.

Our Pegasus satcomm system gives us a steady stream of currency inflow. We have a net trade surplus this year of more than $280 billion. I consider this surplus to be a major advantage in our strategic relations with other Cities.

Tampa isn't a cowardly or stingy place. Our people and businesses are generous and worldly. We'll put our money in other cities. But we'll invest most in those whose stability and circumstances we trust.

And lastly, on the world stage, there is always the question of how our currency is performing against those of other Cities. Here, I simply point again to the exchange rates. This year, the Tampa dollar has outperformed every major currency in the Americas—except the New York dollar and the Houston petro. And our dollars have held value against most of the money center currencies in Asia and Europe.

I have a personal anecdote that works here. My wife was visiting Paris with a group of friends a few weeks ago and ducked into a small shop to buy a cold drink. She was digging through her purse for her money card and the shop keeper saw some of her cash. "Are those Tampa dollars?" the woman asked. My wife said yes. And the woman said "Don't worry about the card. I'll take those."

These are the things that have gone well in the last year. Times are good here. But, like any booming City, we have some problems. In the coming year, we're turning our attention to fixing these.

First, we need to build up our security forces. Our fighting people don't have the state-of the-art equipment and supplies that they need.

We are fortunate to have cordial relations with most of our immediate neighbors—Miami and Havana to the south; Savannah and Mobile to the north. We're working on our relationship with Jacksonville. And, to those citizens worried about that City's commitment to human rights, I say commercial engagement is the best way to maintain a positive influence our neighbors.

Of course, not everything in foreign policy is positive engagement. The recent conflict between Memphis and New Orleans—as well as the ongoing problems in the Great Lakes region—makes me concerned about our ability to defend ourselves from hostile states.

We have so much here that we may become a target. Traditionally, mid-sized Cities worry about the ambitions of the big Cities in their regions. As Tampa becomes the biggest City in our part of the world, I worry that some desperate smaller City might believe a military gambit could give it control of our resources. So, this year, I am going to assess an increased sales tax of one half of one percent—with the additional funds going directly to an increased budget for the City's External Security.

Specifically, the Tampa Security Forces will see budget increases of at least 18 percent this year. Chief Security Officer Bertram Barrett will be personally overseeing the implementation of these additional funds. And he will be reporting back to me on a weekly basis—so that we can all be sure the planes, ground units and weapons tech are all in place and working.

The City's license with Boeing Tactical covers 18 F-1139C Sky Dragons. We've built five. We intend to build seven more this year—and a final six next year. The SkyDragon is the finest security aircraft available today. Tampa has more of them in the air than any other City. And we're going to keep it that way.

Second, like so many successful Cities, we have seen a disturbing increase in the use of illegal nanotech among our citizens and non-citizen stakeholders. Especially among our young people. The risks posed by invasive self-replicating nanobots are serious. If you've ever seen someone with nanotech poisoning, the "gray goo," you know it's a hideous and painful way to die. We've talked about this for a few years—but now we must act. So, I am increasing the criminal penalties for anyone caught selling unlicensed nanotech. I don't care what the intended purpose is—anti-aging therapy, cosmetics, disease treatment—using illegal nanotech is a serious crime. It's equal to selling hallucinogens; and we're going to treat it like that.

These increased penalties will range from 90 days of intense behavior modification for first-time offenders to the death sentence for certain multiple offenders. I am making a special line-item allocation in the City budget to make sure these stronger penalties go into effect immediately.

Also, we're clarifying our City Health Policy on ISRNS symptoms. *Any* person exhibiting symptoms of nanobot replication discharge will be removed to the Inland Health Quarantine Zone until a complete diagnosis and purge can be completed. We're going to enforce a zero-tolerance policy for gray goo. It's deadly and it's contagious and it's a health risk this City won't tolerate.

We need to send a message from the Gulf to the Atlantic Coast—and to the world—that Tampa takes a forceful line against illegal nanotech and ISRN Syndrome.

Third, on the financial front, the greatest risk of the kind of growth we have enjoyed for the past several years is an increase in interest rates for consumer finance and property finance. I am instituting a new communications forum in which banks and finance companies can exchange information and opinion with our CFO's regulators.

I hope that this forum will keep interest rates down, money flowing and avoid any panics or spikes in the financial markets. And, to support the forum's efforts, I am increasing commercial property taxes by one quarter of one percent to fund a special interest management account under the control of the Chief Financial Officer. He will have standing instructions from me: If he sees any increase in consumer interest rates of more than one percent in a 120-day period, he will use special account funds to put more money in circulation. This will help us manage the money supply in circulation and keep all citizens in good shape.

We have other goals. Continuing to help our friends in Miami emerge from their telecom crisis and building on our aid to the displaced people in Chicago and Detroit are two obvious ones. But I put it to you, plainly: security, gray goo and interest rates are the topics to remember for the coming year.

These are our strengths and weaknesses. We have different ones every year. What makes the year ahead look exciting to me is that we have a clear plan for what we're going to do.

We are lucky here in Tampa. Even our problems are really just signs of our success. But there's always work to do. I often recall the words of Tampa's great president Arturo Cruz: "Keeping success can be harder than finding it."

We will work every day of the coming year to keep our success. You'll hear from me regularly, of course. And I look forward to addressing you again one year from now—and I expect to have more good news then.

After everyone left his office, Crowley took a slow drink from his fourth glass of water and stared at his screen.

He knew the report wasn't excellent. But he believed in a different Arturo Cruz lesson, one that managers didn't mention in public very often. "When the City is at peace and the economy is strong, people don't listen to speeches."

He wasn't happy with line recognizing the Jacksonville Human Rights movement. But it was very popular with screen and music celebrities—and he'd always made a practice of embracing fashionable causes sooner, rather than later.

The only part of the report that the Brahmins on the board were going care about would be the interest rate indicators. They looked bad. High interest rates meant a slow economy; a slow economy was *the* unpardonable sin.

He was protected against the worst swings in market conditions. Tampa was famous for being a City with a "weak CEO" system; the Brahmins, led by the Chairman, controlled most major policy decisions through the Board of Directors. It was one of the reasons that he'd been able to get the job at such a young age. The bankers and financial traders knew this…so they looked for subtle signs from the Board as much as public speeches by the CEO.

Still, the speech would affect the markets for a few days. At least.

He got up from his desk and walked over to the wall of glass facing toward the Gulf of Mexico. Whenever he worked late, he tried to take a short break to watch the sun set into the Gulf. It was a small extravagance that reminded him of how far he had come in what he figured was the first third of his life.

One of his oldest memories was of his mother—a sad, confused woman—telling him "You're destined to do great things."

His strongest motivation was to prove her right.

His screen buzzed. "Sir, you have a call from the Chairman."

Two

"...it's never what you think. The smartest guys in the Federal Era thought *their* biggest danger was the Caliphate or the Russians. But their own social welfare system destroyed them. I think about that whenever I drive around. I mean, I'm *sorry* that the U.S. didn't last. Can you imagine one long, seamless highway all the way up the coast? No walls? No security checks? No tolls? Amazing."

"Hailwood, every time the conversation turns to politics, you kick into this nonchalant act. You of all people should give a shit about whether citizens have a real vote in the actions a City takes." Reeser was crude but he made his points plainly. As boozy evenings went on, he usually played a bigger role in the debate. Whatever it was.

Hailwood shrugged his shoulders. "It's not an act, hoss. And I don't see much value in ranting about how Cities are fascist. It's a stale argument. All governments are fascist. Cities *work*. Countries don't. The Reckoning happened because the United States ran out of other people's money to give deadbeat Cities and the wasteland."

He sat back in his chair and drank some of the red wine that was supposed to be very good.

It didn't taste that good to him. But the object of these Friday night dinners was to celebrate a classical vibe. So, wine it was. He tilted his head back and stared at the ceiling. When he was drinking, he thought this was a good way to radiate off the effects of alcohol.

The dining room was a great room—built in the pre-Reckoning days and before the age of pre-fabricated buildings. In its day, the House hadn't been anything special. But time had been kind to it... or, to be more precise, time had been *un*kind to everything else. Hailwood's fraternity had taken care of the House for more than a hundred years while finer buildings around it had crumbled. So, it had become one of the finest old buildings inside the campus walls.

The idea of the Friday night dinners had been to give the House a "correct" social activity that the brothers could point to when the deans pressed them about progressive activities. The College looked at fraternities as a guilty outlet for alcoholism and whoring. The truth was less sinister; the fraternities had become bastions of what young men considered stylish, old-fashioned socializing. Brothers played poker, billiards, chess and other games. Sometimes for money. But the size of the wager was less important than the manner in which the player won or lost. The goal was to show *good form*.

They did drink a lot. And a lot of guys smoked weed or hash. They played beer pong, a distant alcoholic cousin of ping-pong with rules so complex that most brothers couldn't compete until their second year. While the brothers bought whiskey and wine and drugs, they didn't buy beer. They brewed their own. The basement of the House was taken up with small but well-used copper brewing vats that dated back...well, longer than any of the current brothers knew.

Learning how to brew beer was an essential part of initiation.

Though they drank a lot, there wasn't much whoring. At least not in the House. There were places for that—and, even then, most of the brothers were smart enough to be careful about wasteland women. Aside from the usual menu of natural health risks, some of them also carried invasive self-replicating nanobots—and the deadly gray goo they produced. The man-made bugs were a lot worse than nature's.

More often, brothers would bring serious girlfriends to the House on appointed nights. This way, the girls could tell their daughters and granddaughters in years to come that they'd been out to DKE and seen future world leaders forming the real connections that made things work.

"The young brother has a point, Hailwood. You're a sly bastard," This was Taylor talking. He was Hailwood's closest friend in the House, at the College and...probably...in life so far. Taylor was no fool. He was directing the conversation back to something that would keep their guests involved. "You saw more about the inner working of a major City on your way to kindergarten than most people see in their lifetimes. You know what you think. Say it. Be direct. You're amongst friends."

As the invited guests at these dinners, most professors played along the expected lines and showed an intellectual contempt for the fraternities. Hailwood's idea had been to invite one or two of the most contemptuous teachers out to the House for a well-done, old-fashioned dinner. Show the House in its best, clubby light. Maybe counter some of the booze-and-whores criticism.

His idea had worked. The brothers liked dressing up once a week. At least 10 or 12 would show up every Friday; and sometimes, like tonight, even more would show. The professors—whose contempt was often more formal than true—liked the chance to connect with their students outside of the rigid lines College life.

Hailwood had always thought that the students and teachers had far more in common than not. Why else did they all choose to spend time out here in the wasteland? The supposed tensions within the "campus community" were a product of the deans and administrators, who—like bureaucrats everywhere—used trouble to justify themselves.

"Hmm. I don't like to talk about it because the truth is harsh. Democracy has *always* been a myth, Jon. The few times it's been tried, the result has been chaos. The Federal Era was a fluke. Farmers are usually ignorant rustics but, for a few fleeting decades in Massachusetts and Virginia, they were more than that. They were educated, even profound. That was great. Really great. And then their system bankrupted itself."

"So you're saying Tampa isn't a democracy?"

"No. Not really."

"But the citizens vote in elections."

"They vote for executives and directors chosen by the board. Really, all they have is veto power. Which they've never actually used. Look, the goal of a City is to create two impressions among its citizens. First, that they're secure. Second, that they have a say. If people believe these two things, they go to work, pay their taxes and watch their screens at night without making any trouble."

Hailwood was practically channeling his grandfather. No one sitting around the table knew how much. But just about everyone groaned, anyway.

"I don't believe that you believe what you're saying, Terry. And it's not because you're acting nonchalant. It's because you're acting cynical. You're not a convincing cynic." This was Townsend talking. He was the best professor to have over for dinner. On campus, he was a rhetoric teacher who wore his Communist politics proudly.

His impassioned lectures and the shear absurdity of his beliefs made him one of the most popular teachers in the College. "I heard your presentation on the institutional corruption of the corporate City system. It was top-notch stuff. And I don't believe that someone who understands the weakness of our system so well is really so careless."

Hailwood knew something about Townsend, too. His politics were the sort of radical that could only come from a propertied family in New York and tenure at a young age.

But he was a great teacher. He made you want to know more.

Hailwood's opinion of his teacher was affectionate. He admired Townsend's in-the-moment existence and joy for living. He considered Townsend a model. "There's a topic for a colloquium: the different between nonchalance and cynicism. Cynicism is the worst sin, Prof. Townsend. A good man taught me that."

Townsend nodded. Like many of the professors at the College, he dressed flamboyantly. His hair was thick and white and fell six or eight inches past the back of his collar—but his moustache and goatee were still salt-and-pepper. He'd been a handsome man in his youth; but now he was in his sixties—unaltered—and the long hair plus his tweed suit gave him the manner of a wizard from some old children's book.

That was, no doubt, the intended effect.

Hailwood wasn't sure he'd ever pull off dressing so... intentionally. Still, Townsend was one of his favorite people at the College. He lifted his glass and took another sip. After he swallowed, he finished his thought. "That's why I'm here. Not sure I can do anything about nonchalance. But I'm here to purge my cynicism."

"A lofty ambition," Russell, the most outgoing of the younger brothers said as he stepped back toward the table with a bottle of whiskey from the bar. "We whaleshits aren't so grand. I'm just trying to pass rhetoric and logic."

Townsend laughed, mock scandalized. "*Whale*shits?"

"Underclassmen. Nothing lower in the ocean."

Townsend laughed more and shook his head.

Reeser grabbed the bottle, though alcohol was not his drug of choice, "No one cares about your struggles, whaleshit. Seen and not heard. Seen and not heard!"

The older brothers around the table laughed with Reeser. The verbal abuse of younger members was done mostly for show. But there was a vein of verity in it; on campus, students were generally coddled and constantly reminded how precious they were.

Hailwood poured more wine into his glass. "A neophyte's worries, Russell. Trust me. Those will pass and your mind will move on to other troubles. We aren't here to read any particular bit of Cicero or Shakespeare or Kennedy. We're here to strengthen our minds in a more general way."

"You're too profound for me," Taylor said. He was still directing the conversation—even though he didn't say so much. "I'm here because my family believes four years in the wasteland is a rite of passage."

"And a badge of status," Townsend added.

"I guess," Taylor said. "I'd like to think they're beyond that."

Taylor wasn't so good at the give-and-take of these boozy talks. That was why he usually stayed a little in the background, just coaxing things along so that the professors and the younger brothers would be impressed enough with the high-minded exchange that they'd gossip about them on campus next week.

Hailwood held his wine up to the candles in the middle of the big table. Reeser had been a little too harsh with Russell, who was a leader among the younger classes. "Why are we here? An eternal question. My quest to purge cynicism probably means I'll spend my whole life in academia. And that suits my family just fine—kind of like having a priest in the family. Why are *you* here, Russell?"

The young brother took a drink from his glass and made a thoughtful face. "Because it's the best foundation for being an active citizen. No quickie degrees from state schools or online multiversity. Real liberal arts education. My family thinks this is the best way to maintain its resources."

Again, the table groaned. But groaning was the favorite response to anything said in the after-dinner debates.

"A slick answer. A slick answer."

Reeser, back from a quick trip up to his room, didn't think Hailwood was being harsh enough: "Utilitarian, you little bastard."

Townsend poured a few ounces of Scotch into his water glass and cocked his head at the *whale*shit. "You'll find your reason at some point, son. And then, if you're like most, you'll graduate and be gone. But I do hear a hint of higher things in your talk of being an active citizen. The end of the Federal Era was only partly about politics or war. The real reason was the withdrawal of active citizens. Which was, in turn, caused by money. There wasn't enough money to help everyone, so the active ones—the ones who could make a difference and could have saved the nation—drew back, behind their City walls. *That's* why the so-called 'Reckoning' happened."

Without any explicit instruction, the younger brothers were clearing the plates and serving dishes away from the table. This was the order of the night. The Friday dinners were never staffed with servants. The brothers made a point that the youngest among them—who'd also eaten dinner—would clear the table without interrupting the talk. It was considered part of initiation. And, Hailwood thought, a *good* part. He believed strongly that every propertied person should have some experience clearing a table while others talked.

His eyes welled a bit. Hailwood checked himself. This sentimentality was probably just the red wine's influence. He didn't like sentimentality; that was another reason he didn't usually drink wine.

Three

"…but, Mr. Crowley, the markets *didn't* respond positively to your annual report. It's clear that Tampa's net investment in other Cities is seen as a sign of weakness, not strength. And interest rates are continuing to climb."

This sounded bad, but it was actually a question Crowley had requested. The best thing to do when a report or speech tanked was to face the media and get on screens quickly and often. The impression to responding to the criticisms was often more important than the content of the report. Financial markets and the people who made them were emotional things.

"Of course, I understand that some people think the net investment is a bad thing—but there are also people who believe that too many people are a bad thing. I believe in global investment flow and I believe in human capital."

The lights were hot and almost blinding. The make-up stung his eyes. The questions were both simplistic and antagonistic. And he believed that if he catalogued these problems in his mind, he could put them behind him.

"We've been anticipating the interest creep for a long time. That's why I talked about the City capital reserve in the report. If my report serves as the catalyst that prompts some pent-up release, then good. We'll get these adjustments out of the way all the sooner."

He was relieved to get some of these sound bytes out and into the media. After nearly three days of frantic reaction from his staff, *doing something* came as a relief. And, while he wasn't known for his command of the media as some CEOs were, Crowley believed that he was his own best spokesman.

"Sure. Interest rates are market forces. But other Cities include a human face. And the leadership in other Cities—specifically

Boston, Chicago and SoCal—have been highly critical of your argument that investments made there by Tampa citizens are a sign of Tampa's economic superiority. In fact, Chicago's CFO made a speech yesterday in which he raised the possibility of seizing Tampa investments as a financial security measure. What do have to say about that?"

This was the third of four questions. The producers, Crowley's best allies in the media, had agreed to keep the interview brief and direct. He knew that a long-form interview would seem like damage control. A short "hard-hitting" media piece would seem spontaneous.

"The global economy is not a race. Sometimes the rhetoric that people use when talking about global finance makes it sound like one City's gain is another City's loss. But I don't believe that—and I never have. The amazing thing about a booming economy is that it creates new wealth for *every*one. As far as seizing investments that belong to individual citizens…well, other Cities have tried that before. It's usually a sign of economic desperation. And, you can fact check this, it almost always results in worse trouble for the City doing the seizing. My guess is that the senior management in Chicago is going to clarify that point. They don't want to start a panic of foreign investment abandoning their City."

The woman reporter cocked her head back and raised her eyebrows. But she kept even eye contact. She wasn't going to deviate from the script and botch her chance for a future interview with the CEO.

The back of his neck started to sweat a little. That last bit sounded too much like a threat. And threats always meant trouble.

His mind had clouded a little there at the end and his mouth had moved ahead of his thoughts. That was a bad sign. He needed to stay sharp. He'd talk to his doctor about getting his Neuroplex dosage adjusted. But, for right now, the last question was coming—and he needed to end the interview strongly.

"Mr. Crowley, you're well known for being one of the most market-savvy CEOs in the world. But the response to this latest annual report has been unusually critical. Do you have any thoughts about why?"

This woman was one of her network's rising stars. And he could see why. She arrived with only two techs and one producer. Most media people who came to interview him had six or eight assistants.

And she was attractive enough. But her real strength had to be the eye contact. She grabbed it immediately and didn't let go. And she managed to do this without seeming threatening or nutty. She seemed extremely interested in…you.

There was definitely a sexual quality to her intensity. The personal connection suggested that *anything* was possible.

As a public figure, Crowley had groupies coming onto him once a week. Or more often. This was a class above any of that.

"Well, Anna, we live in a dynamic world. There's a lot of good and bad out there—and those two poles are constantly shifting. If I am any good at channeling market forces, that's because I don't try to push or pull them any particular way. A good executive rides waves; he doesn't try to control them. No single person can know why interest rates are rising now…or why global investment is becoming a more sensitive subject. But I do know *this*: Tampa is a world leader. A financial leader. And our words and actions are going to be watched more closely than those of smaller Cities. Once in a while, that means some people are going to react strongly to what we say. So be it. What Tampa's citizens and stakeholders can count on from me is a straight take on the facts as I see them. I'll let the markets handle the rest."

"Thank you, Mr. Crowley." And, for the first time in six minutes, her powerful gaze broke away. "This is Anna Delano Pike for TTVN. Back to you in the studio, Jake and Marla."

The lights waited a few seconds and then shut off suddenly. The crew was packing before Crowley was able to take out his earpiece.

His staff crowded around him. Teresa handed him a tumbler of ice water. He drank half of it at once. This couldn't be good. He was thirsty all the time now. His regular doctor had run every sort of test and assured him there was nothing wrong. He was starting to think about getting a second opinion.

He cast a quick glance at the reporter—who immediately bolted her gaze back on him.

"I am so grateful that you could make time for us, Mr. Crowley. A full segment live during the prime news hour. You certainly know what you're doing."

"Well, let's hope so Anna. If we don't get some kind of grip on these interest rates, I'm going to be out shoveling sand in the wasteland."

Everyone in the room laughed. And their laughter didn't sound nervous, which was a big relief to him.

She thanked him again and backed out of the room with her small group.

Fifteen minutes later, Crowley was in his private office—two doors down from his official office, where the interview had taken place—and Chambers was there, with his young Brahmin aide.

"Forget Chicago. We've got trouble right here at home with SunBank. First thing tomorrow morning, they are going to announce a half-point increase in the standard consumer finance rate. That's going to affect everything. Immediately."

This wasn't good news. But Crowley didn't like the way that Chambers tried to define the terms of discussion.

"Forget Chicago, Chambers. Just tell me what the Old Man is going to say."

Nothing. Practiced calm from Chambers, natural calm from his Brahmin lieutenant.

"You guys must have some idea what the Old Man is going to say when he calls. I mean, SunBank is one of his companies, right?"

"He's an investor. But he doesn't control it."

"He's on the board of directors, right?"

"The board doesn't set interest rates."

"So, the Old Man is on the board of directors of the bank that's running against our interest rate program—and he's going to call me, all pissed off about its actions? Well, I guess that's what Brahmins call *elegant*."

Chambers and his intern looked confused. No one in City government liked the term "Brahmin." It highlighted a social order that wasn't supposed to exist. In theory, all citizens were equal....

But Crowley had more practical matters to consider. The ugly surprise in the days after the annual report had been the "trade war" meme that had been racing through the media—both pirate and official. He'd talked about his plans for more security spending; and he'd talked about global investments. When they'd drafted the report, these seemed like two items on a checklist of ordinary annual report topics. Now, they were the justification for banks to raise interest rates—something they'd wanted to do all along, anyway.

"Well, there's not much we can do. And I certainly don't want to look panicky and fuel any more buzz about a trade war. We'll just have to ride it out. Maybe we can start releasing some of the cheaper paper to the banks to staunch this."

Chambers took a personal screen from the Brahmin aide. They were just going to forget Crowley's little outburst. "I don't know. This boost is pretty bad. We'd tracked them to a quarter-point increase. The half-point will be trouble. The other banks will follow suit. And, as soon as people start getting their new financial statements, there's going to be a lot of unhappiness."

Chambers was starting to sound like a prick. He almost seemed happy about this bad scenario.

"Well, we'll just have to ride it out. What else can we do?"

"We could call Bart Saul. I mean, you could. Or you could have Sandoval make the call."

Bartholomew Saul was the president of SunBank. He was an acquaintance of Crowley's socially and politically; he was a close *friend* of the Shark.

"And say what? 'Please don't raise your interest rates tomorrow.' Don't be ridiculous."

Chambers made some kind of note on his screen and handed it back to the intern. "Well, these higher interest rates are going to put a crimp in everything. We're going to *have* to use our credit reserve to take pressure off of the rates. The good news is that the higher rates should balance out our foreign investment surplus. We'll have capital flowing in from every open City. But the bigger TSF investment's still going to be hard to explain away."

Crowley didn't like the direction this meeting was taking. Chambers was either bringing up side points or talking in circles, looking for a sideways angle to get at something that he didn't want to say plainly.

"Explain away? Why should we do that? Every poll I've seen says that the citizens *want* more money going to the Security Forces."

"It's just that the combination of the higher interest rates and the bigger security budget is going to give these trade war nuts a lot to go on. You said a few minutes ago that you don't want to give them any more fuel. Well, I think you're doing that."

What Chambers was saying made sense. Crowley had been thinking the same thing, himself. But something in his gut told him that this still wasn't what Chambers was really trying to say.

"Matt, I don't understand what you're getting at. This whole conversation has had a strange feeling. Are you trying to circle around to something other than what you're saying?"

Chambers made eye contact—but it was weak. Was he lying about something?

Crowley checked himself. He'd just done an interview with a woman whose eye contact was so intense that it seemed to bore through all personal boundaries. *Anyone*'s eye contact would seem weak after hers.

"Getting at? I have no hidden agenda. You told me you were worried about the trade war talk. I'm worried too. I don't want to be the guy who was CFO when Tampa blew a decade of carefully-managed growth on a financial cold war or a regional hot war."

This still wasn't quite convincing. Crowley's neck was sweating again. And, this time, there were no media lights to blame.

"And I don't want to be the guy who was *CEO* when that happened. So, we're on the same page."

There was a moment of silence that confirmed to Crowley's mind that something was cracked about his CFO.

"Okay, Matt. Thanks for the intelligence about SunBank. I'm not going to call Bart Saul and I don't think Sandoval should, either. We'll just roll with the news a while longer and see where we go. In the meantime, you can get the credit reserve money ready to release as soon as possible."

"Right. How much?"

"The whole thing. I don't like to think of these things in terms of dollars. I like to think of them in terms of response. Once we've flooded out the interest rate pressure, we'll reel the reserve back in a little at a time."

"Matt, your predecessor used to say that the only name any CFO needed to know from the Federal Era was Alan Greenspan."

This was really all preparation for his meeting the next afternoon with the Old Man.

Once a month, Crowley had a lunch meeting with the Chairman of the Board of the City of Tampa Corporation. The Old Man would ask detailed, impatient questions for a couple of hours…and Crowley would usually need a full day to recover.

The Old Man was in his late 80s—but looked 25 years younger and still vibrant because of genetic youth therapy and…probably…

some choice cosmetic surgery. He planned to live 200 years and, if technology could get him there, he'd make it. He had the hard-driven, humorless attitude of someone who was struggling seriously to live forever.

The lunches were the one part of his job that Crowley hadn't been able to master fully. But he was optimistic that he would, eventually. His strongest skill was handling difficult situations.

Two hours—and three glasses of water—later, Crowley was sitting out on the balcony off of his bedroom, staring at his wife.

She didn't think much of his plan to see another doctor. "Michael, I think you forget what a crazy schedule you keep. I don't care how much of a superstar you are, going at full speed 15 to 18 hours a day will kill most people. The fact that your body wants more water is one of the *sanest* things that could happen."

He tried to hold here gaze. But she wasn't inclined.

"That's a nice thing to say, M."

He was doing his best to connect with her after a bad stretch. They didn't fight in the sense that some married couples did. Their version of fighting was long periods—often a week or more—where they wouldn't talk.

It was easy to let a week of silence go by. He'd come back to the house after she gone to bed and be up and gone before she woke. Or she'd stay at the beach house on Sanibel Island. They also had a ski place in Vail. And her mother and brothers still lived in Dallas....

She was a few years older than Crowley. This might have seemed unlikely; but Margot Perot Crowley was one of the most elegant women in the world. She was famous for her style. A Brahmin from Dallas, she looked and talked like a character from a Federal Era movie. Rich and thin. Perfect diction.

She was a major catch for a non-Brahmin—even if he *was* CEO of a major City.

He let the sexrelax pill dissolve a little on his tongue and then swallowed some lemonade to wash it down. At work, he was drinking lots of water. At home, he was drinking a lot of the kids' lemonade.

"The least we can do is show each other a little kindness." She flashed a quick smile and stared out at the Gulf. The sun had set about half an hour ago; but the sky was still colorful twilight and the lights along the coast were just twinkling on.

He knew what she said was a quote from some famous book—but he couldn't place it. And he didn't really care. He'd never tried to keep up with her literary references; he was content to note when she was making them and leave the matter at that.

He'd made the first move this time, calling her and saying that he wanted to spend some time with her. She'd made sure the kids were at friends' houses and everyone except Louisa had the night off.

"So, how much of this trade war talk is serious?"

"Not much. Why?"

"Well, it seems your style. Create the dire possibility and then deftly resolve it."

"I wish I were as scheming as you imagine, M. Most of my day is *re*acting to media and the markets. I don't have so much control."

She rolled her eyes and drank her martini. "You're the man who once told me that the best executive manages the markets ahead of the news."

She was dutiful, if not passionate, about his work. Some spouses of senior managers thought as much about the details of their days as the managers themselves. But he'd chosen a different kind of wife. She would talk with him about work…but she'd rather talk about parties or their children or friends or old books. Family and friends meant more to her than business did.

Fifteen years ago, he'd figured this marriage would be a good stretch for him. He didn't need help managing his career or organizing his sock drawer. He needed someone who would make him seem like an equal among Brahmins, celebrities, top executives and the rest. Not matter how icy things got between them, she'd delivered on that part of the bargain.

"If that's what I'm doing right now, I've gotten to the point where the scheming has become subconscious."

"Sure. That's what they call *mastery*."

"Maybe I'm more in control of all this than I realize."

She looked at him for a moment. This was her way. "Well, cheers to that."

M hadn't always been this cool character. She'd been married once before. Her first husband had been a minor prince from the royal family of the Caliphate. She'd met him when she was a student in Paris and he was spending a lot of time meeting students. She was 22.

The marriage certainly wasn't what her parents had expected when they sent their daughter to Europe for learning and culture. But their worries were just starting. M's newlywed bliss lasted a few months and ended in a scandal when she walked in on the Prince and one of his boyfriends.

She put a bullet in the Prince's thigh and killed the boyfriend.

Crowley would always remember how she explained the shooting, once they'd gotten to know each other: "I always thought that I was more worldly than that. A wife shouldn't be intimidated by a mistress or even a down-low boyfriend. But I just lost my cool. There was something about this little creep that he was fucking that made my skin crawl."

The story made the tabloids for several news cycles. If there was one thing that people everywhere liked to read, it was a Brahmin caught up in a sex scandal. If there was anything else, it was some prince of the Caliphate buggering a boy.

There was some confusion about exactly where the shooting had taken place. No one seemed to know whether the Royal Family's property fell under civil jurisdiction. And, beyond that, Caliphate law was vague about crimes of passion. Which usually cut in favor of angry husbands.

Her father—a Dallas board member—called in some favors. Dallas and the Caliphate may have been competitors for petroleum sales; but, as usually the case, the competitors had more common interests than differences. The sherifs (the Caliphate's version of managers) figured they could get rid of a headache and bank a favor with Dallas by sending Margot home. So they did.

The tabloids lost interest after a few weeks, when the Caliphate authorities said they didn't have enough evidence to prosecute.

Her family was able to get the divorce done quickly and quietly. She spent the rest of her life trying to regain her cool. Gradually, she worked her way back into Dallas society. Her father made sure the fashion screens noted how effortlessly chic Margot was. And she was.

Three years after the divorce, her ex-husband was killed when Caliphate conservatives put a bomb in his car.

Six years after the divorce, she met Crowley at a Christmas fundraiser. He'd come to Dallas to negotiate an extension of the Tampa/Dallas bilateral trade protocols. He was still in his late 20s but already Tampa's CMO. And, in an unusual move, he'd taken over foreign trade responsibility from the City's CFO. Great things were expected of him.

She was one of the best-looking women he'd ever met. Not sexed up and plump, as in the fashion of the time. But clean and sharp and fine. She didn't spend hours making herself look good, but she worked enough to show she gave a damn. His idea of a classic Brahmin. He didn't know anything about her tabloid past when he met her. He just knew she was Marc Perot's daughter and that she'd be a great wife for…someone.

And his strongest skill was handling difficult situations.

Four

Hailwood leaned his head through the open door to Reeser's room. "You ready to go, hoss?"

"Yeah, yeah. Just let me put my shit away." He was breaking down his needle and syringe and placing the pieces carefully into the ultraviolet sterilizer that he kept on his desk.

Neither of them had classes on Thursday afternoons, so they'd made a habit of going into town then. Students were supposed to avoid leaving campus at regular times. But Hailwood didn't give that rule much mind. With a girlfriend in Northampton and a fraternity house full of guys who liked alcohol, fresh fruit, tobacco and drugs, he spent a lot of time in the wasteland.

Reeser pulled on his parka and followed Hailwood downstairs. "We going to drive?"

"Hell no. Look at the day outside. Look at that blue sky! No need to get the rig out to drive 10 blocks. We'll walk."

"Okay. I just thought we were going all the way to the Mall." Reeser always wanted to go to the Mall—about six miles west of campus—because there was a drug shop there that he swore had better stuff.

Hailwood thought that, for Reeser, *better* just meant *cheaper*. "No. Just into town. You're going to have to make your best deal with Hampton's."

"Okay, fine. I'll manage. But *you* pull the fucking sled back."

"We may not need it." It was a nice day. The temperature was in the high 30s and there was no wind. Hailwood didn't bother to zip up his coat or wrap his scarf on the way over to the gate house.

"Really? So, how many orders?"

"Not too many. Russell and the whaleshits want a couple of bottles of bourbon. The Elf has a bottle of some special European

Gin ordered. Taylor wants me to pick up some more wine and some hash. Ding wants cocaine. And then three boxes of Havana *Imperators* for the dinner tomorrow night and whatever apples or pears I can find. I think we can do it with backpacks."

"They're going to have three boxes of *Imperators*?"

"We'll see. If not, we improvise."

They didn't talk any more as the walked past the Old Library, between two dormitories and to the gate house. Inside, a campus security guard neither student knew very well was manning the booth.

Hailwood and Reeser each slid his ID card through the slot. The guard scanned each card, looked carefully at the match on his computer screen and passed the card back without saying a word. He barely looked at them and just nodded slightly and buzzed the door to the locker room.

Their lockers were on different aisles and they were the only two people in the room at that moment. So, Reeser resumed his questions in a loud voice.

"So, what are your plans for the weekend? Is Kate coming over for dinner tomorrow night?"

"No. I'm going over there on Saturday." Hailwood pulled out his winter hiking boots and a shoulder holster for his 9mm Glock.

"What's the deal? Is she mad at us? I haven't seen Kate at the house in weeks."

"Don't take it so personally. She's finishing her honors paper. It's an intense thing." The boots slid over his socks and the bottoms of his blue jeans. They had an old fashioned lace on the outside, which took a few minutes to tighten up to just beneath his knee. Then, they had a Velcro cover over the laces. They were lightweight but rugged—perfect for hiking through unkept snow and ice. His grandfather had said "the Krauts really know how to make winter gear. These things will be perfect for you up in all that snow." And—as usual—he'd been right.

Hailwood checked the Glock and the three clips he'd loaded on his way back from his trip to see Kate the previous Monday night. He loaded one clip in the gun, set the safety and slammed it into the holster, tight against the left side of his chest.

Next, he checked the plasma load on the TAG heavy pistol. This took a little longer, because he hadn't used the gun in a while.

It was at 85 percent. He took out two large charge clips for this gun and zipped them into the sleeve pockets and the pistol into a zipper pocket on the right side of his jacket. The down ski jacket hid the bulky plasma pistol very well.

Last, his Randall blade slid into a similar pocket on the inside of his left boot.

He had a small .22 Ruger with a six-shot clip that could fit in any pocket. But he hadn't used this one in a long time—and he'd have to clean it in order to bring it. So, he decided against.

He patted his shirt pocket to make sure he had his shopping list and his back pants pocket to make sure he had his wallet. "Okay, you ready?"

"Yeah." Reeser had his shotgun holster strapped to his right leg and his pistol—usually a Federal Era police issue .38—on his left hip. Hiding weapons in clothes was expensive and most students at the college, or their families, didn't think it was worth the time and money to do so. After all, the students weren't supposed to *go* off campus.

Hailwood swiped his ID and walked into the exit tunnel. Reeser followed him quickly. A dozen paces trough the tunnel took them under the northern wall of the campus and to a simple metal gate. No card scan here—they just turned the handle and walked out into the wasteland.

The walk from the north wall to the edge of town wasn't long. In a straight line, it was less than half a mile. But the main walking path twisted around a handful of old buildings and squatters camps that dotted the strip of wasteland between the campus and the town line.

The hardest part of the walk was the bad condition of the path. For most of the year—from early September to early May—it was icy. The College and the town didn't get along about much, and the poor condition of the path between the two was an incarnation of their discord. Once or twice, some students had tried to maintain the path with volunteer work crews. But the crews drew anger and gunfire from the squatters in the little camps. They took the message. And wore studded winter hiking boots instead.

The actual townies didn't mind students; in fact, most *wanted* the kids to come in and spend their money. But, to the squatters, the kids maintaining the pathway seemed like a taking. And people in the wasteland hated takings.

This particular Thursday afternoon, Hailwood and Reeser might as well have been walking through the bird sanctuary on campus. There didn't seem to be anyone around—even in the camps. The sun was out, the sky was blue and they made it to the town limits in 10 minutes.

The town limits were easy to see. As they approached, an 8-foot-tall berm of dirty snow rose up jaggedly from the regular white blanket. A slushy section of the path went through the berm. On the other side, the yards and streets of the town proper were neatly plowed and kept. At worst, there might be an inch of clean snow. On this day, the streets and sidewalks were clean and just a little wet. A few parked cars, a few horses breathing vapor at the various hitching posts.

But clean streets didn't mean safe streets. Hailwood and Reeser made a no-nonsense line toward JB's, the tavern and restaurant where they usually ate lunch.

They sat at the bar. The middle-aged man who ran the front of the bar knew them and brought a couple of draft beers. "Gentlemen, what'll you have?"

There was a condescending edge to that *gentlemen*. No townie would call himself a gentleman. But townies did tease and razz each other a lot. And, since Hailwood and Reeser were something like regulars at JB's, Hailwood didn't mind the edge. He ordered a hamburger and fries. Reeser asked what else they had in the kitchen.

The bartender's eyes brightened at the chance to sell his menu. "Well, Whitey's cousin just brought us some clams from Boston. Fresh cherry stones, from out on the Cape. We're frying them, bellies and all. They're big and rich and mighty good."

Reeser said he'd have a hamburger, too, and ordered some of the fried clams to split with Hailwood first.

While Reeser chatted with the owner, Hailwood made a quick scan of the room. Even though he knew the place, he looked for ready exits. They'd made it to JB's between the lunch and dinner hours. It was the best time to be there. Back in the kitchen, Whitey wouldn't be rushed. There were just three other groups in the place.

A boy and girl who couldn't have been 20 were sitting on the same side of a booth, eating what looked like the house-special clams.

Four heavy-set men who dressed like trappers or loggers were well into a lot of beer at another booth. They could be trouble—armed and wasted. But they sounded like they were celebrating some sort of business win.

Finally, two scraggly-looking squatters were sitting together at the other end of the bar. It was hard to tell how old these guys were. Wasteland life made a 30-year-old man look like he was 50; and it was even harder on the women. Townies fared better. But squatters usually had the gaunt look of subsistence living; and they had the nervous shyness that City people called being "broken." No eye contact. And some—like these—had the artificial-looking facial features of shoddy nanobot cosmetic work.

Life in the wasteland had also taught Hailwood that not every gaunt squatter was a trouble-maker. He relaxed a bit, unwrapped his scarf and drank his beer. He'd keep his eye on the two at the end of the bar. But things were probably okay.

In the years before the Reckoning, the town had been home to a big government-run university—in addition to the College. In those days, the town had something like 50,000 residents. After the Reckoning, the university tried to continue as a private institution. But it couldn't make it and closed down.

Boston was an unusual City. It was old and established and famous…but it was poorer than its citizens had expected it to be. So, it had abandoned everything west of Worcester to the wasteland.

This had been hard on the town—in a way, it was as broken as the squatters who lived around its outskirts. Its permanent population shrunk to a couple of thousand. These people did manage to keep some town life, mostly because it was at the crossing of two reasonably well-kept roads, one of which was a major access to the Western New England Tollway.

Also, the buildings north of town—which had been the government university—were one of the largest squatter camps in the area. No one knew how many people lived up there; and the numbers changed dramatically from summer to winter. But there were more people there at any given time than there were residents within the town's limits. Sometimes a lot more.

People from the College visited the squatter's camps for two very different reasons. Some idealistic professors and students would arrange trips up there to offer basic health services and reading lessons. A few thrill-seeking students would go up at night for cheap drugs and even cheaper whores. Hailwood didn't fit in either group. You could get drugs and whores in town—and you didn't run such a risk of dying doing it. The closest he'd ever come to the camps was driving along their perimeter a couple of times, when he'd first gotten to the College and was exploring the area.

"You know, it's an amazing thing. We get the same basic food at home and it tastes like shit. We come into a simple place like this and it tastes really good," Reeser was into his second beer and first couple of fried clams.

Hailwood tried one of the clams. It was good, full of a briny flavor that the clams they served on campus never had. "This tastes like seafood, hoss. The stuff they serve there tastes like rubber."

Both of the students had long ago learned no to mention "College" or "campus" when they were in town. That was the fastest way to start a bar fight. They said "at home" or "back there" instead. A mostly-empty JB's on a Thursday afternoon wasn't such a dangerous place; they probably could have come with Prof. Marshall and had an advanced rhetoric seminar and not been harassed. But one of the bars a little farther into town on a Friday night would another matter.

After they'd finished their hamburgers, the bartender asked how they wanted to settle. Reeser, who'd had five beers along the way, said he had Boston dollars. That was fine by BJ's. They agreed to Bos$15, including the tip.

The girl and the boy had left by the time Hailwood and Reeser were finished. But the other two groups were still there. The mountain men had started singing karryokey to old rock songs. The mangy squatters had barely moved. Or touched their drinks, from all appearances. One wiped his nose with an oily rag. Gray goo. The side effect of cheap nanobot treatments.

Hailwood was glad to be out.

Their next stop was Hampton's, the main liquor and drug store in town. It was an impressive place—but, from the customer's perspective, it was a 10' x 10' plastic box inside of an amazing store.

The owners did a good job of using lighting on both sides of the box to downplay the separation. Depending on where you were standing, you could feel like you were actually inside the store.

Hailwood recognized the old guy they called Fuckin' Ed resting behind one of the two sales windows on at the back of the box—and he headed straight there.

"Good afternoon, Ed."

"Young Mr. Hailwood, a gentleman and a scholar. It's Thursday. Something tells me you've brought a fuckin shopping list."

There was that *gentleman* again. The simplest things marked the difference between the townies and the College students passing through.

"Indeed, I have. Let's start with the most difficult item first."

"Okay. One moment."

He pressed a button that locked the outside doors behind Hailwood and Reeser. This was for their protection.

"We're inviting some professors out to the House tomorrow night and one of these old birds is a cigar smoker. So, I'd like to get three boxes of those Havana *Imperators* that you had here last week."

"Hmm. Mikey will check the humidor. I'm not sure we have three boxes of those fuckers left. But, I'll tell you what. We got in a bunch of Dominican knock-off of *Imperators* that are pretty good. I read a review of them on one of the New York Net sites and sure enough, my guy in New York had some."

Fuckin' Ed always mentioned that he'd read this review or that article about something he had in stock. This was partly just good business, to chat up his existing inventory. But it was also a bit of a boast to his customers from the College. Most people who lived in the wasteland couldn't read.

"Well, maybe. But you know I'm a homer, Ed. If you don't have any *Imperators*, I'll just go with some Ybor City Kings."

"Sure. What's next?"

"Three bottles of Maker's Mark."

"Check."

"Four bottles of Napa Sunset Cabernet."

"Check."

"One bottle of special-order Czech gin for A.P. Hillyer."

"Check on the Czech. Mr. Hillyer called earlier to make sure it was in stock."

"Three one-gram units of Ceballos Major cocaine."

"Check."

"Three one-ounce units of Maui Gold marijuana."

"Check."

Two younger men working behind Ed were gathering the bottles and plastic eggs while Hailwood ordered.

"One of my fellows had asked for a plug of hashish. What decent stuff to you guys have?"

"*Decent* or *good*?"

"Difference?"

"Well, we have some *decent* hash that we got from our Amsterdam source about a week ago. But, frankly, I'm not sure how long it was sittin' around collecting dust there before we got it. On the other hand, we got some *good* hash directly from Istanbul just three days ago. From what I'm told, very strong."

"What's the *price* difference?"

"Let's see. Fifty-eight dollars Boston for the Amsterdam stuff; ninety-six dollars Boston for the Istanbul stuff."

"I'm not the one smoking it, Ed. Let's just go with the Amsterdam."

"Check."

"And let's see, for me...." This was the reason that Hailwood liked to make the trip out of Hampton's. They always featured odd items they'd come across in the course of business—usually alcohol or prepackaged drugs in very small quantities. These oddities were displayed in a tree-shaped wrought-iron unit behind Ed's window. From this tree, Hailwood had picked up a few bottles of real French champagne and other fine things. "Well, look at that. My Kate loves to drink good Tequila and you guys have a bottle of Patron Silver. I'll take one of those."

"Check."

"And...ah...that bottle of Macallan Scotch."

"Very good choice. Now don't be sharin' that fine drink with any of your snot-nosed friends. It's a special occasion thing."

"Very good, then. Toss in a bottle of something I *can* share."

"Glen Ross is a respectable single-malt."

"Sounds good."

"And it looks like we have three boxes of the *Imperators*. But they're the last three. So, your timing has been good."

"Excellent. Now, I'm carrying these fine things back in a backpack. So, please bag them well."

Ed stared at him for a moment. "A backpack?"

"Yeah."

"I've got a better idea." He flipped a switch that opened the pass-throw window to his left. "Pass the fuckin' bag in here and we'll pack it so nothing bad happens to your boodle."

On the other side of the glass box, Reeser was finishing his purchases. Mostly heroin and grass, he'd have a much easier time getting his stuff back to campus.

"So, how do you want to pay for this, Mr. Hailwood? Cash or charge?"

"What's the total?"

"Eleven hundred eight-four dollars and thirteen cents, Boston. Four hundred ninety-six dollars and eight-eight, Tampa." Fuckin' Ed knew the hometowns of his regular customers. And, like most merchants, could do complex currency conversions in his head.

Hailwood had ten Tampa baby bonds in his wallet. He took out five and passed them through the slot in Ed's window.

In the meantime, Ed's assistants placed each item against the glass for inspection. He waved his hands over the items that were ready to pack and made a different gesture over one of the cocaine packets and the hashish.

"Five hundred dollars Tampa. Tenth of a unit corporate bonds. You always make things interesting, Mr. Hailwood. Some day, you're going to bring gold bullion in here."

"And you'd accept it, Ed."

"Fuck yeah. Runs about nine hundred fourteen dollars fifty Boston an ounce as of this morning. But *your* change will be seven dollars and forty-four cents Boston."

Ed put Hailwood's change and the two packets he'd selected in the smaller pass-through window. After Ed shut the door, Hailwood opened his.

He put the money in his pocket and took a testing kit out of his coat. It took just a few seconds to assemble a needle and the testing device. He then jabbed the cocaine packet and waited for the LCD screen to flash the results. It was fine. The chemistry was right— and it was 93 percent pure.

He switched out the needle and jabbed the plug of hashish.

It was fine, too. He put the two packets in one of his inside coat pockets.

"Your lads are impressive, Ed. I could bounce down Memorial Hill and not a thing would be harmed."

"Fuck. You kids from the College are easy. We supply people going as far as Williamstown and Brattleboro. On horses. You're just a walk in the fuckin' park."

Hailwood pulled his backpack out of the larger pass-through window. It was packed with so much cardboard and paper that it didn't feel like anything solid was in it. And, more importantly, it didn't feel very heavy at all. He loosened the straps a bit, so that he could reach inside his coat easily. He tried it a few times, just to be sure.

Reeser was also carrying a backpack. He'd picked up a couple of bottles, too. But Hailwood didn't much care what was in hoss's backpack. The fact that both of them were carrying the things made him less suspicious.

"You fellas be careful out there," Ed unlocked the outer doors and gave a quick wave good-bye. "We'll see you next time."

Their next stop was the fresh produce and flowers store—Valley Greens. It was just a couple of doors down Pleasant Street, past a record store and a gunsmith.

Reeser said he wanted to check something quickly in the music store, so they ducked in there. Hailwood stayed by the front window and scanned the street. The two broken squatters from BJ's were standing out in the front of the tavern. They seemed anxious, like they were waiting for someone. Some did this for money, offering to hold your horse or wash the windows on your car while you went shopping.

At first glance, the two looked like brothers. They were dressed alike, in heavy flannel coats and greasy work pants. They wore their hair and beards long, in the standard squatter style. On second glance, Hailwood could see they didn't really look alike. The taller one had thick, doughy features and a slight hunch in his back; the smaller one had darker skin and sharper features. Like Lenny and George from *Of Mice and Men*.

The shorter one was wiping his nose with an oily handkerchief.

"Gray goo" was the slang name for ISRN Syndrome. Sleazy doctors using unregulated bugs would promise poor, stupid people the same results for a few hundred dollars that rich, smart people got from million-dollar nanotech therapies.

The results of nanotech therapy could be amazing. People with strokes brought back to full fitness. Burn victims made whole, so you'd never know they'd been scarred. Cancerous tumors removed more precisely than any surgeon could cut.

The problem with nanobots wasn't building them or buying them. It was getting rid of them. The reason quality nanotech cost so much was that the best doctors and techs in the big Cities worked hard to make sure their bugs self-terminated after they'd done their work inside the patient's body. If the bugs didn't, they'd usually start replicating faster than the body could purge them. The result was nanotech waste—gray goo. Dead bugs and bug byproduct filling the insides and seeping out of glands and orifices. Eventually, the poor, stupid patient's internal organs would start to fail. It was a painful way to die.

That last thought made Hailwood nervous. He looked over to see what Reeser was doing.

A quorum had gathered near the cash register. Reeser was laying off some of the heroin he'd just bought next door. Hampton's didn't sell single-dose quantities of drugs—but this music store did. Reeser made a habit of selling some of whatever he bought at Hampton's here or at the Mexican restaurant a block up the street. It was a way to get back some of the money he'd spent...and to express his dislike of Hampton's.

Reeser disappeared through a shabby curtain into the back office with the kids. If they were testing the product, they'd be back there for a few minutes.

Hailwood looked back outside. Lenny and George were gone. He relaxed a bit and flipped through some ancient vinyl music records. There were collectors in Tampa who would pay a lot for these things. Someone could buy a few dozen and take them home to resell at a fat profit—but he wasn't organized enough to be that someone.

Who out here valued antique music enough even to support a store? The townies were too practical for such quirkiness. The townies and squatters didn't have the equipment to play vinyl records. Maybe digital discs; they worked on computers as well as music systems. But vinyl?

He walked toward the glass cases in the back of the shop, near the cash register. The real commerce of the shop was drug equipment. Not drugs themselves but every kind of pipe, bong, syringe, transderm patch and carrying case imaginable.

Reeser ambled through the curtains with a lazy smile on his face. "Okay, hoss. I'm done."

Valley Greens had blueberries on sale, so Hailwood bought a five-pound container. And some red apples. He also bought a bunch of tiger lilies for Kate. The girl in the flower section wrapped them in heavy paper and said if he kept them in water they'd last a week.

He paid for the fruit and flowers with Boston cash that he had in his front pocket. Reeser carried the apples. They probably should have brought the sled, after all. Distracted with counting his change and getting a comfortable grip on the blueberries and flowers, Hailwood didn't scan the street as they came out of the store.

Lenny and George were standing on the sidewalk. "You gent'men need some help carryin ya bags?"

Reeser answered, "No thanks. Short walk."

"Then hay bout a dolla for a workin man?"

That "working man" was an insult to the College boys. Actual working men didn't call themselves that; they were just men. Only grifters and trouble-makers *called* themselves working men. Hailwood looked past the squatters: "Sorry. No change today."

"What line of work you fellas in?" Reeser was making a mistake by engaging them. The "spare a dollar" routine was a trouble-making approach. Maybe they weren't broken—just acting.

Hailwood stood up straight, so he could get his Glock fast if he had to. Even though it was packed well, the backpack still made things a little awkward. He scanned the street, as his grandfather's security guys had taught him. He noticed that the smaller squatter was angling himself between Reeser and the curb, funneling Reeser toward the taller squatter.

Reeser kept walking. He was just a step or two from bumping into the taller one and seemed to be challenging him to move aside.

Hailwood didn't like the look of this. "Hoss...."

Reeser turned slightly and moved to squeeze between the two squatters. But this wasn't a crowded party on campus. The squatters might stab him, just for the bag of apples.

Sic Semper Tyrannis

The smaller squatter reached for something inside his flannel jacket. It was an ancient gun. A sawed-off shotgun. He pointed it at Reeser's stomach and hissed, "Jiss stahp, facker." He sounded like his was missing a few teeth. Gray goo was running down from his right nostril.

Reeser didn't stop. Maybe he hadn't heard the hiss. And he didn't see the shotgun. He turned his shoulder into the taller one and spun around, like a happy drunk pressing his way through a crowd. This confused the townies, who weren't expecting physical contact. The taller one grabbed Reeser's shoulders, but without much authority.

More importantly, the smaller one didn't shoot.

Hailwood focused on the hardware. That slowed things down.

The smaller one's hand was covered in a fingerless glove, which probably meant that it had been branded for a felony in Boston or some other City. Its index finger was on the trigger—but didn't squeeze. Maybe no cartridges in the shotgun? There were two or three beats where Reeser was struggling with the taller squatter and Hailwood expected to see the trigger finger twitch. It still didn't.

Hailwood had time to do something. He needed to free his hands. Keeping his eyes focused on the smaller squatter's trigger finger, he dropped the blueberries and the flowers. As gently as he could manage.

No one seemed to notice.

By now, Reeser *did* notice the shotgun pointed at his stomach. He inhaled visibly and twisted his chest backward. Panic.

Hailwood reached into his ski jacket and drew the Glock from his shoulder holster. He flipped the safety off and raised the gun to the smaller squatter's head. He set the man's ear in his sight and squeezed.

The shot was really loud. The smaller squatter's head snapped away from Reeser.

Reeser fell sideways, parallel to the curb. Hailwood drew aim on the chest of the taller squatter. He sighted the second button down from collar on the flannel jacket and moved a few inches to the right. He squeezed and there was another explosion.

The taller one didn't snap so quickly. His doughy face looked… confused. He stumbled back a few steps and then fell on his side—a mirror image of Reeser.

Hailwood looked back at the smaller squatter. He was lying half on the sidewalk and half in the street. There was a burst of blood and brains covering a stretch of sidewalk, an ancient newspaper machine and the front of a four-wheel trailer parked along the curb. His body was twitching.

Hailwood had never noticed the newspaper machine before. And he'd been walking past it for years. His next thought was to avoid touching the smaller one's blood. Gray goo could be contagious. Sometimes.

He closed his eyes for a second. When he opened them again, things seemed to be moving at normal speed. His ears were ringing; he rubbed the back of his neck, which was tight.

Kate's flowers. He looked down. They were fine, barely peeking out of the heavy paper.

Reeser had gathered himself up and was sitting Indian style on the sidewalk. He was talking, but Hailwood could barely hear him.

"…just happened?"

Hailwood answered—but couldn't hear his own words: "You okay?"

"I think so. Jesus. Jesus."

Fuckin' Ed and his two assistants came out from their store. This was the first time Hailwood had ever seen Fuckin' Ed from behind the glass. He was short. Practically a midget. And he walked with a severe limp.

"Fuckin' amazing. Two shots, two kills. Were you in the service, son?"

"No."

"Well, you're a hell of a shot. Ralphie, go get Markie. We need to get these riffraff off of the street."

He could hear himself a little better now. But everything still sounded tinny: "Careful, Ed. Think this one has gray goo."

"Fuckin' hell. Ralphie, Ralphie! Go get the yellow tape from the left side of my desk. We'll mark off this mess."

Hailwood had fired thousands of rounds at gun ranges. Always wearing ear plugs. And a couple of heavily-controlled hunting trips in the wilds around Tampa. But he'd never intentionally killed a living thing. Now, he'd killed two men.

It was easier than he'd imagined.

Five

Crowley's alarm rang at six-thirty and he rolled over the edge of his side of the bed. The night before, they'd been out at a fundraiser where he'd had one martini too many. Drinking those damned things was his foolish idea of grabbing some cheap common ground with M. And she'd seemed to recognize this.

When they'd gotten home, he'd fiddled around online with his growth portfolio. Never a good idea after three drinks.

He looked around and was shocked that she wasn't in bed. He doubled-checked his clock. 6:33. And she was awake?

She wasn't out on the balcony or in her bathroom.

He grabbed his bath robe and headed downstairs.

She was sitting out by the pool in the gray light of a cloudy dawn.

"What are you doing out here?"

"I couldn't sleep."

"Did you take a deepsleep?"

Her chair was turned toward the Gulf. But she couldn't possibly see anything from the angle where she was sitting. "No. I've stopped taking those."

"Hmm. Then maybe it's withdrawal." He pulled a chair out from the glass table, so that it was facing at about the same direction as hers. And he sat down.

"Maybe."

Her screen was playing a talk show hosted by a popular religious guru of a watered-down Zen sort. He was bald, with ink on his face. And he was talking about Human Rights for Jacksonville. But Margot wasn't paying much attention. She was just sitting there in her pajamas, facing the waves.

"I thought you were on the balcony *up*stairs."

She didn't say anything.

49

"Well, I'm going up to shower and shave. Do you want some coffee or juice or something?"

"No. Thank you."

This was starting to bother him. "What's going on, M? Did I say or do something wrong last night?"

She looked at him for the first time since he'd come down. "No. Not all. I just couldn't sleep and thought I'd come down here to listen to the waves."

"Are you sure that's all?"

She rolled her eyes and shook her head slightly. "Not everything is about you, Michael. I just wanted to sit here. By myself."

He didn't buy it. There was more going on; she was angry about something. "Look, maybe I've been more preoccupied than usual the last few days. But the trouble from the annual report is still hanging around and I'm—"

She held and open hand up in his direction. "Stop. I know you're under a lot of pressure. And I know you're working hard to do the right thing. I'm sure that, whatever you end up doing, it will be the best possible solution. But you know I don't really care much about any of that."

"Okay."

She turned back to face the water. "Go take your shower and get ready for the day. I'm going to have breakfast with the kids, as soon as Mrs. Dodds gets them up. Maybe you can have a glass of juice with us. And then I thought I'd go down to Sanibel for a day or two."

"Sure."

He did all that she suggested and was still in his office before eight o'clock. That gave him enough time to scan the news, read his emails and respond to seven or eight of them before his nine o'clock with Andrea Fournier.

She came into office with two assistants. Crowley asked his admin to close the doors and hold incoming messages for 30 minutes.

He got up from his last email response and walked over to the small conference table by the windows. "So, Andrea quick poll results on the League of Cities proposal?"

The younger of her two assistants handed him a screen that was set to Fournier's presentation. Crowley preferred this arrangement—rather than crowding his own infosystem with unwieldy reports, he liked people to bring along a screen he could read that was dedicated to their departments or topics. It was a delegating trick that he'd learned from his predecessor.

"You can see right away that the results are very good. 82 percent respond positively to the 30-word pitch, 56 percent very positively." She was clicking through to datagraphics that showed gender, race and socioec breakdowns. "These are some of the best numbers we've seen on anything in a while. Even demographic spread. Slightly better response among women, as expected. Bell-curve on income, again expected—though I consider that spread to be statistically meaningless. Now, let's look at the background questions."

He lost his focus a bit as she clicked through the questions about why people supported the idea of starting a League of Cities. They all sounded the same. People liked the idea because it would prevent war.

"…as expected, we get a heavy reference to trade wars from the households over one hundred thousand—"

"I've got it, Andrea. What about civic loyalty? Did you hear any worries that a League might lead to federalism or other kinds of nation-building?"

She clicked back and then down into the details of another category. "The resistance to nation-building is a small factor. But an intensely-felt one. Nineteen percent chose it as a reason they might *not* support the plan—and they averaged 8.6 intensity on that issue. If this were an election, I would tell you that's where your opponent would start."

This made sense. The opposition was always smart to begin its attacks on issues that bothered a vocal few the most; then, they would move on to issues that didn't bother people so much but bothered more. "And what would their cross-over issue be?"

She looked at him and raised her eyebrows while clicking back a couple times again. "There is one, Chief. It's not as clear as their starting point but I think it's there. And you're probably not going to like it."

"Who *likes* opposition strategy?" He smirked a bit and Fournier's assistants both took the cue to chuckle.

"Okay. Here we go. The best cross-over issue for your opposition—chosen by 41 percent and scoring 5.0 on intensity—is that you're making the proposal to cover your mistakes in the global investment markets. After that, everything falls off quickly to minor worries about cost. Now, a 5.0 just barely qualifies as a cross-over issue, but there it is. Plus, it's an *ad hominem* issue, which an opposition group would probably like. And it skews heavily among top income households."

His traditional base.

"Well, that's not good. They say the League will lead to nation-building and then they say I'm selling Tampa's sovereignty to bail myself out of trouble with the markets."

Fournier looked quickly at each of her assistants, as if for support, and then back at Crowley. "Something like that. But they'd be fighting an uphill battle. This is a very popular idea. And the intensity on their cross-over issue is iffy. If it were me, I'd think long and hard about going after an 82 percent positive with a 5.0 cross-over negative. The book says that's a losing gambit."

He thought about that for a moment. She was right, of course. But Fournier's flaw was that she was a by-the-book marketer. They were too conservative.

"I do have one question, Chief."

"Go ahead."

"If you do this, who *is* the opposition? We're not near a stakeholder meeting or proxy vote. There are no other ballot initiatives in the works right now. Despite what we found on the negative side of this one issue, your personal approvals are high. Who's going to fight this?"

He looked back at the screen. "Your answer's right here, Andrea. Top income households. Brahmins, yuppies and celebs. Probably my own board. It could get interesting. But I think it's the right thing to do. These were flash polls; how long until we can get some more solid numbers?"

"Seventy-two hours."

He got up and walked back to his desk and his own screen. "Okay. Then we'll meet again Friday and see if our good response continues. I've got a breakfast, so nine's probably out. Does 10 am work for you, Andrea?"

"Absolutely, Chief."

"Good. And make sure that you bring some data on how we should explain this idea, so that we get the best response right from the start. If we could push our initial response number up to 90 maybe we'd convince any naysayers to choose another battle."

"We'll have that data for you on Friday morning."

"Great."

Crowley was beginning to think about his lunch downtown at the Old Florida Club when his admin buzzed through with an urgent call. It was the Chairman.

He'd been expecting this for days. He took the call.

"Michael, how are doing?" The Old Man was eccentric about communication. He didn't like talking on a screen; he preferred the blind contact of a simple audio call. And he didn't like to make schedules, so he called somewhat randomly—though always toward the end of the week. Every call from The Old Man started abruptly.

"Grant. Fine, thanks. What can I do for you?"

"You can lower interest rates, for one. And tell me how the hell you're going to get your ass out of this jam with boys in Chicago and SoCal."

"Our lunch is at noon. Can't this wait until then?"

"No."

"Sounds like you've been watching your screens too much, Grant. The Cities aren't the problem. And I think that Petrella in Chicago has talked himself out of a job. So, I'm not too worried about that."

"Really? Have you ever met the man, Petrella?"

"No, I haven't. But I don't think I need to know him personally to see that he tried to get some cheap publicity for himself and forced his boss to issue a clarification to calm down their foreign investment."

"They're going to try to turn that back around on you. They're streetfighters in Chicago. That's why no one likes doing business with them."

"Maybe. But they're not going to have much success. It takes two sides to fight and we're not interested. Besides, I think they're more worried about their own situation. It sure as hell wasn't me talking about seizing private capital."

Silence on the other end.

Crowley was used to this. When the Old Man was finished talking about something, his verbal blasts just stopped. (Sometimes Crowley wondered whether the Old Man was reading his short chops from cue cards.) "I am more worried about the interest rates. And you know we've got the credit reserve that we've started to release, so the banks stop the consumer boosts."

"I see the news, Michael. You still plan to let it all out and then reel it back in slowly?"

"Yes."

"Well, I guess that's worked in the past."

"And I've got some other thoughts about coordinating monetary policy."

"Your League of Cities?"

"Yes. Among other things."

"Well, I'm on the record being against that idea. Regional groups are just federalism by a different name. Intellectuals always advocating them. Against the weight of history. But I suppose in the current situation, it might be well-received. When are you going to get this golden oldie out of mothballs?"

"I've got a speech at the City Economic Club in two weeks. I thought I'd announce it there."

"But you've already put feelers out your equal numbers elsewhere?"

"Savannah. Mobile. Memphis. Havana. Miami."

"Miami. Hell, that idiot Ramirez would sign a warrant for his own arrest if you told him to do it. What about Jones in Atlanta and Morial in New Orleans? They'll give you more resistance. And that doesn't even get to Jacksonville."

"I'm going to see Harold Jones down in Sanibel next week. But I'm going to bide my time with New Orleans. If involve them, we may need to involve Houston."

"Maybe. Of course, you can say whatever you want in a speech. And you can hold all the informal meetings you like. But if this League is going to have any actual policy-making powers, we're going to need to review the plan. Carefully."

"Of course. And we're probably going to want to put it on a ballot initiative."

"Maybe. Our board next meets in three weeks—a week after your speech."

"Yes."

"You probably planned it like that. We'll have a lot to talk about there."

"As usual."

"Yes. All right, I'll see you at noon at the Club?"

"Of course."

"Very good."

The Old Man was like this—always changing his approach in order to be as unsettling as possible. Crowley prepared his screen as usual for the meeting. The call might mean nothing. The Old Man might have a completely different agenda at the Club.

And he did.

The Old Man spent most of their lunch quizzing Crowley about the new spaceplanes. He had some interest in the speed-of-light tests the Space Agency was planning. Crowley wasn't prepared for that.

He did better when the Old Man's attention returned—again—to interest rates and exchange rates.

Five hours later, Crowley started his last meeting of the day by inviting Bert Barrett into his office and shutting the doors.

Barrett had been Chief Security Officer for long enough that most people in Tampa had forgotten what a controversial choice he'd been when first chosen for the job. Unlike most CSOs, Barrett didn't come from a military background. In fact, he'd never served in TSF or *any* Security Force. His background had been in the technology side of security. This didn't satisfy the public's familiar image of the ideal Security Chief as a gruff former officer.

Barrett was more corporate. He was a smart and obsessively detail-oriented man; and, despite his corporate demeanor, he had a ruthless streak that made him good at security work. He didn't hesitate to use the most effective tactics, people or information— even in ways or situations that would give ordinary managers pause.

When he'd first taken over as CEO, Crowley had had some questions himself about Barrett. But Barrett had steadily put those to rest, starting with a memorable quote from their first private meeting: "I see my job as defending this City's people and assets. I'll bend laws, break bones. But no one's going to harm us on my watch. And I'll count on you and the others to rein me in if I go too far."

That stuck with Crowley.

And, the truth was, Barrett didn't bend very many laws or break very many bones. In the scheme of things, security people were either ruthless or honest—and, though he'd probably hate to hear it—Barrett was honest.

Crowley gestured for Barrett to sit across from him at the desk. "So, what's on you mind, Chief?"

"Three things. First, drugs." Normally, Crowley liked to sit at the smaller conference table near the windows when he met with his direct reports. But he wanted to point out some report data—and Barrett didn't bring dedicated screens to these meetings. So, Crowley turned his screen so they both could see it. "In your last weekly crimestats, I noticed this number: A 70 percent increase in the number of Neurac arrests in the last 90 days. 90 days? There's something going on here."

Barrett took a pocket screen out of his jacket and made a few clicks. "There is. And it's still ramping up. Our projections see the arrests increasing another 320 percent in the next 12 months. And the pounds seized projections are even worse. So, the junkies are carrying more every time we catch them. In terms of pounds seized and arrests, it'll take over as the number one Category A illegal substance early next year."

"What's the explanation?"

Barrett put his pocket screen on the desk. "The markets speak, Chief. Neurac is the 'perfect' drug. It's potent. Relatively few side-effects. Out in the wasteland, no one's cornered production, so it comes in from all over the place. No single source for us to block. And plenty of profit for dealers."

In private meetings, Barrett was a proponent of drug legalization. He thought interdiction efforts were a waste of his department's time and resources. That kind of thing made for interesting cocktail party chatter, but the fact was that most citizens were against legalization. They considered drug laws one of the essential distinctions between life in the City versus life in the wasteland.

"Well, we've got to stay ahead of this explosion. I'll schedule in a public statement about it early next month, after we get the League of Cities plan off the ground. I'd like your crimestats people to get Marketing a complete file on arrests and seizures to date plus your projections, so we can draft the statement. Here comes the memo." Crowley made a couple of clicks and sent a formal request to Barrett and Andrea Fourier and their respective staffs.

"No problem. I can have a couple of narcotics detectives there to back up the image."

"Good idea. Now, on to Topic Two: My memo from last week on the naval hardware. This windfall that the TSF is getting from the special sales tax has got to even the field in the Gulf. I'm worried that your last naval readiness report implies it won't."

Barrett had picked up his pocket screen again as soon as Crowley started the question. "This isn't the kind of problem we can resolve in a few months, Chief. Another attack sub is good. The small hydrofoils help. But what we need are cutters. We'll get the *Javier Perez* in the water this Fall; but the next two are a year off at least. There's no short answer to the fact that we don't have the naval tradition of a Houston or a New Orleans. Are you expecting to go to war?"

The ease with which he moved to that question caught Crowley by surprise. Which, he assumed, was Barrett's goal.

"No. But I want to be sure that Tampa has the first position in the League of Cities that I'm proposing. And, as long as our friends in New Orleans have the Gulfport navy and our friends in Houston have the Galveston navy, it's going to be hard for me to convince everyone else of our primacy on the water."

Barrett rubbed a corner of his pocket screen against his chin. "… and airplanes can't block shipping lanes."

"Exactly."

"The last time you and I spoke about this, I suggested land-based sat-guided missiles. They can easily reach any point in the Gulf."

Crowley hadn't like the missile net idea the first time Barrett had suggested it. He didn't like it ay more this time.

Barrett could see this. "I don't have any other suggestions right now, Michael. If you give me a little while to chew on it, I'll see if there's a viable alternative for our new money. Maybe I can find something on the market in New England or over in the South China Sea. And bear in mind that what's available may be bigger than what we'd like."

This had come up before when they'd discussed buying ships from other Cities. The optimal boats for Tampa's needs were cutters and small frigates. Most of the inventory in the global used warship market was bigger stuff. And the TSF naval officers didn't like the bigger boats.

"Okay. Just make sure you keep this on the top of your list."

"I've got a good procurement guy in the TSF, a young Lt. Colonel named Ruiz. I'll put him on this top priority as soon as you and I are done here. We should have a break-down of what's available in a couple of days."

"That would be good. Topic Three: I've got a board meeting in three of weeks where I'm going to hash out the details of my plan for this League. I've had a couple of quick conversations with the Chairman about the plan. And his response is making me think I've got more trouble on the board about this than anyone has said. I'd like your ears and eyes to make a couple low-key surveys and let me know if I'm right to be worried."

Barrett didn't make any notes on his screen about this request. "Sure. Just focus on the League plan…or a general inquiry in the contentment level of the board?"

It was unusual for Barrett to suggest more intelligence than what Crowley requested.

"Well, shit, Bert. Have you already heard something?"

"Just what everyone who watches the news knows. The Brahmins are worried about a recession."

Six

Hailwood came down to breakfast just a few minutes before the ladies cleaned everything up. Taylor was waiting for him, drinking some coffee and reading his screen. He'd agreed to head into town with Hailwood to pay the assessment for the mess he'd caused when he'd shot the two squatters.

Taylor was a better wingman than Reeser would ever be. Business or pleasure. Taylor was older, more observant. And not a junkie.

"So, you ready to go pay the price of amity?"

"That's a strange way to put it."

"Why strange?"

"Why amity?"

"Well, have you thought through the results of *not* paying?"

"Yes, professor. I don't pay the fine. The Merchants' Association bans me and complains to the College. Some dean—probably Lieber—calls me in and threatens to boot me out if I don't pay. And I can forget teaching or anything else here."

"So you're being a good boy and paying to avoid all of that hassle. Amity."

"I went out with a girl named Amity once...."

This was an inside joke. It was a way to deflate any pompous word. One of the DKE initial rites involved the chant "Prudence or Trust." A few years earlier, when Hailwood and Taylor had been underclassmen, an older brother said "I went out with a girl named Prudence once. Impulsive bitch." He insisted he was being serious—he had gone out with the girl. But the comment was more ironic than he realized.

Now, any time anyone wanted to puncture the pretence of a high-minded word or phrase, he'd say "I went out with a girl named..."

They finished putting on their outside clothes and guns in silence.

When they were walking out into the snow, Taylor started talking again. "There's no justice in the wasteland, Terry. You just do what you have to do to get along. There's no right to property. People with the means arm themselves. There's no free speech. Everyone's too worried about giving offense."

"I don't mind paying the fee. Jon. It's just that the silver lining to the wasteland is supposed to be it doesn't have the sleazy corruption that the Cities do. It's supposed to be clean. But here we go, paying off businessmen. I could have stayed at home and done this."

"Yeah, but you'd never be able to lead the intellectual life you do on campus. You'd be complaining about the vulgarity of City life."

"No…yeah. I would."

Taylor laughed and stomped his boots on the clean sidewalks of the town.

The head of the Merchants' Association ran a ridiculously overpriced pay-per-call telecom store, where townies, squatters and anyone else passing through could rent screens by the minute. He was also the town Sheriff—though he didn't like to advertise this fact.

The store took up an old storefront along one of the side streets in town. It didn't need a prime position on either of the main streets. Using a screen wasn't an impulse purchase. The place was one big, open room with desks set in a classroom-like grid in the middle. It was reasonably clean but smelled bad, with the particular sharp stench of squatters who hadn't bathed in weeks. Or months. Two large townies—probably Sheriff's deputies—lounged menacingly just inside the front door.

Hailwood said he'd come to see the Sheriff.

Immediately, a Yankee twang answered from behind the desks, "Mr. Hailwood? Right on time. Thank you. I'm W.F. McEcknie."

It would have better fit the prevailing attitudes on campus if McEcknie were a porcine sleazebag, wheezing and coughing as he wheedled. But he wasn't. He was a careful, economical man running a profitable business in a wasteland town. He was thin and flinty and small.

The Sheriff invited Hailwood into his "office"—which was really just a cheap, pre-fab desk on an elevated platform near the back of the shop.

Sic Semper Tyrannis

There was only one person using a screen. It was an older woman, who had clearly been crying about whatever was going in the screen on her desk. It was impossible to see the details because each desk was protected on three sides by a 12-inch-high plastic privacy shield. But you could see the shoulders and head of the person sitting there—and the old woman was trying hard to keep her composure. She was dressed a little better than a squatter; but, when Hailwood caught a quick look at her square face, he could see she'd seen some hard living.

Prices for renting screens weren't posted, which meant McEcknie probably used a "sliding scale"—he'd charge different people different amounts, depending on how much money they seemed to have and how desperate they were to make a call. At home, that kind of thing was illegal.

Taylor wasn't paying any attention to the old woman. Or the prices in the shop. He was still keying on the big townies near the front door. Rightly so. They looked like they were used to dealing with trouble.

On campus, the security experts advised students against taking screens with them when they went into town. The main reason that students were robed and killed off-campus was telecoms. In the wasteland, people were starved for connections; they'd willingly kill someone for the few hours or days that they could use his screen before it was shut down.

The Sheriff's desk was very neat. Everything on it was organized into cardboard folder—except Hailwood's paperwork, which lay right in the middle. In plain sight.

"I'm sorry about this, Mr. Hailwood. I understand that these two were trying to rob you. But the fine applies, even so."

"I understand, Mr. McEcknie. Someone's got to pay for the clean-up. Maintaining the streets." That was a fairly true state of his mind.

In the days after the shooting, Hailwood had expected some dread or remorse to come over him. He'd expected his subconscious mind to reach out for justifications or excuses for killing two men. It was self-defense, etc. But none of that had happened. He felt no need for excuses, even to himself. He'd killed the squatters and would do it again, if the situation called. He knew this set him apart from most civilized people, who'd hesitate to kill. And that distinction was neither good nor bad.

"So, the total is $2,346.00 Boston. I can't accept municipal currency or corporate funds. It's got to be gold or an electronic bank transfer."

Welcome to the wasteland. The fine was *valued* in Boston dollars but the town wouldn't *accept* Boston dollars to pay it. And he accepted EBTs, because he had an EBT system as part of his business. No doubt, there'd be a convenience fee of five or 10 percent. Maybe more, for rich College kids who'd killed riffraff.

"Yes. Your letter made that clear. I've got gold."

"Excellent." McEcknie pressed a button or flipped a switch under the desk that locked the outside doors. Hailwood recognized the same muffled click that he knew from Hampton's.

In the same motion, McEcknie threw a stare—and nodded very slightly—to the deputies. They got up and each stood right behind one of the front doors, looking out into the street. Which was quiet.

Taylor looked quizzically to Hailwood. Should he walk over to the deputies or stay close? Hailwood made a subtle gesture with his right hand, palm down. Stay close.

The old woman on the screen in the middle of the room said something quietly to someone…somewhere.

Hailwood reached inside his shirt to the chest pocket of his undershirt. There were five ounces of SunBank coin there, wrapped in heavy paper. "Here are five ounces of first grade. Marked by Tampa SunBank."

He handed the packet to McEcknie, who opened it and placed the coins in a single layer on his scale. "Thank you. This will just take a second. And, if you don't mind, while we wait, I'll ask you to sign the citation. You admit no liability or wrongdoing, you simply agree to pay the fine as a complete satisfaction of any obligations on your part related to the incident last week."

That didn't make any sense. Why should Hailwood sign legal documents in a place with no legal system? The Merchants' Association probably had some sort of operating a agreement or ordinance. But who would enforce that? He looked skeptically at McEcknie but he wasn't sure whether the merchant/Sheriff would understand an ironic quip.

McEcknie slid an old scrib screen across the desk.

Hailwood scanned the screen. It said what the merchant said it said. And that was jibberish. But Hailwood thought about Taylor's talk of amity. He pressed his right thumb in the box at the bottom. He slid the device back without saying anything.

McEcknie looked relieved. Maybe he'd been expecting some ironic quip about the enforceability of a contract in a place with no legal system. Maybe he'd heard it a thousand times from a succession of College boys. He busied himself about the calculations. "Yes, here we go. Of course, the gold is fine. $2,487.13 Boston at this morning's quote. So, let's see, I owe you…$140.87 Boston in change. Unless you'd prefer New York dollars? I'm afraid I don't have any Tampa."

"Oh. No, Boston's fine."

McEcknie made the change in municipal currency out of his store's till. And he grabbed a paper print-out of the signed ticket from his desk printer. "Your change and your receipt. Thank you so much, Mr. Hailwood. And again, I'm sorry about the trouble."

Hailwood and Taylor left the shop as quickly as they could.

Going into town with Taylor wasn't as risky as with Reeser. Taylor had traveled a lot and knew how to keep alert to street traffic, both human and vehicle. Hailwood didn't have to worry quite so much.

"I feel like I need to take a shower, Terry. Can't tell whether it's the Sheriff or his deputies or the crazy woman on the screen."

"Yeah. I wonder when was the last time someone brought $2,500 in gold into that place."

"And he wouldn't take Boston dollars but was happy to give them out as change."

On the main streets, there were more signs of life. It was a cold but sunny afternoon and Pleasant Street had a few dozen people walking up and down. The place had a less sinister feeling than it had had a week earlier.

They kept a fast pace past the shops along the east side of the street, until they stopped for a moment while each looked over the spot in front of Hampton's where Hailwood had killed the squatters. It took them a minute because Hailwood hadn't realized how close to Hampton's it had actually been. Just a few yards away. No wonder Fuckin' Ed and his boys had materialized so quickly.

The details of the shooting had made it all around the campus in the seven days since. Hailwood had told the story dozens of times; Reeser, more. Groups of students from the College—not only brothers from DKE—had walked down Pleasant Street to check out the spot.

There weren't many obvious signs that anything bad had happened. But Taylor did point out a small patch of rust coloring, a couple of inches around, near the curb. From the smaller one. With the gray goo. "I'm still impressed that you dropped them with two shots."

"The tall one wasn't dead right away. He lay over by the bricks over there and coughed up blood for a couple of minutes."

"Still. I think I would have panicked more."

"I was pretty sure they were going to shoot Reeser. If anything, it felt like I was moving too slowly."

They walked a little more slowly after that. And, when they got to JB's, Hailwood looked back at Taylor bent his head toward the corner door.

"You sure you feel like pressing your luck, Dirty Harry?"

"Why not? I'm all square with the Merchants' Association. I've got their change in my pocket. And lighting doesn't strike twice. Usually."

"Okay. Let's get a drink."

Inside JB's, they went to the same spots where Hailwood and Reeser had sat a week earlier. The same bartender approached them. "Gentlemen. On your way back from settling accounts with Mr. McEcknie? Got enough money left for a drink?"

"Yes. We thought we'd duck in for a couple." Hailwood wasn't sure how much tension there was in the bartender's greeting. He hoped that his regular patronage had earned him some good will.

"Your money's good. But the first round in on the house. We weren't no fans of those two squats who tried to rob you."

This was the first time Hailwood had heard anything about the two men he killed. A part of him wanted to ask the bartender more about them. But that wasn't the best way to get information from a townie. Instead, he ordered a bourbon on the rocks and a glass of ice water.

Taylor ordered a dark beer.

When the drinks came, they lifted their glasses to their host.

And Hailwood slipped in a question, as smoothly as he could. "You knew those guys?"

The bartender shrugged. "Don't think there's much to know. Couple of low-life squatters. Not from around here. They came in a few times. We're always careful when squatters come in. I got the 12-

gauge eject button under the bar. But they had cash. And it's not my job to ask a man where he gets his drinking money." And he moved on down to another group of students in town from the College.

Hailwood and Taylor made eye contact with them—three guys and two girls from the second or third year. They nodded back and then huddled together to whisper gossip and figure out their order.

Taylor took a long drag on his beer. "I'm glad we stopped in. I've got something appropriate to discuss off campus. I'm leaving. Come the end of the semester."

"What? Fuck no. You should have at least another year. I thought you were going to hang out."

Like Hailwood, Taylor had completed enough courses to take a basic degree. But they were—or *Hailwood* was—staying two extra years to build enough credits to take an advanced degree. The advanced degree would allow him to teach at a college. Or at a City university, if he wished.

"Ahh, I don't know. The real world is calling. My mom is getting married again and she needs me to come home. Help run things. Take over the board seat. You know."

Taylor came from a propertied family in Cleveland. They'd been minor players during the Great Lakes Wars; and that's how he'd lost his father. Cleveland allied with Detroit, while one of its neighbors—Toledo?—allied with Chicago. Detroit got routed in the Second Peninsula Campaign and Cleveland had to give up assets and land to Toledo. Taylor's father, who'd backed the losing side, was given the choice of banishment or suicide. So, he killed himself and his family got to keep its property and seat on a humbled Cleveland board.

At least, that was Taylor's version.

But Hailwood believed it. "You. Sitting in board meetings."

Taylor shrugged.

Tampa wasn't so Draconian. It wasn't his hometown's style to give someone the choice between banishment and suicide. And maybe it was the worse for that.

Tampa could afford to be more relaxed; it was big and growing. Cleveland had been dying for 200 years. Propertied families in a place like that were much less forgiving about costly mistakes. "Besides, I thought your younger brother was more into the business stuff."

"I don't know. He doesn't want to. And my mom has started using the word *primogeniture* a lot lately. So, it's on me."

"I dated a girl named Primogeniture once...." Hailwood signaled for two more. "Okay. But what are you going to do with your days?"

"Make money. Help the City pay off its reparations. Find a nice house and pretty girl from a good family and settle down. Pattern of the ages."

"And you'll be happy with that?"

Taylor took a long pull from his second pint. Then he shrugged and took another. Then, "I'll read some history from the comfort of my den and contribute an occasional article to this or that journal. Maybe I'll teach a class at one of the City schools. The right kind of scholar."

This was another insider reference. On campus, people talked about deep thinkers who left the College to head back to boring lives in the Cities. The cliché was that they'd say they'd keep up their academic studies as amateurs—"the right kind of scholar." And then only be heard from when donating money.

"Jonnie. You're leaving me out here with a bunch of squatters and junkies."

Taylor had finished his second drink in three quick parts. "You have the passion for this life, Terry. I don't. I mean, I've tried to imagine staying. But I have to train myself to do it. Doesn't come naturally. I've always had it in the back of my mind that I was going back to the real world. I mean, what am I doing here? Studying wonderful shit that has no practical application? Playing beer pong? Fucking around with inch-deep debutantes?"

"Yes. Write that down. Because you're going to come to your senses in that comfortable den in a few years and *wish* you had it all back."

"Maybe." Taylor looked like he was getting ready to leave.

Hailwood signaled for another round. "You're a gentleman, a scholar and a jolly good fellow, Jon. And I've still got a few weeks to convince you that you're making a terrible mistake."

The idea of amity stuck with Hailwood for a few days.

The next day was a Friday and Hailwood had a narrow window of time between the end of his last class and when he needed to be on the road to see Kate. He'd stayed on campus the weekend before because of the fallout after the shooting. So, he had to make sure *this* trip went without any hitches.

Plus, he was giving two underclassmen a ride—which was better than driving alone. But it added two more potential screw-ups and delays.

In the midst of his packing, his grandfather called.

"Grandpa. I hope you don't mind that I pack while we talk. I'm heading out to see Kate."

"Driving?"

"Yeah."

"How's the Badger holding up?"

"Like a champ. I may never drive anything else."

"Glad you like it. Hard vehicle to drive in the City. But some do."

"Yeah. Hey, this is a really clear link."

"The Pegasus satellites."

"Of course. So, what's up?"

"I'm calling to find out your plans for the summer. Spoke with your mother earlier and she says you haven't been in touch."

He could have guessed that was what was happening. This was the first leg in one of his mother's multi-lateral non-apology apologies. She roped his grandfather into offering the olive branch. "Grandpa, you're breaking up a bar fight." One of his grandfather's many famous lines was never to do that. "I spoke with mother about ten days ago. And it ended in a rather hot argument."

"She's worried about you."

"Did you tell her about the shooting?" He'd sent a text to his grandfather, explaining what had happened and explaining that he was going to use five ounces of gold to pay the fine. He explicitly asked his grandfather not to say anything to his mother.

"No, I didn't. Wouldn't disregard your request. She's worried that you're not going to visit at all this summer."

"Yes. I know. That was one of the reasons we had the argument. I'm planning to stay up here and teach a summer course to incoming first-years. And maybe spend some time with Kate and her family in New York."

There was a long silence. Kate had been another—bigger—part of the argument. In her sideways manner, his mother had made some insulting comments about Kate.

"Your mother and I would both like you to come down this summer. She'd like to see you. And I have some family business matters to discuss with you."

He was finished packing. Now, the call was delaying him—but he didn't want to disrespect his grandfather by walking to the garage while the talked.

"No need to sound so ominous, Grandpa. You're okay? Health-wise?"

"I'm not going to be dead this week."

"This summer?"

"Don't think so."

"And mother's okay?"

"Yes. She's fine."

"Good. Of course I'll come down for a visit. But that's all it'll be. A visit. Probably for a week toward the end—mid-August. When it's nice and soupy down there. And I'll probably bring Kate. To be honest, this is where my last talk with mother went off the rails."

"It's no matter to me that you bring your girl. I'll be interested in seeing her again. Get to know her a little better."

"Good. Look, I don't mean to be abrupt, but I've got to get going. I'll send you and mother a note confirming my schedule for the summer term." Keeping the conversation short was the best way to handle the Old Man—but Hailwood realized he was coming across too harshly.

"I can send a plane up."

Then again, there were dividends to coming across too harshly. The Old Man was suing for peace.

Hailwood softened his tone. "Thanks. Let's play that by ear and see how the summer goes. But I'll be down there."

He felt affection for the Old Man and tried to be kind. Someone had to be. The problem was that the Old Man valued a certain hard edge.

"What you can do, if you're feeling generous, is wire a couple thousand into my SunTrust personal account. I don't get another distribution for about 45 days and this thing in town has drained me a bit."

"I'll make the wire this afternoon."

"Thanks much. And, Grandpa, don't let mother rope you into playing the peacemaker. A wise man once told me never to be the guy who tries to break up a bar fight." He was being a little heavy-handed to repeat the point. But, sometimes, the Old Man was distracted and need to hear things twice before they registered.

"Yes, yes. I know. Didn't send you up there to become an expert on bar fights."

"You sure?"

The Old Man laughed a little.

"Anyway, she said some nasty things about Kate. I told her that I expected an apology. And that's where we stand. There's no reason for you get drawn into this."

Another silence, not as long as the first.

"Understand. Have a good weekend."

"You too, Grandpa. I'll talk to you next week."

He got to the garage a couple minutes late—but there was still a little time to show the kids how the Badger worked.

The Mark V Badger was an amazing vehicle. Originally designed as a long-range armored infantry transport, it could move through dense underbrush and shallow river beds as easily as paved highways. Standard ground clearance was 28 inches—but the hydraulic suspension could boost that to 42. It had all-wheel drive and a nine-speed transmission—six forward, three reverse—that gave it its signature versatility. It sat eight people comfortably. The single-axle drive train was enclosed and virtually indestructible. All of its windows were bulletproof and laced with titanium micromesh netting to prevent penetration of just about any sort. And, with everything (except people or cargo), its curb weight was just under 10,000 pounds.

But its two best features were the engine and defense system.

The engine was a 600 horsepower Cummins VHT/Diesel turbocharged power plant. Its torque was so strong that you could put it in first gear and take your foot off of the pedals and climb out of the driver's seat…and it would rumble along at about 2 miles and hour. This was part of the defense system; it meant the driver could focus on the weapons system while the vehicle chugged through trouble. And the VHT technology mean that, in a pinch, the engine could run on just about any standard combustible liquid fuel—gasoline, methanol, synpetro and even rubbing alcohol or cooking oil.

The defense system was like something out of a jet fighter. The Badger had a 360 degree 3-D imaging/infrared recon system with a range of up to three miles in all directions. When the truck was moving, it generated a static electric field on all exterior metal surfaces. This field accomplished two things—it blunted the impact of any object and jolted the body of any person or animal that came in contact.

Finally, it was armed. Two Sanborn .30 caliber machine guns fired through the front grill and two fired through the rear bumper. A Peerless plasma cannon was mounted to a small turret that would rise up from the roof when activated. Plus, it had a Valkrye 60 millimeter mortar cannon that launched through the roof just above the rear hatch. The truck came stocked with a variety of Valkrye shells—anti-personnel, anti-tank, nerve gas, flash grenades and flares. Hailwood stocked the cannon with the anti-tank shells. Any changes or reloads had to be made manually from the rear seats.

This was really the main responsibility that passengers had. If something really bad happened—and Hailwood used more than the eight shells loaded in the cannon, they needed to know how to take the other clips out of the storage compartments under the backseats and load them into the magazine under the back floor.

The two kids riding with him were friends of Russell's. They both belonged to the artsy drug House (as opposed to the *druggy* drug House), which had pretty good relations with DKE. Hailwood recognized the kids vaguely.

"So, you guys ready for a quick drive over to Northampton."

They barked back a security-style "Yes, sir!" Had to be the influence of the truck—Hailwood himself never impressed anyone as a security type.

The kids both sat in the back seats. Hailwood put his jacket and backpack in the front passenger.

He told the kids to belt themselves in while he checked the engine, surveillance, navigation and defense systems. It took about 30 seconds.

The process of passing through the west gate in a vehicle was much the same as through the north gate on foot. They had to swipe their College IDs through a reader and press their right thumbs on a screen. The gate system scanned the barcode parking permit on the Badger's left front bumper and snapped still pictures all around. Finally, the security guard managed to put his screen down long enough to look them over and ask two questions through the speaker.

"Nature of your trip?"

"We're going to Smith to visit some friends for the weekend."

"Expected return?"

"Sunday afternoon."

With that, the gate in front of them and the larger gated doors swung open onto the Campus access road.

"Hang on. I like to drive fast."

He headed north from the College and cut through the town on Second Street—avoiding the Friday afternoon traffic on and pedestrians along Pleasant Street. This move had the added bonus of not passing the shooting scene and resulting in lots of questions from the young Sigmas about what had happened.

From Second Street, he turned west on Hampshire Road. This was a crowded residential stretch for a few blocks—but as soon as they passed the town limits, the sides of the road emptied out. There were just dirty snow drifts and occasional old houses that were either abandoned or used by squatters. Here, Hailwood pressed his speed up to about 60 miles per hour.

Hampshire Road veered southwest. About a mile out of town, it met Old Hadley Road, which was the main east-west artery in the area. As they approached, Hailwood tightened his scanner in to a one-mile radius and brought the closest Pegasus satpic of the streets up on his navmap. The Hampshire/Old Hadley crossing was one of three major intersections along the way—and the one where most accidents happened.

The scanner showed pretty good luck. The closest other vehicle was a half-mile away, heading east on Old Hadley. And it looked like he was leading a parade of cars heading to the College. Bit of a surprise, there. It wasn't football season and graduation was weeks away....

"Dude, when my tour group came up for my college visit last year, we saw the worst wreck up here at the crossing. Two cars just smashed the hell out of each other. And the fucking squatters were crawling all over."

College tours. Of course. That's what the line of cars was. A wasteland college tour, bringing high school kids up from the Cities. Hailwood had never gone on a tour.

"Were they dead?"

"Who?"

"The people in the cars."

"I don't know. They must have been. I mean, I only saw one guy. He was out on the grass and covered with blood. The guys in the other car didn't even get out. And the squatters were like pulling the wheels off the burning cars and shit."

"Welcome to the jungle."

Hailwood interrupted. "We're not going to give any squatters the chance to take a peek at us. See the navmap? The scanner places all the cars on the road. Here and here. And a bunch here."

"Yeah, I know about this stuff. My dad has a Badger Three. But it's got this version navmaps in it."

The turn from Hampshire Road to Old Hadley wasn't a sharp 90 degrees; it was something softer. He'd read somewhere that a good driver in a Badger could take a 90 degree turn at about 40 miles per hour without touching the brake.

He slowed down to about 45 as they approached the crossing. Like most major intersections, it was littered with shacks, horses and other motley animals and wraith-like squatters, ready to beg or burgle as the circumstances warranted.

"Okay. Let's see how fast we can make this."

Both kids screamed as he turned onto Old Hadley at 44 miles per hour, according to his speedometer.

"Damn, man. I thought I was going to shit my pants."

Old Hadley ran in a fairly straight line between campus and the Western New England Tollway. And then another 20 miles or so through another couple of small villages until it connected with the Old Massachusetts Turnpike, which headed into Boston.

Between the College and the WNET, there wasn't much other than the village of Hadley and the Hadley Mall. The village and the Mall were—effectively—one and the same.

The merchant associations in the Hadley Mall and the village both contributed to keeping Old Hadley Road clear and relatively safe. This was important, since they depended on people from Hartford and New York and other Cities to the south who came up to visit the colleges or watch the leaves turn and football games in the Fall. It was difficult to get most citizens to leave the safety of the Cities and venture out into the lawless wilds. So, the merchants had to make the trip reasonably safe.

But it was only *reasonably* safe. Two or three vehicles a month were hijacked along Old Hadley. And, while Hailwood was sure he could fight anyone who tried to hijack the Badger, it was always preferable to move fast and avoid the prospect.

Sic Semper Tyrannis

Hailwood opened the throttle up to about 85 and they blasted past the caravan of cars and small trucks heading the opposite way toward the College. They must have been going 35 or 40. Even with security vans at the front and back of the line, that was too slow to be safe.

"Hey, Terry, do you mind if we stop at the Mall for a bit?"

"I was planning on it. I need to pick up some stuff for my girlfriend and her house mates."

"Cool."

The set up at Hadley encouraged the stop. The town had a local tool booth collecting both ways along the road—but the exit and entrance ramps for the Mall attached to the road on either side. So, if you stopped, you didn't have to pay the toll.

The two kids bounded right out of the truck, as soon as Hailwood parked. He took a minute to call Kate but only got her voicemail. He said they were stopping off to pick up a few things and would be there in about an hour.

He set the alarm and followed the kids past six or eight cars, a dozen horses and a handful of security guards to the entrance. They had to check their guns between the first and second sets of doors.

"Terry, you definitely carry heavy. Why'd those squatters you shot even try fucking with you?"

It wasn't a great idea to talk about shooting people in a Mall.

"Don't know. They tried to rob us. Pulled a sawed-off shotgun on a brother. I waited a minute for them to take the stuff and go. But they didn't. I don't know what they were thinking. They may have been too strung out to be thinking anything."

"No. I mean how did you feel? Scared? Or charged?"

"I don't know. A little scared, I guess. Then relieved. I was glad they didn't shoot my brother. But I'm not even sure their gun was loaded. The main thing is that it's really loud. When you do most of your practice at ranges with ear plugs on, you forget how loud it is."

They didn't ask any more questions.

They agreed to meet back at the weapons check in 20 minutes.

Closer to 40 minutes later, Hailwood pulled the Badger back on to Old Hadley Road and continued west. The two kids were strapped into their seats, whispering to each other and giggling enough that he figured they gotten loaded at the Mall's cheap drug dealer. The one Reeser like so well.

He opened the truck back up to 85 and hoped he could keep the speed up for a while. There wasn't traffic on the road for a Friday. His nervousness to see Kate was picking up.

Then the surveillance scan started pinging. Less than a mile ahead, there was something large that looked like it was blocking the road.

He levered back on the speed—but the ping came into sight pretty soon. It was two or three vehicles that had gotten in some kind of accident. A lot of smoke—which meant burning tires. As they got closer, he could see that the cars had all been stripped already. So it had been a while. But they were still smoking. This must have been what spooked the college tour people.

To his relief, two security cars from the Mall were parked on the other side of the wrecked cars, waving the trickle of cars heading toward the College around the wrecks.

When he got to the scene, Hailwood drove around on the other side—his shoulder and out on the dirt a bit. The uneven ground caused the Badger to list notably to the right—but in a second, the hydraulics compensated for the angle.

Most days, he would have asked the security guys if they needed any help. But, this day, he was in a rush to dump off his passengers and see his girlfriend. So, he just made quick eye contact and nodded. The security guy did the same and waved them along.

"Dude, those cars have been stripped."

"I wonder where the squats are who cleaned them out?"

"The next crossing's just a little up ahead. And there's a camp there. I bet they heard the wreck and came running."

They were right about one thing; the next crossing—which was a road that went north and south through farmlands—was coming right up. Hailwood kept the car at about 35 and moved through it without stopping. But the hair on the back of neck still stood up as they drove past.

The squatter camp at this no-name crossing was big. And it was getting bigger all the time. For no obvious reason. Dozens of shacks. Horses. Cows. Sheep. Chickens. Broken-looking kids. He wondered if the accident behind them had been *caused* by squatters as a ploy to strip the people and vehicles.

Traffic got heavier as they approached the Connecticut River and the WNET. Most of it was moving the opposite direction, but Old

Hadley Road was just two lanes, so Hailwood kept his speed at about 50.

The third crossing was a small farmer's village right before the river. This place was not as dangerous as the other two. Instead of squatters' shacks, this crossing had about six farm stands and a fuel station/general store. He came to a complete stop and waved to the driver facing him across the intersection; a moment after that driver started straight through the crossing, Hailwood eased the Badger across.

A few hundred yards past the farmer's stands, the WNET toll booth blocked the road. Hailwood pulled into the open spot at the gate heading west and its iron mesh doors closed behind him. When the toll-taker—a woman—slid open her window, he rolled down his.

"Hi, honey. Just wait a moment while we run your plates. Are you T.S. Hailwood?"

"Yes, I am."

"Will you please swipe your driver's license and press your right thumb on the screen, as marked?"

He did both quickly and without saying anything.

"Thank you. Please wait another moment."

He put his ID back into his wallet and his wallet back into his shirt pocket. He noticed new signs stacked along the side of the road just ahead of the gate. They read "Caution. Property of WNET Corp." and looked like the might be going up as windblocks or walls to enclose the whole area.

"Are you going to use the Tollway or are you continuing west on Old Hadley Road?"

"We're staying on the Road, through to Northampton."

"Okay, then the bridge fee will be $5 Boston. Would you like to pay that in cash or credit, Mr. Hailwood?"

"Credit please," and he swiped his SunBank card in the same scanner he'd swiped his ID a moment before.

"Yes. Thank you."

The cars heading the opposite way—to the College—were stacking up on the other side. All this traffic couldn't be explained just by college tours. There must have been something else going on.

"Thank you, Mr. Hailwood. Please press your right thumb again on the screen in front of you. Perfect. Here's your ticket and you can get your receipt on the other side."

He drove past the WNET gate at a reasonable pace. Just under 35 miles per hour, the posted speed limit on all entrance/exit ramps and access streets around the WNET. Any faster and the automated machine guns would track the Badger. The main Tollway didn't have speed limits, but the WNET Corp. took the speed limits *around* it very seriously. The speed limits were considered part of the Tollway's security.

The kids in the back kept on whispering and giggling, like they'd been doing since they'd left the Mall.

The signs along the road inside the WNET compound were markets with billboards every few yards. Most of them read "Property of the Western New England Tollway Corporation—Do Not Destroy." The place was cleaner and better kept that the roads and towns in the wasteland.

This crossing area was a little more complex than most simple on-ramp/off-ramp arrangements. The Tollway tracked very closely along the Connecticut River in this area—and the WNET Corp. controlled the Calvin Coolidge Bridge that crossed it River. In all, this meant that the WNET Corp. controlled more than a mile of Old Hadley Road. And it applied its uptight corporate security measures to every inch.

Once the Badger was across the river, Hailwood kept it in the small middle lane, avoiding the two-lane access ramps that veered either south or north.

The vehicles blasting north or south along the WNET were high-rent swells coming up from New York and Hartford into the college area or south from Montreal into the busier Cities. People driving its length—from northern walls of Hartford to the southern walls of Montreal—would go almost all go over 100 miles per hour. High-performance cars would go faster than 150. As fast as they could through the wasteland.

"That sure is fucking loud," one of the Sigmas yelled.

"Yeah. That's why I put down the windows. When you take shuttle through here, you never get a real idea of how loud the Tollway is." This explanation was partly true...but Hailwood had really lowered the windows to drown out their giggling.

"How do the people who work here stand it?"

As soon as they came up from under the Tollway, the traffic was bad. The vehicles heading west from the WNET were mostly likely going to Smith or Williams, which was a couple hours west of Northampton. Hailwood knew some of kids from Tampa who were at Williams, so he'd made that twisty drive a couple of times. But not lately.

While they waited in line to get their receipt and pass through the security exit, Hailwood tried to time the Doppler effects of the vehicles. There was anywhere from six to 30 seconds between the end of one engine scream and the beginning of the next. But it was tough to pace this exactly, because different engines screamed in different ways.

Still, it was a busy day for traffic on the Tollway. Hailwood wondered what the wreck would look like if a guy in a multi-ton truck rear-ended another truck because he was giving it just six seconds of cushion at 125 or 130 miles an hour.

"Hey, Terry. Would you roll up the windows? That noise is starting to bother me."

"Sure."

As Hailwood reached toward the window controls, there was an explosion at the toll gate ahead of them. He looked up in time to see smoke rising out of the car at the gate.

"What was that?"

He closed the windows. Then, he doubled-checked the Badger's defense system and made sure the firing mechanism for his guns was adjusted so that he could start shooting quickly, if he had to.

In the seconds that his double-check took, three WNET Corp. security cars screeched up to the front of the gate. The security guards—there must have been five or six of them—leapt out of their cars, with guns drawn, and approached the smoking car. They barked and nodded among themselves. And one of them squeezed into the tight space between the booth and the car, then leaned in the window.

"What's going on? Is that driver dead or something?"

Before Hailwood could tell his increasingly irritating passengers that he didn't know, his screen chirped and saved the repetition.

"Hey, Terry. Where are you?" It was Kate.

"Waiting to get past the Tollway. Looks like there's some kind of trouble up at the gate. This may take a while."

"No worries. I just wanted to call you back cause I'm out of the shower and getting dressed. You've got plenty of time. Drinks start in Jody's room at six."

"Shouldn't take that long."

"What's the trouble?"

"Hard to tell. I'm three or four cars back. Sounded like there was some kind explosion in the front car."

"Jeez, Ter. Danger man. Don't get yourself shot."

The security guards were making detailed hand gestures to each other now. And another cruiser pulled up.

"Don't worry. I'm hanging way in the back. Low key."

"Yeah, blend right in. In your million-dollar truck. Tell you what. Once you get out of there and are heading into town, give me call. I'll come down and meet you at the Bedford Terrace entrance."

"That would be nice."

The security guards were gathered in three groups, all around the car—which wasn't smoking anymore. After a couple of minutes, a couple of the officers moved the pylons that shaped the lane heading to their booth so that it merged to their right. And a third officer started waving the cars that way.

Hailwood was far enough back that he wasn't directly involved in any of the hood tapping or waving going on in front. But the layout of the different toll booths meant that he'd be just about next to the troubled car when the line moved.

There was no one in the booth for their new lane. So, the Badger ended up stopping just a half-car length behind the troubled car. And—since they were higher than most vehicles—he and the giggling Sigmas could see right inside.

The car was a low-key sedan. Or had been. There had been two people in the car, but their bodies had been beaten and burned into bloody pulps by…something.

Hailwood looked for signs of a bomb. There didn't seem to be any. Instead, the passenger side was pressed inward and back at several dozen points. The windshield and windows were gone, but there was a lot of glass *inside* the car. This didn't look like a bomb. It looked like someone on or near the tool booth had fired a large-caliber machine gun at it.

"They shot those guys."

Hailwood scanned the booth. It didn't have noticeable gun ports. So where had the shots come from?

"Jesus. That's cold-blooded." The giggling Sigmas saw something he didn't.

"What are you guys looking at?"

"That big-ass machine gun on top of the toll booth."

He looked again and saw what he'd missed before. Above the toll booth in their previous lane was a big-ass machine gun on a scissor-style telescoping mount. The mount was also articulated somehow, because it was extended at a strange angle above and in front of the booth. It was positioned to have a clear firing line into the stricken car—through the windshield and driver's window. "That's amazing. It didn't sound like a gun blast. It sounded like a single explosion."

"It's one of those ultra-high-speed TEK cannons that they use on jet fighters. It's so fast you don't hear 'rat-a-tata-tat.' You just hear 'whump.'"

"That's what we heard."

"I wonder what they did?"

"Terry, man, just get us the fuck out of here. I don't care how tricked-out this rig is, if they pull one of those fuckers on us, we're dead."

"Calm down. Not planning on jumping the turnstile. And unless either of you has some bad business with the WNET, we'll be fine." While he said this, he moved his left hand toward the mortar cannon launch keys and pressed the "Arm" button. Just in case there was trouble with the security guys.

"We've got junk, man! From those drug dealers at the Mall."

"These guys don't give a shit about your drugs."

"But I mean we have a lot, more than—"

"Hey, man. Be cool. You heard what he said."

The security guards must have gotten some kind of word from their bosses. They broke up from their little groups and headed in several directions. A couple opened the trunk of one of their cruisers and got out a big yellow tarp—no doubt, to cover the damaged car. Two others climbed the steps up into the toll booth in front of the waiting cars.

Hailwood looked in his rear-view mirror. Cars were backed up on the Tollway exit-ramps from both directions, more so from the south. The security guys had to get the cars moving again before traffic backed up onto the Tollway proper.

Hailwood could see clearly into the toll booth ahead. The two security guards were working there—not toll clerks. That was a bad sign. Maybe they were expecting more trouble.

The gate raised for the first car. Hailwood noticed that one security cruiser was now posted on the outside of the gate, facing the access road into Northampton. Its engine was running. And there were two guys in it. Definitely looked like they were expecting more trouble.

The gate raised for the second car. Two more to go.

"Dude, I think I'm going to piss myself. If those guys find out how much shit we've got…"

This kid was the one who might do something stupid. He was the smaller of the two…and did more of the talking. Hailwood stared at the *other* one in the mirror. "Hey, brother Sigma, you need to calm your buddy down there. These guys. Don't care. About. Your fucking. Drugs."

"I've heard stories about cops pulling people over just to steal their drugs."

"Yeah, and I've heard about sex killers who lop off your head and fuck your esophagus. But that's not going to happen *here*."

When his turn came, Hailwood rolled down his window and handed the ticket to the guard who was working the register. "What the hell happened over there?"

"Securtee matta."

The other guard, who was scanning cars behind the Badger added, "They sure wasn't jess skippin' the toll. Ah tell ya that."

Hailwood laughed, which seemed to put the ticket-taker at ease. He smirked and offered a little more. "Coupla bad guys. Anakists from ahp noath. Tryin to fak up the One-ette. But ya didn't heah that heah. Ya rahceet. Thanks for ya bizniss."

Anarchists trying to blow up the only major vehicle passage in this part of the New England wasteland. Now that was irony. The WNET was the only thread of corporate power…of corporate presence…in the whole region and some shithead radicals wanted to damage it? Their real enemies were the Cities on either end of the Tollway.

And *one-ette*; that was how townies said "WNET." Most City people and college kids said the letters.

"Noss cah."

"Thanks. Good luck with those assholes."

Two miles and one hard curve later, the security officer at the Smith parking lot—a heavyset black woman who'd been working there since Hailwood had first started dating Kate—recognized him and scanned the Badger quickly.

He was able to find a space in the covered part of a two-level lot near Kate's House. This was a rare find for a visitor on a weekend and Hailwood figured it was karmic repayment for a weird and stressful drive. He left most of his weapons in the truck, which had a good anti-theft system and was relatively safe in the parking lot. This way, he had only his Glock to check at the security point at the pedestrian entrance.

He made sure he went first, in front of the Sigmas. They had more to check and—frankly—had a bigger risk of getting their drugs confiscated by College security than by the WNET guys.

He pushed his way through the old-fashioned turnstile and she was waiting for him, as promised.

The things you noticed first about Katherine Kelly Byrne were her height and her red hair. She also had green eyes and double dimples when she smiled…but those things took a little longer to see.

She dressed well. Not as blandly preppy as so many young women at Legacy Colleges. She was from New York and had her City's chic reputation to maintain. Hailwood called her style "eclectic urban couture." A base of classic upper-end fashion, flavored with a dash of gothic romance and a dash or two of bohemian funk.

This day, she was wearing wool, pinstripped slacks under some kind of blue-gray antique military overcoat. A white scarf wrapped tight around her neck and her red hair loose to her shoulders.

And she wasn't a fragile little fashion waif. She was nearly six feet tall and curvy. She'd played field hockey and basketball in high school and still had some of that muscle.

What Hailwood liked best about her were the things that took longer to discover: Her irony and her lack of the usual female neuroses.

He watched her intently as she walked toward him. And when she got close he hugged her hard and spun her around a couple times, without saying anything.

Then: "I feel like Odysseus. It's taken so long and all my psychic energy to wash up on your shores here."

"Well, you don't have any suitors to kick out. But if you'd been another 15 minutes…."

"Please. After the week I've had, don't even joke."

"Okay. Come on, let's get back to the house. We'll have time enough to freshen up a little bit before drinks and dinner."

Freshen up was her code for having sex.

Seven

"...the League will create stability for Tampa and its citizens. It will allow commerce among the Cities around us to go more smoothly and with less risk for merchants and businesses. It will create—"

The Old Man cut him off, "Michael, we've all heard your speech. We know your pitch. This meeting is for something more. What we want to know is what you're going do specifically to get interest rates under control."

Although his mouth and hands moved furiously, the Old Man's eyes stared hard and still at Crowley.

There were many layers of conniving going on in the board room. Crowley didn't want to spend the whole meeting talking about his plans for establishing the League. The truth was that his plans were still not ready for a detailed debate. But he wanted to make the board members think the League was his main priority, so that they would stress interest rates and drug stats—topics he was better prepared to discuss.

"—create more stability, which will calm the fears that some money-center banks have about a trade war happening here. We've been lucky to avoid any serious trade war for almost 40 years. And I strongly believe that the Great Lakes and South China Sea trade wars continue to be a major background cause of rising interest rates."

This point was valid and true. He made it mostly to take control of the meeting back from The Old Man.

Board meetings were usually like this: A battle between the CEO and someone on the board—sometimes the Chairman, sometimes another board member—for who would run the meeting.

Crowley knew of other top managers who just allowed their boards to control the agenda. But those people didn't get much done. Or didn't last long. "Gentlemen, that concludes my brief introduction. Now, if you care to, please see your screens for agenda item number one."

The big screen behind him also flashed the main agenda page. He took a quick drink of water. He wasn't even noticing how often he did this anymore.

"As the Chairman has pointed out, a number of you have let me know that increasing interest rates on all forms of consumer lending are a primary concern. Let's take a look at facts as we have them." He clicked through to detail pages. "Clearly, rates are up. The Tampa Banking Index standard consumer finance rate is 7.75 percent as of today. That's up from 7.25 percent one year ago and 6.90 percent 18 months ago. The trend has been steadily up for six quarters. Before that, we'd been in a tight range of between 6.75 percent and 7.0 for nearly six years. The last time we had a TBI standard rate of 7.75 percent was nine years ago, during the height of the Mississippi River trade wars and our own ag recession. But I'd like to point out—as you can see in figure 1.3—interest rates had been high for almost four years prior to that point."

The Old Man interrupted again, "Bah. We don't need a history lesson, Michael. We need to know what you're going to *do*."

Crowley thought he noticed the Old Man looking at Chambers, as if he could threaten Chambers into taking his side. "Before we drill down in to action points, I'd like to make my case for why I think we're seeing higher rates."

He drank some more water and went back to his presentation. "So, let's go back 13 years ago and see what happened. At that point, almost two years before the Mississippi River wars started and at least a year before our weak ag numbers came in, rates took a climb from the 5.5 percent range to the 8.75 range. At that point, the board's biggest concern was consumer finance defaults. And there was an increase in default rates—but that's not what triggered the recession. It was more like a leading indicator of the trouble that came later."

Crowley took a quick look at the room. They were all—even the Old Man—looking at their screens. That was good.

The Corporation of the City of Tampa had 11 men and women on its board of directors. This was a small number for a large City. Other big Cities—New York, Chicago, Houston and Southern California—had 30 or 40 directors.

Sic Semper Tyrannis

Crowley was always happy about his small board. It meant less corruption and faster decisions. Frankly, it also meant less hassle for him. He could usually count on SunBank Chairman Bartholomew Saul and SpielbergDisney CEO Than Tran Everett. A little less certainly, he could count on support from Mike Baumann, whose family ran BSX Energy Storage, and Cardinal Menendez. The head of the physicians' guild occasionally sided with him, depending on the issue. Finally, two of his managers—Chambers and Sandoval—also sat on the board.

"I think a lot of the same factors are at play in our economy right now. I know that some of you are concerned about default rates going up. And I respect that concern. But bankruptcy and banishment from the City are big incentives for consumers to avoid defaulting. I think that the capital markets are expressing their concern over more general risks."

The Old Man interrupted again: "Bullshit. The major risk is a spike in defaults. I was on this board a decade ago when Harry Turner refused to release the City's credit reserve. And that made the Great Ag Recession worse that it needed to be."

The Old Man's angrier-than-usual behavior made his arguments sound more like a cranky crusade and less like reason.

Crowley's reliable allies gave him a bloc of about half the board. On most major issues, he only had to convince one or two swing votes to support him. (There were also three non-voting members, citizens selected at random for 90-day terms. Permanent members dismissed these short-timers as *stiffs*. But Crowley was good at using their presence to manipulate votes his way.)

The Old Man's complaints had an air of desperation about them. He *knew* that Crowley was well-positioned with the board and he was afraid this meant no one would listen to him about the defaults.

"Again, I think that what the capital markets are really seeing is the possibility of another round of trade wars. I think the heated reaction to some of our recent, and fairly mild, comments about Chicago and the Great Lakes region is an example of this."

The Old Man was making eye contact with Bill Franklin, another old timer and "independent investor" on the board. Franklin had been a lawyer at one time but now he was just rich.

There were several of these deep-pocketed investors on the board. They represented the Brahmins, people and families wealthy enough that they didn't have to work...even as executives. They invested, which meant that—either directly or indirectly—they financed consumer debt. *Unsecured* consumer debt. This was meant loans that covered everything from clothes to personal screens to music to cups of overpriced coffee. Through various convoluted financing schemes, the Brahmins made huge profits underwriting all of the borrowing. But the business left them terrified of interest rate spikes and personal bankruptcies. The things that had ended the Federal Era.

They weren't going to be satisfied with his strategy, no matter how well constructed. They wanted to see one thing.

"As executives, we all know that we live in the present. In order to buy us time to deal with the global issues that are pushing interest rates up, we need to relieve the pressure for Tampa right now. So, please go to Figure 1.7a. Here is my plan for releasing the full amount of the City's Strategic Credit Reserve in the next 15 days."

This was what the old guys wanted.

He drank more water.

"Because I think the upward pressure is global and political—and not based on any specific piece of local economic news—I believe the best use of our money and credit guarantee is to make a bold statement. We'll let the cheap money circulate and do its job against the spike. And then, starting in 45 days, Matt Chambers and I will review the credit flow numbers every week and start reeling our reserve monies back in a little at a time, as needed. To prevent inflation or any other signs of an overheated economy. Any questions?"

One of the three civilians raised his hand. "Why release all of the money at once. Can't you release a little at a time, and see what happens?"

Perfect. The question played right into Crowley's counter-programming against the Old Man's attempts to hijack the meeting.

"That's exactly what my predecessor did 13 years ago. When Chairman Hailwood says that CEO Turner did nothing, he's exaggerating a bit. Turner released small amounts if the City strategic credit reserve. But these small gestures didn't do anything—which made him hesitant to release any more. It made a kind of vicious cycle that eroded the market's perception of the credit reserve's importance. I think, if we're going to have any hope of making a dent in the rates, we need to make a bold statement that we think interest is too high. But, here, let me take this moment to give the podium over to CFO Chambers, who will explain the details of our big release."

After Chambers' talk, they moved on to a discussion of the Neurac problem. Bert Barrett explained the reasons why the drug was booming and said that doling out harsh penalties for importers was the best approach he knew to stunting its growth.

Agenda Item 3 was their plan to use the special tax money to buy a couple of frigates from Macau. Macau needed cash and a temporary lull in the South China Sea trade wars meant it could afford to sell some of its warships. There was going to be some bidding; but Crowley belied Tampa could offer the highest price. Barrett stepped up again for details.

Item 4 was the trouble that some Tampa companies were having with the titles on the real estate in Cuba. Some were saying that any purchase of real estate or assets on the island was potentially fraudulent. The Shark handled this one.

The Old Man didn't like the Shark. So, he interrupted that presentation with impatient questions about "crooks and scammers" all over Cuba.

The rest of the meeting went smoothly, until they came to the last item *Item 9: Plans for Establishing a regional League of Cities.*

"Chairman Hailwood has made the point that you all have heard my sales pitch for the League of Cities. And that's probably true. But I have one piece of information that isn't broadly know. I already have firm commitments from the presidents of Miami, Mobile and Memphis to participate. And I've contacted the presidents of Atlanta, Cuba, Jacksonville and Charleston. If I get those commitments, then I think we have the essential pieces in place."

This time no one interrupted. So, he let his last statement stand for a moment. "We don't need to take any action on this matter now. I'm just making a status report. And I expect that I'll have a document for the board's review at our next meeting."

In all, they'd been in the room for nearly three hours—with only one 10-minute break near the middle. Crowley expected that everyone had either been talked or listened out.

Or maybe not. Franklin, the Old Man's old buddy, inhaled loudly and started talking in his loud monotone: "We hear these plans about trade zones or Leagues every few years. Not from our own President—until now—but Tampa's growing, so I guess it's our turn to take the lead in big ideas. But these Leagues never go anywhere; and I think I know why. Leagues lead to nations. Nations lead to regulations. Regulations lead to conflict. Conflict leads to war. Global war."

No presentation. No data. He was going to derail a major plan with his wrinkled wisdom. This was the arrogance of Brahmins.

"I'm an old man. I've seen a lot. And I know two things. One: Most people will live just beyond their means—no matter what *their means* means. Two: Nations consume wealth. They don't build it or even protect it. A smart investor can make a lot of money from these observations. And a smart executive needs to remember them, too."

Another one of the Brahmins chimed in: "The borrowers usually go for these nation schemes because they think they'll get something free out of it. That if Tampa leads the way, it'll be able to tax Jacksonville and Mobile and Memphis. The problem is Jacksonville and Mobile and Memphis all think the same thing. Someone will end up angry. Memphis will say 'We put in X and only get out Y. We've been robbed.' And they'll declare war. Not trade war. Real war."

"I think we all understand your feelings about nation-building," the woman from SpielbergDisney didn't speak loudly. But she spoke with authority. She was accustomed to people listening to her. "But we have to think about the long term as well as the short. And I think Michael has made a convincing case for City instability being a cause of our steady interest rate creep. It agrees generally with the conclusions that our economists draw. Michael hasn't asked for a formal ratification of a treaty here. He has updated us on his efforts with the proposed League. He has told us to expect a treaty or more formal document for review about the time of our next meeting. On this matter, he has performed his duties as an executive. I think the substantive debate about this League is for another time; but I will say now that the interests of sovereign Cities and global capital flow may not be the same."

The impressive thing about Than Everett was that this wasn't a prepared statement. She spoke like this off the cuff because she *thought* like this. In full paragraphs. And who she was helped quiet the old men. Somewhere deep in their ancient psyches, they felt it was ungallant to interrupt or contradict an attractive, soft-spoken woman.

Half an hour later, Crowley called the meeting to a formal close and had lunch brought in. The menu was seafood salad, chicken cordon blue with mushroom polenta and a pear tarte. Plus wine. The old birds shied away from cocktails at the lunch hour, but they would drink white wine anytime…all the time.

The conversation around lunch turned to much friendlier matters. Gossip about well-known people. Sports. Celebrities. Travel.

Crowley didn't have to do much to shepherd the small talk. It always seemed to manage itself.

He was happy with how the meeting had gone. His plan for managing the City strategic credit reserve had overwhelmed the Old Man's bickering and won unanimous board support in a formal vote. He'd preempted the criticisms of the League, so that they would be positioned to approve its ratification at the next meeting. He'd sounded the alarm about Neurac and gotten board approval for the new war ships. All in all, it had been a successful morning's work.

About 2 o'clock, the executives—the board members with real jobs—started excusing themselves from the table.

Crowley took the chance to go to the men's room with Bart Saul as the banker left for the day.

"So, Bart. How fast will you put this cheap money to work."

"Very fast, Michael. Very fast. This will be a good shot in the arm. But that's not the most impressive thing about this meeting."

"Oh?"

"No. The most impressive thing about this meeting is the way you handle Grant Hailwood. My goodness, man. I don't know what I'd do if I had him nipping at my heels every time I tried to make a presentation."

"Everyone says that. I guess it's all I've ever known."

"Well, one of these days, I'm going to get special dispensation to bring a few of my young execs in here and watch a meeting. You are a lesson in boardroom composure."

By 2:30, the room had dwindled down to the Brahmins and the stiffs. Crowley checked himself and vowed not to use the word *stiffs*—even to himself. Deep down, he liked the idea of opening the board to ordinary citizens.

The Old Man was into his second bottle of wine and deep into his favorite telling of how Crowley was not his first choice for President. "…he was an impressive kid. Bright. Intuitive *and* detail-oriented, a rare combination. Lewis-Lake executive profile ratings through the roof. But he was only 30 years old and was the Chief *Marketing* Officer. The better path is about ten years older and coming out of finance."

"So why did the board hire him, Chairman Hailwood?"

He wasn't sure why, but Crowley always felt obligated to stay at these post-meeting lunches until they were finished. Many times, he'd gone through the ritual of calling a car to take one or two of the old Brahmins home. While that didn't happen at every lunch—he'd gotten better at cutting off the wine—there always seemed the chance. And some of the old guys were pushing 100.

Taking the opened bottles away would seem like an insult to the directors who were still talking. No matter how old they were. So, he sat with them and rode out the last bottles.

Franklin had taken over the story: "Market forces. Houston was talking to him about coming there as President. The age didn't mean anything to them. And then this whole thing started where other Cities—Boston, Seattle—said they'd fire their Presidents to bring him in. We realized that we had more value here than we'd realized. We didn't want to lose him…so, it was up or out. We chose up."

"Well, everyone in world knows you chose right. I mean it's so interesting to hear these stories. I barely remember President Turner. It just seems like we've always had the youngest, most progressive CEO in the world."

Crowley couldn't stand to let this pabulum continue. "I'm far from the youngest. The new guy in Milwaukee is younger. So is the woman in Dublin. And there are four or five in Asia that are younger than *those* two."

The Old Man looked at him and smirked. "You've been much more than anyone might have expected. You know, you may think I don't like you—but it's my job to keep everyone sharp. And that starts at the top."

Crowley poured himself some Pinot Grigio and said "Cheers to you, Mr. Chairman."

The wine tasted terrible.

There was a sailboat cutting a trim figure out in the Bay. His kids would be home from camp the coming weekend. Taking them out on the boat would be a good idea. He wasn't the most attentive father. But he liked having quality time with them.

Eight

"Generally, repetition is overused as a rhetorical device. A speaker who uses it more than once or twice or other than as a thematic link runs the risk of sounding like an evangelical preacher screaming at a tentful of sinners in the wilds of Arkansaw. You have to use it carefully. Think of Cicero's *In Catilinam*. Churchill's *Battle of Britain* speech. Palin's *Against Islam*. In each of these speeches, the repetition is subtle and thematic. The listeners probably didn't even notice the repetition, consciously. But it's there, subconsciously, emphasizing."

The 20 kids in his class were a mix of new students who'd be starting in the Fall but tested poorly coming in and students who'd finished their first year but scored badly on finals. Like most schools in the wasteland, the College had a great reputation and tradition… but actually filling seats was always a challenge. So, sons and daughters of alumni or eminent citizens could send kids who needed extra help. The College promised them admission and a least two years of close support. Getting a degree was another matter.

"Okay. That's it for today. A long Part One recap for a hot Friday morning. As you know, I'm out of town next week. I welcome you all to enjoy some of the time off—but advise you to review your Part One speeches and analysis. The first half exam will be on Monday morning the 10th at nine a.m. sharp. No excuses, no delays, no tales of woe. Repetition right there. Any questions?"

One nervous hand in the back of the room. "Ah, were you serious about us needing to know the Cicero speech in Latin?"

"Well, this is not a Latin course. But it never hurts to take at least a look at a great work in its native language. And, if you're having trouble in Latin, going back over some of the speeches after you've studied them for Rhetoric can be a big help. There usually a lot easier to understand. At least they were for me."

Sic Semper Tyrannis

Hailwood—like all students tapped for the faculty—was taking his first step by teaching summer school. The courses were assigned randomly. Or as randomly as a small department could manage. He'd gotten two Rhetoric classes and one Logic class. He was enjoying the rhetoric and suffering through the logic.

As a student, he'd done better in logic than rhetoric.

"But the test won't reference any Latin in it?"

"No. All the questions will be in English. And I expect your answers to be in English. Have a good week. And I'll see you again in ten days."

When the last student ambled out, Hailwood was done for the first half of the summer and officially on vacation.

In one of his classes, he had a couple of first years who'd been out to the DKE House for parties during the previous year. He'd told Dick Cody—the Composition professor who was his mentor for the summer—that this made him feel a little odd.

Cody had just laughed. "You've got to get over that, Terry. On a campus as small as this one, there's social or sexual incest in every classroom."

That bit had stuck with him. And not in a good way.

Hailwood woke up at about six and climbed out of Kate's bed. The fan was humming but it was still muggy. He was amazed at how hot it could get so quickly, so far north.

Her house was mostly empty for the summer. Like his College, hers stayed open all year long—but most students and teachers followed the ancient tradition of taking the summer off. Kate stayed to finish her honors paper on the neoconservative movement in the late Federal Era. It was supposed to be done at the end of the coming semester, but she'd switched advisers during the year and fallen behind. It was beginning to look like she'd be around one more year.

He put on her bathrobe, grabbed his shaving kit and craned his neck out into the hall. This was as much ritual as necessity. There were only three or our other girls on her floor for the summer. And, at six o'clock on a Saturday morning, it was good bet that were all still asleep. Still, this was a girl's dormitory, so he'd grown accustomed to being considerate.

No one was up.

He ducked into the floor's bathroom and switched on the lights. He had plenty of time to shower and shave uninterrupted.

Fifteen minutes later, he came back into Kate's room and turned on the lights. She groaned.

"Come on. Get up. We've got to be at Windsor Locks in two hours."

"All right, all right. God, you're already showered? Inhuman."

"Just anxious to make a plane. Hell hath no fury like the Old Man if we hold up his jet."

"Okay. I'm up."

And she was.

The night before, after they'd come back after midnight from a boozy dinner with one of her classmates and that girl's finance, Kate had feigned a girly panic over clothes for the trip. This was Kate's sense of irony—to draw contrast to her friend with whom they'd just had dinner. That girl was *really* girly.

"How will your mother expect me to dress?" Even talking about clothes, she was precise.

He shrugged and clicked through some fashion/gossip pages on her oversized wall screen. "Who knows? If you wear a formal dress, she'll be in a bathing suit. If you wear a bikini, she'll be dressed to meet the Queen of England. Just remember: It's hot and humid down there. This is the worst time of year to be in Tampa. We're going to be in the water as much as possible."

He read about divorcing movie stars while she put together a bag.

This morning, after she'd taken a shower, she looked great in a pink polo shirt and some kind of Indian print skirt. Preppy shirt with hippy skirt was becoming her signature style.

"You look good."

"Thanks."

The sun was up and getting hot when they walked to his truck. She stopped for a minute to put on her sunglasses—she'd grabbed a cup of coffee on her way out of the House. He turned back to watch her and made a point to memorize the image.

His expressed anxiety about meeting the plane was only partly right. He was excited about bringing her down. And this excitement had sneaked up on him—he hadn't felt it even a week earlier. This was her second trip down to his home. One trip might be a fluke; two was intentional. A serious thing. Plus, they were going to try to meet his father. Which was a big deal.

When he picked up his gun from the security check, he cleared his mind of giddy happy thoughts and focused on business. The airfield was an hour south on the WNET, past its major crossing with the Old Mass Turnpike. Counting the time on and off the Tollway, they were going to be cutting things close.

Once they were in the Badger, he ran the diagnostics on the surveillance and defense systems as quickly as possible. He cracked his neck while he waited for the ready prompt.

She watched him, bemused. "Terry, calm down. They'll wait for us."

"You're right. I'm just excited to get going. Feels like a proper vacation."

"So the trips into town to meet *my* family aren't proper vacations?" *Town* to her was New York.

"Nope."

"How about the trip last year to the Bahamas with Taylor and Reeser and their girlfriends?"

"No. Wacked-out Spring Break trips aren't proper vacations."

"How about the trip up to the White Mountains?"

"Hiking is also not a proper vacation."

He pulled out onto Northampton's Main Street and east toward the WNET. The roads in town were busier than he'd expected. People were bringing stuff into town for the Saturday farmers' market.

She took a sip from her cup and then said, "It's the plane."

"What?"

"You think this is a 'proper vacation' because your grandfather is sending a plane."

"What? No. It's a proper vacation because you and I are traveling together, like real people. And we're going to have a week together doing nothing but relaxing."

"Maybe we won't like each other so much after a week together."

He shook his head and sped up toward the WNET access road.

There were no misguided radicals delaying things at 7 o'clock on a Saturday morning. Hailwood had the Badger heading south on the Tollway in a few minutes. He set the navmap image sweep for maximum range. There was only one vehicle ahead of them and it was moving faster than they were. He sped up to about 130 and set the speed on cruise control. Next, he clicked up the engine standards—temperature, oil pressure and cylinder displacement. At a steady high speed, these were the most important things to watch.

At this speed, they'd be there in plenty of time.

Kate was looking out her window at the hills to the west.

"What are you thinking about?"

She shuddered a little. "I've liked it here. But lately, every time I go away, I'm not sure I want to come back."

"And if I stay to teach?"

She shrugged. "I don't know. I'll stay. But I want to live in New York. I really think that's where I belong."

"We can do both. There are some teachers who split their week in Boston or New York. Townsend. DeMott, of course. Andy Parker."

"I know. I get that. I don't see how the *others* can live out here permanently. I mean, people at home think that the wasteland is all wild and free. But it's the opposite really. People are only free in Cities. Out here, everything's like a prison."

Another car came onto the navmap from behind. And he was going *very* fast. Maybe a WNET security guy. Hailwood switched into one of the right lanes to give the screamer a wide berth.

"The conventional wisdom on campus is that people burn out on the back-and-forth, eventually. Too much travel."

"Maybe so."

"Sounds like we should take some flying lessons and get a plane."

"See? There you go. Planes again."

"Well, if you want to live the jet-set life, you need a jet. Just make sure you make a good impression on my grandfather."

"I always do."

The car passed them on the left. It *was* a WNET security cruiser, with his lights flashing. And he was going well over 150. Hailwood had read that the Tollway was designed for a top speed of about 150. If you drove any faster, the grooves in the surface and the slight angles of turns could cause your vehicle to lose control. The cop was pressing that limit.

A second car blipped on the radar, going just as fast.

"Jeez." Hailwood pointed to the navmap screen.

"So, what's going on?"

"Lots of cops. Again." He switched on the radio and set it to security band. Then, he pressed the scanner to search for whatever frequency these guys were using. All it found was static.

The second car, also a WNET cruiser with lights flashing, blasted past. Hailwood checked the radar screen again. The blip that had in front of them from the start was still just inside his sweep—the first cop had already driven out of range. So the cops weren't chasing the vehicle in front of him. They were after something farther south.

"I just hope whatever they're chasing is on the other side of Windsor Locks."

"No kidding. Don't like the Tollway having so much trouble."

They drove past the dead city of Springfield and crossed the Connecticut River again. They were starting to get close to Hartford; the Windsor Locks airfield was just outside of Hartford's northern walls.

"So, when should we start the flying lessons?"

"As soon as we get back."

Whatever the cops were chasing was beyond the airfield, because Hailwood and Kate reached their exit without seeing anyone else.

There was no standard security at the airfield. But there was a long, straight access road with a sign that read "Bradley Field. Authorized passengers and guests only" at the entrance and robotic machine gun nests every few yards along the way in.

She sighed as they pulled in. "These things make me nervous. What if there's some sort of computer virus and they start shooting."

He nodded in agreement, "I think that's the point."

The parking garage at the other end of the access road had the usual double gate entry and exit system. And the security guards there took the usual scans and pictures of the vehicle and occupants.

Hailwood was of two minds about what to do with his guns. Even though the parking structure seemed secure, he didn't want anyone stealing the plasma pistol or his antique shotgun. Kate said she could carry her bag to the terminal. So, he packed up his black canvas gun bag with everything, including the small Ruger.

He set the alarm and rigged the mortars to blow 15 seconds after anyone turned the ignition. Even if a thief could hack the alarm, the mortars would be a nasty surprise. He wasn't sure how much of the parking structure would be left.

Like most airports in the wasteland, Bradley Field didn't have any commercial flights. So, the general aviation desk was the busiest part of the terminal. And it was a mess. All three employees were involved in some intense discussion with a half-dozen Asian corporate types whose charter was running late. Finally, a young girl working at one of the freight desks came over to help. She sent Hailwood and Kate to the right gate, where a sleepy-looking young guy said their plane had just called in to confirm approach. They could walk out to the tarmac, if they liked.

They did.

Hailwood didn't recognize the plane that pulled up a few minutes later. It was bigger than the usual jets and hardly made any sound. When the ladder door dropped open, he did recognize the man who stepped out. Steve Masterson had been flying for the Old Man for ten years. Or more. He was, technically, a Tampa Security Forces officer. But you'd never know it. He'd been on permanent detail to the Chairman. His job was flying dignitaries and VIPs around—and, from that, he'd developed the air of a big-shot executive.

"Hello, young Mr. Hailwood. Greetings from Tampa."

"Mr. Masterson. It's been a long time. This is Katherine Byrne."

"Miss Byrne."

The whole conversation took place in yelling voices because the engines of the plane hadn't shut down. But they could hear each other because, even running, the engines didn't make much noise.

"Do either of you have bags that need to be stowed below?"

"I brought my guns." And he raised the black bag a little.

"You can carry them on." Masterson was impatient to get back in the air again.

"We taking off right away?"

"Yes. We got a head's up from Hartford control a few minutes ago that this whole area north of the City is hot for Security action this morning. That's something I'd rather not stick around to hear more about."

"Okay. But don't you need to refuel or something?"

"Nah. If we're running low, we can stop somewhere else, closer to home. And not in the wilds."

They climbed into the plane in front of Masterson and were greeted by a woman flight attendant. This plane was much bigger than the ordinary ones. It looked like it seated more than a dozen people comfortably.

"What's the equipment, Steve?"

Masterson was closing the hatch. "Eccheviera 806. Built down in

Buenos Aires. Logged some hours, but a nice ride. Your grandfather got it about six months ago. Syndicated it as a timeshare with a few other heavy hitters."

This was something the Old Man had been talking about for years. He loved discussing the fine details of financing expensive equipment. Hailwood never paid much attention because it seemed like a sideways kind of boasting—and somehow beneath his grandfather.

"Always working the angles."

"Yes sir. Now, if you all excuse me, I've got to get up front. This is Janice, she'll take care of you."

"Sure, Steve. It's good to see you again."

"Pleasure's mine, Mr. Hailwood. More time to chat once we get wheels up."

He had a copilot up front. And, as soon as Masterson shut the cockpit door, the plane started taxiing.

The baggage compartments were under the sofa-style seats, so Hailwood stowed their bags and buckled himself into a sofa next to Kate.

She just grinned at him and rolled her eyes.

The flight attendant brought them two glasses of champagne and the rest of the bottle in an ice bucket that fit in a lowered part of the table next to their seats. "We'll be taking off in a minute, so I thought I'd bring this to you now."

Kate thanked her. "Happy proper vacation, Terry."

"Happy proper vacation, Kate."

As soon the plane left the runway, Masterson pulled into a very steep ascent. Kate's eyebrows raised well above her sunglasses as she tilted her champagne flute so it didn't spill. After two or three minutes of this, the plane leveled out and banked sharply to make an arc toward the east.

Masterson's voice came back from the cockpit. "Sorry about the sharp take-off, guys. But if you look right below us you can see that something serious is going on down there."

He was right. With the plane banked for its turn, they could see a fire and big plume of smoke right where the WNET ended at the north walls of Hartford.

Hailwood sat up to get a clearer look. It was hard to see exactly what was going on, because of all the smoke. But the fire seemed to be burning right at the last toll gate before the WNET fed into Hartford. And it looked like it was burning the entire gate structure—across all eight lanes, both directions.

Kate grabbed his forearm. "Glad we're out."

Three hours later, they landed at the private airstrip in St. Petersburg. Masterson had made it without refueling. Hailwood thanked him for the flight and said he appreciated the fact he was still flying for the family.

Hailwood had told Kate that he wasn't sure what to expect at the airport. They could be greeted by anything from a complete line of Tampa politicos to…no one.

In fact, Victor—his grandfather's *major domo*—was waiting for them with a car and driver. "Mr. Terry. So good to see you. Or should we call you Professor Hailwood?"

"Not Professor yet, Victor. Not for a while yet. You may remember Katherine Byrne."

"Miss Byrne. Yes. Nice to see you again."

The driver took their bags and Victor gestured toward the back seat of the car. "Do either of you need to freshen up here, before we get on our way? We are about 30 minutes from the House."

Kate shook her head no.

"Looks like we're okay, Victor. Let's go."

"Very good."

Victor and the driver sat in front. The car was more a town car than a limousine; there was no separation between the seats.

"We can stop anywhere along the way that you'd like, Mr. Terry. But we have prepared a late lunch for you and Miss Byrne at the house. And your mother is waiting for you."

"Absolutely, Victor. Let's go home. We have all week to hang out in my old haunts."

He squeezed her hand and she squeezed back. But she was staring out the windows too intently for any small talk.

They drove south from the airfield to the Sunshine Skyway—the signature bridge that spanned the mouth of Tampa Bay. It rose high enough over the shipping lanes that the largest supertankers in the world could come in and out of the Bay without having to lower their masts or interrupting the traffic crossing. The bridge had been knocked down by storms, incompetent ship captains and enemy missiles throughout Tampa's history; but the City had always built the thing back. As his grandfather had always said, "The Skyway is a sign."

Twenty minutes later, they pulled through the electric gate of the house. They coasted up the driveway to the circle in front of the main entrance; it was less than two hundred yards from the gate to the front door. The compound was wide and flat, a boomerang-shaped parcel along the northeast tip of the first island south of the mouth of Tampa Bay.

There were six buildings on the property: the main house, two small guest houses, a detached garage (with a coach house above), a studio-apartment "cabana" next to the swimming pool and a greenhouse that was plumbed and wired. The three houses faced the water. The cabana did, too. Sort of. The garage and the greenhouse were set back from the water, among the Australian pines.

Since he'd been a young teenager, Hailwood had lived in the cabana. He'd move out in a boyish effort to seem more like a man. But the move had gradually become practical. Sleeping with Kate under the same roof as his mother and grandfather would have seemed awkward.

His mother met them in the terrazzo-floored foyer of the main house. "Terry. How good to see you. Please don't be embarrassed by my hug. And, Katherine. You look beautiful. Here, let me look at you. What beautiful skin! And your hair. Now, listen, while you're here visiting during our dog days, I want you to be careful about how much sun you get. Redheads mustn't burn...."

She was wearing a vaguely Asian tunic and slacks in the style popular with middle-aged women. Her hair was up—or maybe it was cut—in a flattering way. Normally, Hailwood liked the look of long hair on women...even older women. But he had a stubborn memory of his mother in the depths of some manic trough or drug bender with her long hair loose, stringy and gray. Not a happy thought.

He'd rather that his mother appeared coherent than attractive.

She'd taken Kate by the arm and was walking her past the dining room and kitchen area, toward the living room at the back of the house. But with the water view.

He'd gotten in a nasty argument with his mother a few months earlier. About Kate. His mother had called Kate "a social climber from New York whose parents sent her to Smith to land someone like you." Did she even remember that she'd said it? She was most vicious when she was loaded on the Neuroplex that her doctors kept flowing through her veins. But she rarely remembered those episodes—or at least she rarely admitted remembering them. So there was a Sisyphusian futility in pushing the points.

He'd tried to roll the rock over her comments about Kate. To no apparent effect. But now his mother was acting the part of a gracious host, so maybe something had stuck. With his mother, who could tell?

He felt it was safe enough to leave them alone for a bit. She wouldn't insult Kate to her face. He ducked back out to the car, where Victor and the driver were just getting to the bags in the trunk. "Victor, you're putting these in the pool house?"

Victor got the point right away and nodded in agreement. "Yes, sir. We'll put the bags in there. I'll make sure it's cleaned up...."

"Clean up?"

"...from last time."

"Last time? I didn't think I left it in that much of a mess."

"Not you, Mr. Terry. You father, Mr. Michael. He was here a few weeks ago."

"My *father*? I don't believe it. Did my grandfather know?"

"Sure. He was here. They had meetings together."

"You must be joking."

"No. Your father was here for a couple of days. And he stayed in the pool house."

"And they didn't try to kill each other?"

Victor hissed out a short laugh. He'd been around for the big fights, in the old days. "No. They talked in private. A couple of times. Didn't seem like trouble."

That was news.

And, as usual, the Old Man seemed to have extrasensory perception. Hailwood had been planning a trip south, so that his black-sheep father could meet his blue-chip girlfriend. Somehow, the Old Man had beaten him to the punch.

For a second, he reconsidered staying in the pool house. He felt a flash of Oedipal awkwardness. But he shook off the hesitation. The pool house was his space. And he wanted Kate to know where he'd lived and slept when he was growing up—so, when he bored her with tales of his youth, she'd have a picture of what he meant.

When he got back to the living room, Kate and his mother were standing next to each other and looking out the two-story windows at the mouth of Tampa Bay. It was the start of a busy weekend and the traffic out on the water was heavy. Sailboats, container freighters, yachts, small fishing boats, hydrofoils heading down to Havana.

Kate was doing most of the talking, explaining her political history/art history double-degree and he plans to work in a gallery in Manhattan—with an eye toward starting her own. It was a familiar plan, but Kate discussed it so well that it seemed original.

"Mother, Kate. Can I get either of you something to drink?"

His mother didn't drink and Kate was tired, so they asked for a cranberry juice and a Diet Coke. He fumbled his way through the wet bar and found what they wanted. And a beer for himself.

He convinced them to sit in the overstuffed sofas that faced each other in the middle of the room. Kate sat on one with him; his mother sat on the other, facing them across the big knee-high coffee table. Everyone was quiet for moment.

"You know, Kate, you might be surprised to hear that I have a Master's Degree myself. In Botany."

"Terry has told me. And why should I be surprised?" Kate was being a sport without seeming condescending. That was a tough balance—and one that had always given Hailwood problems.

"Well, people in Tampa usually keep their children close for university. They don't send them away to the legacy schools up north. I think people here are too practical to see the value in ancient liberal arts."

Kate rolled her eyes. "You make Tampa sound so provincial. I know several young women at school who are from Tampa. And you sent Terry there."

"Well, yes. But the Hailwoods have been going there for generations. If it had been my choice, I'm not sure I would have let him go so far away. And, now look what's happened. He's going to stay up there in the wilds—and I'll be lucky to see him for a few days, once a year."

"Mother, you make it sound like a desert. The country up there is beautiful. And the colleges are little Cities of their own."

"Your mother's never come up visit?" Kate was laying it on a little thick; she knew his mother had never come up.

"Me? Oh, Gods. No. I'm no adventurer. I have my friends and my work at the orchid gardens and walks on the beach. That's my life.

I'm not meant for the wilds. Just promise me one thing, Terrence."

"Yes?"

"Even when you're building a life for yourself as a deep thinker up there, you'll still come down and visit us here. I'm worried that you'll advance and years will go by when we don't see you." Her lower lip trembled in way that struck Hailwood as evidently false. He'd seen that gesture many times before.

"Mother, I'll always come back. Come on, this spot is one of the most beautiful places in the world. And I grew up here. I'd be a fool not to come back and recharge from time to time. Though I should time it better and visit during the winter holidays—when it's a little less swampy."

His mother stared blankly at his for a second and then turned out to the water. She was angry at him about something…or just acting as if. He was out of practice telling the difference.

He looked over to Kate, who was raising her eyebrows in her default look of teasing reprimand. Maybe the crack about swampy weather had come across as too nasty. But it was better not to say anything. Even though he didn't really need it yet, he went back to the little refrigerator in the wet bar for another beer.

While he was gone, they started talking again. He decided to let them go and took his beer out for a walk around the back deck in the swampy afternoon air.

When he came back into the living room, his mother said that Kate was looking tired and that dinner would be at eight.

Hailwood guided Kate around the deck from the main house, past the pool and to the pool house. At one point, the pool house had actually contained the elaborate filter and circulation systems for the pool and outside hot tub. But now that machinery fit into a black box the size of a suitcase stashed to the side of the deck.

Since Hailwood had been a boy, the pool house had seemed like the best building in the place. It was a two-story octagon, with a living room and kitchenette on the first floor and a large wrought-iron circular staircase to the bedroom and bathroom on the second. Both floors had high ceilings—and the ceiling in the bedroom vaulted up to an octagonal skylight 14 feet above the bed.

On each floor, three of the sides facing the Bay were floor-to-ceiling glass. The effect was being in a cabana that was open to the water.

His mother had let him move out here during the summer between seventh and eighth grades. It was the same summer than his father had left for good. He'd lived here through high school and during breaks from college. The first time Kate had visited, they'd slept in separate rooms in the main house. But that felt weird. And required a silly amount of sneaking around. This was better.

After they'd collapsed together on the big bed, Kate said, "Do you have any idea what an apartment like this would cost in Manhattan? Millions. Tens of millions if it was near Central Park."

"Yeah. I've always figured this was a good back-up. No matter how badly I fucked up in life, I could always come back here and be a loser in the high-rent district."

"That means it's your home."

"Yeah."

They screwed around and slept for a couple of hours. A little before seven, they dug their bathing suits out of their bags and went for a swim. They were dressed and back in the living room by 7:30.

His grandfather was already there, sitting in one of the overstuffed sofas with his cocktail, reading his screen. He stood up as soon as they both were in the room. This was better etiquette than the Old Man usually showed. He was behaving for Kate.

He was wearing a black mock-turtleneck shirt, black khakis and well-worn brown leather boat shoes. And he was wearing heavy, black-rimmed glasses that Hailwood had never seen on him before.

This was the weekend look of a 50-year-old CEO trying to act like a 30-year-old up-and-comer. On his grandfather—a 90-year-old Brahmin investor—the outfit looked a little ridiculous. A seersucker suit would have been more age-appropriate.

But age appropriateness wasn't a big consideration for someone who worked so hard to look so much younger than he was.

The Old Man had had so much anti-aging therapy and nanobot work that his face had the generic handsomeness of an animated character on some screen show. It was hard to see what he'd actually looked like as a younger man. He'd recently stopped combing his hair over the bald spot that covered most of the top of his head. Now, he was trimming him hair very short and embracing this naked head. Perversely, this made him look younger—which meant it couldn't have been a spontaneous effect. Some high-priced image consultant had probably recommended it.

Sic Semper Tyrannis

The Old Man's eyes sparkled as he shook hands with Kate. The bastard. All he had to do was get around an attractive woman and his whole personality changed. He went from being one of the most vicious smart guys you've ever met to a conscientious charming guy.

Hailwood envied his grandfather's ability to turn on personal charm like a switch. He hadn't inherited that skill.

While Kate and his grandfather were chatting, Hailwood went to the wet bar and made another batch of martinis with his grandfather's shaker.

"So, Terry. Enough pleasantries. Do you really expect to stay up there? In the wasteland?" Among his many achievements, the Old Man was an attorney who—in his youth—had been a prosecutor for the City. He'd resigned after a few years to manage the family's affairs. But he'd always kept the prosecutor's demeanor.

Hailwood wasn't daunted. He'd been having these talks with his grandfather since he'd been a boy. "Yes I do, Grandpa. I've been tutoring summer school. And they've asked me to tutor two classes this Fall. I'll finish my advanced degree sometime during the coming school year and Jack Townsend is recommending me for one of two tenure-track spots that'll open in the Logic Department next summer."

The Old Man looked tilted his head back and looked down his nose at Hailwood. Standard gesture of evaluation. "Well, congratulations. That's an achievement, I suppose. I've never met Professor Townsend. But, even though I'm not the most enthusiastic alumnus, I try to keep up. I've read some articles he's written—just popular things—and I've read *about* him, of course. From what I understand, a true *prima donna*. With all that that entails. Did you have to kiss his ass to get his support?"

Hailwood didn't rise to the bait. He poured Kate a drink and then one for himself. He offered the shaker to his grandfather, who made a quick *no* gesture with his head.

"I genuinely like the guy—harem of wives and all. And I think I'll be good at the job." He tapped his glass with Kate's and they both drank a little. He slurped a bit. She didn't.

"I don't think that you have to worry about Terry, Mr. Hailwood—"

"Please, call me Grant."

"Thanks. But that would be weird. Terry will make an excellent

105

professor. He's powerfully well-read. And he's absorbed his logic training so completely that he's hard to be around. Sometimes."

His grandfather twisted his neck slightly and made a "charming" smile that seemed a little forced. Looked more like a grimace. "Some say that's a family trait."

Hailwood directed the conversation to Kate and what her plans were. The Old Man didn't seem to mind.

Kate's "Thanks, but that would be weird" was very good. She'd done more with one firm brush-off than the rest of the Hailwood family had done in three generations.

His mother came down around 7:45. She was dressed in loud print dress that was designed to wrap around her like peacock feathers. Again, this was a current style; but she'd looked much better earlier in the afternoon.

Hailwood got his mother a club soda with lemon and a fresh batch of drinks for the rest of them. This time, his grandfather nodded *yes*.

Kate and his mother were sitting in one sofa, talking. Hailwood sat on the sofa next to his grandfather and started his second martini. This one went down more smoothly. "So, Grandpa. How are things going downtown? I don't read the news as much as I should—but our man Crowley seems to like walking on the edge."

His grandfather drank some of his martini and raised his nose. "Very nice. When did you learn mix a drink?"

"Trial and error at the DKE House."

"DKE. I'd forgotten you were a DKE." He drank more. "You're here at an interesting time, Terry. There's something rotten in the state of Denmark. And we're going to have the denouement in the next few days."

"You always make these things sound so ominous, Grandpa. And then I read in the paper that the City's budget projections were off by 0.3 percent or something piddling like that."

His grandfather turned the corners of his mouth down in a theatrical sneer—this was also a familiar gesture. The sneer wasn't really mean-spirited. It suggested secret knowledge (which the Old Man always had but never shared). "T'isn't minor."

Victor announced dinner right at eight. It was a chopped salad followed by stone crab bisque and main course of New York steak and rock shrimp. (His mother had grouper.) There was a bottle of

NoCal red—Hailwood and Kate drank most of it. Dessert was a key lime sherbert.

"Well, Victor has really done it. We've touched all of the bases of the classic Tampa menu for you, Katherine. Anything more and I'd feel like I had to leave a tip."

She laughed a little, one-syllable laugh. "Mr. Hailwood, I don't know where you found you staff. But they are amazing. You mustn't let any of them go. Ever."

"Oh, I know. Victor's going to carry me out of here feet first."

The Old Man offered to move back to the living room but the women both said they were happy where they were. So, after the staff cleared things away and opened the French doors along Kate's side of the room, they had coffee at the table. Hailwood went to the wet bar in the living room and got a glass of Scotch with a big club soda back.

Everyone took a turn, but Kate did a lot of talking. She told them about her family and growing up in New York. They'd heard most of this before. Then, she moved on to some new terrain: how she and Hailwood were trying to figure out how to split their schedules between the College and the Big City.

The Old Man jumped on the idea of flying lessons. "Flying your own plane is a great thing. It's something that more people should do in this life. My first wife—not Terry's grandmother but Charlotte, to whom I was married in my twenties—was a pilot. She was an amazing woman."

"What happened?"

"She died. But not while flying. She died. And then I married Terry's grandmother, Margaret. She was an amazing woman, too. More of calming influence on me. But I always missed the flying with Charlotte."

This was the most direct—and insightful—description Hailwood had ever heard his grandfather make of his two wives.

"I think taking lessons and flying is a great idea. Terry, get the certification first. Then, if you need any help getting a good plane, just give me a call. Hell, you can fly yourself down here for holidays and vacation."

His mother didn't say a word about flying. But she didn't have to. Hailwood knew she would be "concerned" about such stuff. She stayed around for another few minutes and then excused herself to go to sleep.

The Old Man stayed around to talk Tampa gossip. But most of his funny stories were wasted on Kate—who had no idea who most of the eminent persons were.

Hailwood tried to move the conversation back to more general politics—partly for Kate's sake but partly to see if he could coax any more details about this "denouement" from the Old Man.

"Grandpa, don't you ever think about what it would be like if we had real elections? I mean, if nothing else, wouldn't that make all of the intrigue a little more…meaningful?"

The Old Man smiled and shrugged and looked over at Kate. "Katherine, this is an old chestnut of Terry's. He's been bugging me about 'real elections' since he was knee high."

Hailwood copied the Old Man's shrug. Both of them wanted Kate to know this was all in good fun. "Well, there's always been all this gossip and back-and-forth. I think that happens because the political process is controlled by the Board. Politicians want to campaign—but in our world they do it underground."

The Old Man drank some coffee and flashed a steely smile. "Democracies lead to bureaucracies. That's what ended the Federal Era. I'll take anything over bureaucracy. Fascism. Dictatorship. Hell, I'd take a king."

"But Tampa has bureaucracy, Grandpa."

"No. Read your history. Nothing like the late Federal. Nothing. We're small potatoes—a footnote—compared to them. You've been spending too much time listening to romantic nitwits at college. Governments aren't designed to assure individual freedom. They're designed to facilitate an exchange. Physical security for massively concentrated financial power. We give citizens security; they give us the ability to do things that we couldn't do any other way. Cutting edge medical services? Genetic research? The space program? And then, if we're not complete cement heads, we can leverage that concentrated power into control over other assets.

Kate wanted to be part of this exchange. "Mr. Hailwood, some of the early Federal writers said that democracy was the best bulwark against the state."

He smiled again. Less steely this time, back to charming. "My dear girl, democracy is overrated. It destroyed the United States because the people weren't smart enough to recognize their own strategic interests. They were vicious when they should have laughed and elected empty suits when they needed real leaders. They ignored all the signs when their world was falling apart. The Federal Era was a fluke in human history. A fleeting moment.

"In the end, Jeffersonian democracy is inefficient—and that's really the worst sin for any government system. Public votes only reflect people's immediate desires. Or fears. A good manager needs to pay attention to those but, in the end, average citizens don't know what's best for themselves. They're like a colony of ants. Focused on trivia. Oblivious to truth. We have to keep our eyes on the horizon for them."

The Old Man looked eminently pleased with himself.

Hailwood had heard close versions of this speech many times. This retelling was for Kate, not him. Still...there was something harsher in it. It was more damning of ordinary citizens than the Old Man usually liked.

Hailwood sat back in his chair and slowly unwrapped one of his favorite sayings: "There's more real democracy in the wasteland than inside the City walls."

"Maybe. For what little good that's worth. Remember, without the Cities there'd be no banking. No technology. No webs. No medicine. Your impression of the wasteland is very...select."

Around 11, the Old Man made his *goodnights*, took his screen and disappeared upstairs.

While Kate used the bathroom, Hailwood make another Scotch and took one of his grandfather's small cigars—"hand-rolled in Ybor City"—out of the glass humidor above the bar. And couple of wood matches from the box next to it. When Kate came back, he kissed her and took her by the waist. They walked out through the dining room and out the long dock into the man-made lagoon on the north side of the house. Past the Old Man's yacht and to the end of the dock.

"Terry, please. It's really dark out here. I'm afraid we'll fall in."

"Ye of little faith. I've run, walked, skipped and stumbled the length of this dock...since I could run, walk, skip and stumble."

The sat on the end and looked out at the Sunshine Skyway lighted along the eastern horizon in front of them. He handed her the Scotch, which she sipped, and he lit the small cigar and took a drag. Then they swapped.

The night was warm and humid—but nowhere near as muggy as

the afternoon had been. Plus, there was a breeze. The sky was cloudy, but they could see some stars. The boat traffic had died down enough that they could hear insects chirping and an occasional fish jumping.

They swapped again.

"This is very nice, Terry. I'm surprised you ever left."

"Yeah, well. You know how it is. The house can get a little. Crowded."

She laughed her one-syllable laugh again. "I can tell. She's difficult, but I feel like it's the kind of difficult that I know. He's something else all together."

"That's a fact." He took another drag on the cigar. "Guess what happened to his first wife."

"No guess."

"She killed herself."

"No. How?"

"Gun."

"Why?"

"He's never said. Never told me. Not sure he knows."

They swapped again. He rubbed her neck.

"When are you going to tell them we're going to try to see your father?"

"Better we keep that low key. I'll let them know as soon as we get back."

Nine

Crowley had stayed in town Friday night for a long dinner with Andrea Fourier's Asian trade specialist—an ambitious middle-level named Michael Walters—and the trade delegation from Seoul.

The Koreans were scared about the amount of the low-end electronics market they were losing the Malays. They were also worried that the Caliphate would cut back on their petro allowance again, so they were looking for energy storage tech. American Cities—particularly Houston, SoCal and Tampa—made the best heavy-duty batteries in the world.

Their only concept of socializing was the usual Asian companyman excess—drinks at their embassy, top-of-the-menu dinner in a VIP room at ridiculous steak place, more drinks at some trendy club in St. Pete Beach. There was probably a later stage at strip joint in town or a whorehouse out in the wasteland north of the Ocala walls.

Wanting no part of *that*, Crowley had bowed out after the steak place. He hated trade dinners; he'd suggested hosting the dinner at his home, but Walters pointed out that he'd hosted the Seoul group last time. As CEO, he had to suffer one or two of these things a month. The Europeans were more enjoyable—even when they were anxious about their petro allowances from the Caliphate, they didn't exude fear like the Asians did.

But Seoul was a major partner that had grown with Tampa's markets and relatively reliable access to other Cities. And Walters did most of the talking. Impressive chunks in Korean. All Crowley had to do was smile, say a few words and lift his wine glass every few minutes.

The next morning, he woke up late and a little hung-over around nine. The plan was to check in at the office for a couple of hours and then head down to join Margot and the kids at the beach. He had a meeting scheduled for Monday morning with the Board's executive committee—Old Man Hailwood, Bill Franklin, R.J. Rasmussen, Cardinal Menendez and Bart Saul—to talk about three things: his plans for the League, the "special tax refund" that was the Old Man's latest pet project and the draft of a formal succession plan. The Old Man would probably say he'd listed the items in reverse order.

Crowley had never drafted a succession plan. The implicit reason was that a boy genius didn't need an understudy. And there was another reason. Raised in boardroom intrigues, Crowley knew that succession plans meant successors. And successors meant succession—sooner than the succeeded had planned. Even if the succeeded was a boy genius.

But he wasn't such a boy any more; six years into his term, he was running out of excuses for putting it off.

His goal this morning was to take one last look at his memo outlining the steps that the board of directors should take in the event he died unexpectedly or suffered a long-term disability (as defined by his life/disability insurance carrier).

He didn't get into the office until after 10. Since it was a Saturday, almost no one was in—but Jaynice, his third admin, had been running answers to letters from citizens since nine.

"There's only been one call—but it sounded kind of urgent. Bert Barrett called you about 20 minutes ago. He said he'd call back in half an hour. But his voice was a little higher-pitch than usual. And he was talking fast." She was the least-senior of his three admins—but was the smartest and hardest working. She watched educational screens and believed particularly in reading body language.

"That doesn't sound like Barrett. Very observant, Jaynice. Thanks for the insight. I'll check my screen real quick and then give him a call. Let's do it in about five."

"OK. I'll ping you when he's one the line."

He wondered what was bothering Barrett. If it had been something truly urgent, he would have called out at the house or on Crowley's personal screen. He'd done both many times.

There was only one message on his screen that was important. His broker in Geneva was confirming the deposit from Thursday night. With all the focus on his own death or disability—and then the drunken Asians—he'd practically forgotten that he'd made the transfer.

He clicked through to the succession plan.

It was simple. Chambers, the current CFO, would be named interim CEO while the board directors conducted a formal search for his permanent replacement. Crowley's advice to the board was to recruit from another City in the Americas or Europe. And he outlined the specific personality profile and management qualities it should seek.

Without saying a disparaging word—and he reread the document to make sure there wasn't one—he'd let the board know that he didn't think any of his direct reports were ready or able to take over. In the world of politics, the perfect criticism was one which was never actually made. If this memo leaked, his C-levels might be angry; but they would have nothing specific to harbor against him.

The memo ended by saying that it would need to be reviewed and recertified every six months to stay in effect.

"Mr. Crowley, I have Mr. Barrett on your line one."

"Thanks Jaynice." He put in his earpiece and pressed line one. "Bert, what do you need?"

"Michael, you're still putting us all to shame. Are you still planning to head down to Sanibel today?"

"Yes."

"How are going to get there?"

"Tiltrotor. Why? Looking for a ride south?"

"Well, there is something that I'd like to talk over with you. And I don't want to interrupt your plans with your family…."

There was definitely something wrong. Barrett wasn't usually so sideways. "No problem, Bert. Come on over to the office and come down with me. You can stay at our place for the night, if you like."

"Oh no. That's not necessary. Besides, Carla and I have a dinner tonight."

"Well, then swing by here in about an hour. We'll talk on the way down. We can take a walk on the beach, have a quick drink and you'll be back up here before three."

"Yeah. That sounds good."

"Is everything alright, Bert?"

"I'll be at the office in an hour."

Crowley's mind turned back to his succession memo. It was clean. And it said all that it needed to—both directly and indirectly. The Old Man would be satisfied. And one more hurdle in the way of the

League would be removed.

He ran a last grammar and spell check and sent the memo by secure exchange. All of the Executive Committee members received it.

He called Margot to tell her that Barrett would be coming with him for a short meeting. She didn't sound too happy—but she said she'd tell Jella to prep some extra sandwiches.

"I'll be done with this quickly, M. And we spend the rest of the day on the beach."

"Michael, we really need to get past all of the apologies. You do what you do. I do what I do. No excuses."

"Well, what I want to do is play on the beach with Jack and Pea for a few hours. And have us all watch the sunset together."

"We're here."

"I'll see you in 90 minutes."

Next on his list was making some sense out of Chambers' report on the tax refund. It was complex math. As it had to be, because the underlying concept was dubious. The City was still running a budget deficit. But that shortfall had gotten smaller than projected, according to the most recent monthly numbers. And the trend lines looking out 12 and 24 months had suddenly started looking much better. In fact, they would be in the black again inside of two years.

But the Old Man—who was always so fixated on interest rates—was suddenly talking about borrowing against the projected surplus to finance a tax rebate to citizens.

This kind of borrowing was exactly the kind of thing that the bankers didn't like…and would use as an excuse to raise interest rates. But the Old Man insisted that Tampa needed to "stay ahead of the market" and get more spending money into people's hands immediately.

When Crowley clicked through for a risk management illustration, a yellow and blue box appeared in front of his screen. It was mostly yellow.

Chambers had produced a holographic 3-D matrix image that showed possible 12- and 24-month surpluses, possible tax rebate levels and resulting effects on standard consumer finance interest rates. Each of the three axes had four points; the resulting cube was made of 64 smaller cubes—which were the possible outcomes. By his projection, 47 of the smaller cubes would result in lower interest rates (they were the yellow ones); 17 resulted in higher rates. That meant what seemed to Crowley like a reckless move had a 73 percent chance of success.

Not good enough.

He sat back in his chair and rubbed his temples. There was still something about public finance that was just beyond him. The Old Man seemed to know instinctively that borrowing to make a rebate was the right monetary policy. And the number crunchers had validated that instinct.

Crowley figured that the Old Man had just seen so much that he'd internalized more analysis than most managing executives would have until…they had become Old Men.

A 73 percent chance of lower interest rates meant there would be a 27 percent chance of higher rates. And that would be painful—trying to repay the bonds while rates were rising…the kind of situation that could lead to a CEO's ouster.

He checked his screen to see if any of the ExComm boys had gotten back to him about the succession memo. Nothing.

An hour later, Crowley, two security body men and Bert Barrett walked out into the loud daylight on the top of City Hall's west tower. The tiltrotor was screeching and whirring in its distinctive way; its pilots were ready to go.

The four passengers strapped themselves into facing seats and the tech out on the platform slammed the sliding door shut. One of the pilots locked the doors from the cockpit. And the noise was immediately better.

The aircraft jumped off of the roof and up into the sky above Tampa much more suddenly than any jet. The pilot's voice came into the passenger cabin and said that, once they'd reached cruising altitude, he expected to make the trip to the Sanibel house in about seven minutes.

"So, Bert. What's so urgent?"

"Well, it's personal business. If you don't mind, I'd prefer to speak with you once we've landed."

"OK. Sure."

Barrett didn't say anything. He just watched the curved horizon was blue water in the Gulf of Mexico.

There wasn't a proper landing pad at the Sanibel house. So, the security staff had marked a compass-point cross and a most of a circle on the widest section of the serpentine driveway to the house. The pilot dropped square on the cross. Crowley had told to the pilots to shut down and stand by to take Barrett back to the City Building as soon as they were finished.

As usual, the kids ran up to greet him as soon as he stepped away from the whirl of the overhead blades. Christina—whom they called "Pea"—was 12 and Jack was 10. They were both starting to stretch out; but they were both still sweet young kids. Crowley gave Margot a peck on the cheek and invited Barrett inside while he put his things down.

"Thank you, Michael. Margot. But I'm not here to intrude. I'll just pull a chair out on the sand and wait for you, Michael."

Barrett was serious about having their talk out on the beach.

Crowley said he'd be out in a minute or two.

And he was. Margot didn't care enough to ask about Barrett.

Crowley carried a chair out and jammed it into the sand next to Barrett. "Okay, Bert. What is all this about?"

Barrett rubbed his eyes for a moment and then started talking in a carefully-paced voice. "Michael, I think you're in some kind of trouble. And I want to help you. But I need to know exactly what's going on. Which I don't. So, I'm going to tell you what I know and then ask you to help me make sense of it."

"Okay. I'm not sure what you're talking about. But tell me what you know." Crowley had heard this kind of preamble from dozens of managers in his career. Their important news almost never turned out to be as bad as they expected.

Real trouble wasn't announced by senior management.

"Okay. A special prosecutor name Carmine diSousa has been looking at all kinds of Security Department data. On you. Yesterday afternoon, he showed up in my office with a Section 103b4 subpoena signed by the Old Man and the Shark. The subpoena passed all three biometric tests for each signer. And I called the Chairman's office and they confirmed the subpoena by its number."

He'd followed protocol by calling the Old Man's office. And he was bending the rules now, telling Crowley. Without seeing the document, Crowley couldn't be sure, but 103b4 subpoenas were usually supposed to remain secret from the objects of the search.

"They tapped our infobase with two separate systems. Heavy stuff. Hastert Mach 7 CPUs and Ssangyuan 533G data bridges. My

IT director says that with that kind of hardware a search for all the info about *any* one person—even you—should take less than three minutes. They started before four yesterday afternoon and weren't finished until after midnight. More than eight hours as opposed to three minutes. That's a 160-fold discrepancy. I think they were just making a complete copy of all of our files."

The first thought that occurred to Crowley was that Barrett must have prepared this speech. The "160-fold" bit was too precise to be spontaneous. The question was: Had he prepared on his own…or had he been prompted by someone else.

"I've never heard of this diSousa person. But that doesn't mean anything. I don't know every lawyer in the Shark's department. And, if you're going to use the old detective's trick of asking me if I know what he's looking for, I can settle that now. I don't have any idea."

Barrett waited a few minutes before saying anything. He didn't want to have this conversation. But what did that *mean*? Barrett was basically honest. In this moment, Crowley wished that the man were more ruthless; it would be easier to read his motivations.

"I think I know what he's looking for, Michael. Even before the Legal Department got involved, my Financial Security Bureau had alerted me to several wires you made to a bank in Geneva. I didn't call this into Legal. And I don't have a complete trail on the money. But it's suspicious. Can you explain moving cash into an untraceable location?"

So far, both them had been looking out at the water and avoiding each other's direct eye contact. Now, Crowley waited until he caught Barrett's. "Sure, Bert. Margot and I are getting divorced. And I wanted to move some money out of plain sight."

Barrett looked back out at the water and thought about that for a while. "Why would she want your money? She's a Brahmin."

"Brahmins don't stay rich by just walking away from marriages to City CEOs."

This seemed to satisfy Barrett.

But Crowley hadn't decided about Barrett. Was he working for the Shark or the Old Man? Knowingly, with the promise of promotion; or unknowingly, believing that he was doing what was best for the City?

"I don't know the whole equation, Michael. But they're putting some kind of case together."

Crowley's mind was moving fast enough that he was having a hard time paying attention to what Barrett was saying. The *they*—at least as Barrett had described the subpoena—were the Shark and the Old Man. But those two were an unlikely team; they didn't seem to like each other very well. And the Old Man had proved time and again that he didn't care much for expats of any sort. And especially not Cubans.

"Maybe I'm just the excuse, Bert. Maybe what they really want is that complete copy of your infobase."

The obvious thought was that this was the Shark's gambit to become CEO. He was the most presidential of all of the C-level executives. Maybe he had something on the Old Man…or had made some kind of deal with the Old Man.

Or maybe the obvious was too obvious. Maybe the Shark was being set up to set up Crowley. Now, that would be elegant. And it sounded like the Old Man.

Crowley saw no need to confront Barrett about his role. Best to assume he was just doing his job as he saw fit. Acknowledging any conspiracy would do more to legitimize their actions than to undermine them. The best approach was to let the allegations pass through him and find out where—or from whom—Barrett was getting his information. And that wasn't something he was likely to find in one conversation.

"I don't have anything to hide, Bert. One of the few advantages of public life is that it forces an executive to be transparent. My worst failing is that I'm getting a divorce. And that's a personal matter."

Barrett didn't say anything. But, after a moment or two, he got up from his chair and started pacing back and forth in front of Crowley. Maybe he was going to say something more. Though that would be unlike him.

Crowley needed to keep the conversational momentum going, just in case. "What's the matter, Bert. You've done your job well. And, if this is some kind boardroom coup, I've seen plenty in my time. Hell, I've been *behind* them. I have some reliable votes on the board. I can slow the process down enough to get to the bottom of whatever's going on"

"I know you're good at the politics, Michael. And I think you're a fine executive. But people in your position sometimes overestimate their ability to manage their way out of trouble. It doesn't always work like that. *Avoiding* trouble is the only way to get out of trouble."

"Okay, let's assume you're right and there's some major trouble brewing. What would you suggest I do?"

"I'm not a media person, Michael. But I think you need to get out there—soon—and get in front of this. People can sympathize with the CEO having a divorce; they won't be so sympathetic to a husband whose bad behavior *caused* his divorce. They have a lot of information about you—probably a lot of things that seemed insignificant and maybe slipped your mind."

Where was this going? The more Barrett talked, the more it became clear that he was insinuating more than stating facts. Crowley hadn't done anything to cause the trouble with Margot. But Barrett was making wrong assumptions. Not like a detective. Was he involved in the scheme? Not likely. If he'd been involved, he would have been calmer. More certain.

All of this didn't speak well to him as a Security Chief.

"Bert, there must be something else bothering you. I won't be the first CEO—even in this City—to deal with a divorce. If my wire transfers come out, so be it. They're not illegal. CEOs usually survive scandals. You of all people know this."

The sun was starting to come down from its midday height. Crowley was just a few hours away. His favorite part of any day was playing with his kids in neck-deep (for them) water as the sun went down.

"I don't like having some young kid from Legal taking over my department. I don't having to sort through political in-fighting. And the fact that you've let this happen worries me."

"So, take a vacation. This sounds like a boardroom coup. They happen in every City every few years. I'm lucky I got to six years without one. Someone on the board wants me out. Maybe the Old Man, maybe the Shark. Maybe someone else. I'll find out who it is. Don't worry"

"It's Sandoval. This diSousa was at the Security Center within half an hour of the timestamp on the Old Man's biometric strip on the subpoena. That means they had their investigators ready before the subpoena was executed. Plus, Sandoval drafted the subpoena himself. And he signed it before the Old Man did. If I'd drafted the thing, I would have made damn sure to have the Chairman sign it first."

It could also mean that someone had forced the Old Man to sign the subpoena. And Crowley still wasn't certain that *someone* was the Shark.

But this conversation was making him fairly certain that Barrett was dead weight—loyal, perhaps, but useless in a fight.

"Take a week of vacation starting immediately, Bert. Take your wife somewhere far away and let this hand play out. I'll be happy to keep as many of the C-levels as I can untainted by what goes on."

Crowley got up out of his chair and padded across the sand toward the deck that wrapped around the north side of the big house and faced the driveway stretch where the tiltrotor had landed. He made a corkscrew gesture with his right index finger and pointed at Barrett. The two young fellows sitting in the cockpit started getting busy. "Just tell the lads where you want to be dropped off. They can drop you at City Hall or anywhere there's a rooftop pad."

"Thanks. I'm not sure I should be leaving now. I can stay and help you...."

"No. Bert. Take a week off. Steer clear. I didn't get to be CEO of major City by being hesitant. If there's going to be some blood in the board room, I'd just as soon keep your clothes clean. I'll leave any urgent information with your first admin. But I'll try not to do that. I'll see you a week from Monday—the eleventh—and most of this crap will be passed. Now, you'll have to excuse me. I've got a lot of work to do between now and Monday morning."

More than anything, immediately, Crowley was thirsty.

The five minutes with Barrett screwed up the whole weekend. Crowley played with Jack and Pea in the water that afternoon and had dinner with Margot and them on the patio that evening. But he was distracted the whole time. He and Margot watched some stupid comedy later that night—and she fell asleep almost immediately. He drank a few beers and thought about how to handle the Shark's bogus investigation.

He didn't feel focused until he was back in the office Sunday afternoon. And, in truth, even that didn't quash his anxiety. He wanted this confrontation—there really wasn't much more that *thinking* about it could do. But he knew that drama didn't prevail in boardroom battles. Planning did. There were a handful of ways that he could turn the allegations and insinuations against the Old Man and the Shark.

He called Rich Baranski, the best lawyer that he knew personally. "Rich, this is Michael Crowley—"

"Michael? Look. Before you say anything to me, I need to say something to *you*. I've been retained as a consultant by the City's legal department on a matter that makes it impossible for me to render any legal services to you. And, frankly, to speak with you in anything more than just the most incidental social context. I wish you well. And I hope we can talk again at some later point." And he hung up.

Crowley had to make several more calls before he found a lawyer that the Shark hadn't retained as a consultant.

Crowley spoke with Jamie Gaynor for about an hour, laying out the background of what was going on. Gaynor—mostly known as a corporate liability specialist—was excited about being involved. But he asked for a retainer of $250,000. Crowley had to make transfers from two different accounts to cover that much on short notice on a Sunday.

The Executive Committee meeting was scheduled to begin at nine. Crowley had considered arriving very early, to catch the Old Man before the Old Man could catch him. But Gaynor recommended not doing that. He agreed to be at Crowley's house at 7:30. They'd have some breakfast and go over their tactics for handling the meeting.

Gaynor was prompt and had been doing his work the night before. He had public-information files on every board member and legal precedents related to all of the charges that Tampa law allowed the board to make against the CEO or another C-level manager.

"People always assume that—because of the board mechanism—the laws applying to you are different from regular corporate stuff. But they're not, really."

The most noticeable thing about Gaynor was his youth. He was among the youngest and least experienced of the high-profile attorneys in Tampa. And, maybe because of this, he kept a lower public profile than the other heavy-hitters. But his cases appeared on the financial and legal screens all of the time. "They'll drum up some kind of specific crime as an excuse—maybe some kind of fraud or misappropriation—but the bulk of their complaint is probably something they've had prepped for a while. And it's going to be general stuff. Violation of fiduciary duty to the City, negligent management, these things."

Gaynor was small and thin with fair hair and a clear complexion, all of which made him look like a university student. But the thing that really made him seem young was the way he talked. He had a cadence to his voice that almost sounded giddy, like he was close to giggling even when he was sorting through the murk of corporate liability precedents. Crowley figured that this effect must have made his complicated arguments seem easier to follow.

The young-looking lawyer looked up at Crowley, to make sure the client agreed. But he didn't wait too long for his signal.

"We'll be ready for that. Otherwise, the burden is going to be heavy for them. As you say, you lead a pretty transparent life."

"I do."

Gaynor sat back from notes and took in a deep breath. He picked up his glass of orange juice for the first time and took a sip. They were supposed to be eating breakfast, but neither one had touched any food. "Okay, Mr. Crowley. We've got the details wired. Now, my questions for you are the big-picture ones. First and most: What do you want when all of the dust settles here?"

"Want? I want to stay CEO. And I want to clear out the board members behind all of this, so that the rest of the board thinks twice before trying to remove me."

"Understandable. But what if you can stay CEO and the board also stays in place as it is. No changes. Will that be acceptable?"

"I don't think that would be a viable solution."

"No, not for the long term. But would it be acceptable to you right now?"

"Yes. My main goal is to stay in office. I could restructure the board gradually, if I have to."

"Good. That's promising. Now, what if staying in office is not possible? What would an acceptable exit strategy be?"

"I don't have an acceptable exit strategy."

"What if the board offers to drop all charges in exchange for a resignation?"

"I would fight the charges and not resign."

"But you serve at the pleasure of the board. If you fight the charges, board members who would otherwise support you might vote to fire you because you're assuming an adversarial legal position."

Gaynor was doing his job by exploring every scenario. And he was, no doubt, sizing up his client by seeing how Crowley responded. The important thing for Crowley was to appear deliberate and unemotional. "I won't resign. I've considered that scenario. To resign, if they drop the bogus charges, would be to give up my claim to office. The board can fire me. But, if it does that, I can launch a proxy fight and take my message to the people."

Gaynor looked at him intensely for a few beats. "I'm not a political expert. But proxy fights don't usually work. Do they?"

"To keep my moral authority with the board, I need to have that option open. I will not resign."

"What if they offer you a cash settlement?"

"I won't resign."

Gaynor waited for a moment again. "I understand. And I respect your position. Resignation is not an option." He drank the rest of his juice. "Well, we're coming up on it. Is there anything else I should know?"

"I don't think so. I want to do most of the talking. But just make sure I don't talk my way into any corners."

"I'll be watching. And I'll make sure we record everything. But I think you've thought this through pretty carefully."

When they got to City Hall, Gaynor drifted back with the two TSF officers on duty as Crowley's security detail.

They arrived at Crowley's office a little after 8:30 and his first admin said the Chairman had arrived a few minutes earlier with the ExComm in tow. They were all inside.

Gaynor cocked his head slightly, by Crowley just shrugged. This wasn't unusual—it was standard procedure that the Old Man and anyone with him would go into Crowley's office and wait, if he wasn't in.

The two TSF guys went to their desk in the outer office; Crowley and Gaynor went inside to face the ExComm.

Immediately, Crowley noticed that Sandoval and Chambers and a third man—probably the Special Prosecutor—were sitting around the larger table by the windows.

Crowley walked over to his desk, talking along the way. "Grant, gentlemen. You're here early. This is my attorney, Jamie Gaynor. I've asked him to sit in with us this morning. Now, if you're ready, we have a lot discuss. I'll have Shania bring in some coffee and we can get right to it."

The Old Man made a nasty sneer and interrupted. "Your attorney? Well, it looks like we can dispense with the pleasantries. Michael. I'm formally—"

"Wait a second, Grant. Let me make sure that our dictation and security systems are working. And, at my request, Mr. Gaynor will be making a separate record of this meeting and streaming it to the staff at his office." Gaynor nodded. "Okay. Let's call this meeting of the Executive Committee of the Board of Directors to order. Mr. Chairman, you'd like speak?"

The Old Man stared at him for a few seconds.

"You and your lawyer can have a seat, Michael. I'm formally suspending our published agenda and concentrating this meeting on some disturbing news that has come to my attention in the last several days. Now, I'm not familiar with all of the details, so I'm going to ask Counselor Sandoval to make a special presentation to the Executive Committee. Mr. Sandoval."

The Shark leaned forward in his chair. "Thank you, Mr. Chairman. In the last several weeks, Legal Department investigators came across some disturbing news related to financial transactions involving CEO and President Michael Crowley. With my permission, the investigators pursued these transactions and have determined that there are sufficient grounds to appoint a Special Prosecutor to handle an inquiry into possible bribe-taking by President Crowley. This is a violation of OpAg 394.26 and following. Other City laws, too. I have prepared a report that I am sending right now to all your screens. For the moment, Mr. Gaynor, I will ask Mr. Crowley to forward the report to you. As soon as possible, my staff will add your name to all correspondence related to this matter."

"Thank you, Mr. Sandoval. I am sending my contact information to you right now. And please forward to me all correspondence between you and the Special Prosecutor—and keep me copied on any current or future correspondence, as outlined in OpAg 193.57."

"Of course, Mr. Gaynor."

Crowley noticed an interesting visual dynamic between Gaynor and the Shark. They were essentially opposites: Sandoval, the tall barrel-chested aggressor; Gaynor, the small, wiry defender. But Gaynor was holding his own. Maybe their personalities were more alike than their physical types.

Sic Semper Tyrannis

Sandoval continued: "As you can see in the report, the Legal Department has discovered a number of transactions in and out of President Crowley's various bank accounts that establish a pattern—a complex pattern—of moving funds from a group of three Tampa corporations to at least one account at the Union Bank of Geneva.

"Now this group of Tampa corporations is of greatest interest to us. They are: PBK Holdings, Inc., TBIT Corp., Inc. and ASEC Trading, Inc. Quite an alphabet soup."

Sandoval had risen from his seat and was now using the large display screen across the room. Normally, access to the large screen was something Crowley controlled from his desk—though it was no great feat to get access, since any of his admins had the same control. But it seemed like a sign from the Shark that he was taking control.

Crowley thought he should mark this on the recordings, though. "J.C., how did you get access to my display screen?"

"Oh, this? I asked your assistant to connect my screen to the display, so that we would not need to waste any time."

"Hmm."

"So, here we have PBK Holdings. Its corporate listing with the City names one Paholo Baraka Kuk—a citizen of Singapore—as principal and James Evans, an attorney here in Tampa, as secretary. Mr. Kuk is a well-known arms dealer in the South China Sea region.

"Next, we have TBIT Corp., does business as Tampa Bay International Trading. It has two principals, Paholo Baraka Kuk and Mitchell Greider, a citizen of Tampa. And the same James Evans is secretary.

"Finally, we have ASEC Trading. Its listing includes two principals, Mr. Greider and Tampa resident Oleanna Singh. Ms. Singh is a non-citizen who is seeking naturalization in Tampa. In her naturalization papers, she lists Singapore as her place of birth. And James Evans is the secretary. So, I think we see the common thread is Mr. Evans."

The Shark went on to establish a series of deposits from the three companies into Crowley's personal account at SunBank and another personal account—which he used for job-related expenses—with the Tampa City Employees Credit Union. The deposits spanned about 12 weeks and totaled about $2 million.

The accounts were real. But the transactions weren't.

Crowley looked to Gaynor, who shook his head *no* very slightly.

The lawyer was advising the client to stay quiet.

Sandoval was still explaining his case. "What do these cash transfers and the companies from which they originate have in common? We weren't sure ourselves until had a chance to interview Mr. Evans. He explained the connection quite clearly. And I'll let him explain it to you."

The screens shimmered to the image of slightly overweight young man in his late 30s or early 40s. He was dressed in a black suit and wore a goatee and his hair in a spiky flat-top cut. He didn't look like an establishment lawyer.

"I was approached about six months ago by Paholo Kuk. He explained that his government was going to sell two battleships to Tampa and that he was serving as the agent for his City. In the Asian style of doing business, this meant he was going to need to invest some money to make the deal happen.

"He gave me very explicit instructions to set up a total of nine different corporations. And I did this, using the names and personal information from people—mostly non-citizens living in Tampa—he gave me to list as the principals. And Mr. Kuk ended up using all of them for various different business ventures. We received cash infusions from various Asian banks. Then, starting about three months ago, Mr. Kuk gave me instructions to make electronic transfers from three of the corporations to either of two numbered accounts. I was never given the name of the account holder. But, from the bank ID number, I knew the accounts were both at SunBank. I moved a total of about $1.9 million into the two accounts over a six-week period—always moving amounts of less than $100,000, so we didn't attract the attention of the City's Internal Security or Finance Departments.

"It wasn't until recently that I learned that the numbered accounts at SunBank belonged to President Crowley. The entire time that I was making the transfers, I had no idea who was on receiving end. And I had no idea what the payments were for. As far as I knew, they were legitimate payments to security contractors."

The image shimmered off.

And Sandoval took over again. "We have Mr. Evans in custody. He has provided us with receipts and documents that establish Mr. Crowley received the money. City records indicate that Mr. Crowley has transferred about half of that money in several parts—again, all under $100,000, so as not to draw regulatory attention—to the same Geneva bank. Of course, once that money reached Geneva, our ability to follow it ended. But we have other evidence. At this point, I will turn the podium over to Carmine diSousa, the Special Prosecutor who has been handling this case."

diSousa looked and sounded like a miniature version of Sandoval. He was tall, stocky (though a little more muscular than his mentor) and wore a bright blue suit.

"Thank you, Counselor Sandoval. Gentlemen, as you know, the Operating Agreement of the City of Tampa requires a particular process for investigating and prosecuting a sitting CEO or any Department Chief actively serving in the City government. In these cases, the full board of directors of the City Corporation serves as both judge and jury. It is a less-than-desirable situation—but one that is required, in order to keep the City secure.

"I intend to file, within the next 72 hours, formal charges against Michael J. Crowley for consideration by the full board. These charges will include bribe-taking, accepting foreign funds from unconfirmed sources, using public office for private gain, violation of fiduciary duty and abuse of public trust."

The charges were shaping up as Gaynor had predicted.

"My case will be presented as part of a process that is called an administrative review. However, it will look and sound very much like a lawsuit that you might see being tried in any City court. We will expect to complete our case within two days. And will give Mr. Crowley a reasonable amount of time to articulate a defense. For the moment, however, I recommend that you detain Mr. Crowley under a 914(a)i special circumstances binder."

There was a slight delay after diSousa spoke. So, Crowley leaned over to Gaynor. He whispered, "What's going on?"

"They want to arrest you. Keep you locked up until they decide that they have a strong enough case," Gaynor whispered back. "And that day may never come."

Now the Old Man was back at the podium. "Son, you need to make some decisions right here. The best option for you would be accept the following. Sign a complete confession to the bribe-taking and money laundering. If you do this, we're prepared to settle the charges in a way that will allow you to remain a Tampa resident. But you will have to resign as CEO and give up your citizenship. You'll become a legal resident non-citizen. We can even discuss setting you up in a modest job.

"The worst choice would be…well, I guess it would be for you try to run."

The Old Man looked at Gaynor. "And there are various points in between that we might negotiate. But any such negotiations will—in the best case for you—only match the offer we have on the table to you right now. So think about saving yourself and us a lot of trouble and take…"

Gaynor interrupted the Old Man. "Chairman Hailwood, my client has instructed me to tell you and the board the following. One, he did not receive the $1.9 million or $2 million that Mr. Sandoval has claimed was sent by three local corporations. Two, he has never met Paholo Kuk, Oleanna Singh, James Evans or any of the other people you have mentioned as part of this alleged *scheme*. Three, he has never influenced any City decision for his own benefit for by any improper means. Four, he will not admit, accept or for that matter even comment on any charge that he knowingly participated in any illegal or improper activities in connection to his term as CEO. So, a plea bargain that includes any sort of admission of guilt on his part will not be considered."

The Old Man proceeded as if Gaynor wasn't in the room. "Michael, we don't want to drag a trial out for weeks. Make amends—sign the settlement. And you can keep your money and go live anywhere in the world that you wish."

This time, Crowley answered directly: "Grant, this story that these people have concocted can't hold up to the truth. It may take a few days—it may take a few months. But I'll break it down and expose it as a fraud. That's what it is."

Crowley looked over to Gaynor, who shrugged his shoulders slightly.

The Old Man was talking: "…the reason for this argument? Just sign the damned document and you'll be free to go."

That was unlikely. But Crowley had to do something to prevent the Old Man's wobbly logic from being the last word.

"What about the markets? They're not going to like this story you've invented as an excuse to remove me from office."

The Old Man laughed ruefully and shook his head. "Son, the markets *prefer* a crime or a scandal to anything else. Crimes and scandals prove that the flaws in the system are bad humans—not jinxed hardware or overwrought software. Crooked people are an explanation for poor performance that the markets understand. They'll mark you to market before the administrative review is over. In fact, I'd say they've *already* marked you to market.

"You were a good mechanic, son. But you're not a strategist. We're giving you the chance to walk out of this room a free man. If you don't sign the confession, I'm going to swear out a warrant for your arrest right here. Right now." His voice got louder the longer he talked.

Crowley wasn't moved by the Old Man's loud talk. He'd heard it before. Arresting the CEO on trumped-up fraud charges was the kind of thing that sleazy little towns did. Hailwood wouldn't do it because it would be a global embarrassment to Tampa. "I'm not going to sign anything like that, Grant."

"Then you're going to prison."

"If you really think the best thing for the City is to have its CEO arrested and jailed. But I don't think you want the kind of ridicule that minor-league stuff would bring on us."

His heart was beating a little faster. But Crowley knew that he had to do this—to challenge the Old Man's demands. The next few minutes would set up the rest of his term in office.

The Old Man held Crowley's eye contact for what seemed like a long time. Then, he turned his attention to the pocket-sized screen that he'd taken out of his jacket at some point earlier and placed in the podium. Crowley read this gesture as a stalling tactic while the Old Man thought of some diplomatic way to pull back.

Finally, the Old Man started reading. "Michael J. Crowley, under the authority given me—as Chairman of the Board of Directors—by Section 914(a)i of the Operating Agreement of the Corporation of the City of Tampa, I order you arrested and detained while an administrative review of several alleged wrongdoings involving you and your administration is conducted by this board. This is a Civic Security matter."

Suddenly, five TSF troopers filed into the board room. Four were giants carrying plasma rifles; one was an ordinary-size man carrying an elaborate bunch metal hardware over his shoulder. It was restraints. They lined up as far away from the seated board members as they could, along the back wall near the door. They were waiting for further orders. But they were close enough to each of the doors that Crowley couldn't bolt.

The Old Man kept speaking in cautious monotone. "You will be kept in City facilities—separate from the general inmate population—until such a time as the Special Prosecutor either files charges against you or drops the investigation without action. You will be allowed to receive contact from family members and your personal legal representative."

Crowley kept waiting for Gaynor to interrupt. He didn't.

The Old Man wasn't making eye contact. Neither were the other ExComm members.

Crowley couldn't let this go any more. He ignored the part of him that recommended calm: "This is outrageous! I haven't taken any bribes. I haven't failed my duty. Gaynor, do something about this. We need to respond."

Gaynor was busy clicking through his screen, obviously looking for something online. "Chairman Hailwood, a section 914(a)i warrant requires that you have direct evidence of a clear and present danger to the security of the City. Unproven allegations of financial misdeeds by Mr. Crowley do not meet any precedent standard of a clear and present danger. At worst, these are financial disputes. At worst."

The Old Man wasn't prepared. "Sandoval?"

The Shark answered from his seat. "Mr. Gaynor, the Operating Agreement allows the Chairman broad discretion in issuing a 914(a)i warrant. The standard, as defined at the beginning of section 914, is the ordinary business judgment rule, applied to *possible* security threats. But, to add an extra level of certainty to these proceedings, we can have the Executive Committee of the City's board or directors take a vote on the Chairman's warrant. Mr. Chairman?"

Gaynor was still clicking on his screen. He was moving methodically, so he didn't seem to be panicked. That was good. It looked like he knew what he was looking for. From his seat, Crowley couldn't see the actual pages that Gaynor was reading; he assumed they were either statute language or precedent cases.

The Old Man, who'd never left the podium but looked lost in deep thought, snapped to attention. "Members of the Executive Committee, let's take a vote for the record on this serious matter of detaining our CEO. Resolved: That my proposed warrant for the arrest and detention of Michael J. Crowley be implemented immediately. How do you vote? Cardinal Menendez?"

"Yea."

"Mr. Rasmussen?"

"Yea."

"Mr. Franklin?"

"Yea."

"Mr. Saul?"

"Yea."

None of them even looked at Crowley. Their attention was focused entirely on the Old Man.

"My own vote is 'yea.' So, the vote is unanimous—"

"Not quite." Gaynor said this without looking up from his screen. "Mr. Crowley himself is still a member of the Executive Committee. For the record, you need to poll his vote."

"Sandoval?" This time, the Shark got up. He and the Old Man stepped away from the podium and whispered to each other for a few seconds. Crowley noticed the Old Man's eyebrows dart up. Twice. He knew that look. The Old Man had made a mistake. Probably something procedural—and Gaynor had noticed it while researching something else on his screen.

Crowley looked back at Gaynor. He was still clicking intently.

When the Old Man came back to the podium, he was clearly frustrated. He drew his lips tightly against his teeth. "Mr. Crowley?"

Gaynor cut in. "Mr. Crowley votes 'Nay.' And I have sent you all formal Motion to Delay this warrant until Mr. diSousa can present proper legal credentials."

The Old Man's eyebrows shot up. "He doesn't have to present credentials to you!"

"Not to me, Mr. Chairman, to any City court. I'm surprised that he hasn't done so. While the detailed proceedings of Mr. diSousa's investigation may not be for public release, he must present his credentials to a Court of competent jurisdiction. In fact, he was supposed to have done so before he started any investigation with Civic Security implications. And those credentials *are* for public release. They are proof that Mr. diSousa is a member of the bar and can serve as a Special Prosecutor. If he isn't or can't, he's not going to make any presentation to the board and the arrest of my client would be presumed pretextual."

"Sandoval?"

"Mr. Gaynor, a 914(a)i warrant is designed specifically to protect the City against just the sort of legal technicalities that you are offering up here."

"Mr. Sandoval, I have only just started with the technicalities. If the Chairman will withdraw this warrant for the time being, we will be happy to discuss some kind of resolution to our differences in a civil manner. But, if the City treats my client as a suspected criminal, we will proceed in a more adversarial manner. We will respond to the City in the manner than the City attacks us."

The Old Man and the Shark stepped away from the podium again. Crowley looked at Gaynor, who smiled very slightly to Crowley and then went back to his screen.

The Old Man came back to the podium. "Well, Mr. Gaynor, you were right about one thing. This isn't necessary. The Executive Committee has approved my resolution by a vote of five to one. The warrant is issued and Mr. Crowley is under arrest. Bailiffs, please take him into custody."

The TSF soldiers approached him calmly. They didn't use unnecessary force—but they did grab him by the shoulders and guide him up from his chair.

Gaynor looked around and—in a second—seemed to adjust his strategy. "Gentlemen, gentlemen. Please. There's no need to restrain my client. He will cooperate with the bailiffs. Chairman Hailwood, I remind you that I am recording this meeting separately. You have broad discretion in how this 914(a)i process goes. You don't need to humiliate my client. That only adds credence to our argument that this is a personal grudge parading as a security matter."

The TSF soldiers had Crowley standing, with his feet spread to shoulder-width and his hands in front of his chest, ready for the restraints. Again, Crowley was impressed with how smoothly they moved around him. Their handling wasn't abrupt or violent; it seemed as though they were just guiding him into position.

They were well trained. They wouldn't play rough unless he did.

"All right, Mr. Gaynor. You've earned your fee for the day. The bailiffs will not restrain Mr. Crowley, as long as he goes peacefully."

Crowley stared back hard at the Old Man. But the Old Man wouldn't make eye contact. He knew this was a farce.

Ten

The Old Man's yacht was the *Dauntless*. It was a 110-foot cabin cruiser built pre-succession. It had been all around the world—and, before it came into the Hailwood family, it had been owned by various corporate giants. A banker, a software mogul, an arms dealer. A few years after succession, it fell into the hands of a freight baron who lived in the Pacific Northwest.

During the Reckoning, the freight baron found himself out luck, rejected for citizenship by Seattle and Portland. He eventually bought his way into a City somewhere else...and sold his house and big yacht for pennies on the dollar.

The yacht went through the hands of various Reckoning-era entrepreneurs. It ended up owned by a big shot in what was left of the "film" industry in SoCal. That was when Scott Hailwood—Grant's grandfather and Terry's great-great-grandfather—entered the picture. Scott was a banker and, in an auction, ended up taking over the assets of a failed SoCal land bank.

In a story that the Old Man loved to tell, his grandfather had bid on the bank's assets sight-unseen because he believed in the real estate market in what had been San Diego—but was in the process of being absorbed into SoCal. "He made a fortune in SoCal real estate and effectively got the boat for free."

Scott's son Terrence—Hailwood's great-grandfather and namesake—sailed the boat south from SoCal, through the Panama Canal and north into Tampa Bay. He wrote a book about the experience called *The Smoldering Americas* that still existed as an historical site on the nets.

When it came into the Hailwoods' possession, the boat had been called the *Libertine*. But Scott and Terrence agreed that that was an improper name—so they rechristened it the *Dauntless*. It had been the toast of Tampa Bay even since.

It wasn't the biggest boat in the Bay; but it was the finest, with teak and brass appointments that couldn't be replicated for tens of millions of dollars. Many Tampa citizens considered it proof of their City's equal footing with places like New York, Baltimore, Seattle, San Francisco and SoCal. For more than a century, it had led the annual Gasparilla Day boat parade.

Terrence loved the boat; but he died unexpectedly only a year after his father—leaving Terry's grandfather Grant the oldest Hailwood male.

The Old Man was 16 years old when his father died.

He said he'd always hated the *Dauntless*—mostly because it reminded him of arguments between his parents. But he never sold the boat because it was one of his few links to his father. And because of the annual parade.

The story didn't end there. Hailwood's father, Michael, was the Old Man's only child and an avid sailor from a young age. He'd always wanted the *Dauntless*. When Michael was a young boy, the Old Man had said he'd get the boat as a college graduation present. When Michael graduated college, the Old Man said he'd get the boat when he got married. When Michael got married, the Old Man hesitated again. And, soon after that, they had major falling out—for reasons not directly linked to the boat.

The Old Man didn't like to give things up. Even things he hated.

Their falling out culminated with the Old Man calling his son a "spoiled libertine playboy." In that moment, the irony of the yacht's original name escaped him. Later, it occurred to him.

So, Michael left Tampa and bought the boat most like the *Dauntless*—but bigger—that he could find. It was a 140-foot motorized boat that he christened…the *Libertine*.

According to Michael, he wanted Marianne to bring the baby Hailwood and join him aboard the *Libertine* and never set foot in Tampa again. This was not an idea that held any charm for Hailwood's mother. She stayed in Tampa with her son. And with the Old Man.

For the kind of slanted reasons that only make sense within an extended family, young Hailwood grew up with a dread of the *Dauntless*. He believed that, if his grandfather had just given the boat to his father, the family would have stayed together. He didn't appreciate—no one appreciated—the irony of how closely his bad feelings about the boat paralleled the Old Man's.

As he got older, Hailwood realized that his father and the Old Man's problems ran deeper than any boat. But every long-lasting family conflict turns on a single point. The fulcrum of the feud. The boats reflected more about the Hailwoods than the Hailwoods liked to admit.

Hailwood had never taken the *Dauntless* out of its slip. To his knowledge no one had, except for the annual boat parade, in more than a decade. A crew of guys came into the compound once a week to clean the giant from stem to stern.

When Hailwood and Kate planned for their trip out into the Gulf of Mexico, they prepped a 42-foot sloop-rigged sailboat that Hailwood had sailed a lot as a teenager. The sailboat didn't have a name, so they'd always called it by the last two digits of its registration number: *Eighty-Six*. He liked the double-entendre that the number also meant to be thrown out of a place.

When Hailwood told his mother that he and Kate were planning to take the Eighty-Six out, he lied to her. He said they would sail north along the coast toward the sand bar "harbor" near Hog Island off the small patch of Gulf Coast claimed by Jacksonville. That would take about eight hours with good wind. They'd spend the night in the sand bars and then come back the next day.

His mother may have had an idea of where he was really heading—and that he wasn't planning to sail. But she put on a good show of being concerned about their well-being. He assured her that everything would be all right.

They got an early start Wednesday morning and caught a good wind immediately, coming out into the Gulf. The coastline shrunk to a gray blur on the eastern horizon in less than a half and hour. Before it disappeared completely, he turned the truest left that he could make from a compass and pointed his bow south. He flooded the hydrojets while he and Kate dropped and bound the sails. Then, it took about five minutes to drop the mast. They secured everything and had the boat moving south at 35 knots before the sun was high enough to make things really hot. From that point on, he navigated by the navsat system.

His father had given him the coordinates to find the *Libertine* off Key West.

Kate went below for about an hour, eventually bringing up a pitcher of iced tea and lemonade from the galley. She was wrapped up like a mummy in a sarong, one of his white oxford shirts, a bandana around her head and a nose greased up with sunblock. The sun really was rough on redheads—even his mother was right about something once in a while. "So, how long until we get there?"

"About five hours. Maybe a little less. The wind's with us." There were some storm clouds down at the horizon to the south. They'd reach them about the same time that they got to the south Keys. The water would be choppier there; but, for now, it was like glass.

She poured him some iced tea. "It's kind of creepy. I'm not used to engines being so quiet. Just a hissing sound."

"If the chop gets bad, it makes a vibrating sound that gets so loud I'll need to turn on the damper countermeasures. Otherwise, we won't be able to hear ourselves talk. Even if we yell."

"So, he's 100 percent on us coming?" She drank some of her iced tea and then turned her face up to the morning sun.

He inched the master wheel a hair to the east, centering back on his father's bearing. "Yeah. He wants to meet you. He liked to make a good first impression."

"Why does he care?"

"The black sheep of the family? I don't know. I've stopped trying to guess any of this. My father and grandfather couldn't be more different."

"So, where do you fit on that spectrum?"

"You kidding? My earliest memories are of people saying I'm just like the Old Man."

"Yeah." Then a long pause. "Yeah."

They kept the coast in sight for a couple of hours, until they were south of Captiva and Sanibel. Then, they had to drop due south toward Key West and cross about three hours of nothing but blue water.

Before the green/gray stripe along the east horizon disappeared, Hailwood called the harbor master back at the island and reported his current location. Then he pinged the boat's GPS marker and the one that was hidden under the skin of his right shoulder. And he gave them the *Libertine*'s location. If any trouble came along, the guys from TSF/Coast Guard would know where to start their search.

Around noon, Kate took a break from pushing fluids. The

sun was getting to be too much—even with a 40-plus knot wind. Hailwood had the rudder set on autonav and was leaning out in front of the bow, watching a pod of dolphins swimming with the cutting point of the boat.

He always enjoyed watching dolphins. It was amazing how powerfully and precisely they would swim along with a boat going as fast as this. They'd take turns swimming right under the bow, rotating every few minutes like the chamber of a vintage revolver. It must have been a great workout for these animals to keep up at 40 knots—though someone had once told him they sort of "surfed" the bow wave in a way that didn't require as much work as a hairy human would think. With the revolving, it was hard to tell how long any one of them could keep it up; but, as a kid, he'd watched dolphins swim along the front of various family boats for hours.

There was an arcing whistle overhead and an explosion about 50 yards to his right. The *Eighty-Six* caught the spray about halfway down to the water. The autonav slowed the engines to handle the chop and there was a heavy reverse thrust as it did. Hailwood wobbled back to the wheel.

Someone had fired a shell across their bow. They had to be the target. There was nothing else around.

He scanned the horizon to the east and north, behind them. He noticed the orange bump at about eight-o'clock. It was the right color to be a Coast Guard boat...but pirates used orange and white, too.

The autonav system was still chiming the alarm. It was set to do this when any boat came within half a mile. But the chime wasn't very loud and he'd been too wrapped up in watching the dolphins. He hadn't been paying attention. That was bad.

He clicked through the screen to his imaging/IR display. There was the blip heading toward his from the southeast. It was alone and not moving fast enough to intercept. That must have been why they put the shot over his bow. He relaxed a bit. Pirates didn't usually fire warning shots. He set his radio to the standard CG frequency.

"—no-ID vessel at 100.35X by 326.82Y" this is Miami Coast Guard interceptor *Shula*. Please identify. You crossed into Miami water at Marco Island. If you don't identify—"

"Miami CG *Shula*, this is Tampa citizen TA 476.519.86. Again, TA 476.519.86. Read our GPS locator at 156.932. We're out of Anna Maria Island, heading to Key West."

"Thank you, TA 476.519.86. Stand by for ID confirm."

They didn't ask him to stop—which was another good sign. This far out on the blue water, a boat that asked another to stop was presumed to be a pirate vessel.

Kate came up from below. "What's going on?"

"Miami Coast Guard. I hope."

Just to be safe, he clicked through the radar display and ran a quick def systems diagnostic. He was well-armed: 60 rounds of antitank mortar, 12 30-pound floating mines and four nav-guided 75-pound torpedoes. If he activated the nav systems on the torpedoes, the *Shula* would probably pick that up on its scanner. Since they seemed like genuine Coast Guard, he decided to wait and avoid an unnecessary provocation.

Kate had scanned the horizon herself and found the boat approaching them. "Why did they shoot at us?"

"We were going fast and I wasn't paying attention. They're nervous."

"Well, shouldn't you stop?"

"No. That would make them more nervous. Pirates do tricks like that. We already slowed down. The best thing to do is maintain this speed and talk to them."

"TA 476.519.86, we have confirmed the hardware. And we talked to the harbor master at Anna Maria. What password did you leave?"

"Miami CG *Shula*, our password is 'See Dad.' S.E.E. D.A.D.'"

Another silence. If they were pirates, he had the guns to give them a good fight. He'd distract them with shells and then send a couple of the torpedoes toward the blip in the radar. He took a deep breath and tried to slow down his thoughts by focusing intently weapons overlay of the radar display. If they started shooting or told him to stop, he had to be ready to respond.

"Roger TA 476.519.86. We've confirmed your travel plans. You're OK to go. Sorry about the warning, but you were moving very fast. Are you hydrofoil or squirt?"

"We're a Morgan 44 running twin Piersen squirts."

"A big Morgan with squirts? Nice hardware, captain. We thought we were going to have to climb up on our stilts if you didn't check in. Good luck beating those clouds to Key West."

The Coast Guard boat, just now visible on the horizon, turned back toward the coast and fell out of sight.

Kate broke a few minutes of silence. "How close was that to trouble?"

"I don't know. You'd have to ask them."

She didn't like that answer.

"I don't think it was very close."

"But I noticed that you had your weapons system up on the screen."

"Yeah. And if they were pirates, I would have started shooting."

"How do you know all this stuff?"

"The Old Man. My whole childhood was one long training session. How to sail a boat, how to drive a car, how to shoot a gun."

She was quiet again and flipped through a magazine on her screen.

He took the time to check their position by navsat and compare it to his father's bearing. There was the problem. Somehow, they'd drifted closer to the coast he thought. They were supposed to be about 40 miles out into the Gulf of Mexico, east of the Everglades. Instead, they were only about 12 miles out, and farther north than he'd figured. He reset the autonav again to his father's coordinates—which now mean they were heading a little west of south. Their drift was going to stretch the trip by about an hour.

Finally, she broke the silence. "I'm trying to figure out how much that was like the men you shot up at school."

"What? Not at all. What are you talking about?"

"You're confronted by people. You're better armed that the people confronting you understand. In one case, you end up killing the people; in the other, you end up swapping guy talk about your engines. What's the difference?"

"That's a ridiculous question, Kate. Those two in town were squatters. These guys were Miami Coast Guard."

"But they shot at you."

"They shot over the bow. From a distance. That's a standard warning."

"But you could have launched the torpedoes."

"Coast Guard boats have defensive technology that picks up a torpedo guidance system the minute you turn one on. That would have been a provocative act—like pointing a gun at a cop."

"And why wouldn't you do that?"

"Because it's wrong. And stupid."

She was quiet for a minute again. Then: "I don't know anyone else who has killed people at college. No one I *know* knows anyone who has. Other than you. I'm just trying to figure out why you act differently here than you do there."

"I didn't do anything differently. The circumstances were different. There, it was two squatters in the wasteland who might just as well have killed my friend. Here, we're in a City's territorial waters being checked out by legitimate security personnel who are afraid that *we're* the bad guys."

She was quiet again, which meant she wasn't satisfied.

He didn't like the sideways way that she was critical; it was one of her few unattractive traits. He recalculated their remaining travel time, based on their true location and distance to his father's yacht. It was going to be two more hours.

He didn't want silent treatment for two hours. "You think I act differently, Kate?"

"I don't know. I wasn't there when you shot the squatters. But I think everyone acts differently at different times and different places."

"You sound unusually situational today."

"You've said that before."

They were silent again for a while.

The clouds were looking even more threatening when they got to the Snipe Keys, a little north of Key West proper.

Hailwood's father had given him the GPS coordinates for the *Libertine*. He found the big boat easily. It was moored south of the Snipes, with a view of Key West. There wasn't much traffic in the keys, in the middle of the week. On the weekend, boats could make the small islands look like parking lots.

Officially, Key West was part of Miami. But it was a duty-free zone—which meant it had the vibe of a wasteland trading post. A person could get just about anything he or she wanted there. The island itself was a mini-Havana, crowded with casinos, sex clubs of every persuasion and various trendy restaurants. His father's kind of place.

Someone on the *Libertine* noticed their approach and sounded the horn twice.

Kate had wiped most of the sunblock off of her face and was putting her hair into a pony-tail. The change in her hair style seemed to improve her spirits. "So, are you ready for this?"

Sic Semper Tyrannis

"Yeah, I'm fine with my father. My attitude is that he always disappoints, no matter what you expect. Sometimes that means he disappoints by acting completely normal."

Hailwood got on the radio. "*Libertine, Libertine.* This is the *Eighty-Six* out of Anna Maria Island. We're finally here. Read?"

"Roger, *Eighty-Six*. We see you. Our Captain has gone outside to help set up the tandem collar. We suggest that you tack around and approach the rear port for the connection."

"Will do, *Libertine*. Will come around."

He veered off from a direct line toward the yacht. He looked sharp for any markers that indicated turns in the dredged channel or sand bars. The hydrojets helped here—they didn't need as much clearance as a conventional propeller engine. But the *Eighty-Six* was just big enough that it could get stuck on a sandbar even without its propellers engaged.

When he finally pulled up alongside the *Libertine*, two crewmen extended the tandem collar. He killed the engines and the *Eighty-Six* coasted into position. He and Kate each threw a line to one of the crewmen; they pulled the smaller boat into place and dropped the collar onto its deck. The two boats were securely joined.

Hailwood's father arrived just as they were finished with the collar. Dressed in white pants, a pink polo shirt and a navy blue blazer, he looked like a booze ad. He was wearing a New York Yankees baseball cap and a deep tan.

Looks had never been his father's problem—nerves were. He seemed a little jumpy, looking around a lot. And he didn't seem to know what to say, so Hailwood broke the ice. "Permission to come aboard, sir?"

"Permission granted. Come aboard, Terry. Come aboard. Well, you made it down here okay. Not too long on the water. And it looks like you've just beat the weather."

"Yeah. We made okay time. Dad, this is Katherine Byrne. I call her Kate. Kate, this is my father. Michael Hailwood."

"Mr. Hailwood. I've looked forward to meeting you. Thanks for letting us come down for a visit." Kate shook his hand and held his right elbow with her left hand at the same time. She was working hard to get past the initial awkwardness of the meet-the-parents cliché. She was good at this. In an hour or two, he'd be completely warmed up to her.

Maybe too much so.

"Kate. Please call me Michael. You're lovely. And *I* should thank *you*. You've interrupted your vacation to come down all this way to meet the black sheep of the Hailwood clan."

"Well, you can't be too far off—you're wearing a Yankees cap."

"Yes, this. Terry said you live in New York. And I've been a fan since I was a kid. Someday, they'll return to their greatness."

"That's what my father keeps saying."

Michael asked if they wanted to move their things aboard the *Libertine*, but Hailwood was insistent that he and Kate would stay on the *Eighty-Six*. Michael accepted the strong assertion with a shrug and guided them to the front of his boat. Along the way, he gave Kate a quick tour.

The *Libertine* had three decks, though he and his friends only used the top two. The boat had a crew of seven, including the captain and the cook. He kept a full-time personal secretary and a "group of close friends."

The boat could easily sleep another dozen people. And, as the spirit moved him, he would invite more people to stay for a few days. Or a few weeks.

Hailwood and Kate saw crew members but no guests as they wound their way toward the main entertaining area. And the crew clearly made the point of staying out of sight. This shyness had a slightly creepy effect.

When they got to the salon near the front of the upper deck, the view of the small islands and the channels running among them was spectacular. The afternoon sun was still bright, the rain clouds were behind them and water was blue and smooth.

Kate said, "This is beautiful."

Michael laughed in a high-pitched screech that didn't match his appearance. "That's why I don't like to wander too far. We cruise down to the islands and go over to Mexico a couple times a year. But I'd be perfectly happy to just putt around in circles right here. I've seen the world and don't really care to see anything else.

He was warming to her. "Well, come on you two, it's time to meet my menagerie."

He loved calling his group a "menagerie."

They walked into the salon, which opened out to the main dining deck. Together, the salon and deck were probably close to a thousand square feet. The design was Scandinavian minimalist—lots of white and blonde wood, inside and out.

There were four people in the salon and on the deck. Michael introduced Kate to each one. "This is Deb Shamansky. She's been with me longer than any other woman I've ever know. Deb, this is Kate. Terry's friend."

Hailwood had met Deb many times. She was well past 40 but kept in good shape. Her blonde hair was thin but seemed to be natural and she wore it long; she always dressed in sheer clothes that showed off her body. This afternoon, she had a basic bikini top and a white wrap around her hips. Hailwood noticed the freckles on her shoulders and chest. This was a woman who'd been trading on a tanned body for 30 years. Treating her skin cancer was going to make some dermatologist rich.

She was attractive, though.

"This is Katrina Mandlikova. When I first met Trinka—what, two years ago?—she couldn't speak any English. We taught her to speak English and *she's* taught *us* everything else."

Katrinka smiled at Kate and said hello but didn't get up from her deck chair in the sun. She was wearing a black bikini bottom. Or maybe it was underwear. Everything else on her body was ink. The tattoos started above her elbows and wrapped up around her shoulders, down her back and breasts, into her black panties then out again, down her thighs and stopped just above her knees. The colors were brighter than he'd ever seen in tattoos—reds and blues and yellows that combined into complex hues. And the images were animals, human faces and geometric shapes that flowed into one another with strange perspective, like a pattern-recognition test.

In fact, that's exactly what it was. Her tattoos were a pattern recog test.

She had a pierced belly button and both nipples had rings through them. But these piercings seemed like an anti-climax after all of the artwork.

Oddly, nothing pierced on her face—and no earrings.

Hailwood had met Trinka before. But he'd never seen her so close to nude. The artwork was impressive. And it occurred to him that, if Trinka dressed in the right combination of an oxford shirt and Bermuda shorts, you might mistake her for a preppy girl with a big rack.

Sic Semper Tyrannis

The "boys" were inside.

"This is John Michael Marr and Peter Shaye. Boys, this is Kate."

Neither Marr nor Shaye was a screaming queen. But they exuded sodomy. They were both in better physical shape than Hailwood was, even though they were at least 10 years older. Marr—by himself—could pass in most circles as a slightly vain ex-jock. But, once he started talking, Shaye had just enough of a sing-song lilt that no one would mistake him for straight.

And the one's effeminacy made both seem queer. I was rare to see gays outside City walls. They fared very poorly in the wasteland—and Hailwood has always thought of the water as part of the wasteland. But what was this boat, really? Part of the wasteland? A City unto itself? Neither. It was his father's oddball realm.

The boys were friendly enough. And Hailwood had always tried to stay on their good side—this went for all of the creatures in his father's menagerie. He imagined that their bad side was a bad place.

Michael went behind the bar and took drink orders. Vodka tonics seemed to be the consensus choice. All the while, he regaled Kate with various expositional tales about himself. "Years ago, I decided I didn't want to end up like some old corpse, attended to hand and foot. So, I got rid of a couple of crew members and made a rule that we all serve ourselves on this boat. I've got a great chef downstairs—he's Cuban but can cook French or Japanese. And the crew brings the food up. But we eat everything family style. I just felt ridiculous having these guys wait on us when we see each other every day and count on *them* to keep the boat running."

The non-waiter crew brought up a couple of plates of appetizers. Lobster spring rolls and conch fritters.

"We're going to be eight for dinner. I have a personal assistant who works with me here. Really, he splits time between here and small office I keep in Miami. But, the truth is, that Miami office only exists to give him the excuse to be somewhere else a few days each week. He's a serious fellow. And I think our polymorphus perversity here is a little much for his taste." The boys laughed at that. Even Trinka smirked. "But he did want to meet you, Terry."

The food was very good. While his father talked to Kate, Hailwood sat in the chair next to Trinka and tried to make some small talk.

"I never noticed how much body art you have."

"How would you have? We have met twice. Raining both times. It is no reason for sunbathing." She spoke without any trace of accent. But she still had the slightly awkward grammar of a non-native speaker.

"Well, I'm impressed. Some of it looks three-dimensional."

"Yes." She smiled with satisfaction. "*Trompe l'oeil.* Trick of the eye. M.C. Escher, eh? Your father likes it."

"But his talk is cheap. You're the one who has to live with it. Do *you* like it?"

"I *love* it."

He could see why his father had kept Trinka around longer than other young girls he'd picked up and dropped off along the way. She was assertive. Most sex toys looked good but were passive.

Michael's assistant joined the party from somewhere below. Hailwood had expected a middle-aged man—he was off by a couple decades. The assistant looked to be in his 20s—not much older than Hailwood himself. And he dressed more like a Brahmin than a manager. This didn't mean that his clothes were formal. Just simple and well-made.

"Ah, Kate and Terry. Alfonso Herrera. He's the man who keeps my stately pleasure dome decreed. Al, this is my son Terry and his dear friend Kate."

"Mr. Hailwood. Miss."

Hailwood shook Herrera's hand. It wasn't a very strong grip. That *was* like a manager. So what explained the clothes? "Call me Terry. And this is Kate. My father speaks very highly of you."

"Well, thank you. We have had some success in the markets lately. We have a good system. Your father thinks in broad strokes about where he wants to invest and what he wants to do. And I take care of the details." Herrera spoke slowly and deliberatively. And he held very long eye contact…almost strangely so.

"If you've found a good way to work comfortably with my father, you're the only person in the world who has. Except maybe Deb." Hailwood looked over toward her—she didn't seem to be paying attention.

"Well, I find it productive. And I hope your father does, too."

Michael screeched another high-pitched laugh. "Hope I do? Al, you're never going to work anywhere else, for anyone else, as long as I'm breathing." And then *sotto voce* to Hailwood: "Terry, he's quadrupled the high-risk portion of my portfolio in less than two years. It used to be 25 percent. Now it's half—and it'd be more but we keep moving money out to more conservative stuff. And the savvy bastard has put most of his salary in with me."

"So, where did you guys find each other?"

"He emailed me. When he was in college. Tell Terry the rest, Al. I'm got to go make a quick check on dinner."

Trinka followed Michael back and down into the boat.

In his slow, wide-eyed manner, Herrera told the story. He was from a family of managers in Miami but had attended the Wharton School in Philadelphia. Like most of the Legacy Colleges that operated within Cities, Wharton had a relatively large scholarship program; it attracted lots of kids from the management class and even some from the lower classes.

Herrera had been a champion model investor in college and done some kind of research project on pre-Reckoning hedge funds. He decided that he'd rather try some the old investment tactics than take a management job somewhere. So, he did research on wealthy Brahmins who were unconventional enough to try old-fashioned investing strategies. After two weeks of looking, he created a list of 240 candidates—ranked by reported wealth and Herrera's own standard of eccentricity.

To this Hailwood asked, "So few?"

He noticed that Trinka was back, now wearing a black sarong-like outfit that covered all of her tattoos and made her look more like a regular person than a sex toy.

She ducked back against the back wall and changed the music from vintage big-band stuff to modern industrial jazz.

Michael Hailwood was number 26 on the list and the first who answered Herrera's email. "I told your father that I wanted to make enough money for myself quickly enough that I could live from investments by the time I was 30. My offer was the same that I had made to the 25 before him. I would sign a five-year contract to work for him, full-time, where and how he preferred. The contract would be voidable at any time by the employer but not by me. I would take no salary in cash. I would only receive room and board and one-half-of-one percent of the profit that I made from investment funds I managed each quarter. And I would include that compensation in the investments we made during the five-year term. I would only take my money out at the end of the term."

When Michael rejoined Herrera in telling the story, all eight people got food and sat around the big table in the salon.

Michael tested Herrera with a $1 million fund. In the first 90 days, he'd boosted that to $1.4 million. So, Michael gave him more. And a lot more. By the end of the first year, he was managing a quarter of Michael's money. By the end of the second, he was managing half. Now, essentially, all of it.

Michael, cutting into Herrera's story with colorful details while he made more drinks, said, "And I wish I'd given him all of it right away. That ramping-up probably cost me $50 million. And, now I've only got about a year left on the contract."

Hailwood asked what Herrera's secret was.

Herrera answered in what seemed to be an honest effort. "There's really no secret. I invest in stocks and currency. And, on occasion, we have made some short-term commercial loans. For stocks, we start by scanning for fundamental value in the pre-Reckoning Graham model. Then I scan for industry segment volatility, based on published information and my own proprietary formulas. Then I follow a somewhat complex regression analysis of the stock, its sector and its regional economy. This regression analysis is the only intellectually difficult step in the process. For currencies, I use the same system—except I skip the first step. And, for the loans, I use *only* the first step. Plus the understanding that I want companies desperate enough to pay my high fees—but promising enough to pay them and not go bankrupt."

Hailwood couldn't resist testing Herrera's computer-like rationality. "So, how much money have you made from your halves of a percent?"

"Over a million dollars."

This was too modest for Michael: "True but misleading! It's over $5 million. When our contract is up, this kid is going to strike out on his own and leave me in the dust."

"I might be open to an extension," Herrera said, without a trace of irony. "One thing I have learned to appreciate is the leverage you get when dealing with volume of money your father has. I could do well on my own; but, with your father, we have access that I wouldn't. I'm not exaggerating to say that we have as much liquid capacity as some smaller commercial banks."

147

Sic Semper Tyrannis

The three drinks in Michael couldn't let such a bland statement stand. "He's being modest again. We're on the same level with a bunch of small and medium-sized i-banks. We get the same calls from companies and lawyers. Even if we pass on a direct deal, we've got access to the best information. And we can always buy stock somehow related to the deal."

Kate chimed in: "Isn't that illegal? Insider trading or end-running or something?"

"Well, it would be if we were a bank or a brokerage house. But we're not," Michael boasted. "We're a privately-held fund. All we've got to do is pay our taxes to the City and we can do what we like."

"And what City is that? Where you pay your taxes."

"Miami. The fund is based in Miami. But the investments are all over the place. All over the world. But Al spends most of his time in Miami."

"As long as your father and I can talk for a few minutes a day, we can cover the bases. I'm trying to convince him that I can stay in Miami full time—and just call him out here. Or wherever he is. Satphones work anywhere."

Dinner was fried grouper—not a fine fish, but a local favorite—and rock shrimp, one of his father's favorite things. And there were two salads, a fancy potato concoction made with wasabi, some kind of wild rice dish and a steamed green that was like spinach but much more tart.

"But doesn't my father need to sign papers and review documents."

"I can send these online. Or I can sign."

"He's got a limited power of attorney. He can make basic trades himself. And that's usually enough—because we've got to keep a low profile. If a bunch of stock jockeys hear that Al bought this or sold that, they flood in after him. And that grinds down on our return."

Hailwood asked Michael whether he had a lawyer look over the power of attorney.

"…well, I guess you could say that. Al's my lawyer, too."

Hailwood lifted his glass to Herrera, "Don't rob my father blind."

Herrera didn't see any humor in that. "I can make more money for myself keeping him in the life he wants that I could make stealing from him."

Trinka and the boys stepped into the resulting silence and whined

148

that they were tired of listening to business. They wanted to talk about people—even about themselves.

Hailwood took a break from the conversation long enough to notice half a dozen vapor trails slicing across the florid post-sunset sky. They were jets flying south from Tampa and Miami. And a couple coming east from the West Coast. The trails picked up a golden glow from the sun that had already set.

Shaye, the less masculine of the boys, suggested the old game of each person describing himself or herself in a list of eight single words.

Hailwood suggested a less personal game. *Genius or asshole*. It was something that had worked well at their Friday night dinners at school. Basically, one person started the game by naming a person who'd been in the news in the last month. Then, moving counter-clockwise, each person at the table had to say whether that name from news was a genius or an asshole—"no hedging, a choice must be made"—and then briefly explain the choice. The last person who chose and explained got to suggest the next name from the news.

While the game sounded simple enough, it usually worked well at boozy dinners. "I'll start," Hailwood offered. "Mina Potter."

Kate was sitting to his right and she knew the game from the DKE House. "Genius. She's a genius. I've never seen her sitcom. I've never seen her ads. I didn't see the porn vid that was 'accidentally' posted online. And I'm not a snob about what I watch on the screen. But I've never seen any of the alleged work that has made this woman famous. Yet I recognize her instantly in the store or on the news. She's a genius. Michael?"

Hailwood's father thought for a second. "I agree she's a genius. I have seen her sitcom. It's pretty bad. But she does have a sleazy kind of sex appeal. The mystery to me is why she's become such a huge deal on the screens. There are many others prettier. And sexier. Seems pretty random—which means someone's a genius. I'm willing to take a flyer that it's the bimbo herself. Deb?"

She cleared her throat before she said anything. "I'd have to agree with Michael. Anyone who can make herself a household name like that has a genius for self-promotion. The will power to make herself famous is what impresses me."

It wasn't a caustic as the game usually warranted. Hailwood thought Deb's take wasn't bad. He nodded toward John Michael.

"Genius. She's a goddess of bad taste."

Bitchy but succinct. Hailwood nodded to Shaye.

"Genius."

Maybe he was angry about not playing the list-of-words game. Hailwood nodded to Herrera.

"I have no idea who you're talking about. But if everyone else at the table knows her, she must be a genius of some sort."

This wasn't going very well. At school, some of the brothers would pick the unpopular option—just to stir up debate. "Trinka, it's down to you. Someone has to say Mina Potter is an asshole, just to make it interesting."

"Asshole. Because someone has to say it."

"Thank you, Trinka. Now, you get to choose the person."

She shelled a shrimp and dipped it in cocktail sauce while she thought. "I know. Michael Crowley."

"Interesting. If you think I've got any special insider information, you'll be disappointed. He was one of the youngest City presidents in history—that speaks to genius. But, on the brink of a trade war, he gets caught taking bribes. That's definitely asshole. Well, call me a hometown boy, but I've got to go with asshole. He shouldn't have been sticking it to the City. Tampa made him—he owed it clean service. Kate?"

She drank some of the Andean white wine that Michael had opened with the food. "I'm going to say genius. I think he didn't want to be the head guy when this southern trade war started up—so, he orchestrated the bribe allegations. They'll kick his case around for a few months, he'll pay a fine and go become President of some other City. I say genius."

Michael made a face of exaggerated disdain. "My lovely Kate, you're creating conspiracy. I have it on good advice that precocious Mr. Crowley was fighting to keep his job. Still is, in fact. Asshole."

Deb agreed with Michael. "The man is a criminal. That's not genius." The second time around, her earnestness was starting to seem a little dull-witted.

John Michael also agreed. "Asshole. Ick. Asshole."

Shaye also agreed.

Herrera said, "Crowley is a manager. That precludes genius. And he's a thief, so that demands 'asshole.'" And it was his turn to choose a famous person.

The game lost its charge before the choice came all the way around the table. Deb and the boys basically agreed with whatever Michael said. So did Herrera.

This was the drawback to his father's perfect little world. People who put pleasure so far first were basically empty.

Herrera was the first to excuse himself. "Terry, Kate." He sounded awkward, wrestling with the first names. "It was a pleasure to meet you. I hope and expect that we will see each other often in the months and years ahead."

He was trying hard to sound and act like a Brahmin. But those hard efforts only made him seem more like a manager.

The boys made themselves after-dinner drinks and headed down to their room to "get high and watch some movies."

Michael suggested that the five of them who were left move out to the deck for brandy and cigars. They went out into the clear but muggy night—Michael brought out the bottle and four Cuban cigars. Only Deb didn't smoke.

For the first few minutes, no one said much. They just puffed on the tobacco and drank the fancy drink. The lights on the deck were brighter than Hailwood had expected, so sitting around the circular table made him think of a poker game.

Finally, Michael opened: "Kate, I've had the distinct impression all night that you want to say something but have been holding back."

Kate was struggling with a comfortable way to hold her cigar. "Me? No. I'm not someone who holds back. If I wanted to say something, I would."

"Really? Because I notice this eye-roll that you do. Maybe it's just something between you and Terry. But it struck me as holding back."

"Really. I'm not harboring unspoken thoughts. I meant everything I've said. The food at dinner *was* very good. And this boat *is* amazing. And you *do* seem pretty content with the life you've made. So, good for you."

Hailwood fought the urge to step in on her behalf. She could handle herself with his father. Instead, he pushed a granite ash tray her way. And he nodded slightly once toward it. She could just put the cigar on a groove of the ashtray while she talked.

"Okay. I appreciate the effort you made to come down here. I want you to feel free to speak your mind. I want to have a good relationship with you. A strong one. Especially if you're going to be with Terry for a long time. Which I think you are. Terry's been a serious person since he was a little boy. I'm glad he was able to find someone serious to be with him. He's lucky."

Michael took a long drag from his cigar. This may have been why he baited Kate to ask him something—so he could make a long answer.

"But I'm not a City person. Definitely not. I'm a soft-hearted aesthetic living in a hard-hearted materialistic world. Luckily, I have the means to build a life for myself outside of the ugliness. And so that's what I do. And I work hard to make sure that I keep my little hothouse away from the ugly world. I love beauty. I hate ugliness. Call me shallow."

Hailwood noticed Deb's eyes glaze over when his father pulled out his oft-repeated bit about loving beauty. He wondered what she'd had to deal with in his pursuit of "beauty." He imaged that she would happily have been the second wife in a big house in Tampa. Instead, she'd lived 20 years of sexual hedonism—three-ways, four-ways, men, women, close friends, strangers.

The sun set spectacularly over the Gulf of Mexico. And, since the sun had stayed in the sky so late in the evening, darkness fell jealously quick.

"And this isn't a retreat for me. This is my world. My menagerie. We seek beauty and pleasure together. The world forces a choice between the nihilism of the wasteland and the fascism of the Cities. I reject that choice."

Maybe it was the drink. Michael was getting pompous.

Kate pierced that with a question that was more barbed than her delivery. "Is that why you've never divorced Terry's mother?"

His father winced for a second at the question…but recovered quickly. He believed in his image as the worldly playboy and he wasn't going to let her prodding fluster him. "I've never divorced Marianne because she's never asked me to. I think she counts on the coverage of our marriage to live in the same house with my father and not become a social pariah. She cares about things like that more than she'll ever admit. She doesn't go out that much socially, but she cares immensely about status. I don't feel disdain for her. She's a sad woman. I pity her."

"Do you love Terry?"

"With all my heart."

"Do you love your father?"

"I respect the things he has...maintained. But he has some pathetic weaknesses. He's desperately afraid of dying. Despite the nanobot treatments and the gene therapy, he's going to die like everyone else. And he *hates* that. He may be 200 when he finally goes. But he will go. He'll just be such a mummy that no one will even realize it when he breathes his last."

Hailwood didn't like to hear anyone—even his own father—talk about his grandfather like that. It was a strange sensation, rising to the Old Man's defense. But Kate's questions saved him from having to say anything.

"Do *you* want to live a long life?"

"Maybe. But I want to live *well*. I don't want to be some grizzled old piece of protein that they keep having to pump full of nanobots to keep the heart and lungs working. And, when I do go, I want someone to miss me enough that they cry. I like to think my rabbits here on the boat will miss me. And maybe Terry will."

Kate either didn't have any more questions or thought the better of asking any more. "Well, I'm impressed. For a libertine, you certainly seem to know what you want. That's not...expected."

"Thank you. Now that we've shared some intimacies, I'd like to ask *you* a few questions."

"Okay."

"Do *you* love Terry?"

Hailwood had been quiet long enough. "That's a horrible question to ask my girlfriend while I'm at the table. You're putting her on the spot—and may be humiliating me. I think Kate's good for me. In the way I want and need someone to be good for me. She's a decent person. And she and I will figure out how we love each other for ourselves. Leave it at that."

Kate sat back and took a drag on her cigar. Her eyes jumped mischievously. She'd have gone a round or two with Michael—but she was probably glad Hailwood interrupted with the save.

Michael shrugged his shoulders in retreat. "Fair enough, fair enough. I was just asking her the same question she asked me. But I suppose there's a difference in the question. Let me think for a minute." And he sat back with his cigar.

Deb broke the moment of silence. "Kate. Will you live with Terry in the wasteland, when he starts teaching at the College?"

This was her role. To intercede for Michael.

"Well, we've discussed it. I'm from New York. That's the world I know. I've always planned to live there. We might try to split our time between Manhattan and the wilds. Some teachers do it."

Hailwood caught his father's eye, "I've told Kate I'd learn to fly and maybe get a small plane. That would make the commute a lot easier."

Michael's eye snapped out of a late night lull. "Excellent. Deb is taking flying lessons. I think it's something more people should do."

Deb smiled and chatted about her lessons for a few minutes. Her happy chatter had the perverse effect of killing the exchange. Everyone else sat back with their tobacco and liquor. When she was done talking about doing her first vertical take-off and landing flight, Michael was finished with his cigar and ready to go to bed.

"I think I'm going to turn in. You two, thanks so much for making the trip down here. I'm sure you'll have hell to pay when you get back to Tampa."

There was more than trace of self-pity in that response. Hailwood couldn't let it stand. "What are you talking about, Dad? Weren't you just up at the house yourself?"

"So you heard about that? Yeah. I was there for a couple of days. True, true. As much as I may hate the Old Man, I'm his only son. No matter how cranky and dissatisfied he may be, you and I are his blood. Don't ever forget that."

Hailwood found this surprisingly sentimental for his libertine father. He chalked the vibe up to the parting words of the night.

Michael and Deb left. That left Hailwood, Kate and Trinka. The three of them smoked in silence.

While he worked on his cigar, Hailwood imagined taking Trinka back to the *Eighty-Six* with Kate. And talking them into some pornographic three-way sex. But that image didn't hold. The thought of fucking Trinka carried just enough incest to be a buzzkill.

Maybe some other time. And not on his father's boat. And not with Kate.

This reverie made him feel guilty enough that he wanted to say something. "Do you ever want to leave, Trinka?"

She exhaled a small cloud of cigar smoke. "I have left. A couple of times. But I come back."

"Why?"

She stamped out her cigar and finished her brandy. "I admire Michael. He has courage. A different kind of courage, maybe. He seeks pleasure. Most people don't. Even really rich guys. And he understands that pleasure is good. Michael thinks beyond money. He might seem weird to you. But he isn't. He knows what he likes. I'm going to sleep. Good night."

She made a slight bow toward each of them on her way back inside.

So, Hailwood and Kate—the guests—were left to themselves on the deck with the stars out over the dark Gulf. The music was still playing. They both still had cigars and brandy left.

Finally, Hailwood started laughing quietly to himself. Kate looked over to him and then joined in.

"We should make a quick exit in the morning and head back."

"Agreed. But it *is* nice out here."

"Well, yeah. Of course. But living out here makes you strange."

"You don't have to worry, Hailwood. You're no much like your father. I'm not sure I've met anyone who is. He's so…transparent?"

They finished their vices slowly and watched the stars. She gave up on her cigar halfway through and stamped it out. Then she reached over for his hand.

As it got closer to midnight, the stars shined brightly enough that they bounced blue light off of the deck and all furniture on it.

They slept in the *Eighty-Six* and were up an hour after dawn. When they came over the *Libertine* to say goodbye, the only person awake was Deb. She went down and got Michael.

The four of them had a quick cup of coffee and some meaningless small talk. Then, seconds after Hailwood said he and Kate needed to get going, a couple of crew members materialized to help the *Eighty-Six* cast off.

As Hailwood pulled away, Michael waved and yelled: "Take care, Terry. I'd like to see you next time you're down."

"Okay, dad."

It took Hailwood half an hour to plot the course back to Tampa and call his plan in to Tampa Coast Guard. When he was done, he set autonav and sat next to Kate, who was lying on the stern deck.

He didn't say anything, so she finally did. "They're all pretty strange, Terry. But he's the strangest. And he definitely seems damaged. Something fucked him up."

"Yeah. Something did. I mean, I get the impression he was always a odd bird. But for a while he kept it together for a more normal life. Then something pushed him over the edge."

"Something." She opened her right eye at him and squinted through the morning light. "You're the one who says we're all the product of the choices we make, Terry. Just be kind to them and keep them at a healthy distance."

When they got back to the house, the Old Man was gone on a business trip up north.

The next day, Hailwood's mother rode to the plane with them and chattered on about her plans to come up north for a visit. She wanted to see the College campus (she'd never been) and might also include a few days in New York. She was too coy to come out and ask to meet Kate's parents—but Kate took the bait and offered to arrange "a dinner or something" where everyone could meet.

Marianne seemed satisfied with that.

After the bags were loaded on the plane, Kate gave Marianne and small peck on the cheek and Hailwood tried to get away with the same.

But his mother grabbed his shoulders and looked him hard in the eyes. "I'm afraid, Terry. I don't see you enough. And I always fear that when I say good-bye, it's going to be the last time."

He bristled in her grasp. "Don't be melodramatic, mother. I'm not going anywhere crazy or doing anything dangerous. Let's plan for a trip up north—and you can meet Kate's parents. Don't worry."

He hugged her dutifully and climbed onto the plane.

Eleven

The City of Tampa SCSHF—Special Circumstances Security Holding Facility—was in Brandon, a town about an hour south and east of the Downtown Sector. Brandon was an industrial center, notable for the volume of phosphate processing that took place there—closer than most citizens realized to desirable living areas around the Bay.

At some point, the SCSHF had been a school, so it kept a low architectural profile. People drove by it every day, not even realizing that some of the most violent criminals in the City were locked inside it gray walls.

This was all the opposite of Security Prime, which stood tall in the Downtown Sector—a 50-story symbol of the City's power for everyone to see.

Here in Brandon, even an attorney with business in the SCSHF could drive past its main entrance without realizing he'd gone too far. Gaynor was half an hour late for their regular meeting.

He explained the whole story in such a rush that Crowley couldn't understand.

Made a wrong turn off of Old Brandon Road, which set in motion a series of delays. He and his car were scanned at the main gate, then let through. He parked in the visitor's section, handed his keys to a guard who grunted acknowledgement and then waited in a short line of lawyers and family visitors to be scanned on his way into the main entrance.

At the main entrance, he headed for the "Attorneys with Business" gate, where he was scanned a third time.

From that gate, he was escorted by an obese guard down a 90-foot hallway to a gray waiting room. He sat there for a few minutes, while Crowley was brought out from his cell in the Isolation

Containment (Nonviolent) Section.

Finally, Gaynor was scanned a fourth time before he was buzzed into a private room were he could speak with Crowley in what passed for privacy here. Another obese guard stayed in the room with them and the conversation was videoed and audioed.

Crowley had trouble following Gaynor's chatter about his trip in. He was having trouble understanding much beyond the most fundamental declarative statements. He worried that they were drugging his water or food. But he knew it was important not to sound paranoid or delusional.

The room was sparse. Gray concrete walls. One table. Two chairs. Surveillance cameras in all four corners near the white ceiling. The table was a 4-foot by 6-foot metal and rubber box—with a one-inch white stripe painted down the middle, to remind lawyers and inmates to keep to their sides.

One plastic chair was on the prisoner's side of the line and table; one plastic chair was on the attorney's side. The guard in the room stood to the right side of the table, right along the white line. He would watch the conversation like the umpire of a tennis match.

Behind the observing guard, at least two more fat guards watched the meeting through an inch of bullet-proof plastic.

Gaynor set up his laptop, careful to keep it on his side of the table. He did a quick sound and vid check to make sure that it would record everything in the room clearly. And then he waited another few moments.

Crowley had his head shaved again, so the half-inch of graying brown hair that had been there during their last meeting was gone. His eyes looked confused. He was still chewing his fingernails.

But he looked healthy. Not signs beatings or physical abuse. And Gaynor thought Crowley looked better having lost some weight since his arrest.

"If we could get you into court, it might help the case."

"I'd like to be there."

"Well. It's going to be tough. This isn't a regular criminal case. They're wrapping everything up in City Security interests. I'm going to try to bring you in as a witness for your own defense. But that will mean you have to testify. Do you think you could do that?"

Sic Semper Tyrannis

"Yeah. I'm fine. Or as fine as you'd expect. I've had a headache since I got in here. Isn't it a bad sign if you think I need to testify?"

"Sometimes. But the usual rules go out the window in a case like this."

"Right. So, how is our case going?"

"Not so well. But I'm expecting a turn in our favor in the next few days. How are they treating you?"

"They? There's not really any *they*. I see the guards when I'm coming out to see you. I haven't seen another prisoner the whole time I've been here. I can walk the hall in front of my cell for 10 minutes every day at 3:30 pm. That's the only way I know what time it is each day. I never seen anyone other than the guard in the hall with me. There's a window at the end of the hall, so I've got a narrow view of one of the access roads from that. I'm not sure exactly what it is; and no one will tell me. I get sunlight through the window near the ceiling of my cell for about an hour each morning." Crowley realized he was rambling. He licked his lips and looked around for a glass of water. There wasn't any.

Gaynor trained the laptop camera more carefully on Crowley's right eye. The initial questions were designed to measure his overall mental well-being.

"How's the food?"

"Food? It's okay. Twice a day, they knock on my door. I slide the empty tray out and they slide a new tray in. One meat, one starch, one green vegetable. Cup of milk or juice. It's alright."

"Are they letting you read the news?"

"There's a screen built into the wall of the cell next to the bed, so I can read the news or a few books they allow. I get the feeling the news is censored. I haven't seen anything about the trial, which is strange. But I'm about halfway through *Moby Dick*—which I've never read. Mostly I just sit on my cot and try to think. Has Margot contacted you?"

"No."

"Me neither. I hope the kids are okay."

"I haven't heard otherwise. Listen, we need to go over a few things so that I can make the best case on your appeal."

"On appeal?"

"Are you aware that your wife is testifying against you?"

"What?" His pupil dilated and then flashed out of the small

insert screen. He sat forward in his chair. "Why? She doesn't know anything about the details of my work."

"You need to sit back, so I can record this interview, Michael."

He nodded wearily and sat back in his chair. It wobbled a little.

"She's going to testify about money that you transferred through various sham corporations into accounts that you control. Apparently, she's been keeping records for years."

The story sounded right, somehow, to Crowley—even thought he was sure it wasn't true. It was a good plan. If someone wanted to set him up, they'd offer his wife money and then use some of that money as "proof" that he'd stolen the money.

But he couldn't keep his mind focused on the details long enough to make sense of the whole thing. Scenes from the whaling boat in *Moby Dick* kept interfering with his thoughts about business. He knew he understood what was happening, but he was having trouble keeping his thoughts organized long enough to say them to his lawyer.

"Of course. They'd do it like that. Set up fake transactions… and then let her keep part of the money as the pay-off."

"Who's *they*, Michael?"

"I don't know. Chambers? Sandoval? Old Man Hailwood? I don't know. Who benefits from me out of the picture?"

"Lots of people, starting with Chambers. That might be something we can work with. But I'm not sure why Chairman Hailwood would bother with a conspiracy. He could just fire you."

"That's not how he operates. He's behind the scenes. He never wants to be connected to anything."

It felt good to get some of his thoughts out. But the details were fleeing from Crowley's mind as he said the words; he still couldn't keep the whole story in his head at the same time.

He kept thinking about the Indian harpoon throwers from the *Pequod*.

"Well, that might be true. But I suggest that we leave the Chairman out of our counter-argument. It's just going to make you sound paranoid. The Chambers narrative makes sense. He's ambitious. He wants to take over as CEO. He plants evidence about financial crimes—something he's uniquely positioned to do, as CFO."

Crowley couldn't stay focused enough to follow what Gaynor

was saying. His mind had wandered on to the story from the screen about some comedy actress who was getting a divorce from her husband. She was crying because he was having an affair with his costar in another movie.

"Gaynor, I can't follow most of what you're saying. It's really hard for me to focus."

"Hmm. Are they giving you any pharma?"

"No. No pills or shots. But who knows what they're putting in my food."

"I can ask for some blood tests to make sure you're clean."

"Yeah. Maybe we should do that."

"Of course, it might not be any pharma they're giving you. It could be the pharma you're *not* getting."

"Yeah. I thought of that, too."

"Were you taking any Neuroplex?"

"Sure, two 500 mg Clarity pills every morning."

"That Neuroplex is insidious. That's probably what's going on, Michael. They don't have to drug you. You're going through Neuroplex withdrawal."

Crowley was having trouble keeping focused on what Gaynor was saying. He was locked onto the word *insidious*. He couldn't think of what *insidious* meant, though he knew he'd known it at some point. "Withdrawal?"

"I've seen this before with white-collar clients. It can get pretty bad before it gets better. You need to drink a lot of water."

"Yeah. I'm thirsty."

Gaynor stood and whispered something to the guard, who nodded and whispered something into his neck.

"How long?"

"Since you were arrested? Three weeks."

"No. How much longer?"

"I don't know. Maybe another week—or another few days. Let's wait a week before we order that blood work. But, listen to me, you need to drink a lot of water."

"Yeah. Water. Lots of water. Got it. I was already doing that before."

There was a knock on one of the doors and an other guard brought two bottles of water to Gaynor. He thanked the guard—and handed both bottles to Crowley.

"Drink up. Drink as much water as you can stand. I'll send a note to the Director of Inmate Affairs saying that you're not feeling well and need lots of fluids. Now, I'd like to talk with you a little more about what your wife might say when she takes the stand."

It was no use. Crowley was lost in trying to reassemble his thoughts about the set-up. Who else would be involved? The other lawyer—the Shark.

He stopped reading *Moby Dick*. And he started drinking more water—at least one glass an hour. It helped with the headaches. They changed from a sharp pain in his forehead to a duller throbbing in the back of his neck.

It was still hard to gather his thoughts, though. He could hold an abstract idea for few moments—but then it was gone and he'd have to struggle to try to bring it back.

Could this all Neuroplex withdrawal?

He tried to look up "Neuroplex" on his screen. But it resulted in a "Boolean Search Error." That meant his screen was being censored.

But he could watch all the celebrity vid news he wanted.

The guards came to get him for another meeting with Gaynor. Something was different, though. It couldn't have been a week already.

Gaynor was sitting on Crowley's side of the table. That seemed to be a huge difference. Crowley felt a strong urge to get to the other side of the table.

But that didn't make sense. The table didn't matter. Or was he forgetting something?

"Has it been a week already?"

"No. It's just been two days."

"I thought we had our meetings once a week."

"We did, but I'm going to bring you in as a witness. So, we're meeting more often. To get you ready."

"Shouldn't I be in court?"

"We've been through this before, Michael. Normally, you would be. But you've been designated a prime security threat, so you're staying here."

"Prime security threat?"

Sic Semper Tyrannis

"The City hasn't tried a sitting CEO in more than a hundred years. Under the Tampa Security Act, a CEO charged with capital crimes is automatically designated a prime security threat."

Crowley laughed. He'd signed the latest extension of the Tampa Security Act. He could remember the signing ceremony in his public offer. He hadn't supported the extension at first. But there had been some kind of deal.

"—Michael?"

"What?"

"You're acting even more distracted than you were a few days ago. I think I'm going to have that blood test run. Maybe they are giving you some kind of drugs."

"Okay."

"You need to be clear enough to assist with your own defense."

Gaynor looked at him with concern. But all Crowley could think about was the digital signature he'd clicked onto the Tampa Security Act the day he signed it. He remembered that clearly.

For the next few days, the most important thing to Crowley was the shaft of sunlight that passed through his room each morning. It moved slowly down the wall below the thin window near the top of his cell and across of the floor to his bed. Then it stretched across the bed and faded away.

He was fully focused each morning when the light came into his room.

It was hard to focus on anything else. He was tired all the time. Too tired to read the screen.

The guards came in and woke him up. They didn't usually do this.

"Come on. Get up. It's time to go."

"Lawyer?"

"No. You're taking a trip."

"Outside?"

"Yes. It's your lucky morning. You're going outside."

He rubbed his eyes for a second, then the guards took his arms and clicked them behind his back. They also clicked cuffs onto his ankles. Then they slipped his feet into the plastic shoes that he'd been given the first day he'd checked in.

One guard took each shoulder and lifted him up a little.

They slid out of the cell and walked through hallways he didn't recognize. He hadn't been in the place long enough to know where they were going. So, he just relaxed and let the guards guide him. He was groggy and it seemed the easiest thing to do.

After a few minutes of walking, they came up to a large orange door that Crowley found fascinating.

"Wait here for a minute."

It was wider than any door he'd ever seen. It seemed square. It was more like blueprint than an actual door. Its surface looked pitted and rough but the orange paint covering it was thick and solid. How many times had it been painted to get like that?

There was some talk behind him that he couldn't follow. And some electronic noises.

Finally, the guards came back and lifted him again by his armpits. These were rougher than the ones who'd brought him in.

The orange door made a loud buzzing sound and opened by itself.

"Okay. Let's go."

It was dark outside. Crowley had assumed it was daytime. The lighting inside made it hard to know for sure what time of day it was outside.

They put him in the back seat of a regular security patrol car and he waited there for a long time. He noticed that the sky was a little purple in the one direction he could see most clearly. It was above the low wall beyond his left shoulder.

Early morning. He tried to focus on that. Maybe he'd get to see some blue sky today, without having to lie on the floor and twist his neck.

They were moving him. That meant something—and probably something bad. He'd lost track of the days. But maybe the trial was over.

Where was his lawyer?

He needed to focus. If the trial was over, they might be taking him to hear the verdict. Or they might be taking him to his sentencing. That meant he might be dead soon.

The car took off suddenly, with another patrol car in front and another behind.

Their lights were flashing but they didn't make any sound.

Sic Semper Tyrannis

The streets were empty. It was very early. Five o'clock or something.

He tried to pay attention to where they were driving. But it was no use. He couldn't focus on the streets and directions. So, he just concentrated on the screen that separated him from the security troopers in the front seat. Its diamond pattern was regular and soothing.

He was in this car, driving through the City. It was early morning. The security troopers were taking him somewhere. He didn't know where. He didn't want to talk. It seemed so difficult. But he needed to know more. "Where we going?"

He was exhausted, just getting the word out.

There was a short silence, then the trooper who wasn't driving answered. "North Gate 6."

"Lawyer?"

"Don't know about that. We're just taking you to Gate 6."

This was bad. But he couldn't keep everything in his mind at once. His stomach tightened…but he couldn't remember what the biggest problem was. There was something wrong with this. Driving in a security cruiser early in the morning. He was supposed to have his lawyer and a make an appearance in court.

He focused on the screen again and tried to let the regular diamond pattern help him organize his thoughts.

He ended up just watching the street lights go past through the screen. And he fell asleep a little, still sitting up with his hands cuffed.

When they finally stopped, he woke up and didn't recognize the neighborhood. It was rough—warehouses and small wooden shacks. Everything was fenced and gated and barred and locked. In the distance, dogs were barking.

A new set of troopers opened his door and lifted him out of the backseat. They led him to a place on the sidewalk in front of the cruisers and stood there with him in silence.

He tried to clear his mind again. This might be his last few minutes alive. He wanted to know what happening.

They moved him along, through a garage doorway and into a warehouse-type elevator that was like a big cage. Six of them stood in it—and they didn't take up half of its space. There were a lot of loud noises and the elevator started rising.

It was still mostly dark out when they walked him outside from the elevator. But, out past his left shoulder, the sky was lighter purple.

They left him standing alone in the middle of an open space. He was up high, at least five stories. This was probably the City's North Wall. Like the trooper had said, at Gate 6. That would mean they were above the Gate. The walls got taller and thicker at the gates.

Lights flashed on without any warning and he was blinded. Without thinking, he started blinking his eyes because the lights hurt. The blinking made his eyes tear up a little.

"Michael J. Crowley?"

"What?"

"Are you Michael J. Crowley?"

For a second, he thought that if he didn't agree about who he was they couldn't shoot him. But that wasn't how it worked. "Yes. Yes, Michael J. Crowley."

"Mr. Crowley, I am Senior Magistrate L.L. Blaine. I have been assigned to adjudicate the case brought against you by the Board of Directors of the Corporation of the City of Tampa. Do you understand?"

Crowley had known Judge Lionel Blaine but he couldn't remember where or how he'd known him. And he didn't have the time right now that he'd need to piece it all together. He still couldn't see anything. He had no idea whether the Magistrate was standing a few feet in front of him or was speaking remotely through a vid feed.

"I can't see anything."

He was thirsty and his shoulders hurt—just like they had back in the security cruiser.

"We are videoing for the public record. Mr. Crowley, in an open court of public law, you have been found guilty of the following high crimes. Theft of City property valued in excess of $100,000. Conspiracy to steal City property. Dereliction of fiduciary duty. Breach of contract (employment). Failure to identify felonious acts. Theft by deception of more than $100,000. Conversion of stolen property. Conspiracy to advance a criminal enterprise. Use of public assets for private gain. Violation of the Tampa Security

Act. Violation of the Clean Government Act. Violation of the Fourth Government Reform and Maintenance Act. Violation of the Sunshine Ethics Acts. Do you understand what I've explained to you?"

He still couldn't see much, but his eyes were adjusting to the lights. There were a group of people standing behind them. Probably 10 of 15 feet away from him. The Magistrate's voice was coming from among those people. "I didn't do any of that."

"Do you understand that a court of law has found you guilty?"

"No. I didn't do it. Is my attorney here?"

"The trial is over. Your attorney has been released from the case."

"I'll appeal."

"The Board of Directors has already reviewed and affirmed the court's conclusions. There will be no other appeals."

"I didn't do this." His started to shake.

"As ordered by the court, I have informed you of its conclusions."

"No!"

A dull point pressed against his neck and then he felt a jolt of cold running through his body.

He felt woozy, as if he were going to faint.

Then, he heard the Magistrate's voice echoing from a distance.

"Mr. Crowley? Mr. Crowley? Can you hear me?"

He opened his eyes. Two troopers were holding him up by the armpits. He *had* fainted.

"Mr. Crowley, can you hear me?"

He was awake again, but his tongue felt heavy. That made it hard to talk. "Yeth. Ah hear ya."

"Good. By the power vested in me by the City of Tampa, I hereby sentence you, Michael J. Crowley to banishment from the City of Tampa for the duration of your natural life. You may not bring your physical presence within in the City limits. You may not enter or access the City's web facilities in any virtual presence. You may not keep or transfer any monies or financial assets through any bank or financial services firm chartered or based in the City of Tampa. Your citizenship is revoked. Your ability to own property or vote, terminated. Your standing to pursue legal remedies in Tampa courts, terminated. All benefits, salaries, monies or stipends due to you from the City of Tampa are voided and terminated."

Banishment. He was going to be thrown out in the wasteland. Toxic plants. Polluted water.

Crowley tried to say something. But he couldn't move his tongue fast enough to get any words out. One of the security troopers must have hit him with a stun stick. Standard riot gear equipment, he remembered that from a meeting with Bert Barrett. He could remember Barrett's face.

The best he could manage was a sigh that sounded like "Ahh." No one seemed to notice.

"Mr. Chambers, does the executive branch have any intent to pardon this man or commute any part of his sentence?"

"No, Mr. Magistrate, the executive branch does not intend to interfere with the implementation of your sentence. At this point, our only desire is to move away from this episode as quickly as possible."

"Thank you."

There was a short silence. Crowley could hear someone—probably the Judge—pressing buttons on a portable screen. Finally, there was a tone from that screen that sounded like a bell tolling. "It's done. The sentence against Michael J. Crowley has been entered into the public record as of 05:33 am, Thursday the Nineteenth. I hereby declare criminal case # 1148934-705 is closed."

A moment later, the lights all dimmed off and Crowley was blind again.

The troopers let go of his armpits. He tried to stand on his own but wobbled clumsily down into a sitting position. He'd gotten used to sitting on the floor cross-legged in jail. It felt better than standing.

He was very thirsty. But he couldn't talk clearly enough to ask for a drink. So, he just closed his eyes and tried to gather his thoughts. The Magistrate had said "banishment" but there was still a chance that they'd shoot him.

"Michael?" It was Margot.

He opened his eyes. She was standing over him, but all he could make out was the outline of her head and shoulders against the purple sky. "Margot?"

"I'm here to give you this." She dropped some papers in his lap.

"It's the divorce. I'm not sure I even need it now, but I thought it was better to be safe."

The way his hands were cuffed, he couldn't hold the papers. They slipped past his fingers and fell down into his crossed legs.

"I also brought the children to see you one last time." She stepped to the side and Crowley could make out the shapes of Pea and Jack.

"Pea. Ja. How are ya?"

Pea did the talking. "We're fine. We're sorry that you did these bad things, daddy."

He had to clear his thoughts for this. He had to make his mouth and tongue move. They'd have this memory of him for the rest of their lives. "I didn' do it. Loo at me. Both of you. I didn' do these things they say. But tha doesn' matter. The importa thing is that I love you. I love you. And I won't forget you. I'll make some way to see you again."

He looked each of them in eyes as long as he could focus. It felt like a long time. He had to look up at them a little, from his sitting position—but they were almost at eye level. That helped.

Pea looked upset. Jack looked like he might believe his father. Crowley focused on Jack's face and willed himself to remember it. Square for a child. When he'd come in from running or playing on a hot day, beads of sweat would seem to run up along his jaw from behind his ears. Large, bright eyes. They were looking straight back at Crowley. A small nose, like his mother's. His adult teeth were a little crooked, but the dentist had recommended waiting another year or two before getting him braces.

He forced himself to remember Jack's face.

Margot moved them away. "You know, Michael, I knew there was something wrong. I just didn't think it would be *this*."

Crowley tried to fish the divorce paper up from his lap, but he couldn't get enough of a finger-grip on them to pick them up.

"Crowley, I know what a student you are of history. So I thought that we might leave you by reviving and old tradition from the early days after the founding of the City." It was Chambers—but he sounded different. He talked more slowly and with a more noticeable accent. "Officers, will you help Mr. Crowley to his feet?"

The divorce papers fell to the ground. Crowley tried to find Chamber's face—but couldn't. Where was he?

"We used to brand thieves and criminals before we turned them out into the wasteland. We haven't branded criminals in over 100 years. But, since you are a student of history, I thought you would appreciate us bringing the traditional back."

And, in a flash, Chambers was standing right in front of him. He looked amused.

"Gentlemen, please position Mr. Crowley. This will only take a second."

Chambers stepped back and raised something that looked like a sword. But the end was bright orange.

Chambers whispered, from somewhere close behind: "You thought you were so special. That you could force your will on the City. Make this Federal Era league thing happen. But the Federal Era is dead. And one person can never prevail against the power of an institution." There was something strange about his voice.

One of the troopers grabbed Crowley's left ear and pulled his head back against his right shoulder. It hurt the right side of his neck.

Blast of pain on the side of his neck.

Everything else vanished.

The whole left side of his neck felt like it was burning. It made him fell like choking—like something was stuck in his throat. Then, the burning sensation started to shrink. He tried to open his eyes but opening them made the pain worse.

The pain got smaller and started throbbing. The trooper let go of his head but moving his neck back straight made the pain worse. He tried to hold his head back.

The troopers let go of his armpits again and, this time, he didn't have enough balance to sit down. He fell forward onto his side. The right side of his stomach took most of the blow. But he couldn't feel anything except his neck.

He knew he was passing out. It was hard to see. The people were all standing away from him in a dark clump. He felt like he was going to vomit. But he didn't have the energy to roll to his side.

Prevail, Chambers had said.

To prevail, he had to stay alive. That was his immediate goal.

The vid lights were still glowing. And the sky was a lighter shade of purple. Not blue yet.

Twelve

Hailwood was heading down to Tampa himself this time.

Kate didn't want to make the trip. And they'd had a long fight about that. In the course of the fight, she'd said that she didn't like his grandfather and was "creeped out" by his mother. The specifics were new; but the general direction had been like that for a while.

Things between them had been going badly since the start of the new school year. She'd started talking about being accustomed to being the person in charge in the relationship. And then there was the whole "Brahmin" thing. Her family had money, but they considered themselves regular citizens. New York was different, she said. There were lots of people with money, but nothing like Hailwood's family. At least nothing she'd ever met.

He'd started taking flying lessons. She hadn't.

Then she'd started saying that she never really liked his plan for splitting time between the College and New York. And, as that idea was getting closer to becoming reality, she was liking it less.

At some point, in the heat of one of the arguments, he'd said that what she really wanted from life was to be Queen Bee on a cul de sac in Staten Island. She didn't like that at all.

Which only convinced him that it was true.

She was going to spend the break in New York with her family. He half expected that she was going to give him his unconditional release after the break. He wasn't exactly sure how things had fallen apart so fast—and she'd been acting like such a bitch lately he wasn't sure whether the relationship was worth fighting for. He still liked her better than anyone else he'd ever dated. But he wasn't ever going to be the kind of husband she could boss around.

Maybe some time apart would remind her of how much better her life would be with him.

When he was still an hour north of Hartford's walls, a detail of Hartford police cruisers appeared suddenly in his rearview mirror. It was four vehicles driving well over 100 miles per hour with about a foot of space between each; they must have been using some sort of programmed driving system. Manual operators would be too likely to make some minor mistake and cause a pile-up.

He felt the red flash of a datascan around his car. The Hartford cops would have all of his registration information in seconds from the bar codes on his front and rear bumpers.

His screen chirped. Caller ID was unavailable.

"Hello?"

"Is this T.S. Hailwood?"

"Yes."

"This is Officer Jepson of the Hartford Metroplex External Security Force."

"Officer Jepson. Are you part of the detail that just blew past me on the Tollway?"

"No, sir. I'm located in the ESF Regional Command Center. I'm calling to find out whether you are planning to visit the Metroplex today. We don't have any reservation or other information that you should be expected."

"No. I'm not coming inside the walls. I'm using the Windsor Locks Air Field for some private travel. So, I'll be turning off the Tollway just before I get to you."

"Understood. Very good. Drive safely."

Hartford was having a lot of worries. Its west and north gates were under fire from gangs of highwaymen. And its managers were having to deal with encroachment from Boston to the east and from New York to the south. Politicians in both cities had suggested annexing Hartford as a solution to its economic and security problems.

A loud ping sounded from his navmap/targeting system. It had picked up some kind of weapons fire within a three-mile radius. He clicked his steering wheel mouse for details. It was ahead on the highway—no surprise there. But the system couldn't identify the weapons that had fired.

That didn't matter; he could guess that the ESF forces had found someone they didn't like. And he could already see smoke ahead. So, he moved to the far left lane and slowed down a bit.

His grandfather had said that Hartford was widely perceived as a weak and unnecessary City. Fifty years earlier, it had lost significant land and resources to New York and Boston, after the Battle of Long Island Sound. The City of Stamford had disappeared completely in that war and the City Hartford had become the weak sister of the Northeast. The only reason it still existed at all was that New York and Boston couldn't agree how to split it up. Now they seemed ready to finish the job.

With its citizens worried about their security, Hartford had become a more likely target for what managers and diplomats called "merger." And, while Boston and New York were the most likely partners, it wasn't just managers in those Cities who were talking about annexation. Bankers and currency traders had started dumping Hartford currency and bonds. A whole vicious cycle was beginning.

Hartford managers were doing what they could to prevent the death spiral. They clamped down harder on security—and were looking desperately for ways to grow out of their problems. The Western New England Tollway was one of the most profitable wasteland ventures anywhere in the world. In recent weeks, Hartford had decided that the Tollway was a security risk. For the moment, the City was content to increase its ESF presence on the road—but it was clear to all that Hartford would try to take over the whole thing, which reached north up to Montreal.

The other Cities weren't going to like that.

The ESF cars had their lights flashing. They were positioned in a loose square around the burning shell of some sort of van or panel truck. Two officers were standing with strange weapons attached to their shoulders. It didn't look like there were any survivors in the burning vehicle.

They weren't taking any chances with renegade cars.

He double-checked his aud/vid system to make sure he'd have all of this on disc. It was running.

There were three more exits to the Windsor Locks field. Once he was past the burning van, he pressed his speed back up to 100.

Steve Masterson and the plane were waiting on the airstrip when he got there. It took a minute to burn a disc with the vid scenes and the call from the Hartford cops. Then he activated the full alarm system on the Badger and jogged through the terminal.

"Sorry I'm late."

"No problem, sir. But let's get out of here," Masterson said as he locked the hatch and headed for the cockpit. "I don't care what our security people say, I consider Windsor Locks a hot zone."

"Yeah. But give me an extra pass around Hartford at the lowest safe alt. I want to see for myself how much trouble this place is in."

The suggestion didn't go over well with Masterson. He just nodded in noncommittal agreement and told his copilot to start the taxi.

They took a steep ascent to 10,000 feet and circled above the Hartford Metroplex. Most of the City looked like a normal, high-density place. But there were several noticeable empty neighborhoods that looked like a picture of dead tissue in a biology text.

A few weeks earlier, there had been a series of protests about Hartford's tightening security; the managers had responded by calling the protests "riots," cordoning off the neighborhoods and ordering them emptied. It wasn't a good response. Complaints spread quickly and the capital markets hit Hartford's currency and bonds even harder.

This wasn't the Middle Ages or communist Russia. No one could bury bad news.

His grandfather had talked about Hartford in one of their recent calls: "They're in deep yogurt. Just watch. A death spiral doesn't seem so bad at first. It's not linear; it's geometric. Seems like a small problem or a series of small problems. Then it turns deadly faster than anyone expects. Because the real rot has already happened."

The emptied neighborhoods seemed like proof of what his grandfather had said.

"Thanks, Steve. I've seen enough. Let's get home."

The plane turned southeast and ascended to cruising altitude.

There were several reasons that Hailwood was going down to Tampa instead of somewhere else for the break. The most immediate was that his mother had been calling him frequently and talking about how depressed she felt. Despite all, he tried to good be to her. Also, he wanted to get away and figure what he could do…or wanted to do…to keep things going with Kate.

Also, there was also going to be a major Mars mission launch in a few days. He wanted to go over to Canaveral to watch it. Tampa took on a party atmosphere during a big launch; he wanted to be there for the fun.

He'd kissed his first girl and drunk his first beer at moon launch parties. They always lifted his spirits. And his spirits needed lifting.

Once the plane had reached cruising altitude, he got up and made himself a drink and tried to think through why he was feeling so down.

It came down to either Kate or his fucked up family. He didn't think it was Kate. He wanted to be with her because she was a strong personality; she'd always be interesting and their kids would be intelligent. But her strong personality cut two ways. She didn't want to be with him because she'd never control him like she could with some pliant managerial grinder from New York. There wouldn't be so many private planes; but she'd always know who was in charge.

In the end, he just couldn't believe she'd settle for a grinder. He was sure that things would, eventually, end up better for them.

The dread that he was feeling came from somewhere less direct.

He was long past the weirdness with his mother and his grandfather. And he was pretty sure that his recent reconnection with his father was...understandable. But his back tightened up a little when he thought about the three of them at the same time. The dread came from thinking about the family as a group.

What could he do about that? The only advantage he had on his family was time. He had to live his life on his terms and let them live theirs on theirs. And, when they were gone, he could use the family resources as he wanted—and maybe move the family forward morally as far as his grandfather had moved it financially.

Time for another drink.

While he was fixing it, he noticed the lights of a City approaching below. This was unusual; their usual flight plan stayed out over the water until they got to Daytona.

He pressed the intercom. "Steve, what's up? Why are we heading in so soon?"

"We've got clearance from Savannah and Jacksonville to come in over their airspace. And TSA is asking everyone to keep the space over Canaveral clear 72 hours ahead of the launch."

"Wow. Okay. So those guys are giving us clearance now?"

"Not usually. But everybody loves a space launch."

"Guess so."

"I can cut over to the Gulf if you're nervous about the overland."

"No, no. If you've already cleared it in overland that'll get us there faster. How long to St. Pete?"

"Umm...about 50 minutes."

"Great. Time for a drink. Thanks."

"No problem. Cheers."

Tampa's aerospace program was a major asset to the City. It was one of only two cities in North America (the other was Houston) that could put rockets into space regularly and reliably. And Houston only did a fraction of the launches that Tampa did each year.

Plus, Tampa was the only City in the world that had a regular program of putting *people* in space. It was the only City with a colony on the moon; and it was soon to be the only one with a colony on Mars.

Everyone else was content to launch a few satellites a year. Tampa had spaceplanes that patrolled Earth orbit.

Tampa kept the order in near space. Its spaceplanes could repair a malfunctioning satellite anywhere around Earth in a few hours—and they could vaporize a satellite that had fallen into rogue orbit. And Tampa got to define "rogue orbit."

This meant that Tampa had a position of significant power over other Cities, which were forced to work with it to keep their satellites working. No satellites meant no comms, no web, no streaming media on screens—death by modern economic standards.

The Tampa Space Agency was *the* major profit center for the City. And, if it was possible, the Space Agency was an even bigger strategic tool for dealing with rivals. Good relations with Tampa meant easy—if expensive—access to space. Bad relations meant launching your own rockets (costly and unreliable) or dealing with faraway cities like Moscow, Tokyo or Melbourne (costly and unreliable). And even if you managed to get your satellite up, Tampa could shoot it down.

This launch was going to be an important one. A year of unmanned cargo launches had been leading up to it. The specially-rigged spaceplane *Gasparilla* would dock with the main orbital platform, load up with supplies and booster rockets and head on to Mars. There, its crew of 10 would assemble and activate the New Orlando colony station.

A dozen cargo vehicles were stretched out ahead of the astronauts, like camels in a caravan. More would follow. And, six months later—just as the first crew was arriving—another crew of astronauts would take off.

The plan was to keep 20 people at a time at the New Orlando colony. Each mission would be two years—six months traveling there, a year at the station and six months traveling home. The plan was so well organized that it made even someone as cynical as Hailwood proud to be a citizen.

"And," his grandfather had gloated, "if it has that effect on you, imagine what it will do for all the average Jablonskis out there. These space missions work for us on so many levels, it's hard to count."

It was hot. Even at night. On the short walk from the plane to the car, his neck started to get a little damp. He pushed the air conditioning to maximum for the ride south and worked on his thesis the whole way.

No one was home when he got there. That was a little frustrating. His grandfather and mother had been so emphatic about him making it down—and then they each had other things going on.

He waved off Victor's offer of help and carried his own bag into the pool house.

Both his mother and grandfather had been calling more and sounding desperate. His mother with unexpected health problems and the Old Man with sage counsel about business and politics.

And then there was the family dynamic that Kate had seen but not fully appreciated—his father. They'd figured out somewhere along the way that Hailwood had seen his father and was talking to him occasionally.

"Don't be melodramatic," his grandfather had sneered during one vidlink conversation. "I've never hated your father. I'm merely disappointed. He could have done so much more with his life, with his native skills and the resources he had available. Instead, he's made himself into a trivial person. The comedic exaggeration of a dissolute playboy. I hope you don't choose that path, Terry."

But the fact that his grandfather was denying nearly 20 years of not mentioning his father's name made Hailwood pretty sure the Old Man thought he might follow his father down "that path." Perhaps, to the Old Man, there was little difference between drifting around the Keys as the host of an ongoing orgy and teaching Cicero to undergraduates in the northern wasteland.

Of course, the Old Man had encouraged Hailwood to go to the College; so there was some hypocrisy in his current complaint.

They were supposed to talk about that during this trip, too.

Three hours later, Hailwood couldn't sleep. He put on a robe and headed over to the Big House and one of the rocking chairs on the patio that faced the channel. Along the way, he poured himself a glass of some whiskey he'd never heard of and accidentally kicked a footrest in the living room.

When he finally got out to the rocking chairs, he took a long drink of the whiskey and let it burn a trail to his stomach. Then he let the chirps of the crickets and pouring sound of the channel currents lull him into a sense of calm.

From a distance came the faint clip-clop of cars crossing the bridge to the mainland. That was a sound from his youth that he'd never heard in such an agreeable context anywhere else.

That sound—and the fact that people were out driving past midnight—implied a security that the wasteland could never approach. The important thing to people was that Cities were safe.

An uncertain amount of time later, his grandfather slid open one of the glass doors and joined him out on the patio. They both sat in silence for a few minutes.

"Well, I'm glad you're out here. I've always liked this spot at night. One of the nicest in the place. Bit of an underutilized asset."

"You have a particular view of the world, Grandpa."

They went back to silence for a few minutes more.

"Well, I've got to get to bed. Morning meeting tomorrow. How's your girlfriend finding things?"

"She's not here. She went to New York to visit her parents."

"Oh. Didn't like her last visit?"

"Not sure. Some stuff was…an adjustment…for her. She got a little spooked when we went shopping and had one of the security guys go with us."

"Hmmm. Who went with you?" This was typical of the Old Man—the need to know every detail. Like a school teacher.

It took Hailwood a second to remember the name. "Menendez. Like the Bishop. Humberto, I think."

"Sure. Good kid. Savvy. Not your average white socks/black shoes security type. I bet he was fine. What was the problem?"

"No problem. She just wasn't expecting an armed bodyguard."

"Well, hell, people have security in New York."

"Not her people."

"New York liberals, eh?"

"Yeah, I guess."

Silence again for a few moments.

"You don't have to take security with you when you go somewhere in town, Terry. You're old enough to make your own choices about things like this. All I ask is that you keep in mind some people might consider profit in kidnapping a Chairman's family member. For money. Or leverage. It happens."

"Here?"

"No. But other places. It could happen here. We filter immigrants and visitors. We police. But we can't eliminate crime. There's always some risk."

"I understand. I just think you've been inside the City limits for so long, sometimes you have a warped perspective on what's normal."

It was dark, just a few lights from boats in the bay and some ambient light in the sky from downtown. But he thought his grandfather nodded in agreement. This was one of the old man's favorite gestures.

"She's a lovely girl. I hope we see her again." This was unexpectedly…sentimental.

"Are you feeling okay, Grandpa? A little while ago, you were telling me that people are followers who want to be lead by a strong hand. Now you're making it sound like there are anarchists hiding out in gift shops."

His grandfather stood up and walked to the edge of the patio. "Life is confusing, Terry. And confusion may be the world's natural state. Chaos is easy. So, it only takes a handful of dedicated terrorists to destroy hard-won order. *Our* challenge is to make order from the chaos. Citizens have to believe in the illusion of disinterested power. They *need* to believe in it. They want an authority figure. But they respond best to *institutional* authority. If they think that the City is just one man's—or one family's—mechanism for leveraging wealth, they'll shut down. Stop working. Act self-destructively. Not that I care about any given one of them, but societies can commit institutional suicide. That's why it's better to stay behind the scenes. If my life has taught me any lesson, that's it. In your time, I hope you'll see things as I do."

This was what his grandfather wanted out of the trip. It was about whether Hailwood would come back after graduation.

"Institutional authority. I'm sure you're right, Grandpa. But I'm not sure that I want to *have* to see things the way you do. I really think I'm going to stay up there."

"Teaching?"

"Yes. Emerging from the pack up there has been the most important thing I've ever accomplished. I'm pretty sure they're going to invite me to stay on as an instructor after this term. And that's the first step in a career. How can I leave that?"

The Old Man answered his question quickly: "Bahh. I mean, I know you can do it, Terry. Remember, I was the one who first suggested you go up there for school. You could have stayed down here and phoned it in at Harvard or Yale."

"I know."

"I realized when I suggested it that you might love it and decide to stay. Hell, I know that feeling. I felt it myself. But you can't stay up there. Your life is down here."

The Old Man could be a spider—telling people what they wanted to hear and drawing them into his web of negotiation. Hailwood had watched him do this at cocktail parties and public shareholder meetings. Many times. He didn't want to be drawn in here.

"Grandpa, your life is a constant three-dimensional chess game. You work so hard to manage the shares and the bonds. Sweating out a tenth of a point. I know you love it, but I don't think most people would. I don't think *I* would. I'd need more action."

"Action?"

"Sure. Action. Run the City directly and let the markets and the bonds manage themselves."

"You're not going to see much *action* teaching Latin out in the wasteland, Terry. Shooting squatters. I understand the romantic appeal of it, I do. But you're meant for greater things."

"What greater things, Grandpa?"

"Take over from me."

"As what? Chairman?"

"The title doesn't matter. You can run things as the representative of the Office of the Managing Partner and the Hailwood Trusts."

The Office of the Managing Partner was one of his grandfather's proudest creations, a unique legal entity. A corporation controlled by a series of family trusts that was the owner of the single largest bloc of shares in the City of Tampa Corporation. It was the mechanism of his power.

"Behind the scenes, eh?"

"Behind the scenes, in front of the scenes. Whatever you want. But I think in time you'll find out that behind the scenes is the best place to be. The most *effective* place to be. And plenty of action."

"I'm not sure behind the scenes is for me, Grandpa. I like the clarity of connecting my beliefs with my actions. I'd rather not have to negotiate everything through proxies and middlemen."

The Old Man snorted. His signature exclamation—sort of halfway between spitting and an angry laugh. "Don't be an ass. Politics is fickle, Terry. Unpredictable. Even the smartest person with the best plan can have the tables turn against him in the public forum. Let the managers take those risks with their careers. You don't need to. And pretending you do just confuses people. If you joined the civil service, the real managers—who have no choice in what they do—wouldn't applaud your democratic spirit. They'd reject you as a threat to their order."

The Old Man's thoughts were always so specific.

"So, we're back to square one then, Grandpa. I'll just stay at school and teach. I'll let the managers manage and clip my coupons every quarter."

"You'll tire of it. The academic life is essentially false. It's a romantic interlude in a young person's development. But it's not real. Life here is real."

Hailwood had heard the Old Man make this point many times. But it made more sense this time. Academic *was* essentially false. His friend Taylor had made the same point.

"So that's what it call comes down to. That's what people really want. Security?"

"That's why Cities have walls, Terry."

"So the Social Contract isn't a mutual good. Or a set of externalities. Or cultural commonality. It's City walls?"

The Old Man started chuckling at the phrase "Social Contract" and continued for a moment even after Hailwood had finished. Then: "I'm glad you've read Rousseau. But that's the romanticism."

Hailwood felt like the Old Man had put him in check. And that he needed to take evasive maneuvers. "Grandpa, one of my earliest memories is you taking me down to your office and telling me that I was the future of the family. Maybe you laid it on too thick…."

"Are you forging your life's direction on some quibble of developmental psychology?"

"No. But I think your pressure on dad is what turned *him* away from City life."

"I don't think that's true. You don't know the whole story; and it's not important. The important thing is that you're not your father."

"No. I'm not."

"You're very bright, Terry. You see a lot. And you have since you were a little boy. You're not always sure of what action to take, I know that. But you're young. And you're learning. You dropped those squatters and saved your friend's life. Decisive action in the face of harsh reality is what matters most in life."

"Academia is what interests me now."

"Fair enough, fair enough. Well, as I said, it's late and I have a meeting tomorrow."

Before the Old Man slipped away, Hailwood slipped in his question. "Grandpa, I was thinking of going over to Canaveral to watch the *Gasparilla* launch."

"Really? I figured you'd gotten too old for all that."

"You should know me better. It's the real reason I came down."

The Old Man laughed, not a snort or a chuckle this time. A friendlier laugh. "I guess so. Only makes sense. I'll call Jack Simmons in the morning and make sure the box is available. Just you?"

"No. I'll probably go with a few of the old Prep guys. And a few girls. Maybe six or eight of us."

"Okay. But keep your guests in line. We don't need any scenes"

"Of course not. We'll be model citizens. Thanks."

The Old Man had sounded nervous or worried about something. This wasn't a shock. Everyone knew the City was having trouble with senior management. But the unavoidable truth was that the Old Man was getting older. At some point, all this was going to catch up with him. Maybe that was the ambient dread Hailwood had been feeling.

He fell asleep in his rocking chair on the back patio. The breeze and the distant clacking of an occasional car crossing the bridge had always had a hypnotic effect on him.

Thirteen

Crowley was sweating when he woke up. The air was hot and humid. He was lying on dirt and dry leaves.

His neck felt like it was broken. It was stiff and tight. Swollen. He couldn't move his head in any direction without pain. Breathing was difficult. He couldn't fill his lungs.

But he could move his fingers and feet. And he could feel. His clothes were wet and sticky. Especially around his back and the back of his knees. He wasn't paralyzed.

He tried to feel his neck with his fingers. It was hard to move his hand without pulling at least a little on his neck. The pulling hurt, deep into his neck and throat.

The surface of his neck around the burn was numb. But touching it caused a throbbing pain—again, deep into his neck. A second of contact caused 15 or 20 seconds of pain.

To his fingers, the skin felt hard. But there wasn't any blood.

His head hurt. The headache was sharp again and in the front of his skull.

He didn't know where he was. On the ground. In some kind of tall grass. But he was determined to survive. And prevail.

He tried to get up. His legs were strong enough. But he felt dizzy and nauseous as soon as he got to his knees. It took three tries to stand all the way up. And then he only lasted long enough to look around once before he collapsed back to his knees and then his right shoulder.

Which made his neck throb again. He blacked out again for a while.

Was high grass toxic? He couldn't remember the list of dangerous wasteland plants—he just remembered it seemed like everything was dangerous somehow.

He tried of clear his mind enough to decide what to do. Instinctively, he tried to clench his jaw—but that inflamed the pain in his neck. So, he let his face fall slack and tried to "see through" the blackness of his closed eyes. It was a relaxing technique he'd learned way back, as a young manager.

Gradually, his mind cleared. He told himself to be egoless, to let go of his anger and frustration. Anger was pointless here. He had to surrender to his immediate circumstances if he was going recover. Each second—each breath—required his attention.

He was in a little clearing in the midst of some small trees. Maybe live oaks. They had those inside. Probably not poison.

Where was he? Probably somewhere north of the City. There were two wasteland Tollways that headed north from the walls—the Old Florida Highway near the west coast and the Old Interstate 95 near the east. In between, there was more than 100 miles of the nastiest swamps and scrub lands in the southeast. He was somewhere in that hundred miles. Probably closer to the west coast.

There were so many ways that he could die out here. The burn on his neck could get infected. Some bandit or wild animal could attack him. The plant toxins could kill him. The poisoned water could do it.

Water. He was thirsty.

He gathered up his energy and crawled toward the live oaks. It took him a long time to crawl there. He was sweating from every inch of exposed skin. And he was so tired when he reached the trees that he passed out again. Longer this time.

The next few days were miserable. It was hot and humid. He'd sleep fitfully for a few hours at a time. Then move as far he could.

His clothes were the prison-issue jumpsuit and plastic shoes. Cheap synthmesh didn't absorb sweat, so he was soaked. Badly equipped for hiking. But it didn't matter. He could barely stand.

He stumbled and crawled in what he hoped was toward the west. If he was anywhere near Gate 6—as the security troopers had said—then he was closer to the Old Florida Highway. And that should be somewhere to the west. But he knew that he didn't know which way he was going.

The live oak, scrub oak and various thorny bushes scratched his face and hands pretty badly.

He didn't see any people or animals other than birds and bugs.

Sic Semper Tyrannis

He had to keep moving. His memories of Pea and Jack's faces kept him moving. He hadn't been a sentimental parent until Margot had started talking about a divorce. But now, lying in the bushes, he cried for his children. He wanted to see them again. If he was going to do that, he couldn't give up and die in the swampy underbrush.

It rained a couple of times—hard, once. The rain was a welcomed break from the heat. He crawled out from the bushes and lay on his back with his mouth open to catch water. He turned his neck to the rain, to clean out the sweat and dirt.

The rain stung his neck a little. But not as much as his sweat did. And the sting meant his neck wasn't numb any more.

Only during the heavy rain did he collect enough water in his mouth to feel it when he swallowed.

He was into too much pain to be hungry. But he was thirsty all the time. He remembered something he'd read as a boy about sucking on pebbles to ward off thirst. So, he crawled along until he'd found a couple of small, smooth ones. They worked for a while. But they chapped his lips.

When he finally came upon a small creek, he plunged his face in without hesitating. Survive. Prevail.

Of course, he'd grown up hearing how polluted and infested the wasteland water was. But he didn't care. His thirst was stronger than any risk of cancer or intestinal parasites. The water was only a few inches deep—but it was running. So at least it wasn't stagnant. And it was just a little bit cooler than the air around him. He drank so much that he passed out again, on his back in the muddy bank.

This was the first time he slept soundly enough to dream. He dreamed of his mother telling him, "You're meant to great things, Mickey." Awake, he tried not to think about it very much. Her eyes seemed deeply, deeply sad.

Then, suddenly, he was miles up in the sky looking down on himself in the underbrush, crawling in the dirt like worms and bugs. The height made him nervous. But it seemed that, so far down below, he was part of a living system. That was comforting. Very comforting.

Later, when he thought about the flying dream, he wondered if it had been God speaking to him. Crowley had never been a religious man; but the comfort that the dream had given him was like the descriptions he'd heard of genuine religious belief.

The water didn't kill him or make him sick. In fact, he was felling better—though walking more than a few steps was still difficult. Over the next day, he collected dried leaves and built a bed for himself in a shaded bank along the creek.

Crude as it was, the bed made sleeping a long time easier. He could sleep on his side, which was most comfortable. Always had been. And, when he was awake, he didn't do much or even think much. Most of the time, he was content to watch the little ripples in the creek water change their shapes and directions.

That night, he saw his first large animals in the wasteland. A deer and two fawn came to the creek—about eight or 10 meters away from him—to drink. He rolled just slightly in his muddy bed and the deer were gone. Their speed impressed him.

That was also the first time that he was able to breathe normally.

Sleeping more steadily meant he could track time better. He stayed two nights in the mud bed. On the second morning, he was hungry enough that he figured he better find something to eat. He followed the creek for a while, figuring that if he didn't come upon the Tollway soon, he could track back to the mud bed.

He didn't find the Tollway but he never went back to the mud bed. The creek did flow through a small farm.

There were tomatoes near the creek. He climbed through the barbed wire—which wasn't much worse than climbing through the live oak—and ate the ones that were closest to red. They were big and tasted good.

His neck hurt when he chewed. But his hunger was stronger.

He was on his eighth or tenth tomato when a truck pulled up. The farmer stuck a shotgun out the window and blasted at the ground a few feet in front of Crowley.

The ground was soft enough that the shot made a muffled "pomp" sound. And Crowley was more worried about eating than being killed. He was hungry enough that he wasn't scared.

He stuck the last bit of tomato into his mouth and raised his hands over his head.

"Git the fuck off my lan."

"I'm sorry. I'm hungry. I'll work for food."

"Don' need work. Need you git the fuck off my lan."

"Please. I'm starving. I can do work for you in your fields. I can clean up your house. I'll do anything."

"Git the fuck off my lan. If you don' git, next shot's atcha head."

But it wasn't. The farmer gave Crowley time to walk away—which was something Crowley would think about a lot, later. Why didn't that first, angry farmer just kill him? The wasteland wasn't as deadly as he'd expected.

Other farmers would be kinder. But this first experience shaped his impression of the wasteland.

His head was clearer as he climbed back through the barbed wire.

The wasteland *was* more crowded than he'd expected. Long stretches of it seemed like a procession of farms and villages—some walled, some not—with dusty or overgrown roads or fields separating them. And there were more people. You could go a day without seeing anyone. But that was rare.

And it was impossible to go a day without seeing a rusting old shipping container somewhere along the roads or paths. The things were all over the place. People lived in them, villages used them to build ramshackle walls, some people even used them to transport things. Even so, thousands of them sat around rotting in the humidity and heat. People in the Federal Era must have bought and sold an incredible volume of...things.

He reached the Old Florida Highway two days after the angry farmer incident. He couldn't actually see the highway. All he could see was a 10- or 12-foot-high chain link fence with razor wire along the top. The whole thing that gave off the hum of an electrical charge. Beyond the fence was a grassy hill that was at least twice as high. The Highway was somewhere beyond that.

But it didn't matter much that he couldn't get to the Highway. A well-worn foot path—six or eight feet across—ran alongside the fence. It had been worn down so firmly that the packed dirt felt like concrete. The footpath went south and north. South was left to him, north right. South would take him back to Tampa. North would take him to Jacksonville. He headed north. And felt energized.

As he got better, he walked a lot. And he became smarter about picking fruits and vegetables that grew in the wild or on the edges of farms. The edges of farms were the best places to find free food. If you knew how to look, you could find all kinds of produce just outside the fences. Sloppy hands or heavy winds would blow seed beyond the fences.

He learned that, if possible, to ask a farmer about swapping work for food *before* nipping tomatoes or peppers or fruit.

Work was easier to find than he'd expected. Often, asking first meant the farmer would let him stay on the farm for a few days of working and eating. Competition for day-work on the bigger, richer farms was tough; but the people on smaller, poorer farms were more likely to say yes. So, Crowley focused on the smaller farms.

The farmers who said yes usually had some sort of barn or tent set up, where "travelers"—as they called wandering laborers—could sleep. But these quarters were usually dirty and smelly. Whenever he could, Crowley just slept outside.

He didn't have a razor to shave. But most men in the wasteland had beards. And his beard hid the brand on his neck. Partly.

Travelers were usually outcasts from Cities. Like Crowley, they wanted to get back into a City somewhere. But most seemed to have problems—mental problems or violent tendencies—that made return unrealistic. And then there was money. An immigration bond required thousands or *tens* of thousands of dollars or petros, etc.

He fell back into his old habits from his days as a young manager. When he was doing work, he listened closely to what the farmers said and asked questions if he didn't understand something. He didn't pretend to understand things he didn't. Sometimes, he'd take a few minutes to read from an almanac or the instructions to some piece of equipment, because many of the smaller farmers couldn't read. The texts were usually printed on paper, as pamphlets or books.

The small farmers didn't entirely trust his ability to read. They valued his ability to read to solve a specific problem—repair a piece of equipment. They'd even pay him something for the work. But, when that job was done, they'd retreat. Or ask him to move along.

He developed a process for dealing with reading. He'd barter to work. If he saw there was a repair or bit of maintenance to be done on a tool, he'd offer to do it. And barter a price for that. And arrange all of the pieces. Handle everything. Assemble or disassemble what he could by hand and common sense. Then ask for the tools that he thought he'd need. And then, last, ask if there were any documents. Usually, there weren't. But, once in a while, there would be.

And then, he could do a lot. Working on the farms and in the small villages made Crowley appreciate how good owner's manuals were. Especially old ones, from the Federal Era. Exploded illustrations. Well-written instructions. Clear descriptions. All printed on paper or crude screens.

Of course, the reading made him stand out. There were other travelers who could read. The wasteland people called them "scribes." But most of those held themselves apart from other laborers. Crowley's willingness to do work first—and use reading as a tool to get a job done—was rare. When wasteland people saw this, they'd often ask him to take a look at something else. Make a repair on their house. Read a letter or screen about personal business.

Most people in the wasteland were what City managers would have called functionally illiterate. They could figure out road signs and write their names; nine days out of 10, that was all they needed. But most had backlogs of letters, legal notices or catalogs that they needed help deciphering.

A few times, farmers or traders asked him to stay on more than a few days. In the process, he picked up some money—a mix of small-denomination coins from various Cities—but, more importantly, some better clothes and shoes and a sturdy backpack.

His old management training was useful. He'd ask questions of farmers or traders or other travelers. Wasteland people were guarded—but there were safe topics that got them to open up. Road conditions. Local gossip. Stories of cheating wives were especially popular. From this, he started to assemble an understanding of the wasteland.

He figured that he'd need to know the land well if he was to have any chance of getting back to Pea and Jack.

Some of the Tollways and roads followed the old paths of Interstates from the Federal Era; others followed paths that were even older. Some stretches were well maintained by local merchants or villages that were trying to become Cities. Other stretches were abandoned and dangerous.

He learned that the mix changed all the time. A stretch of road between New Orleans and Birmingham would be clear one summer and be full of breaks the next.

But there were other things even more important to know. Experienced travelers avoided major roads, which were dangerous for people going by themselves. In most places, networks of footpaths ran parallel to the roads. And these footpaths were too small for vehicles or bandits—who moved in groups.

Getting around Cities could be tricky. At Jacksonville, there was a wide stretch of swamp around Gator River that was wasteland. Two large Causeways connected the Gulf Coast areas claimed by Jacksonville with the main, walled City. As long as you kept away from the concrete pilings, you could pass underneath without any problems. Electrified fence surrounded the pilings. If you tried to get past it, the machine guns of the automated security system would cut you to ribbons.

He was happy to pass through. Like many travelers, he ended sleeping for a few hours under one of the Causeway lanes. The steady Doppler scream of cars and trucks speeding above was a small taste of City life. It was also intimidating. There was so much economic and technological advantage in a City. It was no wonder they made getting in so hard.

Some travelers talked of being robbed or beaten along the footpaths. Crowley was lucky or instinctively cautious. In his early, walking days, he was never approached by bandits. Later, he'd realize that he'd stayed away from the most dangerous places. It wasn't that he'd understood their danger—it was that his impulse was to stay away from crowds.

They were unnerving. And full of physical oddities. Obese people. Wounded and disfigured ones. People missing fingers or whole limbs. Mental defectives. Gray goo. Strange devices for pleasure or strength or just function, wired crudely into heads and chests and arms. These are all things you didn't see in Cities.

The methods of transport were the same in the wasteland as in the Cities. They were just allocated differently.

A few rich people flew in airplanes. Of course, just like in a City, planes were expensive to buy and even more expensive to keep. You needed a firm base—a large farm or something like that—plus steady income to keep a plane. Also, flying anywhere near a City was dangerous; most Cities' defense forces would shoot down unregistered aircraft that came near their airspace.

Cars also posed problems. A rugged vehicle could navigate the broken cement and occasional jagged rebar of the forgotten roads; a heavily-armed vehicle could fight off the bandits and highwaymen who roamed the major roads. To drive anywhere reliably, your vehicle needed to be both.

When he'd lived in Tampa, Crowley had had a "sport" vehicle for driving through the woods or on the beach. That car wouldn't have lasted a week in the wasteland. Maybe not a day.

There were vehicles built for this terrain. But those cost so much that people who actually lived in the wasteland couldn't afford them. They'd appear occasionally—usually carrying some rich kids from a City, out in the wasteland for kicks. They needed heavy arms because they were obvious targets.

Some wasteland people rode motorcycles. But motorcycles were high profile—literally and figuratively. It was very easy to shoot a solo rider on one. And fuel could be hard to find just when you needed it most. There was safety in numbers, of course; there were motorcycle gangs. Even if they didn't consider themselves bandits, they'd steal when they could or needed to.

Most people with resources rode horses. They were versatile, easy to maintain and liquid—you could buy or sell a horse easily at most farms or villages.

Everyone else walked. Which was fine with Crowley. He considered walking and manual labor as ways to recover.

The Cities were fortresses, inaccessible to wasteland people.

Most were surrounded by concentric rings of villages and big farms. These secondary centers attracted crowds. Travelers and working families would camp around their gates. At sunrise, a raised green flag meant the bosses inside were hiring. A few minutes later, the bosses would appear at the gate, surrounded most of the time by beefy security men. They'd pick the biggest or most assertive travelers, ask a question or two about their skills and offer a day rate. The pay was usually 10 or 20 dollars in coin from a nearby City. If the work was extra dirty or difficult, it might pay a few dollars more. Day workers didn't negotiate.

Working for money meant working hard. Harder than working for food on a family farms. It also meant competing with people who'd fight for the work. And it meant realizing that bandits watched you leaving the big farm at after sunset, with money in your pocket. For Crowley, this meant walking out into the deep wilderness for an hour or more, to get away from the crowds.

So, he waited until he'd recovered to try working at a big farm.

The work usually fell into two types: field work or construction.

Sometimes, he had to wear an armband or bracelet so the bosses could keep track of the outsiders; at the end of the day, he'd give back the marking device in exchange for his pay.

Again, the fact that he could read made a big difference. But the diplomacy of letting the bosses know he could read was different. About half the time, the bosses couldn't read at all; and most of the ones who could read didn't do it very well. But they weren't as defensive as the family farmers and small traders. Crowley learned to say up front that he'd learned to read "in City schools." That would almost always get him chosen—and, sometimes, it meant he'd do less manual labor and more helping bosses read instructions, construction documents and the like.

Like on the smaller farms, these texts were usually printed on paper; but, sometimes, they'd be on screens. The bosses *really* watched him closely if he was reading from a screen. Sometimes, they'd chain him to a tree or keep a drawn gun on him so he wouldn't try to run off with it. A screen that would have cost less than a fancy lunch in Tampa was much more precious to the wasteland farmers.

If he didn't feel up to working a larger farm, Crowley could usually count on doing some scribe work for an innkeeper in exchange for some decent leftovers and a bed.

He also learned that keeping his eyes clear was important. Clear eyes separated rational people from drug addicts and crazies.

Day work agreed with Crowley. People in the wasteland tended to be short. He was tall enough and—in time—healthy enough that he was almost always picked. He'd read if he could but he didn't mind swinging a hoe or lifting some wooden planks. Some days he didn't feel like talking and actually preferred the quiet of heavy labor.

He inched his way across the wasteland, working for a few days and then walking for a few days. His immediate goals were to buy a gun, which he did pretty easily, and a horse, which took a little longer.

He remained egoless. And he thought about the God's-eye dream and why that first farmer hadn't shot him. As angry as he was, he didn't want to kill another man over some tomatoes. That was basically decent.

Crowley thought a lot about that. *Decency*. And his thinking wasn't all positive. Once he understood the rules of how things worked on the farms, he tested the limits of decency. In himself and in others. Somewhere east of Mobile, he earned the trust of a small trader and then swindled him with a few simple lies about how much money the trader had in his till. It wasn't much money—a few dollars in Mobile notes—but it was very easy to do.

He did other things he wasn't proud of. To prove to himself that he could. That he could be as bad as the worst of the wasteland outlaws and bandits. And that, if he was better, it was because he *chose* to be better.

Around New Orleans, he decided to study the "walls" of a big City—and stayed there for a while. The area just outside the walls was almost as busy as a City interior. Except the ring of villages didn't have to follow any of the City's rules. Drugs and prostitution were big business. So were fake identification papers, outlawed medical procedures and untaxed goods and services of all sorts.

Tampa had had some of this; but not as much as New Orleans. Its outskirts seemed like a permanent development.

It was too loud and too busy for him. With no screens or writing, everyone talked. A lot. And most of what they said was worthless. One big rumor was that New Orleans had a policy only letting one immigrant into the City for each that emigrated. Crowley has never heard of such a policy and doubted it was true. But it was a matter of faith to the people desperately hoping to get in.

He wasn't ready yet. He would be someday…but not yet. And, when he was ready, he wouldn't settle for a second-rate place. He'd make his comeback somewhere bigger. After a few weeks, he moved on. Heading north and east.

Somewhere north of Mobile, Crowley did a few days of work helping a devoutly religious farmer with a mid-sized spread repair and run his ancient cotton combine. The farmer figured out pretty quickly that Crowley could read well, so he made him and different offer: Free room and board plus $500 New Orleans at the end if Crowley would teach his two younger boys to read well enough that they could read from the Bible every night after supper.

This time, Crowley did negotiate. He didn't want the $500. He wanted a horse and a decent saddle. The farmer, who had a dozen horses in his stable, agreed.

The boys were 10 and 11—old enough to learn but still young enough that they were eager to please their father. The hard part: they didn't know anything about letters and words. Crowley had helped some adults improve their reading—but those people usually were semi-literate already.

Crowley really wanted the horse, though. He was tired of walking.

He started his lessons by telling the lads that reading was not as hard as some people made it out to be. He, himself, had never been a great reader but he had read many books from beginning to end. And he would teach them how.

"Our Pa wants us to read from the Bible each night to him and Ma," the older boy said. "He said everything a man needs to know in the world is right there. If we read from it every night, by the time we're grown we'll be able to do God's work in the world."

The farmer's wife made things easy by letting Crowley use a slate board and some chalk from her kitchen. He offered to teach her to read, too; but she refused with a nervous laugh. But she usually found some excuse to hover nearby during their lessons.

Crowley thought about calling her out and offering more forcefully to teach her—but every time he tried to make eye contact, she looked away. After several tries, he let the matter pass and focused on his two pious students.

They learned their letters and vowels quickly. They had some problem with words, especially with sounding out multiple vowel combinations. But, one afternoon, he was making a list of words with double vowels for them to sound out and he included "tree" and "wood." The younger boy sounded out each word and said "Oh. I see. 'Tree' is for the tree that grows up from the ground and 'wood" is what you get when you cut down a tree." From that simple little realization, everything seemed to fall into place. Within a few days, they were reading whole sentences.

In the meantime, he ate well and slept in a small, clean barracks with the farmer's three regular workers. Several times, he offered to give lessons to the farmer's older son and daughter—but those offers didn't go any better than the one he'd given the wife. It was just going to be the two small ones.

Of course, they reminded him of Pea and Jack. He tried not to dwell too much on that.

Once they'd mastered their letters and numbers, they worked from the Bible—the only book in the house. Maybe the only book for miles around.

The farmer's wife kept the family Bible in a decorated wooden box. It was the oldest book Crowley had ever held—the front page said it had been published in 1964 of the Federal Era by a company called Gideons. The cover seemed to be some kind of plastic and was remarkably well preserved.

"This Bible was my dowry," the wife told him in a formal tone, one afternoon near the end of his stay. "It has been the property of my family since the Federal Age."

He taught the boys through a humid month—but which one? He'd lost track of time. And the farmer followed a ridiculous version of a Federal Era calendar. They got very good very quickly at sounding out words they didn't understand. (And, the truth was, they knew the Bible stories much better than Crowley did himself. They already knew who Pharisees were—and several of the many words for weapons that the Bible used.)

At the end of six weeks, he joined the farmer's family for dinner in their house. Afterward, the younger boy read the first book of Genesis and the older boy read the first two chapters of the Gospel of Matthew. The family members and the father's regulars all listened to the boys read. It was a real audience, eight people in all. And the boys did well.

Crowley noticed the mother, standing nervously in the doorway between the kitchen and the living room. She smiled and looked down while they read, sometimes mouthing words of passages she knew by heart. Her hands were pressed hard in the pockets of her apron. By the time the older boy was finished, she was wiping tears from her eyes.

The family was satisfied. When the readings were finished, the farmer shook Crowley's hand and said: "Brother Michael, I want you to know how satisfied I am with you teaching the boys to read. It means a great deal to us. And to their mother. Now they can read to us every night. And they can be educated men. Because everything a man needs to be educated and wise is right there in that Bible."

The earnestness of his statement stuck with Crowley.

The next morning, he rode away on a chestnut mare.

Insights often came to Crowley in bunches—and, sometimes, more slowly than he wished. But they would come, often as several realizations, interconnected, all at once. So, it occurred to him a few days after he'd taken off on his horse that it had been the mother of the boys—not the farmer—who'd wanted them to learn to read. And he realized that her desire for her sons to read an expression of self stronger even than learning to read herself. Was this "selfless?" Not really, he thought. Her love for the boys was more like a transcendence of self.

Crowley knew he wasn't usually an abstract thinker. He was a problem-solver, a person with a literal mind. But he recognized something profound in the farmer's wife. She cared about her boys more than she cared about herself, but this deep love was also an expression of self for her. Something about this cycle meant a lot to him. It sparked a strong emotional response in him—almost to the point of driving him to tears.

The citizens of the Cities, at least of Tampa, had lost the sense of connection to others that the farmer's wife felt so strongly for her young sons. This was one more reason that he swore to himself he would see Pea and Jack again.

He rode the chestnut across the wasteland for almost a year. He rode as far north as the walls of Virginia, as far west as the walls of Kansas City. He could have gone farther either direction. But he set his bearings by the Gulf of Mexico and wasn't comfortable far away. He got to know the circuit around the Gulf well. Tampa to Jacksonville to Mobile to New Orleans to Houston. And back again.

Those months were full of cracked concrete, tall grass and the nervous perimeter signs of little villages. And it was miserably hot the whole time. In the Tampa, hot weather had always seemed like a good thing—year-round outdoor activities and no shortages of winter heating fuel that vexed the northern Cities. In the wasteland, the constant heat and humidity were problems.

Men who'd lived in the wasteland for any length of time knew that crotch rot was a problem; it could make sleeping difficult and riding impossible. When he'd been thrown out of Tampa, he'd been wearing a pair of cotton briefs. He was already starting to have problems while he still had that underwear; the problems got worse after those briefs fell apart. Some days, the skin around his balls would get so raw that it would bleed into the crotch of his pants.

He tried to find cotton underwear. No merchants had any... or were willing to *admit* they had any. He was able to find some synthmesh briefs that didn't make the chafing much better.

Sic Semper Tyrannis

Somewhere east of Savannah, the pain had gotten so bad that he'd stopped off in a village that had a nurse/midwife. She sold him a tube of cream that helped almost immediately. And she showed him how to rip a cotton pad out of an old shirt and slide that into his synthmesh underwear.

"This may seem foolish to you but you need to keep your balls and ass from getting too raw. They'll get infected and you'll die from blood poisoning and that's not a good way to die." She'd also suggested bathing in salt water whenever he was around it.

He still had some of the cream left. And he took any chance he could to pick up a cotton shirt. There were some of those around.

How could there be cotton shirts but no cotton underwear?

Having the horse made things different. If he wanted day work, he could get it easily. People in the wasteland assumed anyone with a horse was more than just a traveler. But he did less day labor. More often, he could ride into a village and find paid work as scribe.

Reading and writing had never been his strengths. But he was proud of his ability to survive in the wasteland.

And he realized how much of a child he'd been in his first few days, crawling in the mud. So afraid of toxic plants and poisoned water. There were some of each—but nothing like the scare stories they told in the Cities.

Texas was a different than the rest of the wasteland. First, the roads remained fairly reliable. Second, it still retained something of a state identity. Outside the walls of Houston and Dallas, people talked about Texas forming a republic again. They were better informed than people in other parts of the wasteland. The smartest gossip was that Houston's faceless corporate board wanted to run the whole thing…but "Daddy" John Hanratty—Dallas's charismatic CEO—had a plan up his sleeve to bring Houston into the fold.

In his former life, Crowley had known Hanratty slightly. In person, he wasn't particularly charismatic and he didn't seem like the kind of man with secret plans to make a nation. If Crowley had known Hanratty wanted to establish a republic, he'd have made an effort to talk to him about the League. Back when….

More than anything, though, Crowley had been making his way long enough to recognize the flattering talk of a Big City CEO as the wishful thinking of people desperate to appear in the know. Maybe Hanratty was considered charismatic and visionary because the Texans *wanted* a strong leader.

So, Texas remained...Texas. Crowley had crossed what had once been its eastern and northern borders several times now; every time he had, he could tell when he'd crossed. People *called* themselves Texans, even though they lived in the wasteland. They seemed compelled to add the word to their perimeter signs. "Welcomb 2 Jarvis, Texas." "Ur Intring Bakers Farm, TX."

In Texas, it seemed like every other person was named Baker.

The people talked about living in Texas, even though no one was exactly sure where the borders were.

As he was trained, Crowley thought about Texas in terms of its Cities. There were four—Houston, Dallas, Austin and El Paso. Crowley never rode as far west as El Paso. But he'd spent time wandering outside the walls of Houston, Dallas and Austin. Dallas was different than the others. It seemed bigger than any other City whose walls he'd wandered. And it got cold at night up there.

At each of the three Texas cities he visited, he'd filled out immigration paperwork. In his real name and under a couple of aliases. No replies anywhere. That was the worst part of applying for immigration: you never heard "no." You just never heard.

Texas also had a group of larger villages or towns trying to form into cities. This was a difficult process. The critical step was to convince another City to recognize your start-up with formal diplomatic and commercial relations—but existing Cities didn't have much incentive to recognize new ones. The conventional wisdom among elite managers was there were too many Cities already. No need to dilute dwindling financial resources and add to the political complexity by recognizing new ones.

Still, Crowley had considered that his best chance at citizenship somewhere might be to get inside one of the aspiring Cities and help it win recognition. If he made his case carefully—and if he could find the right sort of people—he had a lot of managerial experience to offer.

He'd been hearing for months that Brownsville wanted to be a City. It was a couple of days south from Houston by horse. So, after another three weeks trying to talk his way into New Orleans, he set out along the old Interstate 10 toward Texas.

The ferry into Texas at the old Interstate had been crowded and pricey, so Crowley rode north a couple of difficult hours to the next ferry, at a village called Hart's Landing. There was no line here; and the two dark-haired teenage boys working the 10-foot tethered barge were excited to accept a silver New Orleans dollar as fare.

The boys worked the tether line harder than Crowley had expected. They were scrawny but strong. As was the custom, the boys slowed down halfway across and waited for Crowley to pay them their money.

He handed the dollar to the taller boy. The smaller one crowded right up alongside, to examine it. Mere friends wouldn't touch each other. They must have been brothers or cousins.

The taller boy muttered something to the shorter, who nodded in quick agreement. Then, they flipped it over and examined the other side.

They turned the coin around several more times…extending the break longer than usual. Crowley watched them while they studied the coin. Their eyes were clear and their faces expressive. They seemed brighter than most of the working children he'd come across in the wasteland—who were, frankly, slack eyed and often junkies by the ages of 10 or 12.

The boys' positive reaction to the coin and nervous flipping meant that they'd never been to New Orleans and probably couldn't read. He pointed to the letters along the upper ridge of the face.

"New Orleans. They say it like one word, but they write it like two. Do you read?" They looked at him and, for the first time, seemed more distrustful than excited.

"I don't read, but I savvy the marks," the taller one said. He spoke quickly. "That one's N for New and that one's O for Orleans."

"Our Nana taught us some of the letters," the smaller one offered. He didn't want to be left out of the conversation. "She's really good to savvy the marks. If we go somewhere, she always knows what the signs say."

Once they'd pocketed the coin and gotten back to pulling, the taller boy seemed determined to say more.

"Signs don't really say nothing. I know that. They don't talk like people. It's just called a figure of speech that somebody says that. They make short-cut ways to name things. But the short-cut ways aren't exactly what they're supposed to be. My Nana told me this part, too. She knows a lot of how things work. She told me that was more important than reading or Army stuff or knowing lots of stories about old stuff."

"Lots of people tell stories about old stuff," the smaller one added. "And some people's just nervous going across this riv right here. So they talk and talk! They talk about Texas and everybody here used to be rich."

Even with the delays—and the weight of Crowley's horse and bags—the barge made it across the river in a few minutes.

"Welcome to Texas, mister," the older boy said when they bumped softly against the wooden bulkhead. "This is Hart's Landing which is the gateway to the Lone Star State."

There wasn't anyone waiting for the trip back across, so Crowley took his time to get back on his horse. He'd used enough village crossings to know that lawmen or highwaymen usually waited for a traveler to dismount. "What do you fellows say to people when you back it across the river going the other way?"

"There ain't so many. More want to go into Texas. And we don't say much to the ones who come out," the smaller one said. "They're usually too tired or in too much of a hurry to listen to Billy's jokes."

The taller one punched him hard on the shoulder.

"Well, I thank you for you ride across, boys. What's the best way to town? I need to get some oats for my horse."

The taller one answered. "Any way gets there. The main path is what most people use. You can also ride along the riv to that first bend and turn in. There's a small path you'll see there and that takes you into the side of town by Jay's Tavern."

"Thanks."

This chitchat had taken just enough time for locals to get impatient and make the first move. Crowley noticed some horses coming out of the scrub brush about 30 meters down the main path.

He was glad he'd stayed on the barge. He couldn't make these boys get him back across the river. He'd have to acknowledge the horses. But he didn't have to do it quickly.

At second glance, they were five horses. One rider clearly in front of the others; the others in two sets of two falling behind him. They had guns. The guns weren't out in front; they were under the coats and hidden in the saddles. But the horses had the plump look of fully-armed vehicles.

The riders' faces were too clean-shaven to be highwaymen. They were some kind of local security. But there wasn't always a lot of difference.

The boys saw him watching the horses come out of the underbrush.

"They're the sheriffs."

He wasn't sure which of the boys said it; he was keeping his eyes on the five horses and their riders. Local security forces were usually killers hired by the biggest farm or factory in a small town. They didn't really enforce any laws. They just snuffed out trouble. And sometimes that meant causing trouble before strangers did.

Crowley thought about doing something—getting off his horse, charging off the barge, bolting backwards into the river. But any fast action would draw fire from the law men. And the dumber they were, the faster they'd draw.

As the riders edged up to the wooden bulkhead, Crowley made sure they could see him looking hard at them. No averted eyes. They were clean-shaven and well dressed, but their faces betrayed a lot of hard living in the wasteland. They looked dull and determined. Veteran killers who'd do what they were told without asking any questions.

The wasteland was full of men like this; but they usually weren't so well equipped.

He didn't want the boys to get hurt. Their bright eyes deserved to stay open. But he did want the protection of the ferry barge. If the lawmen were even a little smart, they'd think twice before chasing him into the river.

He sat as high in the saddle as he could. And he whispered to the boys. "I'm going to try to stay on the barge while I'm talking to these fellows. But, if I do get off, you boys start pulling back right away. You understand?"

"Yes."

Crowley focused on the leader. He was a grayhair. His mustache was carefully trimmed. To Crowley, that meant trouble. Carefully trimmed moustaches meant the worst mix of stupid and vain.

His chestnut wanted to move. He pulled down on the reins to keep her still.

He looked for the lead rider's eyes and tried to size up the man. The eyes were moving fast, all around. Trying to find someone else on the barge? Trying to guess what his own people were going to do? Nervous, anyway. Another bad sign.

Saying something first seemed like the right thing to do.

"G'day."

Their eyes still darted around. The greeting didn't do anything.

After a few long seconds, the lead rider's eyes settled on Crowley's.

"Name's Willard Jackson. I'm the sheriff of Hart County, Texas. These men are my deputies. Who are you?"

Crowley gave a fake name and then some true facts. "I'm from Tampa. And I'm heading to Brownsville. I'm just passing through, looking for a clear road."

The other riders held their places a few steps behind Jackson.

"If you're coming from Tampa, this isn't the fastest way to Brownsville."

"True. But the crowd at the old I-10 bridge was a hundred riders deep. Maybe more. Everyone's trying to get into Texas. I didn't feel like waiting hours, so I just rode up riv."

"Someone who wants to duck out of a crowd so bad usually got a reason. You got any ID?"

"I do. In my right saddle bag here. I can reach in and take it out."

"Yeah. Just do it slow."

A couple of the deputies' horses whinnied and rustled a bit. That meant their riders were shifting their weight…which probably meant they were getting ready to draw their weapons. He had to be careful.

He had a loaded handgun ready with his papers in the saddle bag. He imagined pulling it out instead of the papers. But he wasn't a sure enough shot to take out five men. Maybe one or two. But this group was too many. Good planning on their part.

He'd made his way this far on his wits more than his weaponry. He could talk his way out of this.

He reached past the gun and for the laminated ID sheet. He handed it down to the taller boy and nodded toward the Sheriff. The boy jumped onto the bank and ran the ID to the first horse.

The Sheriff didn't seem so interested in the ID. He looked at it without much focus. That was good. The ID was a high-quality fake, so there wasn't much of chance that a village Sheriff would catch it. But there was a chance, if he looked hard.

"You're riding from Tampa to Brownsville? That's a long way.

Why ain't you taking a plane or a boat?"

"I got into some trouble in Tampa. I'm looking for a new start. Heard Brownsville was a good place for new starts."

"Shit, yeah. Everyone's looking for a new start. Well, mister, we got something in Hart County we call the new start surcharge. Helps us keep our roads clear for people just passing through."

This was bad. The Sheriff was acting more like a highwayman. Once they started like this, they were likely to end up rooting through his gear, looking for things to take.

"I don't have much money, Sheriff. And since I haven't set foot in your county yet, maybe I should have these boys ferry me on back across the river and just look for another place to cross."

"Yeah, you could do that. But we've got all kinds of ways we can work with a good person to help them along. You're a good person, right, mister?"

"I think so. But you're the one with my ID."

The Sheriff handed the ID back to the taller boy, who hurried back onto the barge. "I think I'd like to know why you've got your neck covered up. Why don't you lower that neck piece and let's see if you've got any marks on you?"

Crowley pulled the cloth away from his neck and flipped the collar of his riding jacket down.

He'd had the brand removed by laser treatment in an outside-the-walls clinic near New Orleans. But there was still a patch of shiny skin on his neck. His beard had a kind of bald spot around the patch, so it was noticeable even from a distance.

He'd asked the doctor to make the scar patch larger than the brand had been, so that the original shape and size wouldn't be visible. Still, lawmen and smart citizens could guess that he'd been convicted of something.

"What's the matter with your neck?"

"Burned in an accident."

"An accident?"

"Yeah. It happened a long time ago."

"Before you had some trouble back in Tampa?"

The boys were looking back across the river. They wanted out of this situation. Their bright eyes had seen enough trouble to know when more was coming.

The etiquette of bribes to local law and payments to highwaymen was that you let them ask for something first. But Jackson and his crew seemed as interested in harassing Crowley as in getting money. This could go on for hours.

"Look, Sheriff. Let's just make an easy deal here. I'll pay any reasonable toll to pass through your county. I don't have much money; but I am anxious to get this journey done with. Tell me what the toll is and if I can pay it I will."

His deputies' horses were snorting and screeching more regularly. They were getting as impatient as the boys on the ferry.

"Well, sir, if you had 100 Houston petros in gold, that would get you safely through our jurisdiction."

Of course, Sheriff Jackson's jurisdiction was whatever he claimed. For all the legal authority he had, he could claim the entire wasteland of the North American continent was his.

"Sheriff, if I had 100 Houston in gold, I wouldn't be riding a horse across Texas. I do have a $100 Mobile City bond note. It's yours, if you let me through your county."

The Sheriff laughed bitterly and whispered something to one of his deputies, a Hispanic with a scar that started from the corner of his left eye and sliced down the side of his face. "Here's what we're going to do, mister. We're going to take a quick shot of your right eye. If nothing comes up, I'll take your bond as toll and wish you a pleasant journey. If anything comes up...well, then we'll see."

Crowley had taken his chances with iris scans before and won. Usually, nothing came up. His story was too complicated for the black-and-white priorities of most commercial security database services. But he knew that a few databases had him listed as a felon in Tampa. And, even though most databases didn't have him listed as a felon, some still had old executive data that would prove the ID papers he'd just given the Sheriff were fake.

"Now, step on off that ferry there and let Deputy Gonsalves here do his business. He'll have you look into this pair of goggles for a moment, so we can be on our way."

It all came down to this. He could try to shoot it out. But five of them were two deputies too many. He could try to debate with Jackson—or insist that he take the test from the barge. But all of that would just look suspicious. And it would expose the boys to gunfire.

He pulled up on his reins and gave the chestnut a very slight kick...almost like a rub of his heel.

Sic Semper Tyrannis

His horse clopped off of the ferry and into the light brown Texas mud.

The scarred Hispanic rode up alongside and wrapped his reins around the horn of Crowley's saddle. It was a threatening action.

The boys started pulling the ferry back across the river. This made a comic impression on Jackson and his deputies.

"Well, hell. There goes your posse." And laughter all around.

Deputy Gonsalves was having some trouble connecting the scanning device to whatever kind of computer he was carrying in his saddle or somewhere under his leather jacket.

Crowley concentrated on exhaling fully and remembering the advice someone at New Orleans had given him. "As soon as you look in those goggles, roll your eyes back. Like you're talking to God."

Finally, Gonsalves got his hardware set right. He held the goggles out to Crowley. "Put these goggle up to your eye. Keep your eye open. It'll be black for few seconds, and then quick flash of light. You might be blind for a second but your sight will come back. The most important thing is you keep your eyes open. If you close your eyes or squint or do anything crazy, we have to scan again."

Crowley exhaled once more and lifted the leather and glass device up to his face. There was a flash of light. He kept his eyes open but rolled them back.

South of Houston, Crowley stopped at a trading post to feed his chestnut and pay for a little information about the region. The landscape was greener than he'd expected; it looked like a lot of tomatoes and other vegetables. He'd also seen a few security types riding the perimeters of farms—but not as many as he would have expected for so much food.

He climbed down from his horse and tied her up to the water station. His legs were both stiff. The left one, particularly. It took a few minutes before he could bend his left leg and walk in a manner approaching normal. Luckily, his crotch had stayed dry enough that it wasn't chafing too badly.

He entered the post from its main doors. It was lighted inside, but not very brightly. And it was quiet. No generator hum. That meant it was running on a solar panel system.

"Hey. I'm here to feed my horse and get some directions for Brownsville."

The merchant running the trading post was small and cloudy-eyed. He looked up from an Asian sex comic book. "Howda. Wiccan help ya with that…" He mumbled something about clear riding to Brownsville and that there weren't any highwaymen in the area.

But he did have several motorcycles for sale.

After a little haggling, the merchant accepted eight of Crowley's New Orleans silver dollars for two gallons of ice water and 10 pounds of oats. Crowley tested the water for typhus and cholera and the oats for the standard horse toxins. It all came up clean.

After a couple of pints of water and setting up his horse with a feedbag and some of the oats, Crowley set out around the trading post to stretch his legs. It was a ramshackle place, looking like it had been slapped together from shipping containers and pieces of several different sorts of prefab commercial buildings. He was constantly amazed at how trading posts in the middle of nowhere managed to find enough equipment and supplies to stay open.

Of course, posts made their most of their money from selling alcohol and drugs, not water and oats. And they tended to get busy at night, instead of late morning.

Crowley tried to avoid trading posts at night. He planned on getting back inside City walls…somewhere, somehow. He didn't have enough money or time to spend stumbling around in a stupor.

Sometimes he wondered if it was even a good idea to try to get back into a City. His life in Tampa seemed like a hazy memory. He'd been married to a woman and had two children with her—but he couldn't remember her face. He remembered the kids—Pea and Jack. But he couldn't assemble the face of his ex-wife in his mind.

All the tests he'd taken back in his previous life had said he was a linear thinker, not a visual person. So, maybe it was no surprise that her image had faded from his memory.

He came back to his chestnut and gave it a quick brush. He checked his saddle bags and made sure he had three guns ready on his person and in his saddle. Despite the merchant's assurances, Crowley planned for trouble ahead. As he usually did.

When he'd resaddled his horse, Crowley considered going back in for a real drink and a more useful parley. But another set of riders was coming down the road. It was better to keep moving.

He headed south from the post at a medium pace. A little after noon, he took a break to eat something and check his location.

He activated his electronic map to figure how far he had to ride. Brownsville wasn't a City with surveyed limits and walls; from all he'd heard, it was still a collection of villages trying to establish City structure. There might be some crude version of walls but, more likely, he'd just come upon development that looked like what was on the outside of the walls at Houston or New Orleans.

The trading post wasn't on the map; but, using his own travel numbers since he'd left Houston, he figured he had another 70 or 80 miles. That was a solid day of riding. If he didn't run into any trouble.

The road was pretty well maintained, which meant that it must have been moving a lot of traffic. But he'd seen only a handful of riders since he'd left Houston.

The rich farmland held up for the rest of the afternoon's ride. Crowley wasn't much an ag expert, but he recognized squash and soy beans and cotton. Most of the fields seemed to be divided into mid-sized squares, probably one or two acres each. The security wasn't heavy—usually three or four feet of razor wire with two or three electrified lines running through. There were irrigation control towers spread irregularly, with vid cams on masts above. And, every couple of miles, a stretch of wild woods separated the fields. The woods were probably boundaries of individual farms; they also could have been wind breaks, if the land was controlled by some big ag boss.

There weren't many people working these farms. He only saw a couple of crews actually tending to crops the whole day; and only a few more farmers or security types riding horses through the fields. He'd have expected more harvesting; the crop seasons here were clearly different than in Tampa.

Still, he didn't understand such light security for crops in the wasteland. Significant ag business was usually protected by City walls. All this value was surely vulnerable to bandits, bums or other trouble.

He remembered the teacher from his one ag management course in school saying that soy beans and cotton were like piles of money standing in the sun.

At one point, when he'd taken a break to stretch his bad leg, Crowley walked over to the fence protecting a patch of green and red peppers. The ground had the earthy smell of rich soil. When he got close, he could hear the buzz that meant the electrified lines were hot. But there was easily enough space between the wires to reach through and pick a couple of peppers. He looked around for a moment and didn't see any reason to stop. So, he reached in.

Nothing happened.

He picked two peppers with his right hand and pulled them out.

Walking back to his horse, he cracked open one of the peppers and scraped out the seeds with his thumb. He sprinkled some water on it to wash off any chemicals or insecticides and took a small bite. On first bite, it was spicy but not too much so—but the aftertaste was definitely hot. He drank some water and slipped the second pepper into his pocket. It might go well with the bread and cheese he was planning to eat for dinner. He remembered hearing something years ago about hot peppers being good for making people feel cooler in hot weather.

He thought about going back for more peppers but climbed back on the horse instead.

As the sun started to set, Crowley started to think about what he'd do for the night. His normal procedure was to ride half an hour or so off of the road and look for a reasonably secure location to sleep. He had a few tools for securing his camp. The most useful of these were a battery-powered laser perimeter system that screeched loudly if anything entered and a disposable flamethrower that could burn a wide path through brush—or a narrow one through animals.

The challenge was to find a location that was both clear and elevated. Often, the best spots were taken—fenced off as farm land or taken by some kind of residence or business.

He stayed on the main road until he came to the next stretch of rough woods separating fields of farmland on the east side of the road. This woods seemed a little larger than the others he'd seen. He wouldn't be able to ride very far off the road; the Gulf of Mexico was somewhere less than an hour that direction. But it looked like the best place to turn.

He took a quick drink of water and reined his horse off the road.

The woods were full of underbrush that made it hard to ride, so he kept the chestnut mare near the farmland on the north side of the break. The smell of water, dirt and nitrogen fertilizer was stronger than anything he'd ever known in Tampa. But, again, he'd never been much of an ag person.

The sun was setting behind his back and starting to burn his neck when he noticed a small group of farmers having some kind of meeting among the tomatoes. He flipped up the collar of his jacket and surveyed the scene. The farmer's faces were wrapped in the light scarves that were normal to their trade, so it was difficult to make out who was who or what was going on.

Almost immediately after Crowley noticed them, three of the farmers drew guns on the fourth.

He reined his horse carefully back into the woods and slid down behind a tall pine stump. He was still about 50 meters away, but the brush gave him cover and the chance to look carefully at what was going on.

One of the three farmers who'd drawn guns punched the fourth in the face, knocking him on his back. Crowley couldn't hear much but did get something about "take anything we want including you."

The more carefully Crowley looked at the three gunmen, the more obvious it became that they weren't farmers. Their jackboots were the kind favored by highwaymen. And their jackets were bulging.

The farmer who'd taken the punch was awfully thin for a man. And his hair was long and pulled back in a bun.

He wasn't a *he*.

The three highwaymen were assaulting a woman farmer.

He drew his best pistol from inside his coat. It was a full-size plasma pinscher, accurate to 200 yards and had a laser site to help with his aim.

He didn't activate the site mechanism yet. If the highwaymen were any kind of smart, they'd figure out what was going on as soon as the red dot appeared. He decided to wait a little longer; until they were about to do something to her. Maybe his read was wrong…or maybe they were just delivering a nasty message.

He flipped the safety off of the pistol and drew an unaided bead on the highwayman who was standing over the woman. He could aim at the hand or the head. Most highwaymen wore jackets that contained some kind of bulletproof or impact resistant material.

There was something in the thug's hand; it looked like a knife. He drew in a breath as the thug's arm reached back. And squeezed.

He'd practiced firing this pistol a lot. But this was the first time he was actually shooting at someone. The gun was well made and had a light recoil for a weapon its size. He was comfortable with it. But it still was hotter and louder than he expected.

The thug's head snapped backward and a bloom of blood sprayed out from his temple along his right shoulder.

Crowley exhaled and lowered his weapon, twisting the laser site on. He heard a horse's whinny…but it wasn't his chestnut. It was coming from the direction he'd fired. The two other thugs had dropped to their knees and were trying to locate the site line of the shot. They weren't having much success and yelled at each other angrily.

"Where the fuck did that come from?"

"Shut up! They're in the trees."

Crowley took another deep breath and placed the red dot on the closer thug's nose. He held his breath and squeezed again. This shot struck a little low and to the right, ripping a hole in the target's jaw. He dropped.

Next, Crowley placed the red dot on the third thug. But the woman farmer was already pulling her knife out of his stomach. He fell to his knees and she stepped back several paces.

Crowley twisted the site off and holstered the pistol. He grabbed the reins of his horse and headed out of the narrow woods.

He waited until he was about 20 paces from the woman farmer until he asked if she was all right.

"I don't know. I think so. Did you do…this?"

"Yes. They looked like they were going to kill you."

She didn't waste any time, moving to the body of the first thug and removing his weapons from his jacket. "They might have. Why'd you stop them? Are you some kind of security?"

While she spoke to him, she used one of the first thug's guns to fire a killing shot into the head of the one she'd knifed.

Crowley followed her lead and rolled over the thug he'd shot in the jaw. The entry wound next to the corner of his mouth was small but the exit wound at the base of his skull was four or five inches around. Crowley pulled out three European pistols and a thick wad of small denomination corporate bond notes.

"No. I'm just passing through."

"Well, you might have gotten yourself into more trouble than you reckoned here. These people were part of a brigand syndicate. Their partners aren't going to like this."

Now she was looking off into the woods, a couple hundred meters beyond the tall stump that Crowley had used for cover. He followed her gaze and noticed a vehicle parked crudely amidst the trees.

"Our best plan is to put these three in their truck and then torch the thing. It will make it hard for anyone to figure out for sure what happened."

That sounded like a good idea.

The woman farmer had a gray horse tied up to an irrigation control box a few yards away from where the thugs had been harassing her. That was what he'd heard. She put the guns she'd taken from the thugs into saddle bag. Crowley put his booty into one of his saddle bags and pocketed the money.

With some effort, they stacked all three bodies across Crowley's saddle and led the chestnut over to the truck. That was a lot of weight for his horse.

The woman climbed in the truck and started it up quickly. She drove forward, away from the trees and crushed about two dozen tomato plants, finally stopping about a third of the way into a cultivated section.

Crowley followed the path she'd made and brought his horse up along the passenger side of the truck. She'd already opened the door on that side and, using a sort of flipping motion, they loaded the three bodies into truck more quickly and easily than he'd expected.

"Do you have any explosives or incendiaries?"

He did. He had some K4 dynamite with 120-second chemical fuses that he'd bought for a few dollars on the outskirts of New Orleans. She asked for two sticks.

She led him about 50 meters north and then turned into a four-foot-wide seam that ran northeast between two sections of cultivated field. When the dynamite exploded in the truck, they were a quarter of a mile away. Still, Crowley could feel the ground shudder through his horse's trot.

"Do you want to go back and check that?"

"No. I'm sure it's burning. The worst it will do from right there is burn a half-acre of tomatoes. But if some crops burn, that's okay; it'll look less like a farmer was involved."

"Won't whoever owns those tomatoes want to know what happened?"

"I own the tomatoes."

She invited Crowley to stop off at her home. He could feed his horse and they'd have some time to compare stories, in case anyone ever asked about what had happened.

He agreed, mostly because it was getting dark and he didn't have any place to sleep.

The farmhouse was well protected. First, it was located in a stand of woods instead of amidst cultivated land; so, you couldn't see it from a distance. Second, a high concrete wall—it was 10 or 12 feet, at least—ran around the place. The main pathway into the sheltering woods led to a blank stretch of wall, so the woman farmer turned off of that path and led him through the bush at a canter until they came upon a metal door that was already sliding up as they approached. She must have had a remote control device.

She didn't stop or say anything until they were on the other side of the wall. Once they were, two other young women and a young man in his early 20s met them with rifles drawn.

"It's all right. He's a stranger. And he killed two jacks."

The girls, who wore the same clothes as the woman climbing down from her horse, lowered their weapons. The young man kept his raised. "Let me just get a look at him. Climb on down off of your ride, stranger. And show your arms."

Crowley was more interested in surveying the compound than arguing, so he did what the young man said.

"My name is Michael Crowley. I'm from Tampa. I've got ID. I'm heading for the Brownsville area. Hoping to find some work there." No one seemed interested in his explanation.

The farmhouse was really a compound. One main house and at least four or five other buildings, like a small village unto itself. Several of the buildings were made out of shipping containers welded together. There were other people going about their business on all sides—but they were giving Crowley and his greeting party a lot of room.

"What kind of work you do?"

"I thought I'd try helping them get City recognition."

"People who can help places get City recognition don't usually ride through the wasteland on cheap horses," it was the woman he'd saved. "If you can help them, why aren't they flying you down?"

There didn't seem to be any reason to lie. These people had trusted him enough to let him inside their walls.

"They don't know I'm coming. I got into some trouble in Tampa. I'm kind of looking for a new start somewhere else."

"In that case, I *would* like to see your ID," said the young man. He lowered his rifle a bit but kept it cradled in his right arm in case he needed a quick shot. Crowley had seen legitimate security forces hold their weapons like this. The fellow knew guns.

Crowley told him that the ID was in his saddle bag and proceeded to get it—the one that had his real name. It was an ID he'd gotten for doing work on a big farm north of Mobile.

The young man took the ID and gestured in the direction the woman farmer was walking. One of the younger girls took the reins of both horses and lead them the same direction. Crowley was heading toward a squat building closest to the metal gate, which had closed quickly after he and the woman passed through.

The building was not one of the metal ones. It was ceramic brick and mortar. Crowley and his greeting party stopped in the front hall. Two Hispanic men took the young girls' weapons and, after some whispered instructions from the young man, stood against a far wall with the rifles cradled at the ready. The young man himself disappeared through a door at the back of the hall.

One of the girls was whispering with the woman farmer; the other stayed closer to Crowley.

"There's running water in all of the spigots along the trough. It's clean to drink and you can wash your face and hands. Please keep your weapons out in the open."

Crowley saw no harm in placing his three pistols on a big table that was clearly meant for riding gear. He still had smaller pistols hidden on his shirt and boots, in case there was any trouble.

He also took off his hat and riding coat and loosened his boots. He took her advice and washed the dust from his face and neck.

The woman farmer had started taking off her outer gear while the girl was whispering with her. The woman farmer and the two girls were all tall. Crowley stood almost six feet and all three of them were taller. The girls were both attractive, if a little horsey. Long skinny necks and symmetric features.

It wasn't until the woman farmer came over the water trough that Crowley noticed something odd about her face.

There was a pinkish discoloration around her left eye. Scar tissue. It started from the middle of her forehead and reached across the left side of her face to her ear. This meant no left eyebrow and no hair in front of her left ear. It was the missing hair that gave her face the lopsided look.

While she washed her face, he noticed that her left eye was artificial. The iris and pupil were solid black and the white of the eye had a slight orange glow.

This didn't look like a farming accident. Someone had shot her in the face. Probably with a plasma weapon. But not recently.

The punch she'd taken had done some damage, too. Her upper lip was swollen and the first time she spit out some water, it was red. But she didn't seem bothered.

"Are you hungry?"

"Sure."

"Come on, then. We'll have supper outside with the crew."

Her name was Jana Morrell. The girls were her younger sisters, Toni and Cathy. This was their farm. Jana sat with Crowley at a long picnic table outside the squat building and the two younger sisters brought plates and cups, a pitcher of lemonade, some bread, raw vegetables, cheese and sliced meat. Then, they also sat down and the three sisters said a silent prayer before taking the food.

The two Hispanics also came outside. They kept their distance but kept their rifles cradled.

"You can sleep here tonight, Mr. Crowley. The dorm for our crew is basic, but I think it'll be more comfortable than a bedroll on the ground."

"Thank you, Ms. Morrell. So, how much of the farmland around here do you control?"

"Well, I don't control anything personally. My family has been running this farm for more than 100 years." She looked straight at him for the first time. If not for the scars, she would have been as attractive as her sisters. Maybe more so. "And I'm not sure I should share a lot of details with someone I just met. Even if you did help me with those brigands."

"Fair enough. How about them, then? Why were they attacking you?"

She winced a little when she drank the lemonade and looked at him again. She seemed inclined to talk to him but...cautious.

"Those three weren't anything themselves. They're just part of a group that's trying to take control of working farmland here along the Gulf Coast. They know that we have a cooperative pricing system. But they don't know how it works. So, they don't know who has money. They don't know how to steal from us."

"They're part of a group? How big is the group?"

"I don't know."

"I mean, do they have an army?"

"An army?"

"A large number of security forces."

"I don't know. They act and talk like brigands or highwaymen."

"What you called *jacks*?"

"Yes."

One of the younger sisters said that the jacks traveled in small groups, usually three or four together. But there were many of these small groups. Along the Brownsville road, they might see several dozen different ones every day.

"Do they have any organization?"

"They talk about a man they call *El Jefe* or *Captain*. They pay him tribute from everything they steal."

The young man came out of the actual farmhouse and walked over to the picnic table.

Jana introduced him, "Mr. Crowley, this is my brother. Brian."

His hair and features were darker than the girls'. But he had the same narrow face and intense eyes.

Brian dropped Crowley's laminated ID sheet on the table near his plate. "So, you're Michael Crowley from Tampa?"

"Yes."

"And when did you leave Tampa?"

"Little more than a year ago."

"And did you leave by your own choice?"

"No."

Brian whistled and sat down on the far end of the table, away from Crowley and his sisters. "Unbelievable. Jana, this man used to be Tampa's CEO. He got banished for malfeasance."

She looked at Crowley for a third time. The scarred part of her face was immobile; but the healthy eye looked more interested than upset. "Is this true?"

"Yes. Well, it's true that I was CEO. But the CEO position in Tampa isn't as powerful as in most Cities. I was just a good manager, not a Brahmin."

She ran a slice of tomato through some dressing and ate it, looking at him the whole time. "This is interesting, Mr. Crowley. I'd like to know what they mean when they say *malfeasance* down Tampa way."

"Mostly what it means is my rival needed an excuse to get rid of me. And my Chairman betrayed me. Like they say, there's no room for justice in City politics."

She smiled and passed him some bread. She was pretty. Once you saw past the scars.

Fourteen

Hailwood picked up Chris Stanton and Richie Conroy at Conroy's apartment in St. Pete Beach. When the car arrived, Conroy had some guy from his work and a couple of girls from the beach who wanted to come along.

It was going to be a tight squeeze. Since there was a driver and Bert Menendez—who seemed to be Hailwood's regular body guard lately—in the front, the party had to fit in the back. They had to crawl around a little but eventually made it work. Hailwood, Conroy and the girls jammed into the main bench seat and Stanton and the friend from Conroy's work sat in the jump seats.

In the bench, everyone's hips and hands were touching. But the girls—their names were Angie and Eve—didn't seem to mind. They were going to a Crusader launch in a limousine.

Victor had stocked the cooler with beer and the bar with tequila. And it didn't take long for the guys in the jump seats to start passing around drinks.

Hailwood did some math quickly. Six people here, plus the two security guys up front. Another friend was meeting him at Canaveral with three people—which made a total of 12. That was fine. His grandfather's box held 12. But another friend and his wife said they might drive up. So, that would be 14. And you always had to factor in an extra person or two when it came to big launches.

"We're going to see a Mars launch." One of the girls yelled, right before downing a shot of tequila.

"Go, Tampa!" Conroy said ironically and downed his.

Stanton didn't drink tequila. He was drinking his beer pensively. "How long is the trip to Mars Colony, once they take off from moon orbit?" His topicality may have been the result of not having a beach girl on his lap.

"About six months," Conroy yelled, amid giggles from the beach girl sitting next to him. Among Hailwood's group of friends, Conroy was considered the expert on all things space-related. He worked for Gulf Aerospace, which supplied guidance systems to TSA (and to various aircraft-makers around the world). In terms of sheer IQ, Conroy was probably the smartest of the group. But he was also the heaviest drinker. He was drunk most of the time when they all got together.

"Actually, it's supposed to be 188 days, our time. But there could be some variance, high or low." This was Conroy's friend from work. Another serious guy.

"That's a long-ass time to be weightless."

"True. But these new spaceplanes have magnetic weight grids, where the crew can take turns walking and working out. So, they won't have too much muscle atrophy."

"Well, that's good."

While Stanton and Conroy's friend were having the rocket geek conversation, the beach girl next to Hailwood nuzzled up to his neck and whispered, "I bet fucking in zero g is amazing."

He drank some beer and kissed her. "I bet it's really difficult. Fucking on earth is fine with me."

She giggled and reached out for more tequila.

They stopped four times along the way for food and bathroom breaks. This meant that, even with the driver making his best time on the corridor highway, the trip took almost three hours.

Most of the crowd coming to the launch had arrived hours earlier, in time for plenty of sightseeing and tailgating. But there were still a lot of cars waiting to get through the gates at 4:30 in the afternoon, when Hailwood's car arrived.

They didn't have to wait, though. The car was waved through "official vehicles only" lane and drove under the stadium to deliver its cargo of happy drunks to the luxury box elevator entrance.

"Now, you guys make sure they don't give you any grief about coming up to the box," Hailwood said to the driver, as he climbed out. He didn't know this driver very well; but Menendez was sticking with the party, and Hailwood followed the Old Man's habit of making sure the security guys were treated as well as possible while on duty.

"Don't worry, sir. I'll be up there before the lights go down."

"Great."

The launch was scheduled for 7:00 pm—and, unlike other big public events, it had to go off on time. This meant that the official activities started at around 5:00 pm. The first part, right after the lights in the stadium went down, was the introduction of the crew. TSA worked hard to make its astronauts celebrities. In the weeks leading up to a flight, most of the crew would me on vid talk shows and popular sites. They'd spend as much time talking about their personal lives as on their mission. This human interest content was hugely popular.

By the time the launch came around, the crew—or at least two of three of its members—would be as popular as any vid actor or talk show host. And the stadium would go crazy when they were introduced and gave their waves from the loading platform before climbing aboard their ship.

At the foot of the elevator up to the luxury boxes, there was a small crowd of people surrounding velvet ropes and a security portal. A small middle-aged woman and three large men in headphones stood behind the velvet rope and to the side of the portal.

Hailwood came through the doors at the back of his party—but the woman recognized him right away and told Conroy and the beach girls they could come through the portal, one at a time.

"Mr. H, how nice to see you. It's been a long time."

"Too long, Mrs. T. Too long. I've been working up north and don't get home as often as I wish."

"Well, you've come back on a great night. We haven't had this large a crowd in a couple of years."

"Outstanding. Hey, my driver will coming through in a couple of minutes."

"He's City?"

"Yes."

"We'll make sure he gets through quickly."

"Thanks so much. See you soon."

Hailwood waited with Menendez—who really was a big guy—while the stadium security validated his credentials. The rest of the party lingered on the other side of the portals. After a few seconds, the local security adjusted settings on one portal and waved Hailwood and Menendez through. They could see Menendez's weapons…but no alarms sounded.

The elevator raced several hundred feet up to the luxury box level, which was above and cantilevered in front of the main stadium sections. The effect was impressive: 50,000 roaring fans below and a huge, floodlit rocket ship standing in front of them.

There were some 120 luxury boxes, set in terraces on top of the stadium. Once inside, it was hard to see any other box. And most of the boxes were a combination of a covered room and an open-air balcony. In the box and, especially out on the balcony, you had the feeling that you were floating in the sky above the stadium.

They all got settled on the balcony when the stadium lights dimmed. The crowd started cheering below—and they could feel the rumble through the floor. The beach girls kept hugging each other and squealing "Oh. My. God."

Conroy's friend from work stood next to Hailwood. "You know, this is all just spectacle. These huge rockets aren't necessary to launch a Crusader. In fact, they're inefficient. They burn more fuel and are more dangerous that a piggy-back launch from a heavy cargo plane."

Hailwood smiled at him. "Yeah. But people love rocket launches." And he went to stand with the girls.

After the introductions finished, there was a brief lull in the proceedings. While technicians made sure that the crew was safely and properly secure in the spaceplane, a series of celebrities and City managers gave short talks from the stage in front of the launch platform. This part would culminate in a short speech from CEO Chambers wishing the crew well.

In the main stadium, this was the time when most people went to the bathroom or got more food and drink.

In the luxury boxes, it was the time that people visited each other. Celebrities swapped gossip, executives did business and Brahmins made social plans or married off their kids.

Hailwood wasn't expecting any visitors, so he was surprised when Jack Simmons, the head of the Space Agency, came through the door.

"Terry, how are do you doing?"

"Mr. Simmons. This is a surprise. Thanks for stopping in."

Simmons was followed by a couple of managers in expensive suits.

"No problem. When your grandfather told me you were coming watch the launch, I made a note to myself to drop by and say hello."

"Well, thanks. I should introduce you to a couple of my guests. These are some guys that I went to high school with. This is Richard Conroy. He actually works for you. Indirectly."

"Mr. Simmons, it's an honor to meet you. An honor. I work at Gulf Aerospace in the guidance and telemetry division. I'm just a junior project engineer."

"No such thing as 'just an engineer,' Richard. The guidance systems that you guys build are the reason the world comes to Tampa instead of China or Bangalore to launch sats. People want to be sure their hardware gets where it's supposed to go. And we're the only ones who can assure that. With any meaning. And it's because of your work that we can do that."

Conroy introduced his friend from work to Simmons. And even the friend was drawn into Simmons' charisma. "Mr. Simmons, I got into aerospace engineering because of a speech you gave at USF my freshman year."

"You're a fellow USF alum?"

"Yes, sir."

"Outstanding. Go, Bulls."

While Hailwood introduced Chris Stanton, he noticed Simmons make a subtle head gesture to one of his managers. It must have been a sign that it was time to go. But Simmons turned his attention to Stanton when they shook hands.

Hailwood wanted Simmons to stay for a minute. He was the closest thing that Tampa management had to a celebrity since Michael Crowley had been booted out.

"Mr. Simmons, please settle a debate we've had going on here. The engineers have been trying to explain quantum field propulsion to the rest of us. But they sound like they're contradicting each other about how it works."

Simmons smiled and nodded. "It's the most important project that we have going right now. And it'll be one of the first practical applications of quantum theory. I mean, we could spend hours discussing how it works—but this is the best way I've found to explain it. The system really works like a sail. It doesn't really do much other than catch the quantum field and let that push it along. The hard part is creating the quantum field—which I explain like punching a hole in a water pipe. We punch the hole, the quantum field rushes out like water from a pipe. It fills the sail and moves our craft along."

Conroy's friend chimed in: "But there's no actual sail."

Simmons could see that Conroy's serious friend was kind of a bummer. "No, there's no actual sail. The hardware looks something like a big centrifuge."

Hailwood wanted to redirect the conversation to keep Simmons talking. "And the quantum field pushes the ship faster than the speed of light?"

"Yeah. That's the idea. The main problem in our early development has been trying to control how much faster. We've shot tiny objects using the system. But we can't predict how fast they move. And we can't always measure it. Sometimes they go just faster than sL. Sometimes they go so fast they just disappear. But we're working on that."

"When are you going to start testing spaceplanes?"

"Terry, you sound like your grandfather!"

"Sorry. This is really exciting."

"Don't be sorry. You're right. It is. But we've still got a lot more work to do shooting particles. I'd guess we're a couple of years away from testing practical objects. We've got to find some way to regulate the speed. Right now, it's like opening that sail in the middle of a hurricane."

The managers were making hand gestures again.

Stanton wanted to get his question in. "And what'll it look like when a practical object takes off?"

"Well, there's some debate about that. Some say it'll look like a bolt of lightning. Others say it'll seem to stretch and snap like a rubber band. Still others say it'll just disappear. We'll find out soon enough. No, if you all will excuse me, I've got to get out to the launch platform."

He shook everyone's hand and held the beach girls' elbows when he shook their hands. He was smooth—more like a politician than a manager. But that was how the best managers were.

This was the kind of thing that made Hailwood wonder whether he'd be any good at City politics. Why was Simmons willing to work under a CEO as uninspiring as Matthew Chambers? Most citizens—and, Hailwood assumed, most bankers and traders—would rather have the tech-savvy guy who'd headed up the TSA running the whole City than some shady finance guy who'd ratfucked the old CEO.

The launch was impressive, as usual. The sky was a little cloudy but there were patches of clear sky and stars. Mission control timed the launch to a clear patch by holding the countdown to a few minutes after seven. Once it reached t-minus one minute, the crowd started cheering and chanting.

By the time it got to t-minus 10 seconds, you couldn't hear mission control over the sound system anymore. Fifty thousand people roared the countdown in perfect time.

On the balcony, Stanton leaned over to him around the count of eight and whisper/yelled: "This is fucking amazing. Perfectly in sync."

"Seven…six…"

The sound of the crowd counting down did something to anyone who heard it. This was different than the cheers at a football or baseball game. It rumbled in the base of your spine. And somewhere under your balls.

Angie had missed the point. Zero-g wasn't sexual; a rocket launch was.

The *Gasparilla* was bolted to the top of a Prometheus two-stage rocket. All 12 stories of the rocket were bathed in bright white light. Excess venting from the primer created a misty base near the ground around the rocket exhaust ports.

Around t-minus 30, the last connections to the launch platform had fallen away. So, for the last few seconds, the rocket was standing by itself, pointing toward the sky.

He took a quick look over the bummer engineer who worked with Conroy. Was he getting it now? Why these launches were so important?

It didn't look like he did.

Hailwood hoped that all his schooling and life in academia wouldn't make him like that guy. He preferred the image of Stanton, leaning out above the roar of the crowd.

"Three…two…"

Before the crowd could count down to one, a louder roar drowned out mere human voices. The main fuel feeds on the Prometheus pumped a mix of nitrogen and hydrogen across the primers. Ignition had already happened before the crowd screamed

"Blast off!" That was lost in the light and sound of the *Gasparilla* taking off.

The light was amazing. For some 15 or 20 seconds, the night became day again. You could look down from the box and everything in any available line of sight looked like it had at noon that day.

The rocket started off from the launch platform slowly and gracefully. It always seemed to defy physics—how slowly these huge vehicles left the ground.

The light and roar slowly faded as the rocket left a tail of smoke on the platform. And it visibly gained speed as it climbed higher into the clear patch of sky.

As the roar of the Prometheus diminished, the roar of the crowd took over again. It would keep up for 10 or 15 minutes, until the *Gasparilla* had reached orbit.

After about 90 seconds, there was a flare in the sky—for just a second. This was the first stage of the rocket jettisoning. The crowd's roar faded for a second. They knew the first-stage ditch was a dangerous point of the launch. The image of the rocket on the huge vid screens in front of the stadium showed the flare and the successful firing of the rocket's second stage.

The crowd's roar built up again.

Free of its bulkiest part, the rocket took a noticeable turn to the right and twisted about 60 degrees to head out over the Atlantic Ocean. Now the *Gasparilla*'s own engines were kicking in. Rather than heading upward on a perpendicular angle from the ground, it would rise more like a plane—still at a steep ascent. Once it exited the atmosphere, it would ditch the second stage of the rocket and fly about 30 minutes to the *Atlas* orbital Earth station. There, it would spend a day swapping cargo and fueling up for the trip to Mars.

The bummer engineer had a small point in his grumpiness. There *was* something artificial about all of this hoopla for a first leg of the trip to Mars that would last less than 40 minutes.

But Hailwood's grandfather had told him stories about how important space launches had been in Tampa's history. In its early days, Tampa had lagged behind Cities like New York and SoCal on most metrics. In those days, the Space Agency had been Tampa's main urban asset. The only City that had anything comparable was Houston—but Tampa's program had always maintained a technological and commercial lead on Houston's.

In the old days, space launches weren't just spectacle. They were the City's unifying activity. And, in some ways, they still were.

"So, what do you think?" he asked Angie, as soon as the roars had died down enough for words to work.

Her eyes were teary. "Oh my God. It makes me proud."

She nuzzled her nose against his neck and grabbed his cock through his pants.

A couple of nights later, Hailwood was sitting in a rocking chair next his grandfather on the back porch of the house, explaining what a good impression Simmons had made on his friends. "You're complaining all the time about Chambers. You could replace him with Simmons and I think everyone would be 100 percent happier."

"Jack Simmons is a lovely fellow. Genuinely nice guy. Decent manager. But he'd be far out of his depth as CEO. The bankers wouldn't buy him."

"I don't think that's right. Anyone who can understand and explain quantum field propulsion so well could handle currency exchange rates."

His grandfather looked at him quizzically. This was about as close as the Old Man ever came to considering something someone else said. "Are you sure he really understands quantum field theory?"

"Sure. I mean, as much as anyone does. I don't think he pretends to be Markus Hagel."

The Old Man sat back in his chair. "Well, the currency exchanges are just as complex, in their own ways."

"Okay. I'm just saying…you complain about Chambers a lot. And you complained about Crowley before him. I think you've got too many managers. You say you need them. So, maybe you should look in a different direction for a better solution."

"I should make you CEO?"

"No. You should make *yourself* CEO."

The Old Man laughed and took a sip of Scotch. "Too old. Besides, it would be a step down. Who wants all the nit-picking and babysitting? Better to be a behind-the-scenes guy and maintain you position for years or generations."

"And you're satisfied with that, Grandpa?"

"Hell, yes."

"And you don't want to do more?"

"Hell, no."

"I don't think I'd be satisfied with a behind-the-scenes role." Hailwood sipped his Scotch. He worried a little that the Old Man would be irritated that he kept bringing up the same point. That he'd bolt off, as he often did.

But he didn't, this time. "You say that a lot. But what's your strategy?"

"Strategy?"

"For being a Chairman who's also CEO. Why is it so important? What are you itching to *do*?"

"Take over the closest five or six Cities and form a nation. Like the Asians."

"Nation-building," the Old Man sneered. "Been done here. Doesn't usually last very long. And, again, why? To what end?"

"Restoring true democracy."

"People don't want true democracy, Terry. They want security. Security in an insecure world. That's why—"

"—Cities have walls. Yeah, I know. I'm just trying to figure out some other way. I see people like Jack Simmons and I think it could be possible to run a City without the bullshit politics."

Now the Old Man snorted. "Terry, you're all over the place. One minute, you say you want to restore true democracy; the next, you say you want more efficient management. Those are mutually exclusive."

Hailwood took another small sip. He didn't want to get drunk. And he could see the Old Man had him here. "You're right, you're right. I see your point, Grandpa. I guess I'm saying that if we changed the system, it might—"

"—suddenly start being more efficient? We're losing money, but we'll make it up in volume? No. Something else has to change first. And that 'something else' is human nature."

"That's the trouble with talking politics with you, Grandpa. You've seen and done everything."

"Look, I'm not saying you're categorically wrong, Terry. You may be right. When you take over, you can make Jack Simmons or anyone else you want CEO. You can try to expand the walls. But that's much harder than you think."

"I'll say it again, Grandpa. I don't think I'm made for this like you are. I don't think *anyone* is made for it like you are."

"But you're suggesting CEOs?"

Fifteen

"Go ahead."

She cleared her voice and started. "Mister Jones of the Manor Farm had locked the hen houses for the night but was too drunk to remember to shut the popholes."

Jana could read—she'd surfed the nets and read maps and letters all her life. But she hadn't read many books and felt self-conscious about this. Losing her eye hadn't helped. While the artificial eye could make out letters, she said it caused a kind of vertigo if she read for a long time. So she hadn't done much.

Crowley thought she had a nice voice—low in register for a young woman, but clear and full. And she tentatively admitted that reading out loud took her mind off of the queasiness. So, he'd pulled a couple of dozen "Great Book" texts from a free site that he'd used for quick help back in the old days, when he'd had to deal with intellectuals in City business.

He showed her a few basic tricks he'd learned for using the speech prompter feature of her Apple PowerScreen—he'd had the same machine back in Tampa. With that small encouragement, she'd taken that list and run with it. In a few weeks, she was better-read than he was.

And their free time together became her reading old books out loud to him.

"With the ring of light from his lantern dancing from side to side, he lurked across the yard, kicked off his boots at the back door, drew himself a last glass of beer from the barrel in the scullery and made his way up to bed where Mrs. Jones was already snoring."

She had the screen set to highlight words that she touched. Later, she'd go back and look up each.

"I like the sound of these old words. *Lurked* and *scullery*. You don't hear words like that anymore."

"No. You don't. I heard once that the number of words people use has dropped by more than half from the time that book was written. When I heard it, the first thought that crossed my mind was: Good. Fewer words meant more efficient speaking."

"That's a strange way to look at it."

"Yeah. No doubt helped by the Neuroplex pills. Those damn things just make you stupid."

"Also, it's strange to read words like *drunk* and *beer*. I didn't think they were the kind of words that people would write." She seemed childlike in these moments. In her awkward enthusiasm, Jana was like many wasteland natives; she could ride and fight and talk and gained authority from those things. Reading books was something for priests and scribes.

Or *had been*. She was completely into this now.

"As soon as the light in the bedroom went out there was a stirring and a fluttering all through the farm buildings. Word had gone around during that day that old major the prize middle white boar had a strange dream on the previous night and wished to communicate it to the other animals."

She looked up and stared at him hard. Her lower lip did a kind of quiver…it wasn't crying. In fact, it was the opposite. She usually did it when she was happy about something.

Crowley had never been a visual thinker; all of the various personality profiles he'd had done in his career had pegged him as a numbers person. But he tried to make a mental picture of her in this moment, staring up from the book as she read. If he could keep this image in his mind, through good times or bad…10 years from now, riding through the wasteland, he would remember why he'd fallen in love with her.

"So the animals can talk?" she asked.

"Yes. Just like people. But you're not supposed to take this literally. It's a fable."

And she went back to reading. Her next project was going to be bigger. She was going to read the entire Bible out loud to him.

Crowley had been staying at the Morrell farm for almost three months—longer than he'd stayed at any place during his time in the wasteland. He'd made a big impression by showing Jana's brother some simple tricks for spoofing his way into the nets of Cities like Tampa and New Orleans. This gave Brian an easy way to check prices for his produce and find out what the ag departments were projecting for futures prices. That knowledge made an even bigger impression on the other farmers in the area. They were starved for this kind of specific detail.

Or at least they believed they were.

The strange thing was that these farmers were doing better than people in the wasteland were supposed to. Most had contracts with wholesalers in Houston or Brownsville for crops—and those that didn't have contracts could find one-off buyers riding along the Brownsville Road every couple of months. There was a network of independent wholesalers who would ride a circuit of trading posts and grange coops, looking for crops to sell around—or even ahead of—harvest time.

He'd heard about these secret systems riding his own circuit over the previous year. But he'd always heard about them second- or third-hand, from the jealous perspective of the outsiders scrambling for their next meal. His time at the Morrells' farm had given him his first direct contact with these systems.

There wasn't a formal grange co-op along this stretch of the Brownsville Road; instead, there was a weekly gathering at the Morrell house.

This combination of contracts and one-off sales was more efficient than a City manager would ever guess. But Brian's father had taught him that a farmer could never have too much pricing information, so he was always looking for more.

After the tips for getting into the City nets, Crowley had given Brian and the other nearby farmers something *really* useful—instructions for using their radios to set up a basic triangulation function for their perimeter security system. This was a big deal. Three-dimension vectoring meant they could measure accurately how quickly and from which direction a ping was approaching.

This got him invited to the next meeting. The biggest farmers in the area were called "The Seven Gramps." Brian was the host and a kind of honorary member, having inherited his father's seat.

The method of the meetings was long established. The men gathered in the front room of the Morrell farm house a few minutes early. They might make a few grunts or say quick greetings—but they didn't talk too much. There. They knew each other well enough that they could skip the nervous jabber of salesmen.

When the scheduled hour (usually noon...sometimes early evening) came, some combination of the Morrell daughters would open the old double doors into the dining room and everyone would take seats around the big pine table.

Well into their 70s or 80s, the Gramps were remarkably able-bodied—with one exception. And they were all planning on being around for a while to come.

Jana had told Crowley that each of the Gramps had had some form of gene therapy, either visiting a City or paying a provider to come to their farms.

Gramp Brownlee was the only cripple. He'd had a stroke some years earlier and needed a wheelchair. He came in through the kitchen, where there were fewer stairs; when he wheeled into the foyer, the Morrell girls knew it was time to open the doors.

Crowley recognized this kind of thing from a thousand meetings in Tampa. Gramp Brownlee played power games.

For the noon meetings, there would be simple food—barbecue sandwiches and some beans or potato salad—served buffet style. Pitchers of cold water, fruit juice and whiskey were placed around the table. Each place-setting had a large tumbler glass. Most of the old men drank whiskey and water; some drank water and juice.

Brian didn't drink whiskey at these meetings or anywhere else. Still, he suggested Crowley take a least a little with his water. It would make a good impression on the Gramps.

When everyone had taken some food, the grunts gradually melted into talk. Since Crowley was the new face, he got a lot of questions. This felt familiar, too.

Gramp Simpson—whose farm shared a border with the Morrells' to the south—was the first. "So, Mr. Crowley, I understand we're lucky you happened upon us here. You used to be a big shot down Tampa way?"

"Yes sir. I was a senior manager in Tampa for nearly eight years."

Simpson laughed and drank some whiskey and water. Physically, he was the biggest man in the group—easily three or four inches over six feet. His hair and beard were snow white and thick. He'd been muscular in his youth; his arms and chest still had some bulk.

"You've been staying with Morrells long enough to know we're no fools. Mr. Crowley. You weren't just a *senior manager*. You were the boy genius CEO. And you got fired under some kind of cloud. Some say for stealing; some say for crossing your Chairman."

"Yes. Well, I assure you all, I never stole a thing in Tampa."

"Casting you out was a pretty strong remedy to a policy disagreement, don't you think?" This was Gramp Howard. With his long face, thin hair and pinched expression, he looked like a children's cartoon version of an angry old man. According to Jana, he was the weakest of the Seven—with a relatively small farm that had originally belonged to another family. His question was not as friendly as Simpson's had been.

Crowley looked for the exits, something he'd been training himself to do whenever a situation seemed…like it might mean trouble. One door out to the entry foyer, one door back into the kitchen.

"Well, they loaded a lot of lies into that indictment. But my plan to set up a federation with some other Cities was the main problem. My chairman took it as a personal insult. And my CFO was eager to push me out. The next time I'm in that place again, I'll be more careful about ambitious CFOs."

Most of the Gramps laughed at that—the brass of an outcast thinking about getting back to the top of City government.

The laughter let Crowley relax a little. Howard had been something like an ambitious CFO himself, years ago. According to Jana, he was a local boy who married into a farm family and somehow pushed his wife's brother out. A few years after the wedding, his wife's father was thrown by his horse; a few months after that, his wife disappeared. Some locals said she'd run off; others said Howard had killed her.

Whatever the truth, Howard had effectively taken over the farm. He married a second wife—a woman who'd been a housekeeper for one of the other local families—had his own family and did just enough to be counted among the Gramps.

At the lunch, Howard didn't ask any more questions.

Gramp Brownlee was still interested in what had happened in Tampa, though. He'd wheeled his blubbery self up to the empty space set at the table and eaten quickly. He was ready to take over the talk. "So, it was just politics?"

"I'm not sure I'd call it *just* politics, Mr. Brownlee. In big City government, politics is a lot. Everything, maybe. But, if you're worried about the criminal charges they made, I can assure that those were just drummed up so that Old Man Hailwood could be sure I'd be gone for good. In Tampa, Chairman Hailwood gets whatever he wants."

"Seems to me that a prodigy CEO would know better than to go up against a Chairman who gets whatever he wants."

Crowley took a long look at Gramp Brownlee. He didn't see trouble there; it seemed more that Brownlee was just a tough old bird.

Of course, that's what he'd thought about Old Man Hailwood. A lot was coming back to him.

"I didn't think I was going up against him, Mr. Brownlee. I believed in what I was doing. And I still think that the big Cities are going to have to make some kind of confederation in order for us to do business with the Asians on any kind equal footing. *They* understand the importance of coordination. As long as they're right, groups can do more than individuals."

"You'll have a hard time making that case out here, son. This is the wilds."

The conversation was heading off on a tangent. Brian stepped in, as he'd told Crowley he would. "Gentlemen, let's not waste our time arguing about things that don't bear on the price of barley. This is what I know: We're facing a real problem with a group of brigands trying to form some kind of mafia around here. They think they can use our farms as their money supply. And they're going to get more violent and threatening until we start giving them the money they want. Do you all agree with what I see here?"

The Gramps didn't seem too happy about admitting it—but they did.

"Now here's what I know about Mr. Crowley. He used to be the CEO of a big City. He was formally banished, which is something that Cities don't do very much. So, something really bad must have happened there. Now, I don't know much about City life, praise God; but I do know that there's a lot of money there and the politics is vicious. So, I don't have a problem believing Crowley's version.

"But, most important, I know that his knowledge can help us deal with these brigands. It already has helped us—with him showing

Sic Semper Tyrannis

us how to use our radio systems to triangulate our perimeter radar. I mean, we had these pieces right here all the time and didn't know we could put them together to make a 10-times-better tool. Plus, he showed us how to get into the Houston net for trading prices on our crops. That's real value. Brownlee, I remember you sitting right at this table and saying you wish you could get into the Houston 'net. And now you can. Thanks to Mr. Crowley, here."

Crowley had never heard Brian talk this much before. He wasn't sure he'd heard *anyone* in the wasteland talk this much before. The young man had a touch of the politician in him.

"Now it's clear to me that this man wandered right up to our doorsteps with a lot of knowledge that we need. And maybe he's looking for a chance to recover some of what he had. I'm inclined to accept him as a gift from God and tool for dealing with these damned brigands."

Brownlee still looked skeptical. "One question. What if he's a spy for Tampa or Houston or some other City?"

"Ask him yourself."

"All right. Crowley, I think maybe you and these brigands might all be working for Tampa or some other City. Houston. They're sent here to scare us. You're sent here to work your way into our trust and convince us to pledge loyalty in exchange for protection. And that City will end up taking over our farms. How are you going to convince me otherwise?"

Convince. Crowley had been here before; it was basic meeting management. "I'm not going to convince you of anything, Mr. Brownlee. I'm going to tell you what I see here. And what I know I can do. You and the others are going to decide whether you want my help or not. But let me make one thing plain, right away, so there are no lingering doubts. I'm not a spy or familiar for any City or group. I'm completely alone. And I came here by chance. I was just looking for a safe place to camp for the night."

He let that stand for a moment. Then, "I can help you gentlemen negotiate a favorable security agreement. One that will make sure you keep your farms. And, if what I hear is right, maybe one that will give you some power in Brownsville. As it tries to become a City in its own right."

"And what do you want for helping us like this?"

"Not much. A place to live for a while. Maybe a small amount of money, so I can act properly if I have to go visit the founders in Brownsville. What I want for myself is to get back into a City as a manager. And the best way I can do that is be a good agent for all of you."

As the meeting went on, Crowley suggested that they contact the food wholesalers in Houston about a security agreement…but then take that "bird in the hand" to the people trying to get City recognition for Brownsville.

"You gentlemen have more power here than you realize. The fact that wholesalers in Houston are willing to make contracts with you proves it. Professional managers don't like to make contracts with people in the wasteland—the common wisdom is that they're one-way deals. The outsider can use the contract in a City court but the citizen can't get any justice in the wasteland."

What he didn't tell them was that Tampa had a law stating that only citizens could bring lawsuits in its courts—effectively making contracts with non-citizens useless. Most Cities had similar laws. So, the deals these farmers had with the Houston food wholesalers weren't worth as much as they thought.

"You can use the rise of Brownsville to your advantage here. Use the food people in Houston to put some pressure on the ones in Brownsville. I'm not talking about a bidding war—but just the smart use of competitive pressure. Get them competing to make a security agreement with us. We tell them that we need to get rid of these brigands and whichever one can help us get rid of them will be who we sign with. There will be well-armed security forces out here faster than you can spit."

The Gramps were interested in paying him to make their case in Houston and Brownsville and get a security deal. Preferably, with Houston.

This was a good opportunity. As one of his early mentors had said, "It's always easier to find a job when you have a job."

He told the group that he'd draft a formal request that they could all review. Their response to this idea seemed lukewarm.

Later, Brian would explain to Crowley that only about half of the people in the room could read

Crowley had gotten used to illiterates among the working stiffs in the wasteland. But he still wasn't accustomed to the idea that most of the wealthy, powerful people also couldn't read.

Their explanations were usually the same—almost to the word: "I know I should read. But, when it comes to sitting down and doing it, it just doesn't seem like it's so important. There's so much else going on. I'm just too busy."

Over time, Crowley explained to each of the Gramps that dealing with any City for a security agreement was going to require that they be able to read and write basic business correspondence. He offered to come around to each farmer's house for an hour or two each week and teach them to the point they could read and understand a business letter.

Two of the Gramps accepted on the spot. The others said they'd think about it.

"…no. You're sitting up too straight. Lean against the horn more. You should use the weight of your body to steady the shot."

Jana had insisted that she give Crowley something in exchange for him helping her improve her reading. She'd said it had to be valuable…but not too personal. In other words, not sex. They'd spent several days trying to figure out what that something would be.

Finally, after going through his experiences riding the wasteland for a year and half, he mentioned that he'd never learned to shoot a rifle while riding his horse.

She knew how to do that.

They filled an old 80-pound feed sack with dirt and lashed it against a tall tree stump in the far back of the plum orchard just outside of the compound. He could ride his chestnut to a full gallop in front of the soy field and take shots at the dummy.

His first couple of shots were pretty good, one hitting the sack high and the other, low. But then the shakiness of his style took over and the rest of his shots were way off—usually in the dirt.

She was right. As soon as she said it, he could feel that he was sitting up too straight. But his efforts at leaning into his saddle didn't make much of a difference. His shots were still hitting the dirt.

"Try wrapping your reins around the horn for a second while you square up. That might steady things."

"Really?"

"Yeah. Not a bunch of times. Just once. And keep them in your left hand, too. But a quick wrap should steady your hand and help you lean into it more."

"Okay."

Wrapping the reins was something that he'd learned was dangerous when he'd first started riding. It was also something that experienced riders would do when they were teaching children.

He tried to clear his mind of this. No ego. Just do what she suggested and see if it would make any improvement.

It did. But his shots were still connecting a little low.

The next time he rode out toward her, she looked a little cross. "Where are you aiming?"

"At the heart."

They had pinned a red piece of ribbon near the center of the sack for the heart and an old cloth cotton-picker hat on top for the head.

She squinted at the dummy.

"Let me see the rifle."

Again, he had to suppress the wail of ego.

He didn't say anything and handed her the weapon. It was well-maintained vintage Ruger CTX semiautomatic gauss rifle from the late Federal Era.

There was a long story that he'd never tell her about how he got the gun. He'd traded a weapons dealer outside of New Orleans a half-kilo of Neuroplex/Pleasure pills for it and 200 gold New Orleans dollars the last time he'd been outside the walls there. He'd gotten the Pleasure as payment for killing a drug dealer who'd tried to rip off another drug dealer in some transaction that had happened before he'd shown up.

The killing had been something he'd done to test himself—and because he wasn't getting anywhere trying to talking his way past the gates in New Orleans.

Setting up the hit had been easier than he'd expected. An outcast scribe he met had told him a major drug dealer was looking for a "new face" to do a job no one known in the area could. Within a day, the deal was made.

Crowley used his real name to float the word around a couple of camps outside the walls that he was looking for a large supply of Pleasure. The crooked dealer found him at travelers' inn on the old Interstate about a mile from the eastern gate.

They had a drink in the bar. Crowley said he was going to make a quick flip on the drugs to some City corporate types he still knew.

He said he had $2,000 in City of Tampa bonds to buy in. He said the bonds were upstairs in his saddle bag. He invited the crooked dealer to come up and take pictures of the bonds and their serial numbers so he could verify them himself.

This was the only part of the set up that made Crowley nervous. He was afraid that the crooked dealer would find the story too complicated to believe.

But the dealer agreed to come up and vid the bonds. He told Crowley he was counting on his security men sitting outside of the inn to prevent any trouble.

When they were inside the room, Crowley locked the door. There was no other way out of the room. He pulled his saddle bag out from under his bed, flipped it open and drew the four-inch steel blade from its sheath under the flap. His arm swept up, slashing the crooked dealer hard from his Adam's apple to below his left ear while his eyes were still focusing down into the saddle bag.

Crowley dropped the short blade and drew the 12-inch knife from its sheath along the side of his saddle bag. While the crooked dealer grabbed at the burning sensation on his neck, Crowley stabbed him inside his riding coat, just above his belt on the right side of his navel, and sliced up to the breastbone.

The crooked dealer tried to scream, but the neck-slashing had cut his throat and the gutting had robbed him of breath. The scream sounded like a hiss.

Crowley pushed him back against the wall near the door and took out the 12-inch knife, still slicing up against the crooked dealer's chest on the way out. He dragged the dealer up onto the bed and squared the blade against the man's throat, just below the first slash. And sliced as hard as he could.

Time was an issue. And there was going to be a lot of blood. The mattress of the bed would absorb a lot of it; but, if he wasn't careful, the mess could give him away. He only had 15 or 20 minutes before the crooked dealer's security started getting suspicious. He used the larger blade to cut off the crooked dealer's thumbs and ears. The blade was sharp and did its job well. He wrapped the pieces in a face towel and put that in a small synthmesh bag. Then, he wrapped the body in blankets and centered it on the bed.

He looked himself over to make sure he didn't have any noticeable blood on him. He double-checked his shoes and checked the pistols in his shoulder holster and belt holster and went back down to the bar.

The teenage son of the woman who ran the inn took the leather bag to the dealer who'd hired Crowley.

Crowley waited in the bar. The agreement was that, once the ears and thumbs arrived, the dealer who'd hired him would come to the inn, check the body and pay Crowley.

He didn't drink much, but Crowley had a beer while the boy ran his errand. Two bad things could happen: The dead man's security could come in looking for their boss; and the dealer who'd hired Crowley could welch on their agreement. He was prepared for either.

He looked around the bar for exits. There was the main double door out to the street. A door immediately behind the bar that went back the kitchen. And a narrow hallway that went back to the toilets…and around the kitchen again. That hallway was bad news. The best exit was out the front door. Next best, over the bar and out the back through the kitchen. Part of him wanted to bolt, even without getting paid. But he resisted that.

The dealer who'd hired him showed up quickly with a dozen men. The dead man's security had either disappeared or never been there. Within half an hour, Crowley had traded the Pleasure for the rifle and cash and was riding his chestnut north, making the long trip around New Orleans.

He wasn't proud of what he'd done; but he did feel a kind of… accomplishment…about it. He'd killed a man for money and was confident he could do whatever it would take to climb back.

Jana snatched the weapon from him and raised it to her shoulder. Crowley noticed that she aimed with her artificial eye. She fired twice quickly at the dummy. And then tossed it back to Crowley. It was easy to catch; he just drew his hands into his chest.

"Your shooting isn't so bad. You've just set your sight low. From right here, raise it about a foot on the dummy. Maybe a little less."

She was right.

As his did every Wednesday evening, Crowley rode up to the Simpson farm just as the sun was setting. The main road to the Simpson place approached from west and the Brownsville road, so the golds and reds of the sunset lighted the grand old wood-frame house in rich colors.

Sic Semper Tyrannis

Unlike the Morrell compound, the Simpson house was plainly visible from half a mile in any direction. Gramp Simpson said his best defensive weapon was 360 degrees of clean firing lines. There was barbed wire and some laser-tag mines, of course; but the real security was the fact that no one could reach his place fast enough to surprise him.

As Crowley approached, he could see something was going on at the Simpson house. There were more people there than usual; and something like a dozen horse carts parked in front of the house.

Gramp Simpson was probably the most outgoing of the old farmers; he invited people into his home more often than any other Gramp. He'd been disciplined (more so than the others) about his reading lessons.

But maybe he had forgotten this week and planned some kind of barbecue.

At the main gate into the Simpson compound, Crowley was greeted by Gramp Simpson himself. The old man sat on his horse, flanked by machine gun nests on either side of the barbed wire gate. He was smiling.

"Welcome, Crowley. Welcome. I've decided to act on some of the ideas we've parleyed. So, I thought it best to come out and greet you."

He nodded and the gate whirred open to the right side."

"I see you've got something going on. If you want, we can just wait on our lesson until next week."

Gramp Simpson laughed at this. He laughed at lots of things. "Not at all. These people are here for *you*. Well, for you and a free dinner. I've invited my workers and tenants to join our lessons."

Crowley wasn't sure what to make of this. They hadn't "parleyed" anything—Simpson had simply said that he thought everyone should know how to read.

Something Jana had said stuck in Crowley's mind: Gramp Simpson was so friendly that he got away with being a bigger jerk than most people realized. But Crowley tried to keep his mind open and his mouth closed. He was working on recovering his managerial skills…and he knew that his best skill was keeping his reserve while other people talked and acted.

There were about 20 adult men, in all. And, together, they seemed less shy about learning than wasteland people usually were one by one. Simpson had set up benches in his backyard in a half-circle around a white-board from his study that Crowley had used for their lessons before.

There were another dozen women and eight or 10 teenage kids old enough to pay attention. They were all milling around the benches with their men, waiting to be told what to do.

So, the women and kids were as curious about reading as the men were. This was a good sign. Women in the wasteland were used to being excluded from things. Crowley wasn't any great feminist or intellectual—but all those women seemed like a marketing opportunity to him.

Crowley had never taught a group, so the number daunted him. But he'd believed in facing his fears. "Gramp Simpson, please remember I'm not a teacher by training. Most of my experience teaching reading is one-on-one."

"You're a fine teacher. We've only had a few lessons and I can already read the news from the City Nets for myself."

"But it's like I said. You've probably been reading your whole life and just didn't realize it."

"Well, if that's true for me, it's true for most of these folks."

"Maybe so." Crowley looked back at the benches and drew a long breath. "Okay. Well, then here's my thought. If I'm going to teach 20 men, I might as well teach the women and kids. Let's try and give everyone a bench."

He thought that might be a problem—but it wasn't. They all took their seats, almost immediately. For the rest of his life, Crowley would look back on that outdoor reading lesson and think that Gramp Simpson had foreseen everything.

It was like another famous management lesson: The best ideas are ones that other people think are their own.

"Well, good evening to all of you. Welcome. Those of you who don't know me, my name is Michael Crowley. For a little while now, I've been helping some of the people around the Brownsville Road area with their reading. It's important to know how to read. For lots of reasons. To read screens. To buy or sell things. And, the thing that means most to a lot of people, to read the Bible. Once you know how to read, you can teach yourself just about anything else you need to know. So, it helps balance the power between you and anyone else you come across in life."

As soon as he mentioned the Bible, most of the crown leaned forward.

He started with the alphabet—which most of the people seemed to know, even if they didn't know it in order. And then he singled out the vowels....

There were just 30 minutes until the helicopter was due to arrive and the Tejana girls working on his suit coat weren't finished yet.

Jana tried to be reassuring. "Don't worry Maria J is the best seamstress in the area. She'll have the coat done before you go. I bet this is a lot different than your meetings when you were in Tampa."

"Not really, no. I remember one big meeting when there was a screw up with a new suit that I'd ordered. And it was just like this. Or worse, because it was the pants that were the problem. So, I was standing in my office in my underwear, telling my admin to show everyone to the conference room."

She laughed, but not as much as he'd hoped. He had a hard time predicting what parts of his stories about Tampa she'd find funny.

"Besides, this is just as fancy as anything I ever did in Tampa. I mean, they're sending a tiltrotor and I'm having a custom suit made while I wait."

"Yeah, they've sent tilts a couple of times recently. Once for Brian and Gramp Brownlee, once just for Brian himself. I think they're worried about the Brownsville City thing."

"You're probably right. And we're going to do everything we can to make sure they *stay* worried."

She laughed harder at this.

Maria J had the suit jacket done and on Crowley five minutes before the helicopter landed inside the Morrell farmhouse compound. She snapped it down against his shoulders and studies how it hung.

"'s okay."

She was short and stocky and not much to look at, but Maria J knew how to make clothes. The suit was gray with lighter-gray pinstripes. Boxier than anything he'd ever worn in Tampa. But some managers had worn suits like this, aiming for a retro fashion statement. This was the real thing—old-fashioned, no irony.

Maria J followed him out to the back porch. She wanted to hear what Jana had to say.

Jana cocked her head and told Crowley to spin around. "Muy bueno, chica. Muy bueno."

"'s not too loose?"

"No. I think it looks good. Like on the screens."

"Okay."

Jana hugged Crowley. "I hate when these things come here. They make so much noise. If you weren't going with Brian, I'd be out riding the fence."

Crowley didn't recognize the make or model of the tilt. It looked like it might have started its life as a smaller security troop transport. Now it was marked "Baker Houston Worldwide Foods" along each side of its body.

Jana, Brian and he waited under the covered portion of the back porch until the rotors slowed enough that one of the two pilots folded open the hatch and stepped out. He looked and sounded very official. "B.J. Morrell and two guests for a meeting with BHWF Vice President H.F. Paz?"

Brian answered. "I'm Brian Morrell and I just have one guest today. Our third is ill and can't make the trip."

"Not a problem, sir. Lighter load means we're there and back that much faster. Eye prints, gentlemen. Please." He held out a small biometric scanner that flashed a bright light twice—once for each passenger's right eye. "Thank you. Come on aboard and we'll get started."

Jana squeezed Crowley's upper arm quickly and let go.

The interior of the tiltrotor was more corporate than Crowley had expected. Leather seats for six and wood trim everywhere.

After he'd closed the door again, their greeter gestured to the seats and continued on into the cockpit. A wood paneled door closed behind him.

Crowley and Brian sat in the middle seats, which faced each other.

"Is this what the usually send to get you?"

"Yeah. Well, it's what they've send the last few times. But I wouldn't say usually. Usually, they send a car. Or we just drive up ourselves."

Crowley looked out the window behind Brian. Jana was still watching them from the back porch. They'd discussed the possibility that the biometric scan would show him on some kind of no-fly list. But Crowley was pretty sure that the traditional tensions between

Tampa and Houston would work to his favor in this situation. Houston didn't put much stock in Tampa's no-fly edicts.

The minutes inched by and the rotors didn't start up again. Jana hadn't moved. She hadn't even uncrossed her arms.

Crowley raised his eyebrows to Brian, who shrugged his shoulders back.

"Gentlemen. Sorry for the delay. We're just waiting for final clearance from Houston ATC."

The cockpit must have been watching them. And Crowley suspected the explanation was BS. Vehicles didn't need clearance to take off in the wasteland; they only needed clearance to enter City airspace and land on City property.

A few moments later, the rotors started to whine.

"Gentlemen. Thanks for your patience. We are cleared through to BHWF headquarters. We expect the trip to take about 35 minutes. So, if you'll fasten your seatbelts, we'll get the air."

The flight went smoothly, but it took more than 35 minutes. At the 40 minute mark, the rotors hadn't even tilted back into take-off-and-landing position. Crowley made a circular gesture with one index finger into the other palm. Brian nodded in agreement.

A few minutes after that, the pilot's voice came on again. "Gentlemen, thanks for your patience. We've just been informed by Houston ATC that we're third into the grid for BHWF headquarters. So, we're going to rotor down in about eight minutes and we should be on the ground in about eleven."

Baker Houston Worldwide Foods was a campus style corporate headquarters. The landing pad was on the ground, between two low-rise office buildings. A young woman and two large men were waiting for them in a small covered standing area when they landed.

The same greeter who'd met them at the Morrell compound opened the door for them here. Unlike a regular flight attendant, he exited first.

Outside, the woman did all of the talking. "Hello, Mr. Morrell. Mr. Crowley. My name is Sarbet Howell. I'm Mr. Paz's assistant. And these are Misters Roberts and Kragen. They're here representing the City of Houston."

Crowley recognized Roberts and Kragen immediately as low-level security goons. Thick necks and short hair; loose business suits that very likely concealed guns. He'd dealt with their types many times, inside the walls and in the wasteland. They were tough and even aggressive faced straight on from the front—but usually helpless from the side or behind.

He'd meant that metaphorically but realized it probably worked literally, too.

Sarbet was bright enough not to babble the whole way into the building, as some admins did. Once they got into the elevator, she said that their meeting had been shifted from Bert Paz's office to a conference room on the same floor. "Mr. Paz has asked a couple of additional people to sit in on your meeting."

Crowley recognized one of the additional people immediately. It was Mark Cherbourg, Houston's Chief Marketing Officer. He was a ruthless and ambitious man—either respected or hated for his predatory qualities. Crowley hadn't seen Cherbourg in person in three or four years—years before his banishment. But Cherbourg looked exactly the same. Slicked-back hair and a suit that probably cost $2,000 Tampa.

Cherbourg clearly recognized him but didn't seem surprised.

Paz started the talks, introducing Brian by first and last name to everyone on his side of the table. That included a man named Searle who was Houston's Chief Security Officer. Two C-level managers at a meeting with a farmer from the wasteland..

Then, Brian introduced Crowley.

"Yes, Mr. Crowley and I have met before. When he worked for the City of Tampa. I have to admit, Michael, you look good for someone who's been through so much."

"Thank you, Mark. It's been an interesting couple of years. Mr. Searle, it's an honor to meet you. I'll try not to be offended that you've brought so much security staff to an ag commerce meeting."

"Nothing personal, Mr. Crowley. We all understand there was a…particular…quality to your legal problems in Tampa. But the fact remains that you are convicted felon in a City we recognize."

Brian interrupted the exchange: "Not that it matters to our meeting today, Mr. Searle, but you might want to check your premise. Or talk to your general counsel. By formally banishing Mr. Crowley, the City of Tampa automatically pardoned him of any crimes he might have committed. I'm not an attorney—but I believe the legal reasoning is that if he were a convicted felon, he could appeal his convictions and demand to be readmitted for his court date."

This put Searle on the defensive, where they wanted him to be.

Cherbourg took over for the Houstonians. "Well, you know your partner, Mr. Morrell."

"I'm not his partner, Mark. I'm just serving as a consultant to the Morrells and the farmers along the Brownsville Road while they find a way to deal with some bandits that have been harassing them."

"Well, I'm not sure what we can do about that. When you're in the wasteland, it seems to me that bandits come with territory."

"You know these farmers control some of the richest ag land around. It's the richest I've seen anywhere outside of City walls. And richer than a lot I've seen inside. That's why you sent a tiltrotor down to pick us up for this meeting. Let's not waste each other's time. Baker Houston counts on produce from these farmers; and the farmers appreciate the business. It's a good relationship that needs some support. It deserves some…investment."

Paz, the BHWF manager who was technically running the meeting, didn't like the sound of that. "Investment? Why do we need to make investments? We have contracts for produce from these farmers for the next years."

Cherbourg had the practiced calm of an experienced manager. "I think Mr. Morrell will give us two reasons. First, if the bandits take control of any of these farms, they're not going to care about your contracts. Second, the founding fathers in Brownsville are indicating that they're not going to set reciprocity or extradition agreements with courts in other cities. Which mean *they're* probably not going to honor Houston contracts. So, you need some additional leverage to keep your commercial access." The he turned to Crowley and Brian. "What kind of help are you looking for?"

Brian answered. "About 500 Houston security officers."

"And how will you pay for this?"

Crowley had prepared him for this question. "Thirty days of deferred invoice produce sales to BH Worldwide. You sit on the invoices while we get things started in Brownsville—and make sure that our contracts there will allow us to keep selling produce to you. This should give you guys a nice piece of security that we will be able to work with you, even after the new City is set up. And the security officers will there to look after your interests."

The offer didn't make sense to Searle. he must have been an internal security type. They never liked sending officers beyond the walls. But the offer wasn't designed for him. Cherbourg and Paz understood its value...and, in a few seconds, Cherbourg smiled in a way that suggested he understood the elegant irony of paying Houston to enable the emergence of a rival City.

"Well, that's certainly an attractive offer for BH Wholesale. I'm not so sure whether it's such a good deal for the City. Of Houston."

Paz looked upset. He didn't like the idea of passing up a multi-million dollar credit because a City manager had questions. This was good. It was exactly what Crowley had hoped would happen—he was driving a wedge between his adversaries.

"Mark, do you mind if we take a break for a minute? I know it's kind of early on...but the truth is that we came straight in here from the tiltrotor. I'd like to use the men's room. And maybe we should all take a minute to digest our quick start here."

"Sure. Sure, let's take five."

The secretary outside the conference room pointed them to a nearby men's room. Brian looked a little confused, but Crowley just smiled and shook his head no while they walked into the bathroom. Bathrooms were often bugged.

He was returning to his old form to worry about bugs. It was a kind of achievement. Six months ago, he wasn't sure he'd be alive at this point.

Neither of them had to use the toilet, so Crowley spent a few minutes washing his face and combing his hair in the mirror. He hadn't spent any time looking at himself in the suit the Tejana girls had sewn. He hadn't had time. In the old days, he'd spent hours each week checking his appearance. It felt lumpy. But, in the mirror, it looked pretty good. Definitely minimalist, anti-fashion. As his ex-wife used to say, anti-fashion was the most fashionable approach.

His beard was too long. If he was going to spend time in conference rooms, he was going to have to figure out some balance between the wasteland's standards and the City's.

Back out in the hallway, he and Brian stopped to admire a large mural that showed the idealized chain of food production—Houston farmers leading to Houston processors leading to Houston truckers bringing produce to Houston stores. The mix of smiling races was too perfect to be real. Corporate art was always like this.

"Always take a break when the other side has something to argue about." Crowley spoke to Brian in a quiet, conversational tone.

Sic Semper Tyrannis

Security types rarely bugged hallways—too much ambient noise. And, as far as anyone watching them would guess, they were talking about the mural. "Paz will be going crazy for a month of free produce. He didn't even hear the rest of it. And he'll be pissed about the fact that the City guys came rushing into his meeting, so they'll be on the defensive."

"I thought that the City managers told the corporate managers what to do."

"No, no. City managers are trained from the start to avoid forcing things. One of the first lessons you learn in school is 'persuasion is better than regulation.' It's always critical to make the corporate manager feel like he's in charge. The perfect policy is one that corporate guys think was their idea. Right now, Cherbourg is trying to convince Paz that the deferred invoice is a bad idea."

"How's he doing that?"

"I have no idea."

Cherbourg came out of the conference room with a smile and nod of his head. "Mr. Morrell, whatever your group is paying Mr. Crowley, it's worth it."

"I certainly hope so, Mr. Cherbourg."

"I've got to use the head for a minute. But, while we're on break, you fellows might like to step outside on the balcony beyond our conference room. Believe it or not, we're on some of the highest ground in Houston here. On a clear day, you can almost see Galveston."

When they came back into the conference room, Paz and Searle were both on the comms link. Paz smiled at them. Searle didn't.

Crowley pointed out to the balcony and Paz smiled more broadly, nodding his head in permission.

The view from the balcony wasn't so great. All Crowley could see was an urban sprawl of boulevards and strip malls reaching out to a smoggy horizon. Still, it felt more like home to him than anything he'd seen in the wasteland.

Cherbourg joined them out on the balcony. "I really just have one question, Michael. If they're so far along down there, why are you guys coming to us for security?"

"Because our bandit problem is immediate and Brownsville is still just some merchants with ambitions. Some of the farmers think the bandits may have been sent or at least encouraged by the Brownsville merchants to make everyone along Brownsville Road think they *need* a City's protection. If we can get rid of the bandits now, we'd come into the incorporation talks in a much stronger position."

"I can see that."

"And we'll make sure that ag remains a commercial bridge between our established channels in Houston and our new partners in Brownsville."

Again, Cherbourg looked happy. "I think that's a strategy that will make sense to my Board."

The rest of the meeting drilled down into the details of Paz's trucking schedule with the Brownsville Road farmers for the next several months. Both sides agreed that the deferred invoices would apply to the coming May's deliveries—and the Houston security officers would arrive within 10 days.

Searle agreed that he could mobilize the officers; and everyone else at the table complimented him on his effectiveness. They were condescending him, in a distinctly corporate manner.

Cherbourg said he'd circulate a draft memo within 24 hours and a final memo within 48 hours of that.

As the Houston managers, including their full security detail, walked Crowley and Brian back out to the tiltrotor, Crowley thought about making some comment to Cherbourg about his availability. But something about the eagerness Cherbourg had shown to get them back out stopped him.

Later, on reflection, he'd realize how much of a problem his banishment was—and would always be—for City managers. It wasn't just his long beard. He'd gone through too much to operate within the narrow parameters of City management.

He felt a shortness of breath as the tiltrotor lifted away from the BHWF headquarters. He remembered this feeling, too.

The faces of his son and daughter flashed across his mind. In those foggy first days outside the walls of Tampa, he'd focused on them so much. The drive to see them again had gotten him up, out of the mud. He wanted to see them again; but he was going to have to go about it in a different way.

Sixteen

"Second group nouns follow the same cases as the first group—Nominative, Genitive, Dative, Accusative, Ablative—they just use different endings. Here we go…"

When Hailwood finished writing the endings on the whiteboard, he turned around to see at least three sets of eyes wandering out the windows to his right.

This new section wasn't going so well. He could see it in the underclassmen's eyes by the fourth class.

Because Hailwood's rhetoric section had gone well, the Chairman had given him another section to teach. This time, it was Introductory Latin. This was a big deal. Student instructors were usually limited to one section per term. If he could do well teaching two—as well as finishing up his honors paper—he would be a virtual lock for the tenure track job opening up in the Fall.

Freshmen were allowed to take Latin instead of Spanish, French, German, Japanese or Chinese to fulfill their language requirement. Students with any aptitude for language tended to take one of the Big Five modern ones. As a result, the inept and disinclined drifted toward the Big One dead language. Most thought that Latin would be easy because you didn't have to actually speak the language. They had no idea how much mental precision Latin required.

The majority of these underclassmen would stumble through the four semesters and end up retaining some bits of Caesar's *De Bello Gallico* and Cicero's simpler speeches. After all, this was a selective college—even the dullest students were relatively bright. This would give them a small base of clear thinking from which to draw for the rest of their lives.

A handful would do better and see more. "These," the Chairman had said almost mournfully to him, "are the reason we do what we do. They'll take a real love of clarity back their beaches and board rooms. And maybe they'll instill an appreciation of precision to their kids, so our slender thread of civilization stretches on a little longer."

Here in a stuffy classroom, it didn't seem like the thread was very civilized.

"All right, gentlemen. Let's close our screens for a minute." The change in the tone of his voice drew even the groggiest ones to attention. "Thank you. Now, you may be shocked to find out that Latin 11 is not the breeze that you expected. But I promise you that your two years of study are going to give you two things. One: A strong understanding of the grammar and vocabulary background of English. Two: An appreciation of elegance and clarity in writing of any kind. And I mean that you will appreciate clarity on both mechanical and philosophical levels.

But, first, you have to learn the grammar. And, in order to do that, you need to review noun and verb forms for 30 minutes every night and vocabulary for another 30. And you need to come into this class ready to pay attention and take notes."

He slammed the heel of his right hand down on his lectern. It made a louder sound than he'd intended. Now the kids were definitely paying attention.

"Do this and you'll spend the rest of your life happy that you took advantage of this rare chance to study the nuts and bolts of thinking and writing. Don't do this and you'll have a miserable time for two years. You'll spend the rest of your life complaining about what a waste Latin was. And the people who hear your complaints will consider you an ignorant and boorish individual. So, memorize these works and rules. Pay attention to what I teach you in class. And you'll avoid looking ridiculous when you're an old man."

He meant the harangue to be a little ironic. They seemed to get that…but he wasn't quite sure.

On his way out of New Grosvenor House, Hailwood noticed several concerned-looking students running to their dorms. His wasteland sense told him something bad was going on somewhere.

He picked up his pace toward the House, where Taylor was sitting on his second-floor balcony reading. "Terry, what the hell are you doing here?"

"Coming back from class. Where should I be?"

"On your way to Northampton. Some bunch of bandits is tearing up your girlfriend's school."

Later, Hailwood would wonder why he responded immediately, especially because he and Kate had been having problems. He'd worry that it was just to keep up appearances to friends like Taylor, as much as it was out of any strong love for Kate.

But, whatever the reason, he acted decisively. It only took two or three minutes to get over to the garage where he parked the Badger. A couple of kids with girlfriends in Northampton were waiting at the garage, looking for someone with a vehicle who was heading that way. He recognized one—a freshman who was dating a girl who lived in Kate's house. This would be helpful. By the time he said they could come with him, two more had materialized.

While he warmed up the Badger's engine and ran quick diagnostics on the nav and weapons systems, he tried calling Kate. She didn't answer her screen. No one answered the house comms link in the hallway outside of her room. This wasn't good. But not a complete surprise, either. If something bad was happening, the girls would have headed for the safe room in the basement of their house.

He searched the net for any news. There wasn't much. But the news page on the WNET site did have something about a bandit disturbance leading to heightened security around the Northampton exit. A band of about 120 fighters had ransacked several villages along the WNET and then turned west toward Northampton.

Hartford's CityNews site had a breathless piece about "more armies of bandits moving south out of the Green Mountains, burning a trail toward Hartford's north walls."

Hailwood had a hard time thinking of the Green Mountains as a hotbed for bandit armies. He'd driven up there several times, to go camping or hunting. It seemed picturesque.

Campus security didn't give them any trouble about leaving quickly—on the other hand, none of the security guys volunteered to go with them.

Hailwood asked his passengers what they were carrying, One of the kids—a junior he didn't know very well named Rickey Elliott— had a very nice high-vel plasma rifle. The others just had small-caliber noisemakers.

But they had the Badger. So, as they headed west, he gave the passengers jobs working the vehicle's weapons.

"Do any of you know how to run a detailed triangulated 3D radar scan off of BZX echo beacons?"

No luck. He wished that he'd waited long enough to talk a couple of his brothers into coming along. Taylor and few others would have been helpful. They weren't all ass-kickers but most of them had some knowledge of the Badger's systems.

He thought for a few seconds about turning back. But finding the guys would eat up time; plus, it would mean kicking at least one or two of these kids out. He'd just make do with what he had. Besides, they'd be safe inside the Badger. In nothing went right, he could just park the rig in front of the steps up to Albright House and hold the fort.

He asked Rickey Elliott where his girlfriend lived.

"SoCal."

"Really? So why the hell are you on your way to Northampton?"

"To get laid. I figure there are going to be a few damsels in distress, who'll be grateful for a rescue."

Students from SoCal were like this. Most had been in the security forces—SoCal required all 18-year-olds to serve two years. And, unlike other Cities, it sounded like it really enforced that rule. *Everyone* served, not just guest workers and low rent citizens.

"Well, if you served, you've got to know how to do 3D imaging."

"Sure. I can put together a basic 3D image. But I've got no idea what a BZ whatever-the-fuck you said is."

"They're just echo beacons. Why don't you let one of these other guys use your rifle for the first few minutes when we get there. You'll do us all more good doing the 3D scan."

"Fuck that. Doesn't this rig have AI that can watch the 3D scan?"

"I don't trust AI in real gunfire situations. If you're not willing to do what I ask, I'll drop you off right here and you can walk back to campus."

"No need to get all like that, captain. I'll watch the pictures."

"Thanks."

"But nobody's touching my rifle."

At the Tollway, WNET security cruisers with lights flashing had the on- and off-ramps blocked. There wasn't much traffic; but the goons had a road check set up, anyway.

Hailwood decided to try his luck; he rolled his window down when he passed the one with the most stripes on his leather jacket.

"You guys have any word on what's going on in Northampton?"

"Those hippy bastahds who run that town are gonna be wicked fucked when the smoke cleahs. Our intel says its some bandits from north of heah. There's a lot of 'em. A hundred. Maybe moa. Wha you goin?"

"Girlfriend at the College."

"Shit. Girlfrien' at the College? Well, good luck there, son. Just make sure you don't step outta this vehicle."

"Not if I can help it. Thanks."

The Badger's weapons were loaded and ready when they made the sharp turn into the town. They'd have to drive through most of the town to get to the campus.

All along Main Street, things were quiet. Most of the shops were closed and gated. A few had been broken into and gutted or burned. Of those, the ones that weren't smoking had had their contents thrown out onto the sidewalk and street.

"My God. This looks horrible."

Hailwood didn't say anything in reply. He was dropping a beacon in front of the Town Hall. He hoped it wasn't noticeable. If he did this right, he could set up a large imaging perimeter around this part of the town and Kate's part of the campus.

There were what looked like several vehicle accidents along the few blocks of the main downtown drag. On closer look, the accidents were town security who'd tried to pin brigand vehicles—almost all pick-up trucks—with their squad cars. Apparently, the brigands' response had been to kill the cops and pull them out onto the hoods of their squad cars. There, they'd cut the cops' heads off. Hailwood could guess that the heads were on the front bumpers if the brigands' vehicles.

"A hundred Neurac'd maniacs versus—what—a couple dozen town cops. Those guys didn't have a chance."

Hailwood dropped another beacon three blocks west of the first and then turned right down a side street. "I'm with the security townie at the Tollway. People who run this town are fucking morons. They live off of the table scraps from a famous girl's school and they want peace and love with the world's worst scum. I hope these fuckers cut their heads off, too."

The beacons were a little larger than a golf ball and would emit a radar signature for several days. Each could be identified individually by the Badger's nav system. If he dropped enough of them, they would form a three-dimensional matrix that would make tracking people or vehicles relatively easy. That, combined with sat picts from his nav system, created a reliable 3D image of a several-block area. He could watch the whole place and zoom into a sidewalk or room.

There was still no one on the streets of the town. The sidewalks were empty. The shops and cafes were empty. And the Badger was the only moving vehicle on the street. Hailwood dropped a third beacon three blocks north of the last one and told Elliott to start imaging the 3D scan.

A dull thud vibrated from the roof just above Hailwood's head. Someone was shooting at them. Two more thuds followed. He tried not to get too excited and activated the Kevlar slats as an extra layer of protection for the bulletproof windshield.

Line of sight followed the shots up the hill to the west of the side street. That was the northeast corner of the campus.

He drove another three blocks along the side street, dropped a fourth beacon and turned west, toward campus.

"Have you got anything, Elliott?"

"Not much more than what your nose tells you. It's coming from the campus. Over there."

The Bedford Terrace gate into the College had been breached. It had never been the most secure entrance—but now it was a 20-yard gap of broken concrete, burned wood and smoldering campus security cars. As the Badger approached, there were half a dozen more thuds against the windshield slats and the roof.

"Can you give me a bead on those rifles?"

"Yeah. We've got it. It's in the nav system. You can set your guidance to point of origin. I called it Target 1."

"Excellent. Thank you."

Hailwood inched the Badger through the destroyed gate and into the far corner of the Smith campus. He dropped a fifth beacon.

"You going to give them a shell up the ass?"

"Not yet." A bright flash and loud clang rocked the front passenger side of the truck. "Killing bad guys is more about seeing them than just reeling off blind shots like a junkie."

The bandits had fired some sort of small mortar at them. It didn't do anything to the Badger except make it wobble back and forth a couple of times.

"What the fuck was that?"

"A hand grenade or some piss-ant mortar. That come from the same place, Elliott?"

"Yeah. The top floor of that yellow house over there on the right."

Hailwood was relieved. It wasn't Kate's dorm. He armed and programmed a 90mm Scarab anti-tank smart shell and used the location information that Elliott had loaded from the scan. Here, the Badger's GPS nav system doubled a missile guidance system.

"All right, lads. Here's our first shell-up-the-ass."

The satisfying thunk of the Badger's central launch tube was followed by a faint whooshing sound.

"Keep your eyes on the yellow building."

There were two more thuds on the windshield…and then a bright flash and roar like the sound of a big jet taking off.

There weren't any more thuds.

"Okay. Assuming they don't have anyone else real close, we probably bought ourselves 15 or 20 minutes. Let's try to find the girls and get the hell out of here."

The Badger lurched forward along Bedford Terrace, toward Albright House. He dropped another beacon along the way and—when he got to Kate's dorm—he drove up onto the front yard and parked blocking the stairs up to the front doors.

Hailwood shot a spread of five more echo beacons behind Kate's dorm and toward the central part of the campus. Their signals would give Elliott a larger and more useful 3D image.

He had given one of the kids the responsibility for an infrared scan of the dorm, which was possible because they were very close and the building was a mix of wood and brick. There weren't any warm bodies in the upper floors. Wasteland bandits usually liked the top floors of buildings, so that was a good sign. Maybe they'd left Kate's dorm alone.

Next, Hailwood raised and activated the dual 50-caliber machine cannons on the Badger's roof. He programmed the guns to fire at any motion along a 100 yard semi-circle in front of the dormitory. That would protect the Badger and front door.

Elliott knew how to use the 3D imaging, but he wasn't going to be satisfied staying in the truck. The freshman who had the girlfriend in Kate's house—his name was Mohammad bin Saud, but everyone called him Moto—was also determined to get into Albright. So, Hailwood set up the other two at the 3D screen and the steering wheel. He gave them six weeks of training in 60 seconds. "…look, the upshot is this: Don't put it in gear unless I get on the radio and tell you to."

He took a last look at the kids he was leaving in the truck. They were excited—but their eyes were clear and attentive. They wouldn't do anything stupid. He hoped.

He gave Moto his plasma rifle and a Kevlar vest. He took his impact-resistant jacket and loaded two 10mm plasma pistols. He also took six flash grenades. They were useful for flushing out people hiding in nooks and crannies; he'd read that City security forces liked them for house-to-house combat.

He opened one rear door and sat back, in case snipers fired. None did.

Following their personalities, Elliott went first, Moto went second and Hailwood went last.

At the front doors, Elliott and Moto each stepped to one side and left the entry to Hailwood. He scanned the doors with his bomb sniffer. Nothing. The front doors were closed, but unlocked. Hailwood turned the knob and pulled the right-hand door open an inch. Then he stepped back on Elliott's side. Again, he waited for bullets or concussion—guessing that the bandits might have booby-trapped the door with something his hardware couldn't find.

Nothing.

Now, his concern turned toward the upper floors of the other houses along Bedford Terrace. This might have been a honeypot trap. Dozens of girls in the safe room downstairs as the bait for an ambush. But the only spot that would have been a clear shot to the front doors of Albright House was the yellow Victorian across the street—which his smart bomb had just wiped out.

And he was being paranoid. How could illiterate bandits have guessed that the first armed response would be headed for this particular dorm?

He opened the door all the way and led the other two in. Once they were, he pulled the door nearly closed but left it slightly ajar. No sound and a faster exit, if necessary.

The foyer of the dorm looked fairly normal. The furniture was all in place and there weren't any broken windows or mirrors.

Still, he signaled to the other two to stay still. He took two flash grenades out of his jacket and twisted one until the red "live" light showed—and he rolled it past the grand piano into the living room. He twisted the other and rolled it into the dining room. Then he ducked and signed for the other two to get down.

Five seconds later, what seemed like a bolt of lightning went off in the living room. It was bright and loud, making a sound like shattering glass.

A second later, the grenade in the dining room made the same explosion.

Hailwood stood up quickly but noticed that Elliott was already up with his rifle drawn. Hailwood turned to look into the living room and, on the edge of his peripheral vision, saw a brown wave moving toward him. There was screaming, too.

As soon as Hailwood realized someone was rushing toward him, he heard two loud thuds. The brown wave froze into the form of an overweight man and fell on the ground a few feet in front of him.

The smell of burning rubber meant that Elliot had shot the bandit. And expertly. One shot to the head and a second to the chest. He was good.

The echoes of the flash grenades were still ringing in his ears when he signaled for Elliott and Moto to check the dining room. He checked the living room.

The dining room was clear.

There was a girl's body in the living room. Hailwood didn't recognize her. It looked like she'd been strangled or garroted. And she was naked below the waist.

Elliott and Moto came in with him when he didn't answer their "clear" calls from the dining room. They both seemed too surprised to say anything. So Hailwood did.

"Nice shooting."

Hailwood had been in Albright House's safe room several times, especially when he and Kate had been underclassmen. Since most of the girls living in the house had roommates, it was practically a rite of passage to sneak boyfriends into the basement safe room for "privacy."

The three of them went down the stairs with their weapons raised. There was a fair chance that some horny bandits would be camped out around the safe room.

There didn't seem to be anyone downstairs. Still, to be safe, Hailwood rolled a third flash grenade into the hallway in front of the safe room door.

After the echoes of its flashed faded—and no bandit emerged from any corner—he climbed out from the laundry room, knocked on the door and called Kate's name.

The door was six inches of solid steel hanging on four 18-inch hinges. Basically, a bank vault. Behind it, the girls of Albright House had enough electricity and supplies to last a week or more in cramped but sanitary conditions. They could see what was going on in the hallway through a video feed near the top of the steel door.

Hailwood expected there would be delay from some debate behind the door about whether to open it for a boyfriend some of the girls didn't like. But the door opened immediately.

In the few seconds it took the safe room door to swing open, Hailwood imagined Kate rushing out into his arms and kissing him thanks for getting her out of this chaos.

As his grandfather liked to say, "the truth wasn't quite so Technicolor."

Kate was there. And she was okay. But she looked like she'd seen a ghost. She walked toward Hailwood more exhausted than happy and sighed, "Terry, please get me out of here."

He could tell she'd seen or been through something bad. He hugged her briefly and ran his hands from her neck to her wrists to comfort her.

It wouldn't be as easy as that. The best he could do for the moment was get her out into the Badger.

Most of the girls in the safe room were fine. But two of them—actually, both girls from other dorms that Kate's housemates had found after the trouble had started—were in bad shape. Both had been beaten pretty badly and either raped or beaten around the genitals. The Albright girls had done a good job of cleaning them up; but both needed a doctor.

Moto's girlfriend gave him the greeting Hailwood had wished for himself. And, verifying his reptilian sense of opportunity, Elliott was immediately surrounded by grateful young women.

Once everyone was out of the safe room, they sketched together a plan. Elliott and Moto would confirm that the upper floors were clear and secure the house. Hailwood and some of the girls would get the two injured ones into the Badger, so he and Kate could get them to a hospital.

Moving the injured girls would be relatively easy. Securing the house still might be difficult. Hailwood asked if any of the girls had weapons. He got a lot of cold stares back.

One of the younger girls answered him without irony: "The campus is an anti-war zone."

No one said anything else for a moment.

A thick New Yawk accent broke the silence, "Well, tell truth, I've got a 20-caliber two-shot. My dad told me to keep in my room, no matter what."

This was Hailwood's chance. A two-shot was a tiny gun; but a girl who carried one probably knew how to shoot. "Amen, sister. Dad ever take you to the range?"

"Since I was 10." She was a stocky Hispanic. He'd never seen her before…but he was glad she was there.

"Very good. Here, then you take this. It's a vintage Ruger. Shoots easy, smooth as silk." He stood next to her and lifted his right arm along with hers—the universal weapon instructor position. "Probably won't kick any more than your two-shot. One in the barrel, 16 in the clip. And here are two more clips of 16. Keep them in your front pocket." She was wearing a sweatshirt. "See anything that's got a beard, shoot it in the head. Now, you go with the lads here and show them around your house. We're looking for the best places to set up our defense. Clear lines of sight, front and back."

Hailwood could feel himself playing a part. He knew that he was mimicking his grandfather. The Old Man was a bastard, but people gravitated to him whenever there was trouble. Hailwood had recognized at a young age that something in his grandfather's bastard swagger made people feel safe.

In half an hour, they'd secured the house and moved the injured girls into the Badger. Hailwood stripped his vehicle of weapons and set Albright House up with a decent defense perimeter. The dorm was a squat brick box; but that made it easy to defend.

The girls were so anxious to get the house secure that they didn't even scream too much about the dead girl in the living room. Someone wrapped her in white bedsheets and laid her down by one of the bookshelves.

Hailwood and Elliott dragged the brigand Elliott had shot out onto the street. Hailwood took out his Randle blade and hacked at the dead man's crotch. Elliott looked curious. Hailwood shrugged: "Universal sign of contempt."

"Where did you learn all this stuff, man?"

"Boy scouts. And my grandfather's a nut about personal security."

"So's my dad. But he never taught me this tactical warfare shit."

"Yeah. Well, he should have. Before he sent you out into the wasteland."

"I just thought it was just going to be College."

At one point, one of the house's upperclassmen pulled Hailwood aside and said, "Kate did a great job. She carried one of those two girls in here. I mean, carried her. Over her shoulder."

Hailwood wasn't sure what to say. He thanked her. But that sounded awkward.

They'd set up some of the girls' screens up to read the 3D radar matrix that the beacons were feeding. And they'd made contact with town security, which had contained the bandits in a spot close to the middle of campus.

Incredibly, the College security department—which had authority on campus—was negotiating with the bandits to surrender. Negotiating with murderous rapists, hopped up on Neurac or whatever home-made version they'd cooked over their campfires. At some point, the town or the real professionals from the WNET were going to put an end to *that* strategy.

In the meantime, the town security was sending some of its people around to secure the breach at the Bedford Terrace gate.

Kate didn't want to wait that long. And the bleeding girls probably couldn't. Hailwood agreed to take them back to a safer retreat at his school.

Elliott and Moto agreed to stay and help the girls defend their house. The two other guys stayed, too; their plan was to make their way toward the center of campus to find their girlfriends…as soon as the town security had sealed the breached gate.

If everything went to hell, they'd all head back into the safe room and call for help. But Hailwood was reasonably sure they had enough guns and mortars to protect their position in the House.

The ride back to campus was going to be bumpy, so he folded out the Badger's sick bay beds and injected the two injured girls with a generic sedative from the medical kit. He buckled them in and told them they'd wake up in the College infirmary.

They waited a few minutes, until a town security cruiser finally turned onto Bedford Terrace. The two women in the cruiser were well armed; Hailwood and Elliott walked over to their car and explained what had happened. Hailwood said that he was taking the two seriously injured girls to his campus infirmary.

Kate didn't say a word as they pulled away.

Hailwood was a little nervous to remove the 50 caliber cannons that had been keeping the front of Albright House secure. But the local security forces had to take over. He eased the Badger back through the wreckage of the gate.

He was relieved that there were no sniper thuds against his truck on the way out. In his rear-view mirror, he could see the security cruiser doing its best to block the hole in the wall.

As they gathered some speed heading east out of Northampton, Hailwood tried to break the silence. "Sure you're okay, babe? You seem pretty spooked."

"I'm okay. I just want to go home."

"And you will. Looks like something got to you back there. You can tell me about it. Get rid of it."

She didn't say anything for a while. But, once they crossed the Connecticut River toll bridge, she started…and didn't stop until they were almost back to campus.

"I've never seen a violent crime happen before. And today, on my way back to the house, I saw…I don't know…several? I mean, I clearly saw two people killed. Right in front of me.

"One of those men shot a girl I knew from my Intro Econ class. With a shot gun. In the stomach. She just kind of yelped and fell to her side. She was dead. And I knew it immediately. She was lying just maybe five feet away from me.

"The other was a girl I didn't know so well. But I'd seen her around. I think she was my year. This guy grabbed her hair and started talking about how he was going to fuck her. She said no and he took this baseball bat that he had hanging from his belt. And he just started hitting her with it. In the face. On the head. I don't know how many times. Maybe 10. Maybe more. After five or six, she slumped down on the ground and I knew she was gone. He just kept hitting her.

"And there were more. I just didn't see them so clearly. I know the bandits were attacking people. Raping them. God, 'raping' doesn't even seem like the right word. It doesn't look like much when it's happening. It just looks like people wrestling. Your eyes or your brain don't put it all together. I mean, you're not prepared to see someone doing that to someone out in public in the middle of the day."

As they approached the Mall, six College security cruisers raced past them in convoy fashion—heading toward Kate's school.

Hailwood wasn't sure what six extra cars would accomplish. Maybe help with the wall.

His screen chirped. It was the Assistant Director of Security, in one of the cars heading the opposite way. Hailwood said what he'd seen—and stressed the importance of the Bedford Terrace gate breach.

As soon as he hung up, Kate started talking again.

"I really don't understand why it wasn't me. I mean, it could have been me getting shot in the stomach or thrown to the ground and fucked. I mean, it's just blind luck that it wasn't me."

She'd finally said enough. He let the silence sit for a moment.

"You know the psychology, Kate. Predators are basically cowards. They don't pick strong people to attack. They focus on the weaklings…the runts of the litter. You're a tall, strong girl. You were probably moving with purpose, even if you were scared. These cretins have been spending their whole lives diverting their gazes from women like you."

"Yeah. And for just that reason they could have shot me first."

They were getting near campus. So, he thought it was time to bring her back a little from her dark thoughts. "You know, that Margaret Meehan girl told me you carried one of these girls in."

"Yeah. I don't know her but I think she's from the House across the street. I saw her lying in the gutter of Bedford Terrace. I mean literally lying in the gutter. And she was bleeding from her ear and from her…private parts. First I thought she was dead. But she was crying a little bit. So, I picked her up and carried her up the stairs. I think I was kind of rough with her."

"I don't think she'll mind."

When they got back to the College, an ambulance was standing by to take the injured girls to the infirmary. They would both recover.

The infirmary gave them the usual nanoprevs for AIDS and other STDs. They were both given hypersonic blasts against any pregnancy. The worst lasting injury was that the girl with the bleeding ear had a cracked skull.

At some point later, that girl would recovered from the cracked skull was briefly be engaged to Rickey Elliott—who became a kind of celebrity on Kate's campus.

While Hailwood and Kate were driving away, the town and campus security forces had surrounded the "mountain men" (for some absurd reason, this term was considered less offensive than "highwaymen" or "bandits") near the center of the campus. During the surrender negotiations, some of the mountain men escaped the security cordon and tried to sneak back out through the breached wall at Bedford Terrace.

Elliott had set up a sniper lair in one of the rooms on the top floor of Albright House. He ended up killing 19 bandits—counting the first one in the living room—more than any other person had ever killed in the defense of Kate's College. He would be very popular at parties after that.

(Not everyone was so favorably impressed. At one point, Moto complained to Hailwood: "That guy is a psychopath. He was sadistic. He would shoot the bandits in the shoulder, spinning them around like tops. And then he'd deliver the *coup de grace* with a shot to the head. Laughing all the time.")

Hailwood took Kate back to his rooms to get some sleep. She did…for most of the next three days.

At one point, when he came back from his not-so-great Intro Latin class, she was sitting at his desk in just a long-sleeved t-shirt. He thought she looked pretty fetching.

They had sex. But she was distant and unusually passive the whole time.

After, he offered to drive her down to New York.

"That's okay. I talked to my dad today. He's chartering a tiltrotor to come up to get me tomorrow."

The answer was as cold as the sex had been.

A few days after that, Hailwood was on the screen with the Old Man. "So Grandpa, what's going to happen? Will the wasteland up here empty out? Or will the Cities claim it as their territory?"

"My money's on a joint effort between Boston and New York. They've been looking for an excuse to carve up Hartford. This'll be a good one."

"So they don't mind the bandit attacks?"

"*Mind?* Don't be a twit, boy. Their external security guys probably gave the Mountain Men their guns."

The Old Man could always see the schemes lying behind the chaos and smoke.

Seventeen

Colonel William Tyler of the Houston Security Force was an imposing character, well over six feet tall and thin. But thin in a way that suggested excellent physical shape. He wore his hair in the usual security officer style—shaved close on the sides of his head and just an inch or so on the top.

But he wasn't as uptight as most security types Crowley had known. Tyler acted and spoke more like a manager. When Brian invited him inside the farmhouse, he accepted with humility. He told all but one of his lieutenants to stay on the front porch. Inside, he and his chief of staff sat at the same big table where the Gramps met. He listened intently and held his hands in the steeple position. Sometimes the steeple was an affectation; but this didn't seem to be (though it did highlight his Houston Security Academy ring).

Crowley had first learned to recognize these things in his university negotiating classes. And this knowledge had remained one of the most valuable things he'd gotten from school.

"I can understand your position on this. But, before we get too far into any discussion of our camp location or other logistics, I have a question for you, Mr. Crowley."

"Absolutely." Crowley could feel himself slipping into security vocab.

"What exactly is your position here? My command billet instructs me to communicate with the farm owners south of our City walls. Now, Mr. Morrell introduced you as his scribe; but I'm not sure that I can have formal communications with an informal advisor. And, from what I understand, Mr. Morrell can read and write just fine. So, how should you and I parley?"

He was smart. This question was meant for Brian more than it was for Crowley. But, as long as he directed it to Crowley, it wasn't official. He could decide later whether or not to include it in his report.

Crowley shrugged a little and turned to Brian.

"Mr. Crowley is a trusted advisor," Brian said. "If you need a more official description, you can call him my business agent or counsel."

"Fair enough. And Mr. Crowley is authorized to speak for you and the other farm owners in your group?"

"Well, Colonel, I'm not sure anyone is authorized to speak for the group. You'll find out pretty soon that they're an ornery collection of individuals. But, yes, Mr. Crowley is authorized to speak for me if I'm not available."

"That's fine. Thank you. I'm sorry if my questions seem...basic."

This was Col. Tyler's first hesitation. Crowley decided to step in. "Not a problem, Colonel. I'm sure this is an unusual assignment for you."

"Yes. It is unusual. As you say. Most of my billets outside of the City walls are simple smash-and-grab missions. Over in a few days. We don't usually liaison with property claimants."

Col. Tyler was definitely struggling for the right words. He'd slipped and used the word *claimants*—which was less diplomatic than the term *farm owners* he'd been using before. *Claimants* was a City word. It questioned the legitimacy of property ownership in the wasteland.

Crowley figured that most of Col. Tyler's missions outside of the walls had been to take land that the City of Houston intended to annex. This meant property claimants were usually his enemies. Maybe his victims. "We understand, Colonel. And we understand that some people back in Houston don't believe there's such a thing as land ownership in the wasteland. But these farmers are long established here. I think you'll find they're a lot like any farmers or ag managers you may know inside the walls."

He smiled slightly. "I'm beginning to see that, Mr. Crowley."

Crowley couldn't decide whether Col. Tyler's smile was relieved or menacing. "I think that Mr. Morrell and the other farm owners are savvy about the trade off here."

"The trade off?"

"Between the security support your troops offer and the potential threat they pose to our independence..."

Col. Tyler's smile disappeared.

"…my point is that the owners understand you're here to help get rid of the brigands that have been harassing us."

After a few seconds of thought, Col. Tyler smiled again and nodded slightly. "I see that you appreciate the uniqueness of this assignment, Mr. Crowley. I'm sure there are going to be learning curves for everyone. My orders are to give your farmers complete discretion on whether or where to position our troops. We don't expect to make camp inside your compounds. All we ask is that your farmers cooperate with us in locating our camp somewhere that will give us a defensible position and easy access to the Brownsville Road."

They negotiated for a few minutes and agreed that the HSF troops could make camp in some fallow fields that belonged to the Morrells and sidled right up against the Brownsville Road.

Col. Tyler was worried about making camp right on the Road. He had no desire to maintain a roadblock or even appear to be doing so.

But Brian explained that there was a rise in that section, back away from the Road. "My guess is the crest is something like half a kilometer back from the Road."

"That sounds good."

After 20 minutes of talk, they were done. Col. Tyler invited Brian and Crowley to ride out with him to the camp location.

His riders fell into formation without saying a word. Three rode ahead; three rode behind. The other six formed a rough oval around Col. Tyler.

Along the way, he explained that this was a reconnaissance detail of his most experienced trackers and riders. His complete command was a small company of 88 troops. Most had at least some experience in security assignments outside the walls. They'd been was far as the Pacific Coast.

"Was that when SoCal annexed the last bit of the San Joaquin Valley?"

"You're well informed, Mr. Crowley."

"Well, I know that Houston and SoCal are usually allies."

"Yes. Usually. And, yes, our assignment was to help resolve the border dispute with San Francisco. At least we hope it was the resolution. Reasonable people wonder whether that agreement is going to hold."

Sic Semper Tyrannis

The fallow fields were in the farthest northwest corner of the Morrell property. Col. Tyler's troops would be as close as they could be to their home walls.

As Brian had described, the high point of the area was back away from the Brownsville Road. The peak was not very high—maybe 10 or 12 meters higher than the surrounding land. But that was enough to give them a clear view at least a mile in every direction. And they could move to the Road easily, if they chose.

In fact, Crowley thought the location was a little *too* good. Col. Tyler's billet might also have included instructions about securing the Road for Houston—in case the plan for cooperation with Brownsville didn't work. Or in case the board in Houston changed its mind about cooperation.

Col. Tyler was satisfied. "This should be fine. We'll get started here and have our camp set up by tomorrow."

This wasn't really a conversation. He rode over to his men before Brian or Crowley could respond. The HSF troops moved impressively. Col. Tyler gave a few quick orders and pointed to several spots in the area. The men climbed down from their horses and set to work.

Brian watched it all and made a smirk. "These City security guys. I really get the impression they don't listen to anything anyone says."

"Yeah. But this one's brighter than most. Did you see the ring on his hand?"

"I did. University?"

"Security Academy."

"What's the difference?"

"An Academy is more focused. More intense. University can mean anything. Academy means one thing. Plus, a lot of Brahmins send their kids to Academies. Keeps the ruling class strong. He might come from an old family."

"Or maybe he just tested in." Brian liked to do this—ask a question and then slip in something that showed he'd known the answer all along. His questions were often more about how someone answered than what he said. This was, itself, a favorite Brahmin trick. Brian seemed to come to it naturally.

Managers were more straightforward than this, by temperament and training. Crowley was trying to see beyond his literal approach to things. "Yeah. Maybe that."

Col. Tyler had finished giving his men orders. He and his aide rode over to Brian and Crowley and nodded back in the direction of the Morrell compound. "Maybe we should head back to your house to get ready for the meeting with the other principals."

Crowley sensed that Col. Tyler was more interested in getting them away from the camp preparations than planning for the meeting.

As they rode south, Crowley turned back and saw Tyler's men setting metal pylons around the perimeter of the camp site. They were connected by laser panels. Top shelf technology.

Crowley was beginning to get the feeling that they'd invited trouble.

There'd been a management lesson about this. But he couldn't remember it exactly. Something about how no good commander ever committed his troops without having an exit strategy. What was the exit strategy here?

Crowley rode up to the Simpson farm at sunset again. This time, the sun was low against his right shoulder, rather than square against his back. The year was proceeding.

Other things were different this time. Jana was riding with him, as she did just about everywhere these days. And he had a new horse. Jana and Brian had given him a young black stallion—more fitting to his personality, Jana had said, than a chestnut mare.

The stallion was called Raptor. Jana called him Rap. Crowley wasn't accustomed to calling his horse anything.

The guys working sentry at Simpson's new main gate recognized Crowley and waved him through. "The lady is your guest, Rabbi?"

"Yeah. She's with me."

The outer door was already open, which meant they'd been letting people through. The gauntlet was about 25 feet to the inner door. Simpson's security troops stood eight feet up on the walls along either side. Anyone who looked like trouble would be locked in between the doors, caught in the crossfire of a dozen plasma rifles.

He'd sat through many meetings on security design during his days in Tampa. This new main gate at Simpson's farm was well made.

While Crowley and Jana rode through, the security troops kept their rifles aimed at the sky as a sign of respect. They didn't do this for everyone.

The outer door swung closed with loud metal clang. Then, the inner door slid open.

Crowley noticed that Jana looked a little wide-eyed. She'd been to the Simpson farm many times; but not since Simpson had put in the new gate and never for one of these lessons. "You okay?"

"Yeah. I guess. Is there something secret I should know?"

"No." He gave her a smile. He was proud of how big the lessons at Simpson's farm had grown.

And she knew he was proud. So, she was playing dumb about it. "I'm not afraid of reading in front of people any more."

He laughed. "I know. I know. That's not it. These lessons have become more than just about reading."

When they passed through the inner door, Crowley nodded to Simpson's foreman who was overseeing the crew on the walls.

"Gramp S is waiting for you down by the low hillock, Rabbi."

"Good turnout?"

"There's a lot. We just let in a batch a couple of minutes ahead of you. And there'll be one or two more."

"Okay."

He and Jana rode past the house and down into the shallow valley immediately behind. About half a mile from the house, they crossed a small stream that lead up to the ridge of the hill on which the farmhouse stood. At the ridge, they could look down into the deeper valley that marked the "back 40" of Simpson's farm. In fact, the 40 was more like 400.

And there were a lot of people gathered in the valley.

Because he'd been watching the crowds grow, Crowley was good at estimating how many people were there. He pegged this crowd at about 800. Enough that there were sure to be a few undercover Houston security troops hiding among them.

Jana had no idea how many it was—she'd never seen so many people in one place. "God Christ, Michael. So many...."

Gramp Simpson had a microphone and speaker system set up in the loft the old barn that they used as a stage. This was all right. At one point, Simpson had offered to get a wireless headset from Houston; but Crowley had grimaced and blunted the idea by asking "Is that what we want to be about?" He didn't want to come off so corporate or "City." People in the wasteland were shy enough about learning to read. They already equated it with people living in Cities. Coming off like a high-end motivational speaker would just scare them off.

But an old-fashioned microphone was okay.

They had set up the old barn with lights and a big white board for letters and words. Everything was powered by high density power cells that could keep the operation running for hours, silently. The cells were from Tampa. If those people had any idea....

A couple of the Simpson grandsons had small vid cameras set up on tripods. One close to the speaking platform and one farther back, to one side, in the crowd. They'd record the lesson, edit it into short bits. And post them on the free nets.

Gramp Simpson introduced Crowley to the crowd as "our Rabbi."

Crowley didn't like the nickname. His problem wasn't the religious connection. He knew that, despite (or maybe *because of*) all of the violence in the wasteland, religion was a big deal. Plus, Gramp Simpson seemed so proud to have come up with the nickname that Crowley felt like he'd be a bad sport to complain.

He didn't like the nickname because he felt slightly fraudulent accepting the title of "teacher." He'd done decently in school; but he never been an intellectual. He'd always been a manager—not a deep thinker.

"But it's not about you," Jana had said, a few days earlier. "It's about them. People want a leader. They want a teacher. You know, a person who comes from somewhere else and shows them the way. You fit that perfectly."

So, he'd accepted the nickname. He didn't use it himself; and he didn't encourage it. But he didn't object.

"Thank you all for coming tonight. Welcome. My name is Michael Crowley. For a little while now, I've been helping people with their reading. It's important to know how to read, for lots of reasons. Read screens. Buy or sell things. Read the Bible for yourself. But to me reading's important because, once you can do it, you can teach yourself anything else. This helps balance the power between people. If you can read, you are the equal to any other person you'll ever meet."

He took off the thick leather outer jacket he'd been wearing. Underneath, he had a thin red leather vest over a white cotton shirt.

This had become a sort of uniform he wore for the lessons.

"Now, if it's your first time, don't worry if you feel a little lost. You'll catch on after a lesson or two. And keep this in mind: You probably know more about reading that you think. You've probably been reading things like street signs and money for years without even realizing it. We'll build on that here.

"If you've had reading lessons before, this might seem a little different. There are a couple of ways to learn reading. Any of them can work. We use the system called phonics here. It's a quick way to learn letters and sounds they make. All you need to do is listen and keep your mind focused and you'll be able to read a screen or a book before you know it."

Some people in the crowd joined in parts of his greeting, which was pretty much the same every week. They joined in especially for the line "listen and keep your mind focused." This was another reason Gramp Simpson has started calling him "rabbi." The lessons were part class, part politics and part sermon.

"And one last bit, as we get started. People who've been here a while know that we ask students to give their writing lessons to others. We ask you to pass on what you learn here to your own people—sons and daughters, friends and family. We have reading and writing lessons on the free nets. And, if you don't have a screen, we can give you paper copies. Now, let's get started…."

He'd practically memorized the first 20 minutes of each lesson. It was a quick review of all of the letters; then he went through each in groups of consonants and vowels and covered some simple letter clusters. All the while, he used a steady flow of vocabulary words that illustrated each use. He'd write them on the whiteboard; scribes out the audience would copy them onto big paper sheets, so everyone could get a good look at the words and how a person would write them.

At Brian's advice, he used a lot of Bible words. This tied the lessons back to the only book that most people in the wasteland knew.

After the first section, Crowley would take a break for a drink of water before moving on. The second half of the lesson was different each week, shuffling in more advanced reading and grammar.

During the break, Gramp Simpson or one of his sons would stand up and make the pitch of the crowd. "Every person living in wilds needs two things: a Bible to read the Word of God and a rifle to live by it. The Rabbi will change your life—and he never charges any money for his lessons. But he asks you to donate to the cause. We ask for three things: Bibles, guns and money. If you have any of these to spare, please give them to the young people with the white sacks who are walking out among you. We'll make sure that they get to people who read, believe in God and want the world to be a better place."

Crowley wished that Gramp Simpson did the appeals himself, all of the time. He was the best at it. Maybe because he believed in what he was saying more than any of his sons did. Maybe because he had a warmer personality. Maybe because his white hair gave him more authority.

When he took the mike over again, Crowley made sure thank the ones who'd just made the appeal. But he made sure never to make the appeal directly, himself. He remembered clearly one of the main lessons of good marketing: The effective salesman doesn't make the pitch himself; he makes the close.

"Thank you so much, Gramp Simpson. For opening your home to us to study together in peace and security. For taking care of so many of the small things that make these lessons possible. You are a good man. And a good model for everyone.

"Brothers and sisters, you are smarter and better than you realize. The City people inside their walls have nothing more than you have. They aren't more intelligent. There aren't more deserving. They have some advantages. Some money and some lessons when they're younger. But we're here to bring some balance between the Cities and the wilds."

Most of the time, this speech would focus the crowd's attention back on him. Sometimes, though—if the crowd seemed unexcited—Crowley had a mostly-true color story to add.

"Some of you are fathers. I am one, too. I have a son and a daughter inside the walls at Tampa. Fathers, let me tell you this. There is nothing more important in this life than hearing your daughter read you the Book of Psalms. I challenge you. Not to cry like a baby when she does. It is one of those small flashes of heaven here on Earth. You learn from this and then you go back to your home—and you teach your children!"

Then he dug into the mechanics.

"...not a bad haul. About four thousand dollars in cash and a couple of dozen rifles." Gramp Simpson was happy.

"How many Bibles?"

"Eh. Books are the hard part. You know how it goes. Not many around anymore...and not the kinds of things our people have ever had much cause to need." He took a drink of his whiskey and water. "We've got to stress the Bible on the free nets. These people are just as likely to have a screen as they are a bound book. And maybe we should look into getting some cheap screens made and give them away? Don't the Cities to that?"

The question caught Crowley eating. Lessons always made him hungry. "Um..." he swallowed the fried chicken. "Yeah. They give screens away to kids in school. And they keep the prices down with tax subsidies to the manufacturers. So they're cheap. Simple ones are about the cost of a meal."

"And everyone reads?"

"Well, almost. In Tampa, our literacy rate was something like 97 percent. But these numbers are always a little fuzzy. The bottom 10 percent or so don't read technical stuff or literature. They're mostly using their screens to get porno."

Everyone at the table got a laugh from that. People in the wasteland always liked to hear that people in the Cities acted badly.

"Yeah. I imagine we'd have the same thing out here. But I have to tell you, it would be great to get these people screens. I mean, you can use them for so many things."

"Comms links." Crowley had washed down his fried chicken and cole slaw and was ready to join in the discussion more seriously. "The best management tool is using screens as a comms link. It's old as the moon. People always think that personal electronics are about their own selfish uses. In Tampa, the comms companies ran ads everywhere about their personal devices as fashion, self-expression. Independence. Things like this. In fact, they were the best security system we could ever have. We could locate people easily, and even contact them if we wanted."

"And they had no idea?" Jana was often skeptical of how gullibly Crowley described people in Cities. She couldn't believe people with so much could be so stupid.

"Well, we didn't do anything to hide the security functions. It was

Sic Semper Tyrannis

all disclosed in the user's manuals. But almost no one ever read those things."

Gramp Simpson laughed again. "I'll be honest with you, Michael. There are lots of times that I wonder why they didn't just put a bullet in the back of your head. You know so much. Those guys can't be happy you're out on the loose."

Why hadn't they? "Yeah, I know. I'm sure if I actually had committed high crimes, they would have. The Old Man would have. But they blinked. I think my CFO just wanted to humiliate me and get rid of me. Executive managers have no idea what's outside the City walls. It might as well be death."

"Well, I'm glad they tossed you out our direction. So, you think we should use screens as comms links. I can have Ezra make some calls about prices."

Ezra was the son that Simpson trusted most to take care of business. On his farm or anywhere else.

"It's an idea. We put together a large student body and give the dedicated members screens with a Bible and a farmer's almanac and some basic how-to stuff—maybe basic security for their homes. And we get them used to reading texts. Then, when we need to raise troops, we just send out the word."

The idea seemed to sit well with everyone at the table.

Ezra, who was literally standing behind Gramp Simpson's right shoulder asked: "Where do I start? I'm not sure the guys in Houston will be in any rush to get them for us. And the guys in Brownsville haven't figured out where to put their walls yet."

"Don't assume you have to go through a City commerce department. Just order the screens directly from one of the Asian comms companies and have them send them as an extra destination delivery on their next plane coming to Houston or New Orleans. The Morrells' strip is big enough to handle a standard freight flier."

Gramp Simpson laughed again, and turned back to Ezra. "This is what I mean, see? He thinks like a mechanic when it comes to business. No matter how rich you get, Ez, always keep like that."

One of Simpson's foremen interrupted the table with a request. A couple of farmers from the Tennessee Valley had been to the lesson. They'd ridden three days to learn from Crowley and 'the Brownsville farmers who are telling Cities what to do.' They wanted to talk with the Gramps about setting up their own co-op.

Gramp Simpson got up and marched over to invite the visitors to join them at the table.

Crowley and Brian rode up to the HSF camp a few minutes after eleven. The plan was to meet Col. Tyler and pick an escort of Houston security troops. They had a meeting with the man who called himself the "captain" of the brigands at noon about two miles south of the HSF camp along the Brownsville Road.

The HSF camp was impressive. Within 24 hours of the afternoon they'd picked the site, a steady stream of tiltrotors had brought 14-foot wall assemblies, modular living units, a command tower, two industrial generators and lots of weapons. Col. Tyler's company had arrived—about 30 on horseback and the rest in half a dozen large armored transport vehicles. The men had set up the walls as a perimeter, raised the command tower, hooked up all the power and dug a trench outside of the walls—all in a single day. There were mines in the trench…and maybe elsewhere around. Col. Tyler had told everyone at a meeting of the Gramps that anyone approaching 100 meters of the camp needed to stick to the road.

The sentries were expecting Crowley and Brian. They opened the gate quickly, while the riders got down from their horses. Inside the gate was a secure access pen, much like the one Gramp Simpson had just added to his compound. The sentries scanned Crowley and Brian with a UV flash and then let them into the camp.

The fort didn't look like it was just a couple of weeks old.

Two of the tiltrotors had stayed with the company. They were parked on either side of the command tower. Small groups of HSF troops were huddled around the tiltrotors—no doubt, maintenance crews getting the "birds" ready for their next mission.

The troop vehicles were parked in a staggered pattern that acted as a wall between the gate and the command tower—but the parking pattern also allowed any single vehicle to exit through the gate quickly.

A couple of extremely well-behaved HSF troops took Crowley and Brian's horses. One of the soldiers asked if it was okay to feed the horses water and plain oats. Crowley hadn't heard anyone speak so helpfully since the last time he'd eaten in a restaurant in Tampa.

The command tower was the centerpiece of the camp. It looked like a miniature offshore oil rig. Crowley figured it was two of the modular living units joined together at the top of metal-beam structure at least 30 feet high. A metal-mesh staircase wound it way up, just inside the four main posts and diagonal supports. A cage elevator ran inside the stairs.

"Could Tampa Security do anything like this?"

"Maybe not so fast. Most of this stuff is standard security forces gear. Tampa Security has it, too. But Houston is well-known for its efficiency. And *that's* more about people like Tyler than wall kits or modular living units."

"Speak of the devil...."

Col. Tyler was riding down in the elevator with three other HSF officers. It looked like a tight fit.

"Gentlemen, this is Captain Al Perez. Captain Perez, this is Brian Morrell and Michael Crowley."

They shook hands. Perez and Tyler acted like old friends.

"Captain Perez and some of his men are going to escort you in two of our ATVs to your meeting with these brigands. Since their leader calls himself a captain, I figure we'll show him what a real Captain looks like."

The soldiers thought this was very funny. Crowley and Brian laughed, too. But not as much.

"Capt. Perez has been fully briefed on the situation and understands that he and his men are going along strictly as support for your negotiations with the brigands. No HSF personnel will participate in the parley or initiate any action. They will only take action to protect you gentlemen from actions that the brigands take. And, of course, if those sonsofbitches take any action against HSF personnel or property."

The two Armored Troop Vehicles reached the agreed upon location in just a few minutes, which meant they were a few minutes early. Perez ordered the big doors on either side of each ATV raised, so that the troops could get out quickly—but, for the moment, their orders were to stay in their seats.

Brian and Crowley got out, though; as did Capt. Perez.

The location was one that Brian had suggested. It was out in the open—the fields along this stretch of the Brownsville Road were laying fallow, so there weren't even any plants to use as cover. The closest hiding place for snipers or troops was a windbreak stand of trees almost half a mile further south. It would take a very good sniper with a very strong, zooming sight to make a shot from this distance.

About five minutes after noon, they scanned two small vehicles and a couple of horses coming north. Capt. Perez checked his plasma rifle and whispered something into his headpiece. He took a step back from Crowley and Brian.

Crowley drew the TAG plasma pistol from his belt holster. Drawing it while the bandits were talking would seem provocative. But holding it the whole time would just blend in with the HSF guys' rifles.

The two vehicles were ancient four-wheel-drive light-duty trucks. They'd been well kept. Their shiny black outer panels reflected the sun like mirrors; so, the trucks were hard to see from some angles. Cities spent millions—tens of millions—on electronic camouflage systems…and they didn't do much more than an old-fashioned wax shine.

The bandits kept a slow pace, so that the horses didn't drop behind. Each of the riders had a strip of white fabric tied to his upper arm. Each of the trucks had a white strip attached to one of its antennas. Flags of truce.

Brian snorted. "What are these guys doing flying flags of parley? They think this is movie."

"One of the first management lessons you learn about negotiating is that the aggressor is usually the one claiming to seek peace."

The vehicles and horses stopped about 50 meters from where Crowley and Brian were standing. They didn't seem to mind blocking both lanes of the Brownsville Road. Three horses. Four men in one truck; two in the other. Total of nine. They were all dressed in black, so it was difficult to see the details of how else they were dressed or what they were carrying. But it didn't look like they were wearing much leather. Mostly fabric.

They were older than Crowley had expected. Bandits didn't usually live long. Not many had gray hair. Half of these did. And they all had full beards, braided. High maintenance.

The older ones wore headbands or scarves over their heads. This usually meant they were covering the wires grafted into their skulls for orgasmic stimulation. Neuroplex/Pleasure wasn't enough for some bandits—they'd have their brains hard-wired for pleasure stimulus. This meant six or eight electrodes fed through their skulls, connected to a button on their chests that would give them a jolt of joy when pressed.

Most Cities outlawed pleasure buttons. Even people in the wasteland frowned on the devices. Religious people thought they were wicked; non-believers thought they were dangerous. That left a small group of people with enough money and few enough scruples to have the buttons inserted.

The riders stayed on their horses. The rest climbed out of their vehicles warily. A couple of the grayhairs made eye contact; no one else did.

They huddled with each other for a moment. Then, three walked toward Crowley and Brian—the two who'd made eye contact plus a younger one, carrying a plasma rifle. The younger one still didn't make eye contact; he looked down at the ground in front of him.

The shortest of the three spoke first. "So, yall runs Morrell farm?"

"I'm Brian Morrell. You're Captain Tripps?"

The first time they heard it, Crowley knew that name meant something. But he couldn't place the meaning. Brian looked it up on the Houston net. It was the nickname of a player in a popular music group from the Federal Era. Somehow, along the way, it had come to mean any person who was difficult or dangerous.

The thugs smirked at Brian's mention of the name.

"Yeah, yall kin call me Cap Tripps. These are my men. I got more spread around here sim place. They keepin they eyes on us."

"I'm sure they are. So, what do you want to say?"

"Yall have Houston soldiers backing you. Yall got them killers now. Yall think you get us to move on with them killers."

Crowley studied the talker. It looked like he was wearing some kind of makeup on his face, especially around the eyes and nose. Maybe it was covering up some kind of damage. Or maybe it was covering up the effects of a cheap nanotech cure.

"Your men are stealing our property. And they're harassing our people. We want to you to go."

"Where we go?"

"I don't care where. Just go."

The short one smiled. "Yall don remember me, Mr. Brian?"

"No."

"Just a little? I yusta work Morrell farm."

"Yeah? When?"

"Years ago. Yall a little boy. Yall daddy was bossman. Let me go for lazy."

"He let a lot of people go for that. He wanted hard workers."

"But I warnt lazy."

Brian looked angrily at Crowley. He was frustrated about this brigand blaming the Morrells on his fall into crime. But Crowley had no suggestions—he had nothing to add. He wasn't here to talk.

Finally, Brian turned back to the short man. "You saying we made you a criminal? You could've caught on somewhere else."

The short one looked hard behind them—at Capt. Perez. "I ain't no criminal. This ain't no City. We got same claim to land as you."

"Not so. These farm lands are all claimed, parceled and marked. They're private property."

"Says who?"

"Says I. And says a dozen other farm owners around here. Says the Houston security troops. You and your men need to move along."

"No. We ain't squatters, you know. We're privateers. I have a letter mark from Juarez."

Brian looked back to Perez. He was the only one who could answer a statement like that with authority.

Crowley slipped his finger onto the pistol's trigger.

Perez smiled warily. He didn't want to get involved in the talks. "I'm Captain Javier Perez of the City of Houston Security Force. We don't recognize Letters of Marque. And, if we did, we wouldn't recognize one from Juarez. It's not a City. It's a hideout for bikers and brigands."

The short one smiled back, threateningly. "Well, now we don't like to hear—"

Crowley's first shot struck Cap Tripps in the forehead, just above his right eye. His second shot hit the other grayhair in the mouth.

The younger one raised his plasma rifle, but Perez killed him before it got very far.

The other bandits had drawn and were firing. The sound was louder than anything Crowley had ever heard. It sounded like some combination of an explosion and a wave crashing around him.

Brian dove down to the ground. Crowley took a knee to steady his aim. His hand was shaking.

The HSF troops were firing back intensely. Crowley fired several more time, but he had a hard time focusing. He wasn't sure his shots hit anything.

Next, there were half a dozen loud cracks from the top of the ATVs. They were firing the mid-range light artillery at the tree line to the south.

The ground shook and Crowley fell sideways. He felt heat on his face and another—even louder—explosion. Instinctively, he closed his eyes and waited for the roar to die down.

When he opened his eyes again, the action had stopped and all her could hear was the ringing in his ears.

Brian was lying face down in the grass by the side of the road. Crowley looked for any sign of movement. Brian's shoulder twitched.

Crowley climbed up to his hands and knees.

Then, he heard Capt. Perez's voice behind him just barely over the ringing. "Down! Get back down. Not done yet!"

He dropped back to the ground.

There was a rumbling and then a loud whoosh from above. Crowley rolled onto his right shoulder and looked up. For a second, he thought one of the ATVs was jumping over them—then he realized it was a big tiltrotor flying about eight feet off the ground. It made so much noise that he could feel its engines in his chest; and it moved more slowly than he thought would be possible.

As soon as the tiltrotor move past them, a series of two-syllable explosions started. They came at steady rhythm. Wha-boom. Wha-boom. Wha-boom.

The wha-booms moved south, away from them.

A few moments later, Crowley felt a hand on his shoulder.

"It's okay. You can get up." Capt. Perez's voice still sounded tinny. But it sounded relieved. "You can get up. The hawks are finishing the rest of them."

The troopers were already cleaning up. A few were working on one of the ATVs; a few others were walking a perimeter around where the thugs had been. The ATV looked like it had been hit with some sort of artillery shell. That must have been the explosion that knocked him over.

"Nice shooting, Mr. Crowley. Two clean kills."

"You guys did the hard part."

"We just did our job." And he walked away to talk to his men.

Crowley's eyes were fixed on the windbreak to the south. Two tiltrotors—he assumed the two from the HSF camp—were taking turns dropping concussion bombs into the trees. And they were firing down a hail of plasma blasts as they moved along. Nothing was going to survive that.

He looked back at Brian, who'd rolled onto his back and was being examined by an HSF medic. He'd been shot in the chest. The flak vest that Col. Tyler had given him had absorbed the plasma blast. But his shirt was smoking.

"You okay?"

"Yeah. I think. I'll get up in a few seconds. Feel like I just got thrown from a horse."

"And you're going to need a new shirt."

"Well, at least we got rid of these bastards."

"Yeah."

Now the tricky part would be getting rid of the HSF troops.

The next night, back in the Morrell compound, Crowley had trouble sleeping. He woke up thirsty around three in the morning and got a glass of water from the kitchenette.

He'd moved into a small house near the western wall of the compound because Jana refused to sleep with him in the farm house.

"You're 32 years old," he'd argued. "Why are you uptight about sleeping with a man in your own home?"

"Because I grew up there."

"But you'd sleep with me in your house if we were married?"

"Yes."

"Then let's get married."

"No. Not yet. The time isn't right."

Instead, she'd had his bags moved into this one-room house. It had been a schoolhouse at some point; more recently, it had been a study and workshop for her father. But, for the past decade, it had gone unused.

She'd had it cleaned up and a bed moved in. She was content to sleep with him every night out here...though she wouldn't consider inviting him into her bed in her house.

He gave up arguing otherwise after a few tries. He'd given up trying to convince her of anything different than what she wanted. Being with Jana was going to require deferring to her subtle eccentricities and stubbornness. They came partly from her privileged upbringing and partly from her in-born willfulness.

Her artificial eye gave off an orange glow in the dark. When she was asleep, that eye stayed open a bit. A small, amber light flickered back and forth around her pillow. He'd asked her once if she'd ever wanted nanotech to repair the scars around her eye and forehead. Fix her eyelid so that it would close all the way.

"Why? So I can forget what happened? Why would I want to do that? I want to remember the pain. I want to remember it my whole life."

"Did you like it?"

"No. I never want to feel anything like it again. But if I try to forget it, I'll forget how bad it was."

She murmured a little now, while he watched her sleep. And she made some other noises. He smiled to himself at how different Jana was from Margot. Earthy, and unapologetic about it. When she got her period, he could smell it. Was this the wasteland? Or her?

She rolled over and looked at him, looking at her. She smiled sleepily. He poured himself another glass of water. She asked him what he was thinking about.

"What I need to do."

"Tomorrow?"

"No. Bigger picture. After we get Brownsville set up."

"You're still thinking about staying out?"

"Yeah. I don't think I belong in a City any more. At least not as a manager. And I'm sure that's what everyone's going to ask me to do."

"Well, I say you're a City person."

"Maybe. Maybe not."

She climbed out of bed and pulled on her bath robe. He was awake and she was joining him. "Okay, maybe not. But you're sure as blazes not a farmer."

"No. But I'll become a farmer sooner than I'll go back to working for a City."

"So you want to be a farmer?" She sat next to him, took the glass from his hand and finished the water—all as if in a single motion.

"No. You're right. Probably not." He poured more water into the glass. She was still thirsty.

"So what, then?"

"Not sure. Keep doing what we're doing."

"But you also say you're not a teacher."

"And you keep telling me that I am." He took the glass back and drank some. "Anyway, it's not about the reading. It's about getting rid of the waste. All of these people stuck in their ignorance. I was trained from the time I was a kid to fix inefficiency. I took Neuroplex/Clarity every day for 30 years. I'm sure it changed my brain chem. I hate inefficiency and the wasteland is inefficient."

"And we're going to change all that?"

He poured the last of the water from the pitcher into the glass. He'd had enough but figured she might still be thirsty. "There are farmers all over the place who'd do a lot better if they had half-functional towns where could sell their produce. And workers who knew how to read."

"I don't know. A lot of people think that reading is for City people."

"What does that mean? People who can read are weak? Gay?"

"Gay. I didn't even know what that was until you told me. I don't think it's weak, either. It's just…well, the Gramps and young people like Brian are the ones who read. The rest don't need to."

"You do."

"I'm just trying to say how people see it. They think reading and being smart are for rich people."

"That doesn't make sense."

"I know. But that's the wasteland, babe. Millions of ignorant, pissed-off people."

"The Cities want to keep people out here ignorant because, if they're intelligent and pissed, they'll storm the walls."

"And you want them to?"

"Maybe. Or build their own Cities. Become competition for Houston and Tampa and the rest."

"How are a bunch of raggedy ag co-ops going to be competition for Houston?"

"Food and energy. It's all about food and energy. Always has been. Food and energy. Those are their weak points. The Cities never have enough."

Her eye lit her face enough that he could see her smile.

"Their weak points. You *do* want to tear down the walls."

"It's not about revenge…."

"It's okay, Michael. I trust revenge."

Sic Semper Tyrannis

They saddled up their horses and were riding on the Brownsville Road by dawn.

Brownsville was a three-hour ride south, at medium speed, from the Morrell farm. And Brian felt strongly that they should ride. Anything else would be showing off.

"Downtown" Brownsville was concentrated right on the beach—which seemed like a strange thing to Crowley. From his days in Tampa, he thought of beachfront property in terms of the risks it posed. Whenever a storm came ashore. Tampa kept its most important functions a little back from the water.

The Downtown zone was protected on three sides by a shipping-container-and-fence "wall" that connected three small gates and one medium-sized one. The fourth wall was the Gulf of Mexico. This setup would give any decent security manager nightmares. Of course, the entire population of the town center—several blocks of two-story buildings—could probably fit in one office tower in Tampa. So, there wasn't very much at risk.

To make things even more complicated, Brownsville's the two main commercial powers were not located in the Downtown zone. Each operated behind its own walls—one a little less than a mile due west of Downtown and the other a couple miles south along the coast. These factory compounds operated like their own little Cities. People would gather in the mornings to be checked in at their gates and they'd wander back out again at night.

The companies were a gun manufacturer and truck manufacturer. Solid businesses on which to build a City. Texas American Guns and Gulf Automotive had similar backgrounds. They'd started out repairing and reconditioning their respective products. In time, they'd started making their own.

TAG made cheap guns that knocked off other, more prominent companies' work. But Gulf Automotive was a quality operation with a growing reputation. Its trucks were big, tough and reliable. And it had started making its own power cells, based on a design licensed from a Japanese company. It was a very good product—maybe good enough to challenge the big battery makers in Tampa and SoCal.

TAG was still run by its founder; Gulf Automotive was a family business run by two brothers and a cousin. TAG didn't do much business with City banks; Gulf Automotive did, borrowing significant money from a couple of New York financial houses. Apparently, it did a good job of making the payments on that financing. Various costal Cities were rumored to be offering Gulf Automotive tax and relocation deals to move out of the wasteland. So far, the family owners had resisted. They thought they could do better on their own.

These owners—the ancient gunsmith and the educated sons of the car maker—were the powers behind the move to make Brownsville a proper City.

Crowley realized that TAG and Gulf Automotive were similar enough that they were rivals for the leadership role in the emerging City organization. A year before, Crowley would have jumped into this opening. Now, his guess was the best candidate was the young guy who ran the third-largest employer in town—a liquor distiller that specialized in vodka and tequila.

The distiller was a distant third behind the other two in all the ways that matter to a City—assets owned, revenues earned and jobs created. But he was growing fast. And he'd shown himself to be a smart negotiator. He'd convinced then truck maker to let him share an electrical grid in exchange for committing to a standard monthly payment.

Crowley remembered an old saying from his school days. Something about "When two elephants battle a smart mouse sometimes comes out on top."

He figured the distiller was a smart mouse.

The meeting was taking place at the Gunsmith's beach house.

It was hard to image the place was a "beach house" though. The property was huge—easy two or three town blocks on one side and protected on three sides by a 10- or 12-foot stone wall. Like the Downtown zone, its fourth wall was the Gulf of Mexico.

Automated machine gun sentries guarded each parapet and dozens of actual human sentries paced in between. The gates were both security-grade double-cell locks. Everyone passing through was subject to a better-than-security-grade four-way scan. The place was like its own small City. No wonder this guy wanted to get Brownsville recognized—it would save him a lot of money each month to have a City Security Force protecting his mansion.

Inside, there were more than a dozen buildings, leading up the Beach House—a huge steel and glass structure that started on the sand and reached out into the water.

It seemed to taunt the Gulf reach up and knock it down.

The conference was held in a grand room on the third or fourth floor (Crowley wasn't sure how to count stories in such a place), facing the water.

There were at least 20 people in the room. The brothers and cousin who ran the car maker. The smart-mouse liquor guy. A couple of serious-looking older men who must have been other business owners. A couple of nervous younger men who must have been drug dealers or private security. Each person sitting at the table was shadowed by one or two people standing behind.

The crowd made Crowley nervous. He looked for exists. There were only two, one at each corner of the conference room, each leading to the same hallway. Not good. The best exit might be to shoot the windows out and take your chances with the drop to the sand.

While everyone else was taking his or her seat, the ancient gunsmith was wheeled into the room by two huge bodyguards. He didn't notice any other sun-lined faces. Brian must have been the only farmer in the room.

The gunsmith was the oldest person Crowley had ever seen, much older than any of the Brownsville Road Gramps. He looked like a kid's cartoon version of an old man, with transparent skin and a halo of stringy white hair around his skinny head. Resting against the right side of the wheelchair, his body looked like it could be snapped in half by a strong wind.

But the old man's eyes were clear and blue. And they looked around at everyone seated at the big table.

"Thank you all for coming." The old man's voice was breathy and high-pitched but—like his eyes—it was clear. Everyone in the room could hear and understand him. "We're here today to talk about something that has been on my mind…and some people's minds… for a long time. We're here to set about incorporating the City of Brownsville."

He pronounced the place name as most locals did— brownsVILLE, with the stress on the last part. It was like a secret handshake among people born to the area.

"This is going to cost money and time. Incorporating a City is easy to do—getting other Cities to recognize the incorporation is the hard part. I'm willing to put up a lot of the money, because I have plenty of that. And I'll count on others here to put up time."

Crowley remembered a management lesson about observing the attention of people in boardroom after the first 30 seconds of a meeting. It was a bell curve. Losers and high-performers would be looking around the room, measuring the crowd; mediocrities would be listening to the speaker.

"…I've always considered security to be characteristic that defines a City. Then again, I make my living selling weapons. People focus on the walls, of course. But security is about more than walls. For years, we've been paying privateers for security here. While we inch our way toward recognition. We've never been sure that the money we paid the privateers was well-spent. Some act like professionals. Others are just thugs. But we kept paying. Then I hear the story about these farmers north of us—not soldiers, mind you, just farmers—who called in support from Houston and then shot the privateers in the head. Now, that's not a wall. But that's security."

In a boardroom of 20 people, four or five would be the impatient ones. Of these, two would be problems and the others would be your competition. Either way, those were the people to watch.

Crowley looked around to see who was impatient in this room. No one. There were about 20 people here and everyone was paying attention. Bad data? He had trouble understanding what that meant.

The ancient gunsmith introduced the different people sitting around the table. It was the right mix. Business owners, mechanics, security people, a priest. People with guns, education and money. They had enough here for their board of directors. And if the old man was willing to build the walls, they'd have the foundation.

"You know about Cities and security, don't you Mr. Crowley?"

Crowley was stunned. He didn't think the old gunsmith knew his name. "Well, I grew up in a City, Grandfather."

Another lesson: Good manners were an important tool in negotiations. They bought you more time to gather information.

"More than that. You were the headman in Tampa?"

"Yes, sir. I was."

"So you can tell us a lot about what we need to do."

"Well, there's no book about how to become a City, Grandfather. No formal document. Someone once told me that you measure a City's power by how many other Cities accept its trade envoys."

"And you've already worked out an agreement with Houston that recognizes your involvement in this City?"

"Depends how you define 'this City.' But, yes, our agreement with one of Houston's main food wholesalers anticipates our group's involvement with a City of Brownsville."

The old man smiled and sighed. "You've done our work for us, Mr. Crowley. You've paved the way our first formal recognition."

One of the car maker's sons was worried that the deal with Houston meant that the HSF troops would resist Brownsville walls going up as far north as the Morrell farm. He knew more details about the HSF camp than Crowley had expected. "Are they just going to fold up their camp and let us set our perimeter around the farmers' co-op?"

Brian pointed out that Col. Tyler's command billet was for 120 days. And that was more than half over.

"A security offer's orders can be changed in a minute. They can tell him to stay around longer. You know, just to make sure we don't set our walls too far north."

Crowley agreed. The trouble wouldn't come from Col. Tyler—who, like any good officer, wanted to get home as quickly as possible. Or Paz and the managers at BHWF. It would come from Cherbourg—the City manager they'd met at the food wholesaler's offices. A City bureaucrat's definition of "caution" often meant trouble for everyone else.

Brian defended the deal: "Our contract is with Baker Houston Worldwide Foods. It guarantees Baker Houston very good fixed prices and some valuable benefits during the transition period of our co-op becoming part of the City of Brownsville. The agreement anticipates this. If the Houston Security Forces interfere with our business, we could claim a breach of that contract—and Baker Houston wouldn't get its good prices. As most of you know, Baker Houston has a lot of influence in City politics up there. And I'm pretty certain they don't want to lose those prices we offered them."

Brian made his point forcefully and well; he'd be an effective member of the board.

Still, the car maker was doubtful. "So, even if they don't interfere, we're going to start out honoring a sweetheart deal with the biggest food wholesaler in another City? That doesn't make sense."

Brian shrugged slightly and turned to Crowley.

"Sure it does. You're rushing to a fight where there isn't one. You should want good relations with Houston. Don't assume that you can put up a perimeter and all of the sudden you're on par with one of the biggest and richest Cities in the world. Brownsville is going to be Houston's little brother for years. Maybe decades. Don't get upset about that; make use of it. Invite the HSF troops to stay on and help train the first bunch of Brownsville Security Forces. That makes sense. In fact, it makes so much sense, Houston might decline and call its troops back.

"That's the same reason you keep your deal with Baker Houston and use the leverage to keep some handle on the City managers up there.

"Everyone in this room has a lot in common with the Brahmins in any City. You have wealth and power that you want to keep and increase. That's the same thing propertied people everywhere want. I assume that most of you could buy a citizenship in Houston or New Orleans or Tampa right now, if you chose. But you haven't chosen. You want to keep what you have here. Good for you. Having a City will help you do that. Hammering out your charter and putting up your walls are the easy part.

"It's the City managers that you have to watch out for. The ones from the other cities, sure; but also your own. They'll push for larger borders and commercial boycotts and even security actions. They'll defend their positions with a hundred little reasons that make tactical sense. They'll do that because you'll train them to do that. And you'll train them to have a patriotic loyalty to the abstract notion of the City. But they'll have a poor understanding, if any, of the one big reason a City exists. To protect and increase its founders' assets.

"What I'm saying is that the bureaucrats might seem like a tool for protecting your assets. But I'm not sure they are, really. If you don't rein them in, they become their own constituents. And that's not security for you.

"So, I have some advice that might sound strange at first. Give up a little of your political advantage now. And give it to your citizens as a whole. You're going to want to do something that makes Brownsville stand out from other Cities. I suggest you establish a written Constitution. More than just a charter or Articles of Incorporation. A clear statement of citizens' rights. The people in the Federal Era had that part right. There's value in a written document for people to see. Without that, people sense that the City structure is meant for something other than their interests. And, you know, they're right. What I'm saying is that you think that the City structure is meant for you. But the people it's really for is itself. Which means the bureaucrats. And, trust me, that doesn't do you any good. Where I came from, the Brahmins stayed awake nights trying to figure out how to manage the managers. You're better off in the end setting up a place where people trust the laws and you can keep the managers from becoming their own constituents."

The speech just flowed out of him. He wasn't even sure it had made sense. He'd started out intending to give them a strategic view of dealing with the HSF camp. He'd ended up explaining everything he knew about City politics. And clarifying to himself why he didn't want to be a manager—even the top one—any more.

They took a break after the first 90 minutes, so everyone could check their comms links and use the facilities.

Crowley was still thinking about his speech. He stayed in the boardroom and stared at the water while he thought. After a few minutes, the ancient gunsmith wheeled up alongside him. "Farmer Morrell said we have no chance of convincing you to be our CEO. Now I think I understand what he means."

"Good. You wouldn't want me anyway, Grandfather. To the managers in other big cities, I'm damaged goods. And I don't even know my own mind some of the time. You want someone new. A local native. Keep your CFO your own, too. After that, you can hire your marketing people and security people away from other Cities."

"That makes sense. So does your idea about the written Constitution. We can use it like a recruiting tool for bringing in quality people. Will you at least help us get started?"

"Yes, of course. I told Brian that I would. And I'll always be available to him—and to you—for any help or advice you might need. But you have all the pieces you need right here."

"I like to think we do."

They both watched the water for a few minutes. The sky was blue and the waves were small.

The gunsmith broke the silence again. "So, your plan is to stay in the wasteland, teaching people to read?"

"That's part of it. There's more out there than I ever knew—even with all my City training. I think the greatest opportunity for change in our world is channeling the human assets camped out in the wasteland."

"Ach. The federal system will never come back. Too many promises, too little value."

Crowley thought for a second. "Not a federal system. But something between that and what we've got."

"Why would we want *that*? Son, you just made the smartest analysis of City politics I've ever heard. I think what you said right here makes plenty of sense."

Crowley waited again. The rest of the Brownsville Brahmins were starting to file back into the boardroom. "When I was in Tampa, I used to take Neuroplex to sharpen my tactical and analytic thinking."

"Sure. I give Neuroplex/Productivity to my workers."

"Makes sense. But giving people Neuroplex is dehumanizing—like giving drugs to draft animals. And that's inefficient, in the end. Just like leaving people ignorant and illiterate in the wasteland."

The old man looked confused.

Crowley knew what he believed about Cities and the wasteland. But he wasn't comfortable saying it yet. And didn't say it so well.

"Look, forget that last bit. I'm sorry if I'm being confusing. I'm not a deep thinker, Grandfather. I believe in efficiency. That's how I was trained. It's what I know. And there's something very, very inefficient about the system we've got."

Eighteen

Hailwood walked by himself across campus to Drummond's house. Since Taylor'd left, Drummond had become his closest friend on campus. And Drummond's house was a desirable one, nestled comfortably among the choice faculty residences in a small grid of the campus that looked like something from a vid set. The houses were all vintage New England wood frames, perfectly maintained by the College and usually painted exotic colors according to each occupant's taste.

Drummond's house was not painted exotically. It was olive green with a cream trim. Some of the detail work was painted a dark purple, almost black. The door was glossy red. This color combination was fairly common in upper middle class neighbors just about everywhere. Some years prior, a woman designer from New York had called it the "perfect" color scheme for a wood frame house.

Drummond's wife had decorated their house, inside and out—and just completed it before informing him that she wanted a divorce and planned to move to Europe to be with an Irish political scientist who'd been a visiting professor the year before. Her good taste was one of the many things Drummond was going to miss.

Hailwood was a few minutes late. He'd walked almost halfway across before it occurred to him that he was bringing a bottle of Bushmill's Irish Whiskey as his gift to a man who'd been cuckolded by a linguistic theorist from Dublin. He went back to his room and got a bottle of Russian vodka.

Hailwood and Drummond were alike enough that they might not have gotten along. Drummond was a young professor of Writing/Media with bright prospects that he was working to realize. Hailwood, as a graduating upperclassman and a virtual lock for a graduate appointment to the faculty, was practically competition. Plus, Drummond's field of study was relatively new; Hailwood's was one of the oldest still taught. Many of Hailwood's soon-to-be colleagues in the Classics Department sneered—literally, sneered—at the mention of Media.

But Hailwood and Drummond got along well. Hailwood's first year as a student had been Drummond's first as a teacher. And Hailwood had taken a writing class from Drummond that spring. They shared a sense of time on the campus.

"Hey. I brought something to help you process this transitional phase."

"If you mean you're here to get drunk, come in."

The house was as well-appointed inside as it was painted on the outside. The furniture in the living room matched the period of the house, from the early 1900s. Everywhere else, it was more modern and more comfortable. The kitchen was clean and spare, centered around a large butcher's block table. That's where they settled.

Drummond pulled some pickles, olives and sliced beef from his stainless steel fridge. He had a loaf of bread already on the table. They opened the vodka and started eating and drinking.

"…I guess I don't understand what she wanted, really. I mean, she said she loved living here. Loved academia. But, when I look back on everything that happened between us, there's no way that's true."

There were lessons about his relationship with Kate in all this.

Drummond seemed in decent spirits. So, Hailwood decided to probe his rationalizations a little. "Come on, Craig. She probably does love academia. She didn't leave you for middle-level City Manager or an outlaw biker. She left you for a tenure-track guy from Dublin. She gets to be a professor's wife in a City. That's probably trading up for her."

"Yeah, yeah. But you know what I mean when I say the *academia*. I don't mean one of those diploma mills pumping "management lessons" into the soft skulls of new generations of bureaucrats. I mean the real academic life."

Hailwood drank a shot of iced vodka and thought about keeping his opinions about academic life to himself. But Drummond was a good guy. And close enough to his own station that he should speak freely. "That's a hard balance. I'm having some problems of my own on this count. Not as harsh as yours....but problems, still."

"Really? What?"

"There's this girl I've been seeing. Took her back to meet the folks. The old story."

"This have to do with that rescue mission?"

"Have to do with? It was the whole fucking reason."

"Okay. Very good. Was she all right?"

"She was fine. Got right to the safe room and was there when we found her."

"Okay. So, all's well."

"No. All's definitely not well. She flew back home to New York and wants nothing to do with real academia anymore."

"And that means nothing to do with *you*?"

"I think that's what it means. She hasn't said as much. Calls me every few days to check in. But the last time we fucked, it felt like goodbye."

"I know what you mean by that." Drummond poured them each a new glass. "So, what do you do?" He seemed to be relived to turn the conversation to someone else's life.

"I'm going to see her next weekend, after my meeting with Foster and the other deans. Before rescue mission, we had what seemed like a pretty clear plan to get married and split our time between here and New York. But I think I'm going to have a hard time getting her back to that scenario."

"Maybe. But don't assume the worst. Give her a chance. Hell, they just went through every feminist's worst rape nightmare over there. You can't blame her for being a little gun shy."

"True and true. In fact, I've been thinking the best plan might be to say nothing. At least for a while more."

"Yes. You're right. The low-key approach. That's the one I never get right. Shit, no wonder you're number one with a bullet around here. You're wise beyond your fucking years. Look, we're almost out of this stuff. You want to take a walk over the pub?"

"Yeah, sure. The night's still young."

The letter was on College stationery, with its old fashioned, wide-set all-upper-case header and its elegant, formal type. As a student, you got a letter like this when you were admitted. After that, a letter on this stationery usually meant some kind of trouble.

For that last reason, administration letterhead was often co-opted for pranks and practical jokes. Fake memos involving excessive punishments for minor the infractions of good students or describing outrageous sexual acts in explicit detail. These were most sophomores' favorite brand of humor.

This wasn't a joke, though. He'd been waiting for this letter for more than a year.

Terrence,

On behalf of the College, it gives me great pleasure to offer you the Woodward Family Memorial Fellowship.

As part of this Fellowship, the College invites you to serve as an Instructor in the Department of Classics and Rhetoric for the coming two academic years. During that period, you are encouraged to complete the primary requirements for a Doctor of Letters degree in a subject related to your teaching at the College.

After the two year period as an Instructor, if you have completed the advanced degree work and pass a standard background review, you will be offered a permanent position as a College Professor in your Department.

The Woodward Fellowship is one of the most respected awards that College can give a graduating student. As you know, a number of our most successful faculty members have started their teaching and research careers as Woodward Fellows.

Please let me know whether you will accept this Fellowship by replying to this letter in writing to my office no later than March 23.

On behalf of the entire faculty and administration, I congratulate you on an impressive start to your academic career. We all look forward to welcoming you as a colleague and expecting great things from you as a teacher and expert on rhetoric and Classical languages.

There will be much more to discuss and determine in the weeks ahead if you accept the Fellowship. Please take a few days to consider and reflect upon this offer and all that accepting it will mean for you. It is a decision that anyone should make carefully and advisedly.

I look forward to receiving your reply.

M.G.S. Howell, President

Sic Semper Tyrannis

The first thing that he did, when he got back to his room, was scan the letter and email to his grandfather.

Then, wiped out from a long Monday that had been preceded by a busy weekend, he went to sleep.

Ten hours later, he woke up to a steady pounding on his door.

"Hailwood. I said wake up, man." It was Russell.

"What?"

"Dean Probst's office just called the House comms link. There's some sort of emergency meeting and the heads of the Houses are supposed to be there."

"Shit. Okay, okay. I'm getting up." It was already after 7:30. He had a class at nine.

"The meeting's in 20 minutes."

After a quick shower, Hailwood make it to the Dean's office just a minute or two after 8:00. Probst was the Dean of Physical Plant and Security. He was decent guy—an alum who'd fallen in love with the place and stuck around to keep it going. He did his job well, which meant that students didn't have much experience with him. But Probst had one of the oldest and biggest offices in the main administration building.

Hailwood wasn't the last one in. Probst and his main assistant whispered to each other behind Probst's desk while bleary-eyed upperclassmen stumbled in. At about 8:10, the assistant closed the door and Probst took his seat. There weren't enough seats for all 23 of the House presidents to sit; so, most stood.

This was typical of the petty power games that admins liked to play with students. If Hailwood had been in Probst's position, he'd have stood for the meeting—like everyone else.

"Gentlemen, we have a situation that requires your assistance. After midnight last night, President Howell received an urgent call from President William James at Dartmouth. As you all probably have heard, Dartmouth has been suffering organized attacks from bandits and brigands for several months. Well, last night its campus was overrun. Its security staff has surrendered the campus and is in the process of escorting the students and faculty here as we speak."

This wasn't much of a surprise. Rumors had been circulating for months that Dartmouth was losing control of its walls; students had been transferring to other schools and teachers had been leaving, unannounced.

But, if Howell agreed to take in the students and staff from Dartmouth, it would be the third school that the College had absorbed in less than a year. And the biggest of the three, by far. The campus was running out of room.

That's what this meeting was about. Probst wanted the Houses to take in the transfers.

"I have called you all here to let you know that we need each of your Houses to accommodate incoming students. We're still not sure of exactly how many we're going to admit. But, working from the numbers President James gave to President Howell last night, we expect at least 400 transfers. We will locate half of those in standard College housing. That leaves about 8 to 10 transfers that each of you will need to accommodate."

Hailwood's first thought had been that the College was going to make the Houses take *all* of the transfers. So, the final number wasn't quite so bad. The DKE House could put up another 10... maybe 12...people. And Dartmouth had a DKE chapter, so they'd probably be guys that his guys knew, at least slightly. Who was the president of Dartmouth DKE? Hailwood should have known this but he hadn't been there in a couple of years. He was a little rusty in the inter-chapter relations department. The last time he'd been up to Dartmouth, the head guy there had been a madman they called Buddha. He didn't remember much else.

"To make things as easy as possible, we will try to organize the admissions so that you can take members from the Dartmouth chapters of your groups—if such exist. Otherwise, we will try to match groups with like interests."

Like interests? How would some self-interested admin tool define those? They'd put lacrosse players with Indians because Indians invented the game. Condescending bullshit.

Hailwood looked forward to taking his Fellowship and swapping this for some relatively straightforward academic backstabbing.

The Dartmouth transfers started showing up that afternoon. Some were on horseback, some on foot. Just a few of the most seriously injured came in a handful of vehicles that had made it out. This all suggested they'd been on their way south when the college presidents had spoken. Maybe before. And they were in worse shape than the transfers from Colby or Bates had been. Even the ones who were physically healthy seemed dazed.

The DKE House ended up taking 10 transfers. Eight were actual DKEs—the last eight who'd stayed around. The other two were from the Dartmouth Beta House. Since the College didn't have a Beta Chapter, the deans divided those guys up among other Houses.

Russell and some of the other younger guys took to calling the Dartmouth DKEs "the Elite Eight" and talking up their beer pong skills. It was goofy—but it seemed to raise their spirits some.

Some of the Dartmouth guys talked about what had happened to a few of Hailwood's brothers. But Hailwood had seen enough wasteland violence to know it was a good idea to give the transfers few days to get settled—get their paperwork in and adjust. He set up a cookout and beer pong tournament for the third night after their arrival, where the whole House could get together and hear what had happened to the north.

Buddha had graduated and moved to back New York the previous year. The leader of the Elite Eight was a senior whose name was Bill Rodgers. He knew the pong and cookout was going to be the "meeting" where his guys could say what had happened. After a few games, which the brothers instinctively made sure the Elite Eight won, the group had pretty well assembled. Hailwood called a break in the action and had everyone—including the two Betas who were living with them—down to the Great Room. He introduced the transfers to the few who hadn't already met them and the got right to the point.

"Okay, Rodgers, here's the question I've been waiting to ask: What the fuck happened up there?"

Rodgers looked quickly at his guys and answered: "Our admins fucked up and we fucked up by listening to them."

He and the others took turns filling in the details.

Dartmouth had set itself up for trouble by incorporating the whole town with which it had coexisted for 300 years into its walls. As a result, its security resources were always stretched thin and its administration had to deal with political constituencies beyond the normal mess that colleges in the wasteland had to handle.

"I mean, I didn't go to most of the public meetings. But if

you've seen one, you've seen them all. We're all supposed to be on the same side, inside the walls. But the townies were always paranoid that the college admins were trying to rip them off."

"And the admins had pissed in the water from the start by thinking they were doing the town a big favor by putting it inside. They could never understand why the townies weren't grateful. Which only made the townies resentful. It was a fucking mess."

"Hell, by the end, half of the fucking townies were working with the bandits. Some of them would come right out and say that they had more in common with the bandits than with the College."

"How fucked is that?"

"Yeah. They just shouldn't have put the town inside. Those fucking guys can simmer in their resentment all they want when they're outside the College walls. And they appreciate whatever security the College can provide. When you put them inside, they start to fucking expect complete security. And then they don't like the way you're providing it. You can't win. It's like the fucking Federal Era all over again."

The bandits up around Dartmouth were well organized by a commander who used the name Ethan Allen and called his crew The Green Mountain Men. So, whoever he was, he wasn't ignorant. He knew enough history to pick the right names.

The Green Mountain Men had started a not-so-effective siege of Dartmouth the previous spring. And, even though the siege was raggedy, the Dartmouth admins worked hard to downplay its effects. Even its existence. The siege went on through the early fall. Then, the bandits quit for the winter.

The Dartmouth admins took loud credit for having repelled the bandits. But, privately, everyone on the campus was preparing for another siege the next spring.

Everyone on campus was wrong. Ethan Allen had poured over his notes and didn't come back with another siege. He came back with focused attacks designed to breach specific points along the Dartmouth walls.

"Either he was taking fucking copious vid that first spring or he had really good intelligence inside. Because this spring, he didn't make any mistakes. Every point he hit was a weak one. Plus, he concentrated on the sections of wall farthest away from the College so, when his guys did break through, they were able to hold territory. That's when people really starting bailing."

Once the bandits had breached the walls, the Dartmouth administration tried to set up a new wall around the traditional campus. This pushed the townies even farther onto the bandits' side. And the "new walls" were practically useless. The Dartmouth students joined the battle to defend the new walls—that's how most of the injured got that way. But their efforts were too little, too late. The Green Mountain Men had old weapons but they were positioned perfectly in a semi-circle to lay a field of fire at the new walls.

They breached easily and burned down two classic dormitories. After that, Ethan Allen sent President James terms for surrender. The students and staff had 48 hours to evacuate and the Green Mountain Men would let them go peaceably. If they stayed longer or tried to scorch the earth, the bandits would kill everyone.

Some of the DKEs had been involved in managing the Dartmouth net. "And so, we stripped everything of any value out of the House and helped transfer the complete Dartmouth Archives to media and then blanked the DartNet and headed down here."

"Those assholes got the buildings and hardware, but we completely blanked the net. There's not a fucking byte of code on the whole thing. Tough guys were all threatening about scorched earth; but they were too fucking ignorant to understand that we'd scorched what was really important."

"Nobody's seen James since he made the deal with Howell. Some say he blew his brains in his office; others say a tilt came and carted his ass to New York. Who knows?"

Hailwood asked how much of Dartmouth's security armory the bandits got.

"Well, a lot of the security forces just took off with the cars and light armor units. We took as many vehicles as we could—and there wasn't much left. But the bandits got the bigger stuff. There were four double batteries of 12-inch guns."

"And shells?"

"Yeah. We brought the chemstrike shells with us. There were only about a dozen of those, anyway. We didn't have any nukes. But we left hundreds of basic concussion and incendiaries there. We figured blowing the armory would have gotten us all killed."

That was bad. If Ethan Allen was as sharp a tactical mind as these guys said, he'd figure out all kinds of mayhem to make with 12-inch guns.

The other DKEs asked a few more questions—all getting around to the point of how likely it would be that the Green Mountain Men followed the Dartmouth exodus south. The Elite Eight said what they knew. And they were smart kids; they'd fit in well. But they weren't in the mindset to think strategically. They just wanted to play beer pong and barbecue some meat.

Hailwood and the DKEs made sure they did.

But Hailwood was sure the bandits would eventually turn their attention to the College. It was the best defended campus. But it held the most riches—cash and otherwise. The Green Mountain Men or someone like them would come, sooner or later.

"…I don't know what I'm going to do. I mean Mom and Dad want me to go back to but I just don't think I can handle being out that far. I mean, I can transfer all of credits to Columbia and live at home. My God. That's so much better than having to deal with all of the security stuff out there."

Kate didn't sound like the Kate he knew and loved. She was slipping back into the New York princess that people who didn't know her had always assumed she was.

How did that work? Was she knowingly changing herself into the stereotype in order to justify quitting school? Or was this happening at some level beneath her will?

Hailwood believed that he could keep her from turning herself into a joke. But he had to be with her to keep her from it. And he wasn't with her right now. She was slipping away.

"Kate, you sound terrible. You've got to cut this bullshit out. Come out here for a week and just hang out with me. You can go to classes and hang out at the House. It'll be good for you to get away from the City."

A long silence.

"Valli has been going to Columbia the whole time and she's so happy. I mean, she's going to graduate this Spring. If I'd just gone to Columbia, I'd be graduating, too."

He didn't know who Valli was.

"Babe, if you come back out here you can graduate this

Spring."

"I know. But I don't want to go back out there."

He agreed to come into the City that weekend.

The President's House was the grandest residence on campus. Its front door faced east across the old State Route 116 to the main part of the campus. Its side deck faced west and south down toward the rest of the faculty housing. This was subtle, physical stuff. The President lived literally above the professors and deans.

Part of Hailwood dreaded this meeting. But the bigger part of him knew it was necessary. He had to attend to accept the Fellowship. Formally.

About fifteen seconds after he pressed the button, a formally-dressed butler opened the door. "Yes, sir?"

He handed the butler his invitation. "Terrence Hailwood for President Howell."

"Yes. Come in. Wait here, please."

No matter how fancy his family, Hailwood was still just a junior faculty member waiting in the fine foyer of the President. And the President wasn't going to let him forget this. He spent his minutes like everyone in this foyer did, looking at the pictures of Howell with several CEOs and celebrities. The boozy smiles and indirect site lines of practiced sociability. Howell might be a silly man in some ways, but he carried the reputation of the College with him. And that was something even Hailwood's grandfather respected.

"Terry, welcome!" Howell greeted him personally. The President was sweating just slightly at the temples. He needed something.

Hailwood felt his breath wheeze out of his chest. Howell had no idea how little he could influence major appeals—he was just the well-meaning grandson of a dysfunction family. "Come in. Join us. I'm sure that you know Simon LeDoux, the Dean of Faculty. And Peter Templeton and his wife Marie. And Jeff Gresham and his wife Claire...."

Deans, senior professors and their stout wives.

The Dean of the Faculty would nominally be his boss. But Hailwood sensed that it wasn't going to work that way. This was going to be just like it had been at the prep school in Tampa. His grandfather was too big a deal for anything to be normal.

The white jacketed bartender turned his gloved palms up, open. It was Hailwood's order.

"I'll have an Irish whiskey and soda water back."

A couple of tenured geniuses followed his order. That was a troubling sign. They'd prepared for this.

He'd been stupid. For these few weeks, the Fellowship had seemed like his own achievement. But it wasn't it. It fell in line with all the rest of the bullshit of his life. Purchased, compromised, obscured by his family influence. When he'd been 13 or 14, one of his therapists had suggested the word "obscured" under the theory that the Hailwood influence didn't buy things as much as it blurred them. Maybe that was right.

He'd hoped that the Fellowship wouldn't be blurred. Stupid. And the Old Man had let him babble on about achieving it on his own.

Hailwood had a couple more Irish whiskeys.

President Howell played his hand well. Hailwood didn't even recognize the beginning. He was talking about bidding bridge hands with one of the faculty wives when Howell's talk of needing to "improve our security infrastructure beyond what our operating budget will allow" echoed into the front of Hailwood's attention.

He felt Howell's heavy arm land on his right shoulder. This was high-end fundraising, get the capital commitment with as few details as possible. Which meant Howell figured Hailwood (and, really, the Old Man) either wouldn't understand or wouldn't agree with the details. Logical extension of that: The College wanted to extend its walls around the town.

Like Dartmouth had.

There were a million things that he could have said. He could have been cool and made some ironic reference to wasteland bandits as an effective fundraising tool. He could have been belligerent and called Howell a money-grubbing ghoul. But his grandfather had taught him—and he'd learned for himself—that there wasn't any profit in negation. The immediate satisfaction of mouthing off was like a hit of Neurac, a fleeting high that wasn't worth the long-term cost.

Lashing out at Howell and the College wouldn't be scathing. It would just confuse everyone in the room.

The Woodward Family Fellowship was part of a system. And

he wanted to be part of that system. The system needed money, which the Old Man had. He needed to say something assuring. "This is a great College, President Howell. Now, more than ever, it's important to culture and society. We can't let trouble come to this place."

Howell looked relieved. He smiled and patted Hailwood on the back.

Things had taken a turn for the worse.

The next morning, Hailwood was in the garage at 10 o'clock to prep the Badger for the drive down to New York. Russell was catching a ride with him and arrived early to help with the system checks. Russell was anal-retentive, which made his no-show the night before even more infuriating.

"So…sorry I missed your dinner last night."

Hailwood had been allotted six guests at the dinner. He'd sent one invitation to his mother and actually invited Drummond and four DKEs, including Russell. Who looked to be house President in a couple of years. None had shown. And only Drummond had sent regrets.

"Yeah."

"No, seriously. I'm sorry I missed it. Some of the new guys and the rest of us were playing a pretty intense game of beer pong and time just got away."

"Really?"

"Yeah. Really."

"Fuck you, Dave. Just take your ride. If you lie any more, the shit will start pouring out from your eyes."

"What are you talking about?"

"Don't play stupid. You guys didn't show up to that dinner because you knew Howell was going to put the arm on me for more security money."

"What?"

"Don't play stupid."

"Fuck you, Terry. You're wrong. I'll get another ride down to New York."

Russell seemed about to say something more but hesitated. He just shook his head and left the garage.

Hailwood thought about following Russell back to the House

and explaining why he was so angry. He'd had the same fleeting feelings dozens of times in his life. In those moments, it always seemed as if the dramatic explanation of how screwy his family was would make him the same as everyone else with regular family problems.

But his family wasn't the same and his problems weren't regular. And all of the efforts he'd ever made to explain it away had only made more trouble.

He finished the diagnostics on the Badger's defense systems and they checked out fine. If he set out by noon, he could be to New York's northeast gates by dusk and to Kate's family's apartment in time for a late dinner.

Maybe he could patch things up with her once he got there. A walk down Park Avenue was always a romantic thing. A million miles from a garage in the middle of the wasteland. Maybe Kate was right and the mix was too much.

Once he was out on Old Hadley Road, he synchronized a shot from the Badger's 20mm guns with its 3-D imaging. Straight shot to an abandoned shipping container 600 meters off the road. A small thing, but a good sign.

Nineteen

Crowley watched the riders approach from the east. They looked nervous, even though they were at least 12 riding together. They sat too high in their saddles...and they rode in a near perfect wedge formation. They had the sun in their eyes, but that probably didn't explain it all.

The perimeter guards met the nervous riders at the gate and led them through the camp. The riders had lowered their civic standard but stayed high in their saddles and tightened their wedge. He'd open the meeting with a friendly gambit and try to put them at ease.

Jana was next to him, carrying the baby in the pricey backpack rig that the envoys from SoCal had brought on their last visit. Crowley thought a baby gift was a kind of threat. But Jana liked the thing.

She put Mikey in it all the time. The two of them hiked in it; they rode in it. She did more than recommended with a 10-week-old—but no one was going to stop her. She said the backpack was light for her and comfortable for him. Plus, it had a stiff composite shell that supported his back and neck and covered his face from the sun. Most of the time, he'd fall asleep in it and stay asleep for a couple of hours.

The other times, you might hear him gurgling and catch a flash of his thin black curls.

"These are from Memphis?" she asked.

"No. Mobile." He wiped his neck with the handkerchief that she'd soaked in well water before they'd set out. This place was hot and humid.

"Mobile? Right. Sorry I'm not keeping up."

"Don't worry about it. I don't think this is an important one. They're just coming because they know everyone else has."

"But why are they coming *here*? Camp B is practically in their backyard. Why didn't they visit when we were there?"

"Good question. Maybe they don't know about Camp B. They're so deep in the pocket of New Orleans they may not realize what's in their backyard."

"Why are they riding? Why no tilt?"

"More good questions. It's strange they didn't fly. Maybe they think this makes them seem like jus' folks."

"Why are you watching them so close?"

"They look nervous. That makes us nervous."

She took out her field glasses and followed his. "Yeah, they do. City people don't like lowering their standards in the wasteland. Maybe that's it."

"No. They were riding stiff when they still had their colors up. It's more than the flag."

"What then?"

"Not sure. Maybe Morial and the big brothers in New Orleans *told* them to come here. On horses."

"Why? I thought we were getting along with Morial."

"I thought so, too. I'm probably making something of nothing. I've always had a hard time reading managers from smaller Cities. They get upset about unexpected things. Strange ideas of status, etiquette. Come on, let's get back."

She tipped her hat forward and rode first, as always. He did his best to keep up. He kept his eye on Mikey in the blue backpack and tried not to fall too far behind.

This was Camp A, their main base of operations. It was about halfway between Houston and New Orleans, in what had been for hundreds of years French Acadian country. Crowley liked the fact that the Cajuns had kept their piece of the wasteland much as they had through the Federal Era—even before. Lafayette, the main town, was practically a small City that didn't care about recognition. And, while the Cajuns never put much stock in reading, they understood the value of guns and organization. Many Cajuns had joined the Company early on. They'd told him that setting up here would be a good thing. And they'd been right. The Cajuns in and around Lafayette considered the Camp a good thing. An extra security buffer between them and the ambitions of either Houston or New Orleans.

Crowley and few close aides stayed on the move. They had two other Camps. As Jana had said, Camp B was north of Mobile. Camp C was a couple of hours south Brownsville. They had various ways to get around. They rode a lot. But they also had some trucks. And they could always borrow a tiltrotor or plane from Brian and the Brahmins in Brownsville.

Legally, Crowley, Jana and Mikey were citizens of Brownsville; but Crowley didn't like to draw attention to this fact.

They kept moving because there was a growing number of mercenaries and privateers who wanted to kill Crowley. None of the Cities sending envoys to him would admit it but some of them—probably several, together—had put bounties on his head.

Crowley didn't take the threats personally. The Company was an unknown risk factor to the Cities in the region. Maybe to Cities everywhere. It had grown fast. And his vids were all over the free nets. But they didn't know much about it. He still had enough of a manager's mind that he could see that he was the worst kind of risk to a City manager. An unquantified risk.

It made perfect managerial sense to negotiate officially while funding an assassination through "informal" channels. He'd done similar things when he'd been in Tampa.

He knew something else. City managers tended to overestimate unquantified risks. His main goal these days was to live up to their overestimation.

There wasn't much to worry about when it came to security in the Camps. His students trusted City envoys even less than he did. They would search visitors' horses, vehicles and persons thoroughly—before allowing them onto Camp grounds. The inspections usually took place at gunpoint.

If the visitors objected, they'd never get in. If they tried to resist violently, they'd be shot.

The head guards usually got particular satisfaction from demanding and reviewing an envoy's papers. They'd read the documents carefully and completely. Sometimes out loud. And they wouldn't hesitate to ask the envoys about words or phrases they didn't understand.

Crowley taught his students the old lesson: "There is no such thing as a stupid question." It had always seemed like a trite, throwaway line when he'd lived in Tampa. But he'd realized it wasn't really meant for up-and-coming City managers. It had much more meaning for people who'd spent their lives thinking they were ignorant.

Sic Semper Tyrannis

The close inspection of the papers was good. So was the man-for-man security escort that guided visitors inside. But the real security feature was the number of people in Camp A. There were almost 5,000 people here—about two-thirds were able-bodied men and women, organized into some two dozen operating units. The others were children, old people and the sick or injured on the mend.

The organization of the Camp impressed…or intimidated…most security types. And that was partly the point.

So, if the envoys from Mobile were anxious, it might have been because they'd already heard what to expect coming in.

Camp A was almost 200 acres of secured land. To Crowley, its distinguishing trait was that it smelled of pine pitch. They'd cut a lot of trees to build the Camp; and they burned sap to get rid of bugs.

There were a couple of permanent buildings on the place, but most of the quarters were what the Cajuns called *chambres*. These were something between a Quonset hut and a bivuac tent. The typical *chambre* sat on top of a slab of cement. The building itself was a wood frame base and thin beams, usually hickory slats, holding up tent material made from heavy synthmesh. When the thing was assembled well, the walls and roof felt solid—almost structural. But a tent could be taken apart in a few minutes if a big storm or an enemy security force was coming.

The tents varied in size—but floors were usually about five meters by five. Among the Cajuns, families of five our six would live in a single tent. Most Cajun towns were dozens of *chambres* arranged in a rough circle near some body of water or crossroads. The circular formations were designed to keep intruders or outsiders confused about which tent belonged to what family.

In Camp A, they'd tried to maintain the circular structure. Or, to be more precise, several dozen circles But they had so many tents—almost a thousand, in all—that the circles seemed more like grids.

Crowley had come to understand the need for orderliness. In his prior life, he'd always assumed that security types *desired* order. But, as the Company had grown, he'd realized it was less about desire than it was about need. People in large numbers *needed* organization.

He still wasn't good at the organization. In Tampa, he had been a finance and marketing guy. Here, he was…well, in management terms, he was a product person. Content.

He left the details of organization to other people—the local leaders at each Camp.

An hour after they arrived at Camp A's gates, the envoys from the City of Mobile were lead into to Crowley's personal offices by the ancient Cajun who was the *major domo* of Camp A. The Cajun clasped his meaty hands behind his back; this meant that the envoys had been searched and disarmed. And the Cajun was confident they weren't hiding anything. If he'd been less certain, he would have clasped his hands in front—if he'd been actively worried, he would have rested his right hand on the pistol inside his jacket.

But vieux Guibert was calm. The visitors were *sans dents*.

"Mr. Crowley, my name is Richard Hester. I am the First Vice President of Strategic Planning for the City of Mobile. These are my assistants, James Kloves and Sean Dawson. And we're riding with Captain Matthew Boyette of the Mobile Security Force, commanding a small unit of his men. They're waiting outside the gate."

Hester must have been six and a half feet tall—and maybe taller. He was very thin, with a long neck that made him look a cartoon character. He wasn't a handsome man but he was so tall and so well dressed that he had a certain kind of elegance.

"Welcome, Mr. Hester. We've met before. Several years ago. When I was still in Tampa. You were part of a trade delegation that attended one of Tampa's regional commerce summits."

"I'm impressed that you remember. We did meet briefly at that summit. I was one of several junior managers in our group."

"Well, you stood out. This is my wife, Jana Morrell Crowley. This is William Atell, one of my trusted advisors; and you've already met Jean Guibert, the security director for this place."

"Mr. Atell. Mr. Guibert. Mrs. Crowley, it's a pleasure to meet you. If you don't mind, we'd like to offer you a small token of our esteem and an example of Mobile's economic productivity. It's a bolt of 300-thread count linen, made from Mobile organic cotton."

Other than the baby carrier, Jana didn't like these presents. She said that she thought giving the woman gifts was insulting and sexist. But, ever since the SoCal guys had brought the baby pack, she'd tried to put a better face on accepting them. "It's very nice. I've heard about Mobile cotton. Thank you."

Crowley gestured toward the large pine table in the middle of the big room, "Please, everyone take a seat. Can we get you gentlemen something to drink?"

A couple young Cajun students brought whiskey and chilled water with lemon slices. Crowley had kept the custom of whiskey and water that he'd picked up from his meetings with the Brownsville Road farmers.

When everyone had had something to drink and the welcoming small talk had run its course, Crowley moved the talk to business, such as it was. "Well, I'm sure it's no secret to you that we've had visitors from a number of Cities in the region. And you probably know that they are all interested in whether our Company has political ambitions or poses a security threat to their walls."

Hester nodded and answered: "The purpose of our visit here is to discuss potential commercial or political relationships that we might develop between Mobile and your organization. But we are aware of those other visits. Do you mind if I speak frankly?"

One of the advanced negotiating lessons Crowley remembered from school was that people who talked about "speaking frankly' were usually liars.

"Of course."

"We know that some of the larger Cities are worried about your organization. Except they don't call your organization a Company. They call it a bandit army."

Crowley laughed and Atell and Guibert followed. "Yes. Our bandit army. Mr. Hester, my mission is not to raise an army against anyone or any City. It's to educate and empower hundreds of thousands of people who are living like serfs outside the walls."

Hester let the laughter about his use of *army* pass.

"Do you know what *serf* means, Mr. Hester?"

"No."

"Neither did I. All the years I lived and worked in a big City I never heard the word. The first time I heard it out here, I thought it meant someone who surfed the free nets all day. That's not what it means. It means a person who's a slave to land he lives on. And whoever owns the land owns the person."

"I thought no one owned anything out here, Mr. Crowley."

"Well, that's not exactly true. The smart and the strong own things—effectively. I mean, their claims wouldn't measure up to Mobile's legal standards. But they have effective ownership."

"And they own people?"

"Sometimes. More often, they just act like they do."

"Well, that's bad, Mr. Crowley. We in Mobile don't have slaves. We haven't since we were part of the Federal system. Hundreds of years ago." He didn't seem flustered at Crowley's little bit of misdirection—which meant he was an experienced negotiator. "And we could get behind your efforts to help these people. I never heard that word *serf*. But I do know the word *empower*. It's a good word. But when empowerment means guns in the hands of thousands of angry people, our citizens are likely to see a security risk."

"Do your citizens even know about us, Mr. Hester?"

He smiled a little, thin smile. "The important ones do."

Crowley laughed again. "I'm sure you're right. Well, let me try to explain myself in another way, then. My mission isn't political or social. It's economic. There's massive economic potential out here, Mr. Hester. Massive. But it's lost in disorganization. Chaos. And ignorance. The chaos and ignorance are inefficient. And I hate inefficiency. I was raised and trained as a manager, just like you. I've shaken off the effects of the Neuroplex pills but I still think like a manager."

Now one of Hester's assistants stepped in. "Your students live and train like an army. We've seen it here for ourselves. I mean, it's impressive what you've built. But we'd be foolish not to have issues with this. You call this place a Camp. Your followers call you *Rabbi*. You have to admit that there is a political quality to all of this."

Crowley shot a quick glance at Atell. He understood.

"I'm not sure what you mean by *political*, Mr. Kloves. But let me tell something about my experience in the Rabbi's Company. I'm 46 years old. For 44 of those years, I lived a wasted life. I worked some; I hustled some. I stole. I killed a few people. Wasted more nights that I can remember drunk or high. I'm lucky—just lucky—I wasn't killed myself. I had children with several women. And those are the ones I know of. And the incredible thing is I had no idea what I was doing was wrong. I was just living the same everyone lived.

"Two years ago, I was working on a farm near Brownsville. And I was happy for that because the farm had a barracks where I had my own bed and I wouldn't get stabbed in the middle of the night. I figured I was going to live the rest of life on that farm. And I was relieved to have a warm place to sleep. I lived like an animal, Mr. Kloves.

"Then I went to one of the Rabbi's lessons. And my life changed. I'd seen Bibles and books. I'd heard about the nets. But I'd never understood what any of it meant. Learning how to read changed my life. Reading the Bible and the books the Rabbi gave me changed my life. Learning how to see the news on the nets…I had no idea how much there was in this world.

"The Rabbi says that a person who can read the Bible and fire a gun straight from 100 meters can live any life he chooses. And I believe him. If I'd heard that when I was 10 years old, I'd have lived my life differently."

Crowley had heard this story a dozen times but it still moved him. Atell was always in meetings with City envoys because he told it so well. Visitors who heard Atell's story either warmed to its sentiment or recoiled from its political meaning.

To Crowley, the visitors from Mobile looked like they were falling into the second group—the ones who recoiled. Hester squinted his eyes and looked around the room. His assistants listened, but blankly.

What did this mean? Marc Morial in New Orleans was Machiavellian enough to send his minor league allies to send a message…but why bother? Why not just send his own envoy? Because he didn't want to make a threat under his own standard? That might make sense if Crowley was still the CEO of a City…but not now. City colors didn't mean anything here. No matter how many or well-armed his students were, in diplomatic terms, they were just an informal gathering out in the wasteland. No reason for the CEO of the largest City in the region to worry about diplomacy with them.

Crowley was losing his grasp on the fine points of City politics. Maybe it was no more Neuroplex. Maybe it was thinking more important thoughts. But he couldn't run these scenarios as clearly as he used to.

"It's an impressive story. I can understand how your lessons have caught on out here. Rabbi Crowley—"

"It's just a term of affection. I'm not a Rabbi."

"I'm not so sure. In every sense that I understand the word, you seem to be one." Hester smiled a little differently this time and laughed to emphasize good will. Then, his smile dropped away to a heavy swallow that changed, in a few seconds, to an intense stare. It was a quick change in direction to the conversation. "But I'm here to discuss more worldly things."

"Literacy and guns are worldly things, Mr. Hester."

"Well, it's the guns that we're concerned about."

"Concerned? In what way? And who is 'we'?"

"I have this letter to deliver to you, Mr. Crowley. This copy is sealed for your eyes. But I have a copy that I've read, so I know what it says."

The letter was on heavy cloth stock. The red wax holding the flap closed showed the Seal of the City of Mobile.

"Thank you. If you don't mind, I'll wait a little bit to open this. Since you've already read your copy, please tell me what the letter says."

The request surprised Hester. But it shouldn't have. Crowley was just following a familiar negotiating gambit. When he'd been a CEO, he never read any document anyone handed him at a public event or in a formal meeting. Interrupting a meeting to read some document gave too much power to the presenter. Leaving the letter unopened and unread diminished any power it had.

If Crowley didn't read the letter, he didn't have to respond to anything in it. At least not yet.

Hester recovered from his pause. "Of course. Our Board of Directors congratulates you on the good work that you've done organizing and educating the inhabitants of the wilderness in our region. But the directors warn you that the growing size of your... well, they call it an *army*...is becoming an external security threat to the City of Mobile. In order to avoid any misunderstandings between your organization and the Mobile Security Force, they suggest that you remove your students and standards from any place within 100 miles of the City walls."

"Hmm. A hundred miles is larger than most Cities claim as an extramural zone of interest."

"Sure. You've been gone for a while. The bandit problems in New England the Pacific Coast have changed a lot of things. Most Cities are extending their external security zones to a 100-mile radius."

"From the walls."

"Yes. From the walls."

"I've been doing some work with the City of Brownsville, helping them get up and running. I'm pretty sure they're just claiming the traditional seven miles zone of interest."

"Well, they probably don't have the bandit problem that established Cities have. I'm sure that in time, when Brownsville is more established, it will claim a 100-mile zone, too."

"That's a lot of territory. How are you and New Orleans handling this? A hundred miles from your western walls and their eastern would...overlap."

Hester smiled again. But this smile had lost the flash of confidence. He was nervous. His eyes darted around the room and didn't hold Crowley's stare. "The Cities of Mobile and New Orleans have signed a Reciprocal Security Agreement by which we share external security functions in the wilderness area that lies between us."

"Reciprocal Security Agreement. You know, one of the reasons my tenure in Tampa ended was that I advocated regional security agreements."

Hester nodded. This seemed to be a comfortable thing for him. He was a manager; he'd avoid bad news or confrontation if he could. Even bad news that was stamped with his City seal. "Yes. I remember reading that. You know, your ideas had some supporters in Mobile."

"That's good to hear. I still believe that some sort of confederation is a good idea. It might bring stability and efficiency to the region. And that includes resolving the bandit problems."

"That's an interesting point. Contrarian. Most people in the Cities equate your efforts out here with the rise in banditry. In fact, many think your organization and the bandits are the same. I'm not sure what they would think of you claiming you're trying to *prevent* terrorism."

"That's one of the reasons we don't like the word *terrorism*. Its meaning is too subjective."

Hester smiled again but didn't say anything for a minute. Then: "Our agreement with New Orleans is a bilateral treaty. I think people prefer two-party deals to multilateral ones. Multilateralism reminds people of federalism. And no one wants that."

"I suppose not. Well, is there any more that we need to discuss?"

"I guess not. Or, rather, I think that my Board would like me to come back with some sort of response from you to its letter and its suggestions."

Asking for an answer. Now the power in the exchange had shifted in Crowley's direction. He poured Jana some water...and some for himself. He raised the water pitcher to Hester, who smiled and declined. Finally, he poured a dash of whiskey into his and Jana's water.

"That's another matter. I'll need to read the letter."

He took a long drink from his tumbler.

"I assume that it says all that you say it does. And this raises a lot of questions. And I'm not sure how many of these questions I can answer. First of all, as we've discussed, my students aren't an army. I don't command them. In the wasteland, they live where they choose. Many are farmers whose families have been working their land for generations. If their farms are within a 100 miles of your walls, I don't think they're going to just leave on a whim."

"This isn't a whim, Mr. Crowley. It's a City decree. All over the wasteland, bandits are getting more aggressive."

"I understand that. But my students aren't bandits or terrorists. They're farmers and merchants and laborers."

"Maybe. But that's impossible for us to tell the difference. And, as I'm sure you've heard, some of the terrorists who breached the walls up in Hartford were using your line about reading the Bible and shooting straight from 100 yards. We have to protect our City walls. You of all people out here should understand this."

There was no point in continuing with Hester. He wasn't a negotiator; he was a messenger.

Crowley stood up. "Well, you and your assistants are welcomed to stay here as our guests for the night. I'll send word to your security escort. I assume that they'll want to keep their weapons, which means they'll have to stay outside of the Camp. We'll get them food and anything else they need. And I'll take a look at the letter and talk it over with my advisors. I'm not sure how we'll respond. I'm not sure that any response is appropriate. Let me think about it for a bit. Jean, will you have one of your men show them to a guest quarters?"

"Yes, Rabbi."

Jana followed him out of the tent and across the greens to their personal quarters. "So what are we going to do about this?"

"The first thing to do is figure out whether they're going to try to enforce this with privateers or regular security forces."

"Do they have enough regular security to do that?"

"I don't know. I don't think Mobile does."

"But New Orleans?"

"Maybe."
"Or Houston?"
"Probably."
"And what do we do then?"
"Go to war."

Jana made the face that people who knew her called "that smile." It wasn't really a smile. It was more neutral than that. Really, what she did was just relax of the non-scarred parts of her face. When she relaxed, the scarred part around her eye pulled up a little on the right corner of her mouth—making what looked like a mischievous smirk.

But this wasn't all just an accident of skin and muscles. The spirit behind her smirk had a lot of mischief in it.

She'd fight New Orleans and Houston.

Twenty

Hailwood carried his weekend bag into the charters terminal at Windsor Locks. He'd parked his truck in the secure lot. Again. And it was probably safer than ever now.

Windsor Locks wasn't considered the wasteland any more. Now it was part of the Hartford "Blue Zone" and under the control of the City of New York External Security Forces.

About 20 miles north of Windsor Locks, a series of new signs had appeared along the WNET. They warned drivers about the new security arrangement and stated plainly that the land around the Tollway had been set with mines. Drivers going anywhere away from marked, approved lanes were risking their lives.

Starting about 10 miles north, machine gun turrets marked each quarter mile as the WNET approached Hartford. A checkpoint manned by NYESF troops stopped all traffic just north of the Windsor Locks exit.

Hailwood figured there must have been some friction between the WNET Corporation and the City of New York over all this. The WNET was a for-profit venture, with its own security force; it wasn't likely to hand over its southern line to New York without a fight. Had there been any flare-ups between the WNET security guys and the NYESF troops? All the classic tensions would be there: wasteland boys versus City slickers. Hard-charging entrepreneurs versus bureaucrats. Or had the whole matter been decided in a conference room in Manhattan? Money changing hands. Millions? Billions?

Probably the latter.

The checkpoint included secured booths at each lane of the Tollway. The soldier who tapped his window from the booth was dressed in state-of-the-art battle gear, as if expecting a full-on war.

Kevlar-weave fatigues, titanium composite armor inserts, anti-shock helmet and a black full-face visor.

"May I see proof of ownership of this vehicle and some form of official identification?" It was a woman's voice. That took Hailwood by surprise.

"Ah, yeah. Sure. The truck's registered in Tampa. And my passport is Tampa, too."

Laser scanners checked the barcodes on the front and back of the truck while they had their short exchange.

"Anyone else in the vehicle?"

This was a pointless question. At the same time the lasers scanned the barcodes, various other scans—including a full thermovid—would show her that he was the only warm body in the truck.

"No. I'm alone."

"Purpose and destination?"

"A social visit for the weekend in Manhattan."

"Address?"

"The Plaza Hotel. Is that specific enough?"

"No. Do you have a reservation number?"

"Ah, yeah. Just a moment." He grabbed his screen and checked his reservation. "THX-1157."

"Okay. Wait here, please."

The window of her booth slid closed. Where was he going to go? She had his passport.

Ahead, Hailwood saw the lanes where cars and drivers were being searched. There was also an impound lot where cars that didn't past muster went. And who knew what happened to them.

The window slid open again. This time, the solder had flipped her visor up. She was a young Hispanic girl. In Tampa, people had to be 18 to join the security forces. The rules in New York might have been different. "Are you planning to drive to Manhattan, Mr. Hailwood?"

"No, ma'am."

"Good. Because you can't take an armed vehicle like this anywhere near the City walls. You're flying?"

"Yes. I have a chartered tiltrotor pick up at the Windsor Locks airfield in…about half an hour. And I'll leave the truck in the secured parking at Windsor Locks."

"May I see the details for your charter flight?"

"Right here."

"Also, there's going to be a toll. Separate of the WNET tolls. It's $24. New York. You'll want to get that ready."

"I've got a New York autopay account. It should come up with your scan of the bar codes."

"Outstanding. One more minute, please."

The window closed again.

If the City was charging tolls, this definitely wasn't the wasteland anymore.

Since the troubles in Hartford, it was nearly impossible to drive or ride into New York. When he'd first been at the College, Hailwood had made the drive easily—at least once or twice a semester. Back in those days, it was about an hour to Hartford on the WNET, which had a spur that ran around Hartford's walls so you didn't have check in. The spur around Hartford took another half hour or 45 minutes. Then a little less than two hours from Hartford's southern gate to the Tollway's official terminus at Gate 1A into New York at New Canaan. Of course, traffic got worse once you were inside the walls at New York. But he was a pretty decent City driver.

Now the drive from Windsor Locks to Gate 1A was a maze of roadblocks, checkpoints and security trenches. And, as the soldier had said, they'd never let the Badger inside New York's walls.

Nominally, New York had reached a security agreement with Hartford. Actually, New York and Boston were dividing Hartford's territory and the small belts of wasteland that separated their walls. Just as the Old Man had predicted.

There were colored zones that were supposed to reflect different degrees of terrorist activity.

"Okay. Thank you for cooperating, Mr. Hailwood." She handed back his paperwork. "Please apply this sticker to a visible place on the left side of your windshield. It will let our people know that you have been checked out. They'll leave your truck alone while it's at Windsor Locks field."

"Thank you."

"If you'll wait just a minute, you'll see a series of green lights. Follow them and you'll bypass the rest of the security checks. You should be in plenty of time make your flight."

"Great. Thanks for your help."

"You're welcome. Enjoy your trip."

Her window slid closed again and the green lights went on. He steered the truck hard to the left and avoided the security lanes.

When Hailwood checked in at the charter desk, the clerk said that his tiltrotor was just about to land. Also, two ladies had missed their scheduled flight into Manhattan earlier that morning and were looking to split a charter back into the City. Was he interested in sharing his ride for a two-thirds discount?

"Maybe. Who are the ladies?"

"S. and J. Brownledge. A mother and daughter who came out to look at Legacy Colleges."

"Gutsy. Didn't know anyone was doing that these days. Sure."

"Thanks so much. We were afraid we were going to have to stay the night here in the Blue Zone. And finding the right college is enough adventure for us right now." The mother—Sharon—was a marketing manager with one of the vid channels in New York. She wasn't tall. But she made a strong impression. She shook Hailwood's hand firmly and looked him square in the eye. Her eyes were light blue; her hair was jet black and severe. She was in her 40s but caught a young guy's eye more than her daughter did. All of this was by design. Her ambition was fleshed out by the well-maintained body under her corporate chic clothes.

The daughter—Jennifer—was also petite. She didn't work as hard to compensate for it as her mother did. She was attractive, too; the same blue eyes, lighter brown hair and fine features on a round face. But, standing next her mother, Jennifer was too low-key to be noticed first. Something in the way she suffered her mother's fast talk suggested she understood this was how it would always be.

"We were looking at Smith and Hampshire. Jennifer has the grades and scores for either of those. We've already been to Boston for Wellesley and down to Philadelphia to see Bryn Mawr. But she's determined to attend one of the Legacy Colleges. Not the City versions. And, too tell the truth, I agree with her."

Sharon kept talking through the jerky takeoff.

He'd seen this before among City strivers, a slightly Freudian competitiveness between attractive women and their near-adult daughters.

They weren't sure the daughter's grades were good enough for his College (he was careful to remain vague about what he did). "But, from what we hear, it may end up absorbing every school in the New England wilderness by the time she graduates."

"If there's any New England wilderness left." Hailwood looked out as they rose from the airstrip. The landscape had changed dramatically in less than a year. The walls of Hartford were barely visible anymore. And, rather than a City with some rough spots, it looked like a few developed neighborhoods spread around a security/industrial zone.

"When I was ready for college, my parents didn't give me any choices. I was raised from the start to be a manager—and I was so excited to get into NYU. I was so happy to have a clear path laid out for me that I didn't think twice. But, looking back on it, I wonder if I might have gotten more out of a true college experience. I have the greatest respect for a real liberal arts education. It's so much more than learning managerial lessons."

Sharon's talk was more than just nervous chatter. She was too focused and well-spoken. But her intensity was misplaced. Hailwood didn't give a damn about her journeys of self-discovery. He'd agreed to share the ride with them for the chance that her daughter would be cute.

And she was. But not quite his type.

"My girlfriend was going to Smith until recently. Things have been kind of dangerous there over the last few months. What does your dad think of you going there, Jennifer?"

"Oh, he's okay with whatever I want to do. But we don't see him that often. It's really more up to my mother and stepfather."

"Jennifer's father took a job down in Tampa about 10 years ago. We thought about going with him, but my own career was going well. And I just couldn't see leaving New York. So we went our separate ways. But we're still quite friendly."

Now there were two topics he needed to avoid. The College and Tampa.

"I didn't get married with the idea that I'd ever be divorced. But it was just a thousand small things that caused us to grow apart."

He didn't need to hear anything more to fill the blanks in Sharon's journey. She'd married some guy she'd met at work, a slightly older man in a senior position on the corporate ladder.

They lived on the Upper West Side. They had a beach house in the Hamptons. Everyone got along well.

It wasn't the way that she spoke that sounded stupid; it was *what* she chose to say. Empty words. He could practically hear the Old Man saying that such a chatty, vapid woman was probably a spy.

"What do you want to do for a major, Jennifer?"

"Well, I'm kind of split. My reading skills are really high and I like to read. So, literature is kind of an obvious choice. But I've always been interested in logic. I mean, maybe I ought to pursue my weaknesses instead of my strengths."

He could have kissed her.

Half an hour of Sharon's self-involved talk later, they landed at the helipad on the roof of the Plaza. He encouraged Jennifer to apply to the College. Grades and scores weren't everything. Her idea of pursuing her weaknesses instead of her strengths would make a great admission app essay.

Sharon gave Jennifer one of her business cards and told her to give Hailwood contact information. There was something creepy about that.

Hailwood breezed through the check in and carried his own bag into the room. It was on one of the higher floors, so he could open the window and get some—but not too much—City noise.

He didn't like New York City as much as some of the people he knew from school or from home. He wasn't one of the ones who raved about it. But there was almost always something going on here. He could understand how some people were drawn to the constant activity.

The value of the charter flight in came to a point as he unpacked his clothes. If he'd driven, the security checks would have forced him to leave all of his guns at home. New York gun control laws had been getting stricter. A handful of citizens were allowed to carry; but most were not. And visitors weren't allowed to have guns inside the walls. Legally.

But, coming on a charter right to the roof of his hotel, he was able to avoid all of that and bring both the old Ruger and the 9mm plasma pistol in the leather flap holster in his bag.

Legally, carrying the gun around in New York was a crime. Even if he never fired it. But he considered gun control laws like speed limits; guidelines for acceptable behavior rather than hard-and-fast rules.

He'd leave the Ruger in his bag and take the plasma pistol with him. It was smaller and easier to hide. He could slide it easily into the sewn-in holster in either of the sport coats he'd brought.

He laid out his clothes and then took a long shower. Fancy hotels liked to boast about expensive bed linens or eager concierge services. But, to Hailwood's mind, a strong hot shower was the best luxury any posh place could provide.

This weekend had a strange vibe before it started. Reeser had probably put it best, two nights earlier when—over a game of beer pong—he'd tried to talk Hailwood out of coming. "You're going down there to re-animate the corpse of a dead relationship. If you're not successful, you're going to feel sick. If you are successful, you're not going to have a girlfriend. You're going to having a fucking *zombie*."

"Or a *fucking* zombie," one of the Dartmouth guys said.

Hailwood had been pissed off at the jokey comments at the time. He told Reeser he didn't need another person telling him to bail on Kate.

Then Russell chimed in: "Dude, you're not bailing on her. She bailed on you. It's over. Find someone else."

They were still at loggerheads, from his last trip. Hailwood was having problems with lots of the brothers in his house. It was time to move in with Drummond, over at the faculty houses.

In the rich tradition of DKEs before him, Hailwood ignored the advice of his friends and was chasing a problematic woman.

It was going to be a weekend of him pursuing her, trying to convince her to work things out. And it was all happening on her home turf, with her family and friends around to provide context and support. And he wasn't sure whether that context and support worked for his case or against it.

Kate was ambivalent about their future together. And she'd been plain about this. Her official line was, "I'll always love you, Terry. But I'm not sure that if I'm with you I could have the kind of life that I'd be comfortable living. Your life is just too intense."

He'd dismissed this new-found ambivalence as fallout from the bandit attack at Smith. They'd practically lived together for almost two years. They'd been more places together than most people ever saw in their lives. When he thought about her, he saw a whole live together stretching out to...the end. But his certainty only seemed to make her more doubtful.

Maybe Reeser was right. Maybe this was all bullshit and he had no chance of getting through with any kind of living thing.

Those were the cons.

While he shaved, he went through the pros.

At their best, he and Kate got on seamlessly together. He was as comfortable with her as he'd ever been with any person. He didn't have any secrets from her. He wasn't sure what *love* meant—but, if that word meant anything, he loved her.

And her parents were all for it.

This was the tricky part. At this point, her parents were more excited about them being together than Kate was. He wasn't sure how to play that. She got along well her parents. But pressing too hard on the fact that they were for him might backfire and make her rebel against her parents with one stroke.

The thing that he hadn't admitted to any of his brothers back at the House was that he felt like the losing suitor in some Federal Era melodrama. The tuxedo-wearing schmuck that the heroine rejects for a poor, handsome guy in squatters' clothes.

In their story, who was the romantic lead? She hadn't said anything about another person. Maybe his rival was comfort. She was comfortable with upper middle class life in New York. And he'd just never be that.

So, he hadn't brought any formal clothes. He was packing a plasma pistol. But he couldn't shake the feeling he'd become the odd man out.

She could choose some local guy and settle into a traditional upper middle-class life in the City. Literally, he could provide that for her...tell his family to stick it and take a job as a manager with some New York bank or vid channel.

Maybe that's what she wanted.

This was the same reason he'd used to justify going along with Howell's pitch for more security money back at school. After all the bullshit that he'd put up with being a Hailwood, it seemed stupid to pretend the family money didn't exist. He planned to use it to make the life that he wanted. A life that combined some City living and true academia.

It seemed to him that *that* was the real romantic choice.

Kate's parents understood this…somewhat. They might have put it differently, maybe some cliché about the rich being different. But it was a difference they wanted for Kate. They'd done well, financially. And so, living in New York, they'd seen wealth firsthand. But the Byrnes were still managers at heart. They—especially the father—couldn't give up on the idea of moving their daughter up the social ladder.

Hailwood laughed at himself in the mirror. This really didn't sound good.

On his way out of the hotel, he cashed in for some New York dollars. He wanted to buy a bottle of wine and some flowers to take the Byrnes. And, if he and Kate were going out with friends after dinner, that was going to be pricey…and cash-intensive.

At the front desk, he pulled $1,000 from his main Tampa account. This was probably more than it was wise to carry around in New York. But he was staying in better neighborhoods.

He walked west, across the southern edge of Central Park and north, eight blocks up Central Park West. The weather was near perfect and there was then still some late-afternoon light left. So, he actually cut through the corner of the Park.

The plan was that he was having dinner with Kate's family at their apartment. Then, he and Kate and some of Kate's friends would head out to their favorite clubs.

Tomorrow, he'd spend the day with Kate and her mother, going to a Museum or two and maybe doing some shopping. Then, she and her parents would come down to the Plaza for drinks with him and he'd take them out to dinner.

After that, there was no plan. He and Kate would try to figure out how they were going to proceed.

It was unclear whether Kate was planning to stay with him at the hotel or at her parent's apartment. He'd gotten a big room, just in case.

Their apartment was in a nice, rather generic building in the mid 70s. It was Upper West Side, with all that meant. Since the Federal Era, the UWS had been the place where managers on the rise had lived. It was a safe, status-conscious neighborhood. A cautious executive couldn't go wrong living there.

The doorman scanned his palm and his right eye and let him into the building. The concierge walked him through the arch scanner (it didn't pick up the plasma gun, which made him smile; maybe it was just for looks) and called up to the Byrnes'. In a minute, Hailwood was one the elevator.

"Terry, how are you doing?" Kate's father welcomed him into their apartment. Like the building, it was tasteful and pricey but a little plain. This was how the Byrnes…and all their neighbors… liked things. They had the money to decorate in a more dramatic or original style. But they didn't have the desire. They wanted to fit in. "The gals are just getting ready. How was the trip down?"

"Okay. The flight was smooth. But the Blue Zone north of Hartford is a little surreal."

"Jeez. Let me get you a drink. And tell me more about what Hartford looks like."

Byrne made a couple of martinis and they spun agreeable, just slightly argumentative (her father was all for New York taking over Hartford) chit-chat for a couple of minutes until Kate joined them.

Byrne took the law-and-order line. Hartford had invited brigand attacks because it was badly managed and had famously poor security.

Hailwood made the argument—which he wasn't even sure he believed—that New York was stretching its reach to move so far north. "…one of the main things that I've learned from reading a lot of Julius Caesar and Xenophon is that it's a really bad idea to extend your supply lines too far. And if New York plans to make its walls north of the Windsor Locks airfield…that's more than 100 miles north of here."

"150—but who's counting? SoCal is close to 400 miles, north to south. And 100 miles inland from the Pacific. That's practically a nation, compared to us."

"Hi, dad. Hi, Terry. I see you guys are already mixing it up."

"Well, Terry has always been so low key about the dangers up there in the wasteland. And now that the City is doing something about the bandits, he makes it sound like that's a bad thing."

She gave him a hug and a kiss on the cheek. Not passionate. But happy. Not bad.

"How you doing, Kate?" She looked good to him. She always would.

"I'm doing great. How was your trip?" She squinted her eyes at him. The squint was one of her ways of flirting.

"Good. Short flight."

She was wearing a short, brown and white herringbone skirt over a black body stocking. Her hair was pulled back in a simple ponytail. Almost no make-up, so you could see the freckles on her cheeks. Very Upper West Side.

Not very wasteland.

Maybe her good looks were the problem. At the core, they were what he liked most about her. He'd always told himself this wasn't as shallow as it might sound. Her looks suggested many things to him—the kids he wanted to have, the enjoyable life he wanted to live and the kind of woman he wanted to wake up next to when he was an old man.

Or, if it was shallow, maybe he was just a shallow person. Maybe all he wanted in love was an attractive, educated woman who would provide him a stable, pleasant life. Not the freak show that his parents and grandparents had had.

She'd always seemed a good bet for stability. That's why her recent turn was so disorienting.

Her mother, Mary Beth, joined them a little after Kate had. Mary Beth was the typical Big City career woman. Well appointed and well maintained. Practical, but with a carefully-crafted girlishness. She was smaller than Kate and had finer features. And the differences added up. While she was certainly a good-looking middle-aged woman, Mary Beth's looks had a brittleness that didn't appeal to Hailwood.

He didn't try to develop the flirtatious rap that some guys had with their girlfriends' mothers. And he didn't go for the sugary slop of calling the parents "mom" and "dad." His approach to Kate's parents was straight and unironic. He was interested in their daughter and, to that end, he wanted a good relationship with them. That was all.

Kate's younger brother, P.J., joined them for dinner. Hailwood felt bad for the kid.

Everyone did. He was 15 and hadn't done well in school for the past few years. So, the parents had decided to put P.J. through a radical stem-cell and nanotech therapy that was supposed boost his IQ and improve his mental discipline.

Normally, these therapies were performed gradually on boys with high-risk genetic markers before they reached puberty. The intense regime for older boys was the idea of a contrarian doctor at one of New York's big research hospitals. And there were plenty of frantic, high-achieving parents around to keep his test groups filled.

It was impossible to say whether the cells and implants were making P.J. any smarter—but they certainly did kill his appetite and make him alternately jittery and listless.

The last time Hailwood had come to New York, Byrne and Mary Beth had explained P.J.'s stoned demeanor as a "chrysalis stage" before the therapy took effect and the kid became a razor-sharp go-getter.

The go-getter hadn't yet emerged from the shell.

No matter what anyone else said over drinks and dinner, Kate's father kept bringing the conversation back to City politics. He was fascinated with the annexation of Hartford—through he didn't like the word "annexation." In the jargon of the day, he called it a "security action." And, when Hailwood had said everything he knew about the conditions in Hartford and everyone had had a few cocktails, Byrne moved on to how New York compared to Tampa.

They drifted into the dining room, where their maid/cook had set out a TexMex spread.

Kate's father switched from martinis to beer and kept going with his vid-pundit observations. "...I mean, I have the greatest respect for way your family and the others do business down there. It's like a corporate dictatorship. Or an oligarchy."

"Yeah. That's the word you hear most often. *Oligarchy.*" Hailwood was drinking a lot of water. He wasn't about to get shit-faced drunk at dinner.

This dinner might have been the high point of Byrne's weekend; but it was just Hailwood's first act. He and Kate were going out with her friends later.

"Right."

"But I'm sure that's really accurate—"

"Oh, of course it is. Your grandfather and that board do things right. They make clear decisions. They don't agonize and go back and forth. They stay out of the way of their big companies. They make things work." This wasn't anything like how the Hailwoods were. But he didn't see any profit in correcting his estranged girlfriend's father. "Up here, we're too much of a meritocracy. Too much of a democracy. That's just the way New Yorkers are. But if we can learn a little directness from Cities like Tampa and New Orleans and SoCal, then we'll get things fixed up north."

This is the way her father liked it: He and Hailwood mixing it up, the "girls" chiming in every few minutes with some insight or opinion. For a while, he and Mary Beth had invited various friends to these dinners. But, after one particularly loud and crowded one, Hailwood had told Kate he felt on display. She'd passed the word back to her parents who—to their credit—stopped.

After a few more minutes of Byrne's boozy flattery about Tampa's clarity, he couldn't resist some correction. "My grandfather wouldn't like to hear that you think he 'runs' anything. He believes very strongly that a…a long-term investor should stay in the background and hire executives to set policy and make decisions."

"Well, I'm sure that's what he says. But everyone knows who calls the shots in Tampa."

P.J. was picking noncommittally at his fajitas.

Kate seemed content to play along with her assigned role in her father's production. Hailwood reminded himself to take his cues from that.

"Suppose so, suppose so. He still wouldn't like to admit it." Now he felt like he was selling out the Old Man.

Mary Beth gave him a wan smile when he made eye contact with her.

Kate's friends showed up around 11. There were five of them, three girls and two guys. Hailwood didn't pay a lot of attention to these others—the girls were generically Big City with a dash of goth. One of the guys was a boyfriend; the other was the obligatory gay eunuch type. In Tampa, they called these guys Duckies.

Kate had gone to high school with the girls…and maybe with the Duckie. They were all kind of buzzed and the details weren't very clear. Now, the girls were going to better colleges in New York. Kate was the only one who'd gone away for school. But the group seemed to have digested her recent experiences. They weren't interested in talking about that any more. Instead, it was giggly gossip about people Hailwood didn't know.

They climbed into two cabs and headed to a speakeasy-style bar. In what passed for a shady neighborhood.

In fact, there weren't any shady neighborhoods in Manhattan. Even the worst ones were carefully developed, fully populated and well-policed.

The speakeasy was underneath a diner. In order to get in, you had to go downstairs and walked into the men's bathroom—which wasn't really a bathroom. It was the entrance to a long hallway that opened up into a large wood-paneled room with a great oak bar.

It really looked like a speakeasy from the Federal Era. They'd outlawed alcohol at some point in 1900s—Hailwood had always imagined that period like a throwback to the Puritans and hanging witches. Religious yokels taking power from their better-educated fellows. Now the yokels were banished to the wasteland. And speakeasies were ironic themes.

Hailwood ordered the first round of drinks. Beers and a couple of whiskeys.

The girls headed off to the bathroom at some point and when they came back their gossip was louder and more vicious than it had been before. They were using something, maybe Pleasure. Maybe Neurac.

He'd met these girls before, on previous trips to New York. He'd never thought much about them; and they were past being curious about him.

He tried to make some conversation with the boyfriend. The guy was studying media at NYU. Hailwood said that his degree was in Rhetoric. School talk didn't interest the boyfriend much. He was keeping his eyes on the girl he'd come with. They couldn't have been going out very long if he was still this uptight about her.

Hailwood got another round of drinks.

During a lull in the gossip, he tried to talk to Kate. "Your dad was in fine form tonight."

"Yeah, I'd say. He's been drinking a lot more recently. And my mother is kind of worried. She thinks that he's having problems at work and doesn't want to say so."

He wasn't sure what to do with that. "Well, all managers have stress about work. It goes with the territory."

"I guess so. But they'll put him out to pasture if he has to go to detox again."

Her father had gone to detox for an addiction to unprescribed Neuroplex/Vision pills when Kate was about 10. It had taken weeks to get him off of the illegal pills and back to his right prescription.

"Well, as long as he doesn't drive, it's hard to get in trouble with booze."

"Guess so."

She plugged back into the gossip with the girls. He ordered another whiskey.

The room started getting crowded as the clock inched past midnight. One of the girls said they should go dancing.

Everyone liked that idea.

They managed to hail two cabs—but there were a few minutes in between. Kate went ahead with first group. That left Hailwood with two of the girls. They gave the cabbie the address and chatted nonstop. It wasn't exactly unfriendly. They acknowledged him and even tried to pull him into the chatter.

"...I mean, I'm sure this all sounds so stupid to you, Terry, but people can be such assholes here. I mean, you think someone's you're friend—you've known her for years and years—and then you find out that she's shagging your boyfriend. And why is she doing this? Because someone that she hardly knows says that she's boring and does the right things for the wrong reasons."

What was there to say to that? "Sure. It sounds stupid. But, you know, it never changes—no matter where you go or how old you get. People do damaging things for stupid reasons. For no reason. You just have to let it go. Don't let yourself get so worked up about it. Life is pretty random. Try to avoid the trouble-makers."

"You're so right. Life is pretty random. That's just so right. But you'd hate to think that it gets better at some point. I mean, I wouldn't want to be like my parents age and still have all this BS going on."

"You'd be surprised. Ask your parents next time you see them about what affairs their friends have had. And why."

They both squealed. "I could never ask my parents something like that! I mean, they're so formal and serious about things. I don't think they'd ever just talk about stuff like which of their friends are shagging who."

"No that's not true, Bette. My mother totally told me that Mr. Parks is having an affair with Jess Malanowski's mother."

"What? Ohmagod!"

"Yeah."

"Terry, how old are you?"

"26."

"I mean you're like almost our age but you know things like my parents do."

"And you talk like my dad."

"Yeah, you remind me of dad too."

"Well, there's a big difference between 21 and 26." He had no idea if he meant anything he was saying. It was just bullshit filtered through whiskey (for him) and Pleasure (for the girls).

"No. It's more than that. You're an old soul. That's what my mother calls it."

Thankfully, the cab got to the dance club. The girls slid out to the passenger-side door. Hailwood paid the fare.

Inside, it was another church that had been converted into a dance club.

Were there any more actual churches left in New York?

Kate was standing at the perimeter of the dance floor with the couple and the Duckie. Hailwood gave her quick hug. She kissed him but pulled away first.

It was hard to make out what the music was, exactly. This was true of most fashionable big City clubs. The sound systems played up the base line and drum beat. Melody and lyrics weren't important. So, all the songs sounded the same.

It wasn't Hailwood's scene. The dancers were all bobbing up and down in distracted unison, which meant they were taking Imagery or Happiness or some other trippy Neuroplex. Plus, the crowd seemed too old—most of the people looked like they were in the 30s. And that meant some were probably in their 50s or 60s. So many people in New York were doing age therapy, you couldn't believe your eyes.

Kate wanted to dance. So he did. He was happy for any sign of passion in her. They'd met each other on the dance floor of a party at her college. And they'd always liked dancing with each other.

After a couple of songs, she started talking to him in short bursts in rhythm with the beat.

He couldn't make out everything she said. But it had something to do with Bette, the lesser of the two girls who'd shared the last cab with him.

"...really nervous about it...said I didn't care...she's really sweet...better you than some jerk..."

He shrugged his shoulders and pogoed around in a circle. This was their shorthand for he couldn't understand and didn't want to talk.

After another song, he'd had enough and nodded his head toward the bar. She agreed.

The bar wasn't too crowded. He ordered a couple beers—he was too winded for whiskey—and they faced the room with their bottles.

"So, what do you think?"

"About what?"

"About Bette."

"Bette?"

"Yeah. About taking her back to your hotel?"

"What?"

"She wants to have sex with you."

"Are you joking?"

"No."

"I'm not going to shag some friend of yours." He used the word "shag" because he'd heard the girls using it in the cab.

"I don't mind."

"That's not the point, Kate."

"She's just in a bad place right now and needs some physical affection. That's all. She's sweet."

"What the hell has gotten into you? Why would I want to have sex with someone who's in a bad place?"

"Because she's lonely."

"Well, there are hundreds of guys in this room right now who'll help her with that."

"No. There are lots of creeps here who are her dad's age."

"Maybe she's lonely because she's picky."

"And I don't mind."

"I know. I heard you the first time."

"I don't know why you're being so thorny about this. I thought you'd be excited about this."

"You've got to be kidding, Kate. I came down here to patch things up with you. Not to get involved with one of your friends."

"She just needs to feel pretty to someone."

"I can't believe you're saying this. I'm supposed to spend the day tomorrow with your family."

"We can still do all that."

He looked hard at her. She looked at him weakly and then turned away. Her eyes weren't noticeably dilated. She didn't seem to be sweating profusely. No obvious signs of being high. And her eyebrows had their normal, arched irony. Maybe she was trying to test him somehow.

"Okay, here's what I'll do. If you and Bette both come back to the hotel with me, we can all have sex."

"I'm not gay, Terry."

"You don't have to be. We'll all go together."

"I'm no sure that she'll agree to that."

"Then she's not as lonely as you say." He took a drink of his beer and scanned the room.

There was no way this could be good for patching things up with her. It didn't really matter what either said; the fact she was suggesting he have sex with one of her friends meant she was done with him.

And he was drunk. "You're the only person I came down here to shag."

"We need to see other people, Terry. Our lives are heading in different directions. In order to understand me, you need to lose sometime. And I don't think you ever will."

"Bullshit. You've always wanted to come back here. That's not new. We can still make that happen."

She drained the last of her beer. "I'm going to ask Bette if she wants to dance with us."

He hadn't even paid that much attention to Bette. She was unremarkable in every way to him—medium height, medium build. An ordinary oval-shaped face, buried under a lot of Goth make-up. She'd been in Kate's high school class, which made her 21 or 22; but, in the present fashion, she talked like a little girl.

She fit most conventions of attraction.

It was a little awkward dancing together, at first. But a few shots of tequila took the edge off that.

Hailwood found and focused on Bette's most attractive feature: Her eyes. They were light blue. Like the girl who'd been on the tiltrotor into town.

Some time around two, they stumbled out of the church/club and hailed a cab back to the Plaza. The hotel was surprisingly alive for so late. Welcome to New York.

When they got up to the room, Hailwood poured some tequila and played a mix disc that he'd brought from school. Bette took a vial of cocaine out of her purse—she and Kate had been using at the clubs but she still had a lot left. This was a bigger deal here in town because the white powder was, in theory, contraband. But Hailwood had become so desensitized to drugs at college that he couldn't even pretend to be impressed. At least it wasn't Neurac.

He did take the Viatrate sex pills that she offered.

Bette was aggressive. She took her clothes off quickly, between rails of coke and before her first shot of tequila. She was in good shape but didn't have Kate's natural curves.

It took Kate longer to start taking her clothes off. She needed more coke—and, even with it, she kept her underwear for a while.

When Hailwood started taking his clothes off, Bette was immediately drawn to his plasma pistol. That was *real* contraband in the City.

He let her hold it because there was not chance that she could shoot anyone. It had a biometric safety.

She struck various old-fashioned sexy girl poses around the living room. She and Bette both thought this was very funny. Hailwood laughed to be a good sport. This night was going to be all about Bette.

She kissed him hard on the mouth and grabbed his cock. The sex stims were just taking effect.

Then, she tumbled over to Kate and tried to kiss her. But, high as she was, Kate pulled away. "I don't want to do this out here. Let's go to into the bedroom."

So they did.

Kate liked being on top. Bette liked every position they could think of. Bette kept trying to kiss or caress Kate; Kate kept pulling away. She was serious about not doing anything sexual with Bette. Eventually, she did let Bette massage her back and breasts and she came a couple of times.

Bette screeched and grunted so much, it was hard to tell how many times she came. She was multi-orgasmic…and she didn't want to leave any doubts about that.

Kate was off by a long shot about Bette. She didn't need to feel pretty. She needed to show everyone that she was a freak. Several times, she went out to the living room for drugs and tequila.

With the sex stims, Hailwood lasted about an hour. He could have taken more of the pills—Bette had plenty—but he fell asleep.

He woke up with a pretty bad headache. There was a music video playing on the TV. Loud. How had he slept through that?

Kate was asleep next to him. He hated to get up. The bed was really comfortable and he liked lying awake all morning with Kate. But he knew he needed some ice water.

He switched the TV off on his way out.

It was late morning. Saturday morning was buzzing. By the time he finished his first glass of water, Bette was pulling on her shoes.

"You're a great shag, Bette. Did you get any sleep?"

"A little."

"Where are you heading?"

"Home. Still live at home. And I've got family stuff to do today."

"This was fun."

"Yeah. I'm surprised Kate went for it."

"Well, I think she's in a...transitional place."

She took a shot of tequila. "Transitional place, yeah." She kissed him on the mouth again. She tasted like blue agave and chlorine. "You sound *so much* like my father." And she grabbed her bag and banged out the door. "If you want to do this again, Kate has my number."

He called up a continental breakfast and brought his screen into bed. He read the news while Kate groaned awake. Bette fucked like a hooker. And there was something appealing in that. But it wasn't what Hailwood wanted.

Kate recovered well for the rest of the weekend, which went according to plan.

She went with him to the helipad when he took off Sunday afternoon. And she agreed to come up to the College in a couple weeks—which she did.

But she was right. They were heading in different directions.

Hailwood could pull as hard as anyone. But he was swimming against the tide.

Twenty-one

Crowley, vieux Guibert and Guibert's son Jean Jacques drove with an escort of students about five hours south from Camp A to examine a couple of boats that an older student wanted to donate to the Company.

The roads between New Orleans and Houston were well-maintained and busy. The Old Interstate that connected the Cities' walls was one of the most-used stretches of road anywhere in the wasteland; it was a toll road, operated by a Houston-based company. The same company also maintained two smaller roads that stretched down to the Gulf coast.

Their three-vehicle motorcade was able to make good time on the toll roads, even though the roads got rougher as they dropped farther south from the Old Interstate. They'd started at dawn and reached Grande Isle before noon. By the time they got there, the toll road wasn't much more than a single passable lane.

New Orleans and Houston had grabbed most of the inlets along the Gulf coast, but there were still a few dozen small coves and harbors left to free use. Grand Isle was a village that controlled one of the largest of these. There was room in its harbor for 20 or 30 mid-sized commercial vessels. Right now, that harbor was dominated by two older security boats. Each was docked against a separate pier that otherwise would hold four or five fishing boats. Even so, the security boats didn't really fit in their spaces.

No one in Crowley's group was a naval expert. But Crowley knew a little about ocean-going security hardware from his time in Tampa. And Jean Jacques had a screen hooked up to a satphone. So, he could search the City nets for details on these two boats.

The man who was giving the boats to the Company was nowhere near. He lived on a farm somewhere north of Houston.

Instead, a couple of nervous Cajuns who wouldn't make eye contact led them down to the piers and onto the boats.

Jean Jacques barked orders to the students, who headed out around the boats with cameras and 3-D imaging units that had been rigged up for ultrasound.

The boats were nearly identical—old Coast Guard cutters from the Federal Era that had been converted into missile platforms during the Reckoning. Houston had used them for a few years, then swapped them to a privateer captain for...something...in a shady deal. The privateer captain had used them in the Gulf for a long time, leaving them to his son who—like many sons—drove his father's operation into the shoals. Then, the trail got muddy. The Spanish instructions and warnings stenciled onto the decks and bulkheads suggested that they been used in some official capacity in South America. But someone had cared for them at some point. They'd been refitted with updated hydrofoil propulsion and nav systems.

The missile launching hardware was so old that it was practically useless. But, if they could tear that out and make room for a couple of tiltrotors and troops, the boats might be useful.

Vieux Guibert was not impressed. "There are rusting hulks like these in every harbor on the Gulf, Rabbi. Finding a boat is easy. Fixing it and finding a captain to drive it are the hard parts, eh?"

Crowley stopped near the front of one of the cutters and stared along the waterline toward the aft. It was a big boat and its lines still seemed to be true.

"I know that naval power is considered old-fashioned, Guibert. But most our business is close to the Gulf. I can't help believing that it would be useful to have a good way to move students from one place to another quickly."

"*D'accord*. But you move them through the air."

His son walked quickly down the gangplank and approached them. He was excited. "They're in good shape, Rabbi. Better than they seem. Underneath all of the cheap paint. Very little rust. Good bones, eh? Engines fire up. And the hydrofoil systems look like they work. Need some attention, though."

"Can we move them down to the docks at Camp C?"

"Oh, sure. *No problema*. As long as our channels into C stay clear, these should make it fine."

"Okay, then. Let's get them down there for some work. And maybe some better paint. And I'll put out word to the franchises that we're looking for people with naval experience."

Young Guibert walked his father and Crowley through each of the boats one more time. The father said nothing, which was as close as he'd come to backing away from his earlier doubt. Two hours later, Crowley and vieux Guibert headed back to Camp A. They left half a dozen of students and one of the trucks with the boats and young Guibert. They'd call for another couple of vehicles to bring down supplies and some able bodies to get the boats on their way.

The Company was a decentralized organization. It had units—after a lot of thought, Crowley had landed on the term "franchises"—in various places, but each operated independently. The unifying mechanism was a series of video reading lessons that the Company posted to a stand-alone site hosted by a free net with loose, and deniable, ties to Brownsville.

The vids were their best recruiting tools. And they were the main reason that the name *Rabbi* had stuck to Crowley. The Brownsville Road farmers had started calling him that; a few did on the first vids. And it had taken off from there.

This was an important lesson that Crowley had learned in the last year. Ideas, like people, had lives of their own. He'd decided not to resist that any more. In fact, he tried to follow it. So, even though he was central to the Company, he didn't control it the way a CEO controlled a City.

In the Cities, people responded more predictably; so decision-makers—the people managing people and ideas—could afford to sloppy from time to time. In the wasteland, a leader was more of an instructor who suggested directions than a manager who made decisions.

At first it had been humbling for Crowley. Then, fairly quickly, he'd seen the benefits of the difference. Because the Company had a life of its own, he wasn't so essential to every step and measure. And the politics of the organization wouldn't be as intense as in a City.

For the franchises, he was an advisor more than a boss. And, even among his own students, he tried to avoid giving orders.

But then, just when he was starting to believe that the Company was autonomous, something like the security boats would come along. And he'd buck against the advice of his counselors and force some point because he was certain he knew better.

Maybe they weren't as decentralized as he'd hoped.

For several months, an army of bandits had been gathering in the cypress stands north of Camp A. Crowley's company hadn't paid them much attention, since the bandits talked freely and told vieux Guibert and other locals that they were planning to mount an attack on Houston's northern gates. Their leaders said they'd either breach the walls or take control of the camps outside of Houston.

Like most bandits, they talked tough but had scared eyes. Guibert didn't take them seriously, so Crowley didn't either.

He and Jana and some of the others followed their normal circuit—east to Camp B and then southwest to Camp C. They would have lessons in small towns and villages along the way. And sometimes they'd go out of their way to teach some lessons at farms or villages that had invited them. Crowley would always wear the same white shirt and red vest combination that he's started wearing in the early days along the Brownsville Road. It helped new people recognize him on the barn or trailer or porch—wherever he might be teaching.

A standard lesson would draw a few hundred students. A few of the exceptional ones would draw thousands.

Crowley's program was the same, regardless of the size of the audience. He had six basic lessons, ranging from beginners' letters and phonics to word attack techniques and paragraph reading. For the more advanced lessons, he used the Bible as the text because it was the only book that most people, even in back reaches of the wasteland, had or could find. The Company was doing as much as it could to produce inexpensive screens that came stocked with free net access and the Bible, *Animal Farm* and a few other Great Books. But, no matter how many they had shipped into Camp C or a friendly port in Brownsville, there were always more—and more—people. Broken ones, with downward gazes who'd come to the lessons dirty, hungry and ignorant.

"They're not all going to be Bill Atell," Jana had said, "with wonderful stories about how reading changed their lives. Most will never say anything. Most will take the food and screens and the place to live. And they won't ever know what to say. But you'll make their lives better."

She was right. And she'd essentially restated an advanced management lesson, called the Pareto Prime. You manage for peak efficiency across a population, which often means targeting 80 percent productivity operating at 20 percent capacity. You provide adequate deliverables to your market—and let excellent outliers like Atell emerge from the masses.

But something about this seemed wrong to Crowley.

The reading lessons had become as much about raising money and organizing students as they were about actual teaching. There were dozens of high-quality vids (and hundreds more not-so-high) on the free nets that people could watch. Still, Crowley aimed his lessons at people who couldn't read. Even if some had seen his lessons on a screen, they could use the basic steps as review. And the opening and closing remarks as motivation.

The important thing was that the Company was attracting new people. The troubling thing was that so were the bandit armies. On the low end of the market for wasteland hearts and minds, the Company and the bandits were competitors.

Even thought it was decentralized, the Company was an organization. The bandit armies weren't. But both were growing because they promised people something more than what they had—which was very little. The bandits promised more things. The Company promised more wisdom and a better life...which, frankly, implied more things.

The few times that Crowley had any dealings with bandit chiefs, they seemed too scared and ignorant to offer much. They didn't think strategically—they were, at best, opportunistic. The brown-skin bandits near Camp C ran drugs in the wasteland south of Brownsville. Some of them sold cocaine and Neurac to thrill-seeking teenagers from the City—which was a stupid idea. The Brownsville Security Forces had started running missions beyond its still-new walls burn out bandits because they'd become an external security threat.

Several times, Crowley tried to set up a meeting with *jefe* of the bandits south of Brownsville. But it never worked. Somehow, the *jefe* had heard that Crowley was the man who'd shot Captain Tripps.

When Crowley came back again to Camp A, it had been almost three months. And Guibert was more worried about the bandits there. "They have fine weapons. Brand new guns. As good as Houston Security stuff. I'd surely like to know where these *mal a tetes* get such clean hardware."

Crowley didn't need to hear any more. They had to do something about the bandits to the north.

Jean Jacques had already sketched out an attack plan. Their spies—if you could call them that; the bandits seemed happy to talk about anything to anyone—had reported that the bandit army was organized into three groups that lived in three separate forts. Jean Jacques's plan was that the company would break the bandit army apart, hitting the forts at the same moment and killing as many bad guys as possible. The survivors would be flushed away from one another in different directions.

Two nights later, just after midnight, Crowley left Jana and Mikey in their tent and joined vieux Guibert for the ride north.

"You really must come on this ride. Rabbi? I can't convince you to stay? This is not an important battle. It's a dawn raid. If we do it well, we will be finished in an hour and the bandits will be hiding in the brush."

"I want to see whether they fight. And, if they do, how. I think the success of these bandits speaks to our own shortcomings. We should be drawing their men into our Company."

"Into our Company? *Mais non*, Rabbi. These bandits could not think about Godly things for even a moment. They don't have the minds to learn to read. They want only three things: Drugs, gold and women. If they wanted God or knowledge, they would have found the way into our Company already."

"That's what I used to think about everyone in the wasteland. But I've learned different. I believe some of the bandits are just poor souls who want more from their lives."

"You are a good man, Rabbi. You see the best in bad things."

"I'm not a good man, *pere* Guibert. I'm a bad man trying to do good."

A little before three in the morning, they dropped from their horses, hooded the animals and signaled the students that they'd arrived. Crowley and Guibert were on the high ground—such as it was—of the area. It was hard to see much of the bandit fort. To Crowley, it didn't look like much more than a wooden fence about six feet high.

"There have more than 100 men sleeping in there. Each of their units seems to be 100," Guibert whispered. "They sleep in framed tents, like ours. Johnny thinks some of them *were* students. They've copied too much for it to be chance."

"No surprise. We need to get those back."

"Okay. But you're the one who says a person can't convert by the sword."

"First the sword. Later, the conversion."

"Yes, first the sword. Johnny and his boys are going to start the bombing. So, cover your ears."

Jean Jacques and his students had set up a half circle of mortar nests that would deliver a devastating field of fire on the bandit fort. Most of their shells were simple incendiaries—the lightest to carry and easiest to use. But they also had a few green gas shells to mix in with the fire. Green gas wasn't fatal…but it was toxic enough to set the bandits running for air.

"Will we need gas masks?"

"I think not. But you never know how the wind blows. You should have yours handy."

Right at three, a series of hollow *thonks* sounded all around them. Within 10 seconds, explosions filled the woods. The fence was almost immediately knocked down and burning.

Crowley could hear echo booms from elsewhere in the woods. Other Company units were attacking the other bandit forts.

It was still hard to see much from where he stood. Plus, Crowley had to keep his horse calm—even through the hood, the sounds of the shell blasts were spooking him.

But the explosion flashes gave off a strobe-light effect that, once his eyes adjusted, made some of the scene visible. This group of bandits didn't look like 100; it was probably closer to 40 or 50. They were screaming and trying to get organized…but the shells were making that impossible. The best that the brightest of them could do was find cover.

After a couple of minutes of incendiaries, their gunners switched to the gas shells. The loud bangs and flashes of light gave way to dull thuds and hissing.

It had been years since Crowley had been near toxic gas—but the rancid smell of the green mist rushed straight to the back of his throat. He gagged a little and pulled his gas mask around his neck. If it got any stronger, he'd pull up the mask.

The shelling stopped for a few moments while the gas seeped up around what was left of the fort, probably 100 yards from where Crowley and vieux Guibert were standing with their horses.

They could hear grunts and screams among the bandits on the other side of the smoldering fence.

Some rifle shots clanged out from the fort. Crowley drew his plasma pistol—but Guibert put a hand on his shoulder. "That's not a counter-attack, Rabbi. That's cover. They're running."

A slower procession of incendiary mortars thonked toward the bandits' fort. This time, as they exploded, Crowley could hear and feel the pattern. It started close to them, to his right, and worked north, which was his left. If the survivors weren't already running, they would be now.

After the farthest shell blasted, there was another few moments of quiet. Then Jean Jacques and his unit put on their masks and swept into the fort to inspect what was left.

An hour later, with the first light of dawn just creeping in the sky to the east, they had the survivors from the bandit fort pinned in a small hollow.

Jean Jacques's men recognized their good position almost immediately. They set up laser perimeter pylons in seconds. The pylons gave them triangulation; any time a living creature broke one of the planes, they directed their cross-fire at that point. It took two dead bandits before someone in the bandit crew figured out they were trapped.

In the meantime, Jean Jacques put on a pair of infrared specs and scanned the hollow. He told Crowley that there looked like about two dozen people hiding there.

And the sun was rising. Daylight would make shooting them easier.

"Hello, hello? Okay. We want a parley. We'll send someone out."

Jean Jacques looked at Crowley and shrugged. Crowley shook his head no.

Jean Jacques yelled back. "No parley. You all drop your

weapons and come out to the clearing here with your hands on your heads. You've got 10 seconds. Then we're going to lay down a field of plasma fire and kill all of you."

Nineteen of them came out with their hands up.

The students told them to lie down face-first in the clearing. They did.

Jean Jacques signaled that he saw two more warm bodies in the brush. Crowley nodded.

"We see two more of you still in the brush. Now come on out while you can."

The two bandits started running toward the back of the hollow. They were cut down by a cross-fire of plasma and bullets.

That done, the rest of the company troops moved from their positions.

Again, Jean Jacques's unit moved with impressive speed. The men reset the laser pylons around the prisoners in the clearing—in a circle 25 or 30 feet across. They set up three robotic plasma guns in roughly equidistant positions around the circle. The guns were set, as before, to fire at anything that broke the laser perimeter. The prisoners seemed to have absorbed the lesson that the red light bands between the pylons were deadly. They didn't try to run.

Crowley and the Guiberts, *pere et fils*, spent some time looking over the weapons that the prisoners had been carrying. It was a mixed menu. There were some top-quality plasma weapons, as they'd feared. But there were also some barely functioning projectile weapons that any kid could buy at a wasteland trading post.

Jean Jacques—a slightly taller, 30-years-younger copy of his father—was impatient with the lengthy debate over where the bandits had gotten their plasma guns. "They're bandits. Maybe they just stole the plasma rifles from some citizens out looking for drugs."

His father shook his head. "No. If they came from a City, they would have markings and serial numbers inscribed. If they were smart—and most bandits aren't—they might grind those numbers off. But these rifles are blank. They never had serial numbers. See?" He pointed to the place on the butt where a serial number was normally etched. "This didn't come from Houston or New Orleans or any other City."

That seemed to end the debate. But they still didn't have a good answer for how the bandits were getting high-quality weapons.

"So you mean Peerless or CINCON is manufacturing phantom plasma rifles for bandits? That doesn't make sense. Gun-makers are careful about their contracts with the City Security Forces. They wouldn't risk all of that legitimate business for some measly barter trade with wasteland riffraff."

Peerless and CINCON were the two biggest gun makers in North America., based in Chicago and SoCal, respectively. They dominated the markets for sidearms and personal weapons. It was logical that they were the brands that the Guiberts mentioned first—but they were overlooking the fact that they had a channel for information from that industry.

The old gunsmith at TAG would know if one of his big competitors was making phantom rifles. Crowley didn't say anything—but he planned to contact the gunsmith.

Then again, there was a slight chance that TAG had made these. But Crowley doubted that. Even if the old gunsmith had taken such a contract, he'd have let word of it pass through Brian.

Once more, Jean Jacques wanted the debate to end: "Then maybe these weren't made by one of the big weapons companies. Maybe these are made by some small operator."

"*Non.* This is a Peerless rifle. I'd know it anywhere. Same weight, same scoping."

Crowley sighed and walked to a point of plain sight, a few feet in front of the laser pylons. He told two of Jean Jacques's men to pick one out of the 19 out from the holding pen.

They brought one out and held him up, one holding each shoulder.

Crowley drew his plasma pistol and held it up where the bandit could see it. "Do you speak English?"

"Yes."

"Good. Then listen to me carefully." Crowley rested the charge point of his plasma pistol against the bandit's left temple. "I'm going to ask you some questions. It's important that you answer my questions quickly and truthfully. If you don't…if I think that you're lying or playing games or giving me any kind of partial truth…I will kill you and bring out the next man. Do you understand what I'm saying to you?"

"Yes."

"There's no reason for you hide behind any idea of honor or loyalty to your crew or anything like this. Your crew has been broken up. It doesn't exist anymore. Do you understand?"

"Yes."

"Good. Do you see the plasma rifle my comrade is hold up over there?"

Jean Jacques lifted the phantom rifle.

"Yes."

"Did you use one like this?"

"Yes."

"Do you know what model it is?"

"Yes. Peerless PPW."

"Right. How did you get this PPW plasma rifle that costs something like 3,000 Chicago dollars?"

"Chief give me the gun."

"Why did the chief give you the gun?"

"I'm a good shooter."

"When did the chief give you the gun?"

"I don't know." Crowley twisted the pistol against his head. "I don't know how to read time."

"I mean how long ago did he give you the gun? A few days ago? A year ago?"

"I don't know. I don't know how to read days."

"Well, maybe your chief can tell me when. Is he in the holding pen here?"

"No. Chief is dead."

"Really? How do you know that?"

"Cause one of the bombs killed him and his guards. I saw it."

"Okay. The chief's dead. Are there any sub-commanders in the pen here?"

"Yes."

"Okay, then show me who's in charge."

The two students dragged the bandit along the laser gate until he cocked his head toward a stocky man with fair skin and a long red ponytail.

Crowley told another two of Jean Jacques's troops to bring out the sub-commander. When they had, he moved the pistol to the new bandit's head. "Okay, here's how this is going to work. If you start in with how this guy was lying when he said you were an officer, I'm going to kill both of you and start all over again. Do you understand?"

"Yeah."

"Where did you get these nice guns?"

"The chief got them from some contact he had in Houston."

"What 'contact'?"

"I don't know. No one does. He kept that secret. But it was somebody high up. Every few weeks, the chiefs and the *jefe* would ride out and meet their contact and get some guns."

"How did they pay for the guns?"

"All different ways. Pharma. Gold. Different ways all the time. Truth is I don't know. They kept that stuff secret."

Crowley asked a few more questions about how the bandits planned their attacks on farms and villages—but these were designed to cover the importance of the gun information. He'd already gotten the answers he'd really wanted.

"So Peerless makes some phantom guns as a favor for Houston Security Forces. They hide the phantom guns in the regular shipments to HSF. HSF carts them off to a special program to arm bandits outside the walls. It's an old manager's trick. When I was in Tampa, we called these kinds of bandits 'privateers.' And it was the same idea. We'd give them guns and money to keep order in the camps outside the walls."

"These bandits came a long way from the camps outside of Houston, Rabbi," Jean Jacques said. "Houston wants more than police. They want to create an army to attack us. That says to me that they don't trust their walls to keep us out. *That* says to me that they are weak."

"Yes, they're weak, boy. They know the news. Up north Cities are being overrun. And they blame us for that. Not the bandits."

Crowley, *vieux* Guibert, Jean Jacques and several of his trusted men were having an early dinner at the table near Crowley's *chambre*. They were all tired from the early morning and the ride back to Camp. Jana had joined them. Her nurse was inside the tent, minding Mikey.

"*Privateers* always sounds like something from a children's pirate story." Jana was the most energetic person at the table, she kept the conversation going when the rest of the table got quiet. "Down at Camp C, we've heard stories of Cities making deals like that with bandits."

"These *cretins* did more than just make a deal. They have very good guns."

"Yeah? Well, we have their guns now."

"True." Old Man Guibert got up from the table and stretched his stiff legs. It had been a long day and a lot of riding. "So, what do we do with the prisoners, Rabbi? And then what do we do after that? Go to the other Camps and whip the other bandits? Or bring the other troops here and declare our own war on Houston for arming these?"

"You sound like you want a fight, *pere*."

"You said it, Rabbi. First, the sword."

That gave Crowley an idea for what to do with the bandit prisoners. It also gave him another idea.

Bill Atell wanted to leave Camp A and do missionary work in the East. Atell had risen through the ranks quickly; but, in the last several months, he'd been telling his life story a lot while other students worked their ways into Crowley's inner circle.

"Rabbi, you may have heard that one of my sons came a little while ago to find me and to join the company. We get along well, him and I, and we were thinking that we might go out into the countryside and find a place to set up a Camp ourselves somewhere, teaching and bringing people into the Company."

One of the reasons Crowley hadn't brought Atell into the inner circle at Camp A was that Atell seemed more limited than others by the choices he'd made in his old life. There was anger in him—and a shortage of wisdom or perspective that even some angry men had. But he was a good teacher. And his life story was an effective teaching tool.

Crowley had been sending missionaries out into the wilderness…practically from the first lessons he'd taught at the farms along the Brownsville Road. Some had done very well—like Warren Schaftner's Camp P south of Philadelphia and Hank Pearson's Camp X near Chicago. These missionaries had become prominent and powerful, even wealthy, as they'd drawn thousands of students into the Company. And they sent their tithes—in gold, guns and intelligence—back to Camp A regularly every month. So the senior people in Camp A knew how well these missionaries were doing.

Of course, some of the other missionaries had just disappeared.

"Success at missionary work takes a particular mix of skills, Bill. More than anything, it takes an entrepreneurial temperament. The ability to follow the teachings while making a thousand decisions without any guidance. Now, I believe that your heart is true. So, I don't think you'd give into the temptations of worldly success. But do you think that your mind is well-suited for operating out there on your own?"

"I believe it is. And, where I might fall short, my son Frank will be there to help. He's a bright young man. And he's looking for a new life with me. With his father."

"Is Frank around?"

"Yes, Rabbi. He's just outside."

"Well, bring him in."

Atell bolted up and went outside.

Sending Atell out with a few assistants, some guns and a cart of teaching materials would cost almost nothing. Telling him no would probably damage his effectiveness as a storyteller.

He came back into the tent with a young man who looked in his late teens or early twenties. The son had dark hair and an olive complexion. He looked healthy—but his eyes were hesitant. He wasn't quite broken. But he didn't seem very strong.

"Rabbi, this is my son Francisco Ayala Atell. Frank, this is Michael Crowley."

Crowley stood up and smiled. He reached out for the son's hand.

The son shook Crowley's hand firmly enough...but he looked down while he spoke. "Rabbi, it is an honor to meet you. You are a great man. The Company brought me and my father together."

"Frank. It's good to meet you. Your father has been a big help to me and the Company. His story has drawn a lot of people into our company. And now I understand you want to take him away from us."

The son looked nervous for a second, so Crowley laughed a little to signal the joke.

Then the son laughed nervously. "Well, I never thought about it like that. But we think that we could work well as missionaries together."

"Do you have any idea where you'll go?" The question was for the older Atell.

And he answered, "East. And north. We know there are a lot of people doing missionary work up to New York. We thought we'd go even farther north, around Boston or Quebec."

They'd done their homework. That was open territory.

"Gets awfully cold up there. You ready for that?"

The son answered: "Mortification of the flesh, Rabbi. We should seek more than physical comfort in this life."

"True enough. And that part of world is dangerous right now. Lots of bandit activity and the Cities there are afraid. They'll treat you just like bandits."

The son, again: "But we're not, Rabbi. And they'll see that in time."

Good answer.

"Well, okay then. It sounds like you've thought this through. You have my blessing to ride up into the countryside north of New York for your missionary work. But you'll need to stay far to the north of New York. You might be closer to Quebec than Manhattan. Savvy?"

"Yes, we understand."

"And make sure you take plenty of warm clothes. Go see Phillip Hanson about getting set up with the equipment you'll need. And we'll draft the formal agreement here. That will be ready in a day or two.

"Also, talk to some of the students who've been in that part of the world about when the best time of year will be to get there. You'll probably want to time it so you get there in the Spring so you have as much warm weather as possible right away. And you can put the word out to anyone here who wants to go with you. You'll need a crew of five or six. At least."

He stood up and shook both Atells' hands.

"Thank you, Rabbi. Thank you. This means a lot to us."

"Good luck to you both. Remember that our mission is simple. Give everyone in the wasteland a Bible to read and a rifle to shoot straight."

The son picked up the line: "With those things, a person can do anything."

"Godspeed, Frank."

The trip went by in a blur to Jana.

They'd considered riding but decided against. Too slow and too dangerous. They'd also considered asking her brother for one of Brownsville's tiltrotors—but decided against that. It would send the wrong message. So, Jean Jacques and his first unit drove Jana to Mobile in one of Camp A's armored transports.

The hard part was the first 20 miles of the trip, which meant lots of rough road and several erratic toll points. Jean Jacques usually paid the toll, if it was small enough and the "troll" asking for it was polite. But one of the trolls working one of the gates took a threatening attitude, so they shot him and blew up his toll gate and the house attached.

Once they turned on to the TransTexas Tollway, the driver pressed the transport up to 100 miles per hour and kept it there. They had enough fuel—barely—to make the trip to Mobile without stopping.

It was just an hour to Houston's walls and three hours around them. Then it was three more hours on the Houston/New Orleans Road and two hours around New Orleans. By this point, everyone in the truck was beginning to tire of its cramped space and ridiculously small toilet compartment. But Jean Jacques insisted that they pass on the various rest stops along the way. They only had a few more hours to go.

When they pulled up at Mobile's Gate 12, a 50-troop security detail was waiting for them. The detail had cleared the Gate 12 area so that the envoy and her escort had no problem entering Mobile. Whatever squatters camps were normally outside of Gate 12 were…gone.

The security detail was headed by Captain Boyette, whom Jana had met briefly when the Mobile group and their organic cotton had come to Camp A.

Boyette said that they would have to leave the armored truck in an impound lot near the Gate. But it would be given a complete inspection, any repairs it needed and a full tank of fuel while they were the City of Mobile's guests.

Sic Semper Tyrannis

They also had to surrender all of their weapons.

Jean Jacques asked if he could leave one of his men with the truck. Boyette said that he could—but that the man would not be allowed in the vehicle until they were set up leave Mobile again. They agreed. He told one of the men to stay.

That left five of them to be taken by limousine to a guest house in the historic downtown part of Mobile.

There, the very tall Richard Hester greeted them. His face flushed while he complemented them on their impressively short drive time, on Jana's clothes and on the general excellence of everything their "organization" did.

She didn't remember him being so effeminate. His over-enunciated way of speaking made him sound like a character from a comedy vid.

Jana joined Hester for a small drink of Mobile whiskey. It was so sweet that it didn't taste like whiskey.

Jean Jacques and his men declined Hester's many invitations to join him in a drink. And, when Hester suggested they all go out to dinner, Jana declined firmly—saying that she needed a full night's sleep before the meeting the next morning. This was true.

The blur only slowed a little when she talked to Mikey on the satphone.

"Hi, darling. How are you doing? It's Mommy. Can you hear my voice?"

"Momma. Der. Der. Doh. Momma." Then he laughed a satisfied laugh.

For a moment, she resented Crowley for sending her on this trip. But that passed.

"So, how are you holding up?" he asked.

"I'm fine. I was a little nervous about the thing in the trunk. But I guess they didn't notice."

"Or they noticed and don't care."

"I doubt that."

"Yeah, you're probably right. Well, get some sleep. You'll be done by tomorrow morning and back home soon."

"I sure hope so. I don't think I was made for this."

"No one is. You'll be fine. Have the meeting, just as we've planned. Smile, even if they get nasty."

"*Especially* if they get nasty."

355

"True, true. And when you're finished get back in that rig and get back here. We miss you already."

"You sent me on this trip, Michael."

"I know. You're the best one for the job."

"I hope you're right."

"I am. Get some sleep."

"Okay. I love you."

"I love you, too."

She fell asleep quickly and dreamed of playing on the grass at Camp A with Mikey. He was laughing the whole time. *Der. Der. Doh.*

The next morning, when she got up, Jean Jacques and his men were still standing outside her door. She asked if they'd gotten any sleep. He said they'd sleep when they got home. She knew that meant they were taking Neuroplex/Awake and might be jittery as the trip went on.

She took a quick shower and had a light breakfast. The meeting was set for eight o'clock.

A limousine was waiting for them at seventy-thirty.

The boardroom was just like Crowley had described to her. It seemed to be made mostly of glass.

Jean Jacques and one of his men came into the boardroom with her. The man carried the metal box. The other two stood just outside the main door.

They were there 10 minutes early, but Hester and three other executive types were already sitting at the big table. Their assistants sat behind them, against the walls of the room. The executives carried either nothing or simple tablets; the assistants all wore earpieces and had chunkier tablets that they typed into constantly.

Jana took her seat at the end of the table closest to the door. Jean Jacques and his man stood behind her.

The girl who'd led them in asked if Jana wanted anything to drink. She shook her head and said the glass of water in front of her would be fine.

Hester made some small talk about what she'd thought of the guest house where she'd stayed. He told a story about how visiting dignitaries had been staying there for close to 300 years.

Exactly at eight, the CEO came into the boardroom from the back door—just as Crowley had said he would.

"Ladies, gentlemen. This is a busy day for all of us, let's get this meeting started. Mrs. Crowley, I'm H.R. Clinton. I'm the CEO of the City of Mobile." He was smaller and older than she'd expected. He'd been handsome at some point and he still had the confidence that came from being attractive. "I have to tell you, we originally took this meeting because we expected your husband to be here. We knew him in his previous position."

His eyes kept drifting up to her forehead. Just as Crowley had predicted.

It took her a minute to realize that when he said "we" he meant himself. "He is sorry that he couldn't be here. He sends his regards and says that he remembers you fondly from those days."

Clinton flashed an unfriendly smile. "Lovely. I'm still not sure what I think of a man who sends his wife all this way for a meeting he requested. Call me old-fashioned, but I just think that's not right."

"Don't worry for me, Mr. Clinton. My security escort is very effective. And I think that Michael wants everyone to know what we in the company know—that it's more than just a personality cult."

"You don't need to worry about that. We know your… organization…is more than a cult. So, why are we here this morning?"

She took a drink of water. It was something she'd seen Crowley do. He was always careful not to rush too much. "A few months ago, our troops terminated a brigand encampment near one of our properties. When we examined the camp, we found a cache of these." She nodded to Jean Jacques, who pulled the rifle from the metal box, folded the stock open and placed it down carefully between Jana and Clinton.

While he was doing this, of Clinton's body men drew their weapons. But, since Jean Jacques never raised the rifle to his shoulder, they didn't fire.

The assistants started typing even more furiously and whispering into their comms links.

Clinton acted unimpressed. "Nice work getting that through our security checks."

"We ran the power cell all the way down so that it wouldn't show up on an erg scan. And the ornamental case has some lead and some diffusive composite material that confuses most x-ray and object-based systems. Do you recognize the model?'

"We're not security experts. But it looks like a Peerless."

"Very good. A PPW-H531. It's a new model, this year. We asked ourselves how a bunch of half-starving brigands managed to get their hands on several dozen of these brand new guns."

"Well, they're brigands. They steal things."

"Right. Except these rifles have no serial numbers. You can see for yourself there, on the back of the stock. A blank spot where the serial number is usually etched at the factory. And there are supposed to be other markings, microscopic ones. They aren't there either. You can have this gun. Your security experts can look harder at the weapon. They'll see that we haven't done anything to alter or manipulate this. It's a phantom plasma rifle. Out in the wasteland, we call this a 'drug dealer's dream.'"

"We call it the same thing here, Mrs. Crowley."

"A legitimate company like Peerless isn't supposed to make phantom weapons."

"Yes. Our contract with Peerless states that we'll stop doing business with them if they knowingly manufacture weapons without serial numbers. It's like pharma companies and Neurac. Any of them can make it. But we don't allow the firms within our walls to do so. And we don't allow firms from outside to sell their products here if we find out they make it somewhere else."

"Yet the wasteland is full of Neurac and phantom weapons."

"Yes, it's a tragedy. But what do you expect from us?"

"To enforce your contract and stop doing business with Peerless."

"Well, we make no promises about *that* until we can establish for ourselves that this is all as you say. We have to answer a number of questions before we even approach such a decision. Was this actually made by Peerless? Is it really a phantom weapon? Where has it been since it was built? The manufacture of outlaw weaponry is a serious charge. Please don't take offense, but we won't just take your word about a gun as the basis for terminating a major vendor contract."

"I understand, Mr. Clinton. That's why I'm leaving the gun with you. You can examine it closely."

"All right. Is that all?"

"I suppose so. Though I ask that you consider this matter from our perspective. Organized brigands aren't just a threat to crops. They're a threat to all decent people in the wilderness. And some of these brigands claim to have accords with big Cities."

"That's nonsense."

"We hope it is. Because, if Cities were supporting the brigands, we'll need to reconsider our long-term security strategies. And maybe our short-term. I mean to say that it would create a lot of trouble among our people if it turns out that a City is using phantom guns to help the brigands destroy the humanitarian good that our Company is doing."

"Mrs. Crowley, we can see that you're an intelligent person, so let us speak frankly. There are reasonable people around here who believe that your *husband* is the one arming and organizing the brigands. They believe that he's using them to do his dirty work, destabilizing the Cities. And some of us remember his fascination with starting a new Federal system. External threats of violence certainly make a lot of nervous citizens inclined to agree with that kind of plan."

He hadn't answered her directly. On the other hand, he'd pretty neatly summed up Crowley's long-term plans—though his implication that Crowley controlled the brigands was way off. "My husband didn't create these brigands. And he didn't give them state-of-the-art weapons. No one in our Company did either, either."

"We're glad to hear that. And we appreciate you leaving this weapon with us. We're sure our technicians will be interested in examining it. If they find anything you haven't or reach a different conclusion, we'll get word to you. Now, if this is all, we'll give you our best wishes. Full day of meetings ahead."

She left the rifle on the boardroom and went straight back to the vehicle. She told the driver to get home as quickly as possible.

Of course, this wasn't about hearing anything from them about the weapon. Crowley had said that the phantom rifles were a kind of political hot rock. He could use them to lash out against the Cities...maybe turn the Cities against each other. And, to get that process started, they'd given the proof of City treachery to the most treacherous of the minor Cities.

This might make some immediate trouble for New Orleans and Houston, if either of them were behind the guns.

She could play these political games—but she didn't enjoy them, the way Crowley did. She would rather have been inside the walls of her family home with her son.

Twenty-two

"…so, this is what we come to know as a 'rhetorical question' in common daily conversation. But look at what the rhetorical question requires: Most important, a context so clear that everyone listening to it understands the answer that the questioner seeks.

"That's why so many rhetorical questions fail in modern conversation. It's rare any more that a room full of people will all agree on the answer to any question. So, you can't count on the right answer being implicit. And you have so many speakers who have to explain, 'That was a rhetorical question.'"

Hailwood's workload as a faculty member was a lot more than what it had been when he'd been a graduate instructor. Instead of two courses, he was teaching six. And overseeing four graduate instructors, as well. He worried that the workload was showing in the quality of his lectures. He could feel himself padding them with extra words.

But his personal workload was nothing, compared with the changes going on in the campus.

The consolidation of several schools on the College campus was having big effects on everything.

In theory, each school was operating as a separate entity within the walls of the single campus. But, in a move whose significance no one had appreciated, the deans had decided to allow any student on the campus to take classes from any of the schools.

The result was that the kids from the other schools flocked into the College classes. They were afraid it was going to be the only school left after an inevitable merging and rationalizing of operations—and they didn't want to get caught with shaky credits or being unknown to the department heads.

It was impressive how intuitive kids were about campus politics.

Unlike many of the teachers, Hailwood didn't believe that Howell had been stupid in agreeing to the open enrollment policy. He didn't like Howell's sycophantic style of fundraising—but he thought the man had an instinct for power dynamics and strategic positioning. In this sense, he was smarter than most of the teachers—who considered themselves the smartest people on earth.

Hailwood's guess was that Howell saw a chance to force a complete integration of the schools that would otherwise meet resistance from the faculty and admins from the other colleges. By opening the classroom doors, Howell could present integration as a *fait accompli*.

In the meantime, the campus was living through a logistical nightmare.

When Hailwood had been a graduate instructor, his Introduction to Rhetoric section had had 15 or 16 students. Now the same class had more than 80. Instead of teaching in a seminar room, he taught it in lecture hall. And, because there was a campus-wide shortage of lecture hall space, he had to teach that class three afternoons a week in the Chemistry building. Small, shabby-genteel Grosvenor House wasn't designed for so many students.

And there was no chance any more to get to know all of the students personally. A dozen or so of the smartest and most aggressive stood out. The rest blurred into a cloud of non-assigned seats.

He decided that next semester he'd follow the lead of more experienced teachers and use assigned seating plus a face chart to make sure he got every student in the class involved. But, for now, since he'd started the term with open seating he'd let that stand.

"Cicero counts on his audience to assume that Catiline will go on insulting the citizens unless they take some action to stop him. That's the genius of his question 'how long?' It forces his audience to reach the conclusion that Catiline has to be stopped. If he'd merely asked 'Is Catiline insulting us?' or 'Why is Catiline insulting us?' he wouldn't have forced them to reach a conclusion. Those are questions that other people might answer. But 'how long' forces the question on the listener."

This last bit wasn't very strong. In a smaller seminar setting, Hailwood could have finessed this point by letting some of the kids analyze the form of the questions themselves. In a lecture hall, he had to make his points clearly—and couldn't count on a group effort to smooth out his rough patches. It was a different style of teaching.

He took a sip of water and a quick look out into the hall. Most of the kids were focusing on their screens. They could be taking notes while they recorded the lecture. Or they could be surfing in the nets for porn.

One out of four or five kids were actually looking at him.

He checked his watch. He was running over time, anyway.

"Okay. That's enough for today. The assignment for Thursday is a simple 500 words connecting Cicero's rhetorical questions at the start of the *Catilinam* speech with a modern example of rhetorical questions. You can choose anything you want—a political speech, an ad, a vid. But keep your comparison to something that's been done in the last five years. And let's stick with clear examples. This assignment is about the details of your comparison, not the brilliant obscurity of your choice. If you have to spend too much time explaining your choice, you're not going to do well. Make sure your assignment is in my net file before the start of class Thursday. I'll publicly shame anyone who misses the deadline."

Some hesitant laughs in the cavernous room.

"Very good. See you Thursday."

It was a muggy autumn afternoon and the campus was buzzing and banging with construction. Howell wanted four permanent buildings completed before the winter set in. They copied the colonial style of the campus's least distinguished buildings. But the goal was space, not aesthetic beauty.

As Hailwood understood the history of the campus, it had always alternated between periods of panicked expansion and more careful consolidation—also called *development*. Following that logic, there'd be time for beautiful buildings in a few years.

Even with a simple goal, most of the faculty said the building wouldn't be done on time. The "four boxes" were yet another excuse to complain about the President. Of course, as Drummond pointed out, few of the professors knew how to drive a nail.

Hailwood checked his mail box at Grosvenor House. It was empty. There didn't seem to be anyone else around, so he picked up a couple of books and headed home.

Faculty housing was squeezed as tightly as everything else on campus. But he'd worked out a good solution. He'd moved in with Drummond and, together, they'd managed enough points in the housing allowance system to keep the well-appointed "bad karma" house. Otherwise, he would have had to move into an old resident counselor's apartment in one of the dorms. Or kept living at the DKE House. Neither was an appealing proposition.

Much better to split the bad karma house with his closest friend in the faculty. "Drummond?"

No one was home. Drummond must have taken his dog out for a run—which suddenly sounded like a good idea. Hailwood usually didn't eat lunch on days that he had classes; but he'd made an exception today and had a patty melt on rye bread at the campus pub. It was sitting heavy in his stomach.

His normal running circuit was about three miles, along the edge of campus and around the tennis courts then back down Pleasant Street to the house. That run on this hot day, plus a steam bath afterward, would burn off the lard. After he'd changed into his running sweats, his screen chirped.

"Prof. Hailwood?"

"This is Terry Hailwood." Technically, he wasn't a professor.

"Hi. This is Jana in Dean Lieber's office." She was a student employee. Lieber's regular, bitchy secretary wouldn't have called him *professor*.

"Okay, Jana. What's up?"

"Dean Lieber asked me to call all of the members of the Campus Security Committee and remind them that there's an important meeting this evening with several of the merchants from town."

"Sure. I've got it on my screen. 7:30 p.m. at Converse?"

"That's right."

"Okay. Let him know I'll be there. But, first, I'm just going out for a run."

"Very good. Thank you, Prof. Hailwood. Enjoy your run."

"I will."

He did.

At most colleges, budgets and policies were controlled by committees. All college committees were political—but, since the College was also something like a City unto itself, its committees took on an even more plainly political style.

The Campus Security Committee was made up of three deans, the Campus Security Chief, five faculty members and two students. It controlled a large budget and had a larger effect on campus life that most people realized. Still, it was not a prestige assignment—like the Admissions Committee or the Tenure Committee or the Disciplinary Committee. *Those* assignments were the ones that everyone wanted; Campus Security was one that members accepted grudgingly.

Hailwood had been nominated almost immediately for two reasons. First, it was widely assumed that his family ties to Tampa would help the College with planes or personnel if a major crisis ever occurred. Second, Hailwood didn't hide the fact that he traveled in the wasteland and owned and used guns.

He was a rarity among the faculty in this regard. Few of his colleagues owned guns—and those who did made excuses about needing them for occasional trips off campus. But even that excuse didn't hold up to cocktail party scrutiny. Hailwood had heard dozens of variations of the same statement: "No one needs to own weapons here. You can catch a ride on one of the tiltrotor taxis directly from Memorial Hill landing field to New York or Boston. And no one carries guns there."

Right. He'd quit responding to this stupid stuff. He'd just shrug off the ignorant statements, which allowed colleagues to tolerate his gun ownership with an eccentric-because-he's-rich condescension.

This eccentricity seemed useful for the Security Committee.

The other teachers on the Committee were eccentrics of other stripes. The students seemed a little more mainstream. But none of them—teachers or students—really mattered. The Campus Security Committee was dominated by Security Chief Richard Keyes and Assistant Dean of Students Irwin Lieber.

Hailwood had no problem with Keyes. He was a grizzled old hand who'd spent time in the Hartford Security Force and as a privateer around Hartford and Boston. He acted the part of the world-weary security man. Hailwood's only complaint was that Keyes seemed to be so cautious that he missed some less-obvious risks. It was the old theory about security—that managing chaos required a person who *understood* chaos.

This was really just a small quibble; few security types understood chaos. And Keyes wasn't on the Committee to be a deep thinker. He was there for his practical experience.

Lieber was another matter.

He didn't have security experience *and* he wasn't a deep thinker.

Hailwood didn't like Lieber on various levels. This dislike traced back to Hailwood's student days.

For years, Lieber had been harassing the fraternities on campus as "anti-intellectual" and "elitist." He represented a middle-brow progressive constituency among the faculty and admins. It was a strange vestige of older times that someone living in a walled college campus with robotic machine guns pointed out at the wasteland had a problem with "elitism." There wasn't a great deal of substance to the anti-fraternity arguments; but Lieber took them seriously enough to call in members for occasional "disciplinary interviews."

In his second year, Hailwood had been called in for one such interview, having something to do with anonymous allegations that the DKEs had discriminated against College students who hadn't been admitted to one of the House's parties.

The main thing Hailwood remembered from the interview was Lieber lecturing him, "If you're going to exist on the College campus, you're going to admit all College community members to your parties and social networking events." He'd sounded like he was reading it from a script.

The interview led to a Disciplinary Committee hearing.

Hailwood wasn't an officer of the House at that point and hadn't even been working the door. So, he defended himself pretty easily and was acquitted of any wrongdoing or violation of College policies by the Disciplinary Committee. But his grandfather had been sent an email about the hearing. This notice seemed to have been Lieber's goal—a kind of warning that he could "tell on" Hailwood for belonging to a fraternity.

His grandfather barely noticed the notice, dismissing it with a contemptuous crack about "those half-wit managers have been doing this kind of stuff for years. Just keep out of their kangaroo courts."

The net effect of the whole episode had been to convert Hailwood from an ambivalent member of the DKE House to an active one.

And, as the years had passed, it made him understand first-hand how foolish bureaucratic interference could radicalize people.

Lieber was just such a foolish bureaucrat. He came from a long line of College managers; his family had worked for the College in various capacities for generations. This was a little unusual. Although college managers—*admins*, in the college jargon—were a caste generally, their positions weren't supposed to be specifically dynastic.

But the modern College had always had one or more Liebers on the payroll. And, in the case of this Lieber—he went by the initials I.B.—the family tradition led to an arrogant demeanor rather than a humble sense of duty. Noblesse oblige was a belief for students and teachers…not so much for the bureaucrats who kept the lights turned on.

This distinction occurred to Hailwood often. It struck him as deeply ironic that admins—who were the institutional servants of both students and faculty members in academia—were so often so haughty to the people they were supposed to be serving.

Hailwood had another reason to dislike Lieber. It was campus lore than, several generations back, a homosexual Lieber had had himself cloned to keep the line going. Hailwood didn't have many biases. But he didn't like clones. Like the religious fundamentalists in the wasteland, he considered clones a perversion of nature, though he didn't put so clearly even to himself.

No one in his family shared this view, which made Hailwood's firmness on the matter all the more surprising.

The cloning made all subsequent Liebers suspect, in Hailwood's opinion. And the Liebers knew people suspected them—which explained I.B. Lieber's harassing of fraternities and other "elitist" groups.

There were some Committee meetings in which Hailwood's contempt for the current Lieber was a front-and-center issue. This was not one of those meetings—too much was going on here. A group of merchants from town had asked for the meeting to discuss extending the College's security apparatus to cover their stores.

This was a major concession. For years, the College had offered to wrap the Town within its walls. Town leaders—including the merchants who'd come to this meeting—had always declined. Now, they were not only no longer declining. They'd asked for a meeting in which they could offer to accept.

And, of course, the Town's change of heart was happening just as the College was struggling to absorb all of the recent arrivals.

The meeting took place in the conference room next to Dean Lieber's office in Converse Hall—the oldest building on campus.

Three men represented the merchants: the older townie who ran the bank/comms center (where Hailwood had paid his fine for killing the squatters), the young guy who ran the music store and one of the brothers who owned Hampton's—the favorite liquor store among the College's students. Hailwood had done business with all three. He'd never been ripped off by any of them.

The old man from the comms center started out doing most of the talking for the merchants.

"...this s'nt something any of us wanted to come asking you. But we don't have any choice. The bandit raids are getting worse every week. And the bandits coming in from the south are stirring up the squatters living in the Old University. You know how it is with them—I mean, for years they were quiet, easygoing. Now they're dangerous. Their young kids follow the bandits into town and watch. Then they come back 'round a few days later to stir up their trouble. Tell ya truth, I'm surprised more in't dead already."

Lieber started out doing most of the talking for the Committee. "More? So, that means you've killed some underclass already?"

"Underclass? You mean *squatters*. Yeah, our Deputies have killed a few already. But, I tell ya, it could have been a lot worse."

"I'm not sure what's worse than slaughtering the underclass. You're self-actualized. And armed. They aren't."

"I don't know what you mean, sir. They've got lots of weapons. They're *armed* for certain."

The old townie looked like he was going to cut Lieber's throat. Defending squatters and bandits was absurd. But Lieber was against anything the townies had to say.

Something strange was going on here. Normally, despite his predictable rhetoric, Lieber operated as President Howell instructed—but Howell supported the idea of bringing the town into the College's protection. So, this didn't make sense.

Hailwood guessed that Lieber was free-lancing. So, he decided to step in. "Dean Lieber, I'm not sure I'm following the logic of this exchange. Is the College really going to take the side of bandits against the word of these legitimate business owners?"

He wished that someone else had interrupted. There were other people on the Committee—the facilities guy Probst, for example—who must have seen that Lieber was taking this meeting down a counterproductive path.

"No, Mr. Hailwood. I don't presume to speak for the College. Only President Howell or the Board of Directors can do that. I'm merely trying to establish *why* these business owners find themselves in the position they are in."

"Well, I spend some time in the wasteland. And it doesn't take a security expert to see that the bandits are getting more active all over. What happened to Dartmouth and the emergency actions going on in Hartford are proof of that."

The brother from Hampton's chimed in, "Emergency actions? That's just Big City doubletalk. Let's put it straight. Hartford doesn't exist anymore. It's been absorbed by New York. And let's put *this* straight. That's what we're talking about here. The College has strong security. Everybody knows that. We're asking to join up with the College so that the Town can continue to exist something like it is."

Hailwood gave a hard stare to Probst, who took the cue and said something: "That's a fair request. But there are going to be costs to the College for any expansion of security. Sending our Security Forces on patrol might be relatively easy. But you fellows already have security patrols. If you're talking about expanding the walls. That will be expensive. *Very* expensive."

The Hampton's brother warmed to Probst. It wasn't that his words were any friendlier than Lieber's; but his tone was.

The merchants didn't seem phased by money issue. The Hampton's brother said, "We know it's going to cost. And we're prepared to share the costs with the College. The Merchants Association has been putting together a special fund for financing security improvements. And we're prepared to share revenue for a reasonable amount of time after."

Hailwood couldn't believe this: "You mean you'd be willing to pay a tax to the College?"

"Well, you could call a tax. We'd prefer to call it a fee. But we all know we're talking about the same thing."

There was silence for a moment. This was news. For a hundred years, the local merchants had resisted just about any joint business plan with College because they refused to pay any form of "tax" to the College. The very word "tax" conjured up the most hated elements of the Federal Era and its catastrophic bankruptcies. Now they were backing away from that.

The bandit problem must have been worse than anyone at the

College realized.

Probst broke the silence. "The other thing to consider is that an expansion of the walls is permanent. I mean, you won't decide in a few months that you've overreacted to a short-term spike in bandit activity?"

"We're not overreacting. There are more bandits and they're getting bolder every day."

Lieber came back into the exchange: "And the College is the only solution?" This seemed more like a self-satisfied boast that an honest question. The guy was just a prick.

"We think so. I mean, there's talk of this religious cult calls itself the Company that fights bandits. But the Company hasn't gotten up here yet. And we need a real solution now or we're going to be overrun."

Even Lieber seemed to understand the significance of this. His brow was wrinkled and his mouth turned into a sneer. Admins hated religion; while most teachers kept open minds to matters of faith and God, the managerial class had a visceral hatred of religion. Lieber surely didn't want the townies turning to a religious cult for security.

One of the students on the Committee asked, "So, what's the next step?"

Lieber answered, "Someone's got to come up with a plan for coordination and construction."

The old man who ran the comms center came back into the conversation: "We have something for that. The Merchants Association has come up with a proposal for extending the College's walls to enclose a 16-block area around Pleasant Street and Hampshire Road. That covers most of the Town's commercial district."

He handed a screen disc across the table to Probst, who read it immediately and intensely.

The Hampton's brother spoke as if privately to Hailwood: "It's just a template, mind you. We got some quotes from security contractors in Boston and New York. But those might be a lot higher than the College could get. And we've also got a projection in there for how the fees could cover the cost by three- and five-year schedules."

"That's impressive. You gentlemen came prepared to do business."

"We got to get something done."

President Howell liked the plan as soon as he saw it. Even though the College was busy with its own building program, he agreed with the Merchants that the wall expansion was worth bringing contractors out from Boston to get done fast.

Hailwood was careful not to take too much satisfaction in these developments. It would be like the cagey Howell to instruct Lieber to resist the merchants so that he, Howell, could be the hero in embracing them.

And Hailwood was worried about the Dartmouth model. There, the school had extended its walls to include the town…and that had been the beginning of the end. The comparison wasn't perfect, though. *This* College was bigger and *this* town, smaller. But it was troubling, still.

Having heard through the College grapevine about Hailwood "taking over" the meeting with the town merchants, Drummond was wary about his housemate making an enemy of a Dean. "You keep saying that the guy's never liked you. But this is only going to make that worse. Even if the fix was in on this deal, the meeting was still an embarrassment to him. And you know how much these admins are into status and face-saving. He'll try to get you back for that."

"Who gives a shit? Worrying about him too much is letting him win. He's an annoyance. That's all. An insect." Hailwood noticed that Drummond was shaking his head. "Hey. You're not worried about guilt by association, are you?"

"We're not all independently wealthy, Terry."

A week later, Howell put the town annexation plan to a teleconference of the College's Board, which agreed to put it on a fast track. The plan was to start the construction immediately and press on through the Fall and early Winter. Probst estimated that, on this schedule, the wall construction could be completed by just after the Christmas break. And there was an added plus—by absorbing the commercial zone of the town, the campus would gain about four acres of "dead zone" that currently existed outside its walls. That land would be used for building dormitories and lecture buildings.

But building in the New England winter was an uncertain proposition.

At a faculty dinner a few nights later, Howell cornered Hailwood and congratulated him on taking the merchants' side in the meeting that got the whole plan started. "I know the easy thing to do would have been to reject them or maybe just stay silent. I'm glad there was somewhere there thinking creatively about the future of the College."

Hailwood wasn't sure whether to be flattered or worried. Something about Howell's compliments felt like a set-up. Maybe Drummond was right. Maybe he was just a junior faculty member being played in some larger game of campus politics.

But would Howell really compromise the school's access to Hailwood family money just to screw over one of its members?

Probably not. A couple of events in the next few weeks tempered his worries.

First, the next time Hailwood went in to buy a couple of bottles of Scotch at Hampton's, Fuckin' Ed said they wouldn't accept his money. The Hampton's brothers had set up a tab that Hailwood could "settle later." Hailwood tried to shake off the offer—but Fuckin' Ed wasn't going to give in. The booze and a box of *Imperator* cigars went on the tab.

Second, a week later during his afternoon run, Hailwood heard a series of booms somewhere in the mountains to the east of campus and then noticed a bunch of students in the main quad looking up in the Indian Summer sky. A tiltrotor that seemed to be damaged was circling around overhead. The vehicle was leaving a trail of black smoke as it made a jerky oval a couple hundred feet up.

One of the kids asked him if he thought the tiltrotor was in trouble and looking for a place to land. That didn't make sense. The Memorial Field landing strip was easy to see from above; pilots weren't usually confused.

A couple of more booms echoed from the east.

He called the security chief. "Keyes, this is Terry Hailwood. Have you noticed this tiltrotor above the campus?"

"No, Prof. Hailwood. And I'm too busy to look right now. There's a bandit army trying to make an assault on the East Wall of the campus."

"The East Wall?"

"Yes. The East. Not what we expected."

"How big an army?"

"Hard to tell. Maybe a hundred?"

"And you've got all your troops over there?"

"Yes, I do."

"Could this tiltrotor be with them?"

"Umm...I don't know. Maybe. They're pretty well armed."

"Okay. I'm going to grab a couple of guns and wait and see what happens with this tiltrotor."

"Okay. If they land, hold them there and we'll send some men over there as soon as we get this situation secure."

And the line clicked dead.

The tiltrotor was sweeping down, within 20 feet of the ground, and then climbing back up.

Hailwood noticed a kid from his Intro Rhetoric class among those watching from the Main Quad. The kid's name was Deveare—and Hailwood told Deveare to stay put and keep an eye in the tiltrotor. He was to remember everywhere it flew and swooped.

Hailwood jogged a couple hundred yards to the auto pool at the North Gates. The whole place was deserted. The gates were locked down and the automated perimeter defenses were on—but no one was around. This couldn't be a good idea. If the attack at the East Wall was a diversion, the main gates would be vulnerable.

He went to the Badger and grabbed his plasma rifle and a couple of pistols. The plasmas were fully charged; and he grabbed two boxes of bullets for the standard pistol. Normally, bringing the weapons back into campus would require special permission from the security agent on duty. Not today.

He ran back to the Main Quad.

The smoking tiltrotor was hovering over the Quad, looking like it was gathering up its nerve to land. Deveare said it had stopped the swoops and was just hanging out in one place. Hailwood dragged the kid to the portico of the Old Library about 100 yards away.

"Have you ever fired a pistol, Mr. Deveare?" He didn't remember the kid's first name.

"Yes, sir. My dad taught all of us to shoot. But he said we shouldn't mention it in polite company."

"Do you know what this is?" He held up one of the pistols.

"Other than a pistol?"

"It's a Peerless Hek-9 plasma pistol. I've switched off its safety, so it's ready for anyone to fire. It will site and shoot just like a regular pistol. There will even be a little kick—but not as much as regular pistol. But it shoots plasma blasts instead of bullets. So, you can shoot a lot with this. It will go 80 of 100 rounds before it needs to be reloaded. But don't shoot them all at once. If you do, the gun will get so hot it'll jam. If you just take four or five shots at a time and then give the gun a second or two cool down, you'll be all right. Understand?"

"Yeah. But it's against College policy to have a gun on campus."

"You'll be all right. I've got permission from Chief Keyes to do this."

"Okay. Who are shooting at?"

"Whoever is in that tiltrotor. I think they're bandits."

"Bandits? No shit."

Hailwood switched off the biometric safety and set the pistol so anyone could fire it. Then he handed it to Deveare.

"But we're not going to do anything until it lands. Hear me?"

"Yes."

"I could be wrong. They could just be some regular people with mechanical problems. So we've got to wait and see."

"I understand."

"And you stay in screaming distance of me, you hear?"

"Yeah."

"Good. Now, I'm going over by the vending machines over there by Pratt House. That will give us a crossfire field for shooting any bad guys who come out. You just follow my lead. If I wave my hand like this or if you see me shooting, fire at the tiltrotor or anyone you've seen get out. Understand?"

"Yes. Wait for your lead. Then shoot individuals or the ship."

A crowd of kids was gathering around them. Hailwood told them to be careful—to get behind something solid and watch carefully. There might be bad guys in the tilt.

Then, he nodded to the Deveare kid to follow him. "Now, just take you best cover behind the portico here. And don't get excited about doing anything right away. We're going to give them the chance to surrender or show they mean no harm. Got that?"

"Yes."

"Very good. Now, I'm going over there. You ready?"

"I'm ready, sir."

"Good. Talk to you in a few minutes."

For that few minutes, they just watched the smoking tiltrotor hover. Then, after a sudden jolt, it landed with a metallic thud in the

Main Quad. Not a professional landing. But it did some good by scaring most of the random students away.

The smell of burning plastic wafted through the quad while Hailwood lay down on his stomach and sited the tiltrotor door with the 3D imaging guide on his rifle. It was 126 feet from him. The physics would be easy.

Nothing happened for few minutes. The tiltrotor keep smoking and smell kept getting stronger—which meant something was burning inside.

Finally, the door opened and folded down.

Hailwood kept his eye in the scope.

Three men climbed out. They were older than he expected. And dressed in the shaggy manner that bandits preferred. They were armed with what looked like traditional assault rifles.

Without moving the rifle, Hailwood called out: "You're on College property. It's against our policy to carry arms—"

They lifted their weapons to a spot somewhere between Hailwood and the kid Deveare. The smell or the smoke must have blurred things for them.

They started shooting randomly at the buildings.

Hailwood focused on the first bandit, a gray-beard with lots of tattoos on his arms and neck. He squeezed two rounds and the man's head exploded.

Now, the other two pointed their barrels toward Hailwood.

He moved to the second man out, who wore sunglasses. He fired a shot at the middle of the glasses and the man's head exploded.

He didn't have much time to make his mark on the third bandit. That man's shots were ricocheting behind him. He squeezed two shots at his chest and the third man fell.

The door to the tiltrotor was still open and black smoke was starting to waft out of it. Most tiltrotors that size could hold a dozen people, which would be tough for him to manage. But the smoke was Hailwood's ally. If it got thick and filled the interior, whoever was left inside would have to come out.

Hailwood scoped to the third bandit. He was lying face down on the ground about six feet in front of the hatch. His hands were moving. Maybe trembling. Hailwood wasn't sure what to do. Standard security policy would probably be to finish the man off. But he might be more useful alive, to explain how they'd gotten a tiltrotor.

"Professor Hailwood, do you think it's safe to come out?"

Before he could answer the kid, a strong blast of gunfire came from inside the tiltrotor toward the Old Library porch.

Whoever was inside hadn't been able to see where Hailwood's shots had come from.

He scoped to the hatch and tried to see inside. But he couldn't. It was just dark and shadows. There wasn't even any barrel visible.

Then, for a second, he pulled his head away from his scope and looked for the kid over by the Old Library. He couldn't see him. He'd either pulled back behind the porch for cover or he'd been hit by the blind blast.

Hailwood scoped back to the tiltrotor and saw more this time. The smoke was coming out more heavily. And there was a rifle barrel plainly pointing out, not toward him.

He wasn't sure about the interior layout of this tiltrotor. He didn't recognize the model and didn't know the things very well, even if he had. The person holding the rifle could be standing up, sitting or lying down. All of that mattered to where he placed his next shots.

He remembered something from his Boy Scouts security training years before about firing 18 inches above a rifle barrel if you couldn't see the shooter. That made as much sense as anything, so he squeezed two shots at about that point.

The barrel flipped up and back into the shadows.

He scoped over to the front windshield of the tiltrotor. He could see the pilot and copilot seats pretty clearly—though there was some smoke in the cockpit. It didn't look like anyone was there. He scoped back toward the open door but, just as he moved away, he noticed some movement behind the cockpit seats. There was definitely someone else still inside.

He looked over at the Old Library again to see if Deveare was back in his shooting position. He wasn't.

Hailwood watched the open door for what seemed like a long time. In fact, it might have been five minutes. The smoke thinned a bit. And there was no motion that he could see.

During this break, he noticed booms from the East Wall again. It sounded like the fight was still going on there. If Keyes lost the wall, Hailwood was going to have to get himself and as many others as possible out. And head toward the WNET and Hartford/New York quickly.

After another minute or two, the smoke stopped. This was bad. If there were one or more people holed up in the tiltrotor, they could stay there all day. Hailwood chided himself for not bringing any mortars. A couple of incendiaries would be about enough to destroy the machine.

Maybe he could call Keyes and ask for help.

He noticed the machine tremble just a bit. And then he saw a face just visible in the shadows. It was wearing some sort of vision-enhancing goggles. It was daylight, so they wouldn't have been night vision. Maybe infrared?

He made his mark on the goggles. And then they jerked back away from the door. Why?

He looked out from behind his scope and saw a group of students walking toward the tiltrotor. There were five or six of them, spread out tentatively. "Hello? Is anyone inside? Are you injured?"

Hailwood thought about screaming at them to get back. But he didn't. He couldn't believe that these kids would be so stupid as to approach this tiltrotor—with three dead bandits in front of it.

"Hey, you guys! Get away from that thing!" It was Deveare. He was back in his shooting position by the Old Library. "These people are brigands. And they're armed!"

Eight or 10 shots rang out from the tiltrotor. Hailwood scoped the door again and could see two barrels. He squeezed three sets of two shots in a line about 18 inches above the barrels.

Both barrels dropped to the ground.

Plasma blasts flashed all around the door. Deveare was shooting heavily into the tiltrotor. Some of his shots were going inside, some were flashing against the vehicle's skin. There were breaks in the fire, just as Hailwood had told him. Good boy. If there was anyone left inside, the steady stream of poorly-aimed pistol fire would keep them on their heels.

Hailwood looked out from his scope. One of the kids who'd approached the tiltrotor was crawling away. The others weren't moving.

After a minute or two, Deveare stopped shooting.

Hailwood scoped the door again and saw the goggles back there, just inside the open door. Some talk might draw the goggles forward a little. "You okay there, kid?" he didn't take his eye away from his scope.

"Yeah. I was just spooked there for a second when they shot at me. You think we got them all?"

"Maybe."

The goggles disappeared and were replaced by a rifle barrel. Hailwood squeezed three double shots again. The barrel disappeared.

Deveare followed those shots with a lot more of his own.

Hailwood kept watching through the scope. Several minutes went by with no motion.

Then a scared voice came from out of the tiltrotor. "Parley. Parley. I'm only one left here. Jus' want out."

Hailwood had read that bandits were like this. They kept discipline through competition and shame. As long as two were around, they'd fight. But as soon as one was left, he'd surrender. "Fine. Come on out with your hands up. Walk past those college kids you killed and then turn around and face the tilt. You understand?"

"Yes, yes. I'm comin' out."

"If you try anything funny, you're dead."

"I won't. It's jus' me. I don' wanna die."

"Good."

He was younger than the first three who'd come out. Probably 20 or 25. He was runty and nervous looking, with stringy hair and slight beard that wasn't as intimidating as he'd probably hoped it would be.

He walked past the bodies of the students and his fellow bandits and turned to face the tiltrotor, just as instructed.

"Okay. That's a good start. Now, take off your clothes."

"What?"

Hailwood shot a plasma blast into the grass a foot in front of the bandit. "Take them off."

"Naked?"

"Yes. I want to be sure you don't have any tricks strapped to your thigh. Take off all of your clothes or I put the next shot in the back of your fucking head!"

"Awright, awright."

It took him a few minutes to get all of his greasy clothes off. When he finally did, his tattooed body didn't have any weapons hidden on it. If he had them, they'd been in his clothes.

"Okay, now step backwards."

Hailwood had stood up while the bandit was stripping. Now, he rushed up behind and used his left arm to put the naked bandit in a headlock. With his right hand, he put the barrel of the Ruger against the bandit's head. "Okay. Now we're going back in the tilt and take a look around."

The naked bandit was too scared to say anything. He was just small enough that holding him in the headlock was awkward. Hailwood kept pulling him up, off his feet.

Deveare called over from his position. "Professor Hailwood. You want me come along?"

"No. Stay down. If I'm wrong and these guys are being tricky, you blast anyone you see and call Keyes for support."

"They aren' any tricks, Mista. I'm the only one left. There ain't nobody in there but some bunch of dead bodies."

"Did you guys trap the tilt?"

"Trap it? Nah, sir. We barely could figure out how to fly it. We didn't trap it."

"Okay. Well, you and I are going to make sure. If you're right, we'll be done in a second."

It was difficult climbing in the hatch. Hailwood whacked the naked bandit's knee pretty badly against the side of the opening. He whimpered some.

There was enough room to stand up inside the door; but the tiltrotor had landed at a strange angle, so it was hard not to fall forward. The smell of burning plastic was strong enough to make his eyes water.

Hailwood looked around and counted three bodies. He'd hit the one wearing the goggles in the throat and the shoulder. Maybe later he could figure out what the goggles were. For now, he let the naked bandit go and got a steadier stand. He kept the pistol close to the naked guy's right temple. "Okay. Looks like you were right. Let's go back outside."

As soon as they got back out, the naked bandit started talking. "I didn't kill nobody. It wasn't me that killed those college kids. Jimmy Joe was going crazy because the Boss told us not to lose the tilt. Jimmy Joe figured we were gonna have to blast our way out of the College. We thought all the security was fighting at the Wall."

Hailwood told the bandit to lie face down on the grass and went to check the fallen students. One of them—a girl—was still alive. She'd been shot in the shoulder and the leg but was still breathing. But her breathing was fast and shallow. Not a good sign.

He called Deveare over and a couple of dozen other kids came out of the woodwork. All of the sudden, things got very talky. He told them all to stay back and sent a couple to the infirmary to get help for the girl.

The student who'd managed to crawl away from the tiltrotor was actually standing up. He'd been shot in the arm and grazed on the side of his head. But he was doing well enough to walk and talk—and he wanted to tell anyone who'd listen about what had happened. Hailwood told a couple of the others to walk with him over to the infirmary. "The rush is going to wear off in a few minutes and you're going start hurting and feeling really sick. Get over to the doctor right now."

"Yes, sir. Okay, sir."

He told the naked bandit that he could sit cross-legged on the grass.

And, finally, he called Keyes.

"Professor Hailwood. We've got good news here. We've beaten back the assault. They're running north. How are you doing?"

"The tilt landed but the Quad's secure. A couple of students got shot, though."

"Damn. Okay. I'll have a few of my men over there in a few minutes."

"It was seven bandits. Six down and I've got a prisoner."

"Really? Jesus, Professor. You sound like a City security trooper. Okay. I'll make sure those guys get there quickly." Keyes sounded more interested in the prisoner than he was in what had happened to the students.

"The kids walked right up to the tilt, Chief. They were asking was anyone was hurt. And the bandits blasted them at close range."

"Okay. We've got to do something about what we teach our kids."

"Yeah."

"Okay. Thanks for your help, Professor."

"No problem. My question is how'd these bandits get a tilt."

"Yeah. I know. The ones at the wall here had plasma guns and mortars. I've got another call. We can talk about this more later."

Hailwood relaxed a little.

Deveare's first name was Marcus.

Twenty-three

"How long do you think it will take to get through the gates?"

"Not sure. But not long. Javy and his guys are all peeling away. So, it'll just be us. As long as Brian's left word, we should be okay."

Crowley was driving a light-armor Trailblazer with Jana sitting next to him and the baby asleep in a safety seat behind them. Ana Flora, Mikey's nanny at Camp C was sitting next to him in the back. She was also nodding off. A picture focused tightly on the four of them might look like an ad for the Trailblazer that would be on billboards in any City.

If the camera pulled back, the family-friendly ad image would quickly fall apart. The Trailblazer was a custom rig—fitted with armor plating, bullet-proof glass and automated twin 30mm plasma cannons on its roof. And it was driving fast, squarely in the middle of a seven-vehicle convoy. The trucks ahead of and behind the Trailblazer were even more-heavily armored.

Crowley's screen rang. Jana pressed the speaker button.

"Rabbi, we're getting close. We just got pinged by Brownsville's short-distance radar." It was Hector Tamblin, one of Camp C's senior security officers. He was riding in the lead vehicle.

"Very good, Hector. They expect us; but they're still going to follow their normal security procedures. Tell your troops to treat it like a Yellow Alert. Stay sharp. But don't draw weapons."

"Yellow Alert. *Si*, Rabbi."

"And you should turn off the automated targeting systems."

"Are you sure you want us to do that, Rabbi?"

"Yes. It's standard procedure to turn off the computers when you're within 100 yards of a gate."

"Okay. We'll turn them off when we get there. But is 50 yards okay? I'd feel better about that."

Crowley smiled at the kid's caution. "*Si*, Hector. 50 yards is okay. Just be ready for some nasty looks from the border guards."

"I don't mind the nasty looks, Rabbi."

The students at Camp C, drawing heavily from the Spanish-speaking Mexican population of the immediate area, had taken to "Rabbi" as eagerly as the students at the other Camps. They considered it a point of pride that their leader was something different than the usual bandit *jefe*.

Crowley looked at Jana, she arched her good eyebrow. She was excited. And he stole a quick glance at the baby sleeping in the back.

As Mikey had started saying a few words, Crowley started worrying that his little son's life might end up some strange hash of wasteland politics and tactical planning. He wanted Mikey to have more normal experiences.

And, no matter how much Crowley had traveled and changed, "normal" to him still meant City living.

Lying in bed in their *chambre* one night, he and Jana agreed that she'd take Mikey to her family's farm in Brownsville more often and for longer periods so that he'd have some idea of a conventional home. Crowley said that when Mikey got to school age, maybe he should stay in Brownsville.

Jana was firmly against that. "Michael, that's ridiculous. You're the most famous teacher in the wasteland. Your son should learn to read and write and add and multiply from you. He'll learn more living with us than he'll ever learn from a school in Brownsville."

"I've never really been a teacher, Jana."

"False modesty, Michael." This was a criticism she made of him a lot. "Besides, what kind of message would it send to your students if you send your own son away to learn how to read and write?"

"We focus on basic skills. I'd like him to learn more. He ought to have an education like a Brahmin."

"A Brahmin? Michael! You hate Brahmins."

"I hate their sense of entitlement. I admire their education and background."

"So you want him to go to one of the Legacy Colleges?"

"Maybe. Why not? We've already had a few of our students go to Legacy Colleges."

"This is really something. You do surprise me sometimes."

"I'm a manager, Jana. Everything I ever learned makes me want the best and to be the best. I don't want Mikey to be some arrogant snob. But I do want him to have the best education and training there is. And there's something I kind of admire about the ones that have stayed out in the wasteland."

"I guess. Okay. When he's older, we can send him away to college. Until then, he should be with us. Wherever we are."

What he thought—but didn't say—was that Jana's lack of attention to status and focus on keeping family together is what made her a Brahmin. He'd said things like that to her before. Never went over well.

They approached Brownsville from the south.

Camp C was in a desert coastal region that, in the Federal Era, had been part of Mexico. Also, Camp C was closer to Brownsville than the other Camps were to the nearby Cities. The drive was less than an hour along the southern leg of the Brownsville Road. That Road followed the coast all the way down the Yucatan Peninsula—so, by comparison, Camp C seemed like a suburb of Brownsville.

His screen rang and Jana pressed the speaker again.

"Michael, we're going to be at the gates in five minutes." This was Javier Echevarria. He was the *major domo* of Camp C, roughly equal to what vieux Guibert was at Camp A. "I've called Jana's brother. He's making sure everything is ready; but you're still going to need all of your paperwork handy."

Jana answered him: "Thank you, Javy. But you didn't have to call Brian. I should have done that."

"It's no problem, Jana. I needed to speak with him about some ag business, anyway."

Even more than the other Camps, Camp C grew most of its own food and occasionally had surplus crops that it sold into the Brownsville ag co-op.

"Are you sure you don't want to come into town with us, Javy? I'm sure that Brian would like to see you."

"No, no. I'm busy at home. I probably shouldn't have come at all. But I felt like a drive."

"Right."

Brownsville hadn't been a proper City long enough to attract the crowded shanty towns outside its walls that other Cities had. Some tent villages and semi-permanent shops (operating out of the ancient shipping containers that dotted the wasteland) had gathered along the sides of the Brownsville Road as it approached the South Gates. But there weren't enough of either to be threatening—like the squatter villages that crowed around of Houston and New Orleans.

The scene outside of Brownsville was less ominous. The squatters weren't quite so broken; they seemed like people patiently waiting their chance to get inside. The children didn't have the hollow eyes that kids around bigger cities did. These kids smiled and waved at Crowley's convoy as it approached the gates.

Crowley's screen rang and Jana put it on speaker again. The caller ID showed a City of Brownsville number.

"Michael Crowley."

"Mr. Crowley, this is Lt. Annette Flores of the Brownsville Security Force. I am one of the watch officers on duty right now at the South Gates."

"Thank you for calling, Lt. Flores. We're just approaching."

"Yes, sir. I can see that. Your assistant emailed us a copy of your itinerary. And Director Morrell's office has called to confirm your visit to his farm on the North Side. We have a BSF car standing by to escort you to the Morrell farm. I'm just calling to double check how many vehicles you're bringing in."

"We're just one vehicle. Four occupants. My wife, my son, his nanny and me."

"Okay. Very good. And your vehicle is armed?"

"Yes, it is."

"Okay. We're going to need to take a quick look at that."

"I understand."

"And we're going to ask you to deactivate any automated weaponry systems you have in the vehicle."

"Check."

"And we're going to ask you to have your escort do the same."

"They have instructions to switch off as they approach."

"Very good, sir. When you approach the gate, you will see a series of green lights directing you to Lane 8—the far right of the Security Plaza. You'll have no wait. Just keep to your right and follow the green lights. I look forward to meeting in person in a few minutes."

Javy and Hector kept the trucks in formation until they reached the Security Plaza. There, the trucks slowed to a few miles an hour and took hard turns right and left—creating a sort of gate of their own that Crowley passed through. And the trucks behind him stopped, blocking any vehicle from following. This was a Big City security tactic that Crowley had described to Javy and his men a couple of times. He knew that they had practiced it back at Camp C. but, to his knowledge, this was the first time they'd used it outside.

That's why Javy had come along. He wanted to see Hector's men perform the gate-approach maneuver. He really was like vieux Guibert.

Brownsville's South Gate was, literally, a gate—two 25-foot high steel plates on rollers that parted at 9 o'clock each morning and joined again at 6 o'clock each afternoon.

Like all of the lanes leading to the Security Plaza, Lane 8 went through the gates and under an overpass inside the City Wall that housed hundreds of cameras, several dozen automated plasma cannons and a few live humans keeping their eyes on all vehicles that passed beneath.

Once through the Wall, the lanes were separated by short cement walls for another 20 yards to the Security Plaza.

Crowley's screen rang again. It was Hector.

"That was a nice maneuver. Tell your men they did very well."

"Thank you, Rabbi. We still have you on 3-D image but, if you don't mind, will you keep me on speaker until you're though?"

"Absolutely."

Lane 8 led to a security booth, just like any toll booth anywhere. Crowley stopped the Trailblazer at the booth and the security system automatically ran a multiphase scan.

The comms line scratched static for a moment during the scan but, to Crowley's surprise, Hector was still on the line afterward.

A few minutes after the scan was complete, the small gate blocking Lane 8 slid open and Crowley drove through. A platoon of uniformed security troops stood to one side of the lane, with a smaller officer standing in front of them. They were pointedly not blocking the lane—but keeping an oblique angle to the Trailblazer's approach.

Ana Flora was awake. Mikey was still asleep, making baby snores. Crowley told Jana to get the baby ready to take a little walk.

The small officer walked up to car. Crowley thought about rolling down the window but decided it was a better idea to get out.

"Mr. Crowley. I'm Lt. Flores. It's an honor to meet you, sir." She shook his hand firmly.

"Lt. Flores. Thank you, thank you. The greetings I get from City security officers usually aren't so warm."

"I know how much help you've given the Founders getting Brownsville recognized properly. And, personally, I have sympathy for your efforts to educate the squatters and *wasteros*. I was born in the desert myself."

"Well, that's the promise of a new City. Fresh start for everyone."

"Everyone lucky enough to be inside the walls. We need to get to business, sir. I hope that we'll only keep you and your family here for a few minutes. I'd like our troops to look over your rig. And, when we're finished, we have an escort that will take you up to the Morrell farm as quickly as possible."

Crowley told Hector that they were going to be a few minutes. He told them to stay put on the other side of the wall and that he'd call back when the inspection was over and they were on their way. He kept one eye on the inspection—his only fear was that there would be some kind of "accident" that jammed the plasma cannons or screwed up any of his autonav programs. And he wasn't sure what to make of Lt. Flores. He was encouraged by her professionalism—but was wary of her flattery.

Mikey was awake now and a little grumpy. But he was toddling enough that taking a few steps between "muma" and "dat" occupied his time well.

Lt. Flores' professionalism won out. When their inspection was finished, the Trailblazer was fine.

The lieutenant smiled at Mikey and shook everyone's hand—including Ana Flora's.

"I won't presume to advise you, Mr. Crowley. But, even with your diplomatic permit, those plasma cannons are going to draw attention. So, please try to limit your driving to times when you have a security escort."

"No problem, Lieutenant. We'll make sure we have an escort at all times."

"We'll make sure a security car is outside the Morrell farm at all times."

"Thank you."

The farm hadn't changed much. The store houses that had been old shipping containers had been replaced by larger, prefab steel buildings.

The entire North End of Brownsville seemed much as it had before the City Walls had enclosed it. The farms were critical to Brownsville's economic independence. Even though they were still sending some of their produce to Houston, under the trade agreement that Crowley had helped negotiate, Brownsville counted on the corn, wheat and soy beans. No matter what happened in the outside world, its citizens would always eat. That was a valuable promise.

The ag produce deal with Houston had been the leverage that Brownsville needed to get its first recognition. Once Houston accepted Brownsville, the other major cities had fallen in line.

This made the farmers a powerful constituency.

While the Morrell farm hadn't changed much, Brian Morrell had. He'd converted the old brick barracks into the corporate offices of the Brownsville Road Agricultural Cooperative. This group—essentially, the formalization of the informal meetings that he used to host in his dining room—negotiated price supports from the City. And it also served as Brian's base of operations as one of the 11 members of the City's Board of Directors.

In the first year, Brian had called Crowley every few days to ask his advice or opinion about some fine point of City politics. But Crowley had gotten busier and Brian had grown more confident of his skills and judgment. They spoke less often; but they still shared a good friendship.

Like friends, they slipped back into familiar ways when they met—even if they hadn't seen each other in a long time.

Jana and Crowley stayed in her old room in house. The outbuilding where they'd lived for a while had been expanded into an apartment for their farm manager. Ana Flora and Mikey stayed in the guest room, two doors down. They spent their first few hours just walking around the Morrell compound. Mikey would take three or four steps and then fall on his diaper with pleased thump.

Crowley noticed Jana's good eye getting watery.

In the late afternoon, Brian took his custom-built British sports car out to pick up his girlfriend—an attorney at one of companies owned by the ancient gunsmith.

The ancient gunsmith was still alive. Or at least, that's what his employees said. No one outside his inner circle had seen the gunsmith in months. Brian said he had "attended" the last few City Board meetings by telecom. Some people—even some of the Directors—were beginning to wonder whether the gunsmith was actually alive. "They're trying to set up a public offering for TAG on Wall Street. So, half of the Board thinks his one sharp grandnephew is using CGI to keep up the illusion."

"What does the other half think?"

"That he's a vampire."

On a more vital note, the clearly-living Gramp Simpson was going to join them for dinner. Crowley looked forward to that.

Brian got back with his girlfriend around five. "Brandy Henderson, this is my sister Jana and my brother-in-law Michael."

Brandy was different than Crowley had expected. She was intense, with dark eyes that stared hard at you. She was tall—almost as tall as Jana, but not quite—and sharp-featured. She looked like a New Yorker; but she was a Brownsville native. And she sounded like one. Out of the intense, quick features came a southern twang. "It's so nice to meet you all. I'm still getting used to being introduced to people as 'Brandy and Brian from Brownsville'. People think it's cute, all the B's."

After the initial introductions, she focused on Mikey for a long time. She'd brought him a stuffed doll of some popular Japanese cartoon character.

"Your son is about the cutest little guy I've ever seen. You're blessed, Jana."

"We feel blessed."

Jana didn't talk much to people she didn't know well.

Still, it was a familiar coded exchange between people who believed in God. In Cities—even in unassuming Brownsville—the prevailing belief was non-belief. There weren't any laws against religion here; but the social norms discouraged shows of it. People who believed relied on indirect references to faith.

He and Jana both believed that God existed and that life on earth was a process of experiencing Him through His works in people and nature. But they weren't devout or evangelical—as many of their students were. They felt faith was a private matter, between a person and his or her Creator.

That shocked most people.

The increasingly evangelical tenor of the Company was testing that sense of privacy. And maybe Brandy from Brownsville already knew that. Maybe her comment about being blessed was an effort to play to her assumption that he and Jana were evangelical.

So, Jana's short response was probably the right one.

Brian made whiskey and waters, which they took out on the front porch. A woman Crowley didn't recognize brought out some chips and fried peppers. They talked about Brian and Jana's parents and watched the sun set toward the western wall of the compound.

Near seven o'clock, Gramp Simpson arrived in his new fully-equipped Atlantic Motors Badger. It was shiny and black, with blacked-out windows.

Crowley reached out his hand, "That is some handsome rig, Grandfather."

Simpson hugged him. "Well, Brian over here is making us all rich. And we can take it with us when we go. So what's a man to do?"

He introduced Ulysses, one of his grandsons, and hugged Jana and Brandy. He accepted a tumbler of whiskey and water from Brian. After a few minutes of niceties, his patience gave way. "So, Michael. What word do you have from Mobile and points east?"

"Well, my word is second-hand. Jana went to Mobile in my place. She can tell you directly what Mr. Clinton said."

Jana took a moment to make sure that Ana Flora was okay putting Mickey to sleep. And the rest took that opportunity to move into the dining room.

As soon as she got back, Jana asked Crowley to make her another drink and briefed her brother and Gramp Simpson on the news.

The news they'd all heard about a "star chamber" of big Cities was true. Six of the biggest—New York, Ontario, Chicago, New Orleans, SoCal and Seattle—had formed a committee to draft what it called "the framework for an agreement" granting each administrative authority over its geographic regional "zone." The immediate rational for this agreement was the growing security threats posed by bandit armies and the Company. The managers in the big Cities considered the bandits and the students essentially the same.

"Apparently, they consider Michael the largest bandit *jefe* in the wasteland. And the rumor is that Morial in New Orleans has offered a $100,000 bounty to any privateer who kills him."

Gramp Simpson sneered, "$100,000? That's all? But I s'pose it explains the security car."

Crowley didn't think the bounty was a big deal. "It's loose change because they've got bigger issues than killing me. Mobile is looking to make deal. With us. To blockade New Orleans."

"Those runts want to go to war with their big brother? I've always thought of Mobile as a suburb of New Orleans."

"And Mobile is just figuring that out."

"Are you going to do it?" Gramp was asking a lot of questions.

"No. At least not with Mobile. At least not now. New Orleans is too strong. And too big. And this framework is a mutual defense treaty. They can draw troops from everywhere to break a blockade."

"Not with Mobile. But maybe with someone else?"

"Maybe."

"Come on, don't be so guarded. You're among friends. Give."

"Houston and Jacksonville have both been left out of the framework. They're furious about that. Brian can confirm this. Houston sees New Orleans as a threat in any sort of regional administration plan."

Brian didn't hesitate: "But I don't think they're going to go to war over it. It's not in Houston's nature to fight anyone. They're inwardly focused. They're just going to dig in and not take any orders from New Orleans."

"But Houston may decide that Brownsville is in *its* regional authority."

"Maybe. But, really, that's not their style. I can say certainly that the Board of Directors has heard nothing about any of this from New Orleans or New York or SoCal…or Houston…or anyone. And no official word means that all this talk could just be the paranoia of some smaller cities about what happened to Hartford and Savannah."

Crowley smiled. "Savannah. Now you're getting close. If the Company aligns with any City, it's going to be Jacksonville. They're angry. They think they should be the regional authority."

Now Gramp Simpson smiled. "And they have a sumbitch fascist dictator for a CEO. And they're just north of Tampa."

"My only interests in Tampa are my son and daughter. Beyond that, I don't care what happens there."

Gramp Simpson laughed out loud. "Relax, Michael. Don't be so cautious. People trust revenge. What do you need from us?"

Twenty-four

"Grandpa. It's Terry." He was calling back, after the Old Man had left a message.

"Terry? How are you doing up there? Everything all right?"

"Yeah. The new walls are just about done. Thanks again for the hardware. Probst has them at the new gates. They'll help a lot."

"Well, I don't want to see the College pounded into dust."

"It won't be. So, what's up?"

"Terry, I'd like you to come home this weekend."

"Are you all right?"

"I'm fine. Well, as fine as a man as old as I am can be."

"And you're okay in the boardroom? I'm a little concerned about what I read about boardroom instability in Cities that aren't part of this new Framework."

"You're getting too much of your news from New York. The City's in fine shape. There are just a few things that I'd like to get resolved with you and your…father."

"Dad? You're inviting him?"

"Yes. I'd like to have the three of us together. For a few hours."

"Okay. Well, this is kind of a surprise."

"Oh, for God's sake, Terry. Don't be so dramatic. I'm older than most people. And our family's affairs are complex."

"Yes, yes. You can count on me. I'll be there."

"Excellent. I'll send Masterson up with a fast plane. And everything's going better up there?"

"Yes. Our walls are stronger and we're training the students to think more about security."

The sat connection started getting a little fuzzy.

"Very good. Okay, I'll have Masterson contact you about the schedule."

"Okay. And dad—"

"He's coming in sometime Saturday. But he's staying on his boat. Then we'll get together for a proper family meal Sunday afternoon."

The signaled blurred.

"I'll see you in a few days, Grandpa."

"Yes. Excellent."

The Old Man seemed different than usual. Scared? This had to be something about his health. He'd had gene therapy for youthfulness. And he'd had nanotech to wipe out the cancer. But all of those "cures" came with unpredictable side effects. That's why men over 100 thought about their health constantly.

New York's annexation of Hartford and the WNET had changed travel arrangements a lot. The Windsor Locks airfield was part of New York now; but the Blue Zone was still far from secure. There were bandits and religious zealots connected to the Company battling just outside the new walls. And, when they weren't fighting each other, they were hijacking traffic going in or out. So driving in was dangerous, expensive and time consuming. It was better to hire a tiltrotor to pick up at Memorial Field and then fly into Boston/Logan. Masterson and the other Tampa pilots all liked flying into a large, secure airport better than a small one in a security zone anyway.

To Hailwood, this seemed like the wasteland was taking over Cities, rather than vice-versa. The old-school radicals at the College who complained about "corporate police states" were making more sense lately than they had five or six years before. When it was still possible to drive into Manhattan.

The small tiltrotor picked him up from Memorial Field at 7:00 a.m. sharp, Saturday morning.

One advantage of this new travel arrangement was that he could watch the campus below him as the tiltrotor took off. It was a smooth transition from kids jogging around the sports fields to the clean lines of the new walls. Then the campus and the town faded into the rust and yellow waves of the Berkshire foothills.

It sure was beautiful. Worth fighting for.

The flight took about half an hour.

When he climbed out at Boston/Logan, the jet was waiting for him on the tarmac. This was important. As long as he went straight into his own jet, he didn't have to go through the Boston Security

Forces checkpoint. If he did *that*, he'd have to check his guns. Boston's anti-gun laws were stricter and more strongly enforced than any other big City he knew.

And Boston Security was beefing up after the recent boardroom coup. Boston wasn't part of the Framework. Because of that, the new directors were gearing up for war with New York if New York tried to annex Boston, too. More laws and paranoid leadership. This was the shape of things to come in second-tier Cities.

It was good, as always, to see Steve Masterson in the cockpit.

"Another trip home, professor?"

"Yes. My grandfather calls and I obey."

"It's like that with all of us."

"The older I get, the more I understand that."

"Okay, buckle in. We're going to buzz the hell out of here and get home in time for the end of the Bucs game."

"All right."

He had papers to grade but slept almost all the way to Tampa.

His mother was waiting for him as the car pulled up to the House. She looked a lot different—she'd lost some weight and cut her hair dramatically. She'd gotten some sun and was wearing less or different make-up.

"Honey, good to see you. I was afraid I was going to miss you."

"Miss me? Why?"

"I'm about to leave."

"Where are you going?"

"Europe. I'm going to stay with my friends the Ellegoods in London for a few weeks. And then I'm going to visit my old college friend Liz West in Paris. I've always wanted to have Christmas in Paris. And then the Ellegoods are going to join me again for a trip down to Santorini and Crete. A proper European vacation."

She was high. Even though she looked more relaxed, the manic squint returned to her eyes as she laid out her itinerary. Her sense of self-preservation knew something bad was coming…and she was making sure that she'd be out of ricochet distance.

There was no point in confronting her about any of this. She was probably doing the right thing, in tactical terms.

She'd be traveling with her "friend" Martha Downs. In fact, the recently-retired TSF Maj. Downs was a high-end bodyguard. She was as effective as—and infinitely less noticeable than—two or three muscular thugs.

"Well, your hair looks good."

He was lying. The short hair made her face look mannish. But he'd read or heard somewhere that short hair was coming back into fashion. And he wanted the quickest exit from this conversation.

"Thanks. I just had it cut a few days ago. Apparently, short hair is the style in Paris now."

"Well, you're going to have fun. I can tell. When are you leaving?"

"Tonight."

"That's sudden. You're not staying for this proper family dinner that Grandpa wants to have on Sunday night?"

"No. I've been planning this trip for weeks. And I'm not particularly excited about seeing Michael. It's just a happy chance that I get to see you before I leave."

He took his things out to his room and cleaned up from the flight. Then he and his mother took a walk along the water. Even in October, it was hot.

She chatted nonstop about her plans for seeing plays and eating out at her favorite restaurants. She'd stepped up the regimen of her anti-aging gene therapy for the trip. That was why she'd lost weight. She was planning side trips to Ireland and Scotland when she was in London. And she planned to go to Berlin and Barcelona while she was staying in Paris.

"Maybe you should try to come over and join me for Christmas, Terry. You might find an intellectual French girl to take your mind off of Kate."

"My mind's not on Kate, mother. It's on work. And making sure that the College survives on its own out in the wasteland. In the process, it's practically becoming a City."

"Well, maybe that's the natural evolution of things. And a Hailwood always seems to be in charge. If there's one around."

"Maybe. You're going to have a great trip to Europe. And when you get back, things are going to be back to normal around here."

"Back to normal? What do you mean?"

This was bad. She was playing dumb. Even the ladies who lunched in Tampa's most gilded cages knew enough about world events to understand the bandit problem. And everyone in Tampa knew their City wasn't part of the Framework.

"There's been a lot of anguish lately everywhere about the brigand armies. Politics."

"Really? Well, you know I try not to pay attention to politics. And you shouldn't, either. You should just concentrate on teaching rhetoric to the smartest young people in world."

"Don't get me started on that again, mother. There's more politics in teaching than just about any line of work around."

"More politics in teaching than in politics? Well, that's a shame."

Trying to have a meaningful conversation with her was useless. Trivia was her tactical defense. And her walls were high.

They walked the length of the point and then back to the House. After talking more about the friends she would be visiting, she made an unexpected conversational turn back to him. "I'm really glad that you're settled into what you're doing, Terry. It's a great relief to a parent to see her child on a good direction in his life."

He considered explaining to her how unsettled his life felt. But she wasn't really interested in his take on his life. She was focused on telling him what *she* believed.

"Mother, relax. You're talking in such ominous tones. You're about to take a great trip. Your thoughts should be light and easy. You don't have to sew up everything. This isn't the end of the story."

"Oh, I know. I know. I guess I'm just feeling sentimental about saying good-bye to the House and this place for a long time."

"If you like it, you should get an apartment in London or Paris and go there every Christmas."

"Yes. You're right. I should."

His mother and her friend/bodyguard left a few hours later. Hailwood saw them into the car that would take them to the airport. He hugged his mother and shook the hand of Maj. Downs.

His grandfather was nowhere to be seen.

After his mother had gone, Hailwood asked the staff if they knew where his grandfather was. No one did.

He called some of the old Prep guys and found a party going on in Ybor City. He had the driver pick up Chris Stanton and Richie Conroy on the way to the party. The girls hosting it were from a family of new arrivals from Havana by way of Miami. Why they'd moved to Tampa, no one knew. There was gossip about drug money in the family's past. The father had set up the two daughters in a huge loft apartment and they were having lots of top-notch parties.

Stanton and Conroy had a lot of questions about the College. Stanton, who was a lawyer with SpielbergDisney, had gone to Dartmouth. Like most alums, he was concerned about it surviving as a distinct school. "I mean, is it even going to exist in five years? Or is it just going to be absorbed into the collective?"

Hailwood didn't feel like talking about school, so he gave Stanton the answer he wanted to hear. "The big news on campus is that we expanded the walls to include most of the original town. So, for all practical purposes, we've become a City. There's plenty of infrastructure for the schools who've moved in to maintain their own identities. I wouldn't have said that a year ago. But it's true now. Now, you guys tell me if the bandits are going to attack the north walls here."

Stanton said, "The bandits are bullshit."

Conroy just sneered. He worked for Gulf Aerospace and had strong opinions. "It's not the fucking bandits. They're just cover. The real threat is Jacksonville and these religious freaks who fight for Michael Crowley."

"So, you think he's going to try to come back?"

"His followers think he's the fucking messiah. And everyone knows that Chambers and your, er, grandfather, er, trumped up those embezzlement charges against him. And then Chambers married his wife. The whole thing takes on mythic proportions."

"Mythic proportions don't mean shit against 90-milimeter plasma cannons."

"Yeah, but he has thousands of zealots eager to die fighting for him. And he has Jacksonville's guns and tanks backing them up."

Hailwood had never bought into all the heated gossip about Michael Crowley and "the Company." He'd heard all kinds of talk about the Company, even up at College; but he'd seen little evidence of organization or power. And he had a hard time believing that a born-and-bred manager would suddenly reinvent himself as a desert messiah. "Then the religious freaks are just cover, too. It's all about Jacksonville making a move. They think there's a spot for them at the Big Cities table if they take over Tampa and Miami."

"So why isn't your grandfather making a move against Jacksonville first?"

"He doesn't run things."

"Bullshit." Both of his friends said it together.

Sic Semper Tyrannis

"Okay. Because he doesn't take geopolitical advice from me. He's a deal guy. He'd rather see Chambers make a deal with Jacksonville."

They got to the party around 9 p.m., which was kind of early—but it was already going strong. It took them almost five minutes of Stanton's best fast-talking to get past the security. And he was on the guest list.

Inside, the bars were serving mojitos and cigars, fully embracing the Ybor City *Cubanos* style. Hailwood didn't mind. The drinks and smokes were good.

Stanton introduced him to the Rodriguez sisters. They were unremarkable. Giggly and looking around the room while they made small talk. The older sister was Hailwood's age exactly but he felt 10 years too old for her. Maybe more.

That was fine, though. He wasn't looking to hook up with anyone the night before a serious meeting with his father and grandfather. He thanked his hostesses for their generosity and wandered over to one of the bars for another drink.

The music—Caribe funk trying a little too hard to be edgy—was a little too loud, so he headed toward the balcony at the back of the apartment to smoke his cigar under the stars. It was more like under the clouds. But he was glad to be outside.

And then he saw a woman who grabbed his attention.

She was wearing a red dress. She had dark hair and olive skin. Cuban. And a fantastic body. Curvy. He could tell just from her chest and shoulders. Big breasts but thin upper arms and a lean neck that meant she worked at keeping in shape.

Her face was as full as her body. It was pretty enough. But the hair—thick and jet black, pulled back in an oversized braid that went farther down her back than he could see from this angle—drew Hailwood's stare. Big dark eyes that weren't darting around. They were staring squarely back at him.

She'd caught him looking, so he needed to do something to acknowledge. He lifted his cigar and smiled. She lifted hers and smiled back.

She was sitting at a table with two other women. And the other two were definitely women, old enough to be grandmothers of most of the crowd. No one at the siren's table was talking. They were so out of place that they must have been family. Some relations of the Rodriguez sisters.

Hailwood shook his wrist in the universal drink symbol. The siren nodded slowly while she smoked her cigar.

He ducked inside to get a couple of drinks. Then, it occurred to him that he should get drinks for everyone at the table.

He ran into Stanton at the bar, talking to some tarted-up debutante. Stanton introduced him to the deb—who shook his hand firmly once she heard his last name. "Where've you been?"

"Outside smoking this. Now I'm inside getting a drink for a lady."

"Very good. Who?"

"I saw someone interesting outside. Long black hair. Red dress. Killer body. Any ideas?"

"You just described half the women here."

"No. This one's different. Sense of control of the place. Sitting with two older ladies. I was thinking they're some kind of family of the sisters."

"No idea. You're on your own."

Hailwood had to do some convincing, but the bartender eventually gave him a pitcher of mojitos and four glasses. The tip helped. Managing the drinks, the glassware and a lit cigar was tricky. He ended up holding the cigar and the pitcher in his right hand and the glasses in his left. This was the best way to navigate the crowd.

It took a few minutes to weave his way back to the balcony. He was a little concerned that the siren would be gone—but she and the older ladies were still there.

"Anyone like a drink?"

"Thank you, yes. I didn't realize that there was table service here."

He put the cigar down on an ash tray and poured the drinks. "Well, this is a special service. Easy way to break the ice. I'm Terry Hailwood and I'm looking for a nice place to sit."

The siren smiled warily and nodded to an empty chair.

He poured himself a drink and sat down. "Thanks. Cheers."

"Cheers."

The older ladies didn't say a word. They were either surprised or they'd seen this so often that they were unimpressed.

"So, what brings you to this hipster party?"

"I'm Maria Elena. Sassy and Jelly's aunt."

The two older ladies were Maria Elena's aunts—the girls' great-aunts. Maria Elena lived in Miami. The great-aunts lived in Cuba. They'd all come to visit the girls and their family in their new homes.

Hailwood said he didn't know anything about the girls or their family. He asked the siren for some background. She shot quick looks at the great-aunts and said something about "background not being so easy." Her face was very expressive—in the eyebrows and lips.

She offered some of the story. The girls' father—Maria Elena's brother-in-law—was a banker. He'd set up the Miami office for Havana Merchant Capital Bank and lived there for almost 20 years. Then there was a management shake-up at Havana Merc and he was fired. But he didn't want to leave Miami. So, he started a boutique bank, handling special money for rich Cubans and *Sudamericanos*.

He was retiring to Tampa because it had better security.

"If he wanted better security, maybe he should have retired to Jacksonville." The mojitos were bringing out Hailwood's cynicism.

"Maybe. But I've been to Jacksonville. It's not the kind of place you'd want to retire. It's the kind of place you want to retire *from*. It smells bad."

"Yeah. It does. Always been a big paper town. And making paper stinks."

Stanton stopped by the table with the deb in tow. Hailwood introduced Maria Elena who introduced the great aunts. Stanton introduced the deb and they joined the table. Hailwood went to get another pitcher of drinks. He wasn't sure he had the right amount of cash to tip the bartender again—but it turned out he didn't have to. When he got to the bar a different bartender automatically switched his empty pitcher for a full one.

The first one was the trick.

When he got back out to the table, the older ladies were gone. Conroy, a girl and some other guys had taken seats. Stanton was in the middle of some apparently hilarious story. Their furtive looks told Hailwood he was the punch line.

He poured some more drinks, sat down in the chair next to the siren and grabbed a book of matches to light his new cigar.

She took the matches out of his hand and lit one for him. She had slightly noticeable wrinkles at the corners of her eyes. "So, Hailwood. Your friends tell funny stories about how stubborn you are. What do you do here in Tampa?"

She was older. He was intrigued.

"I visit."

"You don't live here?"

"My family lives here. And I still think of it as my home. But I work up north."

"New York?"

"No."

"Where?"

The noise—music, chatter, ambient humanity—was getting louder, even outside. Stanton flashed a fleeting smile at Hailwood. But he and Conroy were lost in their own hook-ups.

The centrifugal force of sociability was pushing Maria Elena and Hailwood together. This was good.

"I teach at a college in New England."

"Harvard?"

"No. Not Boston. Out in the wasteland."

With that clue, she guessed the College right away.

"Do you know New England?"

"No. But I know smart people. Less boring than *stupidos*."

"It's getting loud. You want to go?"

"Where?"

"Somewhere not so loud. We can get a drink. Or get something to eat. Or go back to my place."

"I thought you didn't live here."

"My family has a place out on the Keys."

"The Keys? Nice."

"Yeah. It is."

He drank some of his mojito. She took his cigar and a drag. When she smiled, the corners of her mouth curled up but the middle stayed still.

He smiled back and looked up at the clouds. They looked like a white blanket. It was the reflection of the City lights.

"Okay. I'll go with you. But I should warn you, I get bored."

"I don't think that's going to be a problem."

He one-button texted the car to say he was coming. He thought that she'd want to say good-bye to Sassy and…Jelly? But she didn't. She headed straight for the door.

He liked walking behind her. She had a great ass. She was short, maybe 5'2" or so. But that figured. Her curves wouldn't hang so well on a larger frame.

He didn't have time to tell Stanton and Conroy he was leaving. Not that either would have cared.

The area around the elevator was jammed with people coming and going, so they walked down the stairs.

"My brother-in-law thinks that it's good for the girls to be in the news as socialites. He has a very American notion of celebrity."

"Maria Elena..."

She turned to hear what he was going to say and he kissed her hard on the mouth. He moved in so quickly that they almost knocked foreheads. But he turned his neck just in time.

He could feel the corners of her mouth curling up as they kissed. And moved his tongue quickly along the back of her front teeth. Next to fucking, this was the most intimate thing he knew.

But there were other people coming down the stairs. And he wasn't trying to make a scene.

"...I don't give a fuck what your brother-in-law thinks."

"Okay."

The stairs let out on the ground floor at the entrance that was only for the sister's loft. The crowd was even thicker here. And there were paparazzi outside.

Some reality star from the vid nets was getting out of her car and the cameras all focused on her. While this photo op was going on, Hailwood and Maria Elena were able to slip out and around, leading a handful of other people who knew what they were doing.

The car was about half a block away. Hailwood took her hand and cut across the street. The driver was at the wheel and Bert Menendez was standing by the door. "Home?"

"Yeah. That direction. Maybe we'll stop somewhere for food along the way."

The doors shut quickly and the car pulled away while the cameras were still flashing at entrance of the party.

The siren started laughing. "I thought we were going to hail a cab. Now what kind of college professor has a car standing by and knows how to sneak past paparazzi?"

"What are you talking about?"

"Give me that cigar."

The drive out to the House took about 30 minutes. It took them about 15 minutes to smoke the rest of the cigar. The rest of the time, they kissed and groped each other.

When they got back to the House, the siren composed herself. And started laughing again.

"What's so funny?"

"I don't know."

"Come on, don't bullshit me, *sirena*. You don't like to be bored. I don't like to be lied to."

"This is a ridiculous scene."

"Hmm. Well, at least it's not boring. I'm having fun."

"I'm having *fun*. But I haven't done this in a long time."

"I find that hard to believe."

"Yeah, well…how old are you, Hailwood?"

"Twenty-seven. Do you care?"

"No."

"Good. Come on, let's have a nightcap and I'll try to convince you to be truthful to me."

They went into the House. Maria Elena laughed quietly each time they walked into another room. It was early—not midnight yet. And Victor and some of the staff were all still up and about. The Old Man was out at dinner but expected back soon.

Hailwood didn't want to go through the hassle of making mojitos, so he poured two big rum and cokes. He offered to get another cigar. But she said she'd had enough. He led her out to the dock. She took her shoes off and they sat down by the water.

"You're rich, professor."

"My family is rich, *sirena*. Does that impress you?"

"I don't know. I guess you didn't seem like this when you looked at me at the party."

"You thought I was poor?"

"No. I thought you were a brash young man trying to act cool."

"That's probably fair. Hey, listen." The whomp-whomp-whomp of a car coming across the bridge echoed over the water. "Do you hear that sound?"

"Yes."

"I love that sound. It means home to me. It means coming back for Christmas and all the best times with my family."

"Really?"

"Yep." He drank the *Cuba Libre*. After the expert mojtios, it didn't taste very good. Too sweet and kind of flat.

"I think you're an eccentric man, professor. You're sitting at the mouth of Tampa Bay, one of the most beautiful places in this world, and you're listening to cars driving across the causeway."

"Well, there you have it, *sirena*. You thought you were going to shag a cocky buck and you've ended up with an eccentric professor."

She climbed into his lap and kissed him. She knocked his glass into the water, but neither of them cared. He slipped his hand into her dress. Her breast filled his palm. He rubbed her nipple with his thumb and it got hard.

So did he.

"*Sirena*, I want to ravage you."

"I would like to see you try."

They walked back along the dock and decks and across the driveway to the guest house. She slipped out of her dress in one motion. He was interested in the garter she wore on her thigh; it carried her wallet.

He took a little longer to get out of his clothes.

She was decisive. And she didn't laugh so much now. She guided his hands and other body parts. She used her hands and fingers on him. And on herself. She was willing to do anything he wanted. And he wanted to do everything. But she wanted him to do specific things to her. She barked "yes" and "no" at different points in different positions. And she did come—though he couldn't keep up with how many times. He came three times. The last, he was on top and drooled onto her chest. She didn't laugh; she rubbed her fingers through it and then put her fingers up his ass.

A few minutes later, when she was on top and came, he put his fingers up her ass and she bit into his shoulder.

That was a first.

"You're a fucking animal, *sirena*. I should put you in a box and take you with me everywhere I go."

"If you try to put me in a box, I will kill you."

He laughed. Figured she might. There was an ancient power in her threat. That was clarity. Do something to me that I don't like and I'll kill you. He laughed, just to hear her laugh too. He figured it was the best way to disarm her.

Hailwood slept soundly and woke up around eight with a slight hangover.

The bed was wreck. Half the pillows were on the ground and the sheets were twisted into knots. She was still asleep. But not curled up sweetly next to him. She was sleeping crosswise, near the foot of the bed. She was on her side, snoring.

He stared at her ass. It was round and muscular, even when she was sleeping. Her skin was olive and smooth—but she had slight tan lies where a bikini would usually be. He tried to guess how old she was. Older than he was but probably not 40. He guessed in her mid-30s. There were older women who used anti-aging therapy to look in their 30s, well into their 50s. But she couldn't be one of those. The body didn't lie—and women who used anti-aging therapy usually had tell-tale signs in their breasts and asses.

He got up, used the bathroom and stared at the bite welt on his shoulder. It was sore to the touch. But it wasn't bleeding.

Then he went to the kitchenette and got them both some ice water.

When he came back to the bedroom, she was awake and sitting at the head of the bed with a sheet pulled up around her. An unexpected bit of modesty from a woman who'd just joined in some of nastiest, angriest and best sex he'd ever had.

"Water."

"Yeah. Very good. Thanks."

The day was already sunny and clear.

"I've got a family meeting this afternoon. But this morning is all ours. You want some breakfast by the pool?"

"Sure."

"What do you like?"

"Anything. Lots of coffee and fruit."

He called over to the main house and asked Victor for some breakfast. Then, he got her a bathrobe and found some sunglasses. An old pair of Kate's. She used the bathroom, came out in her underwear with her hair in a ponytail and wrapped herself in the bathrobe.

They went out by the pool and ate. It was already getting hot.

"You look great. Like an old Hollywood movie star."

"It's the bathrobe and glasses; they make anyone look chic. You've had a woman here, Hailwood. Someone felt comfortable enough to leave hair ties and skin lotion in the bathroom. Do you have a girlfriend."

"Had. At least I'm pretty sure *had*. We were at the point where we were either going to get married or break up. And she said we should see other people."

"I know that conversation. How long ago?"

"A few months—no, almost a year."

"At least she didn't marry you and *then* break it off."

"Well, what's done is done. I'm looking for a new thing now."

They swam and drank ice water and ate fruit until their hangovers eased away. They walked the length of the dock and boardwalk out to the north point—the same walk he'd take the day before with his mother. He did more talking this time.

She made a couple of calls to check in with her family. She needed to get back around noon. At 11:30, he saw her into a car. She was still wearing the bathrobe and sunglasses—plus her heels from the night before. Her wallet and garter were in one of the robe's pockets; she carried the red dress over her arm.

"I was going to fly back tomorrow. But I'd like to see you again, *sirena*. Maybe I'll stay an extra day. Want to do something tomorrow?"

"Sure. A proper date? I haven't had one of those in a long time."

"Yeah. We'll get some lunch, then maybe go out for boat ride or something. Then have dinner. Then fuck each other senseless again."

"There's something relaxing about that, eh?"

"There sure is. I've just got to get something for this welt on my shoulder. So, I'll pick you up around noon tomorrow?"

"Yes."

He kissed her hard on the mouth again and then held her face in his hands for a few seconds and stared hard in her eyes. They were brown. And intense.

"But I'm not sure I'm your new thing, Hailwood."

"That's okay. I'll settle for something relaxing right now."

She laughed at that.

He closed the door and slapped the trunk of the car. The driver didn't need the prompt. It just seemed like the sporty thing to do.

Hailwood took a long shower and organized his thoughts for the meeting with his father and grandfather. This was going to be a rare chance and he didn't want to blow it by just sitting at the table, nodding like a moron.

He worried about something happening to the Old Man. Everyone in the family knew that he'd created a series of trusts that were the legal owners of the family's shares in the City Corporation. But no one else knew the details. And the Old Man was notorious for not writing things down. His notebook was in his head.

When Hailwood walked over to the main house, his father and grandfather were already there.

His father was on the satphone with someone. His grandfather was reading news on his screen on the back porch. "So, you had some company this morning?"

"Yes. A woman who's related by marriage to this Cuban banker who's moved into town."

"Felix Rodriguez?"

"Yes. She's his sister-in-law."

"He's a money-laundering front for brigands and drug lords."

"So, why'd we let him in?"

"Launders a *lot* of money. Plus, strong ties to the Cubans. And he swears he's cleaning up his act. He posted a $10 million immigration bond. So, he's got a large incentive to stay clean."

"New City, new start."

"That's what they say."

His father rang off. "Terry, how are you doing?"

"Fine. How was the ride up?"

"Lovely."

"Where's the boat?"

"I tied it up over by the village docks. My guests are checking out the village and getting some dinner while I'm here." There was no chance that the Old Man was going to host a bunch of his father's whacked-out friends at the House.

The Old Man had other plans. "Well, I'd like to get this show on the road. I thought the three of us should get together because Terry has been bugging me about our family financial plans for a long time. And I've put him off. But there've been some developments lately."

"Are you well, Grandpa?"

"Well? Well, no. I haven't been feeling well for the last few months. And, of course, my first thought was that it was the cancer recurring. But I've been checked out six ways to Sunday and there aren't any tumors or legions anywhere."

"So what is it?"

"My doctor says it's a system-wide failure. The cancer, the nano, the gene therapy—they've all combined to wear down my nervous system. This is apparently happening a lot with people my age. There's some cellular therapy they can give me. But it just makes me feel better. Doesn't actually *do* anything about the nervous erosion."

"Nervous erosion?"

"That's what they call it."

Michael cut to the point: "How long, dad?"

"They're not sure. But, at the rate I'm going, six months or less."

"Jeez."

"Don't worry. I have a plan for dealing with this and I've already put it into action."

Hailwood: "What are you going to do?"

"I'm going to go into space."

"On a Mars mission?"

"No. I'm going to be on board one of the quantum field test ships."

"What? They're putting people on those things?"

"It's not public, but they are. I'll be on the second ship."

"And you're going to be shot out into deep space at some faster-than-light speed?"

"Maybe. Or maybe I'll be killed instantly. But if I'm not—if the flight works as planned—I'll be in space for what seems like a couple of days to me but seems like 50 or 60 years to everyone here. And, when I get back, I hope we'll have some kind of cure for nervous erosion."

This was hard to believe. Incredible. But the Old Man seemed completely serious.

"And it could be longer. From what the TSA techs tell me, they can control where I go. But they don't have any idea how quickly I go there. It could be a little more than the speed of light or it could be hundreds of thousands of times faster. The faster I go, the longer I'll be gone. On the far end, the trip could seem like a few seconds to me and be hundreds of years here."

Hailwood's father didn't say anything. He didn't seem surprised. "Did you know about this already, dad?"

"That he's going up in space? No. I had no idea."

"You don't seem surprised."

"Well, maybe I'm harder to surprise than you are, Terry. This doesn't have anything to do with the markets, does it, dad?"

"No. I wish that I could stay and see everything through this hard patch. But you two are going to have to do that."

His father kept talking in a slow and certain voice. "However you spin this, it's going to sound like you're running away. And that's going to hurt the City." This wasn't like him. It seemed like some kind of power was shifting from his grandfather to his father.

He felt out of place. His father and grandfather both seemed to have better senses of what was going on than he did. "Is there something going on here that I don't know about?"

His grandfather gave him a frustrated look. "Well, we're having major problems with our man Chambers. And we've got an army of religious zealots lead by *Michael Crowley* and backed by the Jacksonville Security Forces making its way toward our northern walls. The New York markets are trading our bonds down by the minute. And I'm leaving you to run our affairs."

"Me? Are you kidding? Why me? And why's this skipping a generation? Dad, you need to come ashore from your pleasure barge and help out here."

His insult seemed to fly past his father. "That's not the plan, Terry. You're the best person to take over here. I'm sorry it's happening so quickly."

"What am I supposed to do about my job?"

The Old Man interrupted him, angrily. "You're supposed to *quit*. Goddamn it, boy, the school is falling apart up there. We can give them all the guns in world—but they're in an impossible situation."

The return of an angry tone of his grandfather's voice was actually reassuring. Anger was the Old Man's normal mode. If he'd been cautious and kind, Hailwood would have been more worried.

"So, what am I supposed to do when I take over? I mean, if Chambers is a problem, my plan would be to fire him and make myself—or the Office of the Executive—CEO."

His grandfather shrugged his shoulders a little. "Terry, soon enough you can fire all the managers and declare yourself CEO or dictator or philosopher-king or whatever you want. But you will find that fronting the City government is not a gentleman's work. I predict that your reign in front of the cameras will be short. I just hope that your reign behind the scenes will be long."

"Grandpa, I think your worries start with the word *reign*. I have equity in the City Corporation. That gives me a bigger right to state my position that other people have. But I'm not a king. If everyone is against me about something, I'd have to listen. And I'm not afraid of admitting that. If working in academia has taught me anything, it's that open negotiations work better than caginess."

His grandfather shook his head. "What citizens want and what the City needs aren't always the same thing. If you were to become a manager and everyone knows your family controls the Corporation, you'd become a slave to the tyranny of the minority. And that's what ended the Federal Era. It doesn't do anyone any good to repeat that."

"I look at it differently. If everyone knew that the CEO controlled a voting majority of corporation shares, anyone trying to cross him would need to have a very strong case."

His grandfather smiled in frustration, baring his teeth. "You can experiment with your political theories all you want. But, remember, you need to keep the trusts from going bankrupt. The trusts are the basis of your authority. They always have to come first."

Hailwood looked over to his father for help.

Michael just rolled his eyes. "Look. Let's keep this away from a debate over philosophies of corporate governance. You two can do that any time. My interest is more getting some personal business straight. Dad, you're talking about these religious freaks backed by Jacksonville. Now, that's a serious problem. If Tampa gets annexed by another City, we're basically broke, right?"

"Tampa's not going to be annexed by anything."

"You said yourself that things aren't going smoothly. So, what do we do if they get worse?"

"You sell your barge and get a job."

"You can't insult me, Dad. If Jacksonville's in league with Michael Crowley, that means they're going to try to annex Tampa. And you're not going to be here. That's a big deal. We need to get everything clear so Terry and I know what to do to keep our assets intact and the money flowing. Because I have no interest in running the City—but a large interest in living my life in my way."

The Old Man got up from the table and poured some coffee. Hailwood tried to figure out what was bothering him. The family strife was the same as it had always been—nothing new. The Jacksonville situation? "The truth is we wouldn't be broke. The recent annexations have taken the form of mergers or acquisitions between the Cities involved. City Directors aren't brigands."

"But brigands *are* brigands, Grandpa. And Crowley's group acts like brigands. He probably wants to burst in and take over. Divine retribution for us kicking him out. Or something. Why didn't you kill him when you had the chance?"

The Old Man looked weary. "Didn't seem to be any need. I just wanted to get rid of him because I…thought Chambers would deliver dividends and not go on and on with all the League of Cities stuff. Look, I made a mistake."

It was the first time Hailwood had ever heard the Old Man say *that*. He felt like he should say something supportive. "So that's one you'd like to have back. So what? Crowley was ahead of his time."

The Old Man sucked in a breath through his teeth. Maybe it was more about Crowley than Jacksonville. His grandfather wasn't used to making mistakes. And he couldn't avoid the fact that kicking Crowley out had been a mistake. That mistake was coming back to attack him. Literally.

Michael stepped in again: "Look, you two. Let's not keep getting off track. This isn't about management philosophy. It's not about politics. It's about making sure the family keeps the cash flowing, regardless of what else happens."

"You're right. We're supposed to be protecting the future. And I shouldn't be talking so much. If I want to run things and shoot managers, I'll do that when my turn comes. I'm sorry, Grandpa."

His father gave his grandfather a nasty look.

Again, Hailwood sensed there was something else going on. "Is there something else here I'm missing?"

The Old Man sat down again at the table and rubbed his temples. "We're going to step back here. We need to take a step back. Tear the house back to its foundation in order to build it back up again."

The three of them sat in silence for a minute. Hailwood thought about saying something—directing the conversation to the mechanics of the family trusts—but it seemed that the Old Man was thinking about something else.

Finally, the Old Man stopped rubbing his head. He sat up in his chair and started talking.

"Terry, I'm doing this. I'm leaving in a few weeks because it's my best chance to go on living. And I'm tired of my life here. So, I'm going to be honest with you. So that you have the best chance of succeeding with everything I'm leaving you to handle."

Hailwood was about to say that the Old Man didn't have to sound so dire. But the Old Man beat him to talking: "The first thing that I need to tell you is that your father isn't your father."

Hailwood's stomach tightened up. This idea had always been

there—in the back of his mind. With his mother living in the House and his father off living some debauched life on his boat. But he'd put the details of how it might work behind him. And, right now, he didn't want to hear a confirmation of his worst fears from the Old Man. Denial felt like a very comfortable option.

Both older men were looking at him, anxious to see what he would say.

He didn't want to say anything. He didn't care about the family's fucked up dynastic dynamics. He just wanted to live his life.

But he knew that saying nothing was the coward's response. "So, who is? You?"

"Well, in a manner of speaking. You're a clone, Terry. You're a clone of me."

That wasn't what he'd been expecting.

Hailwood's first thought was to I.B. Lieber back at the College. *He* was the descendant of a clone. And clones were suspect.

Damn.

The Old Man started talking and Hailwood just tried to absorb everything without comment. The details poured out. Hailwood's father—the man he'd thought of as his father, Michael—couldn't have kids. And wasn't inclined to try. His marriage to Marianne was sinking.

This had caused major problems between the father and son. Grant and Michael.

The Old Man had tried a couple of times to sire another heir by conventional means but didn't have any success. His wife was too old to conceive naturally and wasn't interested in artificial reproductive therapies. The Old Man had tried working with mistresses and surrogates but the anti-aging therapy had wrought havoc on his sperm count.

Plus, clones born from artificial wombs were notoriously troubled.

So, he'd put it bluntly to Marianne. They'd implant the clone in her and she could carry it to term. In exchange, she'd be the legal mother of the Hailwood heir and, no matter what happened to her marriage to Michael, she'd always have a place in the family. She saw the logic in it right away.

After a couple of false starts, she carried the child to term. And the child was Terry.

Hailwood could see the paradox of his still reaction. The situation called for dramatic response. Operatic violence or melodramatic tears. But he didn't feel like doing either. He didn't want to move. He sat in his seat at the table and took in everything the Old Man said.

He didn't judge it or read the Old Man's voice and mannerisms for signals. He didn't question the truthfulness or completeness of what the Old Man said. He just absorbed the facts as presented.

The Old Man didn't dwell on the cloning stuff for long. Soon, he'd moved on to the financial mechanics of the Hailwood fortune.

"Most of our income comes from dividends from three sources. A controlling interest in the City of Tampa corporation. A 15 percent stake in the Tampa Bay Port Authority. And a nine percent stake in Tampa Power and Light Co."

This was news. Hailwood hadn't known that the Old Man had so much money in the Port Authority and the power company. This was more diversification that he'd expected—although it was a pretty narrow kind of diversification. If Crowley and his true believers took over, they might just seize all three entities.

"The shares are controlled by a series of trusts...."

There was cash in New York and Geneva. There were some real estate partnerships. Michael prompted the Old Man through these financial details. "We know *that*, Dad. I think what Terry and I would like know is more precisely how these trusts are set up. And we don't want to hear it from an attorney after you're gone."

The Old Man kept drinking his coffee and staring outside.

Hailwood understood the delay. His grandfather had never wanted to discuss the mechanics of how he controlled the City Corporation and its Board of Directors. These were as much family secrets as who had whose DNA. He'd often said that vagueness was essential to keeping power.

But a small part of Hailwood had always suspected that the Old Man didn't want to discuss the specifics because he wasn't completely in command of them. That thought made more sense than ever now.

This made him want to say something. "Dad's...Michael's...right. Forget the space ship. If you get hit by a bus tomorrow, what's there? We need to know, so we can make sure the family stays in control."

That was it. His interest was in making sure the family stayed in control. Everything else could sort itself out in time.

The Old Man finished his coffee and refilled the cup. Then, he came back to his seat at the table and took it.

"Fair enough. There are a few exceptions—but most of the stock we own follows the same model." His tone had changed; now, he was talking in the well-rehearsed monotone of someone making a boardroom presentation. "There are a total of 12 trusts that own controlling interests in 12 different holding companies. Each trust is the general partner of each holding company. Sometimes the trust is the sole owner of the holding company; sometimes there are minority partners. Usually individuals whose cooperation or alliance we wanted.

"Each trust names one or two family members as its beneficiary. Five name Terry as beneficiary. Four name you, Michael; one names you both together and two name Marianne. So, when I'm gone, some combination of two of you will have to agree on essential decisions.

"I'm trustee of all 12 trusts and—as trustee—serve effectively as the general partner of all of the holding companies. Each holding company owns between two and six percent of the total shares available of City of Tampa corporate stock. So, taken together, the trusts control just under 60 percent of the outstanding shares of the corporation. The same applies to the Port and power company stock; the stock in those is spread around the holding companies."

"Why not have the shares in one holding company?"

The Old Man looked annoyed. Annoyance became him. "Securities laws. Disclosures. Things to be avoided. Since no single holding company owns more than six percent, none gets close to the 6.49 percent threshold when mandatory public disclosure kicks in."

From the way that the Old Man mentioned Tampa securities law, Hailwood could guess who'd drafted that law. The Old Man.

"So, the entire ownership structure can fly under the radar of public reporting?"

"Eh, yes. Under the radar. We can avoid disclosure about the details of who owns the shares or who runs the trusts."

"Why is that important?"

"It gives us some flexibility with regard to tax reporting. It prevents any curious cats from stumbling over exactly how much stock we own. And, most importantly, we can buy or sell shares without drawing attention."

"So, we use the trusts to buy and sell shares?"

"Yes."

"Why?"

"Taxes, again. But also to make sure the market in City stock remains liquid and stays within price ranges we want."

"So you manage the market for the stock?"

"Yes. The term is 'make the market.' But we don't it ourselves. Our brokers do. We just make sure they have enough inventory to keep things where we want them."

"Isn't that illegal?"

"No. There's a loophole in securities law that allows a controlling shareholder in a publicly-traded corporation to 'assure liquidity' in the stock. This makes things safer for individual investors."

"Really?"

"Yes, *really*."

"So, we get credit for controlling the majority of the shares but we avoid the reporting obligations of having more than six-and-a-half percent?"

"Yes. And I'll make sure that we keep it that way."

"I understand. How much of our total holdings do you trade in a given month?"

"Not much. I make sure that we keep the total shares we own in the City Corporation above 51 percent."

"Why 51?"

"Some financing packages and lines of credit that we have require us to keep absolute voting control at all times."

"What do we use lines of credit for?"

"Buy more stock. Take other opportunities."

"Do you use one bank or many for these loans?"

"We have lines available at four local banks. Five more in New York and a few in China. The idea is that we can raise cash quickly if we need it—but no single bank would be exposed to fluctuations in the stock price."

"And the banks know about this?"

"The banks *requested* it."

"Safety in numbers for them, I get it. How much of our stock is security for loans right now?"

"Insignificant amount. Less than one percent. But, we can boost that to almost 50 percent instantly if we need the capital."

"What's the most you've ever pledged at a given time?"

"*Ever?* Well…a long time ago…I took more chances. I went as high as 50 percent when I was younger. But I wouldn't do that again. The most we should encumber is six or seven percent. And then pay that off quickly. That's still a lot of money."

Hailwood hadn't said anything since his comment about the Old Man getting hit by a bus. The whole conversation was going on between Michael and the Old Man. But Hailwood would remember every word for the rest of his life.

"Do we owe any long-term debts or have other liabilities that might interrupt our cash flow? And what exactly is our cash flow?"

"No long-term debts or long-tail liabilities. The City pays a dividend of almost four percent every year. That kind of performance is worth a lot. Hell, it's downright amazing. Those dividends are the engine that drives everything. The rest of this is just minor stuff. Technical tools for financial management."

It was becoming clearer to Hailwood how the Old Man spent his days. Making sure the City's stock price stayed consistent. Borrowing and repaying loans. That's why he didn't handle day-to-day management.

"Who knows about the trust-and-holding-company structure, dad? Chambers?"

"Hell, no! No one involved in City management knows anything about our personal capital structure. They're our employees, for God's sake. The details of our finances are none of their business."

"So, who knows about it?"

"Bill Franklin and our other personal lawyers. With no ties to the City. They can't even take on City agencies as clients."

Bill Franklin was an old crony of the Old Man's. They'd know each other since they'd been young men. Franklin looked the part of the Brahmin professional—he was well over six feet tall with a full head of white hair. If he wasn't wearing a fine suit, he was in a blazer and ascot. He sailed. Sailboats.

"I know Franklin. Your old sailing buddy. Who else?"

The Old Man ticked off the names of six attorneys at four law firms. Hailwood suddenly realized how little he knew about Tampa law firms. He recognized one of the firms. But he'd thought two of the others were a single firm. And he didn't recognize the other at all. It took some effort to move even a little; but he made a file for the lawyers' names and the firms in his screen. He'd check them out later.

"What happens to the trusts when you take off on your trip?"

"Well, now. That's an interesting question. My will states that Terry serves a co-trustee with Bill Franklin on the trusts. Michael, I've never thought you would want this kind of responsibility. And, even if you wanted it, I don't think you have the mind for it. That's just the way I see it."

Michael smiled a little. Despite his tough talk, he *was* stung by the insult. But, in the end, the Old Man was probably right. Michael's interest in these financial matters was intense…but fleeting…as it was in many things.

Hailwood still felt enough filial piety for Michael that he hoped Michael would seize the moment and make a stand against the Old Man's imperious rule. But he didn't.

"I'll live, dad. I think Terry's judgment is good about things like this. Better than mine will ever be. And as long as he keeps our financial resources in order, I'm happy for him to do things as he see fit. But, Terry, the money has to flow."

That summed things up. Michael had the clarity that came from knowing who he was and what he wanted. Who he was and what he wanted were vulgar—but, at the moment, that seemed better than the cloudy confusion Hailwood felt..

The three of them sat in silence again for a while.

This time, Michael and the Old Man weren't looking at him. Or at each other. They both thought they were finished. But Hailwood still had some questions. He took a deep breath and pressed up the energy to ask.

"Okay, so how long until you take off?"

"Unclear. These test flights are done quietly, so they're not scheduled like official flights. At least six weeks; maybe 12. They've got a Crusader set up for the purpose but the propulsion system is all very experimental. That takes some time to get ready. In the meantime, I'll do everything I can to get this matter with Crowley's Holy Army resolved. That should take care of the currency issues and a lot of the pressures we're feeling right now."

"Have you told Franklin about this or given him any orders to keep the trusts operating while you're gone? Or anything like that?" His questions weren't as succinct as Michael's had been.

"No. He doesn't know anything. It's like I've always told you, Terry. You'll be free to run things as you like when I'm gone."

That made Hailwood laugh.

Michael stayed for dinner and sailed out the next morning. He seemed barely concerned about the news—of course, the shocking news for Hailwood hadn't been news to Michael. He and his party were going down to Rio de Janeiro for some kind of festival. The last thing he said to Hailwood was: "I'm here for you anytime you need me, Terry. If you need to vent or talk, just give me a call."

But the statement he'd made earlier about being happy as long as the money flowed was what stayed with Hailwood.

He had to get used to thinking of Michael as a demanding brother rather than as a n'er-do-well father.

Hailwood stayed an extra couple of days. His class schedule meant that, if he missed one day, he could stay two. He saw Maria Elena again. In fact, he spent most of the time with her. He didn't say anything about his news; but she took his mind off of his troubles, anyway.

On Monday night, the Old Man joined them for a drink on the back porch. The Old Man kept one eye on Hailwood but, as ever, he couldn't resist some kind of flirting with an attractive woman. And *la sirena* was definitely that.

Hailwood threw the Old Man a softball by asking why the Cities were getting more belligerent toward each other.

The Old Man hesitated for a second, then swung. "Poverty. Some of the Cities have become poor enough that they're looking for ways to increase their tax bases. It's the weakness that's always at the bottom of land grabs and federal systems. Cities that can't manage their own affairs think they can grow their way out of their problems."

"But they can't."

"I don't think so. But things like this are almost like fashion trends—everyone gets swept along, even if they don't need it. The big Cities will consume nearby small ones and take control of their regions. It'll go for a while like that, then the regional powers will realize they're growth didn't change anything and they're still going broke. Then they'll start battling each other to be in charge of a bigger federal system. And then those fall apart."

Maria Elena asked "What's going to happen to Tampa and Miami?"

"Well, we're both in pretty good financial shape. While I can't speak for Miami, I'd like to see us remain on the sidelines. Neutral. Let the desperate ones play their games. We'll just keep to our own thing."

Hailwood asked "And we'll go to war for the right to stay neutral?"

"If we have to. But, if we use our brains, these things can usually be resolved without fighting."

"And what about Michael Crowley's religious army?"

"Unless he lost his mind out in the desert, Crowley is a rational man. He'll make a deal."

"And if he *did* lose his mind out there?"

"Then someone will need to do something about that. And Jacksonville will have the biggest interest in that, since Nico Karamanlis is doing business with him."

"That's right. They're allies now. Go figure."

"Yes. But, when it comes to Jacksonville, there's no 'they.' Only 'he.'"

"Karamanlis."

"Yes."

They moved on to talking about more philosophical matters—and instinctively spoke in terms vague enough that *la sirena* wouldn't take away anything specific.

"Grandpa, how do you know that you can trust me to make the same choices you would? Do things the way you'd do them?"

The Old Man shrugged his shoulders and took a sip. He was nursing a short whiskey. "I don't think of trust in such narrow terms, Terry. It's not that I trust you to do a given thing in a given way. Hell, I probably don't. But I trust you. Generally. I find it's only meaningful to trust people in broad strokes. I don't trust many people. But I trust you. And one thing or the other that you do won't change that."

Maria Elena made a sound, a kind of sigh, that approved of what the Old Man had said.

Twenty-five

They could hear the SkyDragon approaching through the pine trees long before they saw it. Its roar was closer to a space rocket than the *whomp-whomp-whomp* of a tiltrotor. If it was this loud a quarter-mile away, the machine was going to be deafening when it got there.

There were a lot of people in the clearing. The students at Camp B had never seen a SkyDragon before.

When the machine arrived, it seemed to climb up out of the trees—as if it had been marching through them. In reality, the pilot had been flying low along the tree line. It was the best thing to do, to stay off of the Mobile radar or any listening posts that New Orleans or Houston or Jacksonville might have set up around Camp B.

Still, some of the kids in the crowd screamed and clapped when they saw it. But Crowley could only tell by their motions—the sound of the SkyDragon drowned out any noise they made.

The Boeing B-573 SkyDragon was the jewel of conventional security aerospace tech. It was a stealth jet that could travel at four times the speed of sound, near the top of the atmosphere, and hover six feet off of the ground. It was huge—nearly 100 feet long; it could carry bombs, troops or both and could fly anywhere in the world without refueling.

Its wings had a delta configuration for high-speed travel and could adjust to a "rampant" configuration for hovering, ground support and attack.

SkyDragons were built under license from the Boeing Corporation. And Crowley knew well how complicated these "licenses" were. The Cities buying the bombers would build the basic pieces themselves—or subcontract that work. Then, Boeing engineers would come in and check that the components had been built to specification, oversee final assembly and install the nav and defense systems.

It was that last step—activating the "black systems"—that Boeing controlled tightly. As high-tech as the hardware was, it was useless without the software. It literally couldn't hover or do any of the VTOL maneuvers without the right programming. And the stealth systems wouldn't work.

Boeing was careful about how many of these vehicles it allowed to be built. And under what conditions. Doing so, the company controlled the balance of power among Cities more than most people realized. It made sure no City had an advantage over another…unless Boeing's board decided that it favored one over another.

And Boeing could be ruthless about protecting its franchise. Some years earlier, the Mormons in Salt Lake City thought they had developed their own software for operating an earlier version of the SkyDragon. Its performance was not up to Boeing's standards, but the SLCDragon did fly. For a few weeks. Some managers were shocked that Boeing didn't do anything right away. Then, without any warning, a squadron of some 20 or 30 unmarked SkyDragons—whose performance *did* meet Boeing's standards—attacked Salt Lake City. All of the SLCDragons were destroyed, most while they were still on the ground, and the walls around Salt Lake City were blasted into rubble.

A few days later, the merger between Salt Lake City and Denver was formally announced.

The SkyDragon that landed at Camp A was configured as a troop transport. It had seats for 100 commandoes and their equipment—plus the usual stock of SkyDragon weapons. Brownsville had managed to work out a deal with Boeing for the rights to eight SkyDragons—though it had only announced a deal for six. The additional two were for spywork and "black ops." And this machine was one of those two. Brownsville's clandestine support of the Company was one such op.

The ancient gunsmith had been very good about handling the secretive work of arming and securing the new City. Sixty years of selling guns had taught him the shadowy details of City defense secrets. As Crowley had expected, the gunsmith had been able to help figure out the source of the phantom plasma rifles that the bandits around Camp A were using.

Sic Semper Tyrannis

To Crowley's relief, he hadn't *been* the source.

Brian, the ancient gunsmith and their partners back in Brownsville understood the importance of this meeting. So they were willing to loan Crowley the unmarked SkyDragon. It wasn't the most efficient way to go—even with its high tech engines, this machine would burn as much fuel as six or eight tiltrotors on the trip to Jacksonville.

As soon as the machine landed, the pilot cut the engines. They took a few minutes to quite down. The passenger door folded down automatically and slowly, which added to the drama of the entrance.

Jana was standing at the top of the stairs when they finally touched the ground. She was smiling mischievously and waved once, regally. "What do you think?"

His ears were still ringing a little from the roar of the engines. "You look like an Amazon queen! You're going to knock them dead in Jacksonville."

It was true. She was wearing a robe that he'd ordered for her from a famous old London women's clothes maker. It was meant for horse riding—full-length and dark red, with black velvet lining and a full hood. He thought it would make a strong impression when she entered political meetings. And, if she felt self-conscious about her eye, she could pull up the hood.

"How do you feel?"

"I'm fine. Don't worry about me. Focus on this trip."

"We've got to land just like that when we get there. And, if we can swing it, we should be the last ones to arrive. There are so many details…God, I don't remember everything that we used to do when we set up summit meetings."

"Don't sweat these details, Michael. You don't have to set anything up. They're setting things up for you."

She kissed him and wrapped her arm around his.

"Maybe. How's Mikey?"

"He's fine. He's with Ana Flora. And Brian and Brandy are there. Don't worry about them. Focus on Jacksonville and Houston."

"Oh, I'm ready for them."

"Good."

They timed their arrival well. The managers from Mobile, who were shifting their allegiance from New Orleans to Jacksonville, had arrived the night before. But the groups from Houston, Charleston and Atlanta all arrived at Jacksonville's main landing field around 10 am. They all arrived in executive tiltrotors—as expected at such a meeting.

Crowley and Jana and their party landed in SkyDragon 20 minutes later. The landing field techs guided their landing to an arranged spot, among the tiltrotors. Their vehicle stood out.

While the stairs eased down, Crowley and Jana looked down onto a crisply-organized welcome. The first thing that he saw were three huge banners in turquoise, black and gold—the City colors. They were 10 or 12 stories high, draped in front of each of the three air traffic control towers that were spaced evenly along the face of the main terminal. The banners made the terminal seem like some kind of huge battle fortress. And that was probably by design.

Two of the banners were emblazoned with giant versions of the City crest—a hand holding a hammer in front of a power plant, a crane and group of workers. Very industrial. While most Cities emphasized their brain power, Jacksonville emphasized its manufacturing muscle.

The middle banner had a different image. It was a huge portrait of Nikolas Karamanlis with the words "Patron of Greatness" in huge block letters underneath.

The group of Jacksonville managers standing below them on the tarmac seemed like so many fleas, in front of the banners. Behind them, a small crowd of citizens oohed and aahed and clapped politely.

The air was hot but not as humid as he'd expected.

It was thick with the smell of wood pulp. It was tangy—almost like the smell of an orange, but less natural. Crowley remembered this smell from his last trip to Jacksonville, as a senior manager from a neighboring City.

"Mr. Crowley, welcome to Jacksonville. I'm Will Jansen, Chief Operations Officer. This is Maude Hammerstein, our Vice President of External Development, and Harry Samuelson, our Chief Security Officer." There were eight or 10 other managers in the group, but Jansen only introduced himself and the two others.

"Mr. Jansen. Ms. Hammerstein. Mr. Samuelson. This is my wife, Jana Morrell Crowley." He also introduced the four students he'd brought along. They had important-sounding titles and they were proven bodyguards; but they weren't really significant to the Company. They were practically decoys. Everyone who was important was busy.

Jansen did all of the talking for Jacksonville. "We're glad that you could make it to this summit meeting. Mr. Wilson from Houston, Mr. Phillips from Charleston and Mr. O'Meara from Atlanta have just arrived and are heading to their quarters to rest and freshen up before lunch. President Karamanlis is at his residence, preparing. He asked me to let you know that you can go to your quarters if you'd like or you can go directly to his residence for a quick meeting before lunch."

This was according to plan. Karamanlis was anxious to discuss their next steps against New Orleans and Tampa.

"Thank you, Mr. Jansen. Our trip was short and smooth. And I've been looking forward to seeing Mr. Karamanlis. Let's just go on to his residence."

"Excellent. I know that he's been looking forward to seeing you again, too. I'll call ahead and let him know we're coming directly. Also, it's important that I point out our City ordinances ban gun possession by anyone who isn't on active duty with the Jacksonville Security Force. In recognition of your ambassadorial status, we will allow your party to carry weapons. Our scans show that each of you is armed. That's okay. But, if you draw or fire your weapons at any point, you will become subject to City law and we may have to ask you to leave immediately."

"Thanks for notice, Mr. Jansen. We appreciate your position. If any of us has to fire use our weapons, we will probably *want* to leave immediately."

Jansen stepped away and the rest of them walked across the tarmac toward a smaller, nearby terminal where a half-dozen limousines and three small tiltrotors were parked.

The crowd was well-dressed and well-behaved. That meant it had been carefully chosen. Jacksonville was a tightly-managed City.

And this was an important event. The Jacksonville managers believed they were emerging as the regional power. Some thought that hosting this regional summit would help them gain admission as a participant in the City Framework.

From behind, Jansen said "We'll take the tilt pods. They'll save us half an hour."

Each small tilt could seat four passengers. Crowley and Jana climbed into one with Jansen and one of their students. The other students and the Hammerstein woman got in the second tilt. The Security Chief and staff got in the third. Everyone else went by car.

As soon as they lifted off, the three tilts were surrounded by half a dozen security helicopters. These were cutting-edge models—the kind most Cities used for external security patrols.

"Our escort," Jansen said. "We try not to paranoid about things. But we know Tampa has drone airplanes and extremely accurate smart missiles. We're just not sure when they'll decide to start using them."

He looked like he expected Crowley to reply.

"You're not paranoid, Jansen. But you're probably overreacting. I doubt they'd try to shoot managers out of the sky. They don't think managers are that important. If they make a preemptive attack, it'll be on a landmark or public facility. My guess is they'll want to do something that will scare your citizens."

"Interesting observation. I don't think our citizens scare so easily. And we keep a pretty tight lid on the pop media."

Really, *that* was interesting. Jansen overestimated his management skills if he believed they could control free net access. Most smart managers had accepted external media access as a fact of life.

The ride in the small tilt was bumpy and loud—like riding a motorcycle in the air.

Jana squeezed his hand and nodded down to the City core along the river that wound through the City. It was lined on both sides by oversized buildings like the main airport terminal—and many of them were covered in banners or billboards. It looked like a picture of Nazi Berlin or Communist Moscow in a history book.

Jansen saw them looking. "It's the St. John's River. One of the few great rivers in the world that flows south to north."

Jana answered. "The development of your City is impressive. I'm still not accustomed to the scale of these buildings."

Jansen smiled proudly. "The President's 20-Year Plan for City Development. We'll be finished in two years. When he started, none of those riverfront buildings were there. And everything you see today is designed to last 100 years."

A 20-year plan. Buildings meant to last 100 years. This overriding ambition made Jacksonville's managers sound like small-town rubes.

This had always been their problem. Real, big Cities were more pragmatic. Less controlling.

The trip to Karamanlis's residence took about 10 minutes.

The residence sat on the top of a hill near the coast in Jacksonville. It was a big place, of course. A compound in the modernist style, but without the propaganda that marked the public buildings and City streets. The compound was well positioned on the property to take advantage of the view and—probably—serve the security needs of each part. There were walls; and then the outbuildings formed another ring around the main House.

As they approached, it occurred to Crowley that the hill might have been man-made. Its placement seemed mechanically perfect.

He squeezed Jana's hand.

The three small tilts landed in formation at the pad a little off to the north of the House. The escort vehicles hovered but didn't land. As soon as everyone got out of the small tilts, the escorts screamed away.

Jansen and the Security Chief spoke quickly to the leader of House security detail, who nodded several times and led them inside. It was starting to get hot. Samuelson and his security troops vanished once they got inside.

The conference room was big and clean. Its one glass wall faced the courtyard garden at the center of the House. The real views were probably saved for the living space. Jansen saw them in, asked if they needed anything and then bowed out for a few moments. He left the external development woman—Hammerstein—with them.

She, Jana and the students took seats at the conference table. Crowley, as he usually did, walked over to the glass wall and looked outside.

Jana offered everyone else and then poured herself a glass of water. She made the chit-chat. "So, I saw the staff prepping the lunch as we came in. Looks like we'll be out on a sea-side deck. Very nice."

The Hammerstein woman jumped right in. "Yes. The views from the Mansion are spectacular. It's hard to find nice beaches up here near the Central City. Most of the nice ones are a little south. But the view is amazing. As long as it doesn't get too warm, we'll have a great lunch."

Crowley noticed the tone of confidence in the acknowledgment of the hot weather. It was a small thing—but the kind of thing that builds trust. The woman wasn't stupid.

Jansen came back into the room and Karamanlis followed.

He was older than Crowley remembered, of course. He also seemed smaller. That couldn't be right…but it might be the effect of all the pictures of him. After seeing so many five-story images of his face, you were bound to find him smaller in person.

"Michael Crowley. It's good to see you again."

"Nico. It's been a long time." They shook hands. Karamanlis's grip was strong for such an old man. "A lot has changed since we last shook hands."

"Nonsense. You're simply leading a new organization." He gestured to a chair near his at the head of the table. They didn't sit down yet.

"That's one way to think of it."

"I had no doubt that I'd see you again in a position of authority. Maude, the Security fellows have some things they want you to look over before the rest of our guests arrive for lunch."

"Of course, Mr. President. Mr. Crowley, Mrs. Crowley. It's been a pleasure to meet you. And I look forward to talking with you more." She wasted no time exiting the room.

Karamanlis rolled his eyes toward Crowley's students.

Crowley asked them to wait outside. But to stay near the door, in case he needed them for anything. They knew this meant to size up the security troops guarding the place.

"Nico, this is my wife Jana. She's my trusted advisor. Jana, Nikolas Karamanlis."

"Mrs. Crowley. It's a pleasure to meet you. I've actually heard about you. Your family is one of the founders of Brownsville and you ride alongside your husband everywhere he goes. That's quite impressive."

"Thank you. My husband says that you've been a City CEO longer than anyone else in history. He admires you for that."

Now Crowley and Karamanlis sat.

"I'm glad you were so sure about me, Nico. I had some pretty dark days out there in the wasteland."

"Of course you did. And I've had some dark days here in the lap of luxury. But the point is that a man of quality doesn't stay down. It's impossible. You were bound to come back. And here we are

Sic Semper Tyrannis

again, talking about Tampa's future. But not in a way that that fucker Hailwood would like to hear. Excuse me, Mrs. Crowley."

"No. He's in for a surprise."

"So, tell me: Where are your troops and what's their schedule?"

The armies from Camps A and C had made the long trip and were holding about 50 miles west of Jacksonville's west walls, just off of the old Christopher Columbus Freeway. Karamanlis certainly knew this. Together, they were almost 20,000 troops. They were well-armed and mobile. And they knew their mission was to breach Tampa's walls at the northeast gates.

But Crowley remained vague about the details.

"They're one day from their final staging point north of Tampa. The plan is that they head out this afternoon so that they're in position before dawn tomorrow."

"Excellent. Our external security forces have cleared the path south along the Old 75 Highway, so your guys won't have any bumps along the way."

Crowley's great fear was that the managers in Tampa would be waiting on the Company's arrival. 20,000 troops was a lot—but not the largest army ever gathered. Tampa's security forces plus its reserves would have more than that many bodies. Of course, City security reserves weren't as well trained as his students…but the numbers would favor the City.

"Once they're in place, you and I just need to make our call to Mr. Chambers tomorrow morning."

The killing blow would be if Karamanlis betrayed them. That's why the army from Camp B was standing by, rested and well-fed at home. Strategically, they were supposed to be ready to set a siege around New Orleans and serve as a buffer between the action at Tampa and everything else. But they could also set a siege at Jacksonville—or attack it, if the situation required.

"My plan is to call him a nine o'clock sharp. And I'll be an honest broker, just trying to work out a solution between two well-equipped sides." He winked at Jana.

Crowley's fears ebbed a bit. Karamanlis had more to gain in Tampa's surrender than in betraying the Company. And, as Jana liked to say, self-interest was trustworthy. Even if a person's individual words or small actions weren't.

He had to find his way back to feeling confident in these board rooms. In the old days, confidence had been one of his strengths as a negotiator. He'd been certain that he was good at handling difficult situations; and so he was. Now, he felt like he'd caught the second-guessing disease. And he wished he could get rid of it.

"I still believe we should keep quiet about this to the rest of the summit until they're in place tomorrow."

"I agree, Michael. Happy talk today and general strategy tonight. Nothing inconsistent with our actions—but nothing specific. In fact, I hope that *they* do most of the talking tonight. I'd like Wilson to say something for once."

"Good luck with that."

"Yes, I know. But I'd like to gauge what they think before we drop the bomb tomorrow. These men aren't stupid. They've probably heard about your movements. Hell, I heard you were moving troops a year before it was true. It's what everyone in this part of the world has been fearing."

"I don't make my plans according to what City managers say they fear, Nico. They lie too much."

"You don't make your plans by it. But you listen to it. Their fears tell me that something fundamental has changed. For 200 years, the Cities didn't give a damn about what went on the wasteland. Now, they're worried. Up north, they're making the wasteland disappear. Pushing their walls into each other. Because they're afraid. Of you."

"Are you trying to flatter me, Nico?"

"No. I wouldn't insult you like that. You haven't done all of this yourself. But you've been the catalyst for changes that have been happening for years. The population in the wasteland has grown faster than the populations in the Cities. We knew this was happening 30 years ago. But we didn't do anything. We thought our money and our walls would keep the wasteland out. Tomorrow, you and I are going to put that to the test."

"You don't have to sell me on this. I'm sold. My troops are moving into place. The biggest risk we face now is that Tampa's satellites will pick them up."

"But they're organized to avoid detection."

"Well, obvious detection. But it's hard to hide that many troops completely."

"They'll be fine. Tampa has relied on technology for so long that its security analysts have become dull."

"That's what we're counting on. If my troops do what they're supposed to, everything you've said is true. If they lose, you're wrong and we'll all be sorry."

"I'm not wrong. What happens on the battlefield is always a predictable result of what happens in the board room."

Crowley looked at Jana. She was watching Karamanlis over the rim of her water glass. She didn't look like she bought what the Patron of Greatness was selling—then again, she was probably feeling a little sick. She'd downplayed it with Mikey and she was downplaying it now.

"Okay, Nico. The school books say you're right. All of my management training says you're right. But we live an imperfect reality ruled by imperfect market information. So, I have one simple question for you. Are you aware of any scheme to ambush or betray my troops?"

"No, Michael. You're ahead of everyone."

"Good. Then we're *both* ahead of everyone."

"Is the field commander good?"

"He's the second-best commander I have. I've ridden with him. I've watched him fight. He'll fight until he's won."

"Outstanding. But where's your best commander?"

"With the second-best troops."

The lunch was very nice and strictly social, as such things usually were. This wasn't all good for Crowley and his party.

Crowley had had his group dress in their version of City fashion. One of the early practical lessons he'd learned was that black clothes with simple lines worked in most situations. That's what they (except for Jana, in her robe) were wearing.

But—there were differences. Even though the lines were simple, they were evidently out of fashion with the intricate details of current design. Plus, his students wore jackets that covered their weapons and provided light body armor. Back at Camp, they'd looked like long-time City managers; among long-time City managers, they looked like soldiers.

Many of the aides and staff weren't comfortable dealing with gun-toting people from the wasteland. *They* all recognized each other from conferences and meetings and other summits. They didn't know Crowley, or at least not his students.

The awkwardness would have been worse if the summit had taken place somewhere other than Jacksonville. Its managers and citizens dressed less fashionably than other City dwellers. This mitigated some of the obvious differences between Crowley's students and the rest of the people on the deck overlooking the ocean.

Jacksonville people also spoke and acted in a less gossipy manner than the management elite from other Cities. They were used to having their and conversations scanned. But less gossipy didn't mean *not* gossipy. Elite managers…even ones from police states…traded on gossip.

And the group from the wasteland was cut out from that.

Karamanlis must have noticed the isolation. When he spoke before the meal, he made a point of welcoming "our new allies from the wilds. We hope your presence here is a sign of advantages to come for all of us."

That was as close as anyone came to talking business anyone talked at the lunch.

When they finished eating, a couple of the CEOs came over to welcome Crowley and Jana to the meeting.

T.R. Wilson knew them the best of the CEOs there. He'd met both Crowley and Jana several times. Crowley and the students stood when he approached. They shook hands and Wilson did a kind of Asian bow to Jana. "You look striking in that robe, Jana. Regal."

"Thank you, Reg. I hope not too regal, though. Wouldn't want to be mistaken as anyone's queen. Especially not here."

"Yes. Jacksonville is a workers' paradise. No Brahmins. No money center banks. No queens. But don't worry. The only workers you'll find up here are the ones clearing the plates. Michael, I'll see you downstairs in half an hour?"

"Yes. Time enough for everyone to get on their satphones and fine out what's going on at home."

"Or what's going on in the world at large."

"Exactly."

"See you then. Jana."

The world at large. Maybe he had an idea of what was happening. Houston had satellites, just like Tampa. Maybe his analysts could read the pictures better. Or maybe—as Crowley had long expected—Houston had spies in the Company.

Sic Semper Tyrannis

Crowley had met Phillips from Charleston once, years before. Phillips had done well, keeping his small City relatively strong and independent. Personally, he was a ladies' man who didn't even seem to like the company of men much. There were many jokes that he wanted to *be* the women he was with, as much as sleep with them. But he seemed too comfortable in his persona to have any deep secrets.

"So, most of your troops are located around the Gulf?"

"Yes. Most. But we call them 'students.'"

"But you have outposts elsewhere."

"We call them 'franchises.' And yes, we have franchises on the southeast and up the Atlantic coast. As far north as New England."

"Outstanding."

"There are a lot of people in the wasteland, Larry. And they need so much. We start with teaching them to read and shoot a gun. The rest is up to them."

"You've certainly tapped a growth market, Michael. Good for you. And I suppose you're going to tell us what our plans are here this afternoon." He smiled as he slipped the dig in at the end. Typical management behavior.

"I'm not telling anyone what their plans are, Larry. I'm here to listen to what you City bosses have to say." He winked at Jana.

She looked away.

"And we're here to listen to what the boss from the wasteland has to say."

"I'm hardly the boss. There's too much wasteland. I'm not even sure I'm the boss of the Company. It's a decentralized organization."

"Really? If that's so, it's the only one in the history of mankind. You still pushing the idea of a confederation?"

"Larry, I'm not pushing anything."

"Would you still *support* the idea of a confederation?"

"Sure. For what it's worth. I don't control the kind of assets and infrastructure that even a small City does. The main thing that I have is people."

"Troops."

"They're more than troops. They're an organization with unifying beliefs. They're people who deserve to be treated like more than outcasts and savages."

"That sounds like an army."

"Yeah. Maybe that's what they are. An army." Crowley was more argumentative than he'd planned to be because he was getting tired of the conversation with Phillips.

The importance of the word *army* was that Cities had carefully avoided it since the Trade Wars a hundred years earlier. The series of bilateral treaties that had ended those wars prevented most big Cities from keeping standing armies. The loophole had been to call troops "security forces." These distinctions had seemed logical to him when he'd been a manager; now they seemed pointless.

And that's what scared the managers. That he had raised an army. And that their logical systems seemed pointless to him.

Phillips left to make his calls before the meeting.

Crowley and Jana left, too. She wasn't feeling good and needed some sleep. He sent two of the bodyguards with her in a car. They'd take her to the government house where they'd be staying for the summit. Apparently, it was just a few minutes away.

Crowley didn't have much time before the afternoon meetings started, but he made a call to Jean Jacques.

"How's it going there, Captain?"

"Very good, Rabbi. The road is wide and smooth. We should be at the staging point ahead of schedule."

"Good. But don't rush too fast. You want to have night cover when you get there."

"I don't think that will be a problem. The earliest we'll arrive is midnight."

"Okay. Well, maybe your guys can get a couple hours of sleep."

"My thought exactly."

"Okay. And how have the ex-sec people from this place been?"

"Very good. Very professional. If they're nervous, it's hard to tell. Our sprinters say they're watching us—but not mounting forces in any large numbers. They seem to be keeping their end of the agreement."

"They don't want the Tampa birds picking up any massing."

"The Tampa birds. Or the Houston birds, eh?"

"Yes. Maybe so. Maybe more so."

"We're doing fine, Rabbi. Don't worry about us. We'll be at the right place at the right time. Then it's up to your talks with the big shots. That's what's important."

They agreed Crowley would call later that night, after midnight. Next, he called Brian.

"How's it going?"

"Fine so far. Everything's proceeding according to plan. Our friend sounds assuring."

"Good."

"Your meeting still on for today?"

The Gramps were meeting later that afternoon at the Morrell farm to talk about whether Brownsville wanted to get involved in the Tampa situation in any direct way. Formally, there was a problem: Brownsville's close ties to Houston made it a natural opponent of Jacksonville's rise. At least that's what Wilson would expect. Informally, Brownsville could go on supporting the Company with hardware and logistical support forever. The farmers, conservative by nature, were content with that—even though the Houston trade agreement meant they had to sell some of their produce at below-market rates. (Of course, they were reimbursed for that difference by the City.) But some of the downtown business guys were sick of using Brownsville tax moneys to subsidize produce for Houston. They wouldn't mind forcing some kind of break.

"Yeah, we're still on. Gramp Simpson is all hot and bothered to grab his guns and go shooting."

"He's always been emotional."

"And he's always liked you, Michael. But I'm guessing the other Gramps will rather wait and see."

"No doubt. How are things going at the airport?"

Brownsville Security had loaned the company some tiltrotors—and the SkyDragon that had brought Crowley to Jacksonville. The tilts were standing by at Camp B, with a dozen of the Company's own tilts, to arrive at the staging point at dawn. But Crowley was worried that a couple of dozen tilts wouldn't be enough.

Brian was arranging for Brownsville Security to make another dozen tilts available. But he was starting to get some resistance from the managers and other board members. They were starting to complain that so much hardware was going to clandestine operations far from Brownsville's walls. So, he was having to call in favors to make the additional tilts happen. And he might have to count on favors from his fellow farmers.

"They'll be there if you need them."

That was a guarded response, even in the short-hand that they used for satphone conversations.

At his weakest moments, Crowley wondered whether Brian was really as supportive as he tried to sound. Tampa and Jacksonville were a long way from Brownsville. And Brownsville was new enough among Cities that it didn't need to get involved in foreign wars.

"Okay. We'll know that in about 24 hours."

"Call me any time."

"Okay. How's Mikey?"

"He's fine. He was just talking to Jana."

"Oh? Good, I'm glad she called. She's been feeling a little sick."

"Bound to happen. I'm surprised she made the trip. Guess I shouldn't be, though. I've got to go, Michael. Take care."

He cleared his mind and went back into the conference room.

Twenty-six

The Security Committee's regular "public" meeting was Tuesday evenings at 7 p.m. in the Converse Building Red Room. The room was an old lecture hall; they'd started having meetings there a year earlier, when the consolidation and the expansion of the walls had made a lot of people interested in what was going on.

Even now, months later, students would show up occasionally—stirred by some policy or procedure that they considered a violation of universal civil rights.

This meeting wasn't one of those, though. The only observers there were a couple of people from the Merchants' Association and a reporter from the student newspaper.

Lieber called the meeting to order and read the minutes from the previous meeting. Hailwood laughed at life's ironies. Part of his dislike of Lieber had been based on the man's cloned ancestors. There were plenty of *other* reasons to dislike him.

They moved slowly through new items. Hailwood's proposal was near the bottom of the agenda.

Chief Keyes gave a report on some attacks on the East and New North walls. They were picking up again, after a couple of quiet months.

"The new plasma cannons work real nicely, though. Their range is almost a half-mile and they're true right up to it. It doesn't take more than one or two shots to chase away these bandits. The rest of the time, we keep on top of rogue shipping containers."

"And let's hope that's enough," Lieber added. He was trying to move on.

But one of the underclassmen on the Committee had some questions. "Chief, is there any chance that this spike in attacks could be setting the stage for another coordinated attack?"

435

"Well, of course it could. But we're pretty sure we knocked out the bandit leadership after the last one. It'll take them a long time to develop new leaders."

"What about the religious zealots in 'the Company'? We hear so much about them—but they don't seem to have materialized here yet. Any chance they could step in and fill the void?"

Keyes looked flustered. Hailwood didn't envy his job. "Well, there's always a *chance*. I just don't have any facts to base that conclusion on."

Lieber sighed dramatically. He was reading something from his screen—probably his copy of the agenda. And he wanted to get through it. He was a ridiculous man, dressed in a so-called "solidarity suit"—that was meant to look like an unskilled laborer from one of the big Cities. But sporting a fashionable geometric haircut that no urban working stiff would ever wear. And, through the whole meeting, sighing and sputtering to show his disdain…for Keyes, the closest thing in the room to a real working-class person.

Even with the plasma cannons, he didn't seem how the school could stay here for very much longer. The determination was admirable and even romantic. But it was also railing against the tide. The thugs and squatters had numbers and time on their side; they would overrun the school eventually. Just like they'd done to the smaller colleges.

Almost an hour later, Lieber finally turned to Hailwood. "And our last item for this evening is a new piece of business from Mr. T.S. Hailwood, the rhetoric instructor. Mr. Hailwood?"

Hailwood wasn't sure he was ready for this. But he took a deep breath and willed up enough energy to sound enthusiastic about his presentation.

"Thank you Dean Lieber, Dean Heath. Ladies and gentlemen." He set his screen to prompt format. "What I'm going to propose today is a radical solution to some of the problems we face

"Let me start right away with the most difficult part. I propose that the Security Committee consider the strategic advantages of moving the College, its new subdivisions, its faculty, students and stakeholders to a new location."

"A new location?"

"Yes. A new physical plant."

"Where?"

"Well, that should be a topic of consideration. But here's a starting point: I can offer some space in the southern districts of my hometown, Tampa."

"Tampa?" Lieber stared at Hailwood.

But Hailwood was looking at the other Committee members to gauge their reactions. "We're building a police state to rival Jacksonville or SoCal behind our own walls here, Dean Lieber. And, from the sound of things, I'm not sure whether it's going to work, in the long term. How long before someone among the bandits and squatters out there decides to swarm our walls again?"

This caused murmurs and hums around the table. The sleepy meeting was getting lively. The kid from the paper was recording audio and taking some notes by hand. Hailwood was squaring off against Dean Lieber—and this time, for the first time, it was taking place in a public forum.

"Mr. Hailwood, I'm surprised to hear this from you. You've been such an advocate of the increased militarization of the campus. And now you're comparing the College to a police state?"

"I love the College, Dean Lieber. And I'll do everything I can to protect it. The plasma cannons will help—for a while. But the long-term prospects are bad. Let's start the discussion now about what we'll do when the situation here becomes impossible."

"And that's moving a thousand miles away from where the College has always been?"

"Maybe, maybe not. It may mean agreeing to be annexed by Boston or New York. I'm not recommending any immediate action. But I've texted a copy of the Tampa Plan to everyone on this Committee—and to the President, the Board and the *Daily Student*. You can take a week or two to review it and we can talk more about this next week."

The first sign that something was changing was the trouble he had focusing in class. Through most of his short teaching history, he'd gotten lost in the lessons and discussions when he stepped in front of students.

In the past few weeks, his mind had started wandering.

There hadn't been any noticeable slips—no trailing off in the middle of sentence or calling a student by the wrong name. But he knew he was heading that direction.

He tried running more. He pressed up from two-and-a-half miles every other day to three-and-and-a-half miles every day. That made him hungrier at meals…and he slept a little more soundly. But it didn't do much for his focus in class.

On his daily circuit through the bird sanctuary and around the athletic fields then up Memorial Hill and across the Commons, he thought about talking to one of the analysts who volunteered for Campus Health. But the College was a small place and the analysts were always likely to gossip—so, that meant he'd have to fly into New York to see someone who'd offer a little anonymity.

That would be an excuse to look up Kate.

Which made him think of Maria Elena. They talked or texted each other every few days. But she hadn't come up to visit, as they'd discussed. And it felt like the whole thing between them was passing away. As she'd predicted.

He stopped running at the top of Memorial Hill. It was a clear, cold day. But there was enough color left in the trees that the Valley retained some of its red/gold radiance from the Fall. There sure wouldn't be anything like *that* in Tampa.

"Professor Hailwood?" It was a student, on his was down to the Field House.

"Milo. What can I do for you?"

"Are we having the Sallust class tomorrow?"

"Sure. Absolutely. Why?"

"I got this weird text from the Dean's office saying class was cancelled…."

Hailwood headed straight over to Converse Hall in his running gear to find out what was going on.

Converse had originally been the College library. Early on, it had been converted into the Administration Building. It had been through several rehabs since then—but it always kept the classical colonial lines that made it one of the most recognizable buildings on campus.

As solid and clean as the exterior lines were, the inside of Converse Hall was a mess. It was a hard-to-follow maze of narrow halls and strangely-spaced offices. Hailwood still couldn't find his way around the third floor…and wasn't too certain about the second. Fortunately, he spent most of this time on the first floor and in the basement.

Sic Semper Tyrannis

He went to Carol, Lieber's senior admin who—thankfully—worked in the office next to the Dean.

"Carol, I think I've got a problem. And I know you're the only person who can get to the bottom of it."

She rolled her sardonic eyes his direction. "Mr. Hailwood. Never one who comes here lightly. What's going on?"

He explained the text that Milo and a few other Sallust students had received. Even if only three or four of them had gotten the text message, Latin 41/Sallust was an advanced course only had nine students in it. A handful would be missed.

Carol pressed through some pages on her screen. Finally, she found the message. "Strange. Even though it has the Dean's ID, it has generic settings. Can't trace it to a specific machine. Looks like it went out to all third- and fourth-level Latin students, though."

"Latin not Rhetoric?"

"Right, just Latin"

That was good, because there were only a few third- or fourth-level classes in the Latin section. But it was also bad, because that made it more likely Hailwood's students were being singled out.

"Somebody's idea of a prank?"

Carol was deep into her search. "Could be. But everything's really well secured here. I mean, we even have biometrics on the screens. So, it's hard to use someone's machine without tripping a lot of alarms."

"So, what does that mean? Where did it come from?"

"I can't see. Don't know. The text came through one of the Converse servers. But it's impossible to see which specific screen. Sorry. Maybe it was some sort of prank."

"Really? Have you had other complaints about pranks?"

"Well, umm. No." She said she'd ask the techs to look harder for answers and get back to him.

As the Old Man would say, so *this* was how it was going to be.

When Hailwood got back to the house, he texted all of the students that he knew in the Sallust class. And he asked them to pass the word on to the others that the class was still on.

It was just 7 p.m. That should be enough time.

Then he called Maria Elena in Miami.

"Yes?"

"*Sirena*, you want to fuck?"

"You're a bad man, Professor Hailwood."

"Lot of people up here who'd agree with that, *sirena*. I want to see you."

"I can't leave my work."

"I'll pay you for your time."

"So now I'm a paid escort?"

"No. Of course not. I just thought you were...blunt."

"I am blunt, Professor. And what I bluntly say is that I'm not for you."

"Let's find out. If you head over to Miami/Dade, I'll figure out a plane to get you up here. You can be here by midnight and we can have a nightcap. You can be back in the office by lunch time tomorrow. If you want. Or you can stay the weekend."

Long silence on the other end of the line.

"I've never been in New England. I'll pack a few things and get a cab to the airport."

"Great!"

He called Victor at the House and had the planes set up in five minutes. There'd be a charter jet waiting for her at Miami/Dade that would take her to Boston/Logan. From there, she'd have a chartered tiltrotor that would bring her to the College. The whole ride would take three hours and 40 minutes from whenever she got to the executive terminal at Miami/Dade.

"Just tell the cabbie. He'll know. When you get there, tell them your name and they'll get you to the plane."

"What about security?"

"There's no security. Just tell them your name and they'll get you on the plane."

"No security? What have I got myself into, Professor?"

"A hell of a weekend."

He took a long shower and dressed ruggedly.

He had more than three hours to kill, so he went over to the DKE house and joined the lads for a few games of beer pong. There was something essentially...carefree...about drinking with the boys before meeting a choice girl. He'd done it a hundred times when the choice girl had been Kate. This was the first time in a long time that it was someone else.

He had been the faculty advisor to the House for most of the year. And a few of the older brothers knew him from when he'd been a student. So, they welcomed him with good form.

But things had changed. He could drink with them but he was different now. They were just as intense as his crew had been…but younger by a psychological stretch.

"It's different, Booboo."

"Sure it is. You're a professor now. You're on the other side."

"Not true. I'll never be on the other side."

"Cheers to that, sir."

That was chastening.

"You should see the girl who's coming up here."

"Kate?"

"No. It's not Kate."

"Sorry. Too bad. She's fine, Terry."

"Yeah. She is."

He felt old.

He drained his beer and checked his watch. Still more than two hours.

He wandered back over to Frost Library and read the *New York Times* dedicated screen for a while. Israel was negotiating terms with the Caliphate. The paper didn't seem to hold much hope in the truce. But the *New York Times* was an unflinching advocate for Israel. Through its many wars—right and wrong—against the other Middle East Cities, the paper had always taken Israel's side.

"Nice to know that some things stay the same," one of the student librarians said, as it got close to closing time. He nodded in recognition of the kid's opinion—even if his politics tended to side with Israel. At least the students were thinking for themselves…or at least thinking assertively.

The library closed at midnight, which meant he still had 30 minutes to kill. He walked out to the top of Memorial Hill. The landing strip was down below, near the athletic fields. This late at night, he'd be able to see her tiltrotor coming from a long way out.

The College was the best home that Hailwood had had since he'd been 17 years old. It was a weird island in the middle of the New England wasteland—but it was worth the difficulty. The College had educated five generations of Hailwoods—so it had been truer than most wives or siblings.

And now he was about to abandon the College when it needed him most.

Her tilt approached from the dead east about 12:40. Right on time. It was a nasty-looking ex-security model, dragging a thick stream of smoke behind it. But at least it was on time.

A couple of campus security cruisers pulled up. One of the troopers opened the directory office and hit the landing lights for main strip.

Hailwood watched it all as he walked down the hill from the War Memorial.

The smoking security tilt didn't even stop long enough to slow its engines. The copilot helped Maria Elena out and Hailwood pounced on her while the crew unloaded her single bag.

He held her face in his hands and kissed her on the mouth.

"I don't what's happening to me. But my life is changing. I want you to see this so you know where I came from. But I think any kind of life with me is going to be a lot different than this."

She kissed him back while the tilt took off to go back to Boston. "Calm down, Professor. I'm just off the plane."

He hugged her and picked up her bag. It was light, "Let's go this way. It's part of the way I run."

They walked into the bird sanctuary.

"I can't believe I'm here. At seven o'clock, I thought I was looking forward to a boring weekend in town."

He dropped her bag and kissed her again.

When they got back to his house, they went straight to his bedroom and had sex. For a long time. They were still new enough to each other that there was a nervous energy to the act. And she was still the least inhibited partner he'd ever had.

He'd made a pitcher of mojitos at the house. But they never got around to drinking them.

She wasn't pornographic, which most girls who wanted to seem free would pretend to be. She didn't talk dirty. But she was completely open to whatever he suggested. And she did things without any warning. Which was new to Hailwood.

He figured that her sexual openness came from the fact that she had a great body. She must have always known this. Comfortable in her skin, etc.

The only price of her full breasts and narrow waist was a head that seemed a little too large for her body. But he didn't mind. Her face was pretty to him, so its outsize proportions didn't matter.

He woke up when the sun was high over the woods to the east of the house.

His side was bruised. But the rest of his body felt like it had been stretched to the point of permanent relaxation.

He went to the kitchen and filled a pitcher with ice and water.

When he got back to the bedroom, she was awake. He drank a long draught of water and then handed the pitcher to her. She drank so much that half the water seemed to spill down her chest and into the sheets.

He licked up some of the water from between her breasts and then kissed her on the mouth.

"I could live a whole life with you in this room."

"I could live that life, too. But I think we'd both get bored."

"Yeah. But getting to that kind of bored is the best thing in life." He dropped down next to her on the bed.

"I don't think so. You're talking college bullshit, professor."

"I said I'd never talk bullshit to you."

"Right."

"Only the truth."

"Well, I don't know that you can tell the difference."

She kissed him on the mouth and then moved down.

When she was done, he fell asleep for another hour.

Later than morning, they both got up, showered together and got dressed. He showed her all around the campus and they ended up at a coffee shop in the town for a late brunch. It was hard for him to do justice to how difficult it had been to walk into town—even a couple of years before. He couldn't explain the way it had been when he'd shot a squatter on the same sidewalk where college kids now walked freely.

"Do you think I should care, Terry? That you killed someone?"

"I don't know. Maybe I want you to tell me I was wrong."

"But he drew his weapon first?"

"Yeah."

"Then you did what you had to do." She drank some of her coffee and folded half of a bagel on itself and took a bite.

"I'm glad you think so."

"Fuck you."

"What?"

"You're talking down to me, professor."

"I'm not."

"I think you flew me up here because you need a vulgar woman from Miami to tell you it's okay to shoot someone."

"No…"

"And I don't think it's about the squatter you shot up here a few years ago. You want permission for something you're thinking of doing."

"I don't…"

"Do you want to kill this dean?"

"No."

"Who, then?"

"I don't know. But, if I'm thinking of killing anyone, it's not a dean up here."

"So you think of killing someone?"

"I've thought about killing my…grandfather."

She smiled. "You're not the only who's thought of that."

"No."

She spread cream cheese on another bagel half. "You want permission from a bad woman to do something bad."

"Would you stop calling yourself names? You're not vulgar. You're not bad. And I don't want your permission for anything. I want someone who wants to be with me, regardless. A harbor from my bad actions. Unconditional love."

"I don't know if anyone's love is unconditional."

He drank some of his tea and looked at her intently. "This is College. It's just a staging point. When I leave here, I'll do things that will seem horrible. And maybe brilliant. They will be in the service of protecting my family's interests. Financial. Political. Will you still fuck me like a banshee when I do all that?"

"I never knew you in your idealistic youth. You've been a hard man as long as I've known you."

"And you don't mind being with someone like that?"

"I wouldn't have come here if I minded." She had a spot of cream cheese on her upper lip. He reached over and wiped it off.

They stalled as long as they could, but Maria Elena left Sunday afternoon. She had to get back to work.

The problems with his classes continued all week. Someone in Converse Hall kept sending out texts that seemed to come from

Dean Lieber's office saying that his classes were cancelled. Carol never got back to him with any answers.

Hailwood didn't mind.

He spent a lot of time by himself, preparing for the next Security Committee meeting. And beyond. He put on a good face during his classes, but he knew the direction he'd chosen was moving him away from the classroom.

The next Security Committee meeting was nothing like the previous. Over a hundred people crowded into the Converse Red Room. A lot of students and minor faculty members had come to see a fight. *The Daily Student* had promoted the meeting as a showdown between the Old College Establishment represented by the Dean and the New College Leadership represented by the young professor with the rich pedigree.

All the members of the Committee were there—which was a first, as far as Hailwood could remember. The complete group included Jack Townsend, the lit teacher who'd been Hailwood's idol and model for years.

But Hailwood could tell from the way Townsend avoided eye contact that he was not going support the crazy talk of moving the College.

Lieber took a slow pace through his agenda. He made eye contact with Hailwood from time to time. He seemed to enjoy the delay.

When he brought up the issue of "Mr. Hailwood's suggestion about a consideration of relocation of the campus and physical facility" the audience was anxious enough that half clapped in anticipation. And half booed.

"Now please, now please. This isn't a parliament meeting. We expect stakeholders to show some restraint."

A few more boo's.

As they'd agreed, Lieber gave Hailwood the podium to make his case. Hailwood made his speech, which was improvised more than anyone expected because his path already clear. He'd only come up because the Old Man had suggested he wind up his affairs at the College.

"I love this College. And I want it—and everything that it represents—to continue for another 400 years. The best case will be for it to go on here, where it has always existed. But I think we need to consider the possibility that the changes in the wasteland here may make it impossible to keep the College an independent entity here.

"We can all see what's going on around us. We've survived a coordinated attack on our walls. We've seen the cities of New York and Boston expand their walls to the point that they're pressed against one another.

"We know that groups in the wasteland are organizing and radicalizing the locals into a state of agitation and—maybe, even—insurrection.

"I know that many of our stakeholders here aren't ready to consider drastic reactions right now. But I want to open the dialogue on the subject of moving the College from this chaotic environment to a more tranquil location."

He let the graphics in the overhead screens illustrate the projected move—and the new location south of downtown Tampa.

He could feel the tenor of the audience. They weren't all with Lieber. But they didn't want to be beholden to a City, either. It was a draw—on the Committee and in the audience. In this situation, a draw was a win for the managers.

The College wasn't political, really. It wanted to exist on a level above or at least apart from worldly concerns.

The Committee voted nine-to-four against spending time or money to consider Hailwood's proposal any further.

Townsend shuffled out of the room without saying anything to Hailwood. All he could manage was tired-looking, non-committal nod.

Et tu, Brute?

It was like the passing of a boyhood idol.

Hailwood didn't dwell on the disappointment. He was already gone.

Twenty-seven

"Michael. Michael. It's time to get up."

It was Jana. She was already dressed.

He was in the bed in the house that Karamanlis had given them for the summit. It was still dark out. It was three-thirty. He'd been asleep for about three hours.

He nodded to her and swung his feet onto the floor. His lower back was sore. It was like this most mornings recently.

He had time for a quick shower and shave. In the shower, he let the hot water massage his forehead while he sorted out what he was taking away from a day and half of meetings with the local CEOs.

The summit had served its purpose. The other Cities in the region were moving away from Tampa—leaving it alone to its fate. They all figured that Crowley was looking for revenge…and that his interest in Tampa was unique. He had little reason to correct that misimpression. More importantly, they'd agreed to schedule regular summits, with Karamanlis taking the lead in arranging those. Even Houston's CEO Wilson had agreed. Sort of They'd make their own Framework, with a more regional flavor.

When Charleston's Phillips had asked him during the first meeting why he was willing to meet with them, instead of staying away like New Orleans, Wilson sounded more practical than Crowley had expected.

"You know why Morial isn't here? He's in New York, proving to the Framework Cities that he's *not* one of us and *is* a good little boy. Begging New York and Chicago to take New Orleans in the second round. I'm not that good at kissing ass—and Houston has no chance in the second round or any other. The Framework guys have made their choice in Texas. They think Dallas is best for them. So, I'm just on the sidelines, watching. Maybe looking for weaknesses in their system."

Everything Wilson said appealed to Crowley. And it was probably designed to do so.

"Someone here might make it into Framework—I mean, they're going to have to take on *someone* from the southeast if they want to be like the old Federal system. But my question is why Michael Crowley has joined us. You're in a much different position, Michael. The Framework managers are paying a lot of attention to you and your franchises. From what I hear, they have external security spies in your ranks—"

"As I'm sure most of you do, too."

Some nervous laughs.

Wilson stayed hard on his point. He thought that one of the Framework's priorities was to kill Crowley and break up the Company.

Crowley explained that the Company was organized to survive without him. It was decentralized—with practically no hierarchical management. The leaders of each Camp and each franchise were able—and expected—to operate independently.

"...but what I really want to stress to all of you is that the Company isn't your enemy. As long as our interests are aligned, we're your partner. When I was the CEO in Tampa, I tried to advance the idea of a regional confederation. I pitched the idea to some of you directly. And that's what's emerging right here, right now. It's the right destination, even if the road we took to reach it was...not what I expected.

"The thing that most of the other Cities told me back when I was with Tampa was that the wasteland made things too complicated. That the squatters and bandits in the wasteland were what had destroyed the old Federal system. What I've tried to do with the Company is solve that problem. Organize the wasteland... at least enough to begin a process of creating regional identity."

Mobile's Clinton interrupted him. "That's some smooth talk, Crowley. Of course we're partners as long as our interests are aligned. The important question is: What happens when our interests *aren't* aligned?"

"That's not likely to happen as long as the Framework Cities have shunned you and want to kill me. We need each other enough that we'll resolve our differences." He was going to say more, but he stopped himself. In fact, he tried not to say much more the rest of that first afternoon. He left the others get around to the point of how they'd go about setting up a regional mutual defense agreement. That would take a lot of talk.

Instead, he was going to take action.

That night, he'd talked with Jean Jacques a couple of times. Around midnight, Jean Jacques had reported that some of the lead units had come across a small group of Tampa external security vehicles. They'd exchanged small arms fire and the students had captured the Tampa troops pretty quickly. Now they had eight prisoners and a couple of drivable armed vehicles.

Around 2 o'clock, the forward units has arrived and started digging in at their staging areas. The plan was for them set up in about a dozen locations along the north walls. The first stage of that process would take up to 24 hours to complete. Immediately, they needed Delta Company to get set up so it could start drawing Tampa's attention first. Delta would be the flash point. It would give the others cover and time to get into position.

That morning, at breakfast, Karamanlis had given Crowley an ear piece so that he could listen in on the call. Then, between breakfast and the first summit session, Karamanlis excused himself to make the call.

Crowley took the moment to check the currency and bond markets on his screen. There were no major drops in Tampa dollars or municipal bonds. Each had been trailing downward for several days—mostly because Chambers hadn't been invited to the regional summit. But there was no sign that the traders knew what was going on. Yet.

He poured himself another cup of coffee fit the piece into his ear. This wasn't what he expected—he'd expected to be in the room with Karamanlis for the call. But the earpiece's sound quality was very good, so he decided to believe.

"Chambers, this is Karamanlis."

Chambers didn't sound excited about taking the call. "Nico. How is your summit going?"

"It's going well. Listen. The reason that I'm calling you is that our external security intelligence says there's a tactical presence building just beyond your north walls."

"Excuse me?"

"There's a tactical force gathering outside of your north walls. And it's not ours."

"Our recon sats would have picked up any major bandit activity or movement."

"Recon satellites?"

"I'm sure you knew about them, Nico. Whose troops are they?"

"They're not ours."

"By 'not yours' you mean City of Jacksonville. Are they Crowley's religious freaks? Or are they New Orleans?"

"That's something your people need to figure out. I'm just calling to pass along what my external security people have seen. And to offer my help if you need it."

"Is this an invitation to join your group?"

"No. It's just an offer of help from your neighbor."

"Thanks. I need to ring off now and make a few calls. I'll call you back in a few hours if we need help."

It took almost two hours for the first Tampa external security forces to approach Delta Company. They came in three Badgers and were met with heavy fire. Delta destroyed the vehicles and the Old Florida Highway around Gate 6. Then, for the moment, the action halted.

In the meantime, Crowley and Karamanlis had explained to the summit members what was going on. The Company was setting a siege of Tampa and moving into place to set a blockade around New Orleans in the next couple of days.

Wilson was quiet. But the others reacted more strongly—some followed Karamanlis's lead and were for the first strike, some were against. The ones who were against objected not so much to Tampa being attacked but to not having been told sooner.

Karamanlis predicted that the Company's moves would make an impression on the Framework Cities without directly challenging them.

The biggest risk was that the Framework Cities admitted Tampa and New Orleans immediately or retroactively and turned their collective forces against the Company. But Crowley believed that they would stand aside and let the battles take their own shapes.

As the day proceeded, the other Companies around Tampa reported in. They were almost all in place and digging in.

Tampa had responded tentatively, with high altitude scanners and attack drones. And, importantly, they seemed to focus on Delta Company. Which had been Crowley's plan. Delta was the lightning rod and—if things went according to plan—it would be just the tip of the spear that pierced Tampa's security cordon.

Delta protected itself with anti-aircraft missiles that neutralized the drones before they got anywhere near the ground. It even sent up a couple of high-altitude heat-seekers to try to wipe out the scanners. But it was impossible to tell from so high whether or not the blasts got them.

Crowley figured that his students were too close to the walls for Tampa to consider nukes—even small, tactical nukes. If they were going to engage the Company troops, they were going to have to get external security forces on the ground. And that meant tiltrotors, hundreds of them, operating at maximum efficiency. That would take days to set up.

In the meantime, the Company troops set up their mine fields and missiles. They prepped their EMP projectors. And rested.

Crowley wanted to be there. But the plan was that he would stay at the summit at least one full day.

That day, in the mid-afternoon, Tampa Security Forces landed about 500 troops from several dozen tiltrotors all around Delta Company. A firefight started and went a couple of hours. But Delta held its position.

By that point, the nets were reporting "security activity" outside of Tampa's north walls. The early reports made it sound like just another bandit attack. And that was fine, as far as Crowley was concerned. The bond markets were selling Tampa and other southern Cities and buying New York and the major money centers. The usual retreat to security whenever there was trouble in the world. The markets still hadn't figured out what was going on. He could turn his attention back to the summit for an hour or two.

Meanwhile, Kappa Company launched four Talon Stealth Tactical Smart Nukes from a mobile platform in the wilds north of the walls near Orlando. Tampa's anti-missile defense system tagged two of the Talons in midair. But the other two reached their targets. The first detonated on impact with Tampa Security Forces tower in the Downtown district; the second detonated on impact with Gate 6—near the Delta Company camp.

Tampa Security hadn't responded immediately. Jean Jacques expected them to strike back within 24 hours.

The currency markets started bailing on Tampa dollars and bonds by the early afternoon. And, within hours, they'd fallen far enough that the exchanges halted trading in Tampa instruments before the day officially ended.

When the CEOs gathered back together for their late afternoon meeting, Wilson announced that he was leaving immediately. "The situation near Tampa has become too unstable. From what my intelligence reports one side—and maybe both—have started using tactical nukes. With all due respect to Mr. Crowley, this seems planned to be happening as we're all sitting here. And I know that he has an army based less than a day's drive from my City's walls. I'm not certain that my being here is in the best interest of the City of Houston. I've got to get home and assure the capital markets that our walls are secure."

Crowley kept quiet.

Karamanlis reminded Wilson that the purpose of the summit was to create communications channels and a mutual-defense scheme that would prevent repeats of the Tampa situation. But Wilson wasn't interested. As he left, he said he might be willing to participate in another summit. But he'd have to wait and see what happened with Tampa.

Karamanlis waited a few seconds after Wilson left and then stood up. "Well, gentlemen, that was disappointing but not surprising. We have fully-equipped media rooms set up for all of you, if you'd like to take some time and field questions from your local press of money center media. Please feel free to use the connections and speak as freely as you see fit. We are going to maintain our City Policy of not allowing foreign media into Jacksonville. But you can say anything you wish about our meetings here. What say we meet back here for dinner in…three hours?"

Crowley stayed for the dinner and entertainment at Karamanlis' compound. But he told Jana and, by satphone, Jean Jacques that he'd be in the action first thing in the morning.

Now, six hours later, he got out of the shower and brushed his teeth. He was getting a cavity or something like it in one of his back molars. It was throbbing a little every so often when he pressed against it in just the right way. He hadn't seen a dentist in…

what, almost three years? He'd have to see one soon.

He looked at himself in the mirror. He wore the beard that men from the wasteland did. It was important to his identity as one of their leaders. But the gray in it certainly did make him look older. Could he get away with shaving? Maybe. But this was an issue for another day. His eyes looked clear and focused. He wasn't going to die today. He'd head to the fight and lead his people.

The bodyguards were dressed in full battle armor. A big van was waiting for them outside of the house, with three Jacksonville Security cruisers as an escort. It was early enough that there wasn't much traffic. With the cruisers' lights flashing, they were at the airport in less than 10 minutes.

The SkyDragon took off so smoothly that he wasn't even sure it had. Jana held his had—but wasn't sure when to let go.

"Jana, I don't want you to get out of this plane."

"What?"

"I want you to head straight back home."

"What are you talking about? I'm not going to dump you off into a battle zone and run away."

"This isn't about bravery. It's about security. I don't want both of us exposed to getting shot."

"Neither of us is going to get shot."

"I want you to go home."

She squeezed his hand, "I want to see what it looks like, Michael. I want to see what the students are seeing. It's important."

He didn't say anything. The SkyDragon lurched forward as its wings moved into high-speed configuration. It would only hold this for a few minutes.

Crowley checked his screen—not sure if it would connect to the net from the air. But it did. Tampa's bonds and dollars were in free fall. The markets in Europe were selling heavily; the markets in Asia were buying a little. Houston, New Orleans and Atlanta were all down sharply, too. The Framework Cities were all up.

They'd be thankful to him for this.

His screen's signal dropped. But he'd seen all he needed to.

He didn't think it was necessary to wear full body armor. He was wearing special pants that were made from a light-weight deflective weave. And he had a command jacket made from the same material that generals usually wore in the field. As they got close to the landing zone, he grabbed a full-weight chest plate and strapped it on.

He asked Jana what she was wearing. She lifted her robe. It was a jumpsuit made from the same light-weight material…and a full-weight smock that went below her belly. It was essentially the same protection he was wearing.

"Do you want a gun?"

"Sure. Give me a small plasma pistol."

He walked back to the rolling armory at the back of the plane and got her gun—plus a larger plasma pistol and a bullet gun for himself. The chest plate had two holsters built in; and it hid them pretty well. When he put the command jacket on, it was hard to tell what he was wearing or carrying. Jana looked him over and nodded her approval.

"Rabbi, we're five minutes to landing. There's no fire right now at Delta Company's camp, but we're not going to make any assumptions. Please strap yourselves into your seats."

Jana dashed to her seat and looked out the window. There didn't seem to be anything below but pine trees and scrub oaks carpeting very shallow hills.

Three small tilts took positions around their craft.

The pilot switched his radio onto the cabin speakers.

"Hello, Rabbit 1. This is Captain Shad Clayton, Camp A, Zeta Company. We're going to escort you to the landing zone. The bodyguards looked to Crowley, who nodded as calmly as he could. One of the guards jolted up to the cockpit door and knocked once.

The pilot's voice crackled back over the speakers. "Captain Clayton, this is Rabbit 1. We're following your lead."

Two of the escorts flared away, one up and one down. The other tightened in more closely to the big plane. It stayed close, until it was time to switch to landing mode. And, as soon as they'd both done that, the escort tightened up again and hovered close above while the SkyDragon touched down.

Delta Company's landing zone was barely visible—even from just a few hundred feet directly above. The trees offered remarkable cover.

Jean Jacques was waiting with his aides. He shook Crowley's hand and hugged Jana quickly. "That's a big bird, Rabbi. We're going to have hard time hiding it. Maybe we should move it somewhere farther back. And maybe we should move *you* somewhere farther back."

"I defer to your judgment, Commander. You can move the vehicle. But I thought it would make a good impression on the Tampa managers when they ask for a parley. And Jana and I would like to stay here for a little while."

"Yes. Okay." He whispered something to one of his aides and then pointed west. "We have about a quarter-mile walk to the camp. Is that okay?"

Jana answered. "We'll be fine, Commander. Lead the way."

Jean Jacques had a tent set up for them. And, after giving them a minute, he came in with a table-top screen to brief them on what was happening. His screen generated a three-dimensional holographic map that he could adjust to show the area from different directions and zoom in on specific spots.

They were about a mile from the north walls of the City, closest to Gate 6. And that gate seemed to be the critical point to everything that was going on right now.

The holographic image of the gate was updated as of the Smart Nuke blast. It was a mess, with two large, open breaches— one to each side of the main pile of rubble that used to be the gate.

"This is the troubling part, Rabbi. It's been 24 hours and they haven't done anything to secure that breach."

"Is it safe for people to be there?"

"No. Rad count will be unsafe for at least another 48 hours. But why haven't they used drones or robots to fill in the holes? At least push the rubble around? I mean, we could get guys in rad suits and send them right through."

"They're probably counting on the radiation to keep us out. and they may also be waiting to see how anxious we are to plant a flag inside their walls."

"Yeah. It looks like a trap to me, too. My plan is to let it sit for a while and carry on with rest of our script."

"Sounds good. If we've done our job right getting here, they have no idea how many troops we are. They're probably still scrambling to figure that out. Their assumptions for security planning involve a band of 2,000 ragged bandits. Not 20,000 well-equipped fighters. With nukes. They're probably calling Jacksonville and New Orleans for help."

"And we're in position at New Orleans?"

"Not a complete blockade. But we're blocking the Old Columbus Highway."

"And Jacksonville?"

"They're excited about annexing Tampa's Atlantic coast. And the whole City, if we're not careful."

"Okay. Then, like I say, I'm following the script."

They walked outside and made a circuit around the camp. The bodyguards had moved back to their regular assignments; Jean Jacques and his aides walked with Crowley and Jana. Most of the students recognized Crowley—either from their screens or from live lessons. They recognized him with "Rabbi" or nods. He chatted with a couple who seemed inclined; but he tried not to interfere. He was of two minds about this kind of trip. It was an elementary rule of progressive management to make connections with all people at all levels of an organization; but, since his days as a young manager, he'd been wary of CEOs who acted too chummy with front-line workers. There was something fake in it.

The camp was quieter than Crowley had expected. Platoons gathered and headed out on patrol almost silently. And, when they came back, there wasn't much hooting or hollering. The kids coming back might talk a little but loud and laugh—but it was all pretty low key. Every few minutes, there was the boom of artillery in the distance. But not much more than that.

The students he did speak with were very well informed. They knew Tampa Security hadn't made the expected moves in response to the first nukes. And they knew that Jean Jacques was going to proceed according the plan—even though few of them knew the details of that. But the fact that there was a plan that the Commander was following seemed to be enough.

As usual, a number of the students passed on the best wishes of their parents or spouses or other family members. Some asked to take his picture to send back to family members.

After an hour or so, Jana was starting to get tired. So, they went back to the tent where she could get some rest.

The plan was to move the Smart Nukes east, along the north wall. They'd lob one or two more Smart Nukes into the downtown area—but they'd follow up the near blasts with regular concussion shells. And EMP projectors, which would neutralize any electronics in the area. They'd focus on Gate 6. In 48 hours, if their 3-D imaging still showed no action on the other side, they'd send a few platoons through the breach to check out Tampa proper.

And, if they didn't run into trouble, they'd move Delta Company against the inside of the Gate. That would be a psychological boost to the students and a political boost for the Company.

He'd have to get Jana home by then. If nothing else, she needed to get back with Mikey.

Crowley's screen rang loud enough to rouse him from his nap.

It was vieux Guibert. "Rabbi, we've had a few calls from President Wilson's office in Houston. He wants to talk with you."

"That was quick."

"He says he has a proposition."

"Okay. Get his contact info."

Wilson, like most Big City executives, changed his contact information constantly.

Jana was resting in her cot. "Who?"

"Wilson."

"What?"

"Don't know. But I'm going to make this call with J.J. You just get some rest."

"You've got to be kidding."

They walked over to Jean Jacques's tent. He was eating outside of it with a few of his aides. And talking with someone on a satphone.

"...just hold your position. Don't take the bait. Let them go. Okay. Okay. Call me back in 10 minutes."

He drank some kind of juice from a clear bottle and then nodded to his phone. "Tampa security returned fire against Beta Company about 500 yards from the wall 30 miles east of here. It was hot for about 20 minutes and then the Tampa guys bailed out. Like here. They seem to be daring our guys to chase them back to the wall."

"What are you going to do?"

"Pull Beta Company back and nuke that spot tonight. We're not going to push them back with plasma fights."

"Amen to that."

"So what can I do for you guys?"

"Your father tells me we've had a couple of calls from Houston. Wilson wants to discuss…something. I thought I'd return the call from your tent so we can all hear what he has to say."

This was probably more politics than Jean Jacques would have chosen—but Crowley hadn't just come here for the students. Calling Wilson back from the front would make the right impression.

Inside, Crowley set his satphone to speaker and returned the call. A secretary patched them through.

"Michael, I understand you left the summit this morning?"

"Yes, Reg. I'd said everything I'd come to say and I wanted to get down here. So, I understand you have something you want to discuss."

"Yes, of course. Well, my intelligence reports that some of your troops are massing at the Old Columbus Highway east of Mobile."

"Yes?"

"But they didn't pick up any large troop movements before you attacked Tampa. So, you hid one maneuver but you're showing another."

"I'm not sure what to say, Reg. These are the reports your intelligence unit has given you. You can draw whatever conclusions you see fit."

"Here is the important conclusion we draw. You're not planning to attack Houston. Is that correct?"

"That's correct. We consider Brownsville an ally and, because of your special trade relationship with Brownsville, we consider Houston neutral. In our disputes with aggressive Cities. A friend of a friend. But I've told you this before."

"It has more importance now."

"Fair enough."

"Here's what I propose. The City of Houston remains neutral in your activities east of the City of Mobile in exchange for your agreement to keep your troops at least 200 miles away from our walls."

"The Company doesn't make treaties, Reg. We have no recognition and we seek no recognition. All you'll ever have in any dealings with us is my word. And your own judgment about whether my franchises will listen to what I say."

"I understand the decentralized structure of your organization. I think our neutrality would benefit everyone."

"Probably, probably. How about this: The Company will keep to the east of Houston—but 200 miles is too much. We'll agree that the farthest west we'll go is New Orleans's west wall."

The students fighting under Jean Jacques followed the battle plan closely. After the first two strikes, the Tampa defense system blocked any other missiles from the downtown area. They wanted to avoid lobbing missiles into residential areas, so Crowley suggested targeting the Brandon jail complex and the rest of the industrial sector south of downtown Tampa.

Two days of concussion blasts had opened the breach at what used to be Gate 6 to more than 100 yards across. And the EMP devices wiped anything robotic or automated. Still no Tampa Security forces in sight. And J.J. still thought it might be an elaborate trap. He decided to keep concussion bombing for another day. By then the rad count would be low enough for students to swarm through without needing special gear.

The fighting was more intense to the east. Beta Company at the wall 30 miles east and Kappa Company at the wall near Orlando were still facing heavy fire every day. Even after the Smart Nukes and the electromagnetic pulses. They weren't suffering heavy casualties; but they weren't crossing the wall breaches that the missiles had created.

At some point, they were going to have to take Tampa's bait somewhere.

Tampa Security aircraft—mostly drones, but some tilts and jets—ran circuits over the trees north of the walls. But the Company was several steps ahead. Jean Jacques had set the comms towers and robot plasma cannons away from the camps. Since the Tampa Security forces were trained to locate comms hardware and weapons, they ended up firing a lot at unmanned installations. Even when they hit hard, they weren't as close as they thought.

Still, the sound and vibrations of heavy shell explosions and tactical nukes made it hard for Crowley and Jana to sleep.

By the third morning of the siege, Crowley's second, all nine Companies were in place along the north walls. And they'd landed 3,000 students from Company Mu near the Ft. Myers Gate on

Tampa's south wall. Two more smaller Companies would follow on that side, setting up a two-front war for Tampa Security.

That afternoon, the first students from Delta Company pressed through the breach at Gate 6.

The pessimist manager in Crowley expected the trap to snap shut and the point men to be killed. But they weren't. The 3-D imaging had been right. There wasn't anyone on the other side.

Three days of bombing had fairly well leveled the industrial neighborhood around Gate 6. There were no people and few structures left.

Jean Jacques sent 300 students through and backed them up with tilts and hardware. They moved slowly and used several electromag pulses to disable anything electronic that might be lying in ambush. In a short time they'd located a warehouse about 300 yards from the Gate that was empty and well situated in the immediate area. The rad count there was only slightly elevated. In four hours, they'd established a secure forward post in the shell of the old warehouse.

Late that afternoon, Jean Jacques brought his holographic screen to Crowley's tent for another update and a quick dinner of sandwiches and coffee. The students had secured a 16-block square of burned-out warehouses; more importantly, they'd set up highly precise 3D imaging that gave them a good view of the northwest part of the City. The Tampa Security forces and the people had all evacuated south along the part of the Old Florida Highway that ran from the Gate to the downtown sector.

"Rabbi, our intelligence says that their plan is to make their stand along a perimeter that follows the main loop of the light rail system—about halfway between our forward position and the downtown sector. And they'll fight hard to keep us out of the St. Petersburg sector. But they're just ceding us this…and this…and this. They never should have put their walls this far out."

"It made more sense a hundred years ago. The Old Florida Highway used to be more important."

"Anyway, they're swarming their security forces around the TSA facilities near Orlando. They've assumed that's a major target."

"Don't let them think any different, Jonny. Pound those walls with the Smart Nukes and concussion shells. And keep attacking up to the walls with plasma fire fights. Sneak across here and there if we can—but don't lose men doing it. We'll soften them up for Mr. Karamanlis."

"Aye."

"So, what are you doing this evening?"

"Well, we're securing the walls of the self-destruct arms far enough each direction that we can set up plasma cannons on either side of the breach here—the lads are calling it the Delta Gate."

"Very nice."

"Then we'll try to trigger the self-destructs and collapse the walls a couple hundred yards in either direction."

"Very good."

"And we're moving students into the City. We'll have over 1,000 secure by morning."

"And you—yourself?"

"Oh, I'm sleeping on Tampa soil tonight. You know, I've never spent the night in a City before."

"Excellent."

"And you, Rabbi?"

"I've got to get Jana back to Brownsville tonight. She needs to get back to little Mikey. I'll spend the night there and then come back here tomorrow."

Jean Jacques insisted that they leave before dark, so he escorted them personally to the landing zone. "I think it's better anyway that you two are going. These guys are going to be plenty pissed that we're on their real estate. They're going to be flying bombing runs double-time tonight."

They only had to wait a couple of minutes for the SkyDragon to come over from where it had been holed up for the last two days. During those down moments, Jana asked Jean Jacques were he learned his battle tactics.

"My family has always been fighters. My grandfather used to tell me stories about the old Houston/New Orleans War when I was a kid. And father calls me every hour to check in and give advice. He wishes you'd sent him down here, Rabbi."

"No, Johnny. You're the fist; he's the heart. He needs to be back there keeping the missiles and people flowing."

Two of their bodyguards were already in the SkyDragon when Crowley and Jana climbed aboard. The pilot didn't waste any time jolting right up.

On their way up into the clouds, Crowley and Jana could see the dozens of smoldering columns of smoke on each side of the City wall. And they could see the students bringing vehicles through the Delta Gate and walking patrols along the Old Florida Highway.

"Can't believe they're giving us this foothold," Crowley said, mostly to himself.

Jana answered. "I wasn't sure two days ago. But I am now. They're going to fold, Michael. And you're going to win." She cocked the brow over her good eye and smiled at him.

He laughed and kissed her on the cheek. Then he sat back and checked his screen. The New York exchanges had tried halting trade in Tampa instruments, but the world markets didn't follow. So, the New York markets were allowing limited trading. An hour a day. Tampa's premier bonds were down another 14 percent. There wasn't much farther for them to fall.

Houston's bonds had stopped dropping as soon as Wilson had made his announcement about neutrality earlier that afternoon. And they even recovered a little near the end of the trading day. Between his short sales of Tampa bonds and options on Houston petros, the Company had made almost $100 million New York in less than 12 hours.

The students holding the Highway east of Mobile were free to move now. He sent the word.

The SkyDragon lurched into cruising configuration and chased the setting sun across the Gulf of Mexico, toward Jana's home and Mikey.

Twenty-eight

Hailwood offered to charter a plane from Boston but the Old Man insisted on sending up a special cargo tilt.

"You need something with room enough for your truck. We're not leaving that machine to the savages in the woods up there."

He was right, of course. Boston wasn't about to allow a vehicle like the Badger inside its walls, even for transport to points south.

Hailwood had been talking to the Old Man as much as possible since the religious nuts had started their assault on the City. Several thousand people had been killed. But the Old Man seemed more annoyed than scared. He was sure that their Security Forces would be able to turn back the attack—his immediate concern was keeping the managers from overreacting.

"Crowley's Holy rollers aren't just some rag tag bunch of bandits. They're organized. And they have some heavy weapons. Fairly new smart nukes."

"So why don't you have Chambers nuke them back?"

"He doesn't know what he wants to do. But shooting back is an emotional response. And no doubt what Crowley expects. It won't work for us, though. Their main weapon is *stealth*. They're spread around in the trees, hiding out. Tactical nukes won't do much when you don't know precisely where you're aiming. We'd have to carpet-bomb, which would burn up resources and scare our citizens. These are the tactical advantages of asymmetrical warfare."

Hailwood hadn't liked the Old Man's use of the word "warfare," even in a sarcastic comment. If they were thinking in terms of warfare, they were giving Crowley's zealots more respect than they deserved.

"So, what are you going to do?"

"Honey pot strategy. Draw them in and then squash them."

"Are they stupid enough to be drawn in?"

"Dunno. We'll see. It'll be good to have you down here. Maybe your aggressive take on things will be useful."

The trend was undeniable: People from the wasteland were attacking all over. Hartford. The College. Now Tampa. They were going to have to start taking preemptive actions against them—squash them before they got organized to the point that they could buy and use tactical nukes.

And Crowley…there was no excuse for that. The Old Man had made a big mistake by siding with Chambers in their power struggle. And then he'd made a bigger mistake by allowing Chamber to humiliate Crowley rather than killing him.

And he seemed to know he'd made these mistakes.

The tilt that the Old Man sent up was a giant A-3151 industrial transport. Plenty of room for the Badger.

The A-3151 was too big to land on campus. So, Hailwood made a few last farewells to Drummond and the DKEs and headed out one last time for the Old Hadley Road.

By the time he got to the Hampshire/Hadley intersection, he could already see the tilt straddling Old Hadley Road at the foot of the College incline. It was huge.

And it was positioned perfectly so that all he had to do was drive the Badger up and into the cargo hold.

The security guys tied down the Badger while the tilt wound up its rotors. Hailwood was greatly relieved to see Steve Masterson behind the controls when he ducked his head into the cockpit right on time at 2 pm.

"Steve! What a surprise. I figured you'd be flying missions against Crowley's zealots back at home."

"No missions to fly, sir. Drones are doing all the work."

"Really? That's too bad."

"I agree. Let's get back home and see if you can talk some sense into those people."

"Very good."

Technically, he was taking a personal leave. Howell had insisted that he not quit; this was a common response. The downside of the College was its politics; the upside was its loyal-to-a-fault treatment of students and teachers.

While rotors warmed up and the cargo hold hatch closed, Masterson took a minute to use the bathroom and give the copilot and navigator a moment to make personal calls. But Masterson still didn't set foot on the New England ground. He never had, in all the times he'd come to get Hailwood.

That reminded Hailwood about calling Maria Elena. She'd been back in Miami for awhile. And now, after the nuke hitting downtown Tampa, she wasn't too excited about coming up to see him.

"Yes, Terry. Where are you?"

"I'm just leaving the College. Loading my truck in a giant tilt."

"I still don't understand why this truck is so important."

"When you see it, you'll understand."

"It seems a luxury when your City is being attacked."

"*Sirena*, the Badger is a weapon itself. I could drive it out into the wasteland and make a good run at these religious nuts myself."

"Okay."

"So, am I going to see you at the House?"

"Yeah, yeah. I'm just thinking about the security hassles, though."

"Well, I can remedy that. Why don't we just come down and pick you up?"

"Really?"

"Yeah. It'll take us about two hours to get down there. But if we avoid Miami International, we can drop in easily. Can you drive up to Ft. Lauderdale?"

"Sure."

"Great. I'll call you back in a few minutes with the details."

Masterson wasn't excited at all but he set about charting the extra stop. He called down to Ft. Lauderdale and checked in. They had plenty of slots open. "This'll be a challenge. I've never landed the 3151 at a commercial airport."

"Steve, you landed this albatross perfectly on a country road in the wasteland. Dropping in on a regular airport will be a snap."

Hailwood sat in the cockpit with Masterson and the other fliers. He asked them what had been going on with the terrorist attacks; they'd barely noticed anything. The terrorists didn't have—or, at least, weren't using—any fixed-wing aircraft. It was all missiles and a few small tiltrotors for ground support.

"I don't blame them. Some of those tilts are really nice machines. I mean, they can't move a Badger like this. But some are pretty strong," Masterson said, as he entered the flight plan for Ft. Lauderdale. "Anyway, Main Security has plenty of tiltrotors. And they haven't asked our help for anything yet. We're just spectators like everyone else until they ask us to get involved."

The pilots for the City were, technically, part of the Tampa Security Force. But they didn't like to advertise that fact.

Hailwood said that he'd read on the news sites that there was actually some backlash against the Security Department—citizens complaining that it was more interested in eroding their civil liberties than taking practical steps to prevent attacks religious extremists at the walls.

That didn't make much an impression on the fliers. The copilot said he'd read something about a radical professor at University of Tampa leading some kind of protest. "But that guy's nuts. He's been protesting shit once a week for 20 years."

Earlier that day, Hailwood had made a mental note to pay attention on this departure—because it might be the last time he took off from the northeast. But it had all happened so fast, he had no time to study. Suddenly, he was just gone.

The landing at Ft. Lauderdale was easy. Masterson called it in about half an hour ahead of time and they got their instructions from the tower. They circled around once and landed from the east, over the water.

The ground crew at Ft. Lauderdale seemed familiar with big freighters. Two staffers walked Maria Elena out from the terminal.

She smiled dramatically as she walked up the hatch/ramp. "What kind of plane is this?" She stood up on her toes and kissed him on the mouth.

"It's a classic."

Masterson looked Maria Elena over twice when they all got back inside for the run up to the St. Petersburg landing strip.

"Steve, what's the matter?"

"Do you really want the truth, sir?"

"Yeah."

"Flying into a strip in Tampa right now, even St. Pete, is going to run some risks. I hope that you and your guest understand that."

"Well then, Steve, we're going to sit up here with you guys." He gave her his seat from the ride down and folded out a jump seat for himself. "What's our flight time, Steve?"

"About 35 minutes."

"Good. What's the flight plan into St. Pete?"

"Well, by the book, we're over the wasteland for about 15 minutes. But Tampa has claimed the wasteland all the way to the Miami walls. So, no one's sure what's going on here."

"Who's claimed Lake Okeechobee?"

"No idea, sir. The catfish in the Lake might be the only free agents left on the peninsula." And he lowered the tilt's nose toward the dark patch of the Lake while he said this.

"What's the landing protocol, coming in?"

"Way up and then way down. The holy rollers have set a camp near Gate 15 on the southern wall. So, we have to give it at least 30,000 feet clearance. They're flying all kinds of drones and missiles lower than that. We're going to come in low from the Lake, then roller coaster it up…then drop back down into St. Pete."

He did exactly what he said.

At the top of the climb, when they reached the apogee, there were a few seconds of what seemed like zero gravity. He grabbed the back of Maria Elena's seat and pulled himself toward her to kiss her neck. All of her skin that he could see showed goose bumps. He smiled at that.

Their landing at St. Petersburg was more intense than anything he'd ever been through before. At one point—at what must have been several thousand feet up—he was certain they were going to crash. But Masterson pulled it out.

On the ground, there were Security troops in full battle gear at every main access point inside and outside of the St. Pete airport. And the main terminal was packed with cars and people—which was unusual. It wasn't a major commercial facility. The City had cut way back on the number flights leaving the major airports and stepped up security everywhere, so people were crowding onto charters, private planes and anything they could find to get away.

On the tarmac, Maria Elena made eye contact with him for the first time since they'd left Ft. Lauderdale. "I'm not chic enough to appreciate the zero-gravity. I think I'll take a commercial flight next time."

He put his arm around her waist as the limousine pulled out toward them.

"Not so sure about that, *sirena*. Not sure there are going to *be* any commercial flights for awhile. Besides, if you'd tried to fly commercial from Miami, you'd still be in line."

He was going to push her into the limo—but she pressed against the door and stood up for some fresh air.

He nodded to her and she nodded back.

He left her at the limo for a minute and crossed back toward Masterson. The crew would make sure they got his Badger off of the tilt and back to the House before dawn.

"Don't worry about your rig," Masterson said. "It's safe with us. We'll make sure it gets back to you so you can lead the way to get rid of these zealots."

Hailwood believed that Masterson meant what he said. The people at the top of their fields wanted the City to survive. They had a vested interest in its hierarchy.

He retuned to Maria Elena and they collapsed together into the limo and headed south toward the House. The security troops waved their car through each of several checkpoints.

She rested her head in his lap and smiled up at him. That image stayed with him for a long time.

The traffic was thick for a weekday afternoon. Everyone was trying to get away from the downtown corridor. At one point, she climbed up behind his shoulders and watched all of the cars heading east and south. "They don't believe in the government anymore. This is just like Cuba."

He didn't think so. But he kept his thoughts to himself.

When they arrived at the House, he was ready to fall right to sleep in his bungalow. But she seemed to be getting a second wind. She unbuttoned her shirt and he got hard at the sight of her breasts pressing out from her flesh-colored bra. She climbed on top of him in the bed in his place—and he lasted longer than he expected. It might have been because he was tired. When he finally came, he lifted her with his hips off of the bed. She liked that.

They slept for a little while. But, tired as he was, he was also keyed up by everything that was going on. They pulled on some clothes and walked over to the main House.

There were three Security cruisers in the driveway—one had brought a trailer that was empty. Hailwood guessed there was a missile-to-missile defense unit set up somewhere around.

Two of the troopers were plugged into a couple of screens in the garage; the others were walking the perimeter, just inside the walls. But the House itself was practically empty. The Old Man wasn't around and most of the staff was staying at home. Victor thought the Old Man was downtown at City Hall with the Board; someone else thought he'd gone to a Security bunker inland somewhere.

They had some sandwiches and juice brought out to the back deck. And he called the Old Man—who was at City Hall.

"Terry, are you at the House?"

"Yah. Maria Elena and I got in a couple hours ago."

"Good. I should be back there in a few hours. Tied up in meetings here with the managers. Got to make sure we coordinate our reaction to these God-grabbers better than we anticipated them."

"You want me come over?"

"No. Not now. Don't want to throw them any changes in the thick of things here. Maybe later."

"Okay. Well, we'll just be hanging around here."

"Yes. Don't go anywhere. Best just to stay at the House. You'll be fine there. See you in a bit."

They finished their sandwiches and watched the sun set.

She smiled at him and said, "In this place, you'd never know anything bad was happening."

"Well, except for the soldiers and anti-missile launcher."

"Right. Except for that."

"But you might be onto something. I'm not sure as much is happening as the news pages make it seem."

"Come on, Terry. More than a thousand people died when that missile hit the Security building downtown. And you can't tell me it was an accident that they targeted a Security Department building. They aren't just angry bandits; they know what they're doing."

"Well, they have our former CEO's knowledge of the City. But the Old Man knows what Crowley knows. And more. Their advantage won't last long."

"That's good to hear."

"My only worry is that these brown-nose managers who run everything have never been tested by any kind of real trouble. I hope they're up to the task."

"That's why your grandfather's there."

"Yeah." He didn't say anything about his "grandfather." He'd decided not to tell her about himself. "Come on, let's go back."

He grabbed a couple of bottles of champagne from the bar fridge on their way through the House.

They screwed around and drank champagne. And screwed around more. And drank more.

Around 11, Hailwood went to the bathroom and got some ice water. He drank a full tumbler, intending hydrate so that he could do more. But she was out when he got back to bed. He fell asleep next to her, He slept more soundly than he had in weeks.

He also woke up before she did.

The sun was just rising. He inched away from her, so she wouldn't wake. And he clicked on to the screen in his living room.

It was hard to find any good news on the screen. He'd set it up to access the nets in Tampa, Miami, New York, Chicago, Denver, NoCal and SoCal. The "Battle of Tampa" played out the same way everywhere. Tabloid exclamations on the news pages and then sanctimonious reports about the markets' bad reaction to Tampa in the financial pages. The Big Cities were competitive enough that they usually reveled a little in each other's troubles.

Of course, the economists argued that this competitiveness stunted overall financial growth. But that lesser growth was the price everyone paid for local authority and security.

Most days. Right now, Tampa's City bonds were losing value by the minute. How far could the main operational bonds go? He could buy them and then profit when the City started hitting back. He didn't have much investment capital that he controlled himself—about six hundred thousand New York dollars in a trading account his father had helped him set up when he'd turned 16.

He clicked through to that account and liquidated its conservative mix of corporate stocks. Then he placed an automatic order. If the City of Tampa Central Operational bonds dropped to 27 cents on the dollar of face value, he'd buy immediately.

Sic Semper Tyrannis

He remembered the 27 cents figure from one of his economic history classes. That was the low that Chicago's City Bonds had reached during the height of the Midwest City Wars—and they'd come back with a vengeance when Chicago consolidated its power in the region. That's why so many Chicago traders were rich.

The Tampa bonds were trading at 38 cents now—an historical low. Before the attacks, they'd never traded below 92 cents.

He felt good when he logged out of the trading page. Betting on his hometown was the right thing to do, now.

"What are you doing, Terry?"

"Betting on the home team."

"*Que?*"

"I'm placing a market order for City of Tampa bonds. They're dropping a lot because the markets are overreacting to the attacks. I'm going to take advantage of that. I'll pick them up at what I hope is their low—and then ride them back up when this turns out to be a smaller deal that the news pages think."

"Oh. What does your grandfather say about that?"

"I don't know. I didn't ask him."

"Hmm. I'm going to take a shower." Said like an invitation.

The Old Man was sitting at the big dining room table, drinking coffee and reading his screen. Hailwood sat down across from him. Hailwood was feeling good. He'd walked past his Badger in the driveway; and Maria Elena was taking a bath to recover from the work-over he'd given her in the shower.

The Old Man didn't get up or hug Hailwood. That wasn't his way. He just nodded slightly and said, "Sorry I didn't get back last night. Things are going a little worse than I expected," while his eyes never left his screen.

"What's the problem?"

"Hard to say, exactly." And, for the first time, he looked up. "We underestimated Crowley's army. We'd hoped they were going to try breaching the walls in several places at once. They didn't. We had hoped they'd make a fast start and spread themselves too thin. They didn't. They've been disciplined. They're not taking the bait. And they've set up a fairly secure beachhead near Gate 9."

Hailwood didn't like this hesitation on the Old Man's part. It was unexpected—and coming at the worst time. "You can't let

471

them stay there. We've got to squash those guys. Kill them all. We can't have Crowley sleeping on Tampa soil."

The Old Man rolled his eyes and made a calming gesture with his hands. "It's not as easy as that. They're well-positioned. And they've been very smart about using wall remnants to create a couple of towers that give their plasma cannons 360-degree views of the neighborhood."

"Wall remnants? What the hell does that mean?"

"The walls have been breached up there. Significantly. They've got almost a quarter-mile of open border. But they managed to keep a couple of bits standing—and they have cannons on top of those."

Hailwood whistled at the image of a quarter-mile of breached wall. That was a problem. They could be bringing in all kinds of people and things. "Have you set up a new wall?"

"Yes, yes. This was planned far in advance. We've set up a new line south of Homosassa Springs. They can have the warehouses and crappy golf courses north of there."

"That's not the point. The fact that they've taken our land will sit badly with our citizens. And the markets. And you're the one who's always lectured me about keeping our money accounts in balance. This will jam up all of that. You should just shoot a couple of missiles and nuke them into a cloud of radioactive dust."

"No. If word got out that the City was using nukes, everyone would *really* panic. No, the nukes are what makes these people irrational terrorists."

"Well, then we need to take an army of our own and kill them and secure to our walls."

"We're working on that. But we're not as ready as I thought we'd be. Security can handle guarding our gates and our airports, etc. Since that first missile that got through, our anti-missile systems have knocked down everything else they've fired at us. But our troops aren't accustomed to fighting battles aggressively. Taking the fight to the enemy, as it were."

Hailwood stared hard at the Old Man. "This doesn't sound like you. This sounds like that sniveling little shit Chambers."

"He has a plan for doing something about Crowley."

"A plan? Is it some kind of sideways, cloak-and-dagger plot?"

"You might say that."

"Well fuck *that*. We just need to put our best fighters together and go up there and put a bullet in Crowley's head."

"If he's there."

"Whether he is or not."

"No," the Old Man barked. "I made a mistake letting Crowley get away. This time, here, I want to make sure we kill him. Kill the head and the body dies."

"I know that saying." Hailwood got up to get more coffee. "But I'm telling you, Old Man. If Chambers' plot doesn't work, I'm going to go to City Hall myself and put a bullet in *his* head. Then I'll go after Crowley."

"Agreed. You can do that with my blessing if it all goes to shit. But I'm optimistic that all's *not* going to shit."

Hailwood looked at the Old Man, less angrily this time. He was concerned. The Old Man sounded like he was trying to convince himself of something he didn't believe.

"I have a question, Old Man."

"Go ahead."

"Have you ever killed anyone?"

"No. Not directly. I suppose some would say I've done it indirectly."

"And you went to the College. Lived in the wasteland. Don't you think that the fact I've killed squatters and mountain men attacking the schools means something has changed?"

"It makes me think that New England has gotten a lot more dangerous. And you were smart to get out."

Hailwood felt that he had an advantage on the Old Man here. He'd killed men. Directly. And felt little remorse about it.

"Look, Terry. It's good to have you back. I need someone angrier about our troubles than I am."

"It's good to be back. I just hope these bean-counting managers aren't leading us all down the road to perdition. And bankruptcy."

"I hope not, too."

There was definitely something wrong. The Old Man wasn't the kind who stood around and hoped that other people didn't make mistakes. He'd step in and not let anything else happen until he'd prevented the mistake from ever taking shape.

He decided, in his own style, to let the matter pass. The Old Man had been up all night dealing with mutton-heads.

"I think when I'm done eating here, I'm going down on the beach and shooting guns for a couple of hours. If I'm going to execute some terminations, my aim better be true."

The Old Man was already lost again in his screen. His intensity made Hailwood curious to see for himself what was going on—right that second.

But he let this feeling pass. Hailwood believed to his core that life—from battles to business deals—wasn't won or lost on dozens of nervous decisions make on breaking news. It was won or lost on a few, critical decisions. And these critical decisions were often made far away in space and time from the battlefield.

He cleared his mind and shot guns until his fingers were sore, his ears were ringing and his clothes smelled of gunpowder and burnt plasma. Then he started shooting seriously.

In time, a couple of the security troops gathered around the lower seawall and watched him sniping holographic targets from several hundred feet across the sand.

"Nice shooting, sir. Maybe *you* should be protecting *us* from the terrorists."

"No, you guys take care of the terrorists. I'm aiming lower."

Twenty-nine

They landed right inside the Morrell farm compound—the pilot flying the SkyDragon was getting used to putting it down in tight spaces. He told them he wanted to hop back to the BSF airbase to fuel up and get the engines checked. And get a few hours of sleep.

Jana thanked him and Crowley said they were close but not quite done yet. They had another couple of days of traveling to do. The flier said he'd have the plane back at the compound in eight hours.

Jana was tired. And a little pissed that Crowley had been on a satphone almost the whole way back from Tampa.

"...and I hate the fact that I sound like a hormone-crazed bitch in the middle of such an important week. But I figure it's better to say this stuff and get it out than let it fester."

"That's why I love you, Jana."

They agreed that he'd set up his screen and satphone in her bedroom and work while she slept. She wanted him near.

Mikey shrieked when he saw them and hugged Jana. She picked him up and he butted his forehead against Crowley's.

Crowley let a few minutes slip by playing with Mikey. But the satphone wasn't far from his mind.

Frank Hernandez from Camp B was leading the students from the Columbus Highway toward Mobile. They weren't going to have as much air cover as the students in Tampa had. But they were getting more marine support. All six of the Company's war ships were heading for Mobile Bay. So, the two-front battle in Mobile was going to be from the east and from the water.

The ships were something of an unknown factor. Marine officers weren't natural Company material. They could already read and they were too satisfied with their places in the world to seek much from a just God.

But there were a fair number of captains and experienced ship's officers who'd crossed the New Orleans Merchant Marine Department and lost their command certificates. Some of these officers lost their "tickets" because of drug or alcohol problems; some just had personality clashes with NOMM regulators. They seemed like a political bunch.

The Company had been able to find a small but committed crew of naval officers from these outcasts. And the head man had an even more exotic background.

They'd assembled their small fleet in the same opportunistic manner from gifts and a couple of purchases. They had one old missile frigate whose registry traced back through several refittings to the end of the Federal Era, an old minesweeper (these were the boats he'd inspected with vieux Guibert in Grand Isle), two 55-meter Chinese-made hydrofoil interceptors and two well-armed cutters that had been built for the SoCal Coast Guard but never delivered.

The commander of this fleet was "Admiral Z," a former Chinese Security Naval Officer who'd washed out because of an addiction to Neurac. He'd drifted around, hiring on with merchant ships and dabbling in a little piracy in the Pacific basin.

Then, he'd had a religious awakening in during a bender in San Francisco. His motley crewmates didn't want a believer on their boat, so NoCal Security tossed him out—which meant inland. He had no choice but to sober up and walk the wasteland, praying a lot. He spoke little English and didn't read any. Somehow, he ended up drifting north to the small patch of wasteland between Portland and Seattle—where he learned to read English from a Company franchise that operated in one of the few sections of the Pacific Coast that wasn't part of any City. To the students, he was the old Chinese guy who slept in the mission and cleaned the place for his room and food. When Crowley put out the call for any students with naval experience, Zhyi Hsei Hua raised his hand.

No one had ever asked him about his experience. When Zhyi started talking, the students running the franchise didn't believe him. But he kept offering so much detail about sailing warships that they put him in touch with Camp C.

He turned out to be a real find.

Admiral Z had a very sharp eye for naval skills in other people. If he thought someone would be good, he was rarely wrong. And, if he

Sic Semper Tyrannis

thought someone would be bad, he was *never* wrong. He'd helped set up the deal for the Chinese hydrofoils by putting Hernandez in touch with a broker from Macau who was looking to sell some boats cheap and quickly.

Crowley spoke with Admiral Z often but had only met him once, for a dinner at Camp C. Right away, the Admiral had said, "You taught me to read, sir. I must have watched your vid lessons 100 times. Maybe 200. 'Simple phonics.' 'You are a student your whole life.' 'I am not a deep thinker, I am a practical person. A doer.' Every child should watch those lessons."

Later, when Crowley asked Zhyi why he had been so quiet about his past to the other students in Aberdeen, he said: "I was ashamed of how far I had fallen. I had been a ship's Captain before I had 30 years. And I'd been a junkie, sleeping in streets. Maybe I was still angry. But, most, I think I just wasn't ready. I needed a quiet time to rebuild my spirit. I was happy to sweep and wash dishes. Ride my bike. But, when you called, I answered."

Now, Crowley was talking to the Admiral in the screen next to a sleeping Jana and asking about whether the boats were ready for battle.

"We will be in Mobile Bay at 0600. On schedule."

"So everything's going well?"

"Going well? I don't know what you mean by that, Rabbi. Two of the interceptors have left half their fuel on the water and Albert Einstein himself couldn't keep the reactor on this blessed missile boat running steady. But we will be there with our weapons ready."

Crowley rang off and called Hernandez. "The boats will be there at six. How do you guys look?"

"No problem, Rabbi. The missiles fly at 0555 and we're there on time. This isn't Tampa. We'll have the place secure by lunch time. Get some sleep."

He checked the European markets and called it a day.

Jana was sleeping with Mikey in the bed she'd slept in since she'd been a teenager. Crowley dumped his jacket and pants and shirt and climbed into bed with his wife and child. She'd opened the windows, so a summer breeze crossed the room. It felt very good. He should have enjoyed it more often. He rubbed his toes against the cool sheets and arched his shoulder a little so Mikey could press against his chest. He snored like his mother.

This was so nice. Why wasn't it enough? He could have taken a job working the fields or managing wholesale accounts for Brian? A wiser man would have done that. But he felt compelled to do more. To change things…to control things.

Mikey screamed a little and called for a "ba." Without waking up, Jana reached around for his bottle and pressed it to him. The light from her fake eye make the bed glow for a few seconds.

He was going to die and lose all of this. But he'd considered the facts one way and the other…and always came back to the conclusion that death was coming, no matter how peacefully he lived. So, he'd push to make order from chaos. Maybe he could leave more for Jana and Mikey than just a family farm.

"Michael. Michael, wake up."

"Huh?"

"Wake up!" That one was angrier than others. "J.J. is on the satphone."

It was full morning. The sun was out and the sky was blue. He'd overslept.

"Yeah?"

"Rabbi. It's Jean Jacques."

"Johnny. Yeah. Sorry, I was asleep. What's happening?"

"Nothing. I mean nothing bad. We're fine. But this morning I received an envoy from Tampa."

"An envoy?"

"Yes. He came in a shiny silver tilt."

"What did he want?" Jana gave Crowley a glass of orange juice. He didn't like the juice, normally. But he figured it would help him wake up.

"Are you awake?"

"Yes. What does the envoy want?"

"He has an offer for you."

"For *me*?"

"Yes."

"Okay. What? What's his offer for me?"

"He says he'll only deal you directly."

"Well, tell him he's going to have to wait."

"I did. He said he has your children."

"What?"

"He has your children. Your daughter and your son. But he'll only deal with you directly."

"I'll be there in three hours."

He rubbed his eyes and stared at Jana. She'd heard what Jean Jacques had said. She nodded.

Then he laughed. And she hugged him.

He called the SkyDragon pilot. He had a slight worry that the Brownsville board would want to keep the machine now that it was back on home turf.

"No problem, sir. We're rested and ready. The Black Dragon is fueled and my commander says I'm at your disposal for as long as you say. We'll be at the Morrell compound in 10 minutes."

Crowley washed his face while Jana watched.

"Part of me wants to go with you, Michael."

"I hope it's a small part."

"It's better than I stay here and prepare the House for them. You get the kids and bring them back here to meet their little brother."

This was Jana at her best. She was elegant, in a classical sense. She cut through the layers of neurotic bullshit where a second wife usually got stuck. It was really ridiculous to think of her as a second wife. She wasn't, in any conventional sense.

Jana's take was that the kids were Mikey's siblings. And his home was their home. Again, her strong feelings about family.

The Dragon announced its arrival. He kissed her hard on the mouth and then held her head in his hands and looked into her eyes. The vivid brown of the left eye and mechanical orange of the right. "You are my wife. I love you more than anything in my life. You're the last thing I'll think about the last second I'm alive."

"Just make sure that's not for a long time."

"Okay."

He blew a wet kiss into Mikey's stomach. Mikey laughed.

He watched Jana and Mikey wave at him as the Dragon lifted up into the morning sky. The noise made Mikey lean into Jana's chest. But he kept waving his little hand.

As soon as the Dragon lunged into cruising configuration, Crowley called Hernandez. "Where are you?"

"About 200 yards from their main east gate. We popped one nuke on the wall about a quarter of a mile northwest of here and they're fleeing like rats. I mean it. They're literally coming out through the gate with their hands up, Rabbi. It's like an old movie."

"Well, make sure you have some vid of that. We'll put it up on the free nets."

"Yeah. Already putting it up. And we're setting up a prisoner camp out here. I just hope it's big enough. We're going to take this City before we set foot inside."

"Be careful of a trap, H."

"I hear you, Rabbi. But I don't think that's going to be a problem.'

"Be careful."

"Yes, sir."

"Are you in touch with Admiral Z?"

"Yeah. He's in the Bay. He landed a missile on one of their piers and he says their cutters dropped their flags."

"This is strategic, H. It may be a coup but it may still be a trap. Do you understand what I'm saying?"

"Sure. The connection's not that bad, Rabbi. It's like we discussed in the last briefing."

"Yes. And, like I said, we can't assume the coup will work. Clinton might have figured it out and made a deal with New Orleans."

"I understand. But we're still proceeding to their City Hall, yes?"

"Yes."

"Okay. And the old CEO is Clinton and the new guy is Hester?"

"Maybe. Be careful"

"I hear you, Rabbi. Don't worry. If these people are setting a trap, we'll make them regret their treachery. We'll proceed and I'll check in with you when I'm at City Hall."

"Right. Just keep the gunfire to a minimum. And keep your students calm. We don't want any itchy trigger fingers?"

"What?"

"No nervous shootings."

"Okay. Check."

"I've got to deal with something in Tampa for a little while. Then I'll be heading your way this afternoon."

"Right. This afternoon. Just like we planned."

"But call me again when you're inside."

"Will do."

He called Admiral Z next. "Did you fire a nuke at one of their piers?"

"No nukes. You said no nukes. Two 5,000-pound concussion. They probably wish they'd been a nuke."

"Okay. Very good. No other problems?"

"No problems. Mobile Bay isn't a challenge. I worry New Orleans sending their big boats this way. We need to take the fight to them."

"I know."

"When do we go?"

"Soon, Z. Soon. For now, secure Mobile's docks. Next, it'll be either New Orleans or the Panama Canal."

"New Orleans, Rabbi. The Mississippi River is the key to controlling America. Even a Chinaman knows this."

"Just keep your head down. And try to figure out why your interceptors are leaking fuel."

"Aye, sir."

Crowley checked his screen for the market reports. Word was out. Mobile bonds were down more than 50 percent—and New Orleans almost 30 percent. The other Cities in the region were down… though less. Tampa lost another 12 percent—to 30 percent of their bond's face value. That was, by all standards, a historical low.

Good time to be a bond speculator.

Crowley was watching the New York quotes more, though. The fortune was to be made in betting the small values between where stocks were trading and where they should be. No one of these swings had big meaning in itself; but, taken together, they'd be interesting. And not interesting in a happy way.

Hester had his direct line. He was supposed to call when he'd taken over from Clinton. What made Crowley nervous was that the call hadn't come. He sat back in seat and watched the low clouds over the Gulf. "Harry, ETA?"

"75 minutes, Rabbi."

"Great. Good time. Listen, Harry. There might be a political element to our arrival. I'm going to talk to my guys on the ground there before we land. But we'll probably want to make the most imposing figure we can when we land."

"I understand, sir. We can vent our radiators over the cooling conduits and throw off a lot steam. It's kind of a cheap trick. But anyone who sees it will be impressed."

Exactly 75 minutes later, the Black Dragon landed—with steam spewing out—in Occupied Tampa.

When the landing ramp lowered down, Crowley looked down onto a quarter-mile stretch of the Old Florida Highway. They'd landed on the south-bound lanes of the Highway to the north of three City of Tampa tilts that were parked in a V formation.

Several hundred students were standing in formation on either side of the Highway, creating "walls" between the SkyDragon and the tilts.

Jean Jacques and some aides were waiting at the foot of the ramp. He called attention and the students all presented arms. This was the cue to the envoy in the shining silver tilt—the largest of the three—to come out.

Crowley marched down the ramp. Jean Jacques and his aides closed in behind him.

"Any news?"

"No, Rabbi. They haven't said a thing since I told them you were approaching. The envoy is a cranky old coot."

"Old *coot?*"

"Yeah. Not much of a diplomat."

Crowley had a flash of who the old coot might be.

Just as he was thinking this, Old Man Hailwood climbed out of it with the two children and three…four bodyguards.

Crowley's eyes focused on Pea and Jack again. The dreams of this moment had sustained him through so much pain and so many low points…he tried to focus his thoughts so this moment wouldn't slide past like so many of his experiences in the wasteland.

Pea was taller—but she looked pretty much the same as she did that morning on the wall. Jack was different. He was an inch or so taller than Pea. And thin as a rail.

"Jack. Pea."

He rushed to them and hugged them together.

"Dad."

"Dad."

He pulled back to take a good look at both faces. They were tan and healthy looking. She looked pretty. Her hair was shorter than it had been. And she wore it in a hair band. She looked like a high school girl. Which she was.

Sic Semper Tyrannis

Jack was still growing into his face. And his hair was kind of unkempt. He must have just gone through a growth spurt. They were both wearing tennis clothes. It was normal for their lives—but so different from his life now.

"It's so good to see you two again."

Pea hugged him again and seemed content just to press against his shoulder. Jack looked past him at the big tilt. "Dad. What's going on? Are you the head of another City? What is that plane?"

"It's a SkyDragon, Jack. Carries a lot of people and goes fast. Listen. I want you guys to go back there and walk up that ramp onto the plane. The pilot's name is Harry. And there are some other helpers. They'll get you guys set up. I'll be back there in a minute or two. We're not staying here very long"

They both hesitated a little.

"Go on. Mr. Hailwood and I have some business to discuss for just a short minute. Then, I'll come back there with you."

Jack took his sister's hand and walked with her—pulling her forward a little—toward the ramp.

"This is a sign of good faith, Michael."

Crowley watched his children into the plane and then turned his attention around to the Old Man. He looked the same. But his eyes were a little bloodshot.

"Thank you for returning my children. But there's no need for signs of good faith. We're not seeking any negotiated settlement."

"Look, Michael, I know what a mistake the City made in how we treated you. I know that I've treated you badly. I'm sorry. But we were faced with what seemed like a bad situation. You were losing control of your senior executives and I was worried that your plans for a federation of Cities would drain Tampa's resources—"

"Please, stop. I didn't come here to settle personal grudges. If I did, you'd be dead."

"Don't threaten me."

The Old Man's face was red and his eyes squinted into thin lines. Crowley remembered this face. "I'm not threatening you. And I'm not here to negotiate, so your rhetoric doesn't carry any weight. I'm here because I support Jacksonville's plans to establish a regional confederation of Cities. And, given Tampa's history of resisting such organizations, President Karamanlis and I agreed that I'd come down here and help prepare Jacksonville's annexation of Tampa."

"Annexation?"

"Yes. So, I'm not interested in good faith gestures. I'm not interested in anything that management has to say. There's not going to any merger. We're not going to offer any pay-outs to equity holders or directors. If you want to cooperate, you can announce the bankruptcy and termination of the City of Tampa Corporation."

"We're not going to terminate…"

"About five minutes ago, President Karamanlis formally announced Jacksonville's plan to annex Tampa's territories and assets. We've pledged the support of Occupied Tampa. He's also got the support of the other Cities in the Jacksonville League—and statements of neutrality from those who aren't joining the League."

"Occupied Tampa?"

"We'll let the markets decide what your management is worth. But my guess is that the economics of the situation will make it tough for you to keep quality personnel on your side."

"You bastard."

"While I'm no expert, I suspect Tampa's bonds are going to take a beating in markets. If you're leveraged at all with your own equity shares, you probably started getting margin calls this morning. I don't envy your next few days, Mr. Chairman. But I do appreciate you returning my children to me. My students will honor your diplomatic status until you've returned to your territory. But we will protect our territory and air space from any other incursion. Good bye."

Despite what he had said, that *did* satisfy his grudge.

He walked back quickly. Jean Jacques kept pace.

"Make sure your people dig in deeply. Get the anti-missile systems up and sharp. Maybe move some people back to the original Delta base. They're going to come back with their hardest strike since you've been here. It'll probably be tonight—but it could be five minutes after he leaves."

"We're ready."

"When they start hitting you here, make sure the other companies strike fast at the walls where they are. That will be the best time for them to start moving into Tampa real estate. And use our missile coverage to support those moves. The units here are going to have to rely on the anti-missiles and strong cover."

"I'll make sure they're all standing by."

"Also, they may leave one of their tilts over there. Try to argue that it still has diplomatic cover. Signature Tampa move. If they leave one behind, torch it the second the others leave our air space."

"Got it."

"Okay. I'm going to take these two out of here and then go meet up with H in Mobile. But I'll head back here tonight."

"Okay."

"Tonight will be tough. You may want to spend the night here again. But don't. You need to manage this thing."

"I don't mind the risk, Rabbi."

"I know. But tonight isn't about showing bravery. Johnny. Tonight's about strategy. If you want to spend the night on the front lines, go attack the walls with Kappa or Beta."

"Understood."

"On second thought, don't do that either. Just keep your command post at Camp Delta. I'll be back before midnight."

When he got inside the SkyDragon, he told Harry to head back to the Morrell compound.

He strapped himself into a seat next to Pea and Jack.

"So, when did they tell you two you were coming with me?"

Jack smiled and started to answer.

Pea started to scream. Like she was in pain.

Crowley's first thought was that she scared about the Dragon taking off. He tried to say something reassuring…but her screams only got louder.

She twisted up in her seat, grabbing her right knee and screaming a pattern of noises that took form as "Oh god, Oh god. Ohgod. Ohgod."

He undid his belt and climbed over her. "Pea, Pea. What's the matter?"

Her face was drawn white and severe with pain. She was grinding her teeth and had to gasp to push out a few words of an answer. "My. Leg. Is. On. Fire."

She was rubbing the top of her right thigh, just about halfway between her knee and her hip.

"Mr. Crowley. This is the cockpit. Do you need some help?"

"Daughter's in a lot of pain," he was screaming over her screams. He wasn't thinking about how good the intercom on this tilt was. They could hear everything up front.

"I'll be right there."

Pea's breathing started getting shallow and fast. Crowley knew what that meant—she was hyperventilating. Maybe going into shock.

He tried to move her out of her seat. But her body was rigid.

Harry couldn't do any better when he came back. Pea was too big to move around like a child. It was going to take a couple of people and probably some sedatives to get her out of her seat.

Harry looked at Crowley plaintively.

"Just land at the Delta Company base camp. They have a medical tent there. Go."

Crowley didn't have a number calling the Delta camp directly, so he called Jean Jacques and told him what was happening. Crowley asked Jack if Pea had any medical problems.

"No. I don't know. I've never seen anything like this."

Crowley realized that he must have sounded accusing. "It's okay, son. We'll get a doctor in here right away."

They landed again in about 90 seconds. And a medic team came aboard immediately.

The girl who was the team leader gave Pea a shot and ran her hands quickly along Pea's legs. Pea went limp a few seconds after the shot. "It was her right thigh?"

"Yes. She was rubbing the top."

The medic ran her hands around that thigh. She evidently didn't feel anything. Next, she took a hand-held ultrasound unit out of her bag and ran it back and forth along Pea's thigh.

She ran the ultrasound unit back and forth—and seemed to locate something, right about where Pea had been rubbing.

"There's something in there."

"Something in there? What?"

"I dunno. But it's not organic. Let's get her into the med tent. Dr. Handel is there. She can figure this out and do something."

Jack unstrapped his sister and then Crowley and Harry each took one shoulder and carried Pea down the ramp and followed the medic about 50 yards to the medical tent. She was talking into her ear/mouth piece while they moved.

Dr. Handel was a stout woman in her late 40s. Doctors were hard to find in the wasteland, so Crowley knew her story. She'd been a surgeon in Jacksonville—but had been banished for having an adulterous affair with another doctor's wife. Like so many people, she'd gravitated toward one of the villages outside of New Orleans' walls. She signed on with the Company because it was a chance to work with proper medical equipment again. And, while she wasn't religious, she believed in Crowley's work, teaching people to read.

She had a bed ready. Once they laid Pea flat, she started twitching. The medic prepped and gave her another shot. Handel concentrated on running a larger ultrasound unit along Pea's right leg.

"Here it is, Rabbi. Come look."

Her ultrasound screen was set on a wheeled medical cart. When Crowley got close, he could see a long black rectangle attached somehow to the gray of Pea's femur. The medic was right—it looked too dense to be organic. It looked like some kind of metal stick.

"It will take me a long time to figure out exactly what that is. In the meantime, she's gone into shock because it's done something—"

"Get it out of her!"

"Yes, sir. Medic, please prep the leg. Rabbi, I'm going to ask you and the others to stand back a little while I do this."

She worked fast, putting on a smock that had gloves attached and a face covering while the medic cut off Pea's tennis sweat pants and swabbed her tight in brown disinfectant. Then she strapped Pea into the bed with straps that seemed to appear from nowhere.

The doctor aimed her lights on Pea's leg and then set the screen up high, so she could see it easily without moving her head too much.

She placed a couple of ultrasound markers at different places on Pea's leg. They must have had some kind of adhesive, because they stayed in strange positions. Then, she took a long needle from her cart and inserted into Pea's thigh. She looked back at the screen and sighed. Then she clicked though a couple of menus and sighed again.

"It's a plastic and titanium casing over a bunch of different stuff—including Hydrogen Trinuclear Silicate."

"Hydrogen Trinuclear Silicate? It's a bomb?"

"Seems so. Something went wrong, though and the HTS seeped out into her thigh. That's what causing the pain. It's poisoning her."

The lights flashed a couple of times. This was sterilizing the area around Pea's leg.

"Will she be okay?"

"Too early to tell. Let's get it out of her first. I think I can do this with minimal cutting. I'm going to make a small incision near her knee and an even smaller one near her hip. Then, I'll try to bring it out through the cut near her knee."

"I understand, doctor, Whatever you think will work best."

Handel was already doing the cutting while she talked.

"The real question is did they do something to attach it the femur. Because it seems to be right up against it there. But, if we're lucky, they just inserted really well."

She made the other cut, higher on Pea's thigh and then inserted a probe that looked like a long, skinny spoon into Pea's leg.

"Hey, good news. I can move it. It's not connected to the bone."

She leaned over Pea and twisted the spoon/probe a few times. Then she gave it a steady push. Pea's thigh shifted and the dark tip of the…device…poked out of the incision just above her knee.

"Look at this." Handel grabbed a pair of pinchers from the medical cart and pulled the device out of Pea's leg. It made a cartoonish "shplop" sound when it came out. There was a lot of blood that came out with the thing. But her leg jiggled back into a more normal-looking shape.

Handel put the device on the bed and worked on stapling the cuts closed.

The device looked like an aluminum cigar case. It wasn't a perfect cylinder—it was flat on one side. And, as Crowley looked at the thing, he could see that one end of it was dented and cracked open.

Handel put the device in a clear bag that zipped closed. "Put this inside a lead-lined courier pouch and take this with you, Rabbi. Her signs are all stable. We'll give her enough sedatives that she'll stay asleep for six or eight hours. But you need to get her to a proper hospital. Just to be safe."

"Will do. But before we go anywhere, will you use your ultrasound to examine the rest of her body. I want to make sure there aren't more of those things in her."

"Of course."

"And we also need to check out my son."

Jack looked scared for a second. But he recovered quickly and did everything the doctor told him.

There weren't any other bombs. Each of the kids had an ID transmitter tag in the shoulder. Handle was able to remove those with a pin-point arthroscopic probe; that wasn't much worse than a hypodermic needle shot.

They bandaged Pea's leg and rolled the bed right back onto the SkyDragon.

Crowley thanked Handel and gave her a hug.

"I don't need to tell you this but I will anyway, Rabbi. These City Brahmins are bad people. We really need to bring them down."

"Keep an eye on the news, Doctor. The next day is going to be very interesting like that."

Harry and the other fliers made sure Pea's bed was secure and then headed for Brownsville. Crowley called Jana and told her what had happened. She insisted that they come straight back to the house. She'd have doctors and medical supplies there to meet them.

He also called Brian and told him about the bomb. Brian said he'd talk to the gun-maker and have a couple of TAG's experts come to the house to examine it.

After those calls, Crowley got up and checked on Pea. She was snoring softly and steadily. He asked Jack what he liked to drink; Jack said he liked Cherry Coke. After all that he'd been through, Crowley couldn't deny him a that. They went to the galley together.

Jack said that Chambers and Margot had tried to hide any news about Crowley from them—but, especially in recent months, that had been impossible.

"The news says that you're like a priest. And that you kill people who don't believe in God."

"No. I believe in God a little more than I used to. But I'm not a priest. Some people call me 'Rabbi' but that's in the meaning like 'teacher.' I believe really strongly in teaching people how to read. Most of the people who live in wasteland don't know how. Grown-ups, I mean. I started teaching them. And I'm not even sure I'm that good of a teacher...at least I wasn't in the beginning. Anyway, the one book that most everyone had heard of was the Bible. So, we read that. The people were so happy to learn to read that they started calling me 'Rabbi.' And I read the Bible so much that I've become more religious than I used to be."

"Is that why you decided to go to war against Tampa?"

"Not exactly. That's kind of complicated, Jack. It's not really war against Tampa. It's against the whole City system."

"You want it to be like in the old Federal Era. The United States of America."

"I don't think that can ever happen again. But we might end up with something where we have a couple of smaller versions of the USA. I just think that having Cities and wasteland is...a waste."

"I can see that."

Crowley hugged his son.

Jack said that he and Pea didn't know they were going to meet him. They didn't know exactly what was going on with the war. No one did. But Chambers and Margot had been fighting a lot. "And they fight right in front of us. They don't care. It's pretty screwed up."

"Not any more."

"Anyway, Mom went to the beach house for a few days. Like she does a lot. And Chambers said that Mr. Hailwood was going to ask us to do something important for the City. They're always talking about how lucky we are to live in Tampa and how we should feel duty to the City. Anyway, we thought Mr. Hailwood was going to make us go on the screens and give some speech about how great Tampa was or something. We didn't know what. But when we got in the fancy tilt, he told us we were going to see you again. We thought we were going to fly to another City. Or maybe, ah, to jail or something. We didn't know that your soldiers had already taken over part of Tampa.

"So, when we were waiting for you in his tilt, Mr. Hailwood was talking on the screen with all these different people and just getting madder and madder. And that made me feel happy. I think Patricia felt the same way?"

"Patricia?"

"Yeah. She doesn't like being called 'Pea' any more."

"And she doesn't like Christina?"

"She said she wanted to be called by her middle name. And everyone did."

"I'll try to remember that. Not sure how successful I'll be."

On the way back to their seats, he checked her again. She was sleeping soundly.

Crowley felt proud of Jack, He seemed like one of those kids who'd lived through all kinds of terrible things but managed to come through with a calm personality and a level head.

As they watched the clouds below, it occurred to him that his kids were coming to Brownsville with nothing—not even clothes. "I think you're going to like the Morrell Farm. It's beautiful. Like something out of vid of old-fashioned farm country."

"Is that where you live?"

"Some of the time. But, while I was in the wasteland, I kind of gave up on the idea of having a home in any one place."

Jack accepted that explanation without further comment, and turned back to the clouds below his window.

Jana had what seemed like half of the staff from the North Brownsville Community waiting at the house when they landed. A doctor came aboard with a portable MRI system and scanned Pea in her bed. At the same time, one of his assistants drew blood from her arm and the bandaged thigh.

Pea didn't make a sound the whole time.

"I called Old Man Guibert and he got Dr. Reisbeck in touch with the woman in at the Delta Camp." Jana explained. "She emailed him the details she had."

Crowley looked away from his daughter and kissed his wife. "Thanks. That was good thinking. Jana, this John Alstott Crowley. We call him Jack. Jack, this is Jana Crowley."

He stood up straight and offered his hand. "Nice to meet you, Jana."

She shook his hand and hugged him. "It's good to meet you, Jack. What a day you've had!"

She kept her hand on his shoulder and they all turned back to Pea.

Reisbeck clicked through a screen that hung from a lanyard around his neck. Crowley had never met Reisbeck before, but he'd heard of the man. He was the chief of surgery at the hospital. He told two assistants to unstrap her bed and roll it into the house. "Mr. Crowley. Sorry for being short but I wanted to get a look at your daughter as quickly as possible."

"Of course, doctor. How is she?"

"Her leg is fine. Dr. Handel did a nice job of removing the device with minimal damage. Very little tissue damage. Nice cutting. Next time you see her, give her my regards. I'm a little worried about the toxins, though. Take a few minutes to get to the bottom of that."

They all followed the bed down the ramp and toward the house. Brian and Brandy were waiting on the front steps. Brian said hello quietly and asked Crowley for the device. Jack was carrying it in a lead-lined satchel that one of Jean Jacques's men had given them. Jack gave it to Brian, who disappeared inside. Brandy stayed with rest of them. She smiled at Crowley and squeezed his arm in friendly support.

Reisbeck continued his report. "I've double-checked and looked very closely for any other nasty tricks that might have been put in her or on her. She's got some bridgework on her lower teeth and she has a FemControl bead in her left hip—but, other than that, she's clean."

FemControl was a birth control and STD vaccine device that teenage girls in Tampa were required to have by the time they turned 14. If they didn't, they weren't eligible for free tuition at local colleges. He'd approved the program when he'd been CEO. He remembered wondering briefly how he'd feel about it when Pea turned 14—but he'd figured they'd make the decision about the bead when the time came. It had come more quickly than he'd figured.

"It's the HTS leak that I'm worried about. That's some nasty stuff and it's going to be tough to get it out of her system. I've got a blood cleansing machine set up in the house. And I can give her some antidotes. But there's nothing that's really good at getting HTS out of a person. The best we can do is keep her well hydrated and hope her body washes out the poison."

"What's the risk?"

"Well, right now, she seems to be doing okay. Everything looks normal. The worst case is that the HTS will collect in her liver and cause cirrhosis or in her kidneys and cause renal failure. So, we'll be watching those organs. Her heart and lungs, too; but HTS seems to do the worst to the liver and kidneys."

"How long?"

"Two or three days."

"And then?"

"And then, she'll be okay. Try not to worry too much. You've done all anyone could."

Jana had set up the living room of the house like a room in a hospital intensive care unit. The assistants moved Pea into the "smart bed" that would track her vital signs. And they set up her IV drip to keep the water and meds pumping through.

Brian had come back and watched the last of this. "Michael, why don't we go back to the kitchen for a minute? A couple of friends of ours from downtown are there and they've already got some details on that thing."

Jana and Brandy said they'd stay with Pea.

Brian introduced himself to Jack. "...I'm Jana's brother. So, that makes me your uncle. By marriage."

"When we were coming here, my dad said you run this huge farm."

"Yeah. It's been my family's business for more than 100 years."

"What do you grow?"

"Well, we grow all kinds of things. But mostly soy beans and corn."

"Can I see the crops before we leave? I've never been on a real farm before."

"We can see the crops any time you like, Jack. And I think you're going to have plenty of time. Your father and Jana live here about half the year. We've made a room for you upstairs."

"Cool."

Two young techs—they looked like they were just out of university—had set up a workbench on one of the prep tables in the kitchen. They'd taken apart the device and separated it into component parts. Shell, trigger device and fuel. They had a strange-looking microscope that had a very bright light.

"Michael, this is Cy and Jurgen. They're the explosives geniuses from TAG. Guys, this is my brother-in-law, Michael Crowley."

Cy did most of the talking. "Of course, Mr. Crowley. We've taken a hard look at this little bugger. Here's what we've got. It's a custom piece that we're pretty sure was built by New York Security Forces."

"New York?"

"We're about 90 percent certain. The triggering device is from Assurant Technologies—which I'm sure you recognize as a major arms maker in New York. The shell also comes from Assurant. It's a Model X559, meant for stealthy security work. It usually comes with an adhesive surface along the flat side. But this one didn't have the adhesive."

Jurgen butted in here, "Assurant is usually known for quality work. But look here. This comms link to the trigger was assembled very poorly. Loose connections. As a result, the triggering instructions failed."

"You mean they tried to detonate?"

"Yes. The trigger activated. But it didn't deliver enough of a charge to ignite the HTS fuel. It delivered a very weak charge which caused just enough acceleration to crack the shell and leak fuel into your daughter's leg."

"Any idea how it got from Assurant in New York to Tampa?"

"None. But these types of devices aren't the kinds of things that people like to talk about. Assurant doesn't usually sell X559 bombs to anyone but the NYSF. So, it probably came from NYSF to TSF."

"Any guesses how they implanted it? Or when?"

"Well, we're not experts on implanting bombs in people's bodies. But you'd just use a large-gauge hypodermic—like the things some Cities use to mark prisoners or slaves with tracking devices. The titanium shell is made for use in all kinds of strange places. As long as it was sterile when it was inserted, it could stay inside a person's body for long time."

Jurgen added, "But the serial number on the trigger is pretty recent. It's from a lot...ah, released," he clicked through a portable screen, "well, within the last six months."

"If the bomb was meant for me, they must have done it recently. They weren't even sure I was still alive until a few months ago."

"The dentist..." that was Jack. "Dad! Just like two days ago, Mom took Patricia to the dentist. It was kind of surprise. They said she had a tooth they had to pull and they knocked her out to do it."

Crowley nodded and patted Jack on the shoulder. "I'm sure you're right, Jack. That was probably when they did it."

He asked the gun guys to put the shell back together. He needed that. They could have the fuel and trigger.

He went back out to Jana. She was holding Mikey.

Reisbeck was getting ready to leave—but a younger doctor and a couple of assistants were staying.

Crowley walked Reisbeck out to his car. "So, she'll be okay?"

"She should be. The chances of anything bad happening drop by the hour. We'll keep her asleep for another day or so and then bring her around. Don't worry. With the set-up you have in there, she's probably in better shape than she'd be at the hospital. And I'm 15 minutes away, if there's any problem."

"Thanks. This is happening at a terrible time..."

"I know. I watch the news. Is all of this trouble good for Brownsville?"

"I think so."

"Take care of yourself, Mr. Crowley. And take care of your kids."

Crowley had told Jack that he was going to have to leave them at the farm, as soon as they got Pea settled. Still, he was as worried about doing that. When he came back into the house, he looked in on Pea. The nurses had made the bed neatly around her and were brushing her hair. She looked peaceful. Next, he looked in on the two boys playing with a tennis ball on the floor of the dining room. He made eye contact with Jana, who was standing beside him in a moment.

"I told Jack I was going to leave him here with his sister and little brother. But I was thinking of slipping out now, just to avoid any scene."

"Coward." She slipped her hand into his. "But you be careful. Now you have three to come back to here."

"Four. I'll be back in the morning." He kissed her on the forehead. "Thanks again for doing all of this."

"We owe you a lot, Michael. And you deserve some...stability."

Mikey knew the word "ball" though he said it "ba." He and Jack were rolling the tennis ball around the dining room and Crowley could hear "Ba! Ba! Ba!" as he walked across the lawn to the big plane.

There had been no battle at Mobile. Hester and Boyette convinced enough of their fellow managers to make a deal that the Security Forces stood down when Hernandez's Camp C students arrived. The situation was a little awkward—Hernandez still set up his people and missiles in siege positions. Then he took two companies, totaling about 1,200 students, into the City.

Boyette explained that some of the Mobile Security Forces were holding out and that his troops wanted to take care of them.

Hernandez followed the plan. He said that his troops were going to focus on securing key locations. He suggested that Boyette pin the holdouts into the smallest possible location—and then they would cordon that off and starve them out.

The next few hours went smoothly. Hernandez secured the government buildings, the main telecom facilities and the CEO's mansion. He had Boyette clear out the government building because of a "security drill;" though the allowed a few managers loyal to Hester stay.

Company tech specialists censored all hard-news media outlets, channels and pages in the City—they just ran sports and celebrity news. But he didn't do anything to close businesses or otherwise interfere with the normal work day. Then he and Hester sat in the main government building and discussed what Hester would say.

By five o'clock in the afternoon, a crowd had started gathering around the building. The citizens didn't seem to be violent; they were just curious. On a video call, Crowley told Hernandez and Hester not to worry about the crowd—and that they needed to make sure the Company troops didn't do anything violent. "Just make sure they keep the crowd orderly. No threats. No confrontations. And keep your eyes on the gates and main doors." He gave them various other instructions, including using tiltrotors to make sure that Boyette's troops had contained the hold-outs. And to bring Clinton himself back to the government building. And Hester's skeletal staff needed to arrange a media announcement for around eight.

A few minutes before seven, Crowley called and said he was five minutes away. His pilot was going to land the big plane in the public square in front of the main government building. That would make an impression on the crowd. Plus, he wanted the CEO brought around.

The SkyDragon had the intended effect. When Crowley and his bodyguards walked down the ramp, he saw hundreds of citizens jammed along the sidewalks on the opposite sides of the streets around. But they made very little noise. It was as if some public figure had died.

Inside he asked Hester if he was ready to step forward. He said he was. Then, they went over the prepared remarks for the media event.

When the students brought Clinton into the room, Crowley asked Hernandez and Hester and everyone else to step outside.

Clinton acted calmly. But Crowley could see the anger brewing just beneath the skin of his face.

"Mr. Clinton, I'm Mich—"

"We know who you are."

"Okay. Please, have a seat."

"We prefer to stand."

"Okay, can I get you something to drink?"

"No thank you."

"Okay. Well, if you're going to stand, I will too." He actually didn't mind. All the flying he done had made his legs a little stiff. If he paced while he talked to Clinton, they'd loosen up. "I'm not here to humiliate or insult you, Mr. Clinton. I'll put it you plainly. I want you to sign the letter of resignation. It's short and diplomatically vague about the reasons why."

"What if we don't sign? You'll kill us? We wish you could see how far you've fallen. From a reputable manager to a bandit with delusions of grandeur."

Crowley slid the screen across the table toward Clinton.

"I've killed men before. For money, for a political statement and for principal. But I've come to see now that most of those actions were mistakes. Of arrogance. And I pray to God every morning to forgive me for my arrogance and my mistakes."

"Religion is a crutch for simple minds."

"Yes, I've heard that one before. But you know what? The arrogance that led me to sin was something that I learned when I was a reputable manager. And I can see that arrogance in you right now. It's not strength, Mr. Clinton. It's weakness."

"Your insults are meaningless. And don't lie to yourself. You've haven't killed some people. You've killed thousands."

"Maybe so, maybe so. So, how about this?" He pulled the plasma pistol from the holster in his chest plate. "If you don't sign the letter right now, I'll kill you. Believe me, in the sweep of the changeover, you'll be lost in the details. Don't do that. Resign and live the rest of your life in a fairly normal manner."

"So you're not going to put us in jail?"

"Not unless you commit a crime."

"And you're not going to banish us?"

"Mr. Clinton, there isn't any wasteland left to banish you to."

"And you're letting us keep our money and property?"

"I'm not the tax authority. What you keep is between you and the City of Mobile. Now sign and stamp the resignation letter." He raised his pistol.

The manager in Clinton took over and his anger seemed to diminish. He took a minute to read the letter, signed the box at the bottom and sealed it with this thumbprint.

"Excellent. Now go on and watch the news like everyone else."

Hester did very well at the media announcement. He said that Clinton had resigned, effective immediately. He said that, as interim CEO, he had invited the Company into Mobile help maintain security through the transition—and that he had asked Crowley to serve as a Special Advisor on External Security matters.

He said that his first official act as CEO was to sign the charter of the South East League of Cities and that Mobile would be with Jacksonville, Miami, Charleston, Atlanta, Birmingham and several others to create confederation that would govern the entire region—Cities and "countryside."

Finally, he said that Mobile's board of directors would review all of these developments at its next regularly scheduled meeting in three weeks.

Hester asked Crowley to say a few words.

"I hope that all of you watching this announcement appreciate what a strong vision Richard Hester has for the City of Mobile and the South East League, He is a strong leader—precisely the kind of leader that this City needs in these times of rapid political and economic change. I think he will do very well.

"Why is vision so important in these troubled times? Let me give you an example. Earlier today, in what they claimed was a gesture of good faith, the President and the Chairman of the City of Tampa returned my teenage daughter to me after several years of house arrest with this—" and he held the X559 shell up for the cameras "—implanted in her leg. This is a bomb, intended to detonate inside an airplane that my daughter and I were flying in. It was meant to kill us both, just minutes after we'd been reunited.

"Now, I know that words like *terrorist* and *bandit* are used a lot these days. But, let me tell you something: bandits and terrorists don't always come from the wasteland. Sometimes they come from inside the walls of the world's biggest Cities. What else do you call someone who implants a bomb in a child's leg?

"What we're saying is that it's time to stop thinking that Cities are good and the countryside is bad. We're saying that there's a difference between people like Richard Hester, who's looking for ways to improve the lives of *all* people, and people like Tampa's Grant Hailwood and Matthew Chambers, who are trying to divide people. And trying to kill innocents. Literally. They have more in common with the bandits of the wasteland than they do with this good man."

The speech went over well. He could feel it working as he delivered it.

Thirty

Maria Elena went back to Miami because she liked her job selling ads for the music channel. And, maybe, because she thought it wasn't safe in Tampa. Even in the Hailwood compound.

Frankly, Hailwood was kind of relieved that she'd left.

But now he wasn't sure what to do with his time. Sex was such a great time-killer.

The Old Man had insisted that he stay around the House.

Hailwood talked to the Security guys who were running the anti-missile platform at the House about volunteering to drive supplies up north in his fancy Badger. They didn't take his offer seriously—and immediately he felt stupid for offering.

He knew too much to be a frontline grunt but he didn't have the power to do any practical with his knowledge. He had to patient and wait for the call.

So, he sat on the beach and played battle scenarios in his mind.

After a couple of hours of imaginary war games, he went back to the House and checked the news. The main Tampa bonds had dropped to 19 cents on the dollar. So far, he'd lost over $200,000 from his 27 cents on the dollar "safe bet."

He couldn't believe that the New York markets were taking Crowley's vid rant so seriously. His talk of Tampa spies injecting bombs into his daughter's leg seemed like something out of a cheap screen melodrama. Not the real world.

But the New York traders were just wage slaves—better educated more highly paid that most, but the kind of people who went home and watched melodramas at night. So, of course, they'd get spooked by Crowley's rant. After all, Crowley was one of them. He understood how they thought. Maybe that's what had made him such an effective manager.

Hailwood was sweaty and a little sunburned from the beach. So, he decided to take a long shower. By the time he was done, it would be after 3 pm—and he could call *la sirena*.

He set the shower to 104 degrees and added a little aloe vera oil for his skin. The oil gave the shower a scent that reminded him of Kate. He hadn't thought about her in a long time. Maybe he'd send her an email. That would kill some time.

He and Kate used to have sex a lot in the shower. It was one of the few "wild" kinds of sex that Kate would actually initiate. The thought of her struck some kind of Pavlovian response in his cock. It answered the call of his memories of her freckled breasts.

He really needed to check in with Kate and find out what she was doing. She wasn't that wild in bed—nothing like *la sirena*. But she fit his needs in just about every other way.

"Mr. Hailwood."

At first, with the water running over his neck and head, Hailwood didn't hear anything.

"Mr. Hailwood!"

He pulled his head out of the rush of water. "Who's that?"

It was one of the Security guys. He had a call for Hailwood.

"Hey, I'm just finishing my shower. Can it wait a few minutes?"

"It's Mr. William Franklin, sir. He says it's urgent."

Hailwood shut off the shower and opened the bathroom door just enough to reach out for the screen. Except what the guy handed him wasn't a screen; it was a TSF satphone.

"Hello?"

"Terry?"

"Yeah. Is this Bill Franklin?"

"Yes, it is. Terry. Your grandfather is dead."

"What happened?"

"I'd rather not talk about this over an open comms link."

"Where is he?"

"He's in his office. Look, the security men there will drive you in to your grandfather's office. I'll meet you there."

"I was just in the shower. It'll take me a minute to get dressed."

"That's fine. There's a lot going on. But it's important that we move carefully in the next few hours."

"Yes. I agree. Have you spoken to anyone else?"

"No."

"Who knows?"

"Right now, his secretary and one of my partners. And they're waiting for me at your grandfather's office."

"Good. Please don't say or do anything until you and I can get together and lay out a plan. Will you try to contact my…father…on his boat and let him know?"

"Your grandfather's instructions were very clear. He didn't want your father involved in the estate proceedings."

"I know all about that, Mr. Franklin. And so does my father. We will honor everything the Old Man wanted. But I think my father should know."

"Of course."

The conversation was taking the wrong tone. Franklin was starting to sound like the exasperated advisor to an ill-informed king. "Mr. Franklin. Do you have my personal screen link?"

"Yes. I tried calling there first but couldn't get through."

"That's fine. But I want you to call me back on that line in exactly 15 minutes. I hope that you'll have been able to contact my father by then. When we talk next, we can go over plans for what to do in the next couple of hours."

"Yes. Very good. I'll call you on that line in 15 minutes."

"I'll be dressed and on my way into town."

He handed the phone back to the security trooper. "I'm sorry, what's your name again?"

"Corporal Evans, sir."

"You're the unit leader here?"

"Yes, sir."

"Okay. Evans, we need to get into the downtown area. This is how I'd like to do it. I want your cars downstairs to escort my Badger. And I want one of your guys to drive the Badger, so I can read my screen en route."

He had to get used to giving orders like this. His confidence would instill confidence in others. It was the same dynamic as in the DKE House or in front of first-year rhetoric students.

"Yeah. But I'll need to check in with our commander."

"Go ahead, Evans. I'll be dressed in five minutes."

About 20 hours earlier, Hailwood and the Old Man had been sitting on the big chairs on the back porch, watching the sun set of the Gulf. The Old Man was shaken by the turn of events with Crowley. He'd expected the "good faith gesture" of the kids to work a better effect.

He kept repeating the phrase "good faith gesture." He sounded tired and broken.

The solution came to Hailwood in a flash. "Old Man, it's time for you to go."

The Old Man faced him quickly, with his signature squinting stare. But he didn't say anything. And, slowly, his face softened. "You're right, Terry. It's time."

"How long will it take TSA to get your Crusader ready?"

"It's been ready and standing by for weeks."

"Really?"

"Yeah, sure. I just wanted to get things fixed up…"

"There's no need. We need a radical change to get out of this mess. You know, if were in Sparta or the later Roman Empire, someone in my position might assassinate someone in your position to get things moving."

"Well, thank god we're not in Sparta or Rome."

The Old Man called his personal doctor, who lived nearby on the island, and Bill Franklin. Hailwood called Jack Simmons at TSA and Steve Masterson.

The doctor was at the House in a few minutes. Masterson landed a small tilt in the driveway landing spot about 10 minutes after that. Masterson was the only flier; and there wouldn't be any security escort.

Masterson told Air Security that he was flying on Security business to one of the casinos near Cape Canaveral. Aside from being the Old Man's favorite pilot, Masterson had the reputation for being "fixer" who handled sensitive matters—sometimes sensitive *personal* matters—for board members and other VIPs. So, the guys at Air Traffic Control entered his flight plan and didn't press too hard for details.

The trip to Orlando took about 40 minutes. No one said much during the flight. The doctor asked the Old Man some questions about how he felt and did some simple tests.

But, near the end of the flight, the Old Man looked at Hailwood. "I'm sorry, Terry. I'm sorry for leaving you in this mess."

"Don't worry about it, Old Man."

"And, listen, I want you to promise me something."

"What?"

"Promise me you'll take care of Crowley."

"Say again?"

When they approached Cape Canaveral, Masterson switched his radio to TSA mission control. They gave him landing instructions and said some coded stuff that meant the Crusader was ready.

Masterson followed the instructions and landed next to a dark hangar. One man, dressed in a Crusader flight suit, was standing by the opened doors. He didn't flinch when the tilt rolled up to a few feet from him.

When they climbed out of the tilt, the man in the flight suit approached. "Mr. Chairman, I'm Captain Ryan Eckleson. Looks like you and I are going to be guinea pigs together tonight, sir."

The Old Man nodded. "Yes, Captain. Very much."

"Come with me, sir, and we'll get you squared away."

The doctor went inside the hangar with the Old Man and the astronaut. Hailwood and Masterson walked outside along the tarmac. The Crusader was sitting on top of a modified cargo jet about 200 yards away. The Crusader—which had no name or markings—was modified itself. It had a noticeable bulge near the back, near the base of the rudder.

Hailwood noticed that Masterson seemed unusually impressed. He thought he'd probe the man a bit. "These things always look so big from this angle.

"That's true, sir. From ground level, a few hundred yards away, they seem bigger even than when you're standing next to them on a loading platform."

"You know, the last time I was here was during the first Mars launch. And this bummer engineer in our group was going on and on about how much more efficient it was to launch a Crusader piggyback."

"Well, he might have been a bummer but he was right. There's no need to put a Crusader on top of a Pegasus. No need other than the entertainment value."

"I know, I know. But don't knock entertainment value, Steve."

"I don't, sir."

There wasn't much more time for staring. Masterson climbed onto the cargo puller that was parked inside the hangar and fired it up. Hailwood sat in the front passenger seat. When the other three came out from the changing rooms, the Old Man and the astronaut both had their helmets on and were carrying small metal suitcases. You couldn't see their faces at all. They climbed into the back of the cargo puller and the doctor followed.

Masterson drove around the cargo plane, where a mid-sized loading platform had been completely hidden from view.

Hailwood wasn't accustomed to these platforms being unlit.

Everyone except Masterson got out of the puller and walked over to a big elevator. Jack Simmons and a couple of his managers were waiting for them there.

"Captain Eckleson. Sir. Are you ready to go?"

They both nodded.

The entire group fit on the elevator, which moved slowly up to the loading level. There were a few more techs there.

The techs led the Old Man and the astronaut onto the Crusader which—from this level—didn't seem much different than a regular charter jet. The Old Man's doctor followed. Everyone else milled around near the elevator while the techs ran various kinds of maintenance tests and barked short-hand jargon to one another.

Simmons drifted up to Hailwood. "So, you've come to see our guest off?"

"Yeah. I thought I should."

"I'm glad he told you."

Hailwood looked at Simmons. There was something vaguely condescending in what he was saying—which seemed unlike the man. Maybe the Old Man had been right about Simmons limitations. "Yeah. Well, I'm glad he told me, too."

"As soon as the plane takes off, a few of us are going over to Mission 3 Tower to watch the real launch. Of course, you're welcomed to come along."

"Thanks. I'd like very much to see it."

The doctor came back out of the Crusader and whispered to Hailwood that the Old Man wanted to see him.

Walking onto the Crusader felt exactly like walking onto a charter at any major airport. Inside, though, it felt more like a small tilt than a commercial jet.

The Old Man was belted into the copilot's seat, next to the astronaut. They both had their helmets off. Since the seats were raised from the floor, Hailwood was just about at the Old Man's eye level, standing next to him. "You feel okay?"

"I feel fine. Just some jitters."

They were silent for a minute, while Capt. Eckleson calmly and quietly went through pre-launch prep work with the techs on the platform and at mission control.

"There's so much I want to tell you, Terry. Even though we have had some good talks lately, it would take years for me to think over everything you should know."

"Don't worry. We're in a tight spot—but we'll get through."

"I'm sure you'll do well. I've been sure of that since you were a little child. And I can't tell you what a relief that's been to me. I'm grateful for that relief."

"So, if you could do it all over again...?"

"Ha! You can't trap me with that. Impossible to say."

The astronaut was ready to go.

"Any last advice?"

"Find a good woman and have children. The old-fashioned way. I want the Hailwood stock to be hearty when I get back."

"Words to live by."

"Look. The markets are the best indicator of how you're doing. If City instruments are okay, you're okay. You'll be tempted to think that other Cities are your threats. But they're not. Not usually. Uncertainty is your threat. Chaos."

Hailwood smiled and said something he's been holding back. "You've always been afraid of a revolution, Old Man. Nature of your position. But, if there's one thing I've learned in the last couple of years, it's *be* the revolution. Beat chaos to the punch."

The Old Man looked at him. Skeptical, to the end. "Things aren't always what they seem. Sometimes a peace treaty doesn't make peace. Sometimes a trade treaty loses money. Never hesitate to cut your losses and move on."

"Don't worry. You can trust me."

"I *do* trust you."

"Have a good flight."

The Old Man reached out his hand. Hailwood hugged him.

"I love you, Terry."

"I love you, too, Old Man. But it's a strange thing."

The launch was uneventful—a big charter jet taking off from a nondescript corporate airport terminal.

Hailwood went with Simmons and the TSA managers to a tower a few minutes away from the loading platform. There, they took an elevator (this one like a conventional office building model) up to mission control. Which was not as dramatic as Hailwood had expected.

It seemed like any mid-sized room full of cubicle workstations. But, in the middle of the room, there was one big screen that about half a dozen techs were standing around watching.

Two TSF SkyDragons met the Crusader/cargo jet tandem and escorted it up. Each of the Dragons filmed the ascent.

The cargo jet flew in a wide, cylindrical pattern to an altitude of about 70,000 feet. At that point, its solid fuel engines ignited and took it in a straight line over the Atlantic to about 120,000 feet.

There, the Crusader ignited its engines and broke free of the cargo plane. It gradually steepened its ascent until it was flying almost straight up from the earth.

There was a blackout period of about 15 minutes between the last bit of the Crusader that the SkyDragons could catch on vid and the first bit that the two spaceplanes waiting in orbit could send back. During this part, the vid switched to inside the Crusader. Hailwood could hear the astronaut asking the Old Man for readings and to make various gauge checks. It sounded like he was making sure the Old Man was staying conscious.

And he was.

When the two spaceplanes waiting first got vid of the Crusader, it seemed to be approaching them from an odd angle, turned slightly away even thought it was moving directly toward them.

It came by the other planes pretty quickly and they followed behind.

"It's going to take them about an hour to get to the launch position," Simmons said. "And then another hour or so to get the quantum field system activated. We're going to get something for dinner. Would you like to join us?"

He thought about it for a moment but: "Thanks for the offer, but no. I think I'll stay here and watch them fly."

"No problem. I remember how amazing it seemed the first few times. Can we bring you back something?"

"Sure."

"What would you like?"

"Just a burger or a sandwich or something. Whatever you're having."

"We were thinking Chinese."

"Sounds fine. Chicken. Whatever's good."

It wasn't just because Hailwood had had the bad impression from Simmons that he declined. He also felt that he owed it to the Old Man to watch closely.

He thought about getting word down to Masterson to come up. But there were security clearance issues—this was, even without the Old Man's participation, a secret mission. And he wasn't sure he wanted to share the Old Man's fate with outsiders, even ones he trusted.

An hour and 40 minutes later, Hailwood was finishing his cashew chicken and watching the real countdown to this launch. The quantum field generator inside the Crusader's bulge was humming—literally. And the Old Man was counting down to what they called the FEP or field encounter point.

The crews aboard the other spaceplanes were doing most of the talking back to mission control. Miles away from the Old Man's ship, they were measuring various obscure radiation and particle metrics from the area around the Crusader. And they had it on surprisingly clear vid.

The big screen was split between the exterior shot of the Crusader holding still in orbit while the Earth turned beneath and the interior shot, with both men sitting in their seats.

The mechanical arm from the Old Man's Crusader was holding a small satellite about five meters above its fuselage. Hailwood asked Simmons if the sat was for communication from the quantum field.

"No. Not exactly. It's a capacitor."

"You mean like an energy cell?"

"Yeah. Pretty much. In a few seconds, they'll let go of it."

"What does it do?"

"Watch. When the ship enters the field, there's a large energy displacement. The capacitor absorbs and stores that energy. Most of it, at least."

"And what do you do with it?"

"Keep it. We have a special storage area in the *Atlas* station where we keep the capacitors from our quantum field tests. We study them pretty closely. We think the capacitors may work like tracking devices on the travelers. The energy dissipates from the capacitors at different rates. Which is strange, because the hardware is identical. We think the rate of dissipation correlates to the return of each particular ship from wherever it 'landed'."

Simmons sounded less condescending than he had before. Maybe he realized he'd gotten off to a bad start.

"I remember something about quantum displacement from my sophomore physics class. It's the reason that some people think one object can be in two places at once."

"Very good. It's similar to that theory. Displacement is a critical element of quantum mechanics. It could be that the energy stored in the capacitors is some kind of echo or reflection of the objects we've sent into the field."

"Any chance the energy could be the objects themselves? That you're just zapping the test objects into the containers?"

"Well, anything's possible. But that's not likely. We know there are connections between actions in quantum space—we're just not sure precisely how they measure against each other. But that's what this mission is for."

At about t-minus 30, the mechanical arm released the capacitor, which bent slightly and tilted its mesh dish toward the plane. The arm slithered like a snake back into the plane's cargo hold.

As the Old Man counted down from 10, the astronaut said the field metrics were solid. When the Old Man said six, a whine started up on the audio. The astronaut said all systems were "go."

When the Old Man said three, the image of the plane in the external view began to warp. It looked like its edges were melting forward, toward a point somewhere ahead.

When the Old Man said one, the astronaut said "Hello, tomorrow" and there was what looked like a very straight bolt of lightning in the same direction the melt had been inching a few seconds before. At the same moment, several bolts traditional jagged lightning flashed into the dish of the capacitor. And the Crusader was gone.

The jagged lightning was gone in a flash. The straight bolt faded more slowly. The interior image faded to black at the slower speed. Something about this sequence seemed to support Simmons' belief that the object did, in fact, move elsewhere in the quantum field and the jagged bolts were displaced energy.

The voices from the other spaceplanes kept barking numbers and bits of jargon out busily for several seconds more.

Finally, a voice from mission control said, "Ladies and Gentlemen, Crusader T79 has entered a quantum field. Best wishes for its safe return."

There was some weary applause and a couple of cynical woofs.

Hailwood asked Simmons to make a copy of the split-screen vid of the quantum field launch and send it to him. Then, he called Masterson—who was still waiting with the tilt at the empty hangar.

Simmons' managers arranged a car to take Hailwood back to his tilt. On his way to the elevator, Simmons slipped a vid disc into his hand.

"Good luck in the coming days, sir. If you need any help, don't hesitate to call me."

"Thanks. I may take you up on that offer."

Back at the tilt, Hailwood asked Masterson to wait a minute so he could make a call. That call was to Bill Franklin. It didn't take very long.

"Bill? This is Terry. The passenger made his flight."

"Terry. I'm glad that you went with him. I'm sure he was, too. Godspeed, as they used to say."

"We need to say something tonight or tomorrow."

"Yes, we do. Any preference for which of the options we discussed?"

"I still think the first one makes the most sense, given the news."

"Very good. I'll call you at the House when everything is ready."

"Okay. Thanks."

Masterson had remained standing outside of the tilt, even though Hailwood hadn't explicitly asked him to do so. He was a smart guy, this pilot.

When they were in the air and on their way back to the House, Hailwood asked Masterson if he'd be interested in more than just flying him around.

"What do you mean, sir?"

"I mean, if the situation presents itself, do you think you could change career tracks and advise me on security matters."

"I'm not a politician, sir."

"I know. That's why I'm asking you."

"So the Old Man's really gone?"

"He's gone."

"That's going to leave a vacuum."

"Not for long."

"Well, I guess a smart guy shouldn't be a glorified chauffeur forever."

"Thanks. Now we just need to hope the guys at the House don't have orders to kill me in my sleep."

"Don't worry about that, sir. The units assigned to guard your House are bright young guys, new on the job. This is how your grandfather always wanted it. They don't have established ties within the department; they're not part of any cliques. So they're not likely to be bent."

"Good."

Hailwood shaved and combed his hair, then picked a dark suit out of his carrier. He wasn't sure what the etiquette for a dead grandfather/clone donor was; but a plain black suit seemed like a safe bet. Safer than Tampa bonds at 27 cents, anyway.

Before he put the jacket on, he dug his shoulder holster out of his main suitcase and strapped it on. He checked the charge on his 10mm plasma pistol and holstered it. Then he put on the jacket, grabbed his screen and walked out to the car.

The security troopers were ready to go when he got there. Evans seemed much sharper. Hailwood wondered what had happened to Menendez, his usual body man. He'd been elsewhere this whole trip.

"We're ready to go, Mr. Hailwood. We're heading to City Hall?"

"No. Close by, though. I'll explain on the way."

"Sure. Okay. I'm going to be in the lead car. Private Weatherwax is going to drive your truck."

"Have you even driven a Badger, Private?"

"Not this model, sir. But my dad had an old standard Badger that we used to go hunting down south of the walls."

"You drove an old Badger in the Everglades?"

"Yes, sir."

"You ever get stuck?"

"Lots of times. But we always got home."

"You can get me downtown quickly?"

"Yes, sir."

"You're my man. Let's go."

He climbed into the back of the truck and plugged his screen in to the docking station. The security cruisers in front and behind hit their lights and started off.

"Weatherwax?"

"Yes sir."

"You set the pace."

He checked the news sites. There was lots of coverage of the war—but nothing else. He checked the financial sites for Tampa bonds and Corporation shares. They were down, but there was no action that suggested anything more than the war.

They pulled up at the Gulf Coast Bank building 23 minutes after they'd left the House.

"Good job, Weatherwax. Tell the others to wait here. He's my screen number. If anyone tries to make you move, call me."

"Got it, sir."

Hailwood noticed that Weatherwax and the other security troops could sense something important was happening. Maybe they knew exactly what; maybe they were just responding to his sharp orders. Civilians didn't usually give orders to security officers. Whatever the reason, they responded to him differently than they had before.

There was a steady flow of people leaving the building. It was almost four on a Friday afternoon. The wage slaves were heading out for their weekends. No one in the lobby even noticed him. He had no problem getting an elevator to the 78th floor. No one else was going up at this hour.

When the elevator opened on the executive offices of City of Tampa Corporation, the reception area was empty. This was a little scary. This room was usually buzzing with people.

He walked through the reception area and toward the Old Man's office. Franklin and two others were sitting around the secretary's desk in front of the Old Man's office.

Franklin stood up as soon as he saw Hailwood enter.

"Terry. You made good time. These are a couple of people who are going to be important to you in the next days and weeks. You grandfather's secretary, James Dowd."

"Sure. James and I know each other. How are you doing, man?"

"Well, not so good. As soon as I saw what happened, I called Mr. Franklin and sent everyone home." James was a highly organized, high-strung middle-aged bachelor. The Old Man had churned through hundreds of assistants in his life—but this one had lasted. Hailwood made a mental note that keeping people like James around would be important. Continuity.

"Thanks. That was the right thing to do. Thanks so much."

He hugged James, who hugged him back a bit confused.

"And this is Charles Etheridge. He's a partner in my firm and my main assistant in handling your grandfather's affairs."

"Charles. I'm sure we're going to be working closely together in next few days."

Franklin said they'd been trying to get in touch with Hailwood's father, with no success. He asked if Hailwood was ready to see the Old Man.

Hailwood was. He and Franklin walked through the double doors.

The body was sitting in the Old Man's desk chair, slumped to the left side. Its right hand was in its lap, holding a 10mm plasma pistol. The same model that Hailwood had strapped to his chest. Which was the same gun that the ménage a trois girl in Manhattan had vamped around with his hotel room.

Hailwood walked to the side of the chair. There was blood all over the back and top of the chair. And there was a think spray of blood over the file cabinet and window behind the chair.

He looked more closely at the body's head. The back—what had been thin white hair—was a dark red, gooey mess. The eyes were droopy, mostly closed and the chin and nose were mottled and puffy. It didn't look particularly like the Old Man.

Didn't look particularly *un*like him, either.

His circumstances had surely changed.

The coroner's report would state that the Old Man had put the pistol under his chin and pulled the trigger. The plasma blast had torn apart the back of his head and cauterized part of the wound a millisecond later. That's why there wasn't even more blood.

Sic Semper Tyrannis

"There's a letter here on this screen, Terry."

The Old Man had left his screen on the conference table across from his desk. The unsent draft of an email was on it.

"Have you read this letter, Bill?"

"No."

"Has your partner or the secretary?"

"No. Not to my knowledge. I can ask—"

"No need. I'm going to read it and then we call Security."

"Okay."

Hailwood picked up the screen and read the email.

TERRY—

THIS NOTE IS FOR YOU. I'VE MADE A LOT OF MISTAKES. NONE WORSE THAN THIS LATEST. I TURNED A BLIND EYE TO CHAMBERS BECAUSE I WAS STUBBORN ABOUT THE MISTAKES I'D MADE WITH CROWLEY. I'M JUST TOO TIRED AND NOW I'M TOO EMBARASSED TO STRAIGHTEN HIM OUT. THAT'S YOUR JOB NOW. MY ETSATE IS IN PLACE AS WE HAVE DISCUSSED. SOME BENEFITS TO YOUR MOTHER AND FATHER AND SOME BENFITS TO CHARITY BUT CONTROLLING INTEREST TO YOU.

I HAVE USED SOME OF THE INVESTING POWER OF OUR CORP SHARES TO SUPPORT THE CITY BONDS. I SHOULDN'T HAVE DONE THAT, STRICTLY SPEAKING, BUT I BELIEVED THAT THE BONDS WOULD BOTTOM AT 35/DOLLAR. THAT ALSO FALLS TO YOU NOW. I'M SURE THAT IF YOU ACT DECISIVELY, YOU CAN BRING THE BONDS UP AND MAINTAIN OUR CONTROL OF THE CORP. IF YOU CAN'T, THE CORP SHARES WILL BE WORTHLESS ANYWAY.

I'VE REACHE DTHE END OF MY LIFE IN AN IMPOSSIBLE SITUATION. BUT ONE THAT I'VE MADE. MY EFFORTS TO MANAGE THE CITY FROM A DISTANCE HAVE CREATED A SIUTATION IN WHICH THE CITY IS IN DNAGER OF BEING ANNEXED BY A WEAKER, SMALLER STATE. THIS NEVER SHOULD HAVE HAPPENED. I THINK THAT YOU MAY BE RIGHT. WE MAY BE PAST THE PLACE WHERE EQUITY OWNERS

CAN MANAGE INDIRECTLY.

I BELIEVE YOU WILL FIND A WAY TO FIX THESE PROBLEMS. I BELIEVE THAT YOU WILL SHAPE THE CITY AND THE CORP IN YOUR OWN IMAGE. DON'T GRIEVE FOR ME. I HAD A CALL FROM DR DELA CRUZ THIS MORNING THAT CONFIRMED MANY THINGS THAT I'D BEEN THINKING FOR THE LAST FEW DAYS. I GO TO ENTERNITY WITH A FEW REGRETS BUT NO MORE THAN MOST PEOPLE WHO LIVED IN MY POSITION IN MY TIME.

YOU ARE MY HOPE THAT MY LIFE SPENT TRADING AT THE MARGINS COUNTED FOR SOMEHTING.

Like the body, the note didn't sound especially like the Old Man; but it didn't sound especially *unlike* him, either. Hailwood checked the "track changes" option. There hadn't been any changes.

The email's recipients were Franklin, Dr. dela Cruz, Hailwood and two numbered email accounts. No managers. The two numbered accounts were probably other lawyers…or maybe a judge or government minister the Old Man trusted. All the recipients were listed on the TO line of the email—so they would all see each other. Smart move—it would confirm his last wishes.

But it hadn't been sent. The thumbprint button to SEND was at the bottom of the screen.

Of course. Thumbprint button.

He checked the clock and date on the screen. They were running 16 hours behind. The email would be time-stamped a little after 10 the previous night.

Hailwood reread the letter. It seemed fine. He was ready to do things—and do them differently. The markets were already predicting defeat for Tampa. There wasn't much to lose. Or anything to gain by working in the shadows.

He rubbed his right thumb against his forefinger to make sure it was clean and placed the thumb on the button. He was nervous. Despite what his father and the Old Man had said, he had no physical proof that he was the Old Man's clone. There was a very quick flash of light and the email was sent.

Hailwood turned the screen off.

Sic Semper Tyrannis

He walked out to Dowd's desk as asked him to call Bert Barrett's office. When he did, Hailwood signaled for him to switch the comms link to speaker.

"This is T.S. Hailwood. I'd like to speak with Mr. Barrett. This is extremely urgent. We'll hold while you make the connection."

Hailwood leaned away from the comms link. But Dowd made a cutting gesture with his hand and pressed a mute button on his desk. "Is there something you want?"

"Do you record these calls?"

"Yes. All calls, incoming and outgoing. We keep them here for 90 days and then archive the files."

"Okay. Let's keep doing that. Just, when you archive them every 90 days, send a copy of that file to my personal screen account?"

"Yes. A copy to your account."

Barrett came on the line. "Hello?"

"Mr. Barrett, this is Terry Hailwood."

"Terry, what can I do for you?"

"My grandfather has committed suicide. Please send some officers and a medical crew over to his office right away."

"Of course. And I'll come over myself."

The various family trust accounts owned 58.3 percent of the outstanding City of Tampa Corporation. Normally, the shares weren't connected in any direct way to the dozens of classes of bonds that the City issued. But the Old Man had borrowed an amount equal to about 11 percent of the family's 58 percent to buy City general obligation bonds at an average price of 52 cents on the dollar. His theory—which made economic sense in most situations—was that supporting the bonds would support the price of the shares. Now, those bonds were trading at 18 cents on the dollar. And the fact that the bonds and the shares were both dropping made the problems worse.

"If I can speak candidly, your grandfather didn't fully appreciate that this is a war," Etheridge said. "His financial strategies were for conventional market conditions."

Hailwood tried to think as broadly as he could. "What we need to do is halt trading in City bonds."

"That would be great. But that's not in our control. Even the City of New York doesn't regulate market trading. The exchanges tried halting trades. And they're still limiting them to a few hours a day. But there's not much they can do. The free net markets run 24/7, regardless."

"We could ask the bond exchange to halt trading."

"Of course we could *ask*. But the exchange has no incentive to agree. It operates in cyberspace. And, again, they've got to deal with the influence of the free net markets, 24/7. The traders who run the exchanges aren't going to have any sympathy for the City. They'll just say that your grandfather shouldn't have been trying to support City bonds with his shares."

Hailwood looked back at his screen, which showed the City shares owned by other groups. All of the holders with more than 3 percent were institutional investors—mutual funds and pension groups. Most based in New York, London or Geneva. The problem wasn't that some other *investor* would step in if the family dropped below 50 percent. It had more to do with people using the instability. Chambers might use the war and the Old Man's death as an excuse to call for a vote that let him grab dictatorial powers.

On the other extreme, Crowley's religious zealot armies might win the war, take over the City and the City Corporation would become worthless.

And then there was chaos theory. Interlocking variables. *Both* scenarios could happen.

He clicked through to the roster of senior managers. In three years as CEO, Chambers and surrounded himself with loyal and relatively weak lieutenants. Bertram Barrett wasn't one of those. He'd been CSO back during Michael Crowley's term. And the head lawyer Sandoval was an old-timer.

It didn't make complete sense that Barrett was still around. After the terrorists's early successes—after the Tampa Security building *had been bombed*—the Security Chief should have been fired. Why hadn't he been?

Hailwood sighed and told Etheridge he wanted to take a short break. Franklin was outside, talking to the Security officers and preparing public remarks about the Old Man's death. Hailwood wanted to see for himself what was going on.

He asked Etheridge to prepare a call list of contacts at the various brokerages that they could contact in the morning to negotiate extensions on any margin calls.

When he walked down the hall to the Old Man's office, most of the business was over. The investigators had examined the office, bagged the pistol and the body and sent the body to the coroner's office for an autopsy. Barrett had stopped by—and so had Steve Masterson. Barrett examined things for a few minutes and then, at Bill Franklin's request, left Masterson in charge of the scene.

That made things a little easier. And it suggested against any *sub rosa* ties between Barrett and Chambers. If Barrett had been a Chambers stooge, he'd have fought harder to stick around. Instead, he knew that Masterson was close to the Hailwood family and was willing to respect that.

In the Old Man's office, Masterson and Franklin told Hailwood that they could delay the autopsy for 24 hours while the board of directors discussed how the City should proceed. "We'll do what we can to keep this quiet but, I've got to tell you, the financial media can be as ruthless as the celebrity media when it comes to breaking news. So, don't count on it staying secret for long."

Hailwood wasn't sure whether this was Masterson's real advice or something he was saying expecting to be overheard. And the tension between those two possibilities was instructive for City politics in general.

Franklin said he'd contacted all of the board members. He'd called an emergency meeting in three hours—at 10 o'clock in his office, a few blocks away. Most could make it—a few were going to have to video in.

Chambers would be there because he was on the board. Barrett was going to be there, too; and the lawyer Sandoval would be the C-level executive who'd be vidlinked in from a secure location—standard security procedure.

Hailwood had an idea of how he could announce the new regime dramatically at that meeting.

"Are you feeling all right, Terry? Do you want to go back to the House?"

"Thanks. But there's no time for that, Bill. We need to prep things so that you and Etheridge can hit the ground running tomorrow morning. You're going to need to talk to our brokers—and maybe the directors of the main bond exchanges. I'll just freshen up here and head directly over to your office."

When Franklin left, Hailwood wasn't sure what to do.

He read over the bio's of the directors and the senior managers. The Old Man had stocked the board with allies. They wouldn't be the problem. It was the managers.

And outside forces.

It was hard to form an opinion about Chambers; he'd followed the higher-profile Crowley and, as usually happened in these situations, the successor was—by temperament—a plainer package. But that didn't mean he was plain.

Most of the Brahmins liked Chambers better than Crowley. They hadn't trusted Crowley; he'd been too much a celebrity and not enough a manager. Even before turning himself into a wasteland messiah, his ego had been an issue.

But Hailwood had listened to the Old Man, who'd come to regret chasing Crowley out. This was partly because of the Old Man's inherent bias toward winners. But there were other factors. According to the Old Man, Chambers was a schemer—which had been a surprise. He'd come out of the finance department, so the Old Man had expected a strong mathematical mind and a calm demeanor.

But he should have realized that anyone who was willing to betray his CEO would not make for a loyal performer.

Chambers' own CFO was a recent promotion. Chamber's man. But the CFO hired by a former CFO wasn't likely to be troublemaker.

No. Chambers was the weak point. And that's where Hailwood had to exert pressure.

He felt like taking a walk but he didn't know where to go. He felt like talking but he had no one to trust. He tried calling Kate.

"Yeah?"

"Kate. It's Terry."

"Terry. My God. This is a surprise. Where are you?"

"I'm in Tampa. I came home to help the Old Man

"Are you okay? I mean, from the news here it looks like a full-on war?"

"Eh, you know how that goes. The terrorists made a few marks. But most of the City is operating like normal. Or maybe like normal when there's a hurricane or something." She'd been down during a Category 3 storm. "It's about like that."

"Wow. Well, is everyone okay? Your mom and your grandfather?"

"My mother's fine. She took off on a trip to Paris before the missiles started flying. My grandfather's not doing so well."

"You mean health-wise?"

What should he say? Why had he called her? To boast about his troubles? To boast about taking over the family fortune? For cheap congratulations? This call was a bad idea.

"He's doing pretty badly."

"Oh. Well, I'm sorry to hear that. I always enjoyed his stories about business and politics."

"I'm not sure why I called. I guess I feel like I'm on the edge of some big changes—the terrorists and my job and my family. I guess I just wanted to hear a familiar voice. What're you up to?"

"You're calling from a war zone and you want to know what *I'm* up to?"

"Yeah."

"Is this some kind of perverted Brahmin booty call?"

He laughed at her effort at humor. This was the second time in a few hours that someone had used the term *Brahmin* about him. That wasn't something he'd heard in seven years at the College. "No. I don't think so. No time for that, anyway. There's just a lot ahead of me in the next couple of days and I felt like…. I thought of you."

He was thinking as he talked. And he was talking to himself as much as to Kate.

"Well, you can always call me, Hailwood. I'm not doing much. My dad got me a job at one of the music channels. It's a good job—advertising. I mean, hundreds of people would kill for it."

"But you're not that interested."

"No. I'm not. And I'm seeing somebody. But I'm not really interested in that, either."

"What about school?"

"Well, I'm thinking about it."

'Oh, come on, Kate. You're so close to finishing your degree. If you flake out, you'll end up just one more of those nearly-smart hipster zombies stumbling around New York."

"You know, I ought to conference my dad in on this call. It would be more efficient."

She sounded a generation younger than Maria Elena. Hailwood couldn't decide whether this counted in her favor or against.

"I'm glad you called, Terry. It's good to hear your voice. There's a lot I miss about being with you. Maybe we should get together and see if there's some way we could reboot."

Reboot? That didn't sound like her.

"Give me a couple of weeks to see where my life ends up, Kate. I'm going to have to make some hard choices. And I don't really know what I'm doing. Might end up calling your dad for one of those ad sales jobs."

There was a bit of a pause on Kate's end.

"Terry, you're the perfect person for taking over your grandfather's business. I think everyone who knows you thinks this, even if they don't say it. Your destiny is down there, in the City. Not teaching Latin in the wilds. Everything you've done in your life so far has been preparing you for this."

Was she right? Even if she wasn't, her words energized him.

Etheridge buzzed the intercom. J.C. Sandoval was on time for the meeting, half an hour before the bigger board meeting was scheduled. Hailwood put his suit jacket on—mostly, to hide his gun.

Franklin had offered to sit on this meeting, but Hailwood said no. He thought that two lawyers in one room would be one too many.

Sandoval had the reputation for being a larger-than-life figure. But he didn't seem so when he walked into the side room of the Old Man's office. He wore a double-breasted suit—but many middle-aged Cubans did that. He wore his hair a little long—but many people trying to be fashionable did that.

"Mr. Hailwood. This is an unexpected pleasure."

His manner was colorful, but subdued.

"Thank you, Mr. Sandoval. In about half an hour, we're calling an emergency meeting of the Corporation board."

"Yes. Bill Franklin told me about this meeting."

"And, following standard security practice, one senior manager will stay away from the meeting, comm linked in. Franklin suggested that person be you."

"Yes. I've been the security precaution at quite a few board meetings over the past several years."

Sic Semper Tyrannis

"Franklin told me that."

Sandoval nodded. "I suppose it's no secret. Your CEO and I are not on the best terms."

Hailwood let that stand for a second. It was an interesting opening—no doubt, part of the reason Franklin had suggested keeping Sandoval away. But he wanted to stay focused on the business at hand. "At this meeting, I'm going to announce some news. My grandfather has committed suicide. As of a few hours ago, I own the controlling interest in the City of Tampa Corporation and will replace my grandfather in the Office of the Chairman."

Sandoval thought for a second and then smiled in a worldly way. "My condolences. It's always sad to lose such a forceful person. And at such a critical time. This puts a lot on your shoulders. How can I help?"

"Well, the main thing you can do is just be available. I intend to change some of the things that we do here—and I hope to change the course of our war against these religious zealots and their keepers in the Jacksonville League."

"*Keepers*. Yes, a good way to put it."

"Anyway, it will be useful to have some continuity in our management. Bill Franklin has suggested to me that you're someone who should be part of that continuity. And, from the little I know, I tend to agree."

"Well, I thank you for that confidence. It's been a long time since I have been part of anyone's continuity here. Since the salary episode, I have been the proverbial odd man out."

"Salary episode?"

Now Sandoval looked a little confused. He couldn't believe that Hailwood didn't know about this. Hailwood honestly didn't.

"Several years ago, details of my salary and compensation were leaked to one of the media services. Became a bit of a scandal. It was more than most citizens thought a City Attorney should make."

"Mr. Sandoval, you'll find I put very little value on the tabloid scandals created to generate clicks at news pages."

"That's very good to hear. But I caution you that City politics can be full of these treacheries. Perhaps more than you're used to."

"Try teaching college for a while, Mr. Sandoval. Campus politics are more treacherous than you'd think."

"Point taken."

Hailwood stopped again for a moment. Then, "They call you the Shark."

"Yes. A common nickname for lawyers who are in the arena and considered...flamboyant. But it was a nickname that I was given years ago. This Shark has been lying low lately."

"Sometimes that's the right move."

"Yes, sometimes. Do you mind if I offer you some advice?"

"That's why I invited you up here."

"While I am no friend or ally of Matthew Chambers, let me say this about him. He is a ruthless man and a competent manager. His great strength is that he *thinks* like a manager. And he does that very well. He has thought deeply and carefully about a thousand issues that you or I have not. Immigration policy...but also immigration mechanics. Taxation, down to the small details of income tax brackets. Personnel hiring policies of minor City departments. He is not a visionary; he thrives on the small points of City politics. Systems and procedures. He counts on a man like you to trip over those small points."

"I've known people like that."

"Managers care about process more than outcomes."

"And this City is facing the outcome of losing a war."

"Perhaps he's calculated the odds and his plan is to be the regional administrator for Karamanlis."

"If the terrorists win this war, I expect Michael Crowley to exact some Old Testament vengeance on Chambers. A public beheading or something like this. I understand what you mean about Chambers being a mechanic. And maybe a ruthless one. For that insight, I thank you. I think his problem is that he doesn't have *any* strategy in this war. For himself or for the City. Tampa doesn't need an expert on immigration law or tax policy. It needs someone who will break these terrorists."

"Of course, of course."

"So, I'm asking you to lay low a little longer. But, in a short time, you may be able to swim back up to the surface."

"Thank you for the consideration. Please give my best to Bill Franklin. And good luck in the board meeting."

"Thank *you*. I have a couple of last issues to resolve in my own mind. And a few minutes left to do so."

Sandoval stopped for a second. "You're a thoughtful man, Mr. Hailwood. And determined, I can see. I think this City is worth fighting to save. We were stable and prosperous for longer than any other until this war started. Your grandfather had a lot to do with that stability and growth. I hope that you find a way to recover that. It would be the best way to honor his memory."

Hailwood was surprised. Positively. "I agree with you, Mr. Sandoval. I've been thinking the same thing all day."

The Security guys were waiting downstairs, just as he'd left them. Cpl. Evans had called earlier and asked permission to rotate the troopers through, so each could take a break. Hailwood said that was fine and asked whether any of their superiors had given them any other orders?

"No sir, we reported in when we got here and the shift commander gave us special assignment status. That means we do a location check once an hour; but they probably won't call us until our shift ends at midnight. And Col. Masterson stopped by and talked to us when he left. Our detail is to stay with you. He said he'd arrange our relief but we're to stay on duty until he does."

"Okay. That sounds fine. We should be done with our business by midnight."

They drove the whole convoy the six blocks to Franklin's office building.

Evans followed Hailwood in. In the elevator, he asked "Do you want me to stay in the office area, Mr. Hailwood?"

"No need. I'm sure that Mr. Barrett is going to have people there to keep things safe. You can wait with your unit. I'll call if I need you."

"Yes, sir."

Although it was almost 10 o'clock, Franklin's office was alive. The lights were bright and secretaries and lawyers were all over the place. As Hailwood expected, Barrett had a few uniformed security troops standing outside Franklin's private conference room, which—combined with his office—took up almost half the floor.

Evans followed Hailwood through the offices and waited until Franklin greeted them and Hailwood gave him a nod. Then he saluted Barrett and the other officers and headed out. He didn't waste much time.

It was still a few minutes before 10, but everyone who was going to be at the meeting was in the conference room. Three screens were set up on the conference table, as if the people on them were sitting in chairs. One was Sandoval, one was the Archbishop, one was an old friend of the Old Man's.

The conference table could seat something like 20 people. At full strength, the Board of the City of Tampa Corporation had 11 directors. Right now, that was Hailwood and 10 others. They were seated around one end. The seat at the head of the table was empty. Franklin gestured toward it to Hailwood.

He thought about declining. But, if he didn't take the Old Man's seat, he was going to be half a table away from Chambers. He needed to be closer than that.

The meeting came to order quickly, still a few minutes before 10 o'clock. The doors to the conference room closed and the vid feeds to the screens chimed on.

Franklin did the talking. "Ladies and Gentlemen, I have some terrible news. A few hours ago, Grant Hailwood died in his offices just a few blocks from here. It appears that his death was a suicide. Of course, we will wait for the Security Department's final analysis of all the evidence to make any sort of formal announcement. But I examined the body and the scene myself and it certainly looked like suicide. A single plasma pistol shot under the chin."

Hailwood looked around the room. Seven directors in person, three by video. Barrett was the only one a little removed; he was sitting in chair against the far wall, near the main doors. The other security officers stayed outside. One of Franklin's assistants, watching the formal minutes and taking notes. And him. Nine people in the room. Chambers was seated to his right, about three feet away.

"As you all know, the Chairman's will and estate have been structured for a very clear transfer of interests to his grandson—T.S. Hailwood, who has joined us here tonight. In my capacity as both a director of this Corporation and the Hailwoods' personal attorney, I can assure each of you that controlling ownership of the Corporation passed—at the moment of the Chairman's death—to the younger Mr. Hailwood. Some of the shares he owns directly, others he controls through family trusts of which he is trustee or controlling entity.

"I've called this meeting to confirm all of these facts, so that the board has a clear understanding of what's transpired and so there won't be any more confusion than we've already had in the last few weeks."

"As most of you know, the younger Mr. Hailwood has not been active in day-to-day management of the Corporation. In fact, he hasn't given any thought to our daily business here until today—"

Chambers interrupted Franklin comfortably. "Bill, I've got a number of questions about all of this—starting with how we can be sure that Chairman Hailwood actually did kill himself. Everyone in this room knew him. And I think that we can all agree he was an unlikely suicide."

Chambers spoke with a strange, exaggerated accent that sounded like something out of a bad Southern Gothic vid. Hailwood was no dialogue coach, but he was born and raised in Tampa. Chambers' accent wasn't local. It was some sort of mix of Savannah bluster and Texas draw.

"And then, even if we accept the premise that his death was suicide, there's the matter of Chairman Hailwood's recent investments. Over the last several days, I've heard from several financial brokers both here and in New York who all claim that the Chairman had engaged in an extremely risky strategy of using his equity position in the Corporation to support the market price of the City's general obligation bonds. Now, I appreciate the spirit behind such an investment strategy—but it's clear that recent market movements would hasten the downward spiral of such a plan. And the brokers who've called me say that the Chairman's strategy has imperiled his family's absolute control over the Corporation's voting shares. I understand that several of the Hailwood family trusts have received margin calls and other security demands that will lower their equity position to something like 46 percent of the Corporation's outstanding shares"

Franklin stepped back in. "That's simply not true, Mr. Chambers. As I reported a few moments ago, the Hailwood family trusts give the younger Mr. Hailwood an absolute controlling interest in the corporation. While it's true that the family has used some of its shares as security for transactions involving general obligation bonds, it still owns between 51.8 percent and 54.3 percent of the outstanding shares."

Chambers didn't seem phased by Franklin's correction. "Well, I may have some bad information. Or I may have access to better information than you do, Mr. Franklin. Whatever the case, I think it makes sense for the board to avoid any formal action until the details surrounding the Chairman's death can be firmly established."

Hailwood had been practicing his interruption like a baseball player getting ready to bat might practice his swing against a pitcher's best work. He saw his chance.

"Mr. Chambers, you're fired."

"What?"

"I think you heard me. I said you're fired."

'You can't fire me, son."

"I can. And you are. We're in middle of a regional war with religious terrorists and you're advocating *in*action? Please clear your personal effects from your office and hand over your keys, screen and other Corporation property immediately."

"Is this some idea of a joke?"

"No."

"You can't fire me without the unanimous support of the Board of Directors."

"Not true. That's only for so-called 'for cause' terminations. This isn't one of those. Although it could be—your management of the war against the terrorists has been horribly mishandled. But that's not the reason. You're just fired. No cause."

"I have a contract."

"The Corporation will pay you liquidated damages equal to the amount remaining on your contract."

"Son, you have a lot to learn about how things work—"

"Don't threaten me, Mr. Chambers."

"I didn't threaten you. I don't *make* threats."

Hailwood took a breath and calmed his beating heart. He knew the other board members were watching his response. They were curious about what he would say and how he'd say it.

So, he didn't say anything.

His hand drew the plasma pistol in a smooth move he'd practiced a thousand times. He cleared his mind by concentrating on the hardware, so the moment didn't overwhelm him. Thinking about the lightning-fast firing mechanism inside the pistol and the plasma "bullets" that were really were an incendiary gel made everything else move in slow motion. He drew his mental mark on Chambers' cheek just under the right eye and followed three shots to that point.

Chambers was turning his head to say something to Bill Franklin when Hailwood fired.

The first two blasts hit the soft tissue around the left side of Chambers' mouth. Those shots were barely noticeable. Even from three feet. The third blast sliced through several of the arteries in Chambers' neck and then angled down to hit the wall near the floor. A mist of blood droplets fell over a wedge between his neck and the wall.

Chambers twisted in his seat but didn't gather enough momentum to fall out of it. He ended up leaning on his right side against the right armrest of his chair.

Hailwood knew better than to panic. Chambers was probably still alive. Hailwood stood up from his chair, walked around Chambers' and lowered his pistol to a few inches from Chambers' forehead. It was hard to see whether Chambers was breathing or not. He didn't seem to be. But there was no room for mistakes here. He shot Chambers once more. From so close, the plasma blast burned a two-inch cross into his forehead.

His body rolled back in the chair and his face stared up at the ceiling.

Hailwood looked around the table quickly. No one was making eye contact. He reholstered his gun and rubbed the back of his neck. He closed his eyes for a second and the flow of time returned to normal.

The good thing about plasma weapons was they were quiet, compared to projectiles. His ears weren't ringing like they had been when he killed the squatters.

No one spoke.

"We're going to do things differently. I'm going to step in as temporary CEO to replace him. We have to handle this war with a clear vision."

"What's that?" asked Franklin.

"We want stability and prosperity. Everything else flows from those."

"And how do we measure those things?"

"We follow the markets. We measure stability in terms of stock and debt prices. We measure prosperity in terms of the strength of our currency against that of other cities."

That seemed to satisfy the table. They wanted to know what his specific plans were for defeating the terrorists.

"I'm not sure. But here's what I know. Religious terrorists under the command of a former CEO of this City—in some kind of alliance with our main regional rival—have fired a tactical nuclear missile into a building just a few blocks from here. I know they've taken over a tiny sliver of our land and call it 'Occupied Tampa.' We need to clear out these terrorists—even if that means we nuke them back."

"What do you want from us?"

He pressed a button on the Old Man's screen. "I just emailed all of you a proposal for special executive privileges that I need immediately. These privileges come with a 30-day time limit. I think I can resolve the terrorist problem in 30 days."

And, if he couldn't, one of the special privileges was that he could extend the special privileges.

The Board voted unanimously in support of the proposal.

Hailwood's first action under his special executive privileges was to split the Department of Security into two parts—with Masterson named Director of External Security and Barrett retaining admin responsibility for Internal Security.

Next, he called Simmons and emailed an order that the Tampa Space Administration focus as many satellites as possible on the corridors between the north gates and the closest of the terrorists' permanent camps—which was between Mobile and New Orleans.

Within 90 minutes, he'd ordered the bombing of "occupied Tampa" with tactical nukes.

Thirty-one

Crowley didn't want to watch it. A combination of anger over Jean Jacques's death and contempt for the political ambitions of a Brahmin prince made him not want to see anything the young Mr. Hailwood had to say.

But Jana insisted he watch. "Michael, you tell your students that they need to understand the enemy. This is a prime opportunity to understand the biggest enemy we have right now."

He still resisted. "Jana, I know how these people operate. There's nothing for us to learn from this man. With his prepared speeches and phony Q&A sessions."

"He's more than that, Michael. He's taken strong actions. And the markets are supporting him. I don't think this is another boardroom chess game. He's something different."

After a few minutes, Crowley relented. He couldn't resist his wife's earnest arguments.

He clicked through a few buttons on his screen and they both watched Terry Hailwood hold his first press conference as the Chairman and CEO of the City of Tampa.

Hailwood had the casual attitude of a Brahmin. He wore a business suit. But he put his hands in the jacket pockets in a manner that a professional manager never would. He avoided all technical language. He looked straight at the camera; and he was sarcastic when he answered some of the questions. This combination ran against everything Crowley had ever been taught about media performance; but the media people responded to Hailwood well—that was evident from the vid.

This performance summed up everything that Crowley never understood about Brahmins. They seemed to have a secret signal that appealed to people. It was simply beyond his understanding how anyone could see young Hailwood as anything more than a party boy trying to resolve some family drama. He seemed completely…undeserving…of his position.

Jana saw more. "He's good, Michael. He seems serious—but not afraid. I think he's going to rally his people and the markets."

"When I look at him, Jana, I see the man who killed Jean Jacques Guibert."

"I'm angry about that, too, Michael. But Johnny shouldn't have been staying in the occupied section. That was a huge risk."

"We didn't think it was going to turn out as it did."

"You mean you didn't think that Tampa was going to return a tactical nuke."

"Right."

"Well, that was a mistake."

"Yes. You're right. But what can we do now? Turn tail and run?"

"For now. Yes. Move your students away. I believe him when he says he's going to keep attacking them until they're all dead. Not until they retreat—until they're all dead. And I think we need to start thinking about protecting our Camps."

"That's defensive thinking, Jana. I never meant for the Camps to be permanent facilities. The Camps are supposed to be wherever the students are."

"Well, do you believe he's going to reprogram satellites to find our companies?"

"Yes. That makes sense." He realized, as he said this, that she was moving him toward another point.

"Then we need to think about protecting your students from that."

The first idea that came to Crowley's mind was to move the students to camps right around the walls of allied or neutral Cities. The neutrals, especially. They wouldn't like Tampa sats spying on their walls—that would drive them closer toward the Jacksonville league.

Crowley saved the file of the media conference and, after Jana had gone to bed, he watched it carefully—as they'd done in his media performance classes in school. He believed, as he'd been taught, that a good media performance wasn't magic. It could be explained and understood in specific mechanical elements.

Sic Semper Tyrannis

Hailwood didn't look up for down when he spoke. He looked directly at his audience of media reporters and into the camera. And he didn't close his eyes when he spoke or thought. These were the basic elements of a good performance. But there was something more to the good impression he made.

Finally, after studying the 20-minute vid for more than an hour, he found an image that explained it all for him. Just before answering a question about chasing students to their home Camps, he smiled for an instant before giving his threatening answer. Crowley slowed the vid down so that he could lock onto the smile and then study young Hailwood's whole face. Then he copied the still image.

The smile was slight and lopsided—heavy to the left side of Hailwood's mouth. But it was there.

It was the oldest trick in the performance book. And one that most managers struggled with. Smile when you talk. Hailwood looked like he enjoyed what he was doing.

Crowley didn't usually watch news programs from the Cities. But he did this night, starting with a couple of Brownsville channels and then switching to channels he had from the nets in Houston and Mobile.

The news programs all had experts trying to explain what had happened. They all said that not much was known about young Hailwood. He hadn't apprenticed in any work in Tampa; he'd gone to a Brahmin college in the New England wasteland and became a teacher there. The markets were rewarding Tampa for doing something about the war with the Jacksonville League.

Crowley liked that. They weren't calling his students "terrorists" anymore. They were now part of the Jacksonville League.

The Houston media didn't say anything about young Hailwood actually shooting Chambers himself. The Brownsville and Mobile channels mentioned "some reports" that this new Chairman had summarily executed his former CEO. And one of the Mobile channels noted that the long-term effect might be an exodus of top-level managers from the Tampa.

This was a nice try...but the markets weren't worried about an exodus of managers. Just three days ago, the media was predicting that Tampa would cease to be an independent City. But the tone had changed. The markets were coming back into Tampa instruments. They welcomed long-term problems like manager flight—because those kinds of problems assumed a long term.

A small part of Crowley wanted to concentrate his forces and invade Tampa. But a larger part of him realized the time for doing that had passed. His strategic goal was to establish a regional government and convert his Company into a proper standing army. His own long-term goal was to replace Karamanlis as the head of the Jacksonville League—not to replace an eccentric Brahmin as the head of an isolated City.

Even with the prince in charge, Tampa had nowhere to go.

The next morning, Crowley had a vid conference with Karamanlis. He took charge from the start. "Our new plan with regard to Tampa is containment. I've set up my students in camps anywhere from one to three miles north of Tampa's northern walls. If they do redirect their sats, they won't find anything. And we won't give them the chance to rebuild any sections of the wall we've already taken. Our troops will prevent any significant commerce moving by land. Meanwhile, our naval forces will continue their effective blockade around the mouth of Tampa Bay."

While Crowley spoke, he posted supporting maps and graphics under his vid image.

Karamanlis looked at the maps but didn't say anything. So, Crowley kept going.

"We'll soon control almost all of the Gulf of Mexico region and southern Atlantic Coast. With four major exceptions—Houston, New Orleans, Tampa and Atlanta."

"Michael, those are the four largest Cities in the region."

"Not for very much longer. I'm going to contain all four Cities and use our assets to shrink them like cancer tumors. We'll concentrate at first on Tampa and New Orleans...and maybe the other two will consider joining us."

"This is ambitious talk. The markets are saying that your attack on Tampa has been repulsed but a 27-year-old Brahmin who made two or three quick decisions."

"Nico, before our attack, City of Tampa general obligation bonds were trading at 98 cents per dollar of face value. Right now, they're trading at...52 cents. The markets aren't so impressed with Tampa's prospects."

Sic Semper Tyrannis

Karamanlis looked at the graphics that Crowley was generating and sending while he spoke. This was probably the most valuable skill he'd developed all his years of schooling.

"Siege warfare isn't the same as blitzkrieg warfare, Michael. Are your troops trained to hunker down?"

"Not specifically. But they are trained to be flexible and adaptive. We'll teach them how to build a dead zone around a City. In the meantime, you and I need to consolidate our league."

"Well, I can agree with you on that."

"And I'm going to need to talk to Charleston, Virginia Beach and Mobile about providing ships that can help with the blockades."

Karamanlis clicked on six more images. But he didn't talk.

"Nico. You're not saying much."

The older man took a moment to gather his thoughts. "I understand the logic in not wasting our resources on defeating well-secured Cities. But it's also true that many of the Cities agreed to join the League have done so because they were afraid of your organization's strength. I think that your plan to contain the hold-out Cities while we consolidate is going to sound like a retreat."

"I don't care much about what it sounds like, Nico. It's what I'm going to do."

"But—as you just said—you're going to need help from the Cities with strong navies. And you may need other help. And I've always found it's best to seek help from a position of strength."

"Of course. An essential management lesson. Well, what can I do to re-establish a position of strength?"

"Something that makes it obvious you're not backing away from Tampa. Or New Orleans."

"Missiles?"

"Maybe. If they hit the right targets."

"Okay. I'll do something obvious. Our next summit is in…five days. I'll make sure this something obvious happens in four."

"That would be good."

They talked for another 10 minutes. And then Crowley thought for an hour about whether Karamanlis was pushing him into some sort of trap.

This was the skill that he'd never recovered—being able to read other people's motives immediately throughout a conversation or negotiation. To recognize a change in opinion or sentiments as it was happening. That was real mastery. And it was a skill he wished he'd been able to keep.

He didn't like Karamanlis. He thought about taking a cue from young Hailwood and just shooting Karamanlis in the board room.

But it would never work. He wasn't a Brahmin and this emerging confederation wouldn't survive such an arrogant act.

Crowley needed Karamanlis to help establish the confederation. Once that was done, he could turn his efforts to getting rid of the old dictator.

Crowley had decided that the best time for the missiles to strike was at night. He didn't want lots of collateral damage and "innocent victims" like they'd had with the one tactical nuke that got through the Tampa defenses early on.

This time, they were launching TAG's state-of-the-art Wraith drones for New Orleans and Tampa at the same time. In fact, calling these drones state-of-the-art was exaggerating. This was really something more like a beta test. It would be the first time these stealthy unmanned planes had been used in combat. If they worked, they would be a major victory for the Jacksonville League—and an even bigger victory for TAG. The old gunsmith himself had suggested them for the job.

They'd driven the only two working versions of the Wraiths to Camp A within 24 hours of Crowley's vid conference with Brian and the old gunsmith. The things were smaller than he'd expected—each fit on a single flatbed truck. And they only required three technicians on site. Two weapons specialists for the missiles and a comms expert to make sure the tracking and guidance links stayed in place. The pilots were remote; they worked for TAG and were in undisclosed locations. Presumably, nowhere near Brownsville.

The drones could have launched from TAG's own research airfield—but Brian and the managers there didn't want any part of the project traceable back to their City. Reasonable enough. Brownsville was considering joining the Jacksonville League but didn't want any leadership position in any terrorism or mayhem.

One drone was heading to Tampa, one to New Orleans. Each was assigned two targets. In Tampa, they'd pegged the main airport and the TSA launch stadium at Cape Canaveral. In New Orleans, the main airport and the Gulfport casino strip.

In order to coordinate the strikes, the drone for Tampa had to take off an hour earlier than the drone for New Orleans. Crowley and about a hundred students turned out to watch. He didn't know any of the kids standing with him—the people he knew were all in the field, near Tampa or New Orleans. The last light of the late afternoon was lingering when they gathered at the Camp A airstrip. He made small talk with the kids; as usual, they were eager to meet him and ask questions about whether the League would be a godly venture. He gave them his standard reply: "No venture among men can be godly. The only thing that can be godly is an individual's heart. If enough hearts are godly, then we stand a chance."

They seemed content with that.

The first drone made a lot of noise. Its propulsion system was some proprietary technology. But it sounded like an old-fashioned jet engine.

The take-off was unusual, though. After revving the engines up to a roar, the drone got quiet all of the sudden. It launched like tiltrotor—vertically first and then jolting forward.

The students cheered as the drone darted east.

One of them yelled: "Death to tyrants!"

The others whooped their support.

Crowley watched silently. Jana and the kids had stayed home at the Morrell farm. He wished that he could have, too; but this was going to be something he'd have to get used to. It was good, really. He wanted his work in the Company to feel more like a job and less like a life's mission.

But that meant feeling alone, which he didn't like.

When the second drone launched, it was dark—so most of the students stayed inside. And Crowley was watching the screens intently.

Brian was watching, too, from his office at the farm. So were a couple of the old gunsmith's bright young managers.

When the drones approached the Cities, they dropped low to the ground. Their paths were set by detailed maps plus active 3D radar. The pilots used these tools to keep the drone as tight as 50 feet above the surface. Over the water, this was easy; over land it would be more difficult.

Most anti-missile systems could read to the ground—but they scanned poorly so low. The Wraith's radar signature was the size of a small bird. Put all of this together and there was no system set up to intercept these drones.

Or so the people from TAG had said....

Crowley knew Tampa's geography better than New Orleans', so he focused on that screen. The drone approached the lights of St. Petersburg Beach and the Sunshine Skyway but bolted up before it got too close.

Now something was showing up on the Tampa defense system. But, again, it was too small to draw big attention. The screen went dark and then refocused on the web of lights that was the heavy development around the edge of Tampa Bay. The drone found the airport's beacon signal and locked on that to guide the missiles. It dropped two 10 kilogram tactical nukes on the airport. The screen went white when the warheads exploded.

Then it went dark again, as the drone dropped back down to low altitude. It would be another 15 or 20 minutes to the TSA launching facility.

The New Orleans run was happening in the opposite sequence. The drone had flown out over the water and came in to the Gulfport casino area first. This looked a lot like the Tampa airport strike—except the lights along the coast were concentrated more intensely in a smaller space. The missiles didn't have an airport beacon to lock onto in Gulfport, so the guidance experts used the lights from the casinos as the guides. Again, the first two warheads turned the image of their target into a white blur.

The casino strike was going to create more civilian casualties than any other in the twin attacks. But it was a Wednesday evening, the middle of the week. At least they weren't attacking casinos on a weekend.

The runs between the first and second strikes were going to be the hardest part. They weren't flying low over the Gulf of Mexico any more. Now they were flying low against buildings and houses and comms towers. There were more things to hit. Plus, they'd just nuked major targets. The Security Forces of each City would scramble some kind of response.

Some of the students were scanning the webs for any mention of the first blasts. When the time was right, these same kids would start spreading the word that the Jacksonville League had, in fact, been behind the attacks.

Within five minutes of the first Tampa blasts, locals were logging on and talking about loud explosions and fires visible in neighborhoods near the Airport. *Near.* Near miss.

News of the Gulfport strike took a little longer to appear.

To Crowley, the second targets were more important than the first. He needed these attacks to seem precise and well-executed. Not lucky strikes. That was why he'd settled on two Cities and two targets. Too much detail to be a fluke.

The remote "pilots" had run simulations of these missions dozens of times. They even used real-time weather and commercial activity, so they'd have some idea of the effect of rain or traffic.

The Tampa drone approached Cape Canaveral from the southwest. It bolted up to attack altitude and scanned for anti-missile of anti-aircraft activity. There was none. It prepared to drop its last two nukes from about 15,000 feet. Then it would climb to 60,000 feet for its flight home to Camp A.

They'd specifically chosen the launching stadium facility at the Cape. Of course, Tampa could work around this and be back to launching sats and planes in a short time. Still, the message would be made to Tampa's citizens and managers—and the markets.

But something went wrong. The drone went white too soon, before it could drop its bombs.

"Not good, Rabbi. I think they terminated Wraith 1."

"Any chance that's just the shockwave?"

"If it is, the Wraith fired without orders. And our feedback went dead. I think they killed it."

The New Orleans drone crossed a checkerboard of light and dark patches as it approached the main New Orleans public airport. It couldn't lock on a beacon signal there, so they used GPS nav systems to drop the bombs at the right moment and place. Then, they jumped to a high altitude and returned the drone that way.

The missions were over. It would take a few hours to confirm how successful they'd been. But Crowley had a bad feeling.

He agreed to give an interview to Jacksonville's not-very-reputable news channel. This would be a big coup. For Jacksonville. Even though the channel was predisposed to his side of the story, the vid of him talking would be picked up by news channels and free nets all over the world.

"Our message to Tampa and New Orleans is that they should be part of the League. They are in our geographic and cultural spheres of influence. But, against all logic, their managements resist this simple conclusion. As long as they resist, we will from time to time remind them that we can cripple their infrastructures if we choose."

The original piece also included a long clip from Karamanlis, talking about the League's goal of making the entire region one unified admin district. But he came across on video as scripted and stilted; so, it wasn't surprising that most of the news channels from other cities ignored him. But the New York financial channel included a snippet of Karamanlis saying, "Mr. Crowley speaks for the League in these matters." It was a short snippet, most likely taken out of context—and meant to contradict the League's standard line that each member entity was responsible for its own actions.

This was working perfectly for Crowley. Karamanlis had been the big man in a small market for so long that he made mistakes more polished managers wouldn't.

At the next summit, the other League CEOs would be angry about that snippet. And the old dictator had no experience working with committees. He'd screw it up.

The most satisfying part of all this was that Crowley hadn't had to draw on favors or pay media experts for the favorable coverage. The money-center markets—and their media outlets—*wanted* the League to take responsibility as a group for the Company's actions. The markets didn't like any violent activity but, forced to choose, they preferred war to terrorism.

Some Wall Street traders were predicting a war of consolidation between the Jacksonville League and the Framework Cities over New Orleans and Tampa. But the political pundits said that war was unlikely: The Framework Cities were having trouble coming to terms among themselves as they were; taking on new members wasn't a priority.

Crowley hadn't had to force his spin on the media. He'd just sized up the situation and acted in a way that was most likely to produce the results he wanted. This was good management.

Sic Semper Tyrannis

In the last hour before his flight to Charleston, he sketched out his plans for the summit. He couldn't keep things in his head as clearly as he'd been able to in his Tampa prime but he'd come to accept this. He kept more detailed notes on his screen.

And he watched the Brownsville news channel. The Tampa bonds had fallen off a bit. But not as much as before. The markets expected Tampa to retaliate faster this time.

Nothing had happened by the time Crowley got in the SkyDragon for Charleston; vieux Guibert said the forces scattered around Tampa and New Orleans were reporting in fine. No attacks on either. So, Crowley was nearly certain that the retaliation would come while he was in transit. When it hadn't, he began to think that they had gotten word of the summit and were planning to attack it.

That was the only sense he could make of the silence.

Brian had told him recently that Brownsville could make the unmarked SkyDragon available as long as the Company controlled the balance of power among the big Cities in the region. While it was open-ended, it was definitely a condition added to their standing agreement about the vehicle. And a basic management lesson was that added conditions were the first sign that an agreement was in trouble. Brian wouldn't screw him but the other Brownsville directors might.

He told the pilots to keep the Dragon ready for a quick exit. And to keep checking in with Camp A for any news.

The summit went about as expected. Raymond Briggs' official residence was like a shrine; it dated back to before the Federal Era's Civil War. The formal welcome of the other City leaders was like a grand ball scene from some fairy tale vid.

Through almost two hours of pomp and ceremony, Crowley kept waiting for the explosion. It didn't come.

As soon as the doors shut, the other CEOs took their turns berating Karamanlis. They also dug into Crowley—and a few asked Crowley whether he'd instructed Karamanlis to say the thing about Crowley speaking for the League. This really infuriated Karamanlis. "I haven't taken orders from anyone in 40 years and I'm not about to start now!"

Raising his voice only made him sound older and weaker. And what he said was foolish. Crowley made a note to himself that no manager should ever raise his voice…and no one over 60 should ever—ever—raise his voice.

Crowley didn't say much for the first hour. To him, hitting only three of the four targets was a poor showing. But the others seemed more interested in fighting with each other than focusing on what had happened. So, he let them soften each other.

Finally, after the others had vented, Briggs put the matter to Crowley directly and asked him to explain the second drone and the multiple bombs. They'd all agreed that he would send one missile.

"They treated the first tactical nuke we fired on Tampa like a fluke. I wanted to leave no question that we were hitting them as we designed. That seems to have worked. Now, the fact is, these strikes weren't as precise as I'd wished. But we've been lucky that no one in the media has pointed that out."

Briggs' next question was whether Crowley had given Karamanlis talking points or reached some kind of side agreement with Karamanlis to make it appear that Crowley was the spokesman for the League.

This was a crafty psychological maneuver. The question was absurd. But Briggs was repeating it precisely because it had made the old dictator angriest and would humiliate him further. Maybe to raise another violent reaction. This was no mistake; Briggs was trying to stir up trouble with the perceived leaders of the group.

"That's an insult to Mr. Karamanlis. He doesn't take orders from me. We don't have any side agreement about anything. I saw the vid piece that the Wall Street channel ran. It was pretty clear to me that they ripped that quote out of something else he said. My guess is that he said something about me speaking for the League about wasteland matters—which is something we've all agreed on. Some smart-ass vid producer just took that out of context. And I don't know why anyone thinks I want to be ID'd as the leader of this group. All that does it put a target on my back. It would make young Hailwood come after me first."

"He's *already* coming after you first."

"Well, then, he'd come after me faster."

There wasn't much more to say about the vid clip and the media coverage. Karamanlis was useless for the rest of the meeting, though. He was so angry at having his primacy questioned that he didn't speak. Which may have been Briggs' object all along.

The formal topic of the summit was voting final approval of the mutual defense treaty that would give formal shape to the League. The member Cities would retain their walls and internal security forces; but they acknowledged the League was organized to centralize and coordinate financial, security and public policy among member Cities. As part of this acknowledgment, member Cities would give up any external security functions.

The League itself would administer the wasteland—which it would now call "unincorporated zones"—and its members voted to hand that job to Crowley's Company.

In terms of mutual defense, an attack by any outside entity on a member City of any unincorporated zone would be treated by each member as an attack on its property.

In terms of internal public policy, citizens of League Cities would be allowed to travel in unincorporated zones freely. No one—not even Crowley's Company—could charge any sort of toll, tariff or fee.

Residents of the unincorporated zones could apply for League citizenship and if approved could enter League Cities for short visits or occasional work. And they would be given preference in an application for citizenship in any League City they might choose.

These details had been debated and agreed upon in advance. This meeting was to sign the master document. Everyone did. And the media experts for each City immediately released

That was all Crowley wanted to see. There was another meeting the next morning on coordinating fiscal policy. Since he'd have little to add to that debate, he told his partners that he was heading back to Camp A that night. He could be reached by vid link if his opinion was needed.

They all seemed satisfied with him taking the target on his back away from them. They shouldn't have been.

While Crowley was in the air between Charleston and Camp A, Tampa's retaliation came in the form of missiles falling in both places. And in Jacksonville. And at Camp B. They either didn't know about or chose not to attack Camp C.

The word came across while they were beginning their approach to land at Camp A. Numerous tactical nuke blasts in close order. He knew that meant a multiple-warhead missile. The kind of thing that only a big City could arrange.

The bombs had fallen directly down from high altitudes—so anti-missile defense systems didn't have much three-dimensional flight path to follow. Shooting flak and anti-missile missiles straight up was the least effective way to protect yourself.

"Max, we need to get up and stay up until we know more about what's going on."

"Yes, sir."

They changed their course and went high—beyond the range of any lucky strike.

Word came in. First, from vieux Guibert. That old bird would never die. The staff at Camp A had bunkered down, into the shelters as far down as the local geology would allow. The quick head count in the bunker was over 5,000—which was good news. Few people had been left out.

The word from Camp B was also good—mostly because there was only a skeleton crew on site, anyway.

The trouble was in the Cities. Charleston's defense nets weren't designed to prevent multiple-warhead nukes. They'd flakked off some of the bombs…but several had gotten through. Some of the VIP residences where League CEOs were staying had been hit. That meant some CEOs were probably dead. And the League hadn't formalized its agreements yet.

That wasn't just dumb luck.

The missiles falling on Jacksonville had landed in the residential rings to the west and north of the central core. The City's anti-missile systems had failed almost completely—which was humiliating for them. There was no word yet on how many Jacksonville citizens were dead; Karamanlis' admins would probably try to hide any real reporting. But the final number would be in the thousands, at least. Maybe in the tens of thousands.

Would the League survive this? If it did, would it really be the *Jacksonville* League any longer? There'd be some uncertainty now. Karamanlis's humiliation worked into Crowley's long-term plan.

Young Hailwood didn't miss much. His actions weren't brilliant or inspired. But they came, just like the markets expected. He was reliable. And the markets would reward that. He—or someone close to him—was a good manager.

Thirty-two

Hailwood figured out that he didn't like Old Man's offices. He didn't like the CEO's offices in City Hall, either. He wouldn't get rid of either—he *couldn't* get rid of the CEO's formal offices. But his plan was to use them for ceremonial purposes only. His real business offices would be at the House.

Masterson and a handful of security staffers had come over to discuss planting tactical nuke mines north of the north walls.

"The things are effective. Almost to a fault. They'll vaporize people and hardware in a 200-yard radius and burn hard up to a quarter mile. The fallout is concentrated. It makes a dead zone of about half a square mile with a rad level that's fatal for about three days. Plus there's the cost in political capital."

"What's that?"

"Mines are considered barbaric tools. Very bad PR. Vid actresses leading protests against you and all that."

"I couldn't care less, Steve. We can't afford to have these zealot armies waging asymmetric war on our perimeter. We can't find them. We can't lure them out. They're guerilla fighters, keeping small units in fox holes. I get that strategy. Good for them. So, we'll make the perimeter one big dead zone. If history teaches anything, it's that you nuke guerilas. I say mine the whole peninsula right up to Karamanlis' south gate and then flush those self-righteous sons of bitches back into the mines. We keep the Old Florida Highway clear and patrol the hell out of that."

"So, your order is that we set the mines?"

He typed a few words into his screen. He had boilerplate language for formal memos stored as macros and he was getting to the point that he could issue bureaucratically-compliant executive orders in fewer than 50 keystrokes.

"Just issued the order. Follow the plan that you laid out in your proposal and let's hope Crowley or one of his main guys steps on the first one."

Masterson stayed around for a moment after they were done, so Hailwood invited him to come out for a walk along the seawall.

"What else is there?"

"A couple of things. One strategic. One political."

"Okay."

"First the strategic. If we plant these mines, we're effectively cutting off any sort of random contact with the rest of the continent."

"That's the idea."

"Yes. But the folks down in Miami aren't going to be too happy about that."

"They're already not happy, Steve. Nothing we can do about that."

"But there's that old Memorandum of Understanding that says we won't cut off Miami's logistical access to the rest of the continent."

"And we're not. We're leaving the Old Florida Highway open."

"Sure. But it'll be under our direct control."

"I understand where you're going…but fuck that. Really. That Memo is more than 100 years old. Ramirez can scream all he wants about ground transit. And, you know, I don't believe he will. I think he's going to be happier than ever to be our friend."

Masterson picked up a few shells to skip into the pass. "That guy from Charleston has approached him about joining the Jacksonville League."

"I know. Ramirez and I have a meeting set up for Tuesday morning, right here. We're going to reach an agreement."

"An agreement?"

"I expect that it will be commercial, mostly. But I'm willing to entertain a mutual defense agreement. So you should be here. I think he'll have a few of his guys, too."

"These mutual defense deals seem to be the trend."

"Indeed. But I prefer to make them bilaterally. One City at a time. I don't like gangbang policy."

"I understand."

"Good. So, what's the political issue? City or departmental?"

"Departmental."

"Oh. Damn."

"I know. And I'm sorry. I've done as much as I can to move around Barrett. But he's doing all he can to make things difficult. I mean, it's ridiculous that you have get involved personally in a purchase order for the mines to get this thing rolling."

"Maybe. But I just look at Barrett as a kind of insurance policy. If anything goes terribly wrong, he'll be a useful chunk of meat to throw to the dogs."

"I can see that. But I'm concerned about the institutional damage that he and the rest of the holdovers might be doing every day, when they show up to work and badmouth you and the City and anything else they can."

Hailwood thought about that for a minute. He tried to give Masterson's concerns his complete attention. But he couldn't get past the flavor of bureaucracy in them. He liked Masterson well—and trusted him as much as he trusted anyone—but Masterson was a manager. And Hailwood's strategic take was that having disgruntled people in senior management positions served a purpose he liked: It undermined the whole concept of "professional" managers.

And if Barrett and some other holdovers tried to plot a coup? That would give him exploitable political theater for years.

"Let's just focus on the mine project for now. Don't worry about institutional damage. We can deal with that in time."

"Okay."

> We focus on reading in these lessons. That's the most valuable thing I can give you. But I also want you to think about some other things as we learn together. Reading gives you the keys to living whatever kind of life you choose. And that puts the focus of your life on you.
>
> You are the most important thing in your life. You have the greatest value. You are made in God's image. Everything else in your life—the work you do, the place you live, the people you meet—they are all extensions of *you*. So, you are important. Central. Never let anyone tell you different.

Hailwood had asked one of the intelligence managers working for Masterson to put together a vid of several of Crowley's lessons.

They were all over the free nets—but Hailwood had never watched one. He hadn't realized how much the vids were inspirational stuff. But it made sense. If the vids were just phonics and word-attack skills, they probably never would have become so popular.

Hailwood thought back to the people he'd known in the wilderness—the merchants and the squatters—and wondered whether they would go for this kind of thing. Wasteland people had always seemed rugged and self-reliant to him.

But he realized his experience in the wasteland wasn't typical.

There were other traces of marketing plan in Crowley's lesson. He wore the same white shirt/red vest combo in every vid. And he had a beard, like most men in the wasteland, but it was trimmed neatly. And his hair, too long for City fashion, was also well-kept. He looked like he was from the wasteland…but he might pass as an eccentric intellectual type if he were dropped into a pedestrian section of downtown Tampa.

As the vid went on, Crowley did get into phonics and word-attack skills. But he'd frequently slide in a little "you're important/you're valuable" sermonizing.

That was another thing that struck Hailwood about the vid: There was less God talk than he'd expected. Crowley would mention "God" or "Lord" every now and again; but he talked about "you" much more often. And more passionately.

For a religious zealot, he sounded a lot like a self-help guru. Maybe he believed in "you" more than he believed in an Almighty.

Dowd rang him on the screen line that indicated issues of moderate importance. Dowd was running the official office and doing very effectively. He'd become something between a first assistant and a chief of staff. And he seemed to be enjoying it.

"What have you got, James?"

"Unusual call from New York Internal Security. Matter of someone they have in custody. An H.M. Reeser."

"What do they want?"

"Well, Mr. Reeser is asking for extradition to Tampa, based on a preexisting agreement with this Office. I'm not sure how to respond."

Had he ever promised a "Get Out of Jail Free" card to hoss? He couldn't remember. And if he got involved here, how many more old friends would come out of the woodwork looking for favors or help?

But he was also interested to see how much sway his Office had with one of the Framework Cities.

"Can we find out why he's in custody?"

"Class C felony possession of prohibited pharma. Relatively minor dug bust. He's looking at a three-year incarceration."

"Will New York want something in return?"

"Not on a courtesy extradition. They'll just expect us to honor theirs."

"And do we?"

"Usually."

"What's your opinion on this?"

"Well, a courtesy extradition is kind of overkill for a Class C Felony. But New York Security is probably just as happy to hand off a minor drug dealer. Frees up a prison cot for more serious offenders. I don't know who this Reeser person is or what our agreement with him is...."

"He's an old friend of mine from College. And I'm not sure there's any agreement. But pass word to New York that we'd like the courtesy."

"Very good. I'll send you the doc that you need to execute. And we'll need to send a vehicle up there to get him."

That seemed a bit of a luxury at the moment. But Hailwood was curious about how these diplomatic matters worked. "Okay. Have Masterson send someone up. And make sure they call me before they leave. I'll have some particular instructions for them."

"Will do."

Eight hours later, a TSF tiltrotor landed at the House. It was an hour late—but Hailwood had expected some delays in New York. He climbed aboard.

Hoss was sitting in the seat across from two TSF officers.

He looked bad. He'd put on a lot of weight. His eyes were puffy. His head was shiny with sweat. It was recently shaved—no doubt, when he'd been processed into prison—and his scalp was noticeably whiter than his face or neck. "Thanks, Terry. I owe you one."

Hailwood didn't mind the experiment. But Dowd was right—this much executive power was wasted on such a trivial matter. "No you don't. You don't owe me anything. But I want to say a couple of things to you. First, this is the only time this is going to happen. I won't ever spring you out of some seedy little drug problem again. So don't bother asking. Ever."

"I understand."

"Second, you can't stay here. These guys will refuel the tilt and take you anywhere you want to go. But you can't stay in Tampa."

"Terry, I was hoping—"

"You can't stay here, hoss. We'd be off to a bad start. You'd try to be a good citizen but sooner or later you'd do something stupid and expect me to bail you out. I can't afford that."

Reeser looked like he was about to cry. "I really don't have anywhere to go."

"Go back to school."

"Can't. You don't know what it's like there now, man. It's a fucking police state. Every time some rag-ass bandit shoots a gun at the walls, they pass five more laws."

"Well, have them take you to San Francisco. They have the loosest drug laws. Or drop you off in the wasteland somewhere. Though I'd still recommend somewhere in the West. The holy rollers control all of the wasteland around here. Or Europe. I don't care where you go, hoss. But you can't stay here." He got up to climb out of the tilt.

"We used to be friends, man."

"Yeah. We did. And that's why I did this for you. But never again. You just tell these guys where you want to go. Good bye."

The tilt took off. Hailwood couldn't make a practice of this.

The next day, Masterson sent a secure email saying the first mines had been planted. As per the plan, he was going to plant the mines in 5,000-square-meter fields following a fractal pattern that would be nearly impossible to predict.

It was a great idea. But Hailwood's mind had moved on to other things. The sun was setting. He'd changed his clothes and was waiting for Kate to arrive. The jet he'd sent up to New York to get her had landed at St. Pete; now, she was coming to the House in a tilt.

Hailwood scanned the new sites on his screen. It was Friday night, so they were full of vid reviews and celebrity gossip for the weekend. But the *Miami Herald* did have a piece about him. It didn't mention the meeting with Ramirez directly—but someone must have known. The article sized him up like a baseball team scouting report would size up an opposing pitcher:

> Not much is known about Terrence Hailwood. Until recently, he was a professor of ancient languages and rhetoric at a Legacy College in the New England wasteland. Brought back home by the mysterious circumstances surrounding his grandfather's disappearance, this youngest Hailwood quickly consolidated authority in Tampa's boardroom. Observers say he is more direct than previous Chairmen—and also more ruthless.
>
> According to one source familiar with Tampa politics, the new Chairman "has a specific vision of how a major City should be managed in an era of increasing economic uncertainty. He's going to surprise a lot of people."
>
> No one was more surprised than former Tampa CEO Matthew Chambers, who was fired immediately by Hailwood and has practically vanished from the local scene. City governance experts surmise that Chambers' termination agreement included a requirement that the ousted CEO stay away for a period of time while the new Chairman consolidates his position.

He would have thought that the "someone familiar" was a made-up source, except that Bill Franklin had told him he'd spoken to a reporter from the *Herald*.

The buzz of Kate's tilt echoed back and forth across the pass, announcing her arrival. There was no random air traffic around the House any more.

He walked out onto the back porch and watched the tilt land on the beach strip below. This was one of the small changes he'd made to how the House was run. The Old Man had always preferred tilts to land to the side of the House, on the tennis courts. Hailwood thought visitors would be more impressed by landing on the beach.

And, landing on the beach, the observant ones would notice the anti-aircraft plasma cannons now permanently tucked in along the upper seawall.

He thought about staying up on the porch. But that would be too pompous. He rushed down the stairs to greet Kate on the sand.

The pilot made a dramatic landing maneuver, coming in low across the Bay and then darting up to convert his rotors into landing formation.

Hailwood tried to see Kate inside the tilt but its windows remained tinted. It took a minute for the blades to stop. Then, the passenger hatch in the back opened up.

Kate looked great. She'd lost some weight and her skin was clearer than it had been the last time he'd seen her—in New York, what seemed like a lifetime before. She was wearing a short tartan skirt with a tailored jacket with something that looked like a man's tuxedo shirt. And thick black velvet ribbon in her red hair. A fusion of chic and college. Her best look.

She smiled at him even before he said anything. "You! I can't believe that you've done all this so quickly."

He hugged her and kissed her on the mouth and the eyes—which was something he'd done when they'd first started dating. "I'm really glad to see you, Kate."

"You've got to tell me everything."

Once they got upstairs, he made a pitcher of drinks and talked her through a version of what had happened. Victor was getting dinner ready, grouper, the local favorite fish, and rack of lamb, her favorite meat; but they had some time to kill on the deck.

She listened to what he had to say but the angle of her head said she was impatient with his few details. "In New York, there are rumors that you shot Chambers in the board room. Did you?"

He rolled his eyes and smiled just a little. "Kate, if I did I wouldn't want to talk about it. There's a lot going on that's still... going on. Maybe in a couple months, when the dust has settled, I'll feel better about giving you all the gory details."

She turned her head back and smiled at him. "Okay. I'm sorry. It's just so exciting. I mean, you're President! I knew you could do this. You were born for it. But I didn't think you *would* do it."

He sat next to her in one of the big deck chairs. "I didn't think I would, either, Kate. But the last few months have been very... surprising."

"I'm sure of that. And I'm sorry that I wasn't there for you. I picked the worst possible time to go through some bullshit girl identity crisis." She squeezed his hand. "I want to make it up to you." This was going a little *too* well.

They ate their dinner on the deck and then went upstairs.

An hour after midnight, she was sleeping soundly. He was used to staying up another couple of hours.

He sat up in the big bed and looked out on the pass.

Kate felt familiar. He guessed she always would. Their misfire with the bad weekend in New York seemed millions of miles away.

She was acting like she had when they'd first known each other. Which was good. But he couldn't get over the fact that this felt false. Somehow. The timing was too perfect. Her need to engage him and flatter him, a little too desperate.

She might be a spy for New York—and she might not even know it. The best kind of spy, not burdened by the weight of betrayal. She'd just talk to her mom and dad once a day....

The mines started "popping" almost immediately. Masterson's plan had been to focus External Security attacks at a few points that would drive the terrorists into the fields. But he quickly dumped that plan; the zealots moved a lot without any prompting from the Tampa forces.

TSF troops had planted about 2,000 mines; 31 went off during the first 24 hours. Several more were detonating every few hours. This was more activity than anyone had expected.

Masterson created a tracking map showing where each of the tactical mines had been triggered—and how long its dead zone had until the rad level was safe for unprotected exposure.

Most of the activity was at a point about 20 miles east of the dead zone formerly known as "occupied Tampa." So, they must have moved the bulk of their units over there. That told Hailwood something—Security's conventional wisdom had been that the zealot forces had moved north, along the Old Florida Highway.

And where they'd chosen to hide was some fairly nasty terrain. Swampy. Overgrown.

There'd also been a patch of activity—a dozen mines triggered—around Gate 14, near Orlando and the Old I-95 corridor. That wasn't such a surprise. He'd figured that they'd keep some troops near the TSA launching pads along the Atlantic Coast. But he hadn't planned on patrolling the Old 95 corridor as much as he'd focused on the Old Florida Highway, closer to home on the Gulf Coast.

He emailed Masterson and congratulated him on the quick success. He told him to keep on the schedule for planting the rest of the mines—and asked for an estimate of how many zealots they'd killed. And mentioned his thoughts about patrolling the Old 95 corridor…and asked Masterson for a plan for doing so.

He copied Barrett on the email.

How many troops the terrorists actually had was a constant question. Guerilla armies usually had fewer troops than appeared. Classical siege strategy suggested that they'd troop up before their first attacks and then pull a lot of the force back after they'd established a perimeter.

Crowley or whoever was in charge must have been scrambling. Tampa had broken the siege perimeter with the missiles into the "occupied" zone. And now the terrorists were scrambling into a mine field. Literally.

There other things to consider. If Hailwood broke the terrorist army too quickly, how long until Karamanlis and the rest of the Jacksonville League Cities got involved in a more direct way? The mines were in place, so a land-based response was unlikely. That left air and sea.

Tampa's air defense system was on full alert. And Tampa Bay hadn't been raided successfully in the City's whole history.

He wished he had good intelligence from inside the Jacksonville League and Crowley's "Company." There had to be some way to find out more about their inner dealings. Though he should have considered that before dumping the missiles on their summit meeting. His hope had been that his broadsides would cause them to panic and bicker—and the Jacksonville League would crumble from within. Decent plan, but its problem was that crumbling from within was a hard thing to detect from without.

He made a note to talk with Masterson about developing some intelligence inside the Jacksonville League.

The extra Security troops started showing up at the House the day before Ramirez's visit. They did a double-check of the premises, tested the anti-missile system and installed some temporary monitors.

He'd have surveillance specialists loyal to Masterson check the house *after* the meeting, in case the first crew had planted anything.

For the meantime, Hailwood concentrated on his files on the Miami CEO.

Ramirez was an old-school Brahmin of Cuban extraction. His family had been living in Miami since the Federal Era. They'd made their money in restaurants and alcohol. But like most Old Families, they'd essentially been bankers for generations.

Miami was an older City than Tampa. It had been bigger, a long time ago. But, since the City Era had begun, Tampa had been bigger, richer and better armed. From time to time, there would some disagreements between the Cities—but Miami was generally willing to follow Tampa's lead in most matters of commerce and security. They shared what some earlier CEO called "a special relationship."

That's why Ramirez was the first CEO Hailwood was meeting with formally.

But there were likely to be a few hard topics. Ramirez wasn't going to like the fact that Tampa had planted mines in the wasteland to its north. Legally, there was no treaty or agreement between them that required Hailwood to check in with Ramirez. But Chambers had been more collaborative.

And then there was the matter of Briggs from Charleston inviting Ramirez to bring Miami into the Jacksonville League. This had been unexpected on various levels—that the offer had been made and that Briggs had made it. Hailwood wondered whether this had just elevated a sharper man to the top of the League.

Ramirez didn't like to fly. So, he was driving up in a motorcade that would come up the Old Florida Highway. Masterson's troops were taking extra measures to make sure the Highway was clear and secure. There would be no bandit or terrorist attacks on Ramirez's motorcade.

Normal management protocol was that Barrett would meet the Miami group at the gate. Hailwood considered meeting them himself but decided against. It was better to follow protocol. Besides, welcoming dignitaries and other public events were among the reasons he'd kept Barrett around.

This was Hailwood's version of the Old Man's beliefs about power and indirection. Hailwood would be a public face—but he wanted his true advisors like Masterson to stay out of the public eye. No celebrity managers like Michael Crowley.

By the time Ramirez's motorcade arrived at the House, it was large. Two trucks and three cars from Miami plus four Tampa Security cruisers and two unmarked cars. Getting everyone inside was a bigger production than Hailwood had imagined. But Victor made it go smoothly.

The House had one end of Anna Maria Island to itself—but the south end of the island did have some other houses and the Village, a couple of blocks of shops and restaurants. The Security troops had essentially closed the island to all traffic, which wouldn't make his neighbors too happy. He'd never had much interaction with them, directly. Victor was the one who heard about complaints. And there would be complaints. The neighbors weren't docile proles. They were professionals and high-end managers who took pride in living in a fashionable neighborhood.

Maybe he was going to have to rethink summit meetings at the House.

He stood on the steps in front of the front door and greeted Ramirez. "Mr. President, welcome to Tampa. I'm Terry Hailwood."

Guillermo Ramirez was a company man, a life-long manager who'd gradually gained gathered political capital during more than 40 years of running various aspects of Miami's government. In many ways, he was a typical Miami Cuban. He was formal in carriage and character, carefully groomed and dressed. He'd worked hard to maintain the image of youth. He appeared to be in his late 40s or early 50s, which was impossible, given the length of his career. High quality gene therapy—and a lot of it—kept him looking young.

His managerial assistants dressed just like Ramirez but moved a little differently. More vigorously. They were younger—probably as old in fact as he seemed.

Standing in the driveway, Ramirez acted cautiously. "Yes. Of course. It's good to meet you. It's been a long time since I've been in Tampa. I hadn't seen your grandfather in many years."

"I understand that you don't like to leave your home. So, I appreciate that you've come up to see me here. Please, come in."

Hailwood escorted the older man into the living room. Some of the managers stayed outside; six or eight followed them inside.

Victor had done a good job of moving the furniture so that they could see the pass from the chairs. Ramirez used the bathroom briefly and then they settled down for a brief discussion of their agenda for the next 24 hours. He asked for a glass of ice water. The plan was that Ramirez would stay the night in the guest house. They would discuss the current trade agreement between Tampa and Miami—and a possible mutual defense treaty.

Ramirez wanted to talk about the Jacksonville League.

Although Ramirez was guarded, his attitude improved when they turned to the details of the agreements between the Cities. Hailwood was pleased by this. It was widely known that Ramirez had had a falling out with Harry Banks—Tampa's CEO before Michael Crowley—over what Ramirez considered a defense treaty that was in fact an attempt by Tampa to annex Miami. And it was widely known that he'd dismissed Banks, Crowley and Chambers as "puppets." Presumably, puppets of the Old Man—whom Ramirez didn't like.

So the workmanlike, even cordial, tone of the talks was good thing.

They took a break before dinner, which Victor was preparing for 14 people at eight o'clock. Ramirez agreed to come back half an hour earlier so he and Hailwood would have a private drink.

He was prompt.

Hailwood asked him what he'd like to drink.

"Well, a lady of my acquaintance advised me against your mojitos. So, I'll stay with a martini."

The siren? Hailwood's mind raced through the permutations—and the possible right responses. "Good. I'm much better at those. There's only one woman who'd know how bad my mojitos are. And I'd assumed that meeting her was a happy accident for me. Was I wrong?"

"I have no idea. But, if you're asking whether I sent her, you can rest easy. I did not. Maria Elena is too strong willed to be anyone's spy. I know her brother-in-law, the banker. He was very helpful to me at a critical point some years ago. I'm not sure whether someone like you would ever have need of his services. But I could arrange an introduction if you should."

Hailwood poured the drinks and gave one to Ramirez. He gestured to the chairs in the porch.

"I'll remember your offer, thank you. I suppose you can never have too many bankers. And I also want to thank you for the constructive tone of our talks so far today. I had been afraid that your history with my grandfather might cloud our ability to get things done."

Ramirez took a drink and waited a little while before replying. "Times change. Circumstances change. You are a different man. This is very easy to see. There's no reason to dwell on the past. I'm concerned about the war. The League. The Framework. Tampa will be a part of these developments—either as a partner or as an enemy. I have to make sure that Miami isn't dragged along in the wake. If we go with you...or against you...I have to make sure we do so because it's best for us."

"Understood. But I'm not sure we're *going* anywhere."

"I think you are, whether you wish it or not. We all are."

"Point taken."

"Raymond Briggs calls me every other day, to gossip about business and politics. And to ask me to join the Jacksonville League. He tells me that the League is the best way that I can make sure Miami doesn't dragged into the losing side of your war."

"I hear a lot about Briggs. It sounds like that group has the wrong name. It should be called the Charleston League."

"Not his style. He believes in staying out of the spotlight. Like your grandfather did. And he has a lot of competition for the leadership of the League. Most betting men would put their money on Crowley as the one who emerges."

"I would have thought his prospects worse lately."

"Maybe. Maybe. You've done a lot to break his army down here. But he still has a lot of troops near New Orleans. And still more hiding in the wasteland, I think."

"My next important meeting is with Marc Morial. I suspect he's going to have a lot of interest in what we've done here."

"I understand that Morial hasn't had any luck convincing the Framework Cities to admit New Orleans. It must have been humiliating for him to make all those trips to New York to beg and plead...for nothing."

"I don't care about people's private humiliations. But you're right about one thing: New Orleans hasn't joined the Framework. And Morial's angry about the zealots bombing his casinos."

"Logic says that he'll look for alliance. Either with us or with the Jacksonville League."

Ramirez had said "us."

"Which was *behind* those bombs. Of course, I'm not looking to make an alliance with a City so far away. Our interests might be similar but the geography is against a meaningful deal."

"New Orleans has a large navy and the biggest port in this part of the world."

"And shipping *is* important. But we consider it less important than air power."

"And space power."

"Yes. Our anti-missile shield isn't perfect. But it's been tested. The zealots have fired thousands missiles at us and only a couple have hit anything. Plus, just recently, we killed their drone."

"True. They seem to have gotten lucky early."

"They had the element of surprise. Under my watch, that will never happen again."

Ramirez took another sip of his drink and watched the sunset. He let the conversation stand for a minute. Hailwood let him take the lead.

"I have a blunt question for you, Hailwood."

"Go ahead."

"Did you kill Matthew Chambers?"

Now Hailwood waited. He'd thought a lot about how to talk about this. He wasn't ashamed of it—but he also didn't want to come off sounding like a boastful child.

"Have you ever heard of the Gordian Knot?"

"Yes, of course. The intractable problem. Alexander the Great solved it with a sword stroke."

Hailwood nodded once, slowly.

Ramirez smiled for the first time. "I understand."

"And I think it's had the effect that I intended."

"Maybe more than you intended. Even though the story is still a rumor, people are afraid to be in a room with you. Even me. I'm carrying a pistol right now. And I haven't done that in years."

"You're in no danger here. We want to make deals that will bring our Cities closer together. We're neighbors on this peninsula. It's natural that we should be partners."

"And if I don't want to be your partner?"

"Well, I'll be disappointed. But I'm not going to shoot you." He did a double-take to give Ramirez a sign that he was joking. "I'll just take the time convince you it's in both of our interests that we're partners."

"Your nuclear land mines to the north are isolating us from the rest of the world."

"They're protecting us from Crowley's terrorists."

"Maybe. Do we have time for another drink?"

It was still dawn when one of the Security troops woke Hailwood. It took him a minute to shake the mist that the drinks with Ramirez had caused.

"...sir, Colonel Masterson is on the screen for you."

"What?"

He walked over to his desk and clicked on.

"We've got boats on an attack course for your House."

"Boats?"

"Yes. Six in all. A couple are big enough to be some kind of warships and three are probably escorts—hydrofoils or jet boats. This matches our intelligence on the terrorists' equipment."

"Yeah, I remember. I still can't believe they'd try this. Where are they?"

"About seven miles out in the Gulf. Due west and heading straight for the mouth of the Bay. The only danger they pose right now is that they may have missiles on the bigger boats. I've got the sats tuned in, our hydrofoils heading out and four SkyDragons in the air. We can make short work of them."

"Okay, go ahead. Just make sure we're right about their identity and hostile intent. I don't want to sink some cruise ships that got off course."

"We've been trying to contact them for half an hour. They're jamming all communication. But I'll make sure we get a visual confirm before we shoot."

"Get some sat picts."

"Exactly. I'll have them in a few minutes."

"Okay. Then use your judgment. We sure don't want anything happening while Ramirez is here."

"Yes, sir. I'll call you back in half an hour."

"Good. That'll give time to shower and shave. Hey, tell your guys to try to pick up any survivors. I'd like to hear what the hell they were thinking."

"Check. We'll pick up survivors."

The talks with Ramirez and the Miami group went well. They agreed to resurrect the free trade agreement between Tampa and Miami that had lapsed 20 years earlier. And they agreed to establish a mutual defense agreement that—for the near future—would assure that neither City joined any League or Framework without the other.

This was substantially all that Hailwood wanted. And more than he had expected to accomplish. He and Ramirez agreed that he would come down to Miami for another meeting in about 30 days; at that meeting, they'd review both agreements and sign them.

Ramirez planned to leave at 3 p.m., so he could be back in Miami for a late dinner. But Hailwood said he had something that he wanted to show them.

He called Masterson and had him bring in the prisoner.

"Mr. Ramirez, this Steven Masterson, my Director of External Security. Early this morning, his people detected a small group of security-type vessels approaching us from the east, in the Gulf. We suspected this was the naval unit that the terrorists had assembled. So, we scrambled our ships and SkyDragons and blasted the boats out of the water. Steve, why don't you fill in the rest of the details?"

"Yes, sir. Pleasure to meet you, Mr. Ramirez. Well, we either destroyed of sank all six of the enemy vessels. On Mr. Hailwood's orders, our hydrofoils rescued as many survivors as they could fine. In total, we pulled almost 70 people from the water. Among was this fellow, a man who calls himself Zhang Zhyui Shu. We ran a DNA scan that brought up nothing. It's like that with these zealots—very few of them are in any City database. From the tattoo on the back of neck, it looks like he spent some time in the Shanghai Navy. Anyway, he seems to have been one of the commanders. The other prisoners treat him like the man in charge."

The prisoner stood with an officer's confidence. Even though he was small man, he seemed physically assertive—even with his hands chained behind his back. His face suggested a hard life, though. It was lined and drawn in a past-his-prime way.

"Do you mind if I ask him a few questions, Steve?"

"No, sir. Go right ahead. His English seems good. He speaks without an accent."

"Mr. Zhang, my name is Hailwood. I'm the CEO of the City of Tampa."

"Yes. I know who you are."

"Okay. Good. Now, I'd just like to ask you a few questions. First: Why were you bringing war ships into Tampa's territorial waters?"

"We were testing Tampa's port and harbor security."

"Testing our security?"

"Yes."

"Well, you didn't get anywhere near our port."

"No. Your security network detected us while were still in Gulf."

"Well, you should have expected that. You must have had some other plan of how you'd get closer in."

The prisoner didn't seem to understand the question. Hailwood shrugged his shoulders. That was enough of a prompt.

"I am a tactical commander. And we believed we were going to have bad weather that would give us cover."

"The weather doesn't matter, Mr. Zhang. It hasn't for hundreds of years. Your problems were strategic. So, you never got to the point of proving you tactical proficiency."

"Perhaps."

"Who gave you these bad orders?"

"All orders come from the Rabbi."

"That's Crowley?"

"Yes."

"That doesn't make sense. He would know how quickly we'd find you. I can't believe he'd waste his boats like that. Someone else must have given the order in his name. This is problem with personality cults. How many men did you have on your boats?"

"The total on all eight boats?"

Masterson interrupted. "On all *six*. He keeps claiming to have had eight boats. We only engaged six—and we've scoured the Gulf for any other vessels and found nothing. If you don't mind my saying, sir, it's an old Asian trick to overstate the number of vessels or vehicles or troops that went into battle after a loss. It creates the impression that some got away."

"How many men did you have on the six boats our forces encountered?"

"We had 188 men and women."

"188?"

"Yes."

"Well, we were only able to rescue some 65-odd of those. So, more than 120 of your people died for no reason."

"They died honorably."

"Maybe they did. How a soldier dies is something he controls—and most soldiers who die, die honorably. *Why* a soldier dies is something his commander controls. And I'd like to know why these people died."

The prisoner didn't seem to know how to respond. So, Hailwood just let it stand for a moment. He was about to say something else when the prisoner did first.

"Our mission was successful. We were supposed to test the naval defenses of your City. We found out that they are strong."

"With a 120 men on the bottom of the Gulf, that seems an expensive lesson. If you'd sent an envoy, we would have shown him the range of our sat net and sent him home."

The prisoner grimaced a little while Hailwood said this.

"I have another question for you, Mr. Zhang. Most of the zealots are homelanders or Hispanics. How did a Chinese naval officer end up in charge of their boats?"

"That is an insulting question."

"Okay. Let me restate it, then. How did *you* come to be in charge of Crowley's boats?"

"We all find our own path. I lived a dissolute life when I was young."

"That could describe any of us, Mr. Zhang."

The prisoner wasn't listening. "I squandered great potential. Now I serve the Lord with humility. And I will die at your hands without fear or regret."

"Your fear and regret are your own matters, Mr. Zhang. But you won't die at our hands. You aren't a pirate, from anything I can see. And you don't seem to have committed any war crimes. You were following orders—foolish orders. You are an officer and a prisoner of war. I don't know what you're used to; but we're not sadists here. You and your men will be housed and fed according to Baltimore Treaty standards. Col. Masterson, take this man and his crew to the Brandon detention facility. Put them in the POW bloc."

"Of course, sir. Mr. Ramirez."

When they'd gone, Ramirez nodded to Hailwood. "That was interesting. I've never been in the room with one of them before."

"They act like terrorists. But I'm not going to treat them like terrorists. The last guy tried that and it didn't work. I'm going to respect their position in the Jacksonville League and treat them like prisoners of war. And, by the same token, I'm going to hold the Jacksonville League responsible for the zealots' actions."

Ramirez nodded. "They may not find that so appealing."

"Let's hope not."

"This Chinese didn't seem like an ignorant man. I don't understand all the 'path to God' talk, though."

"I spent some time in the wasteland when I was in college. It's a hard life out there. I think that religion is an important thing to people with few prospects."

"You don't believe in God, Mr. Hailwood?"

"I believe in all of His manifestations, Mr. Ramirez. I believe in the potential of transcendence in the human spirit. But my beliefs are of little importance to our dealings. My interest here isn't in worshipping God. My interest is in making my City stronger and richer. Everything else follows from that. And right now I want to understand why our adversary sent a handful of rickety old ships into the teeth of our defense grid."

Ramirez nodded.

The mines north of Tampa's walls kept exploding more quickly than they'd predicted. Although the trigger rate dropped some after the first few days, it stayed pretty consistently at five or six explosions a day. At this rate, the wasteland would be a dead zone sooner than Hailwood had imagined.

Masterson's men would have to be laying more replacement mines than they'd planned.

Part of the cause of the explosions was the fact that the zealot forces were organized in smaller units that moved more actively than Tampa intelligence had realized. That was useful information.

The other part of the cause was that the squatters and outcasts who'd been living in the live oak hills were leaving. This was a self-fulfilling prophecy: as people considered the wasteland a dead zone, they fled—tripping more mines and increasing the deadliness.

Sic Semper Tyrannis

The *Dauntless* docked at the House for the first time in Hailwood's memory. And Michael came ashore with Deb Shamansky and Trinka.

Michael was dressed like any middle-aged Brahmin on his boat—khaki pants, white shirt, blue blazer and a red cravat. Deb wore a black bodysuit that was too sexy for any middle-aged Brahmin woman; maybe someone in SoCal might try it—but not Tampa. Trinka was wearing blue jeans and a black turtleneck.

Hailwood welcomed them into the House.

"So, where's the rest of your party?"

Michael shrugged. "The boys are in Europe. They go once a year and follow the circuit for a few weeks."

"And how about your financial guru? Herrera?"

"Al's set up permanently in Bermuda. He's running my money from there."

"Bermuda? Why?"

"Well, it's a beautiful island, for one. And there are still a lot of insurance companies there, for two. And Al is investing heavily in insurance."

Hailwood made gin and tonics for everyone. Victor brought a couple plates of stone crab claws and grouper bites out to the back porch.

Trinka camped near the stone crab. As attractive as she as, there was something vulgar about her. The Old Man would have muttered something about "Cossack blood."

"Victor, how are you doing?" Michael yelped. "Are you taking good care of Terry?"

Victor set out the platters and eased away a bit from the scene. After years of working for the Old Man, he'd absorbed some hard opinions about Michael. "I'm very glad that we have Mr. Terry back here full time. Especially with Mr. Grant gone, it's good to have a Hailwood in the House."

Michael bowed slightly. "Well, Terry's going to take Tampa places it's never been. I have no doubt that this House is going to see more activity than ever under his watch."

"Very good, sir." And he was gone.

Hailwood gave Michael his drink, after he'd given Deb and Trinka theirs. "Thanks for coming, dad. I hope that you'll always feel that you can dock your rig up here when you're around."

"Thanks, Terry. You know my feeling on all that."

"Michael, stop being such a cunt," Deb said. "Terry, it means a lot to him to be welcomed here. I promise you—if he won't—that we'll stop by regularly to check in on you."

"Thanks, Deb."

Michael put his arm around her. Just looking at the two of them standing on the porch, a casual observer would be happy to have them as a father and father's second wife. They looked tanned and well-maintained. Magazine ad campaigns were built on images like this.

But the casual observer would have no way of knowing how much strange stuff flowed just under the well-kept surface,

Michael hugged Deb and drained his tumbler. "And it may not be just you. One reason I've stopped in is to ask if you could find an interesting job in the City for Trinka. She's tired of our wandering existence and wants to take a stab at being a career gal."

"Is this true, Trinka?"

"Yeah. I'm ready for a new thing. And I think these two are tired of me. It's time for them to find a new project."

Michael laughed, a little nervously. "Trinka. Like tempered steel. Hard to the last."

Hailwood wondered if their plan was "give" Trinka to him. That would be Michael's style. And he'd thought about what it would be like to fuck this world-class sexual object. But he was trying to simplify his personal life....

"So, what would you want to do, Trinka?"

"Keep an eye on Michael's money, I guess. Represent his shares. Maybe work for the lawyer. Franklin?"

Of course, if she wanted help manage Michael's money, the best for her to do that would be in Bermuda with Herrera. So, something else was going on here.

"Well, I'm sure Bill could find a place for you in his firm. Maybe as a paralegal or research assistant. Keep you in the loop on anything affecting Michael's shares."

"Yeah. That would be good."

Michael stepped in again. "This would mean a lot to me. I trust Trinka. And I trust you, too, Terry. But you have worlds to conquer. I'm sure that she would always keep my perspective on things in the front of her mind."

Maybe he wasn't giving her to him, after all. It sounded more like he was leaving a minder.

"I think I understand what you mean. But I hope you're not worried about me doing anything to squander your equity here. Because it's in the front of my mind that cashflow is the first metric that we use to measure the City's performance."

Deb gave Michael a stern look.

"Terry, of course you're going to do a great job here. You already have. The City instruments are up enough that our equity's in no danger of dilution. If it took shooting Matthew Chambers to accomplish that, you've got my proxy to shoot all of them. In fact, seriously, we've talked about it and I've decided to give you an open-ended proxy to vote my shares in *all* Corporation matters. Just so that there will no questions in anyone's mind about who's running things."

This was news. Michael had never said anything about giving Hailwood his proxy. Hailwood had never thought to ask. His plan had been to make Michael comfortable at the House so he'd come around for board meetings. This proxy would make board meetings a formality.

"Wow. Dad, thanks. I'll make sure we find Trinka a job she likes. Another drink, anyone?"

They all said yes.

Deb spoke up next. "You seem to be doing well, Terry. You're handling so much. How do you feel?"

"Well, I'm okay. I guess." He felt like answering the support she'd shown him. "The strangest thing is that I've looked through old pictures of the Old Man. To see if I can see the resemblance. And I don't. I mean, I think we look like a grandfather and grandson. Related. But not the same."

"Because you're not the same, of course. From your first seconds, the two of you lived different lives. Ate different food. Had different experiences."

That analysis made more sense than any he'd read or heard.

Trinka slept on the *Dauntless* that night, apparently her last with Michael and Deb. The next morning, Hailwood emailed her personal data to J.C. Sandoval and asked that the City Attorney's office prepare her visa, work permit, temporary ID and other legal paperwork and send it over to Bill Franklin's office. Then he called

Bill Franklin and explained the situation. Michael gave Trinka a couple thousand dollars in cash and a pistol. Trinka asked for a ride downtown and disappeared into the City.

Michael and Deb set sail for Port of Spain and points south. Michael said he'd call regularly and that they'd try to stop back again around Christmas.

A few days later, Hailwood had a call from a man named Wellington Frame. He was a Vice Chairman (one of several) from New York. He wanted to set up an appointment to fly down to Tampa and discuss possible strategic relations.

A day after that, while Hailwood was prepping for his meeting with Morial from New Orleans, he had another call. This one was from Michael Crowley. He wanted a meeting to discuss a ransom for his naval troops…and other matters.

Hailwood agreed. And then he went down on the beach and practiced shooting for an hour.

Thirty-three

The losses in Tampa were mounting. And they were causing problems all over the map.

After Tampa Security had nuked the Occupied Zone, Crowley pulled most of the students out. He left one light company—about 1,000 troops—in place, organized in small units that followed a fast-paced hit-and-run strategy around the north walls of the City, making the impression that a larger force was in place.

It was tactical deception—meant to make TSF think they were settling in for a long siege. The change in management in Tampa meant the new regime was going to hit harder, at least for a while. So, it was time to turn the League's attention to New Orleans.

Crowley reminded himself that this wasn't personal. Couldn't be. The plan had been to push Tampa into isolation but look for deals that would bring New Orleans and Houston in. Tampa had fought back more aggressively than they'd expected; but it clearly was isolated. So, the plan was proceeding.

But, since Jean Jacques Guibert had been incinerated in a tactical nuke blast, Crowley had felt like the reins were slipping from his hands. And the Wraith attacks hadn't worked well at all.

In their daily vid conference, Crowley, Karamanlis and Briggs agreed that they'd settle for a draw with Tampa and swarm troops around New Orleans. Then, Crowley and Briggs would meet with Marc Morial to discuss New Orleans' membership in the League.

Crowley had redeployed the students from Tampa to support the units that were already camped about 10 miles east and north of New Orleans' walls. But, since the Wraiths had failed to hit the targets in Tampa, circumstances were turning against them.

First, Commander Z had gone off on his own. Without specific orders, he'd sailed for Tampa to launch short-range missiles during a meeting between young Hailwood and the CEO from Miami. This was an idea they'd discussed in only the loosest terms—and never authorized.

Z's initiative had backfired. Tampa Security intercepted the boats before they'd gotten close enough to fire a single missile. Details were hazy; but none of the boats had crossed back to support the New Orleans siege. And that *had* been Z's priority.

Then, Tampa Security—clearly under new management—had gotten word back through Jacksonville Security that they'd sunk the boats and picked up some survivors.

Second, Tampa hadn't stopped at nuking the occupied zone. They'd planted nuke mines in the wasteland to the north, where the bulk of Crowley's remaining units were scrambling around. In three days, more than 200 students had been killed. Nearly a fourth of the entire force. Plus, the area was poisoned. Moving around quickly was becoming impossible. So was keeping up the impression that they were still more than 20,000 strong.

Third, Morial was being coy about setting up the details of the meeting with Crowley and Briggs. He was waiting to see what would happen in Tampa.

Karamanlis thought that Morial might be talking with Hailwood directly. So not only had the Wraith missiles missed three of their four marks, they had driven Tampa and New Orleans closer together. A double loss.

So, now they were tinkering with the plan. The daily vid conferences were getting longer and less cordial. And Karamanlis was pushing for another summit in Jacksonville.

"There's no time for that right now," Crowley said. "My students are marching through the wasteland or frozen in the woods north of Tampa. If the troops down there make any big moves, even attempt to withdraw, we'll lose the rest of the 1,000. And we can't afford that."

Briggs took over, as was his style lately. "You need to make a truce with Tampa."

"No. That would be a big mistake, *especially* if Morial and Hailwood really are talking. It will telegraph our weakness to New Orleans. And we have to focus on pressuring Morial."

"Okay, but someone needs to get the pressure off of our troops at Tampa. Maybe I'll give Hailwood a call."

There was silence for a while. Briggs liked to take over actions that he'd first suggested for someone else.

"No. If anyone draws a truce with Tampa, it'll be me." He was already thinking of how to do this. He could call Bill Franklin.

Jana didn't like the idea of Crowley going to a meeting with Terry Hailwood. "He's a ruthless psychopath. He might pull a gun and kill you in the middle of a detailed negotiation of right-of-way or ag credits."

"Jana, what's going on? Do you think I'm some sort of idiot? I've spent a big part of my life dealing with people like him. I know who they are and *how* they are. This one's not going to catch me by surprise. I'm going to be armed every minute I'm around him—and so are my bodyguards."

"I don't think you're an idiot. I'm just worried about this meeting. You're not coming into it from a position of strength…"

"I know. But we need to be able to focus on New Orleans now. And I don't want to leave a company of students in the middle of a mine field—literally. We'll make a deal to get them out."

"Can't you send someone else?"

"When have I ever done that?"

"You sent me to Mobile."

"You've got this all backwards, Jana. I *want* to meet him. I mean, it's not like I expect an apology from him. But his family framed me and took my kids away. Our meeting as equals will be an admission of those wrongs."

"Why does that matter to you all of the sudden? You've always said this wasn't about personal satisfaction."

"It's not. But the moral high ground counts for something."

She shrugged her shoulders and sat back. Her artificial eye fluttered a little. The prosthetics tech was coming out to the farm in the morning to take a look at it.

They'd been through this a couple of times. She wanted to make the meeting with Hailwood about some sort of irreconcilable class war between managers and Brahmins.

Brahmins as a class didn't bother Crowley as much as they did some people in the wasteland. He'd grown up working for them. They seemed a natural part of any City—like ethnic restaurants, museums and garbage strikes.

Plus, it seemed strange that Jana should be so mistrusting of Hailwood just because he was a Brahmin. So was she—the literate daughter of a landowning family and the sister of a City's founding board member.

She was usually perceptive about these things. There must have been something else going on with her.

At first, young Hailwood had invited Crowley to come to Tampa—to his family compound on Anna Maria Island. It was, apparently, a signature move on his part. But that was impossible. Among other things, Crowley was still an outlaw in Tampa. Technically, he could be arrested if he returned.

Hailwood pardoned him with an executive order. But Crowley still didn't *want* to come to Tampa. He'd been there recently, on ground that his students had taken. There was no profit in coming to the Hailwood compound—like some kind of guest or subject or supplicant.

He'd suggested that Hailwood could come to Camp A. Hailwood wanted no part of *that*.

Finally, they agreed to meet on neutral ground—Bliss Island, a man-made resort in the Gulf south of Houston. Legally, Bliss Island was an independent property that belonged to a Houston oil billionaire. Houston security patrolled it as a service to the citizen…but the Island was sort of professional neutral site for touchy negotiations, business transactions that required privacy, controversial social events, etc.

It was Hailwood's suggestion, but Crowley agreed that it was an acceptable solution.

Hernandez from Camp C was handling security for the trip. T.R. Wilson's office had sent the technical specs for Bliss Island, so they could locate access and egress points, likely hiding places and other security concerns. This was simply a bigger version of Crowley's information habit—when he entered a place where there might be trouble, he looked for exits and things that he could use as weapons in a pinch.

When he put together his list of staff to take to the meeting, it occurred to him again how much he'd depended on Jean Jacques. He missed having his main lieutenant around. And the haughty young Hailwood had caused J.J.'s death.

But he had to clear his mind of this anger. It served no immediate purpose. He remembered back to his years of City negotiations, on Tampa's side of the table. The most effective negotiator approached things without emotion. Excitement, anger, frustration or happiness made people more likely to overlook some small point and make a bad deal.

In those days, he counted on Neuroplex to keep his mind clear. Now, he had to do it himself.

While he made the list, he tried to see the meeting from the other side. That was usually a good exercise.

Hailwood might blame him for the Old Man's suicide—an unusual humiliation for a Brahmin family. Intelligence from the City said that the Old Man had been involved in some risky trading that was supposed to prop up the City's bonds. He also had cancer, which he'd been hiding. And Crowley knew more than most about the Hailwoods' crazy family situation, the odd relationship between the Old Man and his son's wife. It was easy enough to see that the combination had pushed the Old Man to a desperate act.

The logic wasn't so hard to follow. The catalyst to all those problems was the siege. It had driven down Tampa's paper and crimped its economy. Everything else flowed from that. No matter how grand they liked to seem, Brahmins cared most about money.

Then there was the rumor that young Hailwood had killed Chambers. Literally. What did that mean for their meeting?

Crowley had tried to explain to Jana that he considered young Hailwood an agent of chaos more than a dedicated enemy. If he could find a way to direct the young Brahmin's intensity, he might even be a useful tool.

He made notes about all of this on his screen. The notes had replaced the pills as his means of organizing his thoughts.

When he took a break and walked outside, Pea and Jack were having their Chinese lesson. He walked over and sat next to them, something he liked to do. They'd gotten used to this enough that they didn't stop.

But the young woman who was teaching them nodded a respectful acknowledgment.

"How are they doing?"

"Well, Rabbi, Jack could focus a little more on his characters."

He looked sternly at the boy. But it was hard to be angry.

Brian wasn't against the idea of the meeting with Hailwood. But he wanted to Crowley to take a hard line against Tampa's efforts to set itself up as a leader among the "non-aligned" Cities.

"...he needs to see that he's not going to be able to horde Tampa's aerospace power. Those days are over. He's going to have to do business with us. Or we go to the Jacksonville League or the Framework."

"That's going to be a hard point to made, Brian. He's been raised with the belief in his family's undisputable authority. And he's high on his tactical victories. This won't be like dealing with an ordinary business person."

"Maybe not. But you've got to make that point to him."

"But this may not be the meeting for that. Maybe next time."

"Okay. But next time can't be too far off, Michael."

"Agreed."

Brian had become slightly hesitant about making the unmarked Sky Dragon available. But he couldn't deny it for this meeting. Crowley would take a tilt to Camp A and the Dragon would be there in the morning to take him to Bliss Island.

He packed two days' clothes into the security duty bag that he took to most summit meetings. And he took his Empire Firearms 10mm plasma pistol. It was easy to conceal in civilian clothes and packed a solid punch.

The house was kind of quiet for the middle afternoon. When he walked outside to put his things in the tilt, he could see why. Jana had gotten the kids dressed and waiting for him on the front porch.

Jack asked if he could take the bag out to the tilt. Crowley let him. There was still something a little stilted about the old-fashioned manners that Jana was teaching the kids. It might have had something to do with her transition. She'd expected more time to adjust from being the rebellious daughter to the authority-figure mother. The older kids had forced a faster turn.

By the time Mikey and the new baby were teenagers, she'd have this all down.

But there was something...charming?...about the awkwardness of their current effort.

Pea didn't like to curtsy; she bowed her head instead. "Jana has told us where you're going, dad. You're trying to make a peace agreement for the war in Tampa. She's told us how important that is. I hope it goes well."

"So do I, babe. I think it will."

Jack came back from the tilt.

"The pilot says he's ready to go, dad."

Crowley gave the pilot a thumbs-up. "Thanks, Jack. I'll be back in a couple of days. You take care of things here while I'm gone."

"Yes. Of course."

Crowley kissed Jana and whispered thanks. She smiled, a little nervously. Mikey grabbed his leg and the reached up for a hug.

It was hard to leave this.

The meeting was supposed to start at 10 in the morning. They'd meet for a couple of hours then break for lunch. Then, if necessary, they'd meet for a few more hours in the afternoon. That was all that had been formally planned. But, if things went well, they could have dinner that night before they left the island.

Crowley's plan was to arrive on the SkyDragon at about 9:45 am. That would put him on the Island a few minutes after Hailwood—and make the point that Crowley's hardware was equal to Tampa's best.

The plane was at Camp A at dawn. Crowley waited until 8:50 to climb aboard. Henri Guibert, J.J.'s cousin, was already in his seat.

Houston Air Security was patrolling the air around Bliss Island. A pair of Mach 3 Interceptors escorted them to the landing strip.

An unusual voice came on the SkyDragon's audio system. "Mr. Crowley, this is Ken Jacobs. I'm the Security Director for Bliss Island. Welcome to our retreat."

Crowley clicked the cabin audio feed on. "Thank you, Mr. Jacobs. I'm looking forward to a productive meeting."

"Very good. Your pilot has the landing codes and you can make your approach in about three minutes. Mr. Hailwood's group just landed."

"Thank you."

The SkyDragon lurched into landing configuration and slowed to a hover.

He looked down on the ground. Three small black jets were parked near the terminal. They were arranged in a semicircle with their noses facing the strip. They looked like converted Nippon

Ichiban fighters, top-of-the-line Asian aerotech. And they were positioned for a quick exit.

The SkyDragon landed vertically, also near the terminal and about 100 yards from the black fighters.

Hailwood and two managers were standing on tarmac.

Crowley had four of his bodyguards walk—not march—ahead of him, down the ramp. Henri followed behind him. Everyone else stayed on board, ready if needed.

Hailwood approached, with his hand extended. He was ignoring the political aspect of this meeting and treating it like a business deal. "Michael Crowley. I'm Terry Hailwood. We met several times, years ago now. This is Steve Masterson, my External Security Director. And I think you'll remember Bill Franklin."

He was handsome and well dressed. He was acting like a manager but his hair was longer than any manager would wear it. And he hadn't shaved. All this, plus his body English was typically Brahmin. Casual.

Crowley shook his hand. "Mr. Hailwood. Yes, I remember you as a boy. Mr. Masterson. Bill, it's been a long time. Gentlemen, this is Henri Guibert. His family are some of my closest advisors."

When Henri shook Hailwood's hand, he said "Mr. Hailwood. My cousin died in Tampa."

"I'm sorry for your loss, Mr. Guibert. *Mais c'est le guerre*, eh?"

"*Oui. C'est le guerre.* But my cousin's wife might see different."

"Please send her my sympathies."

"I will. But I'm not sure it will do much good." This was one obvious difference between the cousins. J.J. kept his cool.

Young Hailwood shrugged and looked over to Crowley. Power dynamics. He didn't feel the need to engage an aide.

A man came out of the small terminal and introduced himself. He was Jacobs, the Security Director of the place. "Gentlemen, your rooms are in the Executive Conference Center, just past the terminal. Shall we?"

As they walked, Crowley noticed Hailwood sizing him up—like a school kid itching for a fistfight. Was he going to start swinging? Crowley flexed the pectoral muscle on the left side of his chest to confirm that the pistol was still there. Of course it was.

Then he felt foolish about doing that. He was swinging too high and low. He had to calm down.

The conference room was nicely oriented, with a view of the Gulf on two sides. It was big—and had smaller breakout rooms on the opposite sides. Crowley checked his exits. Two doors. And the big windows would do, in a pinch. It looked like six or eight feet down to the seagrass outside. He didn't need to worry about impromptu weaponry. He had his pistol.

Bill Franklin made the formal introductions.

Once everyone sat down, Hailwood started talking. He looked Crowley straight in the eye. "Mr. Crowley, I appreciate that you contacted us to set up this meeting. I know that it must have been a difficult call for you to make. I hope that we'll be able to make this all worth that effort."

The "appreciate how difficult" was condescending. He planned to control the meeting with his mouth, which meant he didn't have a lot of experience in negotiations. Princes don't negotiate.

Hailwood said that he understood why the Jacksonville League felt it needed to attack Tampa. But his new management team was going to operate differently—and that Tampa and the League had to find some way to coexist: "In many ways, my presence here is the *result* of your attack on the City. It's a new generation of management and we'll need to develop a new relationship."

Crowley didn't say anything right away. In part, because basic negotiating tactics held that silence was the best response to lots of words. But he was also silent because he couldn't decide what he thought about Hailwood.

"I'm here because I'm interested in reaching some kind of truce between your City and my students. And, right now, that means doing something about the nuclear mines that you've planted in the wasteland north of your walls."

"The mines. Yes. It's not practical to remove them, of course. But, more important, it's not in our security interest to do so. But we can talk about making some kind of arrangement to get your troops out of the area with minimal damage."

"Minimal damage?"

"We don't want *anyone* to be killed in the wasteland. If there's a reasonable way, we'll help you get your people to safer ground."

"Where is the ground safer?"

"I'm not sure I can answer that question categorically. I assume that the areas inside the walls of League Cities are safe for them.

And your bases, of course. Beyond that, I assume that the land immediately east and north of Jacksonville is somewhat safe. But I suppose the wasteland will always be a wild card."

"The League is trying to do something about that."

"I'm sure it is. But I've got to say that the wasteland around Tampa is not going to be a safe harbor for *anyone* anymore. We're going to keep it a neutral zone and a security buffer for our City. Not going to expose our citizens to more blind missile lobs."

Crowley decided not to press that point. It meant more to him to get his students out of the mine fields than to debate the diplomatic protocols of using nuclear mines. Besides, young Hailwood didn't seem the type interested in protocols.

The discussion went on for almost two hours. And they agreed to a plan. The students in the wilds north of Tampa could evacuate under a white flag. If they flew that flag, they could withdraw through the Old I-95 Freeway corridor to the east and the Old Florida Highway to the west without any harassment from Tampa External Security. The withdrawal could start immediately and continue for two weeks.

Crowley protested that two weeks might not be enough time. In fact, it was more than they'd need.

Hailwood tried to get Crowley to warrant that all of the League forces would withdraw—but Crowley demurred. "I don't give orders in an organizational sense. I'll tell the commanders what you and I have agreed here. Each of them will make up his own mind about how to implement. Then we'll coordinate."

He didn't say anything about Karamanlis's Special Forces units that were near Tampa's northeast gate. They'd be a surprise.

"Well, we'd like something a little more clear than that. But I suppose the mines aren't going anywhere—so anyone who stays behind will be stuck."

Then young Hailwood suggested they take a short break. He seemed in a rush to make a call on his screen.

When Crowley got back from the men's room, Hailwood suggested they take a walk outside.

Crowley was skeptical about this. He wanted to get a formal memo circulated as soon as possible, so his students could start getting out. But Hailwood didn't seem to be in a threatening pose; he seemed interested in making some sort of personal connection.

Again, amateur strategy.

"Sure. It's a nice day. Let's take a walk for a few minutes."

They followed a boardwalk that wound through landscaped flora and looked down from the cliffs at various points. The staffers and security followed a few yards behind.

Crowley was content to walk the whole island without saying a word. It would be up to Hailwood to start any conversation. After about five silent minutes, he did.

"I wasn't sure that you would agree to meet with me."

Crowley just shrugged. And kept walking.

"Why did you agree? Surely, some of your students advised against this."

"No one close to me was for this meeting. You have a violent reputation, Mr. Hailwood. But a good manager is always willing to negotiate. Especially when soldiers are in the field."

"Right. Negotiate."

They stopped for a bit at a deck overlooking the Gulf. The day was very nice. Sunny, but not too humid.

"I think you hide behind the good manager lessons, Mr. Crowley. In fact, I think you're cagier than that. I think you left fewer troops outside our walls than you imply. I think your real siege is going to be around New Orleans. Your strategy is a feint and parry. Draw attention to Tampa but put the real choke hold on New Orleans. Bring them into your League, with Morial or without him. Which takes an admirable amount discipline on your part, since I'm sure you'd have loved to avenge the shabby treatment we showed you."

Part of Crowley wanted to stay silent; but part wanted to engage Hailwood. "Your instincts are good."

"So are my satellites. Better than most people realize."

"Well, you're right. Strategy is most important. But, honestly, I've gotten most of what I could want from Tampa. I have my children. And the men who treated me badly, Chambers and your grandfather, seem to have exited the picture. Unless your grandfather is still managing things behind the scenes."

Hailwood snorted a laugh. He looked and acted a lot like the Old Man. "The Old Man, now *there* was someone with a strategic mind. He may be pulling strings from the Great Beyond for the next 1,000 years. But, I assure you, he's exited the picture."

"Well, I'm sorry for your loss. Whatever my dealings with him were, I'm sure your grandfather provided well for his family."

"Yeah. He certainly did provide. You know, I know a lot about you, Crowley. More than you might think. I know that you were raised in City schools from the time you were a little boy."

'Yes. I'm a product of Tampa's Public Custody Authority."

"Tell me what you remember of your family."

"That's a personal question."

"I know. Tell me what you remember about your mother."

This was strange. It was no secret that Crowley had been raised in the City orphan welfare system. And someone like Hailwood could easily pull information on Crowley's mother. Did he feel the need to boast about his access to City datafiles? Seemed like a childish gambit. But Crowley didn't see the harm in playing along.

"There's not much to tell. My mother was a troubled woman."

"Do you have any memories of your father?"

"No. I never knew my father. Look, I'm sure you know all about me from City datafiles."

"Yes. But memory fascinates me. What's your earliest memory?"

"My earliest memories are from when I lived at the City Custody School in Ocala."

"Did your mother visit?"

"Yes. And I saw more of her later, when I was out of university. But she died when I was in my early 20s."

"Were you angry at her?"

"Pardon me?"

"For leaving you to the Custody Schools?"

"No. The Custody Schools were home to me. It never occurred to me to be angry about it. And I felt grateful to the teachers and staff. They were kind and considerate. Supportive. Probably more than a biological family in bad circumstances might have been."

"Did your mother ever talk to you about your family?"

"She told me that I was destined for great things."

"Yes. Yes, so did my mother." Young Hailwood seemed genuinely pleased with this silly little similarity. There must have been something more going on here. This must have been some sort of psy ops trickery. The best tactic for dealing with mind games was to change the topic.

"Look, Hailwood. I'm not sure you and I share much common ground here. My mother was a tragic woman. A drug addict. Not a dangerous one—at least not to anyone other than herself."

"But she'd been an athlete?"

"Yes. She'd been a competitive swimmer. But the only thing I connected with my mother was drug addiction. So, I got a prescription for Neuroplex when I was still a kid. It balanced my brain chemistry and helped me avoid worse problems."

"That's what made you stand out from your classmates?"

"No. Lots of kids took Neuroplex."

"True. Ever make any kind of peace with your mother?"

"I suppose so. But I'm not sure she ever made peace with herself. She was educated; and like I say she'd been an athlete at university. I think she was ashamed of what she'd become."

"I see. I'm sorry. *Requiescet in pacem*."

"Thank you. Why are you asking these questions?"

Hailwood stopped walking and stared out at the Gulf for a bit.

"Should we go back? I'd like to get word of our agreement to my company commanders."

"Just a minute." He clicked a few buttons on the small screen that he carried inside his jacket. "There's no need for any joint communiqué. I've sent the instructions to my managers—they'll be posted publicly. Your troops can withdraw in peace."

"Oh. Okay. That's not the conventional way of doing—"

"You have a fascination with protocol, Rabbi. For a terrorist. I don't think even the CEOs of the Jacksonville League Cities would be standing on ceremony to release joint announcements with you. Besides, I want to talk about something else."

"Okay."

"Your mother was Constance Crowley. Actually, she was a two-sport athlete at UTampa. Swimming and volleyball. And a decent student, apparently. Security Sciences major. Never did anything with the degree, though."

"Yes. Why do you want to talk about my mother so much?"

"Several reasons. Like I said, memory interests me. But also, it keeps me from killing you. Which I should do, strictly speaking. As long as you're alive, you're a threat to Tampa's well-being."

"I'm armed and my people are armed. If you try to kill me, we will kill you."

"No. This is a set-up. We've got all of your people in sniper crosshairs. There are explosives under your plane. If I rub my right eye with my right hand, you're all dead in three seconds. Jacobs is prepared for a shoot-out. Wilson is in on it, too."

Crowley felt his heart jump. "Why are you telling me this?"

"What happened to your mother was the Old Man's fault."

"Old Man *Hailwood*?"

"Yes."

"How?"

"He was a ruthless bastard. She got in trouble for using at university and he leveraged that into a bargain. He needed someone to carry his clone. He offered to make her legal problems disappear if she'd have the baby."

"What?"

"You're a clone of Grant Hailwood."

Sweat broke out on Crowley's forehead. "A clone?"

"Yeah. He always had his eye on you. Made sure you were well-positioned and you advanced quickly. But he was…uncertain… about your prospects. He'd had a Mathers Multiphasic Personality Inventory done on you when you were 13. And he didn't like the results. The test found you compliant. Irony in that, huh? The compliant terrorist. Anyway, he was disappointed."

Hailwood looked him in eye again. And shrugged.

"My mother never said anything about this."

"I'm not sure she knew. She probably just thought she was being a surrogate for some VIP couple."

"Does this have something to do with why he backed Chambers against me?"

"I don't know the answer to that. That whole episode doesn't make sense. And he did tell me that he regretted his part in it."

"So this is an apology?"

"Maybe. Though I'm not sure I'm the right one for that. Let's just say it's an explanation." Hailwood smirked slightly. He seemed to be pointing to the absurdity of the situation.

"So, if I'm the Old Man's clone, that makes me your uncle?"

Now Hailwood laughed. "No. There's more. When the Old Man decided you were too compliant, he tried again. This time, the incubator was a Brahmin girl who came to the proposition with fewer issues. Well, fewer *legal* issues anyway."

"Your mother?"

"She's not really my mother. In the genetic sense."

Crowley thought about his mother, coming to visit him at the Custody School on a hot spring day. He'd showed her his high marks and his first-place ribbon from a poster contest. She smiled with her sad eyes and said, "You're destined for greatness, Michael."

She'd been right—but not in the way he thought.

"So we're...what? Brothers?"

"Legally, I guess we would be. Though the whole thing's illegal. Genetically, we're twins. Born some 14 years apart. Spiritually, we're...well, you're probably better suited to tell me about that."

"He told you all of this before he died?"

"Not directly. He wasn't so straight. He gave me some of it. Bits and pieces of the rest. I put it all together after he was gone."

Had the Old Man given *him* hints about this? Crowley couldn't remember many details of their conversations. The Old Man had always seemed harsh and demanding. He never seemed to be planting subtle hints about things.

Crowley looked at young Hailwood. He seemed to be amused by the craziness of the story.

"If I was his own DNA, how could he throw me out of Tampa? Brand me a felon?"

"He didn't do that, Crowley. You know how he operated. He just pulled the strings of the people who did. Of Chambers. Of the lawyers. The Old Man was a behind-the-scenes guy. You said it yourself. You know it better than most."

"I don't remember much from those days. I think the Neuroplex did some kind of damage to my long-term recall."

He remembered that, when he was friendly, the Old Man did act paternally. Called him "son" a lot. But he'd always thought that was just more Brahmin condescension.

"But what you can remember makes you angry?"

"A little. How could he do that to his own blood?"

"You have a more romantic notion of family than I do. The Old Man was like that at the end, too. Sentimental about family."

Crowley stared hard at young Hailwood: "Brahmin trait. They always make a lot of noise about family."

Thoughts of his children had gotten Crowley out of many bad situations. Out of the mud in the wasteland. But something about

Sic Semper Tyrannis

young Hailwood's arrogance and sarcasm bought up a different response in him. He thought about the humiliation and anger that he felt when Chambers had branded his neck and stripped him of his citizenship that gray morning on the wall above Gate 6.

He wanted revenge. He reached for his pistol.

And everything went white.

Crowley made slow, predictable movements. He shook his head and took a deep breath when he reached into his jacket.

Hailwood had drawn before Crowley brought his pistol out. The range—less than three meters—left no time for reflection. His shot hit Crowley in the middle of the forehead.

There was a series of pops back near the conference room.

A few seconds later, Masterson called clear.

Hailwood turned Crowley onto his back and adjusted his body into a resting position, legs straight and arms crossed over his chest.

He wondered if he would look like Crowley in 14 or 15 years. Or the Old Man in 70 or 80. The beard made it difficult to see precisely the lines of Crowley's jaw. But Hailwood could imagine them.

He didn't feel any gut sense of shared identity with this man, though. Crowley could have been anyone—long-lost brother, distant relative, stranger.

Masterson brought two black kits over.

"Loose ends all tied up, Steve?"

"All tied up, sir."

Hailwood took the smaller kit from Masterson and opened it. He activated the device, which was about the size of a deck of playing cards. He placed it in one of Crowley's hands and then stretched the two wires out. Each had a needle on its end. He inserted one needle into Crowley's right forearm, an inch down from the elbow, and the other near his right wrist.

"Okay, Steve. Let's bag him. And then go have a closer look at his phantom plane."

Masterson smiled and unzipped the larger kit.

Thirty-four

"Mr. Crowley. Mr. Crowley..."

The voice brought him out of the white. But it wasn't Jana's.

He opened his eyes. The room was familiar. But he couldn't remember how.

"Mr. Crowley. You're awake. Wonderful. You're going to feel a little woozy for a while. You've been in a medically-induced coma for 13 days. But you're fine. Better than fine, really."

Her voice was low and strong. It pulled him awake.

"Where am I?"

"You're in your home on Sanibel Island."

"Sanibel? How?"

"That's a long story. And the truth is I don't know all of the details. But there's someone here who does. As soon as we get you cleaned up and fully awake, you can have a chat with him."

She guided him up to a sitting position on the bed.

It was his bed. And his room. He could see out the window to the Gulf of Mexico on the north side of the island.

"My name is Amethyst Robinson. You can call me Amy. I'm your nurse. I've been watching over you the past few days and will be with you until you're fully recovered."

She helped him swing his legs over the side of the bed.

"I feel faint."

She started to give his legs a quick massage. "That's normal. You've been sleeping for a long time. But your vital signs are all strong. It's just going to take an hour or so for you to regain your balance. But you'll be back to normal by lunch time. And your appetite will come roaring back."

She lifted his arms and started rubbing his left wrist.

"Coma?"

She laughed. She'd moved up to rubbing his shoulder. And then shifted to his other arm. She knew what she was doing; the massage made him feel better. "They told me you'd be asking a lot of questions. This is what I know. You've been in a medically-induced coma while the doctors cleaned out your system out and ran some nanotech repairs. After everything they've done, you're probably the healthiest middle-aged man in this part of the world."

Clean. They'd removed the tracking chips. "Whose doctors?"

"I'm not sure how to answer that one. It was an all-star team. The best doctors in the City."

"Why?"

"Because Mr. Hailwood asked them to make sure you were fit as medtech can make a person."

"Hailwood. I thought he wanted to kill me."

She laughed again.

Amy helped him into the shower, which also made him feel better. He had some trouble standing; but she'd put a hand-rail device in the stall. He was able to hold that and lean against the wall while the warm water ran over him.

His muscles—especially around his waist and lower back—were stiff and sore.

He tried as hard as he could to remember everything that had happened on Bliss Island. Young Hailwood had told him that he was a clone of Old Man Hailwood. And—this was the part Crowley couldn't be sure of—that he, Hailwood, was also a clone.

And then…he just couldn't assemble how it has ended.

The last thing he could remember was young Hailwood talking to him in a sarcastic tone. Typical. But he wasn't sure what exactly he'd been saying. And then. Nothing. White.

They must have drugged him somehow. Something in the water? But he didn't remember drinking or eating anything on Bliss Island. Something in the air? A dart?

He leaned his shoulder into the side of the shower and rubbed his eyes. That was when he realized he was clean shaven.

After the shower, the nurse helped him get dressed in clothes he hadn't worn in years. They still fit.

He looked at himself in the mirror. He hadn't been clean shaven in so long….

The shiny skin on his neck was gone. It was the same color and texture and the rest of his neck. Nanotech. Sometimes realizations came slowly to Crowley. But this time he thought immediately of Jana's argument for keeping scars to remember what happened.

His teeth also looked whiter.

He asked Amy what else they'd done.

"Well, you had the normal joint erosion of a man your age. Your knees and shoulders had it worst. So, they refurbished your joints. And you had the usual build-up of lead and other toxic junk in your liver and kidneys. Stuff that people who live in the wasteland get. So, they cleaned all that out. And the scarring on the front of your neck and left hand. And then they found some precancerous cells in the skin on the back of your neck and one or two other places, so they got rid of those."

"My beard?"

"Standard procedure for the medtech. Especially with so much going on around your neck. But you can grow it back if you like."

It also occurred to him that shaving his beard and cutting his hair was an easy way for them to change his look. Make him less recognizable to a casual observer. Easier to hide.

"I'd like to walk around a bit."

"Sure. Let's start just slow and easy around the rooms up here. Then, if you're feeling up to it, we can go downstairs. Even outside." She was a very good nurse. Slow and steady and encouraging.

Bertram Barrett was the "someone" that Amy had said could explain more details. He was waiting in the living room when Crowley walked a little slowly down the stairs an hour later.

"Michael, it's good to see you. You look well."

"Bert. I feel pretty bad. But Nurse Amy here says it'll take a day or so to get back to some kind of normal. She also says you can fill me in on what's going on."

"I'll do my best."

Crowley asked to sit in a chair near the water. Nurse Amy said that he shouldn't get too much sun the first day, but he could sit for half an hour. So, he and Bert Barrett ended up sitting exactly where they had four years earlier, when Barrett had tried to warn him of the pending trouble. They put two beach chairs in the sand, right at the edge of the water.

"Well, this has to be a big deal if they sent the CSO."

"They didn't. I'm not the CSO any more. I'm emeritus."

This time Barrett wasn't pacing nervously. He was sitting in a chair next to Crowley. That changed the tenor of conversation.

It occurred to Crowley that Barrett would have done better to sit next to him the first time, too. It might have made his warning more…authoritative.

"Who's Chief of Security?"

"A pilot who used to fly the Old Man around."

"Masterson."

"Yes. Good memory."

"Makes sense. The Hailwoods all trusted him. No experience, though. But what did the Board have to say about that?"

"Things aren't like they used to be, Michael. No one questions young Hailwood about anything."

"Really?"

They sat quietly for a little while after that.

"Not even the woman from SpielbergDisney?"

"No. She left during the zealot…I'm sorry 'the Company' attacks. went to SoCal. And they were getting ready to pull everything out of Orlando. Now they're big supporters of the kid."

"Unintended consequence."

"What?"

The tide was coming in. So, the waves—which were just six or eight inches high—lapped up against Crowley's bare feet. The water was cool and felt good. "We softened up the corporate interests but we didn't break the City completely. That made an opening for a strong figure to come in. Did he know what he was doing? Or was it happy timing?"

"I think the Old Man knew what he was doing. I think he set everything in place for the kid to come in with guns blazing."

"Literally."

"Yes."

Crowley wondered how much Barrett had known four years earlier, when he'd warned about Chambers' coup.

"So young Hailwood really shot Chambers?"

"Right in the middle of a board meeting." Barrett sounded slightly impressed by the absurdity of it. This reminded Crowley of how young Hailwood had talked on Bliss Island.

Crowley laughed. "Shot him dead, in the board room?"

Barrett laughed, too. "Hasn't been another board meeting since."

"What balls."

"It was something to see, Michael. Chambers thought he was flanking the kid. I mean, we all knew that the kid had legal claim to the family trusts and their voting shares. But Chambers thought he could bluff the kid into backing down from the Old Man's chair. He had no fucking idea who he was dealing with. The kid literally drew a gun from his sport coat and shot Chambers. In his chair. It was the damnedest thing I've ever seen. No one knew what to do or say. I mean, the Shark. The marketing people. Me. And he sits in the Old Man's seat and calmly tells us how it's going to be."

"And then he nuked my students."

There was another silence. Which Barrett broke: "The latest news is that we've been invited to join the Framework Cities."

"Tampa has?"

"Yes, Tampa."

"No kidding. Well, that's a surprise. You think the Old Man anticipated *that*?"

"Yeah. I do."

"Impressive. It's the advantage of great family wealth. They do well because they start so far ahead of everyone else. In terms of money—but also information, experience. Intelligence."

"There's more to that story, though, Michael. Rumor has it young Hailwood isn't sure he *wants* to join the Framework."

"He'd be foolish not to."

"He says he's more interested in a plan for what he calls 'aggregating' Tampa's authority in the region. And then he'd give up his operational control to a republic. It's not much different from your old plan."

"I'd say it *is* my old plan. I just didn't have the power he does to force it into being. What are you supposed to do here? Babysit me?"

Barrett laughed again, himself this time. "I wouldn't call it 'babysitting,' Michael. He told me to make sure that you're okay. That you have everything you need. That I answer any questions you have."

Crowley nodded. "Okay. Then I'll take the opportunity to ask everything I can think of."

"I'll answer everything I can."

"Does he plan to kill me?"

"I don't know. I'm not in his inner circle. But I don't think so, Michael. If he wanted to kill you, I think you'd be dead."

"Why did he keep me in a coma for...well, how long was I out?"

"About two weeks, based on what I know about the meeting at Bliss Island."

"Why?"

"Well, I know he had the doctors give you a thorough going-over to make sure you were cleaned out of any toxins or parasites you might have picked up in the wasteland. And they did some nanotech."

"For what?"

"Fix your scars. And some cancer prevent."

"Did they plant anything in me?"

"I don't think so. Hailwood's orders were to clean you out."

"Can I leave here?"

"No. Not now. But at some point."

"I want to see my children."

"He knows that. He told me to assure you that he knows that and will do everything he can to bring your wife and children here as quickly as possible."

"Do people think I'm dead?"

"Some do. Some think you're still with your troops around New Orleans."

"What are they doing, around New Orleans?"

"Not much of anything, as far as we can tell. But they're digging in for a long siege. Not like the hit-and-run stuff you folks were doing here. The squatter villages around the gates there have disappeared. Certainly those people are expecting a long fight."

Long siege. The influence of vieux Guibert. He was out there.

"Does my wife think I'm dead?"

"Well, we can't know that. The kid had the marketers seed the free nets with conspiracy theories that you're not actually dead. Which was really smart. There's so much crazy stuff on the free nets that reasonable people will—"

"—write off anything someone might say about seeing me alive as crazy talk. Yeah, makes sense. Old-fashioned disinformation."

He thought about Jana and the kids for a few moments. He wasn't scared for them. She'd probably keep the kids on the farm,

Sic Semper Tyrannis

safely inside the Brownsville walls. But *she* might feel obligated to lead the Company to some act of vengeance. Or she might cling to the conspiracy talk and try to mount some sort of rescue.

She wasn't foolish, though. She wouldn't act in haste.

Still, he needed to get some kind of word to her, somehow. Tell her to just stay at home with the kids for while. To lie low, until he could get a better sense of what was going on.

But he didn't want to show his priorities to Barrett.

"Not joining the Framework is dumb. Karamanlis and Robert Briggs aren't likely to make peace with Tampa in a regional League."

"Karamanlis has more eternal concerns these days. He's dead."

"Really? How?"

"No one's sure exactly what happened. You know how crappy Jacksonville media is. But the word is that he was killed in a suicide bombing done by an anarchist group based within his own walls."

"Was young Hailwood behind *that*?"

"Some think so. He immediately offered Jacksonville a cease-fire and a peace treaty that offers its board and managers immunity from prosecution or reparations from the war."

"No reparations. Smart. Are they going to accept?"

"They already have—the cease-fire, anyway. They're negotiating the peace treaty. Like I said, the kid doesn't hesitate. But some people think it was Briggs who had Karamanlis killed."

"Briggs. Yes. Keep Tampa the enemy. Keep the Jacksonville League as it was. Maybe the only way to do that is eliminate Nico. Counterintuitive. But maybe…."

"The trouble is that no one knows how these Cities are going to operate without their regular leaders. Karamanlis is gone. You're gone. The Old Man's gone."

"And the Jacksonville League was still just new, anyway."

Now he felt a protective urge toward his students. Someone was going to try to sweep them up. Maybe Briggs. Maybe young Hailwood. It would be a real test of the Company—not being taken over by a City CEO.

He needed to get the Camps the same message he needed to get Jana. Lay low. Don't act in haste. Tend to your own gardens.

That was the basic strategy lesson he'd taught the Company for times of trouble. Don't act on doubt. Dig in, stay with the plan. He had to trust it to stick.

"Kill the head."

"What?"

"Our analysis of Jacksonville was that he'd centralized power so much and for so long that the City was vulnerable to assassination."

"Looks like your analysis was right. Now it's just a question of whether Jacksonville signs a peace treaty that effectively aborts its own League or throws in with Briggs and Charleston and stands up to young Hailwood."

"It's not Briggs. Doesn't have the resources. It'll have to be one of the bigger Cities. New Orleans or Houston—and probably not New Orleans, with all its problems. But Houston doesn't want to go to war with anyone. It's not their way."

He ran through the permutations of City politics and dynamics. It was like saying a prayer that he hadn't said in years. In a place he hadn't been in years. "Young Hailwood has a pretty strong hand."

Barrett laughed again. "That seems to be the emerging consensus."

Crowley had more questions. But he waited for a moment. Then: "What happened to Margot? I mean, I think this is her house, legally. She was supposed to get it in the divorce."

"As far as I know, she did. Right after young Hailwood dispatched Chambers, he called Margot to his compound and later that day she was on a plane for Europe. The word is he gave her money and place to live. In Paris, I think. And suggested strongly that she relocate permanently. She took the hint."

Crowley didn't get any satisfaction from hearing this, which surprised him a bit. "I feel bad for her. She was a prickly character. I just don't understand why she wanted to be with Chambers."

Barrett looked like he didn't want to talk about this. "I dunno, Michael. In some ways, it made perfect sense. She liked being the CEO's wife. She probably thought she was being savvy."

"Probably. Was she involved with Chambers before the coup?"

"I have no idea, Michael. Young Hailwood kept referring to her as 'Gertrude.' And most of us who heard that thought it was some slam on her fashion sense. Then one of the Brahmin interns in the Finance Department said it was from *Hamlet*. I looked it up. Gertrude was the cheating queen."

"We should have studied Shakespeare. Who knew? Has he said anything to you about me? His plans for me, I mean?"

"He told me you're his *heir*."

"Literally?"

"I think so."

"Did he tell you why?"

"No. But I guess it has to do with 'aggregating power' thing."

"Has anyone tried to kill him?"

"No. Not that I know of. He moves too fast, Michael. Most citizens still think he's new to the job. And they're happy that he turned the course of the war. And he's a handsome young guy from a Brahmin family. Royalty, as far as the celebrity channels are concerned. They have no idea how he operates. Most people think the stuff about him shooting Chambers is just urban legend."

"What are his plans for dealing with the Company? I'm sure he has some."

"Probably. But I don't know what they are."

"Will he attack the Camps?"

Barrett shook his head no. "Again, Michael, I'm not in his inner circle. But his focus seems to be on Jacksonville right now. He wants to annex it. He's more about annexing and co-opting than attacking. At least when it comes to Cities or armies or institutions. He's willing to kill an individual person but he seems hesitant to destroy *assets*."

"A true Brahmin."

"Guess so. My bet is that he'd try to absorb the Company."

"They'll fight that."

"You're probably right. That may be why he thinks you're important enough to keep around."

The water felt good on his feet, so Crowley got up and waded a little out into the small waves. He leaned over and splashed some salt water on his face.

Then he turned back to Barrett: "I'd like to get word to Jana. This might work for everyone. If she knows I'm alive, she'll probably be willing to spread the word that the Company should lie low. And she'll stay back on the family farm and wait. If she thinks I'm dead, she might be more inclined to take some action.

"I can see the sense in that. I'll pass word up the channel."

Crowley came back to his chair and sat down again. He was feeling better. Less groggy. But he was still tired.

Barrett looked over to him. "I have a question for you, Michael. Why did you bring the fight to the Cities? And to Tampa? You could have stayed in the wasteland forever. We thought it was your children. We thought that when the Old Man gave them back to you, you'd break off. But you didn't."

"Is this why you're here, Bert?"

"No. I'm just curious. I'm far out of the loop on intelligence gathering these days."

Crowley looked back at Barrett. He didn't completely believe him. But, with a shrug: "Thinking about the kids got me through some low points. Personal low points. But the reason for the Company was something else. For a long time, I said it was about efficiency. That the ignorance in the wasteland was inefficient—"

"That's why they call it the 'wasteland.'"

"Right. You know, I didn't realize that for a long time. And, for a long time, I said that waste irked my manager's sense of efficiency. But that's not it, either. That's not the *real* reason I do what I do."

"What is?"

"Early on, when I was first out there—I mean, before I even had a horse—I was working on small farms for food and a dry place to sleep at night. And on one farm, there were a couple of kids. And the farmer and his wife wanted them to learn to read the Bible. It was really the wife who wanted it. So, I spent a few weeks teaching the boys to read. And, when they had enough to get through Genesis, you should have seen their mother. Her eyes. She was a severe farmer's wife in wasteland—couldn't read herself—and she was crying. So proud of her sons. And proud of *herself* that her sons could read. It was the first time I got a glimpse of it, Bert. A sense of pride in self. People have to have that first, before anything else. Before security or commerce. Or walls. Or anything meaningful in a City.

"We forgot that here. And Cities like Jacksonville? I'm not sure they ever knew it. But Cities have to value that individualism. That self. Or their walls and their security aren't worth anything."

Barrett tilted his head a bit. "I've seen your lesson vids, Michael. You spend a lot of time saying you're not a deep thinker. But you sound like one, sitting here."

"I'm not. I just know a few things."

Amy came out to the chairs. "Okay, you've been out here baking long enough for your first day back on your feet. Time to go inside and try to eat some lunch."

Barrett walked with Crowley back toward the house. But he

stayed outside. "It really is good to see you, Michael. I'm going to head back into town and pass along your request. Maybe we can figure out some way for you to get word to your wife. Or maybe I can help you do it somehow."

Crowley nodded.

Barrett headed around the house, toward the driveway.

Amy had fixed a nice lunch for him on the dining room table, looking out at the water. A roast beef sandwich, a few potato chips, yogurt and some fruit.

"This looks lovely."

"I have you on a high protein menu. We're supposed to work on getting your energy up."

"How long are you going to be watching me, Amy?"

"Until they give me my next assignment."

"Who exactly do you work for?"

"Well, Tampa General. Immediately. But I'm part of a group contracted to the TSF."

"You're former TSF?"

"Yes."

"Are you really a nurse?"

She seemed to take offense to that question. "Yes sir, I can show you my license."

"No, that's okay." He took a bite from the sandwich. It was very good, a little bit of tang in mustard or dressing. His sore molar didn't hurt any more. They must have fixed it when they cleaned his teeth.

After a minute: "What would happen if I took off running down the beach? Or swam out into the Gulf? Or hopped in a car or something?"

"Oh, we're keeping careful eyes on you, Mr. Crowley. We'd scoop you up and bring you right back."

He knew what that meant. The more trouble he made, the more trouble he'd get.

"Suppose I can't use a screen."

"Not true. I have one for you, specially configured. Full access to the Tampa net. No outbound comms. You can read or watch anything you like. You just can't say anything."

"If I hack around the controls?"

"You're welcome to try."

"I'm going to do everything I can to get word to my wife."

"I understand."

One EMP projector and a plasma pistol and he'd be halfway to Brownsville before they knew he was gone.

Or maybe not. If she was ex-TSF, Amy was probably trained in hand-to-hand combat.

"This isn't the first time you've done something like this, is it?"

She laughed. Not in an angry way. "I'd say that each of my assignments is unique. This is the first time I've done something *like this*. But it's not the first time I've had a unique assignment."

He moved on to the yogurt and fruit. She was right. His appetite was coming back. "This still feels like a dream to me."

She laughed again. "It's not. My shift ends at 7 o'clock."

"Who's my night nurse?"

"There are a couple of them. But they're not as sociable as I am."

"I don't like the sound of *that*."

"You'll be fine. And I'm back every morning. With the sun."

She smiled at him genuinely, absolutely certain of herself. He recognized that smile. Neuroplex.

His strongest skill had always been handling difficult situations. He looked around the room for exits. And all the things he could use as a weapon, in a pinch.

His immediate goal was to survive, so that he could prevail.